Colin de Silva was ____ d
grew up there. Dur____ s
a commissioned off____ o
1956 he was a mem____ in
1962 he emigrated

His first novel, *The Winds of Sinhala*, was ____ in
1982 and quickly became an international bestseller, followed by the equally successful *The Founts of Sinhala*.

By the same author

The Winds of Sinhala
The Founts of Sinhala
The Fires of Sinhala

COLIN DE SILVA

The Last Sinhala Lions

GRAFTON BOOKS

A Division of the Collins Publishing Group

LONDON GLASGOW
TORONTO SYDNEY AUCKLAND

Grafton Books
A Division of the Collins Publishing Group
8 Grafton Street, London W1X 3LA

Published by Grafton Books 1989

First published in Great Britain by
Grafton Books 1987

ISBN 0-586-07134-2

Printed and bound in Great Britain by
Collins, Glasgow

Set in Garamond

Dedicated to

| Nala Devayani | Nirmala Cherine |
| my first-born princess | my baby princess |

whose love never failed

Acknowledgements

My deep appreciation and thanks go to:

Grafton Books for its faith in me, particularly to my editor, Anne Charvet, for her unfailing courtesy and professional support; the editorial staff of Grafton Books for excellent editing;

Dominick Abel, my literary agent, for invaluable assistance with a re-write of the original manuscript;

Heidi Helm, for research into Portuguese trading, ships, armament, and dress;

Marcia Krueger, whose devotion to my work once again went beyond the line of duty, in typing several revisions of the manuscript, often meeting impossible deadlines and in making useful suggestions.

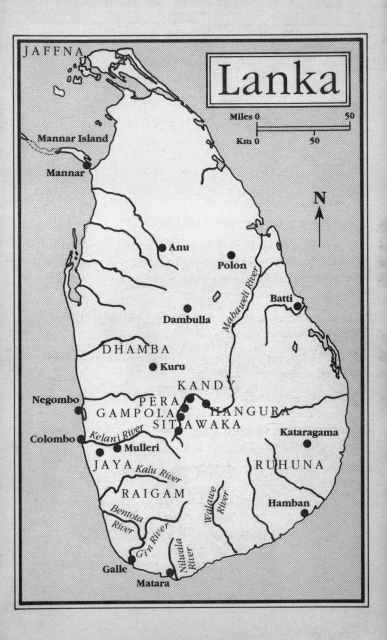

Some Important Sinhala Monarchs

VIJAYA 483–455 B.C.
see *The Founts of Sinhala*

DEVAM PIYA TISSA 247–207 B.C.
Introduced Buddhism to Lanka

ELARA 145–101 B.C.
ABHAYA GAMINI 101–77 B.C.
SADHA TISSA 77–59 B.C.
see *The Winds of Sinhala*

A.D.

QUEEN ANULA 12–16

GAJABAHU 174–196

BHATIKA TISSA 203–227

MAHASENA 334–361

BUDDHADASA 380–409

MAHANAMA 409–431

DHATUSENA 460–478

KASSAPA 478–496

MOGOLLANA 496–513

PARAKRAMA BAHU I 1153–1186
Founder of Polon-naruwa

PARAKRAMA BAHU VIII 1484–1518
Ancestor of:
DHARMA PARAKRAMA BAHU IX
WIJAYO VI
BHUVANEKA BAHU VII
MAYA BUNNE
RAJA SINHA I

PROLOGUE
11 November 1525

Standing at the upstairs bedroom window of his residence on the Mutu Vella hill, Fernao could see the great *nao* warships riding the distant silver waters of Colombo harbour. The power of their huge cannon gripped him again. In 1503, the year in which he had been born, Admiral Vasco da Gama had shown the way to conquest with his brutal bombardment of Calicut. Now he, Fernao, would use Portuguese military might not only to pound out his future but to destroy his arch-rival, the Sinhala Prince Tikiri, some day. He exulted in the savagery that had been let loose within him. It was the antidote to his doubts and fears, suspicion and guilt.

His thoughts flitted to his wife, Julietta, now lying exhausted after her ordeal on the great canopied bed behind him, then to the Sinhala serving woman, Menika, who had been a mother to Julietta from the day she was born. Menika, now an untidy bag of bones and wrinkled skin in the servants' quarters below, awaiting cremation!

Julietta had told him Menika's story, the tragic life of one who could not fight back. Menika had been murdered in her sleep last night by Sergeant Correa, commander of his own household guard.

Colonel Fernao Soarez de Albergaria would never suffer such tragedy. Not yet twenty-two, he was already commander of the Portuguese regiments in Lanka and would always have the character and the power to fight. 'No man takes what is mine with impunity' was the motto of the royal de Albergarias. Prince Tikiri had seized some part of what was his own, his wife's heart. The bastard must pay the price.

Sergeant Correa allegedly abducted Julietta to rape and probably murder her, while he himself had been absent on night duty at the fort. She had been saved by some Sinhala soldiers from the neighbouring governor's mansion. On hearing the news, he had hurried back home in the early hours of the morning, anxious but confused.

How would a trusted soldier of one of the regiments under his command have dared take such a liberty unless . . .? While comforting Julietta, he had questioned her. Had she somehow given cause, even unconsciously, for the abduction? Had the rapist penetrated her? If so, could she have conceived?

He knew he had failed Julietta in her direst hour of need, but he had not been able to control the demon within him. God knew he had tried. Yet, however fair he wanted to be, he could not erase from his mind the smell of a man's emission that had smitten him, no less, when he first took Julietta in his arms. And the feel of her had been different. That's right, some part of her had been withdrawn, as it had been years ago, when she had held back from him because she loved Prince Tikiri. This as much as anything had triggered his responses to her. The woman he was holding in his arms was the old Julietta and yet someone new as well. Had she been this way when he first entered the bedroom and took her in his arms? His mind felt raw with the effort to pierce that veil and cast it aside.

Lying exhausted on the bed, every part of her body aching, her mind screaming, Julietta became even more convinced that she had conceived of Prince Tikiri that night. It filled her with a strange sense of destiny. Though the world, and especially her fellow Catholics, would judge her an adulteress if they knew, she was convinced that the child to be born was a gift from God that some day would bring momentous consequences. The price she had to pay was to keep the knowledge from Fernao and the rest of the world.

The rest of the world! Her own world had just shattered.

Fernao had let her down, shown himself to be self-centred. All the feelings she had been developing for him were abruptly stunted.

And Menika, the earliest mother she could remember, who had begun her world, was dead, foully murdered.

Her mind flew back to when her own world began.

In 1505, the Portuguese naval Captain Lorenzo de Almeida had been blown by a storm into the port of Galle, some seventy miles south of Colombo. He had there erected a great stone cross on a headland north of the Galle harbour carrying the Quinas, the royal coat of arms of Portugal, with a statement that as long as that cross stood, Lanka would be under the divine protection of His Imperial Majesty the King of Portugal. Captain de Almeida concluded a treaty with the Great King of Lanka, including a *sesmaria*, land grant, for a factory in the city of Colombo, and when he finally departed from Lanka, he left behind *a senhor* Duarte de Brito to factor trade and two Catholic friars, Father Juan and Father Perez, to factor religion!

The three men had thereafter been confined to the Great King's palace in Jaya, about seven miles from Colombo harbour. *A senhor* de Brito had fallen in love with a Sinhala woman of lowly estate and married her. Julietta was their baby and therefore a *mestico*, half-caste. Her mother had died in childbirth, so the only mother she had known was the serving woman, Menika. She had grown up in a cottage in the Jaya palace with her father and Menika until the Portuguese returned in 1521; by then she was fourteen and in love with the Sinhala Prince Tikiri, her friend and protector.

Fernao had been a midshipman on the flagship of his father, Admiral Lopo Soarez de Albergaria, who sailed into Colombo with a powerful flotilla of seventeen great *nao* for trade. Julietta recalled their three years of friendship before Fernao manipulated their marriage without her consent. The well-springs of resentment that her marriage vows had dammed for a while came bubbling forth again. She recognized that this was in part a way of absolving herself – though she did not feel she had sinned – but the resentment was just as inevitable. Fernao, like all Portuguese compatriots in this part of the world, played the game.

Memories. Separating her from hideous realities, causing eyelids heavy as chainmail to droop. She was bone weary from the immediate past, but something nagged insistently, something she had to do right now for the future before falling asleep . . . connected with Fernao, the power game . . . something . . . Her mind suddenly grasped it.

Seized by a desperate resolve, she sat up in bed. 'Fernao,' she called softly.

He turned on the instant, his entire being somehow gentling at the tone of her voice.

'Please come, lie down and hold me,' she begged. 'I need your arms around me.'

Her conscience clamoured piteously at the way his eyes lit up.

Dear God, please forgive me, but I must protect my baby's identity even if You condemn me to eternal perdition.

After having avoided Julietta for nigh on four years, the first time I met her again was to save her from rape, brutalization and death in the dark grove on the Mutu Vella hill near Colombo.

I am Tikiri Bandara, son and heir of King Maya Dunne, who rules Sita Waka, one of the three kingdoms of Lanka. Having loved Julietta since my early teens, I continued to love her during all the years when I thought she had betrayed me. I could not stop loving her even after she married Colonel Fernao Soarez de Albergaria. The cause, true love, had produced the effect – my conviction that she

12

remained my responsibility and that it was my duty to protect her from harm.

'Tonight may never happen again,' she had said slowly, her gaze becoming more intense, like that of a woman seer. 'Nor is it a part of my normal life. I need to be cleansed, Tiki-tiki, and only you can do it. I need something that will rescue me from the dragons of fear, uncertainty, anguish and even death.'

'How can I help you?' I inquired hoarsely.

'By making love to me.'

The grove started to spin. I could not believe my ears, but I felt a pounding in them. I had never made love to a woman. My only sexual experience had been the fumbling occasion when I kissed Julietta so long ago. Now this. 'I want no reward for saving you tonight,' I muttered, but still under the wondrous spell of her gaze.

'I am offering you no reward, Tiki-tiki. I am only saying that our love has to be consummated, once and for all time, tonight, while I am Juli and you are Tiki-tiki again.'

I understood what she meant.

Juli and I, a virgin woman, no less, and a virgin man, made love to each other, lying on a soldier's cloak in the semi-gloom of a small glade beneath the Mutu Vella stars. There was no fumbling. It was a perfect union, made in heaven.

Heaven. I looked up at the sky and it had begun to pale, the stars fainter, perhaps three more hours to dawn. Juli must be taken home.

A great sadness, a craving never to let her go, the sick knowledge that I must, churned within me, choking me.

Menika, the dead serving woman, and I, a live prince, had become one through the brief span of our loving and the eternity of our love life; for I knew with certainty that this most precious part of my life had begun and ended in minutes. Menika's travail was over; mine had begun.

What I had known was so pure and right that, as Juli

13

and I lay fulfilled in each other's arms, I wondered what I could give back to it, how I could make it right for a married woman who had broken her vows. In a blinding flash of light, I knew the answer. I had to be true to these moments for the rest of my life.

Silently I took the vow of brachmachariya. *I would never again know a woman in this way, never again, even if I had to marry.*

Thus I gave back to Juli and her God the righteousness and purity of our blessed consummation.

Now the glory of the night had become a cold, bleak dawn. Sleep was out of the question because my heart was thudding and the bliss of sexual communion still coursed through my veins to mingle with the sick knowledge that it was all over, chill and final as the tombs. My mind still refused to grasp that, like Menika, I had lived my lovelife in a single hour; love making equal both serving lady and prince.

Restlessly pacing the boarded floors of my upstairs bedroom, I glanced at the dark grove spreading beneath me. My grainy gaze inevitably drifted to the patches of red-tiled roof appearing through the green slope of branches to my left. Julietta would be there. She was in her husband's residence while I was in the governor's mansion. The distance, a length of rope between fulfilment and despair, seemed almost to strangle me.

Recollection of the punishment I had inflicted on Sergeant Correa intruded.

He had climaxed – what an appropriate word! – his campaign of brutality against women by daring to lay impious hands on my beloved Julietta. But for me, she would be lying dead in that grove at this very moment, despoiled, raped, sodomized. I had decreed that his diseased genitals be cut off . . . he was now probably bleeding to death in the grove. Fierce satisfaction at the justice I had meted out eased some of my anguish, but not for long.

The clamour of birds quarrelling brought me back to the grim reality of the present, the reality of the red roof-top of a residence. Colonel Fernao Soarez de Albergaria would be down there with his wife, my Julietta, at this very instant. Were they in her bedroom ... making ... Dear *devas*, I must not walk that road. I must never, never walk that road. For along it lies madness.

Suddenly, like a sunlit cliff's edge yawning through a mist, the colonel's thoughts became clear to me. He had always been my arch-rival in love, and would be so in war. He passionately hated me. He would do everything in his power to kill me.

My country is divided into three kingdoms, each ruled by one of three brothers: Jaya, under King Bhuvenaka Bahu, still called the Great King; Raigam under the King Raigam; and Sita Waka, the domain of my father, King Maya Dunne. All three kingdoms are threatened by white foreigners with their cannon and muskets. The Fires of Sinhala are being sparked by the invading parangi, *white Europeans led by Colonel Fernao Soarez de Albergaria, and fuelled by our own internal discords.*

From my earliest days, it has been prophesied that I, Prince Tikiri Bandara of Sita Waka, would be the saviour of Lanka. I am the man to put out the fires and restore the Sinhala Lions.

PART ONE
The Royal Lion

CHAPTER ONE

Their love-making on the morning after the attempted rape had been a blind groping of two people for comfort and the need to forget.

In the days following, Fernao wished with all his heart that he had taken a different attitude with Julietta that morning, treating her with understanding rather than subjecting her to an inquisition. But the deed had been done and it could not be altered. His sensitive spirit gave him the sickening message that he had lost some inner core of Julietta again. This was evident, in some subtle way he could sense but not pinpoint, in their love-making. His self-blame heightened as the truth about Sergeant Correa's misdeeds kept coming to his notice. Why on earth had he not exercised more care in the selection of the guard commander of his home? It was due to his youth and inexperience, he knew, but that did not prevent him from castigating himself for having exposed Julietta to such danger. Now he was paying for it.

None of his oft-repeated expressions of sorrow and regret seemed to reach Julietta. She would hush his protestations and she was even more loving and devoted than before, at times even tender. Only someone as perceptive as himself could have identified her subtle withdrawal.

His frustration and guilt slowly produced their own defences. Julietta was being unfair to him. True, she had been through an experience the like of which he could not wish upon any human being, but why take it out on him? After all, it was not he who had tried to rape her.

Somewhere within him a still, small voice intruded questions: Did you not rape her when you plotted your marriage? Would she have mated with you of her own volition? At the very least, did you not seduce her? Is not seduction but a subtler, more despicable form of rape? And did you not rape her spirit that morning after her gruesome experience? Did it have to take confirmation of Sergeant Correa's bestiality to convince you of her innocence?

Then, suddenly, incredibly, Julietta's withdrawal began to dissipate. Each day became an increasing source of joy to Fernao. Oddly enough, however, he had his first setback when Julietta announced two months after the fateful night that she was pregnant. By whom, that evil voice within him whispered, but this time he gave no sign whatever of his doubts. And it had its results, for as he poured out the devotion of an expectant father to her, Julietta drew even closer to him.

Meanwhile, he had flung himself into the only area of his life that was uncomplicated, his work, where the wielding of power had begun to compensate for the helplessness of his personal life. His indefatigable efforts with the Mouro traders Aisha and Abdul Raschid resulted in a vast expansion of trade. Through their connections with Aisha's brother, Paichi Marcar, king of the East Indies commerce operating from Calicut, the soaring profits Fernao had forecast to Viceroy Vasco da Gama in Goa the previous year were soon bettered. He often thought of the Viceroy, wished he had lived to see these successes, but Grand Admiral Vasco da Gama had died on Christmas Day 1524.

In addition to the fact that trade was expanding and profits increasing, Fernao's investigations were now providing him with detailed information he needed to expand the Colombo fort stronghold to the principal coastal harbours of Lanka. He wanted to establish a curtain of iron around the country, Portuguese iron, with virtual domination of the central sub-kingdom of Kandy which gave access to the hill-country fastnesses through the cannon and musketeers he would send Kandy's King Wira when his son, Prince Kumara, converted to the Catholic faith.

His principal driving force remained the overpowering desire to destroy Prince Tikiri and everyone connected with the prince. It remained his secret but guided all his planning. Time and again he recalled that Prince Vidiye had recently married the daughter of the Great King Bhuvenaka of Jaya. Clearly this was an alliance of two men who hated the entire Maya Dunne clan and its staunch supporter, Prince Raigam, who had together prevented King Bhuvenaka from taking over all three kingdoms on the Great King Wijayo's death. And the girl was pregnant. Prince Vidiye, with his great gangling frame, his large rolling eyes, was a man of insensate ambition; there must be some way in which he could be used.

When Fernao learned that Prince Vidiye's wife was with child, he knew how he could do it and decided that the time was right for his next move. As the Great King was in a most amiable mood these days, Fernao's request for an audience, to offer felicitations to the Great King on the prospects of his becoming a grandfather, was readily granted for the morning of the next Saturday.

On 10 February 1525, in the Kandy palace, at a quiet, private ceremony as befitted the Great King Wijayo's widow of one year, Prince Kumara took Queen Anula for his wife. The Court astrologers had waxed enthusiastic when they compared the queen's horoscope with his. Eighteen of the twenty-two compatibilities, especially *yoni*, the sizes and responses of the female and male sexual organs, had matched perfectly. The astrologers had also declared the day *subha nakath*, auspicious, for the purpose, the best time being the end of the third watch after noon.

The marriage followed the traditional form of a Buddhist

21

poruwa ceremony in the king's chamber, attended only by a few chosen noblemen.

Queen Anula looked excitingly beautiful, virginal as only she knew how, with a special magnetism that thrilled him each time their eyes met. Throughout the entire proceedings, Prince Kumara felt his fat, lecherous father, King Wira, envying him and mentally placing himself as the groom. It made Prince Kumara's blood boil. Not so long now, he thought, but his mind, indeed his entire being, was too full of anticipation of the nuptial couch for him to concern himself with other people.

Finally, he was in the queen's bedchamber, which adjoined her waiting room, anticipating the perfect sexual union he had craved at their very first meeting. He would finally probe her mystery.

They lay naked side by side on the pale blue cushions of the queen's bed, beneath its carved wooden canopy. All the tapers and brass lamps were lit so he could see her dusky beauty, the slender features, the large breasts with their purple aureoles, the tiny waist, the full hips and thighs.

Though fully erect, he allowed the moments to pass, savouring them, listening to his wife's breathing, inhaling the fragrance of her skin, without any movement, just thrilling to the touch of her thigh against his leg. She had caught his mood, remained still. He reached out a gentle hand to grasp her fingers. She turned on the instant. Pretending to be worked up, she moaned with simulated passion. 'Touch me, you young stud. Go on, fuck me, I can't stand it any longer. I need you, I need you.'

Sick with disappointment and anger, he sat up abruptly, flinging her aside. She looked at him, startled. 'Why, my prince?' She sat up too, crosslegged on the bed, facing him. 'What's wrong?'

Cool, deliberate, smiling only with his teeth, he slapped her hard across the face. She rocked sideways, steadied herself. She looked at him, fear, anger and bewilderment mingling in her expression.

'That was not an act of punishment, or brutality, but of love,' he declared softly. 'In the past, your men have needed you to satisfy their lust. All they wanted was your body, to move inside you and feel the triumph of their desire for you.' he paused. 'This is me.' He gestured inwards with his fingers. 'I'm different. I love you. It's the real you I need. Now, let us start all over again.'

He gently pushed her back into a reclining position, reached out a tender hand and stroked her face with his fingertips, touched her hair with feather-brush lightness, moving his nails hard enough to excite and caress. Her eyes closed, her nostrils dilated. He touched her all over her body. He kissed each of her fingers slowly, quietly, the sound of each kiss a note of tenderness in the silence of the room. He kissed every part of her body until her breathing deepened, her mouth opened. He brushed her lips with his. A gentle, gentle palm, full of loving, reached out and held the back of his head. Her other hand began to stroke him.

Their union was indeed perfect. She came and came and came, truly, as she had been wont to pretend with others. Finally, she was so exhausted, she looked at him dreamy-eyed. 'I surrender,' she whispered. Deeply thankful that he had reached her ultimate with gentleness and understanding, patience and love, he knew that she had in turn unbared his own mystery.

Saturday, 11 February 1525

Though the audience hall and front courtyard of Jaya palace, seven miles from the fort of Colombo, had been teeming with courtiers, the audience chamber was peaceful as Fernao sat opposite the Great King Bhuvenaka's desk. His black moustache quivering in response on the broad flat face, the ruler was obviously delighted at his new estate as a grandfather-to-be from the marriage of his daughter to Prince Vidiye.

'We hear that you are to become a father,' the Great King beamed.

'Indeed, Sire. My wife and I are blessed by God.' Fernao had selected his lead. 'Which brings me to another reason for my request for an audience. May I mention it?'

The bristly black eyebrows lifted. 'Pray proceed, Colonel.'

'You are well aware, Sire, of the concern of my sovereign lord, His Majesty the King Emperor of Portugal, His Excellency the Viceroy, Captain Oliveira and me personally regarding the recent division of the Great Kingdom of Lanka into three kingdoms. While we have no desire to interfere in the politics of your country, we admire your royal person so greatly as a just and benign ruler that we would have preferred to see you rule the entire, unified country.'

'So would we,' the Great King grumbled. A frown crossed his features for the first time. 'But as you know, we were the victim of other people's ambitions.'

'Precisely, Sire. Which is why I will take the liberty of making some suggestions to you. I hope you will pardon my doing so frankly. My own commander, Captain Oliveira, approves.'

'Please speak freely, Colonel.'

Noting the quickened interest in the beady eyes of the Great King and the tightening of the sides of the mouth, Fernao proceeded smoothly. 'It is essential to break up the power represented by the combined Kingdoms of Sita Waka and Raigam, since King Maya Dunne and King Raigam will always act in concert.'

'Certainly, but how can we achieve that?'

'I propose that as soon as your grandchild is born you apportion to the baby the southern region known as

Billigam Korle, which has hitherto been no-king's-land, declare it a sub-kingdom and give the baby suzerainty over it, with Prince Vidiye appointed its king.'

The black eyes of the Great King widened, then positively shone with delight. 'What a splendid idea. It is worthy of the finest statesman of Europe.' He began communing with himself. 'Yes, yes, Billigam lies between Raigam and the southernmost region, Ruhuna. The move you propose will prevent my two brothers from combining their contiguous territories and acquiring domination of the entire south at some future date.' A chuckle escaped him. 'Besides, this wedge, with the man they dislike, Prince Vidiye, as its ruler, will be a constant irritant to them. As for Prince Vidiye, he will know how to expand the Billigam territory once he is in command. And of course, bestowing the sub-kingdom on our grandson makes it all very proper, in keeping with those *charlithraya*, customary laws, which our brothers seem to worship!' His laugh crackled through the study, then the moon face clouded. 'But if they give us trouble?'

'You are assured of our support, Sire. I also have certain other plans I am formulating which I hope to present for Your Majesty's approval, and the ships and men to support you in this venture.'

The Great King nodded sagely. 'To make it effective, we would even forgo the added delight of having our two brothers experience its discomfiture for that much longer!'

Fernao returned to the fort well satisfied with the results of the audience. He would keep his proposed plan a secret even from Captain Oliveira and Julietta.

As soon as he reached the fort, he sent a messenger to Father Juan in Kandy, so that he could set in motion the other arm of his plan. Not only was the combination of King Maya Dunne and King Raigam in the south too powerful for safety, but the central sub-kingdom of Kandy was too weak because of its division. He had been sparring with Prince Kumara, offering the least support with which he could hope to win the prince's baptism. This had led to the despatch of weak contingents three times in succession, with the prince refusing to budge. He would now send Prince Kumara all the men necessary to support the prince's conversion and the ambitions of King Wira, which he, Fernao, knew would some day accrue to Prince Kumara's benefit. Since Prince Kumara had married Queen Anula yesterday, he would also have the backing of her Kiri Vella clan and could therefore establish a strong, relatively independent Kandy kingdom.

Fernao reasoned that with a strong sub-kingdom of Kandy and four main kingdoms of like power, Jaya, Sita Waka, Raigam and Billigam, he would be able to maintain a divide-and-rule policy.

He found himself exulting in the exercise of power, directly and covertly. At twenty-two, less than four years after he had arrived in Lanka, he was well on his way to wiping out Prince Tikiri.

CHAPTER TWO

Early on the morning of Saturday, 5 August 1525, Julietta was delivered of a baby girl. Standing at the window of the de Albergaria mansion outside Colombo, holding the frail wisp of sleeping humanity awkwardly in his arms, Fernao gazed across the room at Julietta, lying back on the pale pink cushions of the bed on which this miracle of life had been conceived. Her face was much fuller, almost plump, but her expression was one of dreamy contentment, of proud achievement, too. He had heard about these marvels of women, the luminous look of the bride, the winsome expression of the new mother. Now he had witnessed them both in the woman he loved and he thanked God silently for these precious gifts.

They named the infant Julietta Catherina, after Fernao's mother, Menika, after Julietta's adopted mother, de Albergaria. They agreed to call her Catherina.

Monday, 7 August 1525

Nine months after my meeting with Julietta in the dark grove on the Mutu Vella hill, it had become little more than a beautiful dream. Only an occasional sharp thrust of pain from some reminder, a memory at a lonely moment, a disappointment, some need, gave it reality. Fortunately, the pressure and pace of work, day in day out, had enabled me to cope with my loneliness and the sense of loss. But, if only . . . if only . . . persisted.

My father King Maya Dunne and I had barely seated ourselves on the lawn of our mansion in Sita Waka that evening for our regular conference, when we heard the thunder of hooves. A single horseman was approaching at a gallop. We could not see him because recently buildings had sprung up around the mansion's spacious lawns as it was converted to form the centre of the capital within the new fortress of Sita Waka. As soon as the lone rider on the tall bay took the bend in the road, however, we both identified him, riding erect in the saddle, cavalry fashion.

'Why, it's Lord Wickrama Sinha, riding alone!' my father exclaimed. 'He was not yet due back from his official visit to Jaya. He must have urgent news.'

We owed Lord Wickrama Sinha an immense debt of gratitude, for it was he who had organized the Council of Nobles in Jaya to vote against King Bhuvaneka's assumption of power, contrary to the latter's agreement with my father and Prince Raigam when they had deposed their father, the Great King Wijayo, by a display of military force which I had organized. King Wijayo had been mysteriously assassinated that same morning, alone, forsaken, since his Queen Anula, who had set the stage for his overthrow, had fled when she knew that her plan had failed. Using her great beauty and the power of sex, the young Queen had persuaded King Wijayo to adopt her son by her previous marriage, Prince Deva Raja, name him successor to the Great Kingdom with Queen Anula as Regent and plot the murder of the three brothers, the real heirs. These actions, abhorrent to our *charlithraya*, sacred traditions, had caused all of us to rally against the man who was my grandfather, on the understanding that the country would thereafter be divided into three kingdoms until the Council of Nobles determined the succession. But King Bhuvaneka and Prince Vidiye had breached this trust with Portuguese artillery and muskets standing by to support the betrayal. Lord Wickrama Sinha's dramatic assembling of the Council of Nobles who had attended King Wijayo's cremation in Jaya and his brilliant strategy at the meeting finally created the three kingdoms, blunting King Bhuvaneka's betrayal.

So I had heartily approved when my father appointed Lord Wickrama his Chief Minister and Army commander six months before. In the short period that followed, the lord had already proved his worth.

Grooms, clad in our family livery of red and white, rushed up. One of them held the horse's head while Lord Wickrama Sinha dismounted. Though his white pantaloons and tunic were covered with dust and stained with sweat, Wickrama Sinha somehow retained his lean elegance as he strode towards us and gave my father smiling obeisance. 'I bring news of great moment, Sire!' he announced. 'I have ridden night and day to bring it to you personally.'

'It can wait until you have sat down and taken some refreshment.' As usual, my father was very cool and self-possessed.

A man hurried out of the mansion bearing an easy chair, while another came swiftly forward and waited for the lord to sit down before inquiring whether he would like a cup of the hot drink my father and I had been sipping.

This was a black liquid with a delightfully strong aroma brought from the Arabi lands, which, taken with honey, is both delicious and stimulating. The Arabis call it *copi*. They say it is prepared by roasting and grinding the berries of a certain bush growing in their hot climate. They had been drinking it for over a hundred years, though it had only recently been introduced to our part of the world by the Mouro traders, who did not use it for trade but for their private enjoyment and that of kings. We chatted idly until the drink was brought.

Lord Wickrama Sinha took a sip of *copi*. 'Ah, delicious and reviving!' he exclaimed. 'I understand that this has been banned in Europe by the Popes as the Infidel Drink.'

'Naturally!' my father retorted drily. '*Copi* would compete with wine and the Papacy has a flair for banning

29

anything that might interfere with the trade of its sovereign states regardless of the enjoyment of its flock. Besides, any institution that offers instant heaven must surely resort to creating instant sin, else there will be no takers for the offer.'

Lord Wickrama Sinha threw back his head and laughed. 'Which brings me to my first item of news.' He carefully placed his cup on the centre table, leaned back, stretched with a kind of creak of satisfaction. 'Prince Kumara and several Kandyan nobles have been baptized into the Catholic faith.'

'We were expecting that, but what do you think it portends?' My father lifted thick black eyebrows questioningly.

Wickrama Sinha looked grim. 'It means that after several stops and starts, caused by the white-skinned *parangi* trying to get the most by giving least, two companies of *parangi* infantry and a troop of cannon are now in the hill capital at the disposal of King Wira.'

'Ah, the devil's work has started.' My father was speaking almost to himself.

'Very much according to plan, I would say,' Lord Wickrama Sinha responded. 'All this is part of the timed programme which commenced with the marriage of Prince Kumara and Queen Anula. I doubt that the genius behind the moves is King Wira's. It is Prince Kumara who is the master of timing. Baptism added to the marriage will give him the double strength for which he has obviously planned, not for his father the king but for his personal benefit.'

'King Wira's troops can now march against the sub-kings of Pera, Gampola and Hangura?'

'They have already taken over Pera without a single *parangi* musket being fired. After all, the sub-king was King Wira's close relation and near lackey. I suppose King

30

Wira's army will head for Gampola next. But I have other news too, of even greater concern.'

My father leaned alertly forward in his chair, his dark eyes keen. Infected by his mood, I tensed.

'Prince Vidiye has had a baby boy by his wife, your niece, the daughter of the Great King Automatic Bhuvaneka Bahu! They have named the child Dharma Pala. Unfortunately, the lady died at childbirth.'

'Ibey Maha Raja, the Great King Automatic,' was the mock title we had bestowed on my uncle in Jaya, because he had the title without the domains or the power. While my father and I were shocked at the news of the daughter's death, our glance at each other acknowledged our recognition that a male grandson of the Great King added further complications to the political situation.

Then came the cannonball. 'In honour of the event,' Lord Wickrama Sinha continued, 'the Great King has granted suzerainty over the Billigam Korle region to the newborn prince. His father, Prince Vidiye, will rule it with the title of sub-king. He leaves for Billigam with an army soon.'

I grunted with rage, but my father still showed no visible emotion, merely grew thoughtful. The Billigam region lay south of Raigam and extended from the Gin River to the Walawe River. It included the seaports of Galle and Matara. 'This places King Raigam like an areca nut between the twin blades of the cutter, Jaya on one side, Billigam on the other!' I burst forth. 'We cannot tolerate it.'

'Nor we will, Prince,' King Maya Dunne assured me quietly. 'Nor we will.' He turned towards Wickrama Sinha again. 'Do you know what force Prince . . . er . . . King Vidiye will take with him?'

'Three thousand infantry and bowmen, one thousand cavalry and thirty elephants, Sire. They will avoid the Raigam lands, go to Galle by sea in *parangi* ships, land there and join up with a force of five thousand men which

Lord Samara Kon, our sworn enemy in the south, is raising. The *parangi* are obviously behind this plan and will support it to the hilt.' He indicated the pocket of his tunic with a sardonic smile. 'I have all the details of the move here.'

'Trust you!' my father exclaimed appreciatively. 'Such a large force supplemented by Lord Samara Kon's five thousand men will pose an immediate threat to King Raigam and to us. A good thing our gunsmith Palitha has produced one hundred muskets at last.' He tapped the arm of his chair with a forefinger, a sign that he was thinking fast. Lord Samara Kon, one of the leaders of the south and a liege-man of the Great King, was indeed a sworn enemy of my father and King Raigam.

When my father's jaw set, I knew he had come to a decision. 'You and Prince Tikiri shall leave tonight with an expeditionary force against Lord Samara Kon. We must prevent his link-up with Prince Vidiye at all costs. Summon your commanders for a planning session immediately.'

'First, I have one more item of news to report, Sire.' Lord Wickrama Sinha darted such a strange glance at me that it made my stomach clench instinctively. 'Two days ago, Colonel de Albergaria's wife, the Lady Julietta, formerly of the Jaya court, was delivered of a baby girl.'

I had known that Juli was pregnant, but my heart still cried out in anguish, for now she was bound to her husband for ever.

Tuesday, 8 August 1525

The baby was only three days old, but Fernao already found himself looking forward to returning home after work, so he could gaze at the sleeping child with Julietta beside him, watch the baby's eyes crinkle up at the light when it awoke, feel contentment from the sense of family.

This afternoon, when the discussions with Captain Oliveira and the Mouro trader Abdul Raschid were over, he glanced impatiently at the clock hanging on the wall behind Captain Oliveira's desk in the fort. The short arm pointed to four, the long arm to twelve, so it was four of the clock, as the new phrase described it.

Though six feet tall himself, Fernao's long legs made him seem shorter when he sat down, so he felt dwarfed by the other two men in that small office. The afternoon was warm and all three of them were sweating, the captain and the trader more so because of their bulk. It was rather odd, seeing the two shiny bald heads opposite each other across the desk! Outside, the deserted parade ground was silent, the men being at siesta, probably lying bare-bodied on their bunks or in their hammocks, grumbling at the heat. Within the office, the silence that precedes the breaking up of a conference was interrupted by the loud ticking of the clock.

'My lord, the colonel has been terribly strict and ruthless with us these past months.' Abdul Raschid broke the silence in the high-pitched tones which made Fernao think of him as a eunuch, mopped the sweat on his pudgy face with a red linen square. The sides of his small eyes had puckered playfully to rob his words of offence. 'We have had to spend so much money to get things done in record time that we are going to take a loss on this transaction.'

'You Mouro buggers will never lose on any transaction, not even your foreskins!' Captain Oliveira retorted with his customary coarseness. 'As for our colonel, he has changed since . . . er . . .' Captain Oliveira hesitated, then obviously decided to change tack, 'the responsibility became his. If he has been cruel to you, it is in order to be kind.'

'I wish the colonel had not been so kind then,' Abdul Raschid responded, his chubby face creasing. He held out sweaty palms together in mock supplication. 'Less kindness please, my lord, I beg you.'

33

Fernao smiled. 'I have had to push you all beyond the limit to assure our common goals,' he stated. 'You had your direct expenses; we had a tremendous overhead, which required cash flowing in as soon as possible to justify it. This cannot change, because time costs us as much money as your factories and goods. So if we make time together we also make money!' He nodded at the trader, wiped his face with the linen square that was already in his lap.

'Of course, of course, but it is always we traders who suffer most, because, unlike kings, we have to depend on our own resources.'

'The colonel has done a fine job,' Captain Oliveira cut in. 'And you won't get a fucking *cruzado* more out of us, if that's what you're whining for. And if you are hinting that the colonel has treated you differently because you are traders, you are bloody well wrong. His treatment of King Wira and Prince Kumara has been just as firm.'

'I know, lord. We hear the gossip in the market place. Three times the colonel sent his troops by sea and overland to Kandy and three times he withdrew them. If a humble trader may inquire, why?'

'Because the royal personages did not keep their royal promises on which we had agreed to send our royal troops,' Fernao replied. He did not wish to refer to the bargaining he had done.

'Ah yes. I have heard tell. And it was only when Prince Kumara and the nobles were finally baptized, that fourth time, that the troops remained. Now they have helped King Wira take the sub-kingdom of Pera, no? Where next? Gampola?'

'That is our secret,' Fernao rejoined quickly.

'But what does the Great King think about all this? Abdul Raschid inquired.

'The Great King only thinks what we fucking tell him to think,' Captain Oliveira burst forth.

'I heard that your baby is very fair-skinned,' Abdul Raschid volunteered, changing the subject, turning to Fernao.

'Yes indeed,' Fernao responded heartily. 'And she looks enchanting in the pink silk-lined cradle you sent as a gift, for which my wife and I thank you again.'

'All the way from Persia, lord,' Abdul Raschid exclaimed proudly. 'The edge bordered with gold. Sent for as soon as we had the news of *a senhora's* pregnancy, because of the respect and admiration and . . . and . . .' He floundered. 'Everything else.'

Fernao realized with wonder that Abdul Raschid had nearly said 'affection' and was touched for a brief moment. There was some heart beneath the trader's fat after all.

'My wife and I hope you have a good servant for the child,' Abdul Raschid continued.

'Oh yes!' Fernao was emphatic. 'Her name is Maria. She is a widow of Goanese descent. Her husband was a Sinhala trader. She speaks Goanese, Sinhala and Portuguese. Her two children, both girls, have grown up and returned to Goa as the wives of two other traders from there. She is a clean, kindly person, well used to our ways, and she already seems to love the baby. We are very lucky to have found her.'

'Allah only sends such luck to those whom He loves,' Abdul Raschid asserted. 'You have a wonderful lady and a fine nursery governess.'

'Don't forget the beautiful baby!' Fernao reminded him.

Wednesday, 9 August 1525

On the route to Gampola, twelve miles east of Kandy, that same night, Prince Kumara's blood seemed to sparkle in his veins as he rode his tall chestnut on muffled hooves through the darkness, his men following.

So much had happened during the past year. His beloved

mistress, Manel, had died suddenly of a strange stomach disease, taking her unborn child with her. His marriage to Queen Anula had been a tremendous compensation. Then came the moves and counter-moves between himself and the *parangi* Colonel de Albergaria, who had three times sent inadequate forces in the hope of achieving his baptism as a Catholic as cheaply as possible. Only when the fourth attempt brought a large enough contingent had he finally accepted baptism. Pera was immediately annexed to the Kandy kingdom, without a single *parangi* musket-shot being fired. Now, here he was, on the way to taking Gampola.

Even excitement at the battle ahead, the first in his life, could not prevent recall of his wife. He had slept with her every night since their wedding, but had kept away from her bedchamber for the past three days, because he wanted to be physically fit and mentally alert for the military operation. This was a custom followed by warriors in certain warlike societies, he knew.

'You do not love us any longer,' she had complained at dinner last night, the ready tears in her eyes.

'It is because I love you that I want to return from this mission.'

'You do not want to fuck us any longer. Already we have become just worn old clothes to you, which you wish to shed.'

'On the contrary, it is because I want to take your clothes off and lie with you to exhaustion that I want to make sure of returning.'

'We have lost our power to hold you.' A slender hand reached out to fondle his genitals.

'You can see that you have lost none of your power, madam.' He was referring to his instant, rock-stiff erection.

'You are a cad!'

'How else can I show gallantry to such a lusty woman?'

'Good. We lust for you. Be gallant right here and now!'

36

Some deep-rooted instinct for survival had held him firm to his resolve. He did indeed want desperately to return to her, victorious.

He smiled tenderly as his mind went back further to their wedding night. He remembered the stinging slap he had given his wife, not to be brutal, but to bring her to her senses. Their love-making had then become perfect.

It's strange how everything fell into place after I met Anula, he reflected, even Manel's death. The courtesan Manel had been a source of irritation to Anula, he knew, and would have been a serious impediment to his marriage and ambitions; but he had loved Manel in his own way and he still secretly mourned her. She had been the one person in the world who put him before all else, even herself, something of which his wife was incapable. He shrugged as he rode on, but deep inside him, knew he could not shrug off the loss of such a unique human being as Manel, the courtesan.

He sloughed off the memories, returned to the present. The idea of capturing the Gampola capital in a single night raid, instead of by a formal invasion involving inevitable battles, had been his. King Wira, his father, had readily agreed.

The old windbag has no stomach for leading men into action, Prince Kumara thought contemptuously. It's all to the good. I am the Catholic; I am the man who can expect loyalty from the army and from my wife's clansmen; let me also be the one to achieve all the glory. The risk of death, of being maimed for life, was always there, as Queen Anula had fearfully reminded him, but the price of honour is death or the threat of death, as he had retorted.

Here he was leading his raiding party of five hundred fully armed men, the elite army group he had created six months ago. All of them were dressed, like himself, in black. They were following a route he had carefully scouted and with which he had made his five trusted company commanders familiar by taking them over the ground only the previous night. Until these five company commanders issued their orders at dusk, the men had thought their emergency alert was for a night exercise. The need for security was especially vital in the hill-country areas, where secrets travelled faster, it was said, than a young man passing urine!

The entire contingent had proceeded independently in small groups along the Maha Veli Ganga, the Great Sand River, until they came to Pera, where they had crossed the river and met at their assembly point. Here, Prince Kumara had awaited them with the *parangi* detachment, a company of mounted musketeers and a section of cannon. The *parangi* alone had been privy to the proposed action. The wheels of the cannon had been oiled, the rims covered with sacking, to deaden the sounds of their travel.

The column, led by Prince Kumara, included the entire elite army group. A company of one hundred cavalry rode ahead of the *parangi* musketeers, behind whom was another company of cavalry, with the troop of cannon following. Then came two companies of bowmen, each of one hundred, and a company of cavalry in the rear. Two of the company commanders rode ahead to act as scouts and guides.

The route Prince Kumara selected avoided the cultivated lowlands of the valley on either side of the river and kept to the forested hills south of it. This way, they managed to avoid observation, except by a wild pig that snorted and leapt away at their approach and unidentified small animals, probably hare, mouse-deer and rodents, that kept scurrying away through the undergrowth.

It was time to concentrate totally on the objective. Prince Kumara looked up at the sky, heavily overcast, with not a single star visible. The night was cool, but the closeness of the jungle had caused him to sweat so much beneath his leather corselet and thigh greaves, gifts from the *parangi*, that he could not escape the occasional whiff of his own odour. Disgusting.

He thought again of Anula, his wife, lying scented on her bed, and knew a moment of lust. Would his father, King Wira, take advantage of his absence to try and bed the queen?

A surge of jealous anger spouted within the prince. By the devas, I'll carve both his pig-eyes out, rip open his pot belly and eat his liver if he dares lay a hand on her. Then he remembered that he had earned fidelity from her. She would know how to handle the son-of-a-bitch. It amused him to think of his royal grandmother, long dead, as a bitch. Even his own mother had been a Maya Dunne bitch! God rest both their souls, he thought, with spurious Christian piety, and nearly laughed aloud.

One of the horses behind him tripped on a stone, stumbled, snorted. Its rider cursed softly. The rich, cloying scent of ripe *durian* fruit told him they were close to the edge of the jungle, where the cultivated lands began about two miles from the capital. This was the danger zone.

CHAPTER THREE.

Wednesday, 9 August 1525

Once they left the protective cover of the jungle, the only secrecy available would be that of a sleeping countryside. Prince Kumara raised his hand, brought his mount to a halt. He sensed the long column behind him following suit. Two minutes passed, during which the creak of crickets registered in his ears, punctured by the howl of a jackal from a distant mountain top. The two scouts loomed in front of him, visible only as silhouettes. They reined in their horses, their eyes gleamed in the gloom.

'The villagers are asleep and the township is in darkness, lord,' one of the men reported softly. 'All is well.'

'Rejoin your companies,' Prince Kumara directed. He half-turned in his saddle towards the leading commander, the creak of leather audible in the silence. 'Pass the word to remove the muffles.'

Quiet orders started issuing through the darkness. Two grooms came up and started undoing the sacking wrapped around Prince Kumara's horse's hooves.

Ten minutes later, he made the highway, paused and allowed the entire column to fall into line along it.

The capital of Gampola was no more than a township, with the royal palace located in the citadel, a kind of fortress which had been constructed behind earthworks where the river veered from its mountain source as it proceeded downstream. The defences, therefore, ran along the side of the river, the entrance to the fortress being over a bridge which led straight to a single set of gates. The earthworks continued all round the fortress, but it was on the flat lands beyond that the Gampola king had begun assembling his army, in anticipation of trouble from

Kandy. King Wira's wife had been the Gampola king's sister. It was on this lady's death that King Wira had married Prince Kumara's mother, King Maya Dunne's half-sister.

Prince Kumara drew his sword, pointed in the direction of the capital as he eased his horse forward. He broke into a canter, the column following. The clatter of hooves and the thump and rattle of cannon soon caused the air to judder.

The earthworks of the fortress loomed ahead, a huge, squat patch rising above the river. Prince Kumara slowed his mount to a trot, a walk, reined in by the entrance to the bridge. Their approach had been heard, for lights began to prickle the higher ground at the centre of the fortress where the palace was located.

Prince Kumara watched his cannon line up facing the gates, the cavalry deploying in columns of three behind the big guns and the bowmen taking up positions commanding the earthworks. They moved with the ease of practice from mock-ups on the parade grounds. He felt a flash of pride at the way the whole operation was being carried out, hoped the *parangi* officers would admire his skill.

Heads began to appear on the earthworks, dark blobs beneath *chulu*, torchlights held up in vain attempts to pierce the gloom. Stupid men, Prince Kumara thought. They are merely offering themselves as targets.

The mounted *parangi* musketeers formed up behind him.

The tall *parangi* artillery captain, clad in iron helmet and breastplate, stepped forward. 'Aim!' he quietly commanded.

The squeak and grinding of wheels followed.

'Prepare to fire!'

'Fire!'

Eight flashes were followed by a thunderous roar, in which the whoosh of the cannonballs was barely heard.

Wheels squeaked with the backfire. Prince Kumara's ears sang. Smoke puffed, shoving the stink of burnt gunpowder into the air. The tremendous crash of cannonballs against the wooden gates rolled across the river. Simultaneously, a dark flight of arrows arched across the sky like slanting rain.

The *parangi* marksmanship was perfect. Prince Kumara's heart sang at seeing patches of light inside the fort, through the shattered gates. Screams from the earthworks told of the equal skill of his bowmen.

'Prepare to advance!' the prince bellowed. He pointed his sword in the direction of the fortress gates. 'Ad . . . va . . . nce!'

His mount leapt forward. The thirty mounted *parangi* musketeers followed, screaming, the cavalrymen behind them silent, as they had been trained to be. They clattered wildly over the wooden bridge. The shattered gates loomed up.

Bending low, Prince Kumara directed his mount through a gap. When he straightened up, he found himself in the courtyard. The main street led directly to the palace, the two side streets serving the battlements. Enemy sentries turned and fled at their approach. The prince laughed aloud, reined in his mount. Two of the musketeers had swung off their horses and were opening what was left of the gates. The rest of the musketeers rode inside, dismounted, lined up facing the main street. Armed men came rushing down the street towards them. Prince Kumaru nudged his horse back to the lee of the earthworks.

'Prepare to fire!'

The prince sent a fervent prayer, he did not know to whom, for speed. The running enemy were only twenty paces from him. His blood ran cold.

'Fire!'

The muskets flashed. His ears sang again. The charging enemy went down like rice-stalks before the reaper's scythe. Screams of pain arose. A dark figure clutched vainly at spilling guts before collapsing. The enemy in the rear faltered.

'Cha . . . a . . . rge!' Prince Kumara roared.

His cavalry pounded through the open gates, the side columns fanning left and right. As the centre column made for the palace, Prince Kumara shot ahead of it, charged down the central avenue directly towards the palace. A towering guard, spear poised for a throw, stood defiantly in his path. He set his horse at the huge bulk, swerved at the last moment, bending low. The spear whizzed harmlessly by him. A wild exhilaration seized him. He swerved back, his sword sweeping sideways. A mighty stroke. The blade struck bone and gristle. The contact jarred up his arm so fiercely that he thought it would be wrenched at the shoulder. Then he was past, the sword free, a weight in his hand again. His first kill and it had been perfect. He wished that Anula could have seen him. He cried aloud in wild exultation. Dimly, he remembered a civilized, cold-blooded prince.

Another volley of musket fire reached his pounding ears. More dark blobs fell, screaming. The enemy turned and fled.

Prince Kumara thundered along the avenue of torches that lit the entrance to the palace. He ground to a stop before the closed entrance doors. There were lights in several open windows, anxious silhouettes of people peered out. He swung off his horse, tossed the reins to the two ever-present grooms who had raced behind him. The courtyard resounded with the clatter of hooves. As planned and practised, the musketeers lined up around the courtyard. Breathing deeply, the prince strode up to the brown teakwood doors, rapped sharply on them with the hilt of his sword.

'Open up in the name of the Great King of Kandy!' he shouted.

He heard the scrape of bars being moved, the squeak of heavy bolts. He stepped aside in case of sudden attack. Sword ready, he waited in silence.

The doors swung slowly open. Uniformed soldiers with drawn swords packed the entrance foyer. The palace guard, grim, determined men, were ready to die for their master.

Wednesday, 9 August 1525

Galle lay about fifty miles south-west of Sita Waka. The staging area we had selected for my cavalry regiment and our accompanying baggage train before the assault on Lord Samara Kon's forces was a swampy plain known as Habara, lying inland and a few miles south of the port where the *parangi* first landed in the year 1505. The site had been well chosen, for we had intelligence on the way that the enemy were gathering on the great *maidan* north of the Galle harbour.

We force-marched and reached the staging area at dusk. My men immediately commenced setting up bivouacs and field kitchens for the night within an all-round defence perimeter, while reconnaissance patrols punched out in four directions to check on possible enemy activity. Our horses were unsaddled and rubbed down, wood was gathered for the campfires. As darkness fell, the plain was scattered with red-gold glows of flickering flames. Curls of smoke brought the pleasant smell of burning wood, easing the dank, heavy stink of coconut husks rotting in trenches, part of the coir-rope-making industry of the region.

The entire village had turned out to gawk at us from outside the perimeter and ask questions of the patrolling sentries. The village headman begged to see me when he learned my rank. He turned out to be a small, fat man with a protruding stomach and a circular comb on his silver and black hair. I knew as soon as I saw him that he was one of Lord Samara Kon's men and that he would lose no time informing his master of our presence and our strength.

After the headman left, I removed my leather armour and made the rounds of the encampment to ensure that the men were comfortably settled. I then returned to the solitary tree at the centre of the camp where my aide, Captain Wickram, had set up headquarters. The captain was exercising beside a merrily blazing campfire to ease the stiffness of his joints from having been in the saddle almost continuously for two days. I joined him briefly in his bending and stretching. We both smelled high from riding in our leather armour!

We finished our exercising, sat on the grass, palms on the ground, legs outstretched. Firelight flickering on our faces made the whole situation so peaceful that it took an effort to realize that battle and death lay ahead on the morrow.

'I wonder why Lord Wickrama Sinha's messengers haven't arrived as yet.' Captain Wickram echoed the question in my mind.

'They should have got here before us,' I responded.

Knowing that Lord Samara Kon's troops were converging on Galle to join King Vidiye's force when it arrived by sea, our plan had been to move our own forces to Galle in two columns. My cavalry regiment of one thousand men, with the one hundred musketeers and our baggage train, had taken the most direct route from Sita Waka, through the forested mountains and down into the flatlands so as to approach Galle from the south. Lord Wickrama Sinha's two thousand infantrymen, five hundred bowmen and fifty musketeers took the southern pass through the mountains. They were to commandeer rafts at the source of the Gin River, float down to the mouth of the river about three miles along the coast from Galle and attack Lord Samara Kon's men from the north.

'What will we do if Lord Wickrama Sinha doesn't arrive in time, Prince?' Captain Wickram inquired.

'Attack alone.'

He cocked an eyebrow at me. 'We shall be heavily outnumbered. And we have no infantry or bowmen.'

'We had best get used to fighting against odds,' I retorted grimly. 'At least we have the musketeers.'

Namothassa bagavatho arahato . . . The words of the chant that commences the taking of *pan-sil*, the five precepts, wafted through the night air. Another sharp contrast with our warlike intent. The more devout of the men had gathered around a nearby campfire. They were obviously preparing themselves for tomorrow, when some of them would lie in untimely death. Beyond, a dome-shaped white *dagoba* was etched towards the west, the direction in which we would ride before dawn. Its pinnacle and spire thrust upwards to a night sky burnished by low clouds, an invitation to holiness and peace. *Anicca, dhukka, anatta,* impermanence, sorrow, intangibility.

I shivered as a gust of wind cloaked me with the warmth of the campfire.

Wednesday, 9 August 1525

The palace guard, determined men in leather corselets, packed closely in line, stood silently in the foyer, spears poised for throwing. Prince Kumara stepped well away from the doorway. The enemy were led by a giant captain in the centre of the group. Prince Kumara recognized the bristling beard. This was Captain Ratwatte. The tall, handsome man to his right with enormous shoulders was Ehelepola. The torches in the courtyard hissed before a gust of wind.

'Fire!'

Prince Kumara could not count the flashes, but the rattle of the muskets across the confines of the courtyard was deafening. He watched the results of the volley with curious detachment. His blood was up and the fight had been too brief. The tight line of men in the foyer sagged and collapsed, a mess of bloodied fronts and shattered limbs. Groans and curses echoed through the singing in his ears. Ratwatte and Ehelepola lay askew, as if smitten by an avalanche.

As the stench of burnt gunpowder from the volley was wafted to Prince Kumara's nostrils, the command resounded again. 'Fire!' More men fell; others tried to scramble away, some on hands and knees, some dragging maimed bodies.

A great elation filled Prince Kumara, and a mad urge to rush in with drawn sword, to slash away at enemy bodies, for the foyer was suddenly empty, save for the sprawled corpses and groaning wounded.

Bloodied sword still in his hand, Prince Kumara strode to the doorway, paused to look at the men on the blood-soaked floor. Captain Ratwatte suddenly half-rose, clutching a gaping red wound in his stomach, holding back his guts. His eyes were glazing over, but they caught Prince Kumara's figure in the entrance, identified him briefly. The trembling lips formed the words, 'Foul traitor!' Then the captain slowly keeled over in death.

'What pariah dogs dare desecrate our palace and our royal home?' The words, uttered in stentorian tones, slashed through the clatter of the attackers rushing into the building.

Prince Kumara glanced up in the direction of the speaker. The King of Gampola stood on the landing at the top of the stairs, a couple of scared attendants hovering behind him. He was a tall, well-proportioned man, fair of skin, with dark eyes and silver-grey hair and moustache. Balancing on feet spread well apart, arms akimbo, he was fully dressed in a white ballooning *dhoti*, the eighteen yards of cloth assembled at the waist to give him the *thalasthani* worthy-look, and a black tunic waistcoat embroidered in silver and gold. He cut such an imposing figure that the men behind Prince Kumara hesitated.

Prince Kumara was, however, in no mood to give ground before someone else's majesty. 'There is only one pariah dog here,' he shouted back. 'And it is he who desecrates this palace and even his own person.'

The king's upper lip curled in scorn. 'On the contrary, nephew – for we now see that it is indeed you in fancy dress! – we understand you are the dog who wags his tail at his new masters, the *parangi*, a race of men who do not wash their defecation, but merely wipe it.' He scornfully sniffed the air. 'The odour emanating from all of you tells us that you are indeed worthy dogs of your masters. Stop your play-acting and begone now.' He shook his head sadly, turned on his heel and started walking away.

With a cry of rage, Prince Kumara sprinted up the stairs in pursuit. He felt the movement of air, heard the whoosh, then the thwack of impact and halted. A great gasp escaped the king. He staggered forward, groaned once. He paused in his stride, a spear quivering in his back.

Prince Kumara turned, looked down at the crowded foyer. The man who had thrown the spear was a tall, swarthy Kandyan noble. His grin through a black beard was devilish with anger. 'No man calls me a dog and lives!' he shouted.

A crash on the landing made Prince Kumara swing back sharply. The king lay sprawled on the wooden floor, an untidy heap where once had stood a gallant man. The sight brought immediate reason back to the prince. I cannot blame you, my comrade, for what you did to the king, he thought, for I was ready to do it, too. Yet the *devas* saved me from stabbing the Gampola ruler in the back. I would readily have done so, but how could I then have had the respect and support of the people of a country that I expect to unite under my rule?

48

The heat of battle clothed his body, but Prince Kumara felt a shiver run through him.

Thursday, 10 August 1525

When Lord Wickrama Sinha's messengers did not arrive by the commencement of the pre-dawn watch, I gave orders for our group to strike camp and move to the attack.

After a forced march, the first rays of sunlight creeping behind us over the tops of the coconut groves and the harbour bazaar buildings caught us moving in orderly fashion to take up positions facing our enemy. Lord Samara Kon's men were assuming offensive positions to the blare of their trumpets and conch shells. As I had expected, he had decided to give us battle on the green *maidan*, expecting to use his vastly superior numbers to good effect. The spreading ranks of brawny pikemen now lining the *maidan* were like a moat with spikes somehow turned horizontally in our direction. Masses of infantry, cavalry and bowmen were already in position. Hardly a welcoming party!

I glowed with pride as I observed my regiment moving with unerring smoothness and precision, like the well-oiled wheels of a rice mill.

I saw Lord Samara Kon, standing on a mound, towering over his troops, and I suddenly had the strangest reaction. The host of five thousand men before me, their weapons, the aura of kill that emanated from them, were concentrated in one single person, their giant leader. I had met him only once before, several years ago. I didn't like him then. I hated him now. I hated him with a passionate, all-consuming hatred that found expression in such a crazed desire to kill him that my nostrils dilated, my breath caught and my body trembled.

When my troops were in position, I eased my black war-horse, Rama, forward to the head of the centre group of cavalrymen, who were spread out in three lines, one behind the other. An aide rode up and handed me a lance, the pennant carrying our family colours, red and white. The blare of our trumpets immediately slashed through the screams of the enemy champions, sending a flock of crows soaring into the pale blue sky. The enemy replied with fierce yells of defiance, but my own men were trained to silence. They left it to lesser breeds to shake away fear and generate valour with curses and cries.

Our drums gave a single roll. The lines of musketeers and their targe-bearers jerked and commenced advancing steadily towards the enemy. On a sudden hush, I heard a great twang as of a single mighty bow-string. A tremendous flight of arrows arced from the enemy ranks, patterned through the blue sky, whooshed at my advancing men. Great thwacks resounded against the shields. The two targe-bearers directly ahead of me cried out, stumbled and fell. I could not see the arrows that got them. Our advancing musketeers never faltered, but I wished Lord Wickrama Sinha would arrive with our own bowmen to give us cover.

The enemy trumpets broke out, the battlefield became a din. Our musketeers halted, aimed and fired, the reports of their weapons shattering through the welter of sound. Three enemy champions fell, and many pikemen, some clutching bloody wounds. Merciless, exhilarated, I watched the front rank of our musketeers reloading. A second volley of enemy arrows arced into the sky. The stink of burnt gunpowder assailed my nostrils. Strangely, incongruously, in a few moments of silence, I heard the crash of surf.

Then, 'Fire!'

As the second volley of musketfire rattled, the enemy front rank was shattered, many crying in agony. I heard sharp orders from their commanders to advance. Their ranks seemed to consolidate, then began a surge towards us. I urged Rama forward so that all my lines of cavalry could see me. I raised my lance aloft, its red and white pennant fluttering. I couched my lance and dug my heels into Rama's flanks. He leapt forward like a bolt from a catapult.

'Cha ... ar ... ge!' I screamed the words as the wind started whipping my face.

'Cha ... ar ... ge!' my men echoed, as we broke through our musketeers and thundered across the green grass.

Through gaps in their pikemen's ranks, I saw the enemy infantry marching steadily forward ... a lean, tall, dark-skinned man brandished a spear, the face of a beardless youth was set in a bestial snarl. I hurled Rama dead centre to the enemy. Then we were on them. My lance pierced a pot-belly, the head above it jerked violently. The man went 'Hu ... unh!' then his face burst into sweat. His eyes bulged before he was flung aside by my momentum. I let go the lance to avoid being dragged with it.

My blood was up. I drew my sword and charged into the wall of men before me. A wide, mowing slash severed a bull neck, a backward sweep bit deep into a leather corselet, spun the soldier against his comrades. I hacked my way through the human mass by sheer ferocity. Rama shared my madness, pounding on, trampling bodies that scrambled to get away from his hooves. I saw fearful eyes, laughed at the spears flung against me, their range too close to be effective. This is the way of the invincible in battle, I thought, then took a sharp spear jab in my left thigh. Barely noticing the pain, I swung my sword back over Rama's neck, crossing it over my left hand in one mighty stroke, smiting the head of the man who had struck me, then viciously tore my sword loose from his cloven skull.

Rama began losing his momentum. It was time to wheel away from the engagement, join the rest of the cavalry group and return to our positions, so our next rank could make its charge while we seized new lances for a second

51

charge. Suddenly I knew that I simply would not turn around. Some tremendous compulsion stronger than me had taken over, forcing me onwards to find Lord Samara Kon. All I wanted to do was to savage . . . kill, thrust . . . kill, slash . . . kill . . . until I got to him.

Then it was too late to turn back anyhow. I was surrounded by a host of angry men, desperate men, terrified men, screaming, cursing, brandishing their weapons, trying to get at me. Clutching hands reached out to grab my legs. I kicked away, realized that, mounted, I was a target for too many, my power to strike limited. I swept a leg over the saddle, dismounted into the mêlée, laying about me so fiercely with my sword that men leapt out of my way like rabbits, only to be pushed back by the crush of their own comrades. I was alone now, wielding my sword like a scythe, a space cleared around me, a dozen slashed or cloven men fallen. Bearded warriors, beardless boys, sweat-strewn skins, terrified eyes. Not people. Not Sinhala fellow-countrymen. Just the enemy.

Men quailed and cowered before my ferocity. In seconds, the clear space around me widened. Miraculously, Rama had followed me, protecting my rear. Slipping on bodies, I cut and chopped a passage over blood-stained grass in the direction of that mound, heading inexorably towards my target.

'He's a *mara yakka*, a death-dealing devil!' . . .

'I've had enough!' . . .

'Get out of the way!' . . .

The words penetrated a roaring in my ears. The mass of enemy now appeared through a red blood-haze. Sweat drops clung to my eyelashes. But I was invincible. 'I shall eat your leader's liver!' I screamed through bared teeth. A great animal roar escaped me. I felt the terror of those around me and knowledge flashed across my mind.

I am Sinha, the lion, invincible.

Suddenly the crowd in front of me parted, like mud

52

before a plough. Someone shouted, 'Make way for Lord Samara Kon!'

Was this a battlefield or a court? Everyone paused except for the giant swaggering towards me, a massive sword in one hand, shield in the other. He had obviously dismounted to take me on in single combat. I had only my sword.

He halted within six paces of me. He was fully eight inches taller than me and twice my girth, but I had eyes only for the head above his bull-neck, observed his wide-boned face, the black beard, the fierce bloodshot gaze. A single thought struck me: I shall send this head to my father.

Lord Samara Kon jabbed the point of his sword on to the green grass. 'How dare you invade our territory, *para balla*, accursed dog?' he snarled. His voice was deep, strong as his huge body.

Suddenly the hot rage left me, to be replaced by a cold anger. Breeding, contempt for this upstart, took over. 'There are no dogs on this battlefield,' I retorted. 'You face a royal horse, Rama, and a royal prince, Tikiri Bandara, son of King Maya Dunne, by whose command I have come to take over your land and rid it of the jackals banding into a pack against us.'

His eyes flamed with anger. 'I shall chop you to pieces and feed you to the jackals of the Deniya jungles!' he bellowed.

I eyed him scornfully. 'Know before you die that I intend sending your jackal head to King Maya Dunne as a gift,' I quietly stated.

One moment he stood before me with hate-filled eyes. The next he was on me in a single bound, the mighty sword upraised to cleave me in two. His speed was incredible for such a huge man. I leapt aside twisting, felt the wind of his sword slashing past my face. He arrested the blow, lashed sideways before I could recover. The flat

53

of his blade slammed violently against my left arm, sent me sprawling on the ground.

With a roar of triumph, he spun towards me, raising his sword aloft.

CHAPTER FOUR
Thursday, 10 August 1525

With Prince Vidiye and his expeditionary force safely on their way to Galle, packed into the *nao* like a shoal of small fish, Fernao's horizon was clear but for one factor. He had failed to take into account the economic results of the political forces he had let loose. Firstly, Prince Vidiye had insisted that all local profits from trade channelled through the ports of Galle and Matara should accrue to his Treasury as King of Billigam Korle. Secondly, the Great King had blandly indicated that he would need a similar monopoly of trade going through the ports of Colombo and Negombo, seventeen miles north, in order to support the expenses of the campaign which he had undertaken at Fernao's behest.

King Wijaya had tried to enforce a similar plan the previous year. The Raschids would be hit hard.

When Fernao bade Abdul Raschid take the seat across his desk in the small office room of the tower in the Colombo fort that morning, he did not know whether to be glad or sorry that it had fallen to him to convey the bad news to the Mouro trader so soon after their last discussion, since Captain Oliveira had suddenly been stricken with dysentery.

Barked commands, the stamp of feet, the squeak of wheels from the garrison drilling on the parade ground reached inside the room, while Abdul Raschid eased his bulk into the settle. 'A beautiful morning outside . . .' He breathed hard, fleshy nostrils distending with the slight exertion. 'Getting too fat, lord,' he observed, with a grin. 'Too much *pilau*.' He ran a palm over his shiny, bald head.

Too much prosperity, Fernao thought cynically. He

recalled his first visit to Abdul Raschid's mansion, in the Muslim quarter bordering the lake about half a mile from the port of Colombo on his father's flagship, and it had resulted from a written invitation delivered by the Raschids' son, Ali, then fourteen. He had been invited to keep the beautiful boy with golden skin and the mother's delicate features – but with large black eyes that warned of latent ferocity – as hostage against his safe return, but had taken the boy with him instead, along with an escort of thirty musketeers. He had been impressed by the pink, flat-roofed Moorish-style mansion, set in green, tree-shaded lawns that sloped down to the silver waters of the lake. Fernao remembered the coolness of the huge centre courtyard. It had marble floors, a great turquoise bathing pool and a fountain, all shaded by orange, tangerine and *jambu* trees in which mynahs, grey doves and bee-eaters nested, with the women's quarters barely visible at the rear, from which only Aisha, Abdul Raschid's chief wife, and her maid, Sabrina, could emerge with any regularity. Aisha Raschid had her own reception chamber at the front of the mansion with entrance to the main courtyard; it even had an aviary of yellow and blue and white parrakeets to lend music to the residents.

From the negotiations of that first visit had emerged the exclusive trade arrangements with the Abdul Raschids which had been increased later as Fernao expanded the Portuguese plans in his moves to get a grip on the entire island of Lanka, and with a great extension of the Raschids' infrastructure. Yes, the luxurious reception chamber with its floors of pink and white squares of marble, filigreed marble screens lining the back wall, green and red Persian carpets, green and white silk divans and low ebony tables inlaid with mother of pearl, had seen the beginning of Portugal's trading history in Lanka. While Fernao felt guilt that the trading arrangements would now have to be sharply modified, he could not commiserate unduly with

Abdul Raschid, who had been enormously wealthy before the Portuguese flotilla ever sailed into Colombo harbour. The past could not be permitted to stand in the way of the future in spite of the still small voice within him that breathed of the code of the *cavaleiro* and of honour.

He came to the point abruptly. 'What I summoned you for may mean less *pilau*,' he stated in deliberate tones.

Abdul Raschid's small eyes widened, then the beefy shoulders beneath the black waistcoat shrugged. 'Fat, lean, *pilau*, *kurakkan*, hunger! They are all the will of Allah.' He placed pudgy hands on fleshy thighs, awaiting Fernao's news fatalistically.

'The Great King's expansionist plans are forcing us to modify our own,' Fernao proceeded. 'When Prince Vidiye becomes king of the Billigam Korle, he will control the ports of Galle and Matara. He insists on a monopoly of all our local trade through those ports. Similarly, the Great King needs money to pay for the southern campaign and the maintenance of full sovereignty in that region. His one source of ready revenue is trade with us, so he will monopolize all our trade out of Colombo and Negombo.'

For a moment, anger flamed in the Mouro's eyes, to be quickly replaced by a look of pleading. 'Like father, like son,' he stated bitterly, referring to King Wijayo's former plan. 'Where does that leave us, lord?'

'You will continue to have the trade from all other ports, principally from Batti, in the east.'

'Our promises, our agreements?' The pudgy hands were raised helplessly.

'Must be set aside before the exigencies of the situation. Trade agreements are always subject to change.'

'We trusted you, lord. We have spent much money, devoted much time to establishing factories along the coast, building up the trade.'

'You have made much money too in this short time.'

'We have honoured our word to the letter, lord.'

'So have we, right down to the huge advance of gold *cruzados*.'

Suddenly Abdul Raschid straightened slumping shoulders, became invested with a new dignity. 'Forgive me, lord, but those have become a pittance. And under the circumstances, are they not merely thirty shekels of silver?'

Fernao felt himself reddening. 'Listen, Mouro, you'll get nowhere with insults.'

'I have got nowhere, even without them, today.' A sudden grin creased the chubby cheeks, made them shine. 'I beg my lord's pardon. I hope you'll forgive me.' He hesitated. 'After all, you are but carrying out the dictates of your masters' policies. Can we not find some areas of compromise?'

'Such as what?'

'Such as our continuing the trading, giving the Great King a percentage.' A gleam of hope sped across the Mouro's eyes. 'Perhaps Captain Oliveira can arrange something.'

Fernao had already conditioned himself to taking a cold, hard stand, the only way in which he could banish his conscience. As the political plan was his, he felt responsible for letting the Mouro down. 'There is no possibility whatsoever.'

'The warehouses, the ships. You will need them from us.'

'The Great King will commandeer your warehouses. It is up to him to pay you compensation or not. As for the ships, we shall supply them.'

'Dear Allah! We shall be ruined.'

'Not ruined, Mouro. Merely become a little less rich.'

'Does the captain approve this . . . this betrayal?'

'Captain Oliveira is stricken with dysentery. He will return home to Portugal as soon as he has recovered.'

'But he will give the orders till then, perhaps. I would like to appeal to him. Everyone has the right of appeal.'

'I am the chief factor here. I make all the trade decisions.'

When she heard the discreet knocking on the door of her waiting room that morning, Queen Anula thought it must be a messenger from Prince Kumara and her heart beat faster. She had been up most of the night wondering how her husband had fared on his Gampola raid. It was a totally unfamiliar role for her. There were moments when she imagined that her prince was dead. Panic seized her then, a cold sweat broke all over her body. She loved her husband, desired him, felt emotions for him that were foreign to her, but she also needed him for her security and her future.

She nodded to her attendant, indicating that the visitor might enter, settled herself more sedately on the settee.

The door opened. To her amazement, the obese King Wira waddled in. Recovering quickly, she rose to give him the obeisance of a daughter, her new estate.

'Ah! Surprised you, didn't we?' the king wagged a pudgy finger playfully at her while his pig-eyes swept the room. 'We have never been here before. Quite a pleasant place.' He glanced through the window at the trees of the Highland Forest mountain rising fresh green to meet a clear blue sky, then looked about him and found a spittoon. He walked up to it, spat a stream of red betel juice expertly into it.

'Pray be seated, my lord.' Queen Anula indicated the settee opposite that which she had just vacated. Why had the king invaded her quarters? Did he have news of Prince Kumara?

The king eased himself into the settee, wheezed once, smoothed his blue pantaloons. 'You sit down too ... er ... daughter,' he bade her.

She bowed her thanks, sat down, straightened her shoulders and folded her hands primly on her lap.

'You may leave our daughter and us,' the king commanded the attendant, who had been hovering about the entrance door. 'We have private matters to discuss and we are not to be disturbed. We shall send for you when we need you.'

A tremor of apprehension flickered through the queen. Did the king have ill news? Or was she finally to face the advances she had been expecting for some time now? 'Would Your Majesty like Nona to bring some refreshment?' she inquired.

'No, no! We have already eaten.' He waved his hand impatiently at the attendant, who beat a hurried retreat, closing the door behind her.

'That's better!' King Wira inspected her with lecherous eyes. 'This is also the first time we have been alone with you. You look even more beautiful . . . alone.' His glance, now positively lascivious, slowly crept over her full breasts, slender waist, generous hips. 'You are quite a figure of a woman, Anula.'

'We are glad your daughter pleases you.' She laid emphasis on the word 'daughter', thought quickly, decided to change the subject. 'Do you have news of our husband, your son, lord? Perhaps that is why you decided to honour us with a visit? Was the raid successful? Is Prince Kumara safe and well?'

He was taken aback. 'Yes, yes, indeed. The raid was a total success. The Gampola buffoon is dead. We are now the Great King of three sub-kingdoms. Tomorrow it shall be the whole *uda rata*, the day after, all of Lanka.' A dribble of red juice appeared on the side of the small mouth. 'So come over here and sit down beside us.' As he patted the seat of his settee, she noticed how small his hands were. 'We have waited a long time for this moment, ever since we first gave you sanctuary. You can now fulfil your implied promises and share in our glory.'

Your glory, yes. Your bed, never, she thought coolly. I'll slit your fat throat first. She decided to take the horny bull by the horns, bring it all out into the open. 'Lord, that

60

would not be proper,' she replied, feigning demureness while giving him a flirtatious glance. She sighed ostentatiously. 'There is nothing we would like better than to repay you for your many kindnesses.' She fixed him with a brilliant gaze. 'We too have waited long for the opportunity. When you did not create it, we wondered whether you did not find us attractive any more. You are so . . . so . . . magnificent, lord. What woman could resist you?' She knew that all he wanted was a quick fuck on the settee, but the thought of any physical contact with him filled her with disgust.

Something between a gasp and a croak escaped him; lust entered his eyes. He made to rise.

She held up a warning hand. He flopped back on his seat. She sighed more heavily. 'But it cannot be today, lord.' She deliberately dropped the royal plural. 'Alas! What a miserable creature I must be to miss this glorious opportunity to know a man who is a real man, a glorious king, a *maha raja.*'

'What do you mean?' he demanded hoarsely.

'We would dishonour you by offering ourselves to you today.' She shook her head sadly. 'We started our monthly period last night and it is really flowing,' she lied sweetly.

Thursday, 10 August 1525

Her husband, Prince Kumara, returned in triumph that evening. After dinner, he lost no time in taking his wife to bed and she gave herself to him completely as always.

Awaking from the first beautiful sleep that always followed their lovemaking, she lay relaxed in the darkness for a few minutes. The scent of the queen-of-the-night made her glance through the window. The darkness of the mountain ended abruptly at the glowing skyline. She could see a solitary star in the heavens. She listened to the sound of her husband's breathing. Suddenly it seemed as if it were one with the eternal creak of crickets and the beating of her heart. It was all part of life . . . and death.

She thought quietly of the people she had killed. A husband, a lover, Prince Kumara's mistress. Perhaps she had also caused the death of her late husband, the Great King Wijayo. She was excited by the brilliant future that was about to open for Prince Kumara. She would help him become the Great King of Lanka some day. There was, however, a long way to go before he reached that goal, so the first important step had to be taken without delay. Her ambitious young husband needed no urging, but impetus always helped.

She turned on her side. The prince was lying on his back, his hands crossed over his chest, his breathing deep and regular. She propped herself on an elbow and looked at his face. Even in the gloom, the regular features, black hair and tight-drawn golden skin were obvious. She was fortunate to have a handsome young stud, with a promising future, for a husband. She had listened enthralled, during dinner, to the details of the raid, including his reactions and exploits, all told with his usual inverse modesty. How proud she was of all he had achieved so far.

She reached out and started stroking his face very gently, until he finally stirred. She half rose and pressed her naked breasts on his bare chest, kissed him on the mouth, grabbed his organ. It was already erect and hard.

He awoke with a start. 'What? What is it, Anula?'

'I have something important to tell you.'

On the instant, he was wide awake. She quietly told him of the morning's incident with King Wira.

He listened without comment, but she could feel the pent-up rage within him and she gloried in it.

He cursed softly when she finished. 'Damn him! Damn him! I'll have his guts.' He pushed her aside, sat up sharply. 'You're sure you did not give yourself to that fat pig?'

'How could I? He believed that I had my period.'

'What would you have done if he had wanted to lay you regardless?'

'Listen. Your father is the kind of man who would fuck a cow when the lust is on him. Then it's just the sensations from moving and the orgasm. What he wants of me is different. It's my beauty. Fucking me is incidental to his conquest of my beauty, a sort of seal or symbol of his manhood. Many physically unattractive men are like that. Your father would not want to take my beautiful flesh when it is blood-stained, soiled, especially because he is the kind who would want to eat it. He has lust without passion, so your question is hypothetical.

'You still have not answered it.' She could feel the coldness of his state even in the dark.

'I would have slit his fat belly before I allowed him even to touch me. I'm for you alone.'

'Good.' His body relaxed. He reached out a gentle hand and caressed her breast, pulled her on to him again. She felt the beating of his heart against her chest. 'We have three days in which to act,' he finally stated, very, very quietly.

Her own heart stated pounding with excitement. 'What d'you mean?'

'Your period will end in three days, will it not?'

The words came out so gently, she trembled. 'I was hoping you'd say that,' she whispered.

Thursday, 10 August 1525

Aisha Raschid had been visiting friends in the coastal town of Beruwala, some thirty miles south of Colombo, and she was unaware of her husband's interview with Colonel de Albergaria when she returned home the next morning. Abdul had asked to see her immediately she arrived, so it must be something of dire importance. She felt a instinctive clenching of her stomach at the thought of a crisis. But, as always, the crisis brought out the blood in her. My brother,

63

Paichi Marcar, emperor of Moorish trade in the Indies, and I are descended from Mahmud of Ghazni, who swept into India hundreds of years ago and conquered much of it with strength, ferocity and cruelty, she thought. We have also inherited the qualities of our later ancestor Mohamed Ghuri, who trained bodies of mounted archers to wheel, feint and retreat, then circle around the triumphant enemy for surprise flank attacks. Yes, of Mohamed Ghuri who bestowed such a crushing defeat on the Rajput armies of India at the battle of Tarain that the Muslim historians recorded 'a hundred thousand grovelling Hindus swiftly despatched to the flames of hell'. I fear no man, no situation.

She stood up when her husband waddled into the reception chamber, only three inches shorter than his six-foot-two-inch height, conscious that her slim figure, with its perfectly white skin, the slender, delicately boned face and large black eyes hid an indomitable, more than masculine spirit as effectively as the brown *chador* and veil disguised her body. Though she interpreted the rules of *purdah* to suit her own belief that she was an instrument of Allah, specially endowed to fulfil His will, which must take priority over interpretations of the Koran made by mere men, she was a Muslim first and last. She recalled her words from over three years ago.

'. . . *we have given the world its first real civilization, the sciences of mathematics and astronomy, the Arabic script, the cultured arts. Here in Lanka, we even supply the Sinhala with food from abroad, because internal wars and the invading Cholas have made them dependent. We have governed the lives of all in Lanka because Allah gave us the material resources and the will to exploit them* . . .'

She knelt before her husband in the traditional greeting when he paused at the entrance to her reception chamber.

'We are ruined! We are ruined!' Abdul Raschid's normally high voice was pitched higher than ever. He hastened to his divan, automatically reached for a Turkish delight before he even sat down.

Having discovered that his favourite seat on the divan and the compulsive eating of sweetmeats in her chamber somehow gave her husband strength, instead of loathing the habit, Aisha had come to feel a strange sense of protectiveness towards him. She now loved this man, not in any romantic way, but with deep affection, respect for his abilities and appreciation of his kindliness.

'Put not your trust in princes. They are scum, vermin, pig's offal. They deserve each other.' Abdul was mouthing the words through the salivated Turkish delight, with sucking noises in between each phrase. His cheeks were trembling, his small eyes a mixture of concern and anger. 'May Allah strike them dead. May He give me the power to cut off their balls and place them on their eyes.'

His flood of anger abated. Suddenly he grinned wryly, that puckish, childlike grin peculiar to fat men and, as always since her feelings for him had changed, it went to her heart. A couple of love-birds in the cages outside started whistling and twittering.

'You must be wondering what this is all about,' Abdul resumed quietly. His cheeks stopped quivering, a reflective note entered his voice. 'Strange, how I can bring it all out in your presence, wife of mine, and become calm again. Your strength gives me strength.'

'We are one family under Allah. Nothing can ruin us so long as we have each other.'

'True, true.' A tender expression crossed his face. 'You are Allah's greatest gift to me.' He paused, eyebrows lifted. 'Captain Oliveira is sick with dysentery. Apparently he is under orders to proceed back to Portugal, removing our one reliable supporter. Well, at least we have ensured a comfortable retirement for him.'

'Who will succeed him?'

'For the present Colonel de Albergaria is in charge.'

'He is our friend.'

'Yes, but he is an even closer friend of his ambitions. As you know, he has changed considerably from the young lieutenant who first came to this house. I rather suspect that the attempted rape of his wife did something to him. I sometimes get the feeling that some pain is eating into him, making him like the elephant in *musth*.'

'How can you tell?'

'A truly happy family man has something totally free inside him. You may call it a trusting, loving heart. Why has family life and the birth of his daughter not preserved the colonel's compassion? What makes him almost vicious at times? It can't be ambition alone. As I said, he is like the elephant in *musth* . . .'

'What are you, my husband? she inquired mischievously, still bent on calming him.

'You make me a camel in heat.' His eyes crinkled, then grew serious. 'Here is my news.' He reached for another sweetmeat. Aisha noted with satisfaction that he drew his hand back empty, looked her in the eye and quietly launched into his story. 'I have not yet estimated the losses to us, since I hastened to come to you,' he concluded. 'But they could be enormous.'

She had heard him out with the familiar cold anger rising within her.

More words from the past flashed through her mind.

'*Then came the Portuguese. They are worse than the ravening Mongols of the east. Having taken over our influence in the entire ocean by sheer force, they are now here in Lanka. I am a Ghazni and a Ghuri. I can match the accursed of Allah in strength, ferocity and cruelty.*'

She began assessing the financial impact of the new situation. 'I beg to disagree,' she countered. 'The advance paid by the *parangi*, which you so wisely insisted upon, will more than cover the capital costs we have incurred. The private trade we had before the *parangi* came can now

66

be resumed. Our only losses are the anticipated profits from trade with them. How can we lose something we never had? Meanwhile we have each other and our son, Ali, can come back home from the provinces.'

He looked at her in astonishment, then that high-pitched giggle escaped him. 'You are so right,' he declared. 'You have the rare ability to shear through mist, to reduce everything to its simplest terms.' His massive jaw tightened, he ran a palm over his shiny, bald head. 'But we cannot leave it at that, you know.'

Aisha thrilled at the note of menace that had entered his voice, an echo of her own private reactions. 'No, indeed, we cannot. It will take time, but there is much that we can do.'

'Like what?' he inquired blandly.

'First, we must alert my brother, Paichi Marcar, so we can evolve a plan to continue using our factories, warehouses, ships and contracts, but to *compete* with the Portuguese. His last letter speaks of another European nation that has finally observed the wealth that Portugal has developed through its trade with this region. While England, France and Spain, even Venice, have been blind, this new race of European traders called the Hollanders have been increasing their regular trading operations and are now casting eyes in this direction. My brother has contacted the Hollanders. It is only a matter of time before their ships appear in Indian waters. The other European powers will follow, like jackals seeking the lion's kill. While the Europeans blast each other off in our part of the world, as they are doing in Europe, we shall prosper.'

'We shall then use the facilities for which the Portuguese have paid so we can trade with a competing nation. Brilliant! Absolutely brilliant!' Abdul laughed out loud. 'What sweet revenge.'

'It will take time. We may not even live to see it, but we

can indeed laugh at the knowledge that we have made it inevitable.'

'While enriching ourselves.'

'While moving, though more slowly than we had thought before, towards that end.'

'And what about the Great King whose ambitions will have cost us so dear?'

Aisha knew immediately that her husband had already made plans on that score. 'Did not another Great King attempt such a move against us before, husband of mine?'

A pleased grin wreathed his chubby face, the double chins began to shake with silent mirth. 'I was hoping that you would remember that!'

'Allah always helps those who do not depend only on His grace.'

'The enemies of our enemies are our friends.' Abdul Raschid quoted the expression almost dreamily.

'Yes ... The Great King's actions of recent times, especially his appointment of Prince Vidiye as King of the Billigam Korle, his formal adoption of his infant grandson and now his desire to strengthen his Treasury, obviously to build up a strong army, cannot make his brother, King Maya Dunne, his friend. So we must be more cunning than the most cunning. We must support the Great King's enemies and meanwhile plan to have him ... er ... eliminated.' The old implacable, ruthless determination had seized Aisha's spirit. I am a Ghazni, she thought.

'Vengeance is the first law of our people,' Abdul responded. 'It is essential for our survival.'

Aisha drew a deep breath. 'There is one more act of vengeance we must perform.'

'What is that?'

'As you know, my brother and the Zamorin of Calicut have slowly been building up the strength of their own guns and ships. I have come to the conclusion that the only way in which we will ever have the assurance of permanent trade directly with the *parangi* is with a Great King who is not greedy and has too much pride to become a trader.'

Abdul Raschid's small eyes widened. 'And who would that be?' he inquired, but Aisha knew that he already had the answer.

'King Maya Dunne,' she asserted. Noting his comprehension of the truth of her statement and the slow nodding of agreement, she proceeded. 'We must solve our problem from its origins. We want the *parangi* here, but only for trade, not to be dominant politically and militarily. King Maya Dunne can become the Great King if he has outside military support to counterbalance the power of the *parangi*. I suggest that you leave on our ship that sails for Calicut tomorrow. A visit from you to my brother, Paichi Marcar, is long overdue. Meanwhile, I shall ensure personal contact with King Maya Dunne to discover whether he would be open to an alliance with the native ruler of Calicut, the Zamorin, what support he needs and how much he is prepared to pay for it. His treasury is full.'

'*You* are *my* treasury!' Abdul Raschid exclaimed impulsively. That roguish smile creased his plump cheeks. 'I shall not part with you for anything.' He grew serious. 'What sort of support do you think the Zamorin would be able to give?'

'I have thought about that for some time now, though this decision of the *parangi* has hastened the need for our action. The Zamorin can keep the *parangi* fleet tied up in his waters, which would of course be helpful to him too, and provide sufficient naval vessels to beat off any attempts by the *parangi* to bring reinforcements into Lanka once battle is joined here. As far as local support from the Zamorin is concerned, it would seem to me from all the information we have of the strength of the armies of the kings, that ten thousand cavalrymen and foot soldiers of the Zamorin's best-trained troops would be satisfactory.'

'What will it cost King Maya Dunne?'

'You expect me to know too much, husband of mine.'

'Then let me guess.' He placed his pudgy hands on his ample stomach. 'I would say that the Zamorin would be prepared to contribute freely towards a cause that would keep two *parangi terco* – regiments – and several warships tied up here while he engaged their bases along the west coast of India.' He pursed his small lips. 'The only assistance he would provide without direct benefit would be the troops for use in Lanka. I should try and obtain that for a small cash payment and the costs of providing billets, food and pay for the troops while in Lanka.' He paused. 'How will I know whether King Maya Dunne will even be prepared to accept such support? I mean, would it not be better for me to make sure of that first?'

'So it might seem; it would be more effective with such a ruler as the Zamorin if we could make him a solid proposal rather than talk in vague terms or ask him questions. And time is short.'

'You are absolutely correct.' He pondered awhile, absently scratching his cheek. 'I suggest that you have your contact sound King Maya Dunne out in time to send me the message through our son, Ali, on the ship that sails for Calicut next week. In that way, having already prepared the ground in Calicut, I shall be able to return within four or five weeks, hopefully with firm proposals.' His eyes went moist. 'Four or five weeks.' he repeated, almost to himself. 'I have never been parted from you for more than four or five days. I shall miss you.'

CHAPTER FIVE
Thursday, 10 August 1525

For the split of a second, I watched Lord Samara Kon's huge sword-blade poised above me, heard his shout of triumph. The sword flashed down. I rolled desperately sideways. The air from the mighty stroke slashed across my face. The great thwack of impact made the earth shudder. I had escaped by a hair's breadth. There was no time for fear or relief. Using the leverage of my roll, I leapt to my feet with a wrestler's spring. The two seconds while the giant tugged at his sword, his shield down, were all I needed to swipe my own sword upwards at his face. He jerked his head sideways, took the blow on his helmet, grunted. Then his sword was out and he parried my backswing. Sparks flew from the clang of our blades.

We began circling each other. Having no shield, I was at an added disadvantage, but I noticed with fierce joy the weal my slash had left on his massive face.

He lifted his sword, leapt in, smashing downwards, then upwards. Our swords clanged and clanged again as I parried and parried. He was so strong, his blows juddered through my whole body, vibrated into my brain. He had brute strength. How could I overcome it? Miraculously, in that instant, across the centuries of time, King Abhaya Gamini's boyhood tactic came back to me: 'Power can overcome brute strength.' Where did my power lie? In stamina and brains, technique and patience. I became cool as spring water, leapt back to disengage.

Lord Samara Kon paused, breathing hard. He was not in good condition. I would allow his strength and physical power to sap him. I heard his mocking words. 'The young pig is not ready to fight a lion!'

'The old pig is tiring already!' I taunted him.

With a roar, he rushed at me again, but I danced away and he struck empty air again and again. I laughed aloud, infuriating him. Slow minutes passed while we kept repeating our dance.

'Fight like a man, damn you!' His breathing had begun its first rasp. He leapt in suddenly, thrust, cavorted, slashed downwards, sidestepped and swiped. A tremendous sequence in the approved manner, with speed and agility remarkable in such a huge man. He struck only empty air each time. Each minute of his powerful attacks drained him more. His taunts had turned from sneering to imprecations and now to growling rage. 'Fight, damn you! Fight, you coward!' his breath came shorter, his recovery from each mighty stroke slower.

Finally, the time was right. I danced away from a downward swing, deliberately turned quarter circle so the risen sun was full in his eyes when he swivelled round to face me. He blinked against the glare as I knew he would. In the instant, my sword in both hands, I leapt inside his guard, swinging the blade sideways before he could raise his shield. One tremendous neck slash. He jerked convulsively with the blow. I back-slashed him before he could recover. He jerked again, like a huge tree before the axe. His great arms slackened. Blood gouted, a red necklace on his bull neck. His face contorted with pain. In a trice, I gripped my sword more firmly with both hands, raised it aloft and brought it down with fiendish strength. One great thunk, the metal grinding through leather and bone. The blow jarred up my hands, ran up my arms, almost loosened my grip. Then its mighty force brought the sword-point down his forehead. Slicing between his eyes and nose, it stuck there quivering like a spear on a boar's back.

The shock of the blow killed him, but he remained upright. Then his sword and shield clattered to the ground.

He tottered, a giant tree being uprooted, then suddenly crashed to the ground, wrenching my sword from my grasp.

I had been conscious of nothing save the fight. Now I heard the breathless hush that filled the air as I placed a foot on the fallen leader's chest and tugged my sword away.

Cries of alarm resounded. I came on guard, ready to defend myself. The crackle of musket-fire penetrated my fogged senses, the thudding of hooves arose behind me, a thunderous clanking of metal to my right. In a trice I realized that Lord Samara Kon and I had fought through the second and third charges of my cavalry who were now pressing home the advantage.

Above the din, I heard the cry: 'A Sinha to the kill . . . A Sinha to the kill . . .' from a thousand throats. My ally, Lord Wickrama Sinha, had arrived.

The prospect of victory drove me berserk. With a wild shout, I plunged into the shocked enemy, wielding my sword mightily. New life surging through me, I killed or laid low all who stood in my path. I slashed, cut, parried, chopped, endlessly. A way cleared before me like magic as men cringed, ran away from my insanity. Through sweat-dimmed lashes I caught a glimpse of the blue-green ocean.

The enemy were fleeing or throwing away their arms, pleading to be spared. The dead lay thick about me, the screams and groans of the wounded rose above the dying clamour of battle.

Sword at the ready, I paused, sweat dripping, lungs pumping, desperately trying to regain my breath. Only the ocean spread before me, glinting in the sunlight, calm save for serried ranks of white surf sweeping towards the black rocks on the shore. It should have brought the dank odour of seaweed, but I had only the stench of blood and sweat in my nostrils.

Starkly etched against the blue-green ocean, I saw the

great grey stone cross planted by Captain Lorenzo de Almeida, the first *parangi* to land on our shores, twenty years ago to the day.

As I gazed at it, spellbound, the sky began to turn blood-red, the light faded from the sun. Lightning flashed, thunder rolled and crackled. A man's form appeared on the cross, hanging limply from it, lit by fitful flames of torches held by soldiers in armour. A spear flashed through the gloom. It struck the crucified man on the side. His body jerked, stiffened. The head, bearing a crown of thorns, sagged. Blood gouted from the spear wound, its stench in my nostrils. My eyes dilated, my heart thudded against my ribs. This was Jesus of Nazareth, crucified again.

'Father forgive them, for they know not what they do.' The words were a hoarse whisper.

The flashes of lightning behind Jesus suddenly emerged from the mouths of big guns, the thunder from a belching cannonade and the rattle of muskets. Bloodthirsty screams arose and the agonized cries of dying innocents.

Vivid scenes from the past snapped on and off in the foreground of my vision. The merciless state of my tutor Father Juan, the body of a prostitute mutilated by the pervert Sergeant Correa, Palitha's father Kodi tortured to death, gunfire pounding innocent civilians outside the Jaya gates, Portuguese soldiers marching in Kandy. All the arrogance of military might which caused today's battle and would soak my country in blood.

The flesh of the man on the cross began to dissolve, to shrivel, leaving him a skeleton with horrible socket eyes. This was no Saviour but a man made hollow by his followers, a man betrayed, his message of peace and love delivered with sword and gun. A man nailed to the Cross daily by those who claimed to worship him.

Suddenly, I knew the meaning of it all. The conquest of nations can only be achieved through love. Followers of religions that preach love with weapon in hand, Christianity, Islam, make a mockery of the truth. None of it would be for me. If my father sought the spread of Lord Buddha's Doctrine with a battle-cry, I would echo it, but my only religion would be the duty of my office and the call of my destiny.

If this Cross before me were a true symbol of the principles for which the Son of God was nailed to it, I would be the first to worship it and spread the Word throughout the land.

I raised my sword aloft and shouted wordlessly in impotent rage.

The cannon fire merged with the pounding of the surf. The sky paled, turned white, then blue. Sharp-etched against it once more, the great stone cross rightly bore no Christ. The blood stench of his wound remained in my nostrils.

I saw the truth of that cross as man had made it, a symbol of the *power* of the Church, no longer of its *love*, a symbol of the domination of Portugal and of the white man, a symbol that stood in the way of free people.

I picked up a fallen spear and rushed forward to the cross. 'Follow me, all true Sinhala,' I cried.

I started to dig around the monument. Other patriots joined me. Laughing, weeping, we attacked the base of the cross, hacking away, digging out the soil with our bare hands. My fingernails tore and bled.

We had dug deep enough. We leaned against the cross. We pushed and shoved, straining with might and main until it began to give. We redoubled our efforts, sweating, groaning. U . . . unh . . . unh . . .

The cross teetered. 'One more time, all you true Sinhala!' I screamed. Through a mist of sweat drops I read the words etched on the base, I saw the royal coat-of-arms of Portugal. While it stood, this cross extended to Lanka the protection of the mighty Portuguese Empire. And this was the symbol of the man of peace? Surely He would say with me, To hell with it!

One final maniacal shove and the huge stone cross keeled over. We leapt aside as it dropped from the headland to strike the ocean with a tremendous splash, sending up salt spray on to our faces.

Saturday, 12 August 1525

Captain Oliveira's condition had worsened and the physicians had suggested that he proceed to Goa, where better medical facilities were available, on the very next ship. Fernao had therefore assumed complete command of the fort. He was busy working on budgets for the forthcoming year when the door swung open. To his surprise, Father Juan stood at the entrance, unannounced, an apologetic Aires, Fernao's soldier servant, hovering in the background.

Fernao rose to his feet and saluted. 'Father, what a pleasant surprise. I didn't know you had come down from Kandy.' Fernao nodded a dismissal to the orderly.

'I had no intention of coming down, my son, but our protégé, Prince Kumara, seized the Gampola kingdom by a brilliant raid three nights ago and I decided to bring you the news personally.'

The friar's narrow face was less sallow than it had been when he lived in Colombo. The cooler hill country air was responsible. Fernao thought fleetingly of taking a holiday in the hills with Julietta and the baby, then noticed that the friar's well-kept russet beard seemed to be bristling, anger lurking within the pale yellow pebbles of eyes. He felt a spurt of alarm, for only twice before had he seen Father Juan this way and both times it had meant bad news, in more senses than one.

'Please sit down.' Fernao deliberately injected a note of calm into his voice, indicated the settle across his desk.

Father Juan stared at him a moment, sat down abruptly. Obviously attempting to control himself, he came straight to the point. 'One victory for Our Lord, but one for the heathen too,' he stated, his unusually loud voice booming through the small room. 'Holy Church demands immediate action.'

'What heathen? What victory, Father? Would you please start at the beginning and tell me what this is all about?'

The friar took a deep breath to steady himself, his thin nostrils dilating. 'I came down joyfully from Kandy to inform you of Prince Kumara's victory and to ask you for more of our troops to support his incursion into Hangura, which will require a greater show of force. I arrived at our seminary in Jaya late last night. As I was about to leave for the fort early this morning, one of our sp ... er ... converts in Galle arrived with terrible news.'

Fernao tensed. Prince Vidiye and his force, having set sail for Galle on the Portuguese *nao*, were due to land there around noon that day.

'I warned you about Prince Tikiri!' the friar burst out. 'He force-marched his cavalry regiment across the mountains to attack Lord Samara Kon's troops before Prince Vidiye linked up with them. Meanwhile, an infantry group under Lord Wickrama Sinha floated down the Gin River in rafts to take Lord Samara Kon in the flank, but was delayed in making the rendezvous. Prince Tikiri struck on his own. The battle took place on the Galle *maidan* north of the harbour. Though outnumbered five-to-one, Prince Tikiri killed Lord Samara Kon in personal combat and routed his army. Lord Wickrama Sinha's men effected the link-up at the last moment, so our enemies are on the Galle *maidan* in full strength.'

Fernao's tension turned to alarm. King Maya Dunne had obviously taken the initiative to prevent the squeeze on King Raigam. 'With Prince Tikiri on the *maidan* adjoining the Galle harbour, King Vidiye's forces will be destroyed piecemeal as they go ashore in boatloads this afternoon,' he declared, suddenly feeling helpless to do anything about a force he may have sent to their deaths.

'Don't worry, Colonel.' The friar's smile was smug. 'Holy Church has already looked after it.'

'Looked after it? . . . I mean . . . How?'

'Some of our strongest converts are fishermen in the coastal areas. Our contact near Galle, Father Philip, arranged for fishing boats to go out to the *nao* and warn Prince Vidiye.'

'Thank God.' Relief flooded Fernao.

'It was God's will that the Church should have Catholic allies in the right place at the right time,' the friar responded ponderously. 'It shows what we can achieve when the State co-operates with the Church.' His look was as pointed as his remark.

'Prince Tikiri's victory will have instilled fear into the minds of the nobles of the region, so even those who would have joined King Vidiye may hesitate.' Father Juan was echoing Fernao's own thinking. 'They would not wish to invite Lord Samara Kon's fate or what Prince Tikiri did with the corpse.'

'What did he do?' Fernao demanded.

'He decapitated it and sent the head, suitably preserved, to his father as a token of victory.' The friar gave a bitter laugh. 'My former pupil.'

'How barbaric!'

'I warned you the Sinhala, though an ancient civilization, are capable of savagery.'

'Like all races.' Fernao resented Father Juan's superior attitude.

The friar's reaction was unusually violent. 'Like all races?' The booming voice had risen more than a tone. 'How dare . . . how can you compare these heathens with us, the chosen of God?'

'I thought the Jews were the chosen people!' Fernao exclaimed drily.

Father Juan paused, took a deep breath, exhaled bad breath loudly. My punishment for the remark, Fernao thought with disgust.

'I bring you news of supreme importance, Colonel, and all you can do is to make clever remarks,' the friar complained.

'On the contrary, Father, I'm still waiting for you to complete your news, so I can decide on the action to be taken. I can tell there's more you have left unsaid.'

'You are right,' Father Juan declared, simmering down. 'But the final items of news are quite shattering. First, Prince Tikiri's forces include over one hundred musketeers.'

Fernao was appalled. 'Musketeers? How on earth . . .? D'you mean they have finally mastered the art of making muskets? The skill of the gunsmith was the one resource we were determined to keep from them.'

'It would seem so,' the friar said regretfully. 'Sinhala craftsmen are very clever. They'll be manufacturing cannon next.'

Fernao was now thoroughly alarmed. 'Any other news, Father?' he inquired, controlling his concern.

The friar straightened up, inhaled deeply and Fernao steeled himself for the blow, of bad breath too. 'The heathen, the barbaric Sinhala, led by Prince Tikiri, uprooted the cross that Lorenzo de Almeida planted on the headland in Galle in 1505 and hurled it into the ocean.' Father Juan's voice dropped to a whisper. 'I saw that cross being hewn from stone. I helped raise it. I picked up earth with my own hands to plant it firmly in the soil of this heathen land.' He raised his palms, lowered his head to gaze at skeletal fingers, then lifted his eyes to penetrate Fernao with the flaming glare of the fanatic. 'That cross was a symbol, not only of Holy Church and our mission for it. That cross, while it stood, promised the protection of our sovereign lord, the King of Portugal, for this barbaric country. He lifted his head, pointed a shaking finger upwards, his pale yellow eyes making him a figure of menace. 'That divine protection has now been removed by the hideous sacrilege of Prince Tikiri's action. I nursed that viper in my bosom. Holy Church demands that you avenge the insult to us all, that you destroy this upstart prince before we lose all the ground we have gained through years of patient toil.'

Fernao was strangely unmoved by the news. So a bunch of heathens had uprooted a cross that should never have been erected in the first place. 'What do you consider we should do in Galle?'

'Smite the heathen hip and thigh, punish him, burn him,' Father Juan's voice rose passionately. 'Introduce the Holy Inquisition here. Treat the Sinhala as we treat the Jews in our motherland, cleanse them by *auto-da-fé*.'

'Father, you have been many years in this country,' Fernao replied gently. 'The first sixteen of them must have been hideous, because you made so little headway in spreading the Word of God. Now you stand on the threshold of success. I ask you, what could be more appealing to the Sinhala than the message of Christ's love, at a time when their leaders are warring with each other, at a time of cruelty, bloodshed and death?' He was testing the friar.

Only yesterday, the mail packet from Goa had belatedly brought him a gift which Admiral Vasco da Gama, before he died, had ordered for his 'new-found friend, whom I would have been proud to call my son'. The gift was a copy of the Psalter originally published in Mainz in 1457 by Fust and Schoeffer, the first book printed in movable type to bear its printers' names. The accompanying preface acknowledged their debt to Johann Gutenberg of Mainz, who introduced printing to Europe with a Papal Indulgence of 1454, to the Korean people who had made movable type in moulds at the beginning of the century and to the Chinese who had invented printing centuries earlier with seals and stamps for making impressions in clay.

The gift had touched Fernao, handling it had reached somewhere deep inside him, rekindled his hopes of becoming a writer some day. The dead Admiral had known of his aspirations, had reached across the grave to touch the right chord in him.

'Do I hear you right, Colonel?' Father Juan demanded angrily. 'Do you not recall that Our Lord berated the Scribes and the Pharisees and scourged the moneychangers who defiled the temple?'

Fernao shook himself free of a spell. 'I apologize for trying to preach the gospel to you, father,' he said firmly. 'I am in command of His Majesty's forces in this country. Be assured that as soon as I have the fullest intelligence, I shall take all necessary precautions to safeguard his Majesty's interests.' He hesitated. 'And to ensure the well-being of Holy Church.'

'You have a plan, Colonel?'

The gall of the friar riled Ferneo into saying more than he intended. He wanted to put the man in his place. 'Yes, I have a plan,' he almost snapped. 'Once King Vidiye establishes control over Galle, I shall obtain a land grant from the Great King and build a tremendous fort there, operating as a trading station but manned in sufficient strength to exercise power.' With an inner sigh, he remembered his father's words to him on the day they first arrived in Colombo. 'We can then proceed to establish similar forts in every major seaport of this island.'

Father Juan's eyes widened. 'It would serve as a base for us to convert the heathen by the hundreds. You're a visionary, Colonel.' There was excitement in the booming

81

voice. 'Why, the entire coastline would be ringed with the faithful.'

'Not to mention the iron of our military might.'

Father Juan pondered awhile. 'I have long thought of another plan by which we can convert the natives.' A crafty gleam flickered in his pale eyes. 'And thereby ensure loyal subjects for His Majesty, our most noble King Emperor. Once the forts are established, you can refuse to buy spices or goods from anyone other than a Catholic.'

'Oh no . . .' Fernao began, sick at the suggestion.

'Oh yes. If you do not do so, Holy Church will intercede with His Imperial Majesty to pass such a decree. Also, with a live military presence in all those areas, you can commence a system of land registration. Those who register their land must be Catholic, when they will automatically have a Christian name, or take a Portuguese name for identification by our officials.'

'To what end?'

'First, to ensure converts. Second, to induce the leading families to adopt foreign names; by taking Portuguese names these families will be diluting their national identity. Third, to aggravate the caste divisions that exist among the Sinhala. People who are identified by name as being of lower caste will rush to take new foreign names.' He grinned smugly. 'Divide and rule does not merely apply geographically and ethnically, Colonel, but must extend to every possible facet of life. Then, as I said before, you will buy only the produce of loyal Catholics, confining your purchases to those whose names you can identify. After all, most Sinhala names are difficult for Europeans even to pronounce.'

'How would a man become a loyalist merely by taking a Portuguese name?'

'We of the clergy have been encouraging the natives to follow our enlightened Western ways. I have observed a sort of fashion, almost a cult, developing among certain of the leading families of the country, to ape our manners and customs. We must destroy the manners and customs of the natives if we are to serve their best interests. He beamed his triumph. 'Another divisive factor.'

'But their own manners and customs are ancient and enlightened.'

'The only true way is the way of the West, the Christian way.'

'But how will a change of name . . .?' Fernao repeated.

Father Juan's smile was almost malignant. 'Take away a man's ancient family name and you destroy one of the fundamentals of his existence, an ancient identity.'

Saturday, 12 August 1525

Prince Kumara had told no one of his plan; it was so simple that he did not need to take anyone into his confidence. He had timed it for the dusk watch, because most people in the Kandy palace were then relaxing over dinner.

Except for the usual bare-chested guards and an occasional attendant, who saluted him, the palace verandahs, pungent with the odour of their flaming torches, were almost deserted as he strode towards King Wira's chambers, followed by the armed escort he had hand-picked from his new personal guard. The fountain in the main courtyard splashed merrily beneath the tinkle of a *venna* from one of the chambers, the notes silvery as the twinkling stars he could glimpse in the deep blue sky. He brushed aside the young guard who stood at the entrance to the king's chamber with a haughty wave of the hand and lined his men two-deep in front of the door. Like the attendants, even these men merely imagined that they were there because the king for some reason needed a guard.

He raised his hand to rap on the brown teak-wood door

and paused to steady his breathing and the beat of his heart. Within seconds now, there would be no turning back. Forcing himself to a calm confidence, he rapped on the closed door. It was promptly opened by the ancient attendant, who recognized him, made obeisance. He pushed his way past the kneeling man.

The smell of curry hung in the air. King Wira was seated as usual, cross-legged on the gold divan, absently scratching the black hairs on his chest. His small eyes narrowed, flashed angrily at his son's unceremonious entrance. He belched involuntarily. 'Is your head so full of one small victory that it has no room left for decorum, not to mention good sense?' he demanded, his high-pitched voice ominous. 'Or must we have it taken off?'

Prince Kumara glanced at the attendant, dismissed him with a jerk of the head. 'Leave the door open, *kollu*,' he directed. 'I want our king to see the present I have brought him.'

The old man made obeisance and backed out of the room.

King Wira stared at his son a moment, then through the entrance. His small eyes widened in surprise at seeing the guard lined up on the verandah. 'What the fuck . . .?' he began.

Prince Kumara carefully closed the door behind the attendant, turned to face the king. 'From this moment, you cease to be king,' he stated flatly.

King Wira laughed shortly. 'Stop this *nadagam*, play-acting, else I'll have you flayed alive, bathed in honey and fed to the flies.' For all his bold words, there was unease in his voice.

'This is not play-acting. If anyone is to command torture and execution, it shall be I.' Prince Kumara's smile was grim. 'Or should I say, "We"?' He paused, deliberately injected a deadly seriousness into his voice. 'And if anyone is to suffer such punishment it shall be you. So move yourself off that seat, get to your bed-chamber and pack your belongings. You shall tell your guards that you are taking an unexpected trip to Jaya. We have a suitable escort waiting outside the gates for you, ten of the palace cavalry, one hundred infantrymen, even six elephants, suitably caparisoned, with *sesath* bearers, all as befits your former rank. We have included with your entourage a wagon containing some treasure, ostensibly gifts for the Great King, but really to set you up wherever you want to live outside the Kandyan kingdoms.'

'And if we do not leave?'

Prince Kumara's voice was chill, his expression evil. 'Would you like to take the consequences?' He himself did not know what they were if his bluff failed.

King Wira glared at him challengingly. 'Yes!'

Prince Kumara's heart missed a beat. Betraying none of his apprehension, he drew his sword in one clean sweep, half-turned towards the door. His heart had begun to pound now.

'On second thought, perhaps it may be timely for us to pay our cousin the Great King in Jaya a visit,' King Wira interjected.

Relief flooded the prince like a great white light in darkness. 'Good timing is one of the essentials of wisdom,' he declared.

'Our time will come. King Wira's voice held menace. 'For now, you would not dare lay hands on your father, lest it spoil your image.' He shook his head in disbelief. 'How could we have failed to see what lay beneath your *ahey raja*, yes, my lord, your unctuous outward appearance?' He nodded slowly. 'Well, it's done now, but never fear. We shall return.'

'The only way you will return to the *uda rata* is in a coffin. Our first decree as Great King of the *uda rata* is that you are banished from these territories for ever. As to our reason for sparing you, yes, we are doing so only for the purpose of maintaining our image. But do not push us too far.'

'Our friends the nobles will not permit . . .'

'You have no friends who will support you in adversity,' Prince Kumara interrupted cynically. 'Surely you know that to be one of the prerogatives of the *uda rata*, up-country kings!'

'The people will rise against you once they know the truth.'

'The people are a rabble to be roused only by the clamour of their bellies. You know that too. Besides, you have been so far removed from them that they may not even know that you exist except through your tax-collectors, who bleed them.'

'You have all the answers, haven't you?' A reflective expression crossed King Wira's pudgy features. He smiled wryly. 'Can't we work this out? After all, you want power. You shall have it.' He was almost pleading. 'We shall appoint you prince regent and you can rule . . .'

'We can rule as Great King, without you,' Prince Kumara interrupted, contemptuously now.

'We played into your hands. We see it all at last.' King Wira stared into space. 'Your becoming a Catholic, the support of the Church and the *parangi* musket companies and cannon, your five hundred cavalry men, even your marriage. You waited for the right moment. Indeed, your timing has been perfect.'

'More perfect than you think.' Prince Kumara's tone was suddenly as merciless as he knew his eyes to be, as the whole of his being felt.

'How so?'

'My wife, the queen, has just finished her pretended period. You dare even cast an eye on her ever again and I'll have your liver, you fat womanizer. During your long hours in lonely exile, you can reflect with regret that it was your own lack of judgement and sorry timing that brought you to this pass sooner rather than later.

Saturday, 12 August 1525

One hour later, Queen Anula glanced up as her husband entered her chamber. She could not tell from his expression whether his mission had succeeded or failed. He stood before her, slim, tall, unusually serious-faced. She could not help noticing how beautifully his fair skin contrasted with his dark-blue tunic and pantaloons. 'Do I greet you with obeisance as the Great King of the *uda rata*, or hide you beneath my skirts because your mission has failed?' she demanded.

His face broke into that devilish grin she adored. 'We would hide beneath your skirt, whatever our condition, to gaze at the glorious flower of your womanhood, breathe its fragrance, imbibe its honey, O Great Queen,' he responded.

His words told her of his new estate. With a happy laugh, she sank in obeisance before him. She rose to feel his grip strong on her arms. He pulled her to him, kissed her on the lips. Long heavenly moments passed. And she, lost in his spell.

She pulled herself out of it, gazed into his eyes. Her dream had come true again. Power, position were within her grasp once more, a far cry from the helplessness of the widow who had sought sanctuary in the Kandyan court less than eighteen months before. Revenge too. 'We cannot say we love you more than ever,' she whispered. 'But we have never been more proud of you, or of anyone, in our entire life.'

'I love you,' he responded, and she noted with delight that he had omitted the royal 'we'.

'I love you.' She paused. 'Now please sit down and tell me all about it.' She took his hand, led him to the settee.

'There's not much to tell that you don't already know.'
He laughed shortly. 'The trick was to make the entire
operation seem normal until we could get to my father,
then bluff him into leaving by the show of force from our
escort, who did not even know what it was all about until
he was outside the palace, being conducted to Jaya by the
entourage we had provided ostensibly at his own command.' He chuckled. 'He would not dare question those
accompanying him and they would not question him
either, even if they thought the whole operation odd. By
the time they exchange information, they will not know
what support, if any, they would have if they returned.
Before the night is out, I shall pass word around the palace
that the king has voluntarily abdicated in favour of his son
and heir. As you know, most people will support an
incumbent king!'

'You are so clever it's frightening.'

'Good. But now that we are the Great King, we will
have our immediate reward.'

'And that, lord?'

'A right royal bedding from the queen of the *uda rata*
kingdoms.'

CHAPTER SIX

Monday, 14 August 1525

The past year had been eventful for Julietta. First, her marriage, then the attempted rape, Menika's death and finally the baby. Now Captain Oliveira had left Lisbon, a very sick man, and Fernao was appointed to succeed him as head of all the Portuguese operations in Lanka.

A few days before Catherina's birth, Julietta's father, Duarte de Brito, had died of a sudden heart attack. He had been Portugal's factor on the island for twenty years, but Fernao decided not to appoint a replacement; he would act as factor himself and thus retain the whole of the commissions.

It took the finality of her father's death, the more poignant because he would never see his grandchild, for Julietta to realize how greatly she had depended on him as the one root in her life. Now he was gone, her last link with her past was severed. She had not heard from Prince Tikiri, her only remaining link with her childhood, even when her father died, and assumed this was because he did not want to embarrass her with Fernao. Also, Prince Tikiri must be deeply hurt by the birth of her baby. He could not even guess that little Catherina was his child, not Fernao's.

Part of Julietta had wanted the baby to be a boy and to look like Prince Tikiri. So often she visualized Prince Tikiri's slim, six-foot frame, the hard, muscled body which she had known so intimately just once. His hair was glossy and black, the face well-chiselled, the features elegant and cast in the Arya mould, with tight muscles and a straight nose, the nostrils lightly flaring. The cleft chin gave firmness to his jaw. His colour was Sinhala gold, all of him so like his father, except that King Maya Dunne was taller, broader and his hair shot with silver.

But it would never do for her baby to grow up looking like Prince Tikiri. There were times when that possibility made her panic. The child's paternity should never be betrayed, so it would be best if Catherina grew up to look like her, especially since Fernao had told Julietta that she reminded him of his mother. Julietta could believe this because she herself bore some resemblance to Fernao. Many people fall in love or become friends with people who look like themselves. Julietta supposed that this was an expression of self-love. She and Fernao had the same fair skin and dark hair, while Fernao's fine facial bones and straight nose would have made him look feminine were it not for the ice-blue eyes of the de Albergarias and the innate strength of the features.

A source of comfort to her from the past was Appu, her *major domo*, who turned out to be Prince Tikiri's man. It was Appu's vigilance that had first uncovered Sergeant Correa's foul intentions. Despite her terror and loathing of the rapist, a vague, brutal figure in a dark grove, she could not help a shudder each time she recalled his fate, for his stinking corpse had been found in the same grove two days later, dead from stab wounds. But Appu was a watch-dog rather than a tangible connection with Prince Tikiri. Would Appu ever become a tangible connection? She cast aside the question each time it arose in her mind. That was more than unlikely, it was impossible. And yet, some intuition remained as she watched the rose and flame which heralded dusk in the western sky, always spectacular from the Mutu Vella hilltop, especially when seen from her upstairs bedroom window.

The sunset was especially vivid this evening. The *nao* in the harbour were sharp-etched on grey-gold waters, their bulk dwarfing a solitary catamaran slowly sailing out west. The movement of a flock of seagulls wheeling above the warships brought the desire, but only half-hearted, to paint the scene. The connection between artistic delight and its expression had somehow been severed on the night of the attempted rape.

She walked back from the window to her favourite chair beside it. She heard the twet-tvee ... twet-tvee ... of an oriole from the red-blossomed flamboyant tree on the lawn beneath her. How wonderful it would be if one could incorporate sounds and scents into the sights of a painting, she thought.

She recalled her pregnancy. When it became obvious to her that she was going to have a baby, she knew beyond doubt that Prince Tikiri, not Fernao, was the father. It made the inner withdrawal from Fernao that had commenced on the morning after the attempted rape even more difficult to overcome. The knowledge that she was safest when Fernao was around – the house was guarded by Captain Rego, who had been best man at their wedding, during Fernao's turn of night duty in the fort – helped greatly and in a few weeks she found herself getting over her withdrawal. It had taken many months, however, to overcome the sheer terror that would grip her at times when she was alone. She had been sleeping so peacefully in that very room, on that very bed. And Menika had been asleep on her mat on the floor beside her, to guard her. Poor Menika had been unable to protect herself. Julietta's eyes drifted to the space by the bed. She remembered Menika's wrinkled skin and frail body, the intense kindliness in the brown eyes, and her own eyes prickled with tears. Such a dire night and with the dawn Fernao had arrived to fail her in her direst hour of need. A voice whispered of her own guilt, however, and she dried her tears.

After the baby was born, Fernao's obvious love for the child these past few days had caused her to start melting towards him again, within the bond of family magically created by the birth. Her dominant feeling, however, was an even fiercer protectiveness towards Catherina. She would save her baby at all costs from the shame of being known as a *mestico*, half-caste, of bastard birth. She would keep that secret from everyone, including Prince Tikiri and especially Fernao, whatever the price. The pretence tore her, but Fernao must continue believing that he was the baby's father. God forgive her the sin.

For some reason, which she could not identify, the feeling of guilt became strong as she watched the road leading to the mansion for Fernao's return home this evening. He was unusually late and she discovered that she missed him. It brought the recollection of how kind Fernao had been to her. He had defied his father, even sacrificed his birthright, in order to uplift her to an honoured place in society. He really loved the baby. Could it possibly be that he was the father? Her woman's knowledge told her that he was not. Surely her husband deserved far more than betrayal and deceit. Yet, what could she do?

Her eyes lifted to the heavens for succour and God seemed to answer. You are right to save Fernao from this knowledge, my child. It caused her to smile with thankfulness, closing the ears of her mind to that little voice within her, questioning: are you not creating God in the image necessary for you to justify your sin?

The baby's whimper broke the stillness of the room. She glanced towards her, relieved when the whimper turned to sucking noises and ended beneath the harsh evening caws of crows suddenly intruding from outside. The odour of the child's excreta reached her nostrils. She had best change its napkin immediately. The last thing Fernao needed was an offensive smell to greet him on his return from work.

Immediately she started removing the soiled napkin, the baby awoke, crying petulantly at being disturbed. O . . . yaa . . . O . . . yaa . . . Catherina was fully awake by the time Julietta finally picked her up and hushed her. Such a pretty rosy-cheeked mite, with dark hair, normally even tempered, but capable of being imperious. Like her royal father, Julietta thought.

She carried Catherina to the window and resumed her seat, cradling the baby on her lap. Was I as good as this when I was little? Poor *o pai*, you had to cope with me by yourself, since I had no mother. You did not even live to enjoy your granddaughter. Why did you have to die so suddenly? Did you know you had a weak heart? Were you afraid to die?

She would never be with her father again. Never, never. The stark finality of it caused the tears to flow once more. What's wrong with me that I have become such a cry-baby? *You* are responsible for my condition, you wee one! She hugged the baby, then took out her white linen handkerchief, blew her nose, dabbed her cheeks. Fernao must not be greeted with tears either. He had worries of his own.

The baby's eyes, wide open now, lifted to hers. The glancing sunlight caught them at an unusual angle. A chill had gripped Julietta's stomach. The dark brown eyes had blue rims. Only two people in the world had such eyes, Tiki-tiki and his father, King Maya Dunne.

Julietta stiffened, peered closer at the baby's eyes, praying that it had been some trick of the light. That chill hand of fear became certainty, coldly gripping her, tightening, tightening. The baby was fair-skinned, looked very European, but would her eyes betray the secret to Fernao and the world? Her intensity frightened the little mite, caused her to start wailing loudly. She kissed the tiny puckered face, flushed so red, began rocking the baby, hushing it again. But she was trembling inside.

The clip-clop of horse's hooves trickled into her consciousness like steps of doom. She glanced down at the cobbled road, knew relief at seeing that it was not Fernao, but a Portuguese soldier on a chestnut mount, trotting towards the mansion.

Minutes later, Maria, the child's nurse, entered. 'Lady, a messenger has come from the fort to say that Master Fernao will not be home till late. He has gone to the Jaya capital for an unexpected audience and dinner with the Great King.' Maria smiled, removed the baby's soiled linen and departed, a plump comfortable figure.

Julietta felt the need for prayer.

She walked across the room, placed the baby back in her silk-lined cradle, hushed her with a finger to her lips. She went to the little altar on the far side of the bedroom. She knelt on the *pri-dieu* before the blue and white statue of the Blessed Virgin Mary.

'O Mary, Sweet Virgin, O Mother most mild
'With eyes full of mercy watch over thy child . . .'

Monday, 14 August 1525

Flushed with our victory over Lord Samara Kon, the news that the *parangi* ships had veered off the coast of Galle, heading back towards Colombo, was a bitter disappointment to me. I had expected to destroy Prince Vidiye's forces when they attempted to land in the Galle harbour. Now they remained a potential threat. Lord Wickrama Sinha's arrival in Galle had been delayed because the river upstream had been dammed by enemy nobles in the area and he had to land from his rafts on three occasions and fight his way through. Only total victory over Prince Vidiye would have brought such opposing nobles to our side.

When it became evident that the *parangi* ships bearing Prince Vidiye and his men would not return – fishermen had observed them well on their way back – I decided that my presence in Galle was no longer necessary. Two older Sita Waka princes and their contingents, who had formed a part of Lord Wickrama Sinha's forces, had already left for home, bearing Lord Samara Kon's head, preserved in medicinal herbs, as my gift to my father. Leaving Lord Wickrama Sinha and his men behind, I proceeded back with my regiment to Sita Waka, taking the musketeer company with me. News and details of our victory had therefore preceded me and I was greeted as some kind of hero all along the route. Like my father, I found such adulation embarrassing. After all, the real heroes and victors were my troops.

It was late evening, four days after the battle, by the time I clattered at the head of my cavalry escort between the flaming torches lining the driveway leading to our palace in Sita Waka. Cheering crowds had assembled between the torches. Their cries of *'Jaya-wewa! ... Ape Kumaraya Jaya-wewa! ... Triumph! ... May our prince triumph ...'* rang through the darkling sky. Lamplight glowed from all the palace windows. To my amazement, for the first time since he became king, my father, surrounded by courtiers in magnificent attire, stood at the entrance verandah to greet me. He was richly dressed in white satin tunic, pantaloons and turban with gold shoes and jewelled ornaments. His slim, tall figure, one hand lightly on the holt of his sword, was more than dashing, it was regal.

Wishing that I was not so sweaty and dirt-stained, I quickly dismounted, handed Rama's reins to a groom. A gleam of amusement crossed my father's chiselled features as I smoothed back a forelock in a subconscious attempt to appear neater. When I knelt before him in obeisance, he reached out a hand and laid it gently on my bowed head. Thrills ran through my body at this rare contact. I rose to my feet. He gripped me firmly by the hand and drew me to his embrace.

Confused, my heart pounding, I let him hold me, unused to exhibiting emotion, embarrassed by its public display, reluctant to touch the king, not wanting him to release me.

During those moments, I smelled the clean, sandalwood scent of my father and breathed the essence of his *prana*, life-force. Surprisingly, I found loneliness and a strange mysticism in him.

My father released me, raised his hand to silence the cheers that had broken out. 'Our loyal subjects and devoted friends, hear your king on this auspicious occasion.' He pitched his voice so the crowds on the lawn could also hear. 'You have all heard of the victory we have won in Galle over an arch enemy. You have also heard of the courage and daring of the troops we sent out to battle. But they will be the first to admit that none can match their leader, this prince whom we are proud to call our son. Two of our Arya cousins who were present, having retailed the story of his ferocity in battle, added, "It is not merely a son you have bred, Sire, but a royal prince who will devour lions." Our pride at hearing these words made us pause and think. Prince Tikiri Bandara is not only a great soldier, but is also our heir. It has been foretold that he will reign over a free, united Lanka, which we ourselves have pledged our life and our sacred honour to create.'

My blood quickened at hearing his pledge. The cheering on the verandah hit the rafters of the palace, outside it reached for the heavens.

My father raised his hand again for silence. 'As you know, this prince was named Tikiri Bandara because he was the youngest of our three sons. Loku Bandara, our eldest son, and Medduma Bandara, our middle son, are long gone to other life-forms in the cycle of Samsara. It is not fitting that a devourer of lions should retain the name of his babyhood. What name would honour such a prince, the most royal of lions?'

The crowd gave back their answer. 'Raja Sinha . . . Raja Sinha . . . the royal lion, the royal lion!'

My breath caught, the blood pounded in my ears. Through a haze, in a sudden profound silence that had fallen, I heard the words of my father, King Maya Dunne. 'Prince Tikiri Bandara of Sita Waka, as your father and your king, we hereby confer on you for ever the name and title you have achieved, Raja Sinha. May your *kharma* and the blessings of the Triple Gem crown you with achievements worthy of that name throughout your life and in your wanderings through Samsara. You shall henceforth be known as Prince Parakrama Bahulage Maya Dunne Raja Sinha of Sita Waka.' He paused, a prophetic note caused a tremor in his voice. 'Some day, you shall become the Great King Raja Sinha I of Lanka.'

Monday, 14 August 1525

For the Great King's dinner at the Jaya palace that evening, Fernao wore a white silken uniform, which he kept in his quarters in the Colombo fort for such unexpected events. Having received the invitation only that afternoon, he had deduced that the occasion must be personal and an emergency. Regardless, he went prepared to expose his own plan to the king, even taking with him the necessary documents.

There was no evidence of anxiety in King Bhuvenaka's behaviour when they sat beside each other in the dining hall and enjoyed a sumptuous meal consisting of Sinhala curries and Portuguese delicacies. Two hours of the customary Sinhala entertainment followed. While he enjoyed the dancing, drumming and chanting, Fernao was anxious to get on with the business for which he had been summoned at such short notice. Since the Sinhala were too conscious of form to mix business with hospitality, there had been nothing but small talk throughout the meal and entertainment. He was relieved therefore when the Great King finally invited him to the audience chamber for a 'quiet chat'.

The Great King sat at his ebony desk, gestured to Fernao

to sit opposite him. The fragrance of the devil's brew, *copi*, which had been banned by His Holiness the Pope, clung to the air, mingling with the sharp camphor scent of incense smoke from the brass burners placed before the two gold Buddha statues on alabaster stands at the wall behind the desk to give the room a sense of unreality.

'A fitting end to a great meal,' the Great King remarked, lifting the lightly steaming cup. He pursed his lips and took a sip of the *copi*, slurping a little to avoid its heat. 'What a pity it has been banned by your Church, Colonel. *Copi* has such a settling effect on the stomach.'

'So has *hashish* on the mind.' Fernao smiled to rob the words of offence. 'They both come from the same heathen source and are inspired by the devil.'

The eyes of the ruler twinkled. 'Mathematics, your script and astronomy also came from that heathen source,' he observed drily. 'Surely all things from that region are not of the devil?'

'All that you speak of came *before* Muhammad, Sire. *Copi* came *after* the prophet had re-infected his followers with ancient hatreds and roused the devil in them.'

'*Copi* is new, but *hashish* is older than the prophet, is it not? And is not hatred the oldest of all evils?' The dark eyes twinkled again. 'And is not religion the *hashish* of the masses?'

Fernao was seeing the Great King in a new light. He seemed knowledgeable and possessed of a keen mind. Why then was he always so dependent on others to achieve his ambitions? A good thinker but a poor performer, perhaps? Though he did not wish to waste more time debating philosophical issues, Fernao felt constrained to counter his host's theses. 'Being a true believer, I am guided by the dictates of Holy Church, as you are by the Doctrine of Lord Buddha.'

'Well put, Colonel. But it makes us glad that we do not believe in the devil.' He took another sip of the *copi*. 'Mmm

'. . . Delicious. It is laced with honey. We hope you will be permitted by your Church to try it some time.'

'For the present it is as abhorrent to me as alcohol is to good Buddhists.'

'Ah! Now you admonish us, no?'

'No, Sire. I am merely making my excuses for not accepting a royal suggestion.'

'Well, at least the meal was a good one, was it not?'

'The best, Sire.'

'And you are sure you would not like some port?' King Bhuvenaka, who, like all good Buddhists, did not take alcohol, was obviously trying to display his civilized tolerance.

Fernao held up his hand. 'No, thank you, Sire.'

The Great King lifted a shaggy eyebrow. 'These beautiful customs, of any race, are so important in today's world, which has no respect for rank, station, or circumstance.'

'I entirely agree.' Fernao decided to direct the conversation to more official channels. 'Why else would a young prince go out with an army and give battle to the nominee of his uncle, the Great King?'

'Right, Colonel. We are told that after five days at sea, Pr . . . er . . . King Vidiye is expected back in Colombo tonight.'

'Yes, Sire. It was to hear what plans Your Majesty might in your wisdom have and what assistance we can provide that I was about to request an early audience with you when your gracious invitation to dinner arrived.'

'Tell us, Colonel, what do you advise?'

Fernao decided to be cautious. 'The actions of King Maya Dunne and Prince Tikiri as well as their prowess in battle have greatly exceeded our assessments. This victory and the desecration of our cross, to which I shall presently allude, will increase their popularity in the Sinhala Buddhist area. Therefore King Vidiye should only return to

99

Billigam Korle with sufficient strength to establish mastery over the region.'

'How can that be achieved?'

'I commend to your royal notice that we, the Portuguese people, have established a domin . . . er . . . strong presence in Colombo by building our fort and erecting a factory.' He leaned forward to give emphasis to his words. 'There is an area of land on the headland in Galle, on which Admiral de Almeida erected the stone cross, that is ideally located for the creation of a strong fort, which could support King Vidiye in that region. It is bordered by the ocean on its west side, the harbour to the south and a stream to the north. We are prepared to build such a fort there if Your Majesty would give us leave.'

The Great King let out a 'Ha!' and slapped a plump thigh with the palm of his right hand. 'You are a superb strategist, Colonel!' he exclaimed. 'How did you guess that was the plan we had in mind?'

'Because I know you to be an even greater strategist, Sire,' Fernao responded, lying gallantly for his country. 'I take it then that you will bestow on us the necessary land grants for this purpose.'

'Of course we shall, for our partners in trade, with whom we shall have an exclusive supply agreement.' The Great King was cleverly imposing a condition.

Fernao was not surprised at the reminder that the Great King would expect to be the exclusive buying agent for the commercial part of the enterprise. 'We must act fast to prevent the enemy strength from growing and ours from being eroded,' he declared. 'There is also a matter of pride and prestige on which we require Your Majesty's support. I refer to the desecration of our cross. Those who committed the terrible sacrilege of pushing our cross, the sacred symbol of our religion, into the ocean must be punished immediately. Please treat this as a formal protest on behalf of my King Emperor and Holy Church, Your Majesty.'

'Be assured, Colonel, that such barbaric acts are foreign to the *charlithraya*, traditions and religion of the Sinhala people, whom you well know to be tolerant of and respectful towards other religions. The vandals will indeed be punished ... and swiftly ... er ... with your military help.'

'Our friars ...'

'We fully understand,' the Great King interrupted, raising his hand. 'Our *bhikkus*, monks, are also like that. Always trying to interfere in the business of ruling the realm. Our brother, King Maya Dunne, listens to them, hoping for their support, but we stand firmly by what is right, not by who is right. We would rather depend on friends, such as you, than on a bunch of ignorant priests. Talking of which, how do you plan to deal with the Catholic prince ... er ... King in Kandy, Colonel?' The Great King had adroitly closed the subject of the desecration of the cross. 'You must surely be aware that he seized power from his father in a bloodless action? *Cha*, not good, no?'

'I heard of the event this morning. Please understand that the prince's actions fit in well with our plan.' Fernao's tone was smooth, soothing. 'You and I both need a united, strong hill country kingdom against King Maya Dunne. Since King Kumara's new territory borders the Sita Waka kingdom, he will seek to expand towards Sita Waka. We will support King Kumara in this objective, because it will compel King Maya Dunne to direct his resources to a new direction, thus helping ensure the security of your own rule.'

'Tchk!' the Great King clucked. 'We do not trust Kandyans, still less a man who can throw out his own father ...' He paused, grinning wryly. Obviously remembering that he had deposed his own father King Wijayo, he added '... without cause.'

Fernao decided to change the subject and to make his

major move. 'As you know, Sire, I am but the representative of my government. While I proffer advice, I'm here to carry out the dictates of my king, which are communicated to me by our Viceroy. One of the strongest influences on His Imperial Majesty is Holy Church.' Fernao paused to ensure that he had the Great King's total attention. 'There is one way in which you can ensure the unqualified support of Holy Church and my government.'

The ruler's face tightened; the dark eyes became watchful.

'Since you have no sons, you might wish to name your grandson, the baby born to King Vidiye and your daughter, who, God rest her soul, so unfortunately died at childbirth, your heir.'

The dark eyes blinked once, a hand instinctively stroked the black moustache. Fernao pressed home his point. 'You might then send an embassy to His Majesty, Dom João III, in Lisbon, requesting the Emperor's divine protection for your heir.'

A slow smile crossed the broad features of the Great King. 'A wonderful idea, which but supports what we had already considered,' he declared loftily. Fernao hid his amusement at the pomposity of kings who must never acknowledge an original idea which they had not already thought of themselves.

The Great King reflected a few minutes, drummed a rapid tattoo with his fingers on the ebony desk. 'As a matter of fact, we had thought of an improvement to that idea,' he lied. 'We shall make a gold effigy of the baby, Prince Dharma Pala, and send it to His Majesty your King Emperor for a pre-crowning ceremony in Lisbon. Your sovereign lord will thus always have a valuable reminder of his gracious agreement to extend his divine protection to the rightful heir to our throne.'

A bribe of gold, Fernao thought cynically. Why not? 'A splendid thought,' he declared. 'Since you are a life-size monarch, I'm sure you will want to make the effigy as near life-size as possible.'

'Yes, yes. The eyes shall be brown tourmalines, the mouth shall be of red rubies, the ornaments of the *navaratna*, the nine gems. We shall also send other fitting presents of great price to your Emperor as a mark of our esteem. You will write a suitable letter to His Majesty in your language, conveying our sentiments?' The lifted eyebrows invited an answer.

'Certainly, nothing would give me greater pleasure,' Fernao responded. He hesitated, then decided to take the plunge. 'Here is where the much-needed backing of Holy Church comes in, Sire. It would help enormously if you informed my Emperor that the baby will be taught the Catholic religion.' Noting the shaggy eyebrows rise again, he hastened to add, 'It will compensate in some small measure for the desecration of our cross in Galle.'

Open admiration filled the Great King's face. 'A brilliant suggestion. We are delighted to find that you appreciate the finer points of the *manta yuddhaya*, diplomatic battle, which we enlightened Arya monarchs have favoured over physical battle for more than two thousand years.'

'You are most kind, Sire. I am honoured by your approval and inspired by your praise.' Fernao decided to clinch the argument. 'May I also respectfully suggest therefore that you request my Emperor to bestow on the baby prince a royal Portuguese name. It would certainly create greater personal feelings.'

'A Portuguese name? What for?'

'We live in a time when the more names a man has, the nobler is his station.' Fernao did not want to admit that having considered Father Juan's suggestions, he had decided that, if the Sinhala people were going to be coerced into changing their ancient names, it had better start at the top. 'In your country, low-caste people, like the Rodiyas, have only one name. People of higher caste are permitted the *ge* name, or the name of their house. Those of higher caste yet are permitted the name of the village or district as their *ge* name, while nobility and royalty have their own distinctive names in addition. We shall shortly institute a system of land registration in the areas in which we trade, so that our agents, most of whom do not speak the local languages, can identify our suppliers and ensure the quality of their produce. We will buy only from people who have registered Portuguese or Spanish names. Catholic converts will of course already have their baptismal Christian names. It would give tremendous encouragement to all your people if you set the example with your own grandson and heir.'

Fernao had observed, with dismay, the smile slowly leave the Great King's face. He now noted the big jaw tighten. 'That would begin the destruction of our age-old systems. We cannot permit . . .' The Great King paused, thinking deeply. His fingers drummed a quicker tattoo on the desk, an echo of Fernao's increased heartbeat. Finally, the Great King nodded slowly. 'That may not be such a bad idea after all,' he mused.

'It could cause a change of heart among some of those who now support your brother, Sire,' Fernao volunteered boldly. 'If you give the plan your royal blessing, you might consider extending the policy to all areas of the country, certainly the coasts. The more Sinhala Catholics you have, the fewer Sinhala Buddhists for King Maya Dunne. By providing the leading families with a means to extend their grand, titular names and by affording those of lower castes a means of disguising their caste, you would acquire tremendous support at all levels, as an enlightened monarch.'

'True, true. A capital policy indeed.' So capital did the Great King seem to think it that for once he failed to capitalize on it as his own. The broad features relaxed in a smile again. 'We invited you to dinner tonight, Colonel, because we desired to savour with you the bitter fruit of the Galle defeat and to make immediate plans to sweeten it.' He paused, a sincere note entered his voice. 'You have brought us instead the sweeter prospects of future victory.'

'A just dessert, Sire.' Fernao completed the metaphor. 'Now as for Galle, here is my plan.' He told the Great King what he intended. For long moments after he had finished, the Great King remained lost in thought.

'Building a new fort will cost you many gold *cruzados*, will it not?' To Fernao's relief there was no opposition in the Great King's voice.

'Indeed it will, Sire. The fort will be constructed primarily of wood, clay bricks and mortar.' Inspiration seized him. 'We shall need large, solid timbers for the fort.'

'You can have them from the mountains of our very own Sinha Raja, royal forest, nearby. We shall have the timbers floated down the river to its mouth, Gin-tota, from where our royal elephants can haul them to Galle.' The Great King bared white teeth beneath the great black moustaches. 'At our minimal cost of course.'

'You are most gracious to help, Sire.'

The Great King nodded amiably. 'You are a clever young man. You shall also have a land grant ... er ... at our minimal cost.'

Fernao grinned. His planning had been perfect. He reached into his doublet. 'I have already brought three documents for you to sign and have your seal affixed to, Sire,' he declared, placing the parchments he had prepared that very evening on the desk.

The Great King was taken aback. Then a guffaw escaped him and he shook his head from side to side. 'You white men, when you want something, you waste no time with protocol.' He paused. 'But why three documents?'

'The first is the land grant, the second is your royal endorsement of our land registration system in the coastal areas of our trade, the third is your request to my King Emperor that he extend his divine protection for your grandson and heir, Prince Dharma Pala, on whom will be bestowed the royal Portuguese name, Dom Juan of Lanka, with his father, King Vidiye, to be Prince Regent in the event of your demise, which God forbid, while your heir is not of age.'

The Great King stared into space. He was not communing with the past, Fernao knew, but searching the future. Finally, he heaved a great sigh. A strange sadness surfaced in his eyes. 'We shall match your promptitude and sign the documents immediately our advisers have reviewed them.'

The conversation drifted back to the pleasantries which begin and end such discussions. The Great King proudly described his grandson, then questioned Fernao closely on the appearance of his daughter. 'Does the baby have blue eyes?' he inquired. 'We think blue eyes are beautiful. Does she have a very fair skin?'

'No, Sire. As you know, these infants spend most of their time sleeping, but *a senhora* and I have agreed that our baby's eyes are dark brown. Her skin is as fair as her mother's.'

'That is good. A wise *bhikku*, monk, once told us never to trust people with pale brown eyes or those whose eyes have rims that contrast with the eye-colour.' He seemed about to say something, smiled rather awkwardly, hesitated. 'We can share this sad confidence with you now that we are such close allies. You may not have noticed it, but our brother, King Maya Dunne and his son, Prince Tikiri, both have the same unique eyes, possibly a throw-back on our Aryan heritage. The colour is dark brown, but the rims are blue. Quite attractive really, but if what the *bhikku* told us is true, this may be evidence that – or perhaps the reason why – they are not to be trusted.'

Monday, 14 August 1525

Later that night, after our guests had departed, my father, King Maya Dunne, and I retired to his study in our Sita Waka residence, now its palace. As usual, he sat behind his *nadun*-wood desk and I occupied a settle to one side of it, leaning back against the wall. The hush of approaching bedtime had fallen over this part of the palace, though the servants were doubtless still busy in the kitchen quarters.

'When we were young, we won many a battle against the Cholas,' my father stated, after I had given him all details of the Galle operation. 'Today we face more powerful enemies, especially the *parangi*. It is obvious that they are exercising power from behind the scenes, using the weakness and ambition of men like the Great King and Prince Vidiye for their own purposes. The sad part of it all is that the Great King, Prince Vidiye and Prince Kumara are trying in turn to manipulate the *parangi* strength for their own ends. Having tasted power, the *parangi* will go after it to promote their trade interests, not least because they are enjoying a lifestyle that they could never hope for in their native Portugal. As you know, they live grandly in Colombo, in a manner in which even their great disciplinarian, Vasco da Gama, could not stop in Goa. Some of the men have now started to use their money to keep harems of local women. They will breed children of mixed blood with loyalty only to them. Worse, they have infected our people in Colombo with their manners, customs and culture, not to mention the pox, so that many Sinhala have become brown Portuguese.'

'Then let us attack the *parangi* instead of fighting against our fellow Sinhala, Sire.'

He shook his head, a sad smile touching his fine features. 'Easier said than done, *putha*, son. Lacking the firepower, we will need to wait until their forces here are depleted. Meanwhile, once the nation is reunited, we can oppose anyone. Remember though that such attempts to unite the country have their own consequences. War costs money. It is a drain on the people and on all our resources.' He paused. 'Also, being a small island, we fear we are fated to keep on fighting to defend our independence, for ever. Our concern for you, as a sentient being, relates to your *kharma*.'

I hated it whenever he talked like this . . . 'sentient being' . . . '*kharma*', such words of *bhikkus* have no place in the vocabulary of warriors and freedom fighters, but as always I refrained from making any comment. 'What are you trying to tell me, *tha*?' I inquired.

He gathered his thoughts. 'Would you consider that your feelings in the heat of battle were those of a warrior, or those of a killer?'

The unexpected question jarred me, plunging into my mind with the force of a dagger thrust. 'I . . . ah . . . that is . . .' I paused helplessly, then started furious introspection.

He placed his hands on the desk, calmly awaiting my reply. The seconds passed by. Finding myself in the closest, deepest self-examination I have ever made, I subconsciously noted the sand slowly running out in the sand-clock. Damn you, *tha*, I thought, but with affection, you have made me probe too much and it is more difficult than planning or fighting a battle.

He sensed my thoughts with his uncanny perception. 'We warned you that the battle of the senses is the most difficult of all.'

'When I rode into battle, I was a warrior,' I replied. 'Then I saw Lord Samara Kon towering over his men. I remembered my vow to myself that I would send you his head on a pike. Something snapped inside me. I was completely engulfed by deep, all-consuming hatred, his and mine. I wanted to kill him, to feel the joy of my sword in his fat belly, to watch his blood and entrails gush out while I hacked him to death.' I paused, sweating now at a recollection that was nonetheless a revelation.

'There is within you then a product of your past *kharma* which has the *vipaka*, effect, of making you a killer. Only the Doctrine can save you. Try always to be the warrior, even the executioner, without tainting your *kharma* by letting loose the mentality of the killer which is inherent in us all.'

I did not want to hurt him more by telling him of the lust I had felt at killing my enemies, so strong that it was almost sexual, so sexual that I could feel it in my loins. Instead, I wondered dismally whether killing and battle were not meant to be my only sexual experiences, since I had taken the vow of *brachmachariya* after my union with Julietta. Was it for this too that I would remain celibate, my *lingam* – phallus – the sword?

'You have no cause to worry,' my father assured me, misunderstanding my reaction for once. 'The Doctrine provides us with the remedies for what is a *kharmic* manifestation within you. Your salvation lies in Right Mindfulness, Right Concentration, Right Meditation at all times, reinforced by the regular observance of *pan-sil*, *ata-sil*, *dasa-sil*, the five, eight and ten precepts. You must learn to kill without being a killer.'

I appreciated his words and their source, his deep love for me, but inside I was impatient of such sentiments. I had no great affinity with the Doctrine. The Hindus, especially those who follow god Siva, have the right idea, total dedication to *dharma*, the duty of one's station, even if it means killing one's opponents. Buddhism could only make us such slaves to self-improvement that the national cause would suffer.

I had a purpose, a destiny to fulfil, which made me invincible in battle. I would accept any religion that would propel me, without hypocrisy, to that destiny. At that moment, Hinduism seemed to offer a better way to it than Lord Buddha's Doctrine.

CHAPTER SEVEN

Tuesday, 15 August 1525

Having returned home to the Mutu Vella mansion long after midnight after dinner and his audience with the Great King, Fernao slept late, but still did not want to sacrifice the time he spent each morning with the baby before leaving for the fort. Breakfast over, while Julietta remained downstairs organizing the morning's shopping detail, he went upstairs to her bedroom. The room adjoining the bedroom on the north side of the house had been converted to a nursery and the baby slept there in its crib at night, looked after by Maria, but occupied Julietta's bedroom during the day.

To Fernao's delight, the baby was awake, trying to focus her teetering eyes here and there. Smiling to himself at his expertise as a ten-day-old father when he had been so scared even to touch the child on the day it was born, he bent down and lifted it from the cradle. Holding the baby in the crook of his right arm, he used his left hand to wrap the pink cover around a tiny foot that had poked through. Humming an improvised lullaby, he walked to the window, so Catherina could see the blue sky, the green tree-tops, the mynahs, magpies and doves flitting around, shrilling, trilling or cooing. 'See . . . e . . .' he half-crooned. 'Can you see the pretty birdies, darling?'

Realizing that a baby might not be able to see that far, he felt rather foolish. Swaying from side to side, he held Catherina up, hoping that she would at least see the bright, silver sunshine.

The baby eyes moved towards the light, squinted against the glare, then opened wide, shifting sideways. Fernao's breath caught. Did the black-brown eyes have blue rims?

A knife-edge of anxiety slashed through him. He peered more closely at the eyes. No, they did not even have rims. A gush of thankfulness swept through his being.

A gardener called to his mate, the harsh cawing of a crow broke through the bird-song. The baby eyes shifted again. The thin rims, barely perceptible, were unmistakably blue.

How could this be? Did Julietta secretly love Prince Tikiri so much that she had re-created his eyes, the gateway to his soul, in childbirth? No, that was absurd. How then could his baby have the Maya Dunne family eyes? His pulse racing, the question ran like a burning fuse to the powder keg of Fernao's earlier suspicions, which had lain dormant, so deep, deep down inside him that he had almost come to forget them . . . and caused an explosion.

Some wisdom acquired from the price he had paid for mishandling Julietta on the morning following the attempted rape jerked Fernao into a cold awareness that he must not rush to conclusions, still less accusations. He had to be calm, wise, even cunning about this.

Barely conscious of the baby now, he ran over the facts. Julietta Catherina Menika was born on 5 August. He counted back rapidly. She must have been conceived during the first or second week of November. He had made love to Julietta on the day of the attempted rape and more than usual during that time, so she could get over her ordeal, reasoning that she should get back in the saddle and ride the horse that had just thrown her. So he could definitely have been the father. A jagged flash of recall slaked through his relief. The raw smell of a man's emission . . . Julietta inviting him to make love to her that dreadful morning . . .

But how did it all connect with Prince Tikiri? He looked down at the baby again. She had pursed her little mouth and made a spit bubble. She looked so adorable that he felt the warmth of the tie. If she were not his, he would not be able to respond to her, but might even want to throw her out of the window. He could feel no antagonism at all towards the mite. He must be the father. Yet he felt a sort of hopelessness and the stirring of indeterminate rage.

He started reasoning again, coldly now. King Maya Dunne could not possibly have fathered the baby. For Prince Tikiri to have done so, he would have had to be in Colombo at the time. But he had been in Sita Waka . . . or had he?

Nonetheless ashamed of his groundless suspicions, Fernao kissed the baby's soft, pink cheek, held the tiny body warm and close to him, rocking gently from side to side.

Tuesday, 15 August 1525

The Great King kept his promise to match Fernao's speed. The three treaties which Fernao had handed to him the previous night were delivered to the fort the following evening, duly executed by the Great King and bearing his impressive seals. Fernao was elated. Such treaties normally took months to obtain, were frequently altered, amended or modified and sometimes were never even executed.

But it was not elation at the treaties alone that drove him to summon his regimental commanders and the captains of the six great square-rigged *nao* and three fast caravels comprising the flotilla that lay anchored in the Colombo harbour for a staff conference in the large briefing room of the fort that very evening. He was excited by the exercise of power, the prospect of singular achievements ahead, including the construction of a new fort that might give him a place in history. This was the first time that he would be issuing direct orders to all the older men under his command who were very senior to him in service. He felt a momentary qualm because he was only twenty-two, but his self-confidence, and the remembrance that many of the world's great generals, such as Sikander the Great, had been very young, caused him to overcome it easily. Above all, it was the prospect of striking back at King Maya Dunne for having foiled his plan in the south and at Prince Tikiri for somehow coming between him and Julietta that swept him to immediate action.

Despatching a flotilla of nine ships on such an operation some seventy miles from Colombo would require close planning. Though all the naval captains and army commanders assembled within the hour, Fernao sent word to Julietta through Captain Armand Rego that he would not be home that night; Captain Rego would remain in the house for her protection until morning.

The briefing room was part of the barracks, so it was warm and close inside, but since Fernao had already set up the necessary maps and plans and the men sitting around the plain yellow-jak-wood table were all professionals, the session went smoothly. As an infantry landing was part of the phasing of the operation, Colonel Felipe Gonzales, the senior regimental commander, was to be in overall command.

The tactical position of the selected site on the headland was ideal, with the harbour waters to the south, the ocean to the west, a stream to the north and an open *maidan* to the east. All operations could therefore take place under the protection of the big guns of the warships. Apart from the actual landing, the speedy establishment of a wide enough beach-head with perimeter defences supplemented by cannon off-loaded from the ships, was deemed to be essential. The proposed fort would be staked out by the surveyors within this perimeter, into which arms, supplies, and stores could be off-loaded. Construction would proceed thereafter as with the Colombo fort, except that this one would be mainly of earthworks and timber.

The conference yielded 29 August, two weeks away, as the earliest date on which the flotilla could sail, the delay being primarily due to the need to obtain the necessary provisions and stores so the ships and the men could be self-sufficient until they had established themselves in Galle.

It was almost midnight before the conference ended. Fernao's staff officers would draft orders the next day, after which the commanders concerned would brief their own staffs and perfect their individual planning.

When the officers had departed, Fernao stood alone outside his quarters, enjoying the cooler, fresher night air, experiencing a tremendous exhilaration at all that had been accomplished. He knew he had acquitted himself extremely well at the conference. He had even sensed admiration in many of those present and a change of heart in those who had doubted his competence. The parade ground was deserted, the fort was in darkness except for lights in the windows of the tower. Even the sentries patrolling the ramparts and the quiet wash of waves fitted into the total picture of stillness. He heard an apologetic cough and turned around in its direction. His man, Aires, had emerged from his quarters, a lean shadow silhouetted against the pale glow of lantern-light behind him. He raised a finger to his forelock, smiled.

'Ah Aires, did you wait up for me?' Fernao inquired. 'You really shouldn't have, you know.'

'It be my duty, sir.' Aires paused, shifted his feet. He obviously had something on his mind. 'I thought to go to residence to help look after *a senhora*, Colonel sir, but did not have your permission. I hope *a senhora* will be safe.'

'Oh, I'm sure she will be all right. I sent Captain Rego to remain in the house tonight.'

'I hear tell, Colonel sir.' Aires shifted his feet again, looked awkwardly at the ground. Then the words came out in a rush. 'Colonel sir, begging your pardon, it be my duty to confess something.'

'What is it, Aires? You know you may speak freely to me.'

114

The dark eyes of the soldier servant, now raised to meet Fernao's gaze, glistened in the gloom. 'Wondering if *a senhora* is safe tonight with the colonel away, sir, made me think of night when Sergeant Correa kidnap her. I feel so bad I think I must tell sir all about it even after so many months.'

Fernao froze. 'Ye-es.'

'That night you stay in fort on duty, so when I finish seeing you to bed, I go visit my Sinhala woman, who live on far side of Mutu Vella hill. I start back to fort by shortcut and see Prince Tikiri men near mansion gates. I go behind them quietlike so they not see me. I know Sinhala language from my woman. The men tell of *parangi* pig who kidnap my lady. Prince Tikiri had them cut off his privates to punish him. They think this is very good. *A senhora* is safe and they have left Sergeant Correa in grove. I am very angry, Colonel sir. I run to grove. I search and find Sergeant Correa, bleeding to death. I take out my knife. I stab and stab him.' Aires paused, breathing heavily. 'Mebbe you punish me now for killing Sergeant Correa, sir.' A fierce note entered his voice. 'But if it happen again, I do it again.'

Prince Tikiri's men, Aires had said . . . Prince Tikiri's sentence . . .! The news pounded into Fernao's brain like thudding cannonballs on ground already pulverized by his suspicions about his baby's eyes. It was not the governor's men, but Prince Tikiri's men who had rescued Julietta that night. It had been on Prince Tikiri's orders that they had cut off Sergeant Correa's privates. What had they been doing there? When had these orders been given? Where had Prince Tikiri been? He stared bleakly at Aires, his brain raw, noted the man's discomfiture and returned to the present. 'You are not to blame, Aires,' he responded quietly. 'Thank you for being man enough to admit the truth.'

'You do not punish me, Colonel sir?'

'Of course not. Sergeant Correa deserved all he got, not because of what he did to *a senhora* alone, but because he had a bad record of perversion and murder. That does not condone your taking the law into your own hands, but since all you did was to hasten Sergeant Correa's death, your act may even have been merciful.' He nodded encouragingly, though his mind was in turmoil. 'So it shall remain our secret.'

'Thank you, Colonel sir.' Aires bobbed his respects. 'Thank you, indeed. I be so glad you know at last.'

The need for confirmation pushed Fernao. 'Tell me, though, did you say it was Prince Tikiri's men who rescued *a senhora*?'

'Indeed, sir.'

'Not the port governor's guards?'

'They work for governor, sir, but they be really Prince Tikiri's men.'

Fernao struggled to set aside his seething suspicions, his brain raw with the effort. He recognized that it did not matter to whom the rescuers owed allegiance. One fact alone was important. Where was Prince Tikiri that night, in Sita Waka as he had thought, or in the governor's mansion?

'Thank you again for being honest with me, Aires,' he said. 'You may go to sleep now.'

Fernao stepped past the man and entered his quarters. He could not wait for tomorrow to start finding out the answer to the burning question hammering at his mind.

During the days that followed, Fernao maintained a calm exterior, did not voice his suspicions to Julietta and acted as the devoted husband and father. There were a few times when he was tempted to burst loose and shout his accusations to Julietta, but he held back with a superhuman effort. He discovered that each time he held back, it became easier to do so the next time. I'm growing up, he thought.

116

But the harrowing doubts, the hideous suspicion, the hurt, the grievously injured pride kept eating into him.

Meanwhile, his inquiries as to Prince Tikiri's whereabouts on the night of the kidnapping had to be made slowly and carefully through his spies and trade contacts; so despite his impatience the passage of time enabled him to decide what he would do if Prince Tikiri had indeed been in the port governor's mansion on the fatal night.

The evidence he had so far seemed flimsy at times. Julietta's childhood love for Prince Tikiri, the walls she had built around herself in consequence, her inability to feel romantic love for him, Fernao, the colour of the baby's eyes and Julietta's rescue by Prince Tikiri's men. What would Prince Tikiri's presence in Colombo at the time the baby could have been conceived prove? That his beautiful refined wife was a slut who had foisted a bastard child on him? Never. There must be dozens of people in Lanka who had brown eyes with blue rims because of their Aryan ancestry. Why, he had even heard of an entire village, named Waha, a few miles north-west of Kandy, populated by people with blue eyes.

But there were the other times, especially when he awoke during the still watches of the night, when the evidence he already had seemed so overwhelming that it expanded until his brain seemed fit to burst with shame, while the grisly dishonour gnawed at his vitals. At those times, he asked himself what his options were even if Julietta's infidelity were proved to his complete satisfaction. He loved Julietta. He could not create a scandal. He would have to make the best of the situation. At those times, he wondered whether he should not give up the search for Prince Tikiri's whereabouts that night. But some inexorable, unconquerable urge, strong as a death wish, drove him on.

The one thing he did resolve was that, in the event of proof, he would ease his hurt, overcome his shame, by wreaking vengeance on Prince Tikiri. By God, he would destroy the prince with all the power he wielded.

Wednesday, 23 August 1525

The courier who had ridden post haste from Colombo to Sita Waka was one of our master spies who headed contacts in the Jaya palace, the Colombo port and the *parangi* fort. He reached our palace in the evening and was immediately conducted to my father, King Maya Dunne, who was in his study. Lord Wickrama Sinha and I were present, seated side by side on settles in the golden glow of the lamps that had already been lit. Smoke curling from the braziers matched the grey of the sky outside. Distant sounds and tinkle-curls of *veena* strings spoke of the peace of the people's lives outside the room.

The messenger had with him all details of the treaties between the Great King and the Portuguese. We studied these in shocked silence.

'These treaties are a greater betrayal of the Sinhala peole than the acts of our father, King Wijayo,' my father observed soberly. 'They will destroy the fabric of our Sinhala society and turn us into a race of bastards. The *parangi* will want to implement their plans soon.' His dark eyes shifted to the courier's face.

'Sooner than soon, Sire,' the courier responded. 'Immediately.' He drew a sheaf of papers from inside his tunic. 'They leave for Galle in six days.' He proffered the papers to the king, left hand to right elbow, in the approved manner. 'Here are summaries of their plans, Sire.'

'Good man.' My father studied the plans grimly, handed them to Lord Wickrama Sinha. I looked over the lord's shoulder and my blood began to boil. What the *parangi* intended was an invasion of Galle, no less. We stared at each other in sombre silence.

'Once they establish a fort in Galle, they will give Prince

Vidiye command of the south,' my father stated at last. 'Lord Wickrama Sinha, you and Prince Raja Sinha will lead an expeditionary force without delay, to join our existing troops in Galle. You will reach Galle in time to oppose the *parangi* landing at all costs. We will need to retain sufficient strength in Sita Waka to meet any threat from the Great King or King Kumara. This will limit your own force. Also, you will need to ensure that your attack on the *parangi* is timed to prevent your being decimated by their ships' cannon.' He rose tall to his feet and we all stood up with him. 'Summon your commanders to a staff conference in the war room one hour from now.' That devil-may-care smile chased across his face. 'Meanwhile, gentlemen, let us have dinner. It's going to be a long night.'

On 26 August, Fernao learned through the Great King's spies that an expeditionary force consisting of Prince Tikiri's cavalry regiment, one thousand bowmen and two thousand infantry was due to leave Sita Waka that day to reinforce King Maya Dunne's victorious troops who still remained in Galle.

Two days later, Fernao finally discovered through Abdul Raschid that Prince Tikiri had indeed spent the night of Julietta's kidnapping in the port governor's mansion on the Mutu Vella hill.

The news ate into his brain. He decided to sleep in the fort that night.

He paid a brief visit home with Aires the next morning, so the servant could pack his seabag. He saw Julietta and the baby, played the loving devoted husband and father, but with sick rage ready to explode within him. How could Julietta, whom he had raised from being a despised half-caste to high estate, on whom he had showered his love, have done this to him? Pleading the excuse that conflicts between the commanders had made it imperative that he take personal charge of the invasion of Galle, as he called it, he soon left for the fort.

On 29 August 1525, with the great square-rigged *nao* *Flower of the Sea* as his flagship, Fernao sailed for Galle with his flotilla of nine warships, the blue of his eyes reflecting the murder in his heart.

Tuesday, 29 August 1525

Driven by aftwinds to speeds approaching ten knots, the flotilla which had sailed with the dawn tides from Colombo reached Galle shortly after dusk. The six great square-rigged *nao* and three fast caravels, which carried a complete infantry regiment of one thousand men, plus spare cannon, building materials, food supplies and water, rode the swells outside the harbour easily on their sea-anchors.

After dinner, Fernao stood alone on the poop deck of his flagship, on which the great Admiral Albuquerque had once sailed, staring across the dark waters towards the dim lights that pricked the darker land mass in the distance. Since he decided to lead the expedition to Galle he had been filled with a deadly chill of purpose which, for the present, stilled the cries of the grievous wound he had suffered. He prayed that he would face his mortal enemy Prince Tikiri, the man who had cuckolded him, at long last.

Though he was outwardly controlled, the gentle creak of the ship's timbers and the light land breeze tinged with the scent of cinnamon, a caress on his face, were in sharp contrast with the emotional upheaval within him. Hands lightly on the rails, poised on the balls of his feet to balance himself against the rolls, Fernao remembered Vasco da Gama's merciless bombardment of Calicut the second time the admiral sailed the Indies. The great explorer's captains had to beg him to cease fire because they feared that their ships' seams would come apart. He also recalled Admiral

Alfonso de Albuquerque's eight-day pulverization of Goa from the very ship on which he now stood.

He thought he had made his decisions as to Julietta's infidelity and what he would do about it, but he now found himself thinking agitatedly again, searching for some possibility that his life had not been shattered. He recalled Julietta's sudden withdrawal from him on the morning following the attempted rape, then of the love-making. Could the cause of both have been the same? Contact with Prince Tikiri? Even if Prince Tikiri had been with the rescue party, how could he and Julietta have had the opportunity to make love? Did the colour of the baby's eyes prove anything, especially with Julietta's Sinhala ancestry? He needed so much to have faith in her. The sick questions multiplied, like baby cobras from their mother's womb, until the bile rose bitter in his throat.

How would he ever learn the truth? Never from Julietta. He recognized her quiet inner strength once she made up her mind. Not from Prince Tikiri's men, nebulous figures in the darkness of a night on the Mutu Vella hill. Not from the dead Sergeant Correa. Certainly not from Prince Tikiri.

What was the time frame? How could he establish a time frame? Impossible. He pounded the wooden rail impotently until his hand hurt.

Why had Julietta not told him that it was the prince's men who had rescued her? Perhaps she had not known, because she was so distraught. Prince Tikiri need not even have been present in the grove.

O Blessed Virgin, I thank thee for this gleam of light in my bleak darkness. Help me to cast aside these base suspicions and enjoy my family, which is all I have in life.

What family? An illegitimate child? Was not honour part of the code too? Vengeance against any man who took your woman? And what about the de Albergaria family motto? *Let no man seize what is mine with impunity*.

Deliberately, he brought the picture of the baby into

focus in his mind. The same dark chestnut hair as Julietta, the same fair, delicate skin, the promise of his own small, elegant facial bones. Try as he might, he could not picture the eyes. The eyes were blank, dead eyes in hollow sockets.

CHAPTER EIGHT

Wednesday, 30 August 1525

The first glimmering of dawn enabled Lord Wickrama Sinha and I to distinguish the nine ships that were anchored in line just outside the Galle harbour.

We had split our forces into groups in order to meet the *parangi* wherever they landed, our object being to deny the enemy a beach-head.

Easing myself on my black mount, Rama, I surveyed the scene once more. The harbour was really an inland bay. The narrow entrance was flanked by a long hilly headland which contained a single, small white sand beach that rose sharply from the water to sprawl ashore. Foreign sailors had called the headland Buena Vista, 'the good view', because the white sand beach had fresh springs for the watering of their ships. Since it was unlikely that any large-scale landing would be effected on that side of the harbour, I had concentrated one group of our forces along its northern edge, with another group lining the western ocean shore in case boats attempted a landing across the reef. The third group, including my crack cavalry regiment, was in reserve, behind Lord Wickrama Sinha and me.

Having had sufficient time to prepare for the operation, our bowmen had measured distance on both flanks to provide effective fire against any boat-loads of *parangi* that attempted a landing. Our musketeers, divided between the first and second groups, were up front on the water's edge.

Lord Wickrama Sinha stiffened in his saddle, pointed a finger in the direction of the ocean. 'Look, prince. The ships are moving.'

I stared across the water. White sails were beginning to unfurl, tauten and billow. 'They have no intention of landing!' I exclaimed. 'What can they be up to?'

'They probably have pilots to guide them into the harbour,' Lord Wickrama Sinha said in disgust. 'Look, they are still in line but slowly moving closer inshore.'

Minutes of silence passed by as we stared at the ships. 'They're coming!' I heard one of our men exclaim. I could sense the tension in our ranks.

I saw the flashes first, like jagged lightning spread horizontally across the ocean, followed by puffs of smoke, then heard the thunderous peals rolling across the water, causing my ears to sing. A succession of great geysers of spray suddenly erupted just off the beach.

'They are bombarding us!' Wickrama Sinha shouted. He turned to our men. 'Back! Back! Out of range!'

'Regroup in the same formation at the farther end of the *maidan*!' I shouted to the officers behind me. 'Rush orders to our harbour force to do likewise.'

Commands started ringing out. As our men began an orderly retreat, I berated myself for having exposed my troops as cannon fodder to the broadsides from a hundred guns and more. The fact that I had never experienced a cannonade before was little excuse. Good commanders must anticipate every possibility.

As I wheeled Rama round and urged him forward, the next thunderous roar came bellowing across the ocean. Pounding like bolts from heaven, the cannonballs fell at the head of our retreating troups. Men's agonized screams and the shrill neighing of horses filled the air.

'They are straddling their barrages to obtain the correct range!' I shouted to the officers nearest me. 'Extend our infantry into line and wheel to the left.'

It was like trying to push a great river sideways but the infantry finally made its wheeling movement and proceeded northward at a run.

I actually saw the next salvo hit. Cannonballs pounded into our men, smashing some to pulp, shattering limbs, spewing blood, guts and bone shards on the green grass. For two seconds that excluded the babel and confusion around me, I recalled the day I held a cannonball in my hands for the first time and felt the tremendous power it exuded. That had been in the Mutu Vella grove, which had demonstrated another kind of power and beauty to me not one year ago.

The present intruded fiercely. I saw our decimated troops again, heard their screams and groans. I wheeled Rama round to face those devil ships, shaking my fist impotently at them. 'You fiends!' I screamed. 'I shall have your livers some day!'

'Come, prince. We must live to make that possible.' The command in Lord Wickrama Sinha's voice penetrated my consciousness.

I turned to stare at him. My mouth was parched, my throat dry, my ears were singing. His lean features tight-drawn, he reached out to grip my arm, gently guided me away.

'Our men,' I began, glancing dazedly at mangled bodies on the green, a man sitting up, staring at the bloody remains of a shattered leg, a headless corpse lying flat on its belly.

'Don't look there,' Lord Wickrama Sinha urged. 'Look to where our living are your inspiration.'

My eyes flickered to our troops trotting across the green in orderly lines, at the medical orderlies who were rushing forward to help the wounded, regardless of their own safety. Another great salvo resounded from the distance. Cannonballs whispered, whooshed and pounded the earth as if with hammers of the gods. 'Their guns have found the right range, but we have left them no targets!' Wickrama Sinha exclaimed triumphantly.

I relaxed the reins, squeezed gently with my thighs. Rama moved automatically forward. 'Rejoin our men,' I directed Lord Wickrama Sinha. 'I shall follow.'

Marvelling at the quiet courage of my horse, I rode him towards the wounded.

Over two dozen of our footsoldiers lay dead, about one hundred were wounded, and there was no help I could give here.

I remembered my father's warnings and splinters of guilt splattered my mind. I was responsible for the plight of the wounded and for all the corpses strewing the *maidan*, I, recently named Raja Sinha, the royal lion! I twisted my head round and glared wildly at the ships, now more sharply etched against the lightening horizon. Somehow I knew that, in spite of the earlier plans of the *parangi*, my arch enemy and rival was in the lead ship, all puffed up with the destruction he had wrought, gloating over his victory. Violent loathing for him seized my entrails, hardening them, extending through my whole being. Somehow, some way, even if it was to the smallest degree, I had to hit back.

The ships, still in line, were making a turning movement. Realizing that this would enable their starboard guns to fire as well, I suddenly knew that they planned to sail up and down the coast bombarding us and the town at will. How long would they do it for? I recalled to my horror tales of other Portuguese bombardments in the Indies.

My eyes fell on the point of land that held the cross which I had flung into the ocean. The first salvo had turned it into a heap of rubble. The message of the Cross, I thought savagely.

As I trotted slowly back to my troops, cannonballs thudded upon the earth around me. I ignored them. I knew they could not harm me.

Fernao was driven by overwhelming forces within him, raging devils he could not control.

Leading his ships up and down the coast the whole day for his gunnery officer, Lieutenant Nantes, to unleash salvo after accurate salvo from the big guns to pulverize Galle, he was filled with a sense of power. The country had never known anything like it. Indeed, this bombardment would place him in history along with Admirals Vasco da Gama and de Albuquerque. His personal life being in ruins, only shattering of the enemy mattered. His flagship, *Flower of the Sea*, shook and bucked with each salvo. The reek of gunpowder hung heavy in the air, the noise was so deafening that his ears were permanently singing. The vibrations of each blast quivered in his bones long after the eruption.

The bombardment was systematic. First the *maidan*, then the waterfront, next the bazaar running along it, finally the houses on the seashore. Over and over again.

As he watched the havoc wrought by the cannon, buildings crumbling, earth spewing, trees falling, he knew that he was destroying innocent civilians. He dimly realized that he too was a victim, consumed by a blazing urge to pound and pound again until his enemies, the Sinhala, were ground to the dust. Then alone would his honour be avenged, then alone would Julietta be his exclusively and for ever. He loved Julietta beyond counting, and measured his hatred of Prince Tikiri against that love.

And what of the bastard child? he asked himself time and again.

I am a soldier. I do not wage war against babies, came the reply.

And what of your immortal soul? a still small voice within him whispered.

I dedicate this mission to God and to Holy Church. These people are being punished for desecrating the Cross.

And the real devil within him, beneath all the other raging devils, laughed so quietly that he barely heard the sound.

He knew that what he was doing went far beyond the scope of what the Great King had expected, but he did not care. To hell with the Great King. To hell with all the Sinhala. He would assure Portuguese dominion, *his* mastery, over any part of this land to which he decided to extend it.

Finally, when night came, he ordered the bombardment to cease and the ships to anchor once more. A hush fell on the dark ocean, but all the vibrations of the day's incessant thunder remained shuddering in the air.

Standing on the bridge, hands on the rail, he stared across at a township that displayed only scattered fragments of light. Was Prince Tikiri dead? Wounded, maimed? If not, where was he?

The singing in his ears slowly gave way to the splash of waves slapping against the sides of the ship, but the stench of gunpowder remained in his nostrils. He became aware of the hushed voices of the men on the deck below him. Slowly he realized that they were talking about him, seeing him in a new light, as a harsh, cruel, ruthless commander. The devil within him laughed, this time so loud and clear he found himself exulting.

I have won. I have smashed my enemy. All that matters in life is victory.

Sunday, 3 September 1525

During the first dreadful bombardment, four days earlier. I had seen the white sand beach of the Buena Vista headland as a symbol of peace and purity. A few hours later, when all our forces had been withdrawn inland, realizing that there was no way in which we could oppose a landing, even if we had a hundred times our number of troops, in the face of such merciless cover from the warships' cannon, recall of that white sand beach brought inspiration and hope. If we could not prevent the *parangi* from landing, we could at least strike a telling blow against them. They would anchor their ships in the harbour, effect their landing and at some point of time send boats to that white sand beach for fresh water, fearing that the water in the town might be poisoned.

If they came at all, it would be at dawn. Lord Wickrama Sinha and I stood side by side on a small hillock immediately above the white sand beach. Having withdrawn our entire force well inland, this was the third morning in succession on which we had arisen to the crowing of the jungle cocks that abounded on the heavily wooded headland. Even today, all we could hear was the quiet splash of ripples on the shore. As the waters began to gleam with the first hints of the sun stirring in its bed far away beyond the trees to our left, I could sense the alertness of the men around us.

'I wonder why this headland was never inhabited?' Lord Wickrama Sinha inquired, his voice low.

'Probably because the land rises so sharply from the water that no one can build on it. Also, the only water available comes from the natural springs on that tiny beach below.'

He changed the subject. 'I still can't believe that the Great King, one of our own Sinhala, would not only permit the *parangi* to slaughter us, but would actually provide them with timber to build their fort.'

'The Great King would wear a donkey's head if that is what it takes for him to remain in power.'

'At least this barbaric bombardment will rally patriotic Sinhala in this region to our cause.'

'Never forget, however, that while we offer those patriotic Sinhala liberation and sacrifice, the *parangi* will

129

extend work and trade opportunities to them, wine and music, a seemingly happier way of life.'

I came alert before he could respond. Had I heard the faint creak of rowlocks and the splash of oars?

The air had lightened faintly; birds had started their first tentative whistles, chirps and twittering overhead. The call of a *koha* . . . ko-haa-a . . . resounded above the creak of a parakeet. I tried not to inhale the stink of some dead, rotting animal brought by a land breeze as I peered intently in the direction of the sounds.

My eyes were drawn to the movement of the boats, eight dark silhouettes, their dipping oars raising light splashes on the ocean. I quietly reached out and touched the arm of my aide, Captain Wickram, who had been standing silently at my left. He nodded his acknowledgement of the signal, passed it down the line. My heart started beating faster. The rowboats loomed larger as they drew close to the beach. I strained to catch a better glimpse of the occupants, counted ten blobs of heads in the lead vessel. Each boat would be manned by two men at the oars, four to carry the water casks slung between two poles and four musketeers as escorts. That meant a total of eighty enemy. I ran my tongue over lips suddenly gone dry, for there were two hundred of us.

The lead boat touched the beach, ground along the sand. I could make out the *parangi* now, pale faces, blond and brown beards beneath iron helmets, bodies looking huge in their armour. Two men leapt ashore and held the boat while the four musketeers clambered out, weapons at the ready. As they surveyed the beach and the little glade, only the sounds of the woods greeted them. They jerked their heads at those in the boat. Four water carriers hauled the casks out of the lead boat, as I had guessed they would.

The remaining boats ground and scraped along the beach. The musketeers fanned out, moved past the springs and pools to take defensive positions around the glade, and they were now so close to us that I felt I should hold my breath lest they hear me. I avoided directing my gaze towards any one of the enemy, for there is nothing worse than eye contact, even though one is concealed, to alert an opponent's inner instincts, draw his own gaze to the source of the contact. Armed with muskets, shortswords and daggers, these men could be formidable if they were prematurely warned.

It was almost light by the time the group, now under command of a man who stood apart, a long sword at his side, swung into a brisk routine. The water carriers, having filled their casks at the pools, grunted as they hefted their loads.

By the time the second set of casks had been hauled to the boats, the *parangi* had relaxed so much they even started talking to each other. One of them made a joke and those around him laughed.

I could distinguish faces more clearly now. A swarthy, bearded water-carrier with a scar slash down his cheek reminded me of the beast, Sergeant Correa. A fair, beardless youth had the pale blue eyes of a killer. When the sentries turned to start exchanging pleasantries with the water-carriers, shredded sunlight faint on their faces, I knew the timing was right. I gave the wood-pigeon's call, heard the scrape of tinder, saw the tiniest flare of the matches on either side of me.

The *parangi* sentries, instantly alert, turned to stare in our direction. Too late. Fifty muskets shattered the stillness. That first volley was directed at the sentries, who fell in the mass execution, some screaming in agony, some with gaping holes in their stomachs, some with torn limbs. A giant tottered briefly on lifeless feet, a body with his face blown apart. The remaining sentries threw down their muskets and raced for the beach. The reek of burnt gunpowder streaked into my nostrils.

The officer drew his sword, held it aloft, issued a rallying cry, turned towards the beach. Our second line of fifty musketeers had already run forward in an arc into the clearing. Tinders scraped, matches flared. The next thunderous volley, unmuffled by trees overhead, tore through the glade. The officer dropped his sword, his hands reaching up to the back of his head. His helmet askew, he collapsed in an untidy heap. The marksmanship of our musketeers was remarkable.

There were barely thirty survivors on the beach. The sixteen boatmen, who had frantically pushed the boats into the water, now held them for their panic-stricken comrades to tumble inside. I stepped forward from my cover, drew my sword, raised it aloft, screaming. 'Cha . . . rge!' Ninety Sinhala infantrymen, forty-five on each flank, responded as a single unit.

Uttering wild cries, we raced for the water-carriers who had been cut off from the boats.

We arrived at the water's edge too late. The beach was strewn with bloody corpses, white sand soaked red with blood. Our flank troops had massacred the remaining *parangi* to a man. They now seized the eight boats, dragged them into deeper water, held them firm.

Lord Wickrama Sinha and I stood side by side, panting. 'A signal blow against the enemy which will resound throughout the country!' he exulted. 'Eighty enemy dead and not even a single scratch on our men.'

'It will produce reprisals,' I commented grimly.

Our ten hatchet men who had remained in reserve ran past us. The air was rent with the sounds of iron shattering wood. Soon, gurgling sounds arose from the boats. They began rocking, then settled slowly into the waters.

'Back now, men!' I roared.

'Look, lord,' one of my men cried. 'We have made history. Look at the first *parangi* blood to stain our sacred waters!'

Laughing exultantly in response, I raced back to the cover of the jungle, filtered into it. We were half-way up the hill before we heard the thunder of the answering cannonade from the enemy ships in the harbour. Cannon-balls whispered overhead.

As you anticipated, the *parangi* were alerted by our musketfire and are pounding the beach and the hill-top!' Lord Wickrama Sinha was breathless beside me.

'While we are well spread out, headed back to camp,' I replied, grinning. 'We have taught them a lesson they will never forget. We have proved that they are not invincible!'

Still, my mind warned me that the war had only begun.

CHAPTER NINE

Wednesday, 13 September 1525

King Kumara's character had been formed long before he seized power from his father, King Wira. So when he became king, he continued making his own decisions, convinced that anyone, especially a ruler, should act independently. Other people, including ministers, military commanders and heads of departments, were there to provide him with the facts; he alone would decide what to do. Insofar as he trusted anyone, it was his wife, not only because it was not in her interest to betray him, but also because he knew she had more brains than all his other advisers put together.

This afternoon, he hastened to his wife's quarters because he wanted her to be the first person with whom to share the news he had just received.

Even though it was the siesta hour, Queen Anula attended him immediately. 'To what do we owe the honour of this unexpected visit, Sire?' she inquired when they were finally seated, she on her ebony settee and he on his usual settle across the room. 'It's a pleasure to see our lord and master at any time, but a break from his sacred schedule merely to see us is indeed a privilege.'

Whenever she used this tone, King Kumara never knew whether she was bantering, baiting him, or serious. 'Since today is Sunday and we are good Catholics, it seemed a proper extension of our having attended Father Juan's Mass this morning and taken the Blessed Sacrament to visit you and worship at your shrine.' He bared his teeth. 'Servicing you religiously is more important than any religious service.'

She dimpled, her white teeth showing in a smile that

made him tender towards her. 'We are indeed uplifted by your attention, Sire, for we have come to worship you. We are most grateful for your visit. Your unification of the *uda rata*, hill country, sub-kingdoms under your suzerainty have assured you a place in history. Your raids on our person assure you a place in our heart!'

'It is important that we have more than just a place in your heart, madam.'

'You have all of it, Sire, for it enshrines you.'

His eyes shone, then he suddenly became pensive. 'Two things mar the perfection of our achievements.'

'And what are they?'

'First, we keep wondering even this long after the event, why did we allow that fat pig, our father Wira, to outsmart us in the end? He not only took the elephants we permitted him, but sneaked away with the royal tusker. He not only carried away the royal treasure, but stole the royal crown! Damn him! He must be laughing each time he talks about it in the Sita Waka court, where he has been given sanctuary by King Maya Dunne.'

'King Maya Dunne has only provided your father with a place in the mountains, where he lives in virtual exile and where he will remain, harmless and ineffective, until his benefactor chooses to use him. Meanwhile, King Maya Dunne will have him make Sinhala Buddhist noises against you and the *parangi*, thus deriving more support throughout the kingdom that is dedicated to Buddhist compassion.'

'Correct. King Maya Dunne's grand gesture will endear him to the crowd of Sinhala Buddhists who worship compassion in the hope that it will be bestowed on them.' Observing the little laughter lines crinkling on either side of her mouth, he nodded sagely. 'Yes, indeed. The *bhikkus*, the *ayurvedic* physicians, the school teachers will become more vociferous in their support of the emerging Sinhala Buddhist champion, King Maya Dunne. And what do *we* receive for being a good Catholic?'

'What, my lord?'

'We are sure that the bombardment of Galle by the *parangi* and their successful landing there in order to build a fort was done to support the Great King Bhuvaneka Bahu, though it was made out to be a reprisal against the desecration of their . . . er . . . our Cross. All this is part of the plotting of the Church, led by the Arch-Devil, Father Juan. Never trust a man with pale brown pebbles for eyes.' A wolfish grin streaked his mouth. 'Well, the latest news is that Prince Tikiri struck back and killed eighty Portuguese who had been sent by Colonel de Albergaria on a water detail. The colonel then seized eighty civilians in Galle and had them publicly hanged on the *maidan* in reprisal. He appears to have changed recently, perhaps because he is now in sole charge of his government's operations in Lanka. This ruthless act will harden the resistance of all true Sinhala against him in particular and against Catholics in general! Since King Bhuvaneka would appear to have condoned the act, it will probably turn people against him too, creating a demand for a saviour, the role which King Maya Dunne desires to play. It will be interesting to see how far the *parangi* push Prince Vidiye in his own role of King of Billigam Korle.' He paused, reflecting. 'Prince Vidiye is such an ambitious man that he is a danger to all of us kings. He is the real threat to King Maya Dunne because he has remained an ardent Sinhala Buddhist.'

'But surely the *parangi* will win anyway? Even a hundred thousand Sinhala Buddhists are nothing against a hundred cannon and a thousand muskets.'

He smiled appreciatively. 'A nice turn of speech, my dear, but while armaments may subjugate a country, they can never hold it. And as we also know, King Maya Dunne has some muskets and may even have cannon soon. The *parangi* have now promised us all the troops and fire-power necessary to proceed against King Maya Dunne, but once committed to such an action, we would be totally dependent on their firepower. Can we trust them?' He paused to stretch his long legs, glanced reflectively out of the open window. 'We have decided not to accept their offer of help. Instead, we shall consolidate our gains in Pera, Gampola and Hangura and attempt to win over the remaining dissident elements in the *uda rata*. We shall not pull jak seeds out of the fire for the *parangi*.'

'Foreign invaders never have any concept of what the indigenous people are really like, but what about you, my lord? Do you care about the people?'

'Only to the extent necessary to perpetuate our own domination,' he declared seriously. 'One thing you may be sure of is that we shall always do what is right – to gain power! Consistency is self-defeating in a ruler, because it makes him predictable and therefore vulnerable. You know of the treaties signed by the Great King permitting the *parangi* to trade only with Sinhala who register their land with the *parangi* and take Portuguese names. We shall not adopt this policy in our kingdom – not because we have suddenly developed a passion for principle but because we need the principle to obtain the support of those dedicated to national sentiment.'

She eyed him admiringly, then her expression suddenly changed. Her large, dark eyes widened into a stare that glazed over him. 'You remain the most delightfully amoral man ever. It makes you strong, like air, which is the strongest substance in the world. You punch air and it gives, but moves back into place the instant you withdraw your hand. Yet it can also accumulate tempest force to destroy cities, to create storms and tidal waves, to rule over the other strong elements, water, fire and earth. If you ever weaken, or change, I do not know what I shall do.' She had deliberately dropped the royal plural to give effect to her words. 'Loving you as I do, I would want to protect you even from yourself, from any human weaknesses such as consistency, loyalty, integrity, which would destroy you

137

as a person. I would rather you died cynical than remained on this earth a believer.'

Her words sent a chill tremor through him.

Wednesday, 13 September 1525

On the very morning of our successful raid on the *parangi* water detail, Colonel de Albergaria had sent out a detachment of his troops who seized eighty Sinhala men from the town at random and hanged them on the green *maidan* fronting the *parangi* beach-head. Henceforth, a life for each Portuguese soldier killed by you, was the word he had passed on as a warning.

On receiving news of the executions, Lord Wickrama Sinha and I had made our way from our encampment in Habara to the *maidan* in Galle to view the tragic sight. From eighty improvised gibbets, eighty sagging corpses were slow-turning in the wind. Rage made my stomach quiver, filled the depths of my being. We had not dared go close enough to register the faces of the dead, but if all true Sinhala felt the same bitter outrage as I did, Lanka would surely be freed of foreign domination in a day. My frustration had bordered on despair. What were we, a slave race, that we could not respond to such a barbaric act of oppression?

Look to the people for support, I thought. But it was ten days before the oppressed dared respond to our repeated requests for discussions. When they finally did, it was in the form of a deputation from the townspeople of Galle. Led by their elders, whose head was a tall cadaver of a man with a gaunt face and long grey hair, they called at our encampment in Habara well after nightfall. We met under the spreading *cassia* tree where Lord Wickrama Sinha and I had set up our headquarters. It was a still, gloomy night, with the sputtering of the campfire around which we were seated on the grass breaking through the incessant croaking of bullfrogs.

Instead of offering to join us in our struggle, they implored us to leave without giving the *parangi* further cause for such reprisals. The stink in my nostrils did not come from the rotting coconut husks in the swamp-pits, but from the dead sea of my contempt for these cravens moved only by a single current, of compassion for the families of the dead.

'Ours is a freedom struggle,' I tried to reason with them, though passionately. 'Many will surely die. The soldiers who perish on the battlefield are no less innocent victims of the invader, no less human beings with families and friends, than the poor corpses. I feel for you. Can you not see that it is to end such acts of *parangi* depravity that we are here and in need of your support?'

But I could not convince them. All they wanted was for us to leave immediately. 'Better a live slave than a dead one, for we are slaves anyway,' their leader declared.

Heartsick, I watched them depart into the darkness from which they had emerged. So much for the support of the people. In despair, I decided to teach these locals a lesson by staying on with my army in Habara regardless, but my plan was interrupted by an unexpected summons from my father.

We had ridden to Galle, the scene of our former victory, with great hopes. We returned from it now in the bitterness of defeat. We force-marched back to our capital, the advance guard of my cavalry reaching it on the afternoon of 16 September, by the Christian calendar. I discovered that my father was away visiting Lord Madu Wan of Panamure, one of the most powerful nobles in Sita Waka, and was not expected back till late afternoon.

My very first glance at my father, seated behind the brown *nadun*-wood desk in his study that evening,

139

revealed a new man. His eyes were alive, his whole body seemed to vibrate like a warhorse before a charge. I knew in a flash that dramatic events were impending.

'Good news, *putha*.' He came straight to the point. 'We know you must have been disappointed at being summoned back when your successful ambush of the *parangi* seemed to reveal the way to deal with them, but more important work has arisen here.' He paused. 'First, your report.'

He listened attentively while I recounted the details of events in Galle, from our withdrawal under bombardment to the ambush. Though he already knew of the hanging of the eighty men, when I gave him the grisly details, his body grew tense and he gripped the edge of his desk so tightly the knuckles turned white. I went on to tell him of the reaction of the townsmen and he shook his head sadly.

I finished my report and gazed at him expectantly.

'I believe we have the means to avenge those innocent men and their families,' he stated grimly. 'Abdul Raschid's wife sounded us out through a trustworthy contact over five weeks ago, inquiring whether we would consider an alliance with the Zamorin of Calicut to contain the *parangi* and establish a united Lanka. We did not wish to divulge this to anyone because it was very theoretical at the time, but were more heartened when we discovered that Abdul Raschid had already left for Calicut; as you know, his brother-in-law, Paichi Marcar, is one of the most powerful figures in the Indies and has direct access to the Zamorin at all times. We responded that we would indeed be open to such an alliance and were delighted to learn that Abdul Raschid's son, Ali, also departed for Calicut immediately afterwards. We have long known that the brain behind the political machinations of the Rachids is the woman, Aisha. True enough, she remained our channel of communication after her husband and son left. Well, they both returned the day before yesterday and I had their news last night.'

He paused, his eyes glowing, deliberately keeping me in suspense.

'What was the news he brought back, Sire?' I cried impatiently.

'The Zamorin will soon engage the *parangi* warships in his waters. He will also send part of his navy to our own waters to prevent *parangi* reinforcements from reaching Lanka.'

'What is the price, Sire?' I inquired, fear of what it would cost us cutting across my own rising excitement.

'Nothing, except that we will be committed to keeping all possible *parangi* military forces tied up here. Now here is the best part. The Zamorin will send us ten thousand crack cavalry and infantrymen, all Rajputs, for centuries the fiercest fighters in the world, and two hundred chariots. We will pay all expenses of that contingent, including the cost of billets, food and wages, while they are here. For the present, all that the Zamorin requests, as an earnest of good faith, is an advance payment of one hundred elephants plus two shiploads of rice as soon as he has demonstrated to our satisfaction that the troops will be available to us. Once we have become the Great King, he will also receive from us two shiploads of rice and of the best cinnamon annually for five years.'

'Why do we need mercenaries, Sire?' I was disturbed by the news though my father had expected me to be elated.

'We need the strength. We have given ourselves six months to increase our own armed forces. You yourself will commission and train nine new regiments of cavalry, which alone will put your total at ten thousand men and therefore equal in size to the mercenary force, apart from our other cavalry regiments, infantrymen and bowmen. Since we have the musketeers too now, we need not be afraid of the Indian mercenaries, as you call them, especially as they will be here as our allies.'

'But, Sire, throughout our history, it is loyal patriots who have freed the land from foreign domination.'

Disappointment clouded my father's face, then it became animated with purpose. He leaned forward in his chair. 'Do you approve of the Zamorin's fleet taking on the *parangi* ships in our waters?'

I hesitated, knowing the direction in which he was heading.

'Is there not the risk that a victory for the Zamorin might tempt him to take over the *parangi* position in Lanka?' he went on.

'Yes, Sire,' I replied, uneasily.

A knowing smile relaxed his chiselled features. 'Yet you would be prepared to take that risk to achieve your goals?'

'Yes, Sire.'

'Well, what's the difference between that and having mercenaries paid by us, rather than by a foreign power, mercenaries under our direct command and control, men whom we can dismiss simply by paying them off, fighting for that same cause?'

I looked down, having no reply, realizing that it was only some instinct, some pride that had moved me.

'You know, *putha*, there is nothing, absolutely nothing, we would not do to rid our sacred soil of invaders, to ensure the liberty of our people and the triumph of the Doctrine.' The king's voice rang out so strongly that I automatically raised my eyes to him. His face was alive with an almost fanatical light. 'We both have the same goals,' he continued. 'But there is a basic difference between us. You will rush in, unheeding, to achieve your goals, trusting to abstract principles of loyalty and patriotism. We, on the other hand, move according to the principles of politics, diplomacy and military strategy, because we are totally unprincipled as to how we win.'

I was shocked by his words. But I saw them immediately as the truth, realized with certainty that I would never forget them. Yet my instinct still told me that liberty could only be achieved by patriotic freedom fighters.

Oddly, my father echoed some of this sentiment. 'As you may have deduced, the reason for our visit to Lord Madu Wan today was because he is the one certain source from which we can obtain the one hundred elephants. As the *devas* have obviously decreed, he is due to hold his once in five years *kraal* to entrap wild elephants this year. What a fine omen! As we told you, we have six months during which to raise our army to full fighting strength. We need patriots from the areas that provided freedom fighters for the kings of old, doughty warriors from Ruhuna, such as those who fought with Abhaya Gamini, and from the Raja Rata, like the victorious forces of Parakrama Bahu the Great. Your orders, commencing immediately, are to raise your cavalry corps to ten fully trained and equipped regiments, mainly from the Ruhuna area, and to add a new regiment of two hundred chariots and four hundred musketeers to your army group. Lord Wickrama Sinha shall be commanded to bring our infantry forces up to thirty thousand men.'

Suddenly I heard the rumbling of distant thunder. I glanced through an open window to find only the golden sunlight of evening splashing the lawn.

My father observed my look and a smile twitched his lips. 'You are wondering about thunder on a clear day?'

'Yes, Sire, but it is not an unusual phenomenon at this time of year.'

'This particular phenomenon is not merely unusual, it is unique,' he replied soberly. 'We have decided to bring our cannon out into the open, closer to home, and it is their first practice salvo you are privileged to hear. The day of catapults flinging stones is over for us Sinhala!' He smiled at my start of delighted surprise, but could not know that my mind had also shot back to the morning of my sixteenth birthday, when I first heard the distant thunder of *parangi*

143

cannon from Father Juan's room in the Jaya palace on a clear day such as this.

I was consumed with excitement. 'When do I start my own mission, Sire?'

'Immediately. Time is short.'

'I sincerely hope we will not have a repetition of our recent experience with the town-leaders of Galle.'

'Do not worry about that. Townspeople, being concentrated, are vulnerable to reprisal and therefore more afraid. Our peasantry will be different.' He smiled. 'You need not leave for Ruhuna yourself for another two weeks. Send your aide, Captain Wickram, to prepare the way for you. Meanwhile, start your enlistments with as many loyal men of our own kingdom as possible, men who will not leave the service temporarily to go back to their villages for sowing, harvesting and the attainment of maidenhood by their daughters! Also, we desire you to attend the *kraal* which Lord Madu Wan of Panamure is organizing shortly, to provide us with the one hundred elephants we need for the Zamorin.'

'You have wasted no time visiting Lord Madu Wan.'

'Indeed. We also wanted his backing for the new appointment we have made.'

'What appointment, Sire?'

'Yours, as General Raja Sinha, Commander of the Mobile Forces and Musketeers of Sita Waka.'

I gasped in surprise, rose to my feet, knelt before him, my head bowed. 'Sire, I am your servant.' I found myself stammering, so I composed myself. 'I shall follow you to the death.' In a flash, I recalled similar words I had uttered to the Great King Parakrama Bahu IX in the Jaya palace on the day this all began. I suddenly thought of Julietta. I wish . . . oh, how I wish . . .

'You offer us your allegiance anew and we are moved by it, General, but you have not yet inquired as to whom we intend taking on in battle,' he stated softly.

Flushing, I raised my head. 'I assumed it was the *parangi*, Sire.'

'No, General.' His voice was firm. 'We shall march on Jaya, against the Great King.'

Monday, 18 September 1525

Two days later, King Maya Dunne's messenger reported his agreement to the Abdul Raschids through their trusted intermediaries.

Having received the message late in the evening, Abdul Raschid, back from Calicut, carried the news to Aisha in her chamber. He kept giggling happily as he sat opposite her, never once reaching for a sweetmeat.

When he had finished, she looked at him with a tremendous gush of love within her. 'As you said over four years ago, we make a fine team, husband of mine,' she declared.

'You plan it and I execute it.'

'Now we have our son too.' Her smile beneath the *yashmak* was grim. 'Since the Great King and the *parangi* have combined to deprive him of a job, we shall have to give him one, won't we? He shall be our courier to and from Calicut, someone we can trust completely.'

'He will act independently too, never fear.'

'It is all the will of Allah. Especially that Lord Madu Wan's elephant *kraal* should fall this year.'

'Allah has His instruments.' Abdul Raschid's grin was mischievous. 'How do you think the question of elephants in part-payment arose?'

She pointed a finger at him. 'You mean, you . . .'

He shrugged, embarrassed now. 'The Zamorins have always coveted trained elephants. Remember how the former Zamorin wanted Vasco da Gama to seize a Sinhala ship that was carrying elephants? Well, I remembered that and offered him the bait, which he took!'

'A rather heavy bait!'

'But easy enough for King Maya Dunne to find this year.' He paused, his pig-eyes became loving. 'Do you think I have been clever?'

'Indeed, I do.'

'May I then have some advance payment in my wife's bed tonight?'

CHAPTER TEN
Tuesday, 19 September 1525

Fernao had been gone exactly three weeks and she had not heard from him once during that time. She had hoped for a letter each day, but there was nothing for her in the caravels that shuttled regularly between Galle and Colombo.

Walking the lawn of her residence on the Mutu Vella hill this morning, Julietta could not help remembering once again that Fernao had written to her every day the last two times they had been parted, first when he went on the mission to Jaya and later when he went to Goa, even though some of the letters from Goa had arrived after his return. Oh, well, he had only been a young lieutenant then, whereas he was now the colonel in charge of the Lanka garrison, leading an important mission seventy miles away. But surely he could at least have sent her a brief note. So much had changed so drastically since those early days.

She glanced at the pink-lined cradle placed in the shade of a red-blossomed spathodea tree. Catherina was sleeping soundly after being up all night, grinding her gums. She was much too small to be teething, but then she was precocious in so many ways. Like her father, Julietta thought and trembled. The baby's tiny pink face was relaxed in sleep. She would be lulled by the hum of insects that could not get through the fine muslin drape. Julietta's heart went to her baby, so tiny, so helpless, so dependent on her. From the days she had carried this child in her womb, it was her life's sustenance that had nurtured it. Remembering touched off the sense of miracle within her, brought a great surge of protectiveness.

Her mind flitted to the news she had received from

147

Galle. Prince Tikiri's successful ambush which involved the massacre of eighty Portuguese was somehow easier to condone than Fernao's bombardment of the town followed by those terrible reprisals. How could her husband, the gentle, sensitive man she still loved, have ordered such dreadful deeds?

Her eyes turned to the distant south, across the red and white roofs of homes, the shimmering lake. Somewhere out there the two men in her life, one whom she was in love with and the other whom she loved, were in a life and death combat. Suddenly, she felt responsible, because she was the prize at least so far as her husband was concerned. Oh God, help me, she prayed, for I am but the innocent victim of Fernao's love for me. The old resentment against him for having forced marriage on her boiled up for an instant, but was soon replaced by gratitude for his goodness to her and guilt at having given her husband a child conceived through another man. What could she do? Only hope that Fernao would never learn the truth.

As the answer to her prayers, she suddenly knew that she had to protect both men as best she could, regardless of her conscience or normal concepts of right and wrong. Fernao especially needed that help at a time when his conduct in Galle revealed that he was placing his immortal soul in jeopardy. A great calm settled over her. I thank Thee for showing me the way, O God.

She wished that Fernao would come back soon so that she could start her new mission to make him feel a truly loved, cherished husband.

Hearing the sentry's loud challenge at the entrance gates, she turned. The gates squeaked open. The clatter of urgent horses' hooves reached her. A black military carriage drawn by two greys swung round the bend in the driveway. Even before it reached her, she knew that Fernao was back home.

It was so totally unexpected, something broke loose

within her. 'Fernao! Oh Fernao!' she cried and started running across the lawn, regardless of deportment.

The carriage wheels screeched to a stop on the cobble-stones. Fernao, lean, bronzed, gallant in his white uniform, dismounted. She flung herself into his arms. Startled, he held her close. 'What? What is it, Juli . . . Juli, darling?'

She buried her face on his broad chest, felt the scrape of the gold braid on it. 'Nothing, Fernao . . . just nothing! . . . only that I'm so thankful to have you back.'

His arms tightened fiercely around her. His lips sought hers eagerly, almost feverishly. As he kissed her, she felt him trembling and glimpsed the demented soul of him, the utter loneliness of his spirit. She knew with the force of a thunder-clap that she alone had caused his dreadful atroci-ties. Fear gripped her stomach.

Minutes of desperate reaching for each other passed. Finally, she pulled away to look at him. Her fingers reached gently for his face, touched the gold crucifix he always wore around his neck. The startling knowledge seared through her brain that she had crucified him. Yes, she had crucified Fernao, her lawful wedded husband, whom she had sworn before God, sweet Jesu and the Virgin Mary to cherish, to love, honour and obey, to look after in sickness and in health, for richer for poorer. She had resented him for forcing their marriage on her. She had secretly disowned him, pulled away from him, dis-honoured him, then tried to blame him for it.

Fernao gazed down at her anxiously. 'What is it, Juli, my love?' It was as if he too had set aside all restraint and was miraculously his gentle, tender self again.

'Nothing . . . nothing, Fernao.'

She knew her role with certainty. What she and Tiki-tiki had was not of this lifetime, except to create the single new life that lay sleeping peacefully in its cradle. From now on she would love and cherish her husband, Fernao, she would honour and obey him until death parted them. Thereafter, in heaven, she would return to her Tiki-tiki, the God-given love of her immortal soul.

Tuesday, 19 September 1525

Fernao had returned to Colombo on the *Flower of the Sea* only after the fort had been staked and construction had commenced, and when it became evident that the Sinhala forces had pulled back towards Sita Waka. During the past three weeks, he had alternated between studied calm, the urge to extract the truth from Julietta and the inevitable pangs at wondering whether he had done right to bombard Galle and hang innocent civilians in reprisal against Prince Tikiri's ambush. He had heard that the prince was now named Raja Sinha, but he would never think of him as anything but Prince Tikiri.

While most military commanders would have exercised ruthlessness without concern, there was a sensitive part of Fernao that posed questions of morality, chivalry and honour. There was the honest part that sometimes clamoured in protest before the knowledge that his cruelty had not been caused by the need to achieve his objectives but by a wounded heart. It was easier for him to sweep these questions aside because he received the praise of his officers, the undisguised adulation of his men, and could also see that all his objectives had been achieved, including the withdrawal of the Sinhala forces.

If Julietta would only tell him the truth, confess, he would forgive her and they could start a new life together, however difficult, based on restored confidence in veracity. After all, honesty was the most important ingredient in a marriage. That same honesty questioned him, Can you sustain the truth, when the very thought of your wife in someone else's arms drives you wild?

All in all, this had been a period of intense turmoil for Fernao. He had given the order to sail the flagship back to

Colombo during one of those moments, when he needed to escape from it all and return home.

When his carriage drove into the mansion on the Mutu Vella hill that morning and he saw Julietta alone on the lawn, with the baby beside her, she seemed so pure, so clean, such a contrast with the muck and slime of his soul, that something snapped within him. He immediately saw her as the refuge of his ravaged spirit. Here was the perfect wife and mother, devoted to her duties and responsibilities. Then she came so naturally into his arms, and as he held her, it was as if he had been rescued from a black, stinking, stifling swamp that had almost engulfed him. The exquisite face, the white skin, the auburn hair, the dark eyes, were those of a Madonna. Yes, a Madonna. How could he ever have doubted such a person? He needed to absorb the purity of her, to be cleansed physically. He needed to feel the power of making love to her, so he could be certain of how much he possessed her. Yes, indeed, he needed to heal his sick spirit!

He gripped her by the arms, held her so he could take in all of her. His eyes lingered on her face, her shining hair, then swept past her slender neck, took in the rising breasts. She blushed at that, the two tiny laughter lines on either side of her mouth crinkling. 'Oh Juli, Juli, I've missed you so much, not just for three weeks but for so long now. It's so good to be *us* again. We must never, never more be parted in spirit. Please forgive me for whatever I have done, for whomever I may have been that caused you pain. Let's start all over again.'

Her large blue eyes glistened with tears. 'No, Fernao, the fault has been mine. I know you have suffered and I understand what you must feel to have let loose all that violence in Galle and how dreadful it must have been for you afterwards. Yes, my heart has truly bled for you. Please forgive me too, but . . .'

'Hush, my beloved.' He had placed a finger on her lips.

'Let's not talk about it any more. Let's face the future and make today even better than our honeymoon.'

Her gaze was as of old. 'Just you and I, Fernao,' she whispered. 'Let us exclude the rest of the world.'

'You and I and our baby now, remember?' he corrected her, tenderly.

Her face crumpled; the tears began to flow. He counted them his reward, kissed them away. He removed the white linen square from his pocket and gently wiped her face. 'There now!' he declared, replacing the linen in his pocket. 'You are fit to present me to our daughter.'

She dropped him a curtsy, pretended to inspect him thoroughly. 'Ah! The noble Colonel Fernao de Albergaria, handsome and immaculate as usual. I have the honour to present you to the Lady Julietta Catherina Menika de Albergaria.' She turned and gestured with slender fingers towards the cradle, then clasped his hand. 'This way if you please, sir.'

He stode light-heartedly beside Julietta towards the spathodea tree, feeling the sun warm on his face, joy warming his heart.

He paused at the cradle, looked at the frail body covered by pink linen lying peacefully inside it. This was *his* baby. Surges of love and tenderness began to fountain within him. His baby, flesh of his flesh, blood of his blood, bone of his bone. The sunlight suddenly brightened and the baby opened her eyes. Without realizing it, he noted their colour, dark brown, almost black, with the beginning of blue rims around them. It connected with the images he had been conjuring on board ship, when he had felt raw from his efforts to *see* the baby's eyes with his mind's eye. He began sinking, sinking into that hateful, black slimy swamp again. He heard a despairing cry, knew immediately that it was from within his soul and had never been uttered. Something was about to burst within him.

Some miracle of love for Julietta, some instinct for

survival, restrained him. He gulped, took a deep breath, fiercely pulled himself away from the danger. And in doing so, he emerged sweating, his chest tight but victorious.

'Fernao, what's happened? What's wrong?'

He had been under such a strain. Yet the bewilderment and despair in her voice made him reach out for her again. 'Nothing is wrong,' he breathed hoarsely. 'Everything is right now that I'm back at home.'

His eyes closed, he held her to him for long moments, the coldness in his heart slowly warming like his face from the sunshine. Then he released her, placed his hands beneath the baby's armpits and lifted her gently to him. The baby started crying before bawling so loudly that a bare-chested Sinhala gardener who had been working at the side of the mansion came out to investigate, then scuttled back to his work.

'You have been away so long, she is unused to you,' Julietta teased. She took the baby from him, hushed it. 'There! There!'

The desire to be soothed as well gripped Fernao. He waited until the baby's crying subsided. At that moment, inspiration dawned. He would impregnate Julietta again and again. This time, when she had a baby, he would be sure it was his. 'Ask Maria to keep the baby and come upstairs with me,' he quietly bade Julietta.

In the bedroom upstairs, they made love as never before, trying to reach each other through the mists of circumstances, needing to live for a few moments in the eternal so they could forget the past. Each of them was still caught in the reflex of old fears. For each of them, in their own way, the coming was part release, part thrilling, part pain, not complete fulfilment.

When it was done, Fernao rolled on to his back feeling curiously empty. Within minutes, the doubts began creeping back. The baby's eyes ... had Julietta even once this morning called him the baby's father, or referred to the baby as his? He went over their conversation on the lawn, found his recall jumbled, tried to get it into the proper sequence and failed. He could not remember Julietta's exact words. He turned towards her. She too lay on her back. Her naked white body half covered by a pale blue silken robe, she stared at the ceiling. He knew that, being perceptive, she had guessed at his reactions on the lawn. Poor Julietta. He had not been fair to her.

He sighed, reached over, drew her to him. As he cradled her head on his shoulder, she raised her aquamarine eyes to him. They had the same haunted look that he felt in his spirit.

Perhaps we have found common ground at last, the rock bottom beneath the suffocating swamp.

CHAPTER ELEVEN

Tuesday, 19 December 1525

It took three months for Lord Madu Wan, the Dissawe, or high chief, one of the most powerful nobles in the country, to get the elephant *kraal* organized. Since his domain spread over thousands of acres of land, much of it hilly, some mountainous, with great areas of jungle in which wild elephants abounded, he held a *kraal* once every five years, during which he captured between fifty and one hundred elephants. We were lucky that this was the fifth year. My father believed it to be an auspicious sign that his need for one hundred tamed and trained elephants as an advance payment to the Zamorin of Calicut should have arisen at the same time. He had readily agreed to attend the *kraal* and I shared his excitement at the prospect.

The site for the *kraal* was far removed from the chieftain's fine mansion and had been selected centuries ago. I had never met Lord Madu Wan. Since his residence lay about twenty miles due east of Sita Waka, it was mid-morning by the time my father and I, dressed in brown silk tunics and pantaloons for the occasion, reached the Madu Wan mansion, accompanied by our mounted escort.

We were greeted at the entrance to the village by Lord Mola, a nephew of Lord Madu Wan, and the traditional procession, led by whip-crackers and trumpet-players, followed by drummers and dancers. We rode after them slowly, beneath silver sunlight punctured by occasional patches of shade from the branches of tall flamboyants overhead. The brown dirt road had been tamped down by elephants, so it was firm beneath our horses' hooves as they walked quietly between neat, white-washed houses with roofs of yellow paddy thatch or white country tile, bordered mostly by red hibiscus, the bright green paddy fields beyond.

The road was lined with villagers and retainers, all shouting '*Jayawewa . . . Maya Dunne Raja-thuma, jay-awewa.*' Guiding his mount with his knees, my father acknowledged the cries with smiles and the palms together greeting. Seeing the smiling faces, most of them fairer-skinned than the Sinhala in the lower country regions, the stalwart bare-chested men in brightly coloured sarongs, I realized that this was the heartland of Lanka from which we would have to pluck our future warriors. The customs of centuries had made an orderly people. Neatly dressed children sat, squatted or knelt in the front rows, women in red, green or blue cloths and jackets stood immediately behind them, with the men in the rear. Apart from an occasional sickly child with gaunt cheeks and large staring eyes or a bulbous stomach, the young ones seemed very healthy, their pink cheeks glowing, dark eyes sparkling.

The two-storey granite Madu Wan mansion lay sheltered in a grove of jak trees, coconut, kitul and areca palms. Its red roof combined pleasantly with the sunlight and shadow around it, the greenery above and a blue sky dappled with white clouds.

Seeing Madu Wan standing at the entrance of the mansion, dressed in formal clothes to receive us, relations and retainers crowding behind him, reminded me that such ceremonial, good manners, *charlithraya* – tradition – are necessary to maintain the structure of society and the place of the individual in it. Even when a person belongs to one of the so-called lower orders, a phrase and institution which I secretly loathed, he could bring dignity to it by behaving according to the code, in a well-mannered, refined way. By according dignity to his so-called superiors, the source of his security in society, he reaped the benefit of personal dignity and created a cycle that gave stability to life. He knew his place and was therefore contented. It is the people who have an insatiable hunger for more who are dissatisfied and therefore unhappy.

Having said this, I must confess that I did not dare open my mind or my imagination to what it must be like to be poor and lowly. I had of late begun to rebel against the prostrations and genuflections commanded of men. Was it not a sign of weakness in rulers or gods when symbols of servility were demanded to demonstrate a respect that may not be in the human heart?

There was no sign of weakness in Lord Madu Wan, a lean, tall man, over six feet in height, gorgeously turned out in the eighteen-yard white *dhoti* to give the *thalasthani*, worthy, look to his lean figure. His high chief's padded jacket and three-cornered hat were of purple with gold embroidery, as were his shoes, curving to a point. I was immediately struck by his dignity and proud bearing, which combined with neatly combed white hair, moustaches and long beard that contrasted strongly with a well-tanned skin to make him the perfect image of the legendary hill-country chieftain. His fierce dark eyes, set in a hatchet face, were now crinkled in a smile. The drumming and trumpeting stopped abruptly, in the middle of a cadence. 'You are most welcome to my humble abode, Sire,' Lord Madu Wan declared in deep tones, as soon as we had dismounted and the grooms led the horses away. He made obeisance. 'I am honoured by your presence.'

'Indeed, it is we who are honoured to be extended the hospitality of your roof, Lord Madu Wan,' the king responded.

'Would you like some refreshing *thambili*, king coconut water?'

'That would be delightful. Riding can be thirsty work.'

We were given our choice of refreshments in the great hall of the mansion. The long wooden table, covered with a white linen table cloth, was laden with clay pitchers containing sweet coconut water, pomegranate juice, melon juice with kitul honey and a dash of lemon juice. An array of *rasa kavili*, sweetmeats, on huge platters included the traditional *kavung*, oil-cakes, which one may not refuse without giving offence, crunchy *kokkis*, *aggala*, the delightful white *aasmi* with honey poured on it and even *kalu dodol*, solid black jelly from distant Hamban in the south.

Then, since we were to proceed directly to the *kraal* site, Lord Madu Wan and his nephew changed into clothes more suitable for riding while my father and I rested in our rooms. It was so good to be able to stretch away the stiffness from the ride, which the rules of decorum prohibited my doing publicly.

My father and I met Lord Madu Wan and his nephew by the entrance to the mansion at noon. We mounted fresh horses and set off side by side at a brisk canter towards the *kraal* site. This was higher up in the mountains. We first followed a meandering stream, rippling over black rocks, riding through pleasant villages in rich green valleys, their neat white-washed houses set in large patches of light green paddy field. Curious women and children emerged from their noontide activity to stare at us. We passed brawny, bare-chested men returning from the fields, shovels on tanned shoulders, who fell to their knees on recognizing their lord. Only the dogs were no respecters of persons, occasionally yapping and barking almost beneath our horses' hooves.

When we reached the jungle land, the road became a track which began winding around a steep hill. We climbed several hundred feet before the burnt blue sky broke through the dense overhanging branches of the jungle. Finally we reined in our horses on a rocky eminence devoid of trees. This had to be the platform of the gods. Hills of black granite with sharp, sloping sides enclosed a huge, deep basin of dark green jungle, through which a broad stream ran, splashing merrily in the sunlight.

Lord Madu Wan eased himself in the saddle of his chestnut, pointed downwards. 'You see that stream, Sire? Strangers imagine that it is a work of Nature.' A note of pride entered his deep voice. 'In truth, it was created by my ancestors, who discovered perennial springs beneath a rocky bed and harnessed them into that stream which now irrigates several dozen villages. Wild elephants have known from time immemorial, long before my forefathers came, that water existed here, so the stream has remained their *watering point* in dry seasons such as the present one.' He looked at me, his twinkling eyes telling me that his choice of words was a compliment to my ambush of the *parangi* at the Galle watering point.

My father's laugh rang out. 'Well put, Lord Madu Wan, but pray tell us, do not the elephants, which are such wise animals, recognize this as dangerous ground because of *kraals* you and your ancestors have held for centuries? After all, the elephant never forgets!'

'Five years is a long time, and we never kill, only capture the animals, so we leave no taint of blood down there. Besides, when the creatures are stricken by the thirst of the dry seasons, they are probably driven here willy-nilly by the stronger urge to survive.'

We rode down the side of the hill until we reached the basin below and came upon the stockade, which encompassed a rectangular space of about five acres. It consisted of huge, weathered, satinwood logs, the strongest wood in the region, each about two feet in diameter, placed about three feet apart and held by great cross-beams tied to each post, with supporting beams outside.

'Can *that* hold back huge elephants?' my father demanded incredulously. 'And how do you get them inside?'

'An elephant in full charge could demolish it,' Lord Madu Wan replied. 'But remember the space in the stockade is so confined that maximum speed cannot be achieved.

As for getting the creatures inside, we depend on the fixed routine of all animals. Elephants feed and drink mainly in the evening and night, then retire to the thickest jungle between the end of the first dawn watch and about three hours after noontime, to get away from the heat, sun and flies and to enjoy their afternoon naps. We therefore tackle them as they emerge in the evenings. You will see how it is done.'

'How many men do you use for this operation?'

'Normally about two thousand mahouts and watchers, but this time we have about five hundred extra in the hope of rounding up more animals. The groups stand outside the stockade about ten yards apart, with fires burning, during the hours when the elephants will emerge. Every twenty-two men are under the command of a headman, but two of them are cooks and water-carriers for the group. At night, the men are on constant watch, carrying nothing but burning brands and spears.'

'Oh yes, elephants fear fire,' my father recalled.

'Also, reportedly, ants and mice!'

The lord had arranged a meal of rice and curries in a small temporary building of brown coconut thatch close to the entrance to the stockade. After the meal, we rested on mats and cushions in the building, sweltering in the heat.

Four hours after noontime, we all arose. Lord Madu Wan and his chieftains and retainers went into the stockade and made offerings to the *devas* of the jungles, to the elephant god Ganesh and to god Kataragam, praying for the success of the enterprise. One hour later, Lord Madu Wan led us to a *massa*, tree house, set high above the entrance to the stockade. My father, Lord Madu Wan, and I climbed the makeshift ladder to reach it. We were followed by two armed retainers, one of them, Banda by name, a renowned 'elephant man' well versed in the elephant language. From this vantage point we could see the fires of the mahouts glimmering through the trees and hear the quiet crackle of the fires nearer us. These had been lit within the stockade, about three yards apart, and were guarded by bare-chested watchers bearing blazing brands, shadowy shades lighting the way between the fires of the elephants' hell.

Darkness fell quickly, as if the jungle had shut out the sun. The whole scene suddenly became unreal as a ghost-watch. Yet the scent of wood smoke was pleasant to the nostrils, erasing the foetid jungle smells of rotting leaves and carcasses.

The night meal, again of rice and curries, was served us on the *massa*, in the light of the flaming torches tied to the rail. We ate in a silence that was slashed only by the bark of a deer, the *ho-ro-ho-ro* of a monkey and the eerie screams of a peacock.

We had barely finished eating when Lord Madu Wan came alert. 'Hush!' he commanded, his lean body tensing.

The drums and cries of the beaters and a slight rumple of undergrowth in the distance reached us. A sudden shrill trumpeting crashed through the jungle, startling me.

'Put out the torches. They are coming.' Lord Madu Wan stared in the direction of the sounds. 'The watch-fires hem them in, the beaters, with drums and firebrands, are channelling them towards the stockade entrance. Ah! Here they are, the lords of the jungle!'

Great, grey shapes tracked by drumbeats and flaming brands moved hurriedly towards us. The crump, crump, crump of their tread became audible. I saw the creatures as a bewildered stream, seeking a safe outlet. They found it in the entrance to the stockade and the illusion of silence within it. I counted twenty-eight ghosts streaming beneath me before the grey line ended leaving behind the smell of fresh elephant dung.

One of the groups of beaters rushed up to place great beams across the entrance to the stockade. The herd was trapped inside.

'Success tonight!' Lord Madu Wan exulted. 'The next stage of the operation will take place tomorrow, when we will noose and capture the elephants to start the taming process, before returning to round up more and more until we have at least your one hundred.'

'Won't they try to break out tonight?' my father inquired.

'Some will try. Our watchers with the blazing brands will discourage them. Most of the creatures are, however, bewildered, and will choose to remain within the stockade because it seems a greater refuge than the jungle outside now offers them.'

With the elephants trapped in the stockade, there was no more to see. After one last look at the mass of grey huddled together, we climbed down the ladder and made for the temporary building.

In the pale light of dawn the next day, following an early breakfast of rice cakes, eggs, curry and fruit, we climbed to the *massa* again to watch the next stage of the operation.

Expert mahouts in white loin cloths and red turbans, each with a spearman as guard, rode eight large tame elephants to form a barrier outside the stockade entrance. Beaters then removed the beams that had blocked the entrance the previous night, and the mahouts rode the tame elephants into the stockade. They were followed by thirty bare-chested spearmen on foot, after which the great logs were firmly tied back into place. The entire group within the stockade advanced on the great, grey cluster of wild elephants, the mahouts holding the heads of their mounts ready to meet a charge. The wild elephant herd closed ranks and wheeled to face the approaching group. It was a breathtaking moment. Would the herd make a concerted charge? If they did, the intruders would be smashed out of the way. With a twinge of pity, I noted that the herd was merely huddling closer together in bewilderment, the larger ones up front to protect the rest.

Suddenly, to my horror, a single bull broke ranks and began a charge. A gasp escaped me, turned to relief when the bull stopped short, backed into the herd again. This was the signal for the entire herd to veer off and flee. The newcomers started in pursuit. Round and round the stockade went the herd, trampling bushes underfoot, even knocking down trees. After circling the stockade several times, they suddenly turned and charged the pallisade logs. But to no avail. My heart went out to the poor, trapped beasts, the once mighty lords of the jungle, especially when their stampede began to slow and they finally paused, flanks pumping, totally discouraged. Now they were so fearful of the noise and confusion, the shouting guards and brandished torches that they would not even move. A bearer carrying a stout rope about ten yards long, a noose on one end, clambered over the palisade. He ran up to the largest of the tame elephants and fastened the rope to its harness. He picked up the noose and walked towards the palpitating herd.

My chest grew tight with excitement and I gripped the rail of the *massa* hard as I watched the bearer attempt to get the noose around the rear leg of one of the wild elephants. He darted forward; the elephant he had chosen backed away, then paused and made a short charge. The bearer beat a retreat.

It took three tries before the bearer finally succeeded in noosing the animal, which became infuriated by the restriction. The bearer darted away, while the tame elephant took the strain of the tugging and pulling on its harness. It was strange and even pitiful to see how little power a massive wild elephant has in just its rear leg.

The tame elephant and the wild one pulled hither and thither, the tame animal, directed by its mahout, moving to get the rope around a tree. The mahout being an expert, this was achieved within minutes. Two more tame elephants were promptly urged forward by their mahouts and placed on either side of the noosed wild elephant, so it could not move sideways. These two elephants then helped to back the wild one against the tree, manoeuvring it until it was harnessed with only about one foot of play on the rope.

All the tame elephants were immediately moved away and the wild one stood there alone, trumpeting and screaming, straining vainly to break free.

My mouth was dry, my heart somehow sick.

'Now it is only a matter of time,' Lord Madu Wan stated, a pleased note in his voice. 'Regular food and water, the sugar cane and stick approach, will complete the process of taming that one. We will repeat the process with each elephant in turn today.'

I saw too much of a parallel between the ensnaring of elephants and the enslaving of a people to enjoy the rest of the day, filled with the pounding of mammoth feet, shrill screams of frustration, trumpets of rage, squeals from the younger elephants. I could almost smell the fear emanating from their great, grey, wrinkled bodies.

When night fell again, in the lights of flaming torches, I thought I was witnessing the pachyderms' hell. The noblest, freest of earth's creatures were being robbed of their natural dignity and subdued. Thus are whole nations enslaved.

CHAPTER TWELVE

Monday, 14 May 1526

For eight months after Fernao returned from Galle, he bided his time, preparing his troops for a confrontation with King Maya Dunne, which would of course inevitably involve Prince Tikiri. Meanwhile, his spies kept bringing him word, which Father Juan and the Great King confirmed, of the build-up of Sita Waka forces, and he awaited only the parallel build-up of the forces of the Great King and Prince Vidiye before setting into motion a new plan he had conceived for challenging King Maya Dunne in the south. The fortress in Galle was already one-third complete and would soon be secure enough for use as a base of operations. Although the warships frequently went out on patrol, he still had the six *nao* and three caravels at his disposal.

More recently, news of the massing of a great war fleet by the Zamorin of Calicut, assisted by the king of Mouro trade, Paichi Marcar, brought reports of counter-moves by the Portuguese East Indies Fleet. These made Fernao somewhat apprehensive as to whether his flotilla might not be withdrawn, so he accelerated both his own efforts and the pressure on his allies to give effect to his plan in Lanka. Too young and inexperienced to face up to the worst that could happen, he proceeded on the most optimistic assumptions, for he had grown accustomed to thinking of those nine warships as the Portuguese Lanka Fleet. After all, he had repeatedly been promised the fullest support for his policies by his superiors, and they would all work unitedly for the greater glory of their King Emperor and the country they loved, Portugal.

When he received the promise of six more *nao* already

on the way from Goa and carrying six additional *terco* – regiments – Fernao had finally fixed the following Monday as the date for implementing his plan to invade Galle.

Now here he was, being rowed to the mail packet *Berrio*, which had just anchored in Colombo harbour, and apprehension was churning in his stomach. He surveyed with dismay the *Berrio*'s shattered mast, shredded sails, splintered rails. The ship, a smaller, slower and less well-armed vessel than the *nao*, had taken a tremendous beating. This was especially evident in contrast with the sleek lines of the sloop *Curaçao* anchored next to her, immaculate after a peaceful voyage out of Java.

Ferneo was piped aboard the *Berrio* and greeted on deck by Captain Morales, a swarthy half-Spaniard. He noted that the decks too had taken a pounding and that the men were solemn as he followed the captain into his cabin.

No sooner were they seated across the built-in table than the captain told Fernao his story. 'As you know, Colonel,' he asserted grimly, 'we routinely make this trip without escort. By the grace of the Blessed Virgin, His Excellency Don Garcia de Noronha, our Viceroy, being aware of the Zamorin's fleet movements, decided that this time we should sail under protection of the six *nao* heading for Colombo, led by Admiral Miguel Ferreira, to reinforce your present strength.'

'Admiral Ferreira? I thought he had retired. He must be seventy years old.'

'The admiral is still an old sea-dog.' Captain Morales smiled briefly, shrugged his shoulders. 'He will never retire. As a matter of fact, it was only his superb naval strategy that saved us. We were off Cochin when the Zamorin's fleet, consisting of twelve warships, appeared on the horizon. We never dreamed that the enemy ships were equipped with cannon.' He leaned back with a bitter smile. 'I suppose they were provided by those sneaking jackals, the Hollanders, who have started providing arms to others to fight their wars. Having joined battle, we fought all day, avoiding close encounter. The admiral's tactics enabled us to sink four enemy warships, but we lost two of our own. When darkness began to fall, the enemy disengaged, veered off and headed back east. The admiral assessed the damage to the *Berrio* and commanded me to proceed alone to Colombo for repairs and to deliver this despatch to you.' He handed Fernao a rolled-up parchment lying on the table.

Fernao's heart had been sinking as he listened to the captain. He now unrolled the parchment and rapidly scanned its contents. It briefly explained the background of the naval situation in the Indian Ocean and gave some details of the Cochin battle. It ended:

In the name of His Excellency the Viceroy, I have made the following decisions: (1) I shall return to Goa with my flotilla, now consisting of four ships and four *terco* augmented by the survivors of the lost regiments whom we were able to pluck from the waters. (2) You shall retain the flagship *Flower of the Sea* for the protection of the Colombo fort and the warship *São Maria* for the protection of the Galle operation. (3) You shall retain the *Berrio* in Colombo for repairs. (4) *Curaçao*, on her return from Java, shall assume mail packet duties. (5) You shall, in your sole discretion, make such military and strategic decisions as you deem fit for the combined operation against Galle and the southern region of Lanka. (6) You shall temporarily return our remaining seven warships and two *terco*, infantry regiments, to Goa immediately, to join the fleet we are assembling for an all-out attack and final victory over the naval forces of the Zamorin . . .

Betrayed! Let down! Months, almost years of careful planning and diplomacy sunk. The entire future of mighty Portugal at stake. How would he explain this betrayal to his local allies after all his grand talk?

The cabin seemed to go black before Fernao. He clenched his fists beneath the table to prevent himself from pounding it. His hopes of a massive victory over King Maya Dunne, King Raigam and Prince Tikiri had been shattered by the Zamorin's naval cannon. With only two warships and one infantry regiment, the entire position of Portugal in Lanka would be back where it had been in 1521. Jaya and Colombo would now have to defend instead of attacking. Galle could barely hold its own. He could have wept with impotent despair.

God, why did You do this to me? Why have You smitten me down when I had almost reached the heights?

How to deal with the situation? Knowing that Captain Morales was watching him intently, he outwardly maintained an iron calm. How could he still invade Galle? As the thoughts raced, an idea flashed into his mind. Yes, that was it. He re-scanned the despatch. There were the words '. . . return our remaining warships and two *terco* to Goa *as soon as possible* . . .'

From the time he bid Captain Morales goodbye, even before his barge touched the wharf, Fernao had worked out details of a new plan. As soon as he reached his office in the fort, he shouted for Aires, whom he had recently promoted to corporal. 'Have the unit commanders assemble here at the double,' he ordered. 'Ask the captain of the sloop *Curaçao* that just arrived from Java to report to me immediately. Send a messenger to the Great King and King Vidiye in Jaya to say I shall be calling on them in the palace this afternoon on a matter of great urgency. I shall need a fast horse and an escort of ten men under your command.'

'Yes, sir.' Corporal Aires' eyes were sparkling at the prospect of action. He saluted, turned smartly and hurried away.

Fernao gazed grimly at his orderly's retreating back. He would give the Great King and King Vidiye news of the battle off Cochin. He would say that the promised reinforcements would be delayed until a great naval battle, for which Admiral Miguel Ferreira was assembling the entire

Portuguese East Indies fleet, was fought and won. Rather than await that event, their plans should be accelerated to avoid the temporary absence of the flotilla at present in Galle harbour. Meanwhile, he would send the *Curaçao* with a message to the captain commanding the flotilla at Galle to return to Colombo and ferry the assault forces to Galle before departing for Goa. It was a gamble, perhaps desperate, but one last devastating blow at the enemy before his forces were depleted would buy him the time he needed.

He had no doubt whatever that the promises of massive reinforcements would be fulfilled very soon. The ill news aroused more patriotic feelings within him than he had ever experienced before. Portuguese military might had never before been challenged in the Indies. This setback made him fiercely determined to preserve the power of Portugal at all costs. He loved his country. He would do anything for her.

Thursday, 17 May 1526

It was one of the rare occasions when Queen Anula could join her husband, King Kumara, for the noon meal in the king's dining room of the Kandy palace. They had just finished eating when Father Juan was announced.

'We shall receive him in the reception chamber,' King Kumara directed the kneeling attendant. He turned to his wife. 'This may be important, so you shall join us.'

Seated on her usual settle in the reception chamber, Queen Anula recalled the first day on which she had occupied the very same seat, alone, frightened, her entire future shattered. She glanced beyond the verandah at the sunshine lying bright on the courtyard. 'It was on a day such as this that you brought the first ray of warm sunshine to our bleak, clouded heart,' she told her husband.

'Not to mention light and life to your one-time frigidity!'

She felt herself blush. He could make her feel like a young girl with such words. 'That too!' she readily agreed. 'You restored security and hope to a woman stripped of everything.'

'Save your clothes, madam,' he remarked drily. 'Thank the Christian God.'

Knowing that this was his way of covering up emotion, she smiled gently. 'You stripped off our clothes,' she remarked, then sighed.

'Why the sigh, madam?'

'We do not know why, lord. It escaped us, perhaps because of our physical condition.'

'You are not sick, are you?'

She detected with pleasure the note of concern in his voice. 'A different kind of sickness, lord, that of impending motherhood.'

She had expected him to light up with joy. Instead, he looked at her in stunned surprise. 'Are you sure?' he demanded. 'Perhaps . . .' He hesitated, confused for once.

'Perhaps, what, lord?' she inquired, disappointed. 'What could be more natural, since we are fertile and you are so potent?'

'We had assumed that, having escaped conception all these years, you were probably . . .'

'Barren?' she was stung to inquire. 'You certainly do not seem to be overjoyed that we are not barren.'

'No, no! We are delighted. Our concern is for you. Nine months of child-carrying, discomfort, the dangers of birthing. You are too precious to lose.'

Somehow his words only sent a flicker of alarm through her. 'Will you cease to love us when we are fat and heavy with child?'

'Madam, your beauty is constant under all circumstances.'

170

The alarm turned to a chill tremor as another thought intruded. 'Will you turn elsewhere for your pleasure when we cannot service you as before?'

'That's an ugly, uncouth word for our acts of lovemaking,' he rejoined firmly.

She felt some slight reassurance, but the fear remained. 'A man needs an outlet,' she began.

'We are not a man, madam, but your husband and lover.'

The wrinkled old chief attendant stood at the entrance, made obeisance, ushered in Father Juan.

'You take another woman and we shall kill you,' she hissed so only her husband could hear.

His face was inscrutable, the brown eyes slightly mocking. 'It is not you but we who should now fear a rival,' he replied softly.

A flood of understanding engulfed her as she watched the friar enter and bow low. Her husband was already jealous of the child she had in her womb. She was hardly addicted to motherhood, had even gladly left her only son, Prince Deva Raja, once named heir to the throne of Lanka, to be brought up by relations in her native Kiri Vella so that she could be rid of the responsibility and enjoy her husband and her position in the Kandy court to the full. She and King Kumara had been perfect for each other, because there was no one else to demand personal attention from either of them. Her husband was obviously worried that a baby might divert some of the total attention she had given him. Should she try to get rid of the baby? Eating raw pineapple was supposed to do it. There was also a midwife, but the last woman to seek that remedy bled to death. She hardly heard the formal exchange of pleasantries between her husband and Father Juan, but kept nodding and smiling at the appropriate places, an attribute of those trained to the world of diplomacy.

'And to what do we owe the honour of this visit,

Father?' King Kumara's question jolted her back to complete attention.

'I bear some ill tidings, I'm afraid, Sire.' The normally booming voice was couched deliberately low in the manner of official mourners at a bereavement.

'And what are they?'

'The Zamorin of Calicut assembled a large naval force and gave battle to a flotilla of our warships under the command of Admiral Miguel Ferreira off Cochin six days ago. The battle was inconclusive, our forces sinking four of the Zamorin's warships with the loss of only two of our own, but the admiral decided to withdraw to Goa and assemble our entire fleet for a major decisive battle with the Zamorin. Colonel de Albergaria directed me to come post haste to Kandy and convey to you personally the gist of the orders he received from the admiral.'

Seeming very calm, King Kumara indicated with a lift of the chin that the friar should proceed.

'The colonel is to return seven of the great *nao* presently under his command to Goa, along with two of the *terco*, infantry regiments. This leaves him with only two *nao* and one *terco*.'

'Where does that leave us?'

Father Juan shifted in his seat, stared at the king, the black pupils of his eyes hard as agates. 'The colonel will not withdraw the company you have in Kandy. He will protect our interests in Colombo and Galle with one *nao* and one company of infantry in each city, depending upon their land guns to defend them.'

'That leaves one more company of infantry. What does the colonel propose to do with that? Move it to the defence of Jaya since it appears that the military build-ups that have been going on in Jaya and Sita Waka for months have reached their climax? How will he protect those he encouraged to prepare for war against the power of an attack

172

from Sita Waka? And what about those secret plans we have been hearing of for another operation in Galle?'

The friar raised his hands in protest. 'So many questions, Sire.' The pale eyes gleamed, one hand reached to stroke his copper-brown beard. 'First, the remaining infantry company will be moved to Kandy for your protection and use.'

'A generous gesture indeed.'

'Surely.' The friar fell for the trap, as the queen knew he would. A triumphant note entered his voice. 'With two companies of our infantry and your army of ten thousand men, two cavalry regiments and one hundred elephants, you can easily accomplish your mission against King Maya Dunne and seize the Sita Waka kingdom while he is engaged against the Great King in Jaya. Colonel de Albergaria also has another plan, which will be divulged later, but which will keep the Sita Waka forces fully occupied.'

'How do we attack without the two entire regiments we were promised from the reinforcements the colonel expected out of Goa?'

'There will be problems, Sire. But remember there is no great opportunity without risk. Already you are king of the entire *uda rata* because of our help. Be assured that our future help and protection will make you the Great King of Lanka. That is the intention of Holy Church, since you are the only Catholic king in this country. I would therefore respectfully remind you to fulfil your own obligations to support the spread of the Portuguese Christian empire.' The deep voice boomed passionately. 'We will extend the gospel through the length and breadth of this kingdom of Lanka and over the entire East Indies. Already more soldiers of Christ, the Franciscans, are getting ready for voyages on the greatest evangelical mission the world has ever known. Your position in Kandy will be safe while you are away, Sire, because there are so many Christians here who will martyr themselves for the cause.'

'That is what we fear, Father.'

'What do you mean, Sire?'

'You know what the word Sinha means, don't you?'

The friar was obviously taken aback at this unexpected response to his inspiring evangelical call. 'Why ... er ... certainly. It means lion.'

'So the Sinhala are the lion race?'

'Why ... yes.'

'Remember, Father, ever since the days of ancient Rome, wherever there are lions the Christians will be thrown to them.'

Friday, 18 May 1526

When we learned of the naval battle off Cochin, we were elated. Immediately afterwards came the news of the imminent depletion of Portuguese naval and military forces in Lanka and we decided to strike immediately. We were at fault not to have wondered why the latter information reached us in Sita Waka so easily. We should have suspected a trap, but eager to attack before the monsoon rains commenced, we surprise-marched on Jaya. To our amazement, we encountered no resistance whatever, not even when we surrounded the city on the evening of 17 May. Despite the enormous strength of our army, both my father and I found this ominous. We could understand the Great King holing in, like a frightened hare, but King Vidiye?

Now it was evening, twenty-four hours later, and being firmly enough entrenched, we had sent the Great King a message demanding surrender. Sitting our mounts in the same grove from which the *parangi* had first fired their cannon on the Lanka capital five years before, we stared across the shining waters of the moat. The rampart walls beyond glowed pink in the slanting rays of the setting sun.

Black dots, lining the walls in close array, told us they were fully manned.

As I gazed at the golden light cast by the evening sun on the swamp waters, the reeds and the moat, my father turned and gestured with his arm at our men making camp in the grove, lighting fires, rubbing down their horses, cleaning their muskets. 'Here we are at long last,' he observed soberly. 'The greatest Sinhala army assembled in over a century. Twenty thousand infantrymen, five thousand cavalry, two hundred charioteers, two hundred musketeers, an entire artillery squadron of twelve guns. Men, nobles and princes from Ruhuna, Raja Rata, Raigam and Sita Waka.'

My elation made me interject. 'You forgot the one hundred elephants and a thousand Rajput mercenaries, Sire.'

Knowing that I was not in favour of the mercenaries, he frowned; then his laugh rang out. 'Well put, Prince.' He paused, raised a finger. 'But don't you see that it proves my point? Neither the elephants, nor the horses, nor the mercenaries, nor even our camp followers and baggage train, this entire force spreading for miles around the capital city, are here to vindicate a principle. They are all here for a cause, or by virtue of a cause, even when it is only money.'

'What is important, Sire, is that we are all here because of your foresight and wisdom. If it takes a cause rather than a principle to place us on the threshold of a great victory which will permit the establishment of all our principles, so be it. We shall prevail. The *parangi* are in the valley of despair, while we are at the heights, looking at the promised land. I confess it was worth waiting for.'

His face clouded on the instant. 'Remember always, however, there is no such thing as final victory,' he warned.

'It is victory enough that we have the Great King in his

175

funk-hole and the *parangi* on the run. You are a master strategist.'

'Taking Jaya will not be easy, for unlike the *parangi* we have no intention of using cannon or muskets against innocent Sinhala civilians to establish our cause.'

A squeaking and creaking shuddered through the air. My father paused, glanced alertly in the direction of the entrance gates to the capital. They were slowly opening. 'Ah, now here comes the Great King's response.'

Friday, 18 May 1526

When the huge city gates were fully open, my father and I gazed in astonishment at a solitary figure that stood framed for a moment within the dark yawning gap of the entrance. The thousand watchful eyes of our men were also intent on the figure as it stepped into the dwindling sunlight. The man who started to walk towards us was clad only in a white waistcloth, the dark upper body bare. This was no king's messenger. Before he even reached the further edge of the causeway, the gates creaked shut and my father and I both recognized him simultaneously.

'Dharma!' my father exclaimed. 'What on earth could he want?'

We had sent secret word to the holy man who had been my childhood mentor and friend to come to Sita Waka and meet us when we first formulated our plans, because we wanted his support, but had been told that he had gone on a pilgrimage to Buddha Gaya in North India. We watched in silence as he now drew closer. Calm and fearless, he reached the grove and was quickly surrounded by a group of our soldiers, who led him to us. He had not changed at all. The broad, cleanshaven features were still classic, the teeth white in their smile, the dark eyes compelling, the well-muscled torso gleaming with health. When he made obeisance to my father, it was as before, an act of pride not of servitude.

'We are glad to see you!' my father asserted, returning the salutation from his saddle with the palms together greeting, the hands a little higher than he would usually place them for one of like rank. 'We sent word to you months ago, but were told that you had gone to Buddha Gaya. We hope the pilgrimage was a rewarding experience for you.'

'Indeed it was, Sire.' Dharma's voice was as deep and gentle as I recalled it. 'A timely reminder of the real rewards of life and the true sanctity of territory.'

'Ah, yes. The sacred gardens, the sacred shrine, the sacred *bodhi*-tree under which our Lord Buddha obtained Enlightenment and died.'

'No, Sire. We refer to the inner sanctity of the lands which the Enlightened One blessed by his Doctrine of non-violence.'

I had thought he came to pledge his support to us, but somehow his words were not giving me that impression.

'The sanctity of any territory, whether physical or spiritual, has to be secured through violence at times,' my father replied gravely, understanding.

'Such is not the Doctrine of the Noble Eightfold Path.'

'Such is the way to freedom and national unity.

'What good is either at the expense of spiritual values? The end justifying the means could augur no lasting good for anyone.'

'Yet you once supported violence for a cause.'

The answering smile was white and gentle, the words uttered with compassion. 'On the contrary, Sire; if you will recall, I led a non-violent movement to achieve that for which you were about to resort to violence. There was only one person killed in the attempt and that was by Prince Tikiri, who now bears the name Raja Sinha because of his prowess in the physical battle, with the added

177

distinction of being the first Sinhala to have a fellow Sinhala or a *parangi* killed by a firearm.'

I experienced a spurt of anger and noted the flashing of my father's eyes. 'Your point is well taken.' My father's voice had grown surprisingly hard and resolute. He will not take criticism of me, I thought with a thrill of pleasure. 'But we are here now and we intend taking Jaya by physical force, if necessary. We will not insult you by explaining why this step should be taken. If you oppose the means we shall employ, then use your influence to have the Great King abdicate his throne so that we can restore the Sinhala race and the Buddha's Doctrine to its rightful place.'

'The Great King must abdicate his throne when the forces of *kharma/vipaka*, cause and effect, dictate it. At the very latest, this will happen when his own *kharmic* forces are extinguished by timely or untimely death. Why do you, a *dharmista* ruler, invite the effects of these violent causes upon your own *kharma*?'

My father's smile was almost cynical. 'Perhaps it is because the Great King's *kharmic* forces are nearing exhaustion that we are here. Or perhaps it is because we have not reached a stage of *kharmic* development that would dictate otherwise. Or perhaps again, we are here because we believe that the performing of *dharma* the duty of one's station,' he nodded slowly at this use of the word that is the name of the man he is addressing, 'is the highest form of *kharma*.'

I was stunned to find my father pointing in the direction of my own recent thoughts, but he immediately set me straight. '*Dharma* is in order to establish a cause, not as a principle of itself,' he added.

Dharma's eyes became luminous with compassion. 'The sun is just setting, Sire,' he stated. 'See how darkness begins to creep upon the earth. The sounds of the day's end are emerging. Soon, somewhere, the scent of queen-of-the night will tinge the air. All around us is cause and effect as

178

ordained by the *kharmic* laws. Man alone has the choice of altering his *kharma*. So the campfires of your soldiers will blaze around the capital city, soiling the air with wood-smoke. Your cannon and muskets are being primed for tomorrow's deadly task, blasting your fellow-countrymen for the first time since the *parangi* laid them low at this very spot. Listen! One of your men is singing a *siyupada*, poem. How peaceful, when the smell of gun-oil will disturb the perfumes of the night and the defecations of your encampment will pollute the boundaries of a city within which helpless men, women and children live in fear that you will pound them to death. Do you know why, Sire?'

My father continued to eye Dharma grimly, but I could tell that he was slowly burning with anger.

'Since you will not answer, let me tell you,' Dharma continued. 'It is because the people are not yet ready to fight for your cause. When they *are*, you may not need your soldiers, or your weapons. I shall not be there to lead them then as I did once before, because I am departing again this week for Lumbini where I shall end my days in Lord Buddha's grove, but the people will gather round your banner, never fear. You will certainly not need foreign mercenaries then! Realize, Sire, that it is not enough for *you* to have a cause. The *people* must have a cause. They will rise against a tyrant, but never against a ruler merely because he is weak.'

A thoughtful expression had crossed my father's face. 'The Great King has been more than weak,' he countered. 'He has slowly been delivering our country to the foreigner. You must surely be aware of the three treaties he executed with the Portuguese, whereunder our sacred land, culture and religion are attacked. He has even placed his heir under the protection of a foreign king.'

'Do those acts entitle you to remove the Great King when that removal might cause the foreign ruler to extend his so-called protection fully to this country, Sire? Surely it would be better to await the event before confronting it.'

'No,' my father firmly countered. 'The truth is that we are here today and in sufficient strength to establish a new order in the country.' He paused, eased himself in the saddle, looked in the direction of the city, now being slowly enshrouded by dusk. He dropped his voice. 'For your information alone, we have the cannon, but we shall not use them against any Sinhala unless they get in our way.'

'You have other plans? You will perhaps have the Zamorin's ships blockade the ports on our seaboard and starve the capital into submission?' Dharma obviously did not lack strategic insight. Getting no response save for an inscrutable look, he shrugged his broad shoulders, then suddenly became very still and relaxed.

As I watched closely, Dharma's whole body began to glow faintly in the near-dark, his eyes took on an unnatural sheen, as if mirrors had covered the eyeballs. His face dissolved into a mist so that when he spoke, his voice seemed to rumble through clouds. 'Eighteen hundred years ago, a certain *bhikku*, the Venerable Sri Suman, warned Prince Sadha Tissa on the Culan plain in Ruhuna that, having won a first encounter, he would not win his final war against his older brother, Prince Abhaya Gamini. Blessed with the gift of inner sight, I warn you likewise, King Maya Dunne. You will not win this battle against your older brother. He has another *vipaka*, of which his own actions will be the *kharma*, cause. Nor will the *parangi* be held back from their greed and ambition. Depart now in peace and return when the forces of *kharma/vipaka* make it right for you.'

'How can you be so sure?' my father demanded, his expression sardonic.

Dharma had returned to our world. 'I am sorry to be

the bearer of ill news,' he stated quietly. 'But you are not in the position of strength you imagine.'

'Because we do not have the people's support?'

'No, Sire. Because the *parangi* Colonel de Albergaria has out-smarted you. Upon receiving news of the naval battle between the admiral's flotilla and the Zamorin's fleet off Cochin, it seemed that the colonel withdrew his *nao* and his regiments from Galle in order to return most of them to Goa. The truth was that he did not.'

Dharma paused for effect and my blood ran cold.

'Within a few hours of the arrival of the damaged mail packet in Colombo on 14 May,' Dharma continued, 'the colonel despatched a sloop that had just sailed in from Java to Galle, with instructions that all the *parangi* warships stationed there, save one, were to return to Colombo empty except for a false show of infantrymen on the decks. The reports he caused to be sent to you were equally misleading. You may have wondered why you have been unopposed so far. Just before you reached Jaya, King Vidiye's force of over five thousand men and one *parangi* regiment were secretly placed on board the ships at night for transportation to Galle. You were tricked into concentrating on your purpose! I have just learned from my sources that the colonel's plan was to land these forces in Galle, have them and the *parangi* infantry take the city and destroy Prince Raigam in a surprise engagement. The *parangi* ships and infantry regiments would then proceed directly from Galle to Goa while Prince Vidiye's victorious troops brought the south under his dominion.' He shook his head sadly. 'So you see, Sire, when you ignore the dictates of *kharma/vipaka*, you end up in the wrong place at the right time, or in the right place at the wrong time!'

CHAPTER THIRTEEN
Saturday, 19 May 1526

The Raschids had at first been elated by the turn of events. The naval battle off Cochin, followed by the withdrawal of the Portuguese flotilla from Lanka, meant that the Zamorin's naval forces could blockade Lanka effectively. One regiment of the Rajput mercenaries had been landed in Negombo, some seventeen miles north of Colombo, and were already serving with King Maya Dunne's men who had invested the city of Jaya. But the rest had gone down with the Zamorin's ships that were sunk by Admiral Ferreira's flotilla.

Now the Raschids were seated in Aisha's chamber, gloomily discussing the latest reports they had received of Colonel de Albergaria's plan to seize Raigam and deliver the south to King Vidiye. With their spy system in the Colombo port, they had been aware of King Vidiye's sudden departure but not his destination and purpose.

'King Vidiye will end our trading in the south,' Aisha declared.

'Bribe him!' Ali interjected quietly.

The boy's frankness made her pause . . . 'Very well then, we can try,' she asserted. 'But our real enemy will remain the Great King.'

'We shall have the Great King killed,' Ali stated. His pale brown eyes were expressionless. He might have been talking of cutting the neck of a farmyard cockerel for *pilau*. Aisha could not resist a shudder.

'It will take time, but I shall start work on the assignment tomorrow,' the young man added.

Aisha was taken aback, but only momentarily. She was growing accustomed to her son's ruthlessness. A thought struck her. 'Should we not have a contingency plan against the possibility of our security here in Colombo being threatened?' she inquired.

Her husband's brows furrowed. 'How could that happen?'

'The Great King and Colonel de Albergaria must surely suspect that we are acting as intermediaries between King Maya Dunne and the Zamorin. The belief that the Zamorin is assembling a huge war fleet only for his own ends will be diminished when he imposes a naval blockade on Colombo and more of his troops land to support King Maya Dunne. If King Maya Dunne is successful, all will be well. But if he fails, we will be in considerable danger. I believe Colonel de Albergaria will support us through loyalty and because we can further his trade interests, but we must face up to the real possibility that the Great King will at least accuse us of treason. Even if he does not have sufficient evidence, he would gladly do so to remove us from trade.'

Her husband blanched, but her son's eyes only glittered. 'What sort of contingency plan do you propose?' Abdul Raschid questioned.

'One that takes into account a truly desperate situation, when we are due to be arrested and our possessions seized.'

'You think of everything,' Abdul Raschid declared admiringly.

'It is the only way to survive. We must be prepared to leave hurriedly through an escape route, with sufficient funds to get us to the east coast. A vessel should be ready there at all times to carry us to Calicut where my brother will look after us.'

Saturday, 19 May 1526

In the days that followed the arrival of the orders from the Viceroy, Fernao had had cause to reflect that when adversities strike they do so in armadas. It had been on his advice that King Maya Dunne had been permitted to invest the capital city of Jaya unopposed, so as to divert him while King Vidiye took control over the south, but he could not get over the setback to his original plan to destroy King Maya Dunne's army through Portuguese might. The long months of careful planning had been wasted and now he could only hope for good news from his bold strike in Galle.

If his military ambitions had been dashed, however, he was happy at home. Julietta had been a model wife, never failing to respond to his loving moments. He recognized that her attitude was based on a decision she had taken and came from a surprising inner strength and resolve.

When he had remarked on it one day, she had smiled her sweet-Madonna smile. 'Fernao, I'm your wife, aren't I, for better, for worse, until death do us part?'

Tonight he had rushed home from the fort, sparkling with news, and he was ecstatic when he faced Juli in the lamplight of her bedroom.

'I heard you gallop in Fernao, what's wrong?' She searched his face, caught his mood. Her eyes brightened.

'Nothing's wrong,' Fernao cried. 'Everything's right. Oh Juli, everything's going to be all right.' He reached for her and held her soft, yielding body.

Finally, she looked up at him, the familiar roguish smile causing the tiny crinkles on either side of her red mouth. 'All right, Fernao, I'm dying to hear your news.'

'Come sit beside me and I'll tell you.'

They sat by the window, he on the chair, she on the floor looking up at him. 'See, there are fireflies on the tree-tops, Juli,' he said softly, wanting to savour the moment first. 'They are a reminder that beauty can always remain in our life.'

As she turned her head towards the dark branches below them, he became aware of the delicate scent of the lilac perfume she was wearing, a present he had given her, imported from Lisbon. The faint sound of Sinhala drumming beneath a flute, haunting in the night, reached his ears, a reminder from Juli's past. He pushed it deliberately from his mind.

'Now for the news,' he began. 'A real break in the gloom of the past week.' He told her of the success of his plan in Galle and the south.

'Oh, Fernao, I'm so proud of you,' she declared when he had finished. 'Is that *all* your news?'

'Isn't it enough?'

She sat up, faced him squarely. 'Not when I have good news for you too, Fernao, my husband. In about seven months, I shall present you with another baby. I hope to make it a boy this time.'

His heart leapt. Now Julietta and he were indeed inseparably one.

Saturday, 19 May 1526

The promised company of *parangi* musketeers had arrived late that evening and were installed in their barracks in the city of Kandy. After interviewing his secret emissaries, in accordance with the schedule of Aryan monarchs, King Kumara had his second bath and received his army commander's daily report. By the time the burly General Dunu departed, the king was almost ready for bed. A feeling of restlessness made him hasten to his wife's quarters instead of observing the scheduled hour for meditation. One of his departures from the regular schedule of Aryan kings was that he slept with his wife, who serviced him every night, even when she had her menstrual period and her impurity forbade normal intercourse.

As she rose from making her obeisance, Queen Anula seemed listless and pale in the golden lamplight.

'What is wrong, beloved lady?' he inquired solicitously. He sat on his usual settle, stretched his slender legs out

185

while the queen resumed her seat opposite. 'You do not look at all well.' He slapped both hands at a whining mosquito, but it got away. Even a king cannot execute a mosquito, he thought idly.

'Nothing, Sire.' Her voice was less strong than usual. A shiver escaped her.

'Are you getting the shivering sickness? Should you not have some *kottha-malli*, coriander tea, with lots of ginger and garlic? Shall we summon the palace *veda rala*, physicians?' Neither of them had been sick since they were married and he had come to think of her as incapable of any illness.

She smiled rather wearily. 'We are not ill, lord, merely sick.'

'To your stomach?'

'We doubt it goes that deep. The sickness is mostly in the throat. You know its cause.'

'We do not know of such things,' he muttered. 'We thought that pregnant ladies had such sickness only in the mornings.'

'Remember, we are different!'

'Well, to business then,' he stated briskly.

She came erect with an effort of will, slim shoulders straight, palms together on her lap. 'We are ready, Sire.'

He gave her the news of the investment of Jaya and King Vidiye's landing in Galle. 'So it would seem that Sita Waka is now open to attack,' he ended.

'What if King Maya Dunne abandons Jaya and marches on Kandy while you invade Sita Waka?'

He gazed at her approvingly. 'A very shrewd thought indeed, lady of our dreams. We did not say that we would invade Sita Waka, merely that it is open to attack. The timing must be right for us to make any such move.' He felt his penis harden at the mind-power behind her flawless beauty. A sudden thought struck him. 'It is a good thing you have no aspirations to being a ruler.'

'We must confess to having such aspirations, Sire,' she responded demurely, eyes downcast.

He was shocked. 'What?' he demanded.

Her smile was sweet. 'We wish to rule your heart.'

He heaved an inward sigh of relief. 'And you do, indeed you do, beautiful wife and queen of our heart.' He held her gaze adoringly till the air between them became tremulous.

'I love you,' he added.

'I love you,' she whispered. 'Oh, how I love you. I would give my life for you.' She paused, then the words seemed to tumble out of her, willy-nilly, as if some force more powerful than herself ejected them. 'I would take your life for you.'

Apprehension gripped his guts. He covered up. 'Now, why would you say that?' he inquired blandly. 'You have already taken our life!'

'I do not know.' She shook her head like a puzzled child, her beautiful large eyes brimming with tears. 'The words just came out. You are so beautiful, lord,' she murmured. 'So totally strong, so completely sure of yourself, so natural. If anything happened to weaken you, to change you . . .' Her voice trailed off, as if it journeyed to meet her eyes that stared through him into a far distance.

Her words reminded him of the need for resoluteness. He wiped the frown from his brain. 'Well, as to that, you can come out of your trance,' he declared, a merry twinkle in his eyes. 'We shall never change. You should look to retaining your own strength, which we regard as equally essential.'

'You are right, lord. Neither you nor we have room for any weakness in our life together.'

He grinned cheerfully. 'Spoken like the lady we love.' He paused deliberately. 'So for now, here is *our* strength.' He stretched out his legs, unfastened his pantaloons, popped out his taut penis. 'Now show us *yours*.'

She rose to her feet, came swiftly to him. She knelt down and grasped his penis. She fondled it till he felt it almost at bursting point. She looked up at him, eyes luminous, deliberately allowing him to see her full beauty. She relaxed her soft, red lips, bent over, kissed his penis so lightly he grunted in delight. This was sheer ecstasy for he was a worshipper of the perfect beauty of image that was now combined with the perfect sensuality of experience.

She opened her wet mouth slowly to take the throbbing penis in. Her lips were warm, soft. A groan escaped him. Unexpectedly, she gagged, moved her mouth away, quietly retching.

He stared at her aghast, in frustration and dismay. For once, the incredible beauty of their unions had ended abruptly, with an almost obscene reaction. The faint odour of the vomit in her throat reached his nostrils. It was as if he had been gazing at a beautiful scene in a mirror only to have the glass suddenly stained.

Sunday, 20 May 1526

I was three days too late to help my uncle, King Raigam, as my father had commanded. By the time I crossed the Gin River with my six cavalry regiments and reached the battleground, a plain surrounded by hillocks on the south bank of the river, hundreds of carrion crows cawed and wheeled overhead, shrouding the blue morning sky in their search for the remnants of corpses. The plain bore ample evidence of the dreadful, tragic disaster, countless piles of ashes from the funeral pyres in which the villagers of the area had mass cremated the thousands of brave Sinhala who had died with my uncle.

According to the local headmen, a joint force of thousands of Sinhala and *parangi* troops, the latter armed with muskets, had encircled and trapped King Raigam's army of five thousand men in that basin, appearing suddenly on the hillocks while King Raigam's men were on the plain. The *parangi* muskets had done their deadly work. Most of King Raigam's men, fired by his example, had fought to the death. The enemy had taken no prisoners. This I could believe of the *parangi*, but not of King Vidiye of Billigam, as he had declared himself. Yet why not? That gangling giant frame, the long ape-like arms, the black skin and large, staring eyes, fierce as a lunatic's, surely spoke of cruelty and ambition.

It was impossible to identify which were my uncle's ashes, so there was no tangible part of him that I could take away for commemoration. Heart-sick, spirit-weary, utterly dejected, I tried to console myself with the thought that his valour would be his finest memorial. Barely hearing the soft murmurs and exclamations of my men thronging behind me, I stared in silence at the grey-green waters of the river. I swore to avenge my uncle's death and to erect a fitting memorial in his honour some day on that very plain, in a free Raigam Korle. A still small voice within me inquired, what of the other thousands who died so gallantly beside King Raigam with so much less to die for? My grief-filled heart could find no space for an answer. Suddenly, I caught a glimpse of the futility of it all. The lowest moment of my life overtook me.

Wednesday, 23 May 1526

As commanded by my father before I left on my rescue mission, I returned to Jaya immediately, reaching our encampment in the evening three days later. I was told that the King could be found at the edge of the grove facing the west gate. One look at his drawn face and I knew that he had already received the tragic news. I could sense his spirit's anguish as we stood silently at the edge of the grove, staring across the swamps at the darkening mass of the city walls. Bullfrogs had begun to croak and marsh stench was heavy in the air. I noticed these things as a sort of excuse for not immediately broaching the dreadful news I had to give him. Then I squared my shoulders and told him all I had discovered. He listened without comment.

Long moments passed when I had finished. Finally, he nodded in the direction of the capital. 'Now, only the three of us are left,' he observed sadly, 'My brother the Great King, you and I.' The direction of his thoughts amazed me. What he said was true. His mother died when he was but a boy. He lost his only sister, King Wira's wife, King Kumara's mother, not long after. My older sister, Princess Mala and my two older brothers were both dead. His father, King Wijayo, was murdered in that very capital not long ago. Now this!

At that moment, I realized that this self-sufficient man, my father, standing so straight and tall beside me, his chiselled face still set in devil-may-care lines, had always been touched by a loneliness of spirit. I was reminded again of the futility of it all.

We made forays almost daily against Jaya, but were unable to force a passage into the city, because my father was determined not to use our few cannon. Our only hope was to starve the defenders into submission. The Rajput mercenaries, thirsty for blood and plunder, soon became restive. Our own troops seemed discouraged. Meanwhile, we received news of victory after victory achieved by King Vidiye against those nobles who dared oppose him in the south. He had quickly added to his reputation for being a magnificent warrior, daring in battle, and a great general. With King Raigam gone, he was slowly expanding his hold on the south. My father repeatedly refused my requests to be allowed to go out and give him battle. 'Once we smash the serpent's head which is right here, the body will die,' he had forecast the last time I had begged him.

'Let us hope that King Kumara will not strike at Sita Waka in our absence,' I had responded.

'No fear of that. He will move when he is sure of victory, a trait inherited from his father perhaps, who is living a life of idle indulgence in the sanctuary we have provided him.'

During those weeks, I came to suspect that it was just as much brotherly love for King Bhuvaneka as a reluctance to pound a Sinhala capital with cannon and risk destroying innocent civilians and their homes that moved my father. He seemed to feel some bond, brother to brother, that I had never suspected in him.

We had sat around the capital for four weeks before the monsoon that sweeps in from the south-west broke. The whole earth was perpetually darkened by clouds. Lightning flashed and thunder rolled, rain poured down incessantly in bucketfuls. The swamp waters rose. Our men were soaked to the skin, for there was no way to remain dry in our tents. Sniffles commenced, turned into nasty colds and hacking coughs everywhere in the encampment. Huge cauldrons of *kottha malli*, coriander tea, steamed day and night above glowing fires shielded by hastily erected roofs of coconut thatch. Some of our troops had the shivering sickness, said to be common in areas of stagnant water. To crown their misery, the monsoon had broken just before the great Buddhist festival, Poson, which falls on the first full moon day aftger Wesak, and commemorates the birth, Enlightenment and death of Lord Buddha. They had been disappointed enough at having to be investing Jaya during Wesak instead of in their homes celebrating the event, but this compounded their misery. So there were no *pandals* for them this season, no making of Wesak lanterns, no hanging of coloured festoons, no traditional sweetmeats. Even the observances of *dasa-sil*, the ten precepts, and the *bana* preaching had to be curtailed. But it was the mercenaries who grumbled most. I was sorry my father had ever hired the miserable wretches.

'This expedition is accursed,' I overheard a trooper complain quietly to a comrade one day. The remark told me that the morale of our troops was ebbing. Something had to be done – and done quickly – to stop the termite rot within their spirits. But what?

Conditions improved only after the rains petered out and ceased altogether. Soon, golden days of clear sunshine revealed a green earth that seemed to ask, 'Who, me?' amid a chorus of bird-songs, the stink of rotting leaves, of drowned carcasses and stale mud.

Sunday, 1 July 1526

Dawn had just broken when I heard a commotion and emerged from my tent, pitched next to my father's. It was just getting light, so I could see dew glistening on the reeds at the edge of the grove, hear it dripping quietly from the dark branches on to the dead leaves below. A bird whistle-trilled, the sound emerging sweet and clear as 'Victo . . . rious . . . victo . . . rious.' Another replied 'Shut up . . . shu . . . ut . . . up . . .'

Around our headquarters, camp activity was just commencing, the scent of rice being boiled for the morning meal filtered between the trees. The guards who had escorted the messenger stood around the small clearing, trying not to betray their curiosity.

My father smiled at me, broke the seals off the scroll which the kneeling messenger had proffered him. His face turned grave as he read the message. He reached the end, read it again, glanced at me and silently handed the parchment to me. 'A message from Abdul Raschid,' he commented tersely.

The words swam before my eyes. Abdul Raschid had received the news from the captain of a small Mouro trading ship, which had just put into port in Colombo. The Zamorin's fleet of 51 ships, with 500 guns and 2,000 men, which had helped provide our naval blockade, had encountered the consolidated Portuguese East Indies fleet, under command of its most brilliant naval officer, Admiral Martin Alfonso de Sousa, despatched from Lisbon as soon as news of the build-up of the Zamorin's fleet had been conveyed to the King Emperor. The action had taken place off Vedalai, near Rames Waram on the south-west coast of India. The Portuguese had totally routed the Zamorin's fleet, even captured a beautiful silken umbrella hung with pearls which the Zamorin had sent as a present to his 'friend, brother and ally, King Maya Dunne of Sita Waka, soon to be the Great King of Lanka'. The captain of the trading ship warned that the Portuguese fleet would be heading for Colombo once they had finished active pursuit of the Zamorin's scattered warships.

'Too late,' my father muttered. He turned to me. 'We put it off too long.' He turned and walked slowly back inside his tent. His head was erect, but I knew his heart was sunk in the depths.

At our best in a crisis, however, neither my father nor I took long to recover from the first shattering effects of the news. Within the hour, Lord Wickrama Sinha, my father and I were seated at the rough table of white *gini sapu* wood in my father's tent, my father's face calm. 'We expect the *parangi* will land at least ten regiments complete with artillery support in Colombo,' he stated. 'We can attack Jaya with our cannon immediately and force an entry, but this may take time and we would in any event be faced with an attack from the Portuguese. Our best course therefore is to withdraw to Sita Waka immediately. But we cannot ignore the total picture, so both of you gentlemen shall leave again for the south today with your strike forces. Your object, to seek out and destroy King Vidiye and his army.'

I glanced quickly at Lord Wickrama Sinha. His lean, handsome face was so tense the fair cheeks looked pinched and pale. 'Supposing the *parangi* and the Great King join in an invasion of Sita Waka, Sire?' he inquired. 'Would it not be wiser for us to avoid splitting up our own forces?'

My father shook his head with certainty. 'It would take some powerful persuasion to make our brother, the Great King, invade our domain, especially since he knows he could never hold it for long. On the other hand, your mission, Lord Wickrama Sinha, will be to prevent King Vidiye from uniting with his allies and presenting us with really overwhelming odds.'

'Supposing King Kumara decides to throw in his lot with the Great King and the *parangi*, Sire?' I demanded.

'That is a contingency we have to face when it arises. It is such a pity that King Raigam's ... King Raigam's ...' He paused, shrugged to control himself.

By unspoken consent, Lord Wickrama Sinha and I decided it was time to leave. I craved the king's permission to withdraw. We rose, made obeisance and walked outside. The sun had refused to emerge.

Thursday, 12 July 1526

Unseasonable rains in the mountains had flooded the three rivers we had to cross on the way to Galle, so it took us five days to get to the outskirts of the city. Our spies informed us that King Vidiye had proceeded south with his army to Hamban, seventy-two miles away, to quell a major uprising. If he succeeded in doing so, it would bring the independent region of Ruhuna under his control.

Having no desire to expose ourselves to the *parangi* cannon, we made a great detour around Galle. With three more river-crossings and the last thirty miles through the

194

appalling heat of dense jungle, we finally reached the ocean-front sand dunes and salt pans of Hamban on the eleventh day after our departure from Jaya and encamped on an open plain by the seashore. We were well enough west of the town to have early warning of any threat from King Vidiye's troops.

Since we had no time to organize a supply train before leaving Jaya we had lived off the land. Although we paid for our food, it was not easy to feed six thousand soldiers on the move. Even if the headmen and friendly nobles did not mind doing so, many villagers resented having to give up their stocks of rice. After all, they could not fill empty bellies with money in seasons of drought or flood. We were thankful therefore to be near the town of Hamban, where rice, vegetables and salt were in good supply. A strong Mouro population also provided mutton and hunters brought in venison. The men welcomed the pause and the prospect of a good meal followed by a full night's rest.

We camped in the open scrubland, organized an all-round defence perimeter and sent our patrols towards the town to obtain intelligence as to King Vidiye's troop dispositions. We had been almost totally without news since we left Galle and Matara.

Meanwhile, the off-duty men were enjoying a quick dip in the ocean. Hundreds of bare bodies glistened in the evening sun, packed the shallows like a pilgrim picnic at a mountain stream. There was much shouting, snorting and splashing, the few good swimmers trying to show off in the deeper waters. It was all so peaceful. I recalled that we were not far from where our magnificent King Abhaya Gamini enjoyed his boyhood eighteen hundred years before and prepared for war.

Our first reconnaissance patrols returned within the hour. Lord Wickrama Sinha and I received them on the white sand beach fringed with green groundcover where our tent had been erected.

195

'Several great *parangi* warships sailed in and anchored off the roadstead at Hamban Bay yesterday morning,' the patrol leader reported excitedly. 'King Vidiye's entire army boarded the ships and sailed away by evening! Knowing you were tracking him, prince, the king left a message for you with the district chieftain.' He bowed and proffered an *ola*, left hand to right elbow in the approved manner.

I glanced at Lord Wickrama Sinha, noted the inquiring look on his lean face. I dismissed the patrol leader, opened the *ola* scroll and read loud enough for Lord Wickrama Sinha to hear:

'To Prince Tikiri Bandara, now known as Raja Sinha, Vidiye Bandara, King of Billigam and Raigam, sends greetings.
　'We regret that our encounter has had to be postponed for a more pressing reason.
　'Never fear, we shall return. It is in the stars that we destroy you some day, if you survive long enough . . .'

I clutched the scroll, squeezed it in anger.

'What do we do now?' Lord Wickrama Sinha was smiling his sweet smile. He was a man of action not of words.

'We have no option but to return to Sita Waka,' I replied.

'What about another raid on the *parangi* in Galle, prince?'

'We cannot risk another bombardment of the town. Besides, we should hasten to join King Maya Dunne, for he may be needing every bit of support he can get on the home front. Colonel de Albergaria is a shrewd strategist, capable of incredible timing. Once reinforcements arrive in Colombo, he will have a more powerful force of his own people than he has ever had before. It will make him deadly dangerous. We shall therefore leave for Sita Waka at first light tomorrow, carrying one day's field rations. We shall follow the shortest route, which is along the Amban river then up through the hill country. Have the commanders assemble within an hour for their orders. Meanwhile, our outposts and pickets may stand easy and our patrol activity may cease.'

Monday, 16 July 1526

Four nights later we encamped in a long stretch of open glade running along the south bank of the Menik river, so named because gemstones roll down it from sources in the high mountains. Dark trees, running down from the slopes, pressed to a halt around the glade. The still of the night was punctured by the splutter and crackle of damp logs from our long lines of campfires. We had placed the fires closer to each other than usual, as protection against the leeches that abounded here, so our fires warmed the cool mountain air. A jackal howled from the distance. Our men were mostly silent, contemplative, like me, as I lay on my blanket, looking up at the stars glistening in a dark blue sky.

I raised myself on one elbow at the sound of voices. Two guards emerged into the flickering firelight, escorting a dark figure. As they came closer, I distinguished a lean, tall man in a black tunic coat and white pantaloons. A brown woollen shawl covered his head and shoulders, so his gaunt face, dominated by a high-bridged nose and high thin forehead, looked like that of a Catholic friar. He removed his shawl as a mark of respect and made obeisance to me.

One of the guards introduced the newcomer. 'This is Banda, prince. He says he is the headman of Embil, the village between here and Sita Waka. He claims to bring news of grave importance.'

'You may speak,' I directed the headman.

'I heard from a carter journeying through my village that you were on your way to Sita Waka with a great army,

197

lord,' he quavered. 'So I thought I should bring you the stirring news myself.'

'What news?' I demanded.

Hearing the crunch of footsteps, I turned my head to find Lord Wickrama Sinha coming towards us. He nodded a greeting and stood beside me.

'A great host of *parangi* joined the army of the Great King of Jaya and made a surprise incursion into our kingdom,' Banda proceeded. 'King Maya Dunne, may the blessings of the Triple Gem always be on him, advanced against them yesterday with his entire army. A tremendous battle took place. We heard its distant sounds all the way to our village, like the war of the rain gods in the skies when the monsoons arrive. The firing of the cannon guns such as we have heard of recently went on all afternoon and into the evening. Such a portentous event.'

'What was the result of the battle, man?' I interrupted him impatiently, making the give motion with my fingers. 'Who won?'

'We have no final information, lord, because we are so far away, but word in the village is that King Maya Dunne was victorious.' His tone was emphatic, his grin almost triumphant. 'How else could it be?'

I almost turned aside in frustration, but thanked the man instead, directed that he be given a gift of money and sent on his way. Lord Wickrama Sinha and I finally stood alone. 'If I may make an intelligent observation, we have either won, or lost!' Lord Wickrama Sinha stated. 'If we have won, we need not speed to the rescue. If we have lost, we had better not charge ahead.'

Tuesday, 17 July 1526

I rode through the next day in a kind of daze, because the earliest reports we had from passing wagoners were that our army had been defeated in a great battle and had retreated under command of my father, the king. I thanked the *devas* that he was reported safe, but there were tears in my spirit at what that proud man, once invincible, must be enduring under the ignominy of defeat.

'At least they can make a stand within the city, which is fortified,' Lord Wickrama Sinha, who was riding beside me, commented, his face grave. He eyed me thoughtfully. 'You are probably wondering whether our presence with the king might have made a difference to the outcome of the battle. I beg you to realize that we too might have been helpless before the firepower of the Portuguese.'

I nodded my agreement, but my heart was full of gloom. As we drew nearer our destination, the news became worse. Men in the villages and passing travellers told of a crushing defeat of our army, which had been decimated by an artillery barrage more fierce than the thunderbolts of all the worlds and by the savagery of the *parangi degredados*. Somehow, all else, including the deaths of thousands, the fate of the country and my destiny, paled into insignificance before my heartsickness at my father's situation.

The first physical evidence of a real disaster more catastrophic than I had ever imagined was a strange odour at dusk, as we neared the approach to the mountain pass that overlooked the city. Lord Wickrama Sinha sniffed the air and remarked, 'I would swear that is the smell of burning.'

'Burning!' I exclaimed.

As one, we spurred our horses to canter up the dark trail running between tall timber shadowed by dense branches. Seeing the angry red glow in the sky before we reached the crest of the steep slope, I broke into a gallop. As we neared the gap of the pass, pluming black-grey smoke appeared in the distance.

We broke through the gap, reined in our horses. I stared aghast at the scene below.

Less than a mile into the valley, the entire capitol of Sita

Waka city was aflame, a great square of raging red, soaring upwards, violently pushing smoke towards the heavens. A roaring as of the rumbling of the earth before it quakes rolled towards us, bringing a blast of heat which hit the mountainside. It would return in a great wind to fuel the flames from which it had first emerged. Tiny black dots of people, silhouetted against the glare, scurried around. I thought I heard their cries. The dreadful smell of burning was now so harsh that it scratched my throat.

My whole life has gone up with those flames, I thought. My birthplace, my home, my few treasured possessions, my past. Even my present and my entire future.

I heard Lord Wickrama Sinha cursing softly.

He muttered, 'Never has this happened in the history of our country, except when the invading Cholas burned Anu and Polon. Only the *parangi* could have done such a terrible deed.'

I could not speak because I had no words. My entire will was directed to keeping back my tears. Oh yes indeed. I did have tears to shed.

I heard the rustle of undergrowth on the side of the trail. My heart beating faster, I whipped out my sword and turned Rama to face the sound.

A man on horseback broke through the trees. I would have recognized that figure anywhere. My father was walking his bay towards us. He was alone, his head swathed in a white bandage, his right arm in a sling. Lord Wickrama Sinha and I watched in petrified silence as he drew closer. He was bathed in sweat, bloodied, weary. But his head was unbowed.

CHAPTER FOURTEEN
Tuesday, 17 July 1526

At the same time that night, standing on the open verandah of a large homestead located on the opposite mountainside, overlooking the city of Sita Waka from its western approaches, Fernao faced the wrath of the Great King Bhuvaneka Bahu with an obviously amused King Kumara looking on. They were alone in the quiet of the living area of the lodging commandeered for the Great King. Attendants bustled in the kitchen quarters, but the smell of smoke struck from the burning capitol, wafted up by hot winds. The sharp barking of frightened dogs, the shrill neigh of terrified horses and an occasional scream told of a city in confusion.

'Colonel de Albergaria, you have violated one of the most sacred tenets of the Sinhala *charlithraya*, tradition. When King Maya Dunne draped his palace with white cloth and withdrew from his capital city this afternoon, it was the symbol of his call for a truce. We told you this afternoon that the truce should be honoured and that we should await emissaries from our br. . . King Maya Dunne, in the same way that the Europeans would honour the white flag of surrender.' The Great King's moustache was positively bristling, his plump cheeks quivering with outrage. 'Now your men have burned down King Maya Dunne's palace, which was also our own family house. It held many memories for us.' A tremor had entered the high, raspy voice. 'Yet that is not what evokes our outrage. Rather, it is the offence against our sacred code, which every true Sinhala will abhor. And what will history say of us?'

'That we were ruthless as conquerors and that no man,

be it king or prince, nobleman or commander, dared to cross us,' King Kumara observed with a cynical grin.

Fernao thanked King Kumara with a sidelong smile, but he was hot and tired from forced marches and battles. His face, blotched with soot, was sweaty and his body itched, his iron helmet felt heavy as an elephant's tread and the metal jacket he had worn since dawn hurt his ribs. All he wanted was a bath, food and sleep. His irritation made him decide that the time had come to be firm with the plump ruler who had ridden with his army but had taken no part in the actual fighting. 'King Maya Dunne did not raise the white flag of surrender, Sire,' he retorted. 'He merely signalled his desire for truce talks, and even if his gesture had been a symbol of his desire to parley, we are in no mood to accept anything but unconditional surrender. Remember, the king escaped with his cannon, muskets and gunpowder intact. He also emptied his treasury. Remember too that, before landing in Colombo, most of my men had ridden the ocean waves for four days and participated in the great naval encounter against the Zamorin's fleet, one of the most massive ever assembled in these waters, at the battle of Vedalai. Immediately after they landed in Colombo, they hastened to your rescue in Jaya, then proceeded without pause on a two-day forced march, carrying muskets and accompanied by cannon. Finally, they fought a whole day's land battle yesterday, against an enemy equipped with firepower, elephants, chariots and cavalry. They have had comrades wounded and killed. Their blood is up. They cannot be held back either by white drapes in a palace or some nebulous custom.'

The Great King's jaw dropped, his face, glistening with the heat arising from the blazing capitol, became contorted with rage. He pointed a shaking finger at the flames roaring beneath them. 'You order such a deed and dare talk to us in this manner?' he demanded.

'Listen to me, Great King,' Fernao directed, his pale blue

eyes frosty. 'The time has come for you and me to understand each other. This entire operation was conceived at a period when you were locked within your city walls and in desperate straits. It was planned by me and supported by my government.' He gestured inwards with his right hand. 'My men and I have risked our lives to get here. For what? We do not wish to alter the Sinhala way of life, but we will only honour your customs and traditions as long as they do not clash with our interests. My men are paid wages and provided with food, clothing and shelter. Their hope of a peaceful retirement, however, lies in the spoils of war. When they found that the palace, the capitol and the treasury had been stripped by King Maya Dunne before he withdrew, it was I who held them back from giving vent to their frustration by raping women and looting civilians. I made an example of the first *degredado* to attempt rape by having him flogged in the presence of his comrades. He now lies at death's door. My troops set fire to the capitol because they were enraged at finding it bare. I did nothing to prevent it because it provided them with an outlet which destroyed the scorpion's nest.'

The Great King's eyes had begun to bulge with wrath, but King Kumara intervened. 'Perhaps the lion's den might be a better analogy,' he observed urbanely, then turned to survey the mountain slope, pretending to be preoccupied by the Portuguese soldiers stalking about the torch-lit glade immediately below them.

'Whatever the situation,' Fernao stated, 'we shall always give you the respect due your position, Sire, but never deference to your desires against our better dictates.'

To Fernao's surprise, the Great King suddenly composed himself. He actually smiled, not with his eyes but with his teeth. 'Very well, Colonel de Albergaria,' he responded pleasantly. 'We thank you for your timely reminder. Let us make sure that we do indeed understand each other.' He paused. 'You speak thus obviously from strength, but remember that your military strength is only maintained to promote trade, which in turn supports you and your military. It is we, the kings, who command the produce you so badly need to fill your coffers, manufacture your ships and weapons, pay your soldiers. It is we, the kings, to whom the people will give loyalty and support, which is moral strength. You have just assumed a position of authority, but you will never be able to dominate the whole island of Lanka without more military strength than your entire country possesses.' He turned towards King Kumara. 'As for you, cousin, we are not surprised that you feel no outrage at this terrible deed. After all, you are not renowned for your morality.'

King Kumara smiled. 'Nothing would cause us more outrage, cousin, than to be accused of morality. Since you treasure the concept, however, ask yourself about a Great King who sells his country to a foreign power in order to retain his sovereignty. Bah! What have you in fact retained, cousin? As for tradition, it is no more than slippery okra, which winners cast in the path of victims to ensure their enslavement and losers hurl at a victor's feet to make him slip on his own advance! We heartily agree with the colonel. After all the great conquerors throughout history, Genghis Khan, Mahmud of Ghazni, Sikander, not to mention the Crusaders, have repeatedly destroyed the centres of opposition and enjoyed the spoils of war.'

A scornful expression crossed the Great King's face and his chin lifted. 'Ah, spoken like a good Catholic,' he retorted. 'But beware, you may be heading for the hell of your own professed beliefs.'

'On the contrary, cousin, we are here in the heaven of victory.' As King Kumara paused, a twinkle in his eyes, Fernao warmed towards the man. 'Of course, it is possible that hell is heading towards us. After all, heaven and hell are not that far apart.' He shrugged lithe shoulders. 'But that is a phenomenon all men face and we would rather hell came to us, so we could welcome it, than that we should go to hell!'

At a loss for words, the Great King could only glare at King Kumara.

'Be reasonable, cousin,' King Kumara continued in soothing tones. 'Colonel Fernao de Albergaria brought about our present situation almost single-handed. He ensured the despatch of reinforcements from Portugal, had them sent on to Lanka, created our cousin, King Vidiye's, diversionary tactics and rushed to your rescue. It was the colonel's brilliant plan that forced King Maya Dunne into open battle on a broad plain where the king's elephants were terrified and his chariots and cavalry rendered helpless by an artillery bombardment such as this country has never before experienced. It was the colonel who had your army attack on the flank while his own regiments attacked frontally and secretly arranged for our Kandyan army group to appear on the battle scene, completely unexpectedly, to take King Maya Dunne on the other flank. It was his unique idea to leave the rear open, so the enemy could flee, which they did after a whole day's gallant fighting that nonetheless produced casualties of over ten to our one. If you had not cried halt, we would have driven the enemy further and further east, right into the arms of King Vidiye, advancing unknown to them, from Batti. Oh, and let us not forget the way in which the colonel softened King Maya Dunne's strength by disposing of King Raigam and his army. You owe the colonel everything and your brother, King Maya Dunne, nothing. The colonel is the man of the hour and you should extend him every support and co-operation, not to mention admiration and some honour.'

'Would you say we must also wash the colonel's arse?' the Great King demanded harshly.

Fernao was taken aback at the crudeness of the question, completely out of character with the Great King. 'We have all been through rough times,' he intervened in more gentle tones. 'What has been done cannot be undone. Let us sleep on it.'

'Let us indeed,' King Kumara agreed with great humour. 'Our cousin, the Great King, is so preoccupied with the nether regions tonight that he is having the devil's own time in a hell of his own making.'

'You are clever with words,' the Great King retorted.

'We trust we have also proved clever with deeds, especially on the battlefield.' Fernao knew this last to be a pointed reference to the Great King's lack of participation in the fighting while King Kumara had proved himself a superb commander and a champion warrior.

'What do you propose doing in Sita Waka, Colonel?' the Great King demanded, abruptly changing the uncomfortable subject.

'Departing soon, leaving behind an occupation force.'

'Of your own men?'

'No, of your men and King Kumara's, with token support from us.'

'The occupation force should be ours alone,' King Kumara broke in harshly. 'That was our contract, Colonel. We were to attack Sita Waka and, once victorious, remain as its king, by right, because our mother was a Maya Dunne.'

'Never!' the Great King demurred vehemently. His fierce glance turned to Fernao. 'Was that your plan? If so, please understand that you may not dispose of Sita Waka on your own authority. It is part of Lanka and we are the Great King. Only *we* have the power to appoint new kings.'

'You certainly did not appoint us in the *uda rata*,' King Kumara interjected with unwonted vehemence. He looked at Fernao for his support.

Fernao was nonplussed. He was being forced into the strait before he was ready to cross it. He thought quickly.

'The contract with you, King Kumara, depended upon your making an independent, diversionary attack on Sita Waka. Nor did it specify a timeframe. Don't you think that it would be premature for you to attempt to rule this kingdom?'

'Nothing is premature for those who dare,' King Kumara retorted.

'It is not a matter of whether King Kumara is ready or not,' the Great King interrupted. 'We simply will not permit it.'

The air had become charged with conflict. Fernao felt he had to relax it. 'Now, now, let us not have dissension in our ranks,' he requested, raising his palms in a call for calm.

The Great King's face was set. He straightened his shoulders, stood with his feet firmly apart. 'We have not yet abdicated our throne,' he declared steadily. He glanced down at the flaming buildings, then up at the smoke billowing towards the clouded sky. His bulging eyes suddenly turned sad. 'King Maya Dunne is our brother,' he said. 'He has been robbed of his capitol and his dignity today. The kingdom of Sita Waka is not a commodity for contract or barter, like fish on the beaches or cinnamon in the market place.' He glanced contemptuously at King Kumara. 'Or even queenly flesh. We have gone far enough. Our commands shall be obeyed, on pain of death.'

King Kumara clapped his hands in mock applause. 'A splendid performance, cousin,' he said. 'You play the part so well it sounds almost authentic. All it lacks is realism, a commodity of which you are temporarily out of stock.'

'Perhaps we have been out of stock of courage as well up to now,' the Great King snapped. 'The colonel's actions have given us back some supply of both commodities.' He turned full face to Fernao. 'Do you intend leaving a garrison in Sita Waka, Colonel?' The question came out imperiously, with a proud lift of the head.

Fernao could not help a surge of admiration for the sudden dignity of the man before him. Years of submission to authority took over. 'No, Sire,' he replied. 'I cannot spare the men and some of the warships and regiments must be returned to Goa, once this expedition has been successfully concluded.'

The Great King smiled blandly. 'We put it to our cousin here.' He merely jerked his head towards King Kumara, not deigning to look at him. 'That it is he who is in short supply of realism. Sita Waka, Raigam and even the *uda rata*, which our cousin presently rules, are parts of our domain.' His mouth twitched with amusement. 'We understand that ex-King Wira resides in these parts. Perhaps King Kumara should seek out his father while he is here. If he can find the man, King Kumara may recover the Kandyan crown and return it to his own kingdom, as a king indeed instead of a usurper without a crown.' He paused, eyes flashing. 'We shall not permit him to rule Sita Waka. If he is realistic, he will accept the fact that once you leave, Colonel, we will outnumber him three to one, even excluding King Maya Dunne's army and that of King Vidiye which is on its way. As for King Maya Dunne, we shall deal with his future ourselves. This audience is terminated. We bid you both *ayubowan*.' He turned round abruptly and stalked inside the house.

Fernao found King Kumara's blazing eyes on him. 'And what do you say to that, Colonel?'

'I say that my government and I are on your side.' Fernao could not bring himself to look the disappointed king in the face. 'But timing is most important. We have established your presence here today as one of the great victors. That gives you national recognition. As I told the Great King just now, we cannot maintain an occupation force in Sita Waka, so we cannot back a seizure of the throne by you. The moment we leave, the Great King's army will be able to cut you to pieces. If he joins forces with his brother, which he will certainly do if we compel him, you will be hopelessly outnumbered.' He paused, then dropped his voice. 'Remember, though, that the Great King is old and you are very, very young. Also, kings die.' He looked meaningfully at King Kumara. 'This one will be succeeded by a puppet, his grandson, Prince Dom Juan. We will then help you expand your rule of other kingdoms, I promise you.'

'That is as good a promise as that of virginity from a whore!' King Kumara's voice was a combination of controlled venom, disgust and scorn. He became thoughtful. 'Is this your final word, Colonel?'

Fernao shifted uncomfortably on his feet. He had juggled sub-kingdoms before, but he was not used to the role of king-maker. He spread the palms of his hands in a gesture of helplessness. 'What else can I say?'

'Use your present strength to follow the remains of King Maya Dunne's forces and destroy them all.' A cunning gleam entered King Kumara's brown eyes. 'Including the untouched cavalry corps and infantry regiments of your rival, Prince Raja Sinha.'

Fernao recoiled as if he had been slapped across the face. How did this young devil incarnate know of the wound in his heart? 'I cannot use the forces of His Imperial Majesty for such a purpose,' he rejoined. 'My orders are to re-establish the suzerainty of the Great King over his domains and return most of the military and naval forces to Goa.'

'We obviously have no place here, now that you have achieved that limited objective which you so cleverly hid from us, Colonel.' The handsome face was set in tight lines. 'We are not beggars to sue for favours, least of all from those who have no real sense of loyalty and honour. We are an independent ruler. We shall issue orders for our army to depart for Kandy at dawn tomorrow.'

Fernao flushed, restrained the urge to strike the king

209

across the face. 'With or without my two musket companies?' he demanded.

'That is up to you, Colonel.' King Kumara turned, clumped down the verandah steps, then walked across the glade in the direction of his cottage.

Fernao gazed up at a sky obscured by smoke clouds of his making. He was suddenly out of his depth and very tired. Dear God in heaven, give me Thy strength, he prayed.

As if in answer, the thought of Julietta with his baby in her womb flashed into his weary brain. Nothing else mattered, not even the possibility that Catherina might be a bastard child. His wife now carried a part of him that would be perpetuated for ever, within her, the woman he loved. All he wanted was to leave tomorrow with his troops, to get away from the charred remains of the Maya Dunne capital and back to the quietude of his own home on the Mutu Vella hill.

Concealing his rage and frustration, King Kumara strode across the glade. This was not a good time in his life, he decided. First, the disappointment in the Kandy palace when his queen had gagged and vomited when taking him into her mouth had affected him curiously. He knew that a normal man would have understood and accepted it, especially if he loved his woman. But he was a not normal man. He was a finely tuned, sensitive aesthete, to whom beauty was as important as the act or the person. Now, the victory over King Maya Dunne had turned to dust and ashes in his mouth. He was left with the need for some release, some outlet. His thoughts turned to sex. He could do with a woman tonight. He stifled the temptation. He loved Queen Anula and wanted to give her fidelity. After all, what he had known with her was superb, unmatchable.

His two aides, who had been waiting in the shadows, saluted and fell in behind him. He returned the greeting absent-mindedly, stalked up to the waiting horses. A member of his escort, having remained in attendance, held the head of his grey. He mounted, eased himself in the saddle, gave the horse its head. The animal began picking its way down the track, its hooves clipping and clopping on the small stones. The escort followed in single file.

The entire armies of Kandy and Jaya were encamped in the great bowl of the plain in which the city lay, with the Portuguese on the nearer western side of the pass. The Kandyan army commander had selected the parklands flanking the city for his encampment. Sounds of revelry, a drumbeat, the tinkle of a *sitar* followed by a song reached King Kumara through the stifling smoke. Strange how people found time for being their normal selves even after military action. He coughed, realized that he was very alert, his mind sparkling with anger though he should be weary from the gruelling day. His thoughts drifted again to Queen Anula. What was she doing at this moment? He realized that he was thinking objectively about her for the first time since he met her. Why? In the past, he had associated her with sweet scents, a clean body, the poetry of motion even in their sexual unisons. Now, the smell of her vomit intruded. What kind of person am I, he asked himself for the first time in his life. Am I incapable of true love? Do I love the image, not the person?

A woman's shrieking followed by ribald laughter of men crashed through his reflections. He glanced in the direction from which the sounds had come, a modest house, lit by flares. He glanced back at his aides. 'What was that?' he demanded.

'Probably a woman being . . . er . . . difficult,' the aide replied with a sly grin.

'Whose men would they be?'

'Probably the Great King's, Sire.'

'Follow me!' King Kumara directed. He turned his mount, urged it through an open gateway, clattered up the short entrance walkway and ground to a stop. He dismounted in an instance, drew his sword, rapped insistently with its hilt on the closed door.

The shouts within the house were suddenly hushed. The woman started shrieking 'Help! Help!' But her screams were immediately stifled.

'Open in the king's name!' the aide behind King Kumara roared. He had already dismounted and the escort was filing into the garden.

King Kumara drew back his booted foot, slammed the sole hard against the door. It gave slightly. He kicked again and the door swung in. He stood back from the entrance and surveyed the scene. Three soldiers without pantaloons, penises erect, stood around a naked woman who lay on the ground. In the light of an oil-lamp, the scene was poised before him for a few seconds like a still-life drawing.

Then it burst into action.

One of the soldiers, a great, brawny man with a black beard and vicious eyes, leapt for his sword, seized it and lunged towards the door. King Kumara merely stood his ground, disdainfully parried the thrust, shifted his grip, the point of his sword circling around his opponent's blade. Right knee bent, he leaned gracefully forward and his opponent ran into the classic thrust. The sword sank in between his ribs, clean into the heart.

The man grunted, gave. His jaw dropped open, his sword arm sagging with it. Red blood gouted from the wound when the king withdrew his blade. The man's eyes crossed. He gave a kind of sigh. His breath rattled. He was dead before he collapsed. His sword clattered on the flagstone floor.

The other two men had seized their swords in a single move. They came swarming towards the door, but were impeded by the body of their dead comrade. King Kumara did not make the mistake of enetering the room. He let the men jostle each other at the doorway. Another classic

212

thrust went through the stomach of the man in the centre, the already blooded sword sinking in smooth as a plough-share. The man screamed, clutched wildly at the sword, screamed again as the withdrawal of the blade sliced his palms. He sank to the ground.

In a single bound, King Kumara was inside the room. He moved with lightning speed to his left, swinging round to face his opponent. One look at his grim visage, the deadly purpose in his eyes and the man paused. His eyes shifted to the king's aides rushing through the doorway. He dropped his sword and fell to his knees.

'Take him away and hang him!' the king commanded his aides.

'But, Sire, they are all the Great King's men,' one of the aides stammered.

Hang the Great King too, King Kumara thought. Aloud, he said, 'Hang him on a royal poinciana tree then. Attempted rape is a crime anywhere on our island. Remove these two corpses and hang them too, as an example.'

He moved forward to a settee on which a blue robe had been flung, picked up the garment and threw it towards the naked woman, who was now sitting up, knees drawn to her chin, trying to hide her large creamy breasts with her hands. 'Here, hide your nakedness,' he directed. 'Did they succeed?'

She shook her head. 'No, lord. You arrived in time.' She rose to her feet, draping the robe around her, eyes still on him. 'And I bless you.'

Only when the aides had hustled the rapist outside and dragged the corpses away did King Kumara look at the woman. He was stunned by what he saw. Not much more than twenty years old, she was the living image of his dead mistress, Manel. She had the same fair skin, now shiny with sweat, large, dark almond-shaped eyes, high cheek-bones and a classic mouth. His eyes travelled down, noting the same terrific breasts, slim waist and plump thighs.

'What's your name?' he demanded.

'Sita,' she replied. Fear and horror were slowly leaving her eyes. 'May I inquire who my rescuer is, lord?'

'We are King Kumara of the *uda rata*.'

Her eyes widened. She sank to her knees in obeisance, remained there, forehead to the ground.

'Stand up and tell us why you were here alone,' he directed.

She rose gracefully to her feet. 'This is home, lord,' she stated. 'I am from Ruhuna but my husband, Ravi, was a captain in King Maya Dunne's army.'

'Was?'

'Yes, lord.' The words came out in a hoarse whisper. A sob escaped her and tears filled her eyes. 'I was told this morning that he died in yesterday's battle, killed by the soldiers of the Great King.'

'We are sorry.' Somehow, he really felt for her.

In that instant, he recognized that the feeling came from his own pain and disappointment, which had linked with hers. He remembered Anula's words, 'There is no room for weakness in our love.' Somehow that was not right. This woman, Sita, was weeping because she was weak before her love and the need for her husband.

Some part of his feelings must have reached her, for she stared at him in a strange, bewildered manner.

'You and I are both in need of comfort tonight,' he declared, deliberately dropping the royal plural. 'Would you like someone who needs you to comfort you?'

She pulled back afraid, searching his face. He smiled wistfully at her. 'If you would rather not, I shall understand and let you be, leaving some of my men behind to protect you while you sleep tonight. Give me your decision when I return. This has been a dreadful experience for you.' He wiped his bloody sword on his large linen square, sheathed the weapon and strode outside. He rode on to his headquarters, where he gave his army commander, General

214

Dunu, orders to organize the move of the entire Kandyan army back home the following morning.

When he returned to Sita's house, accompanied by two of his most trusted aides, she opened the door at his knock. He paused at the entrance, gazing at her with gentle inquiry.

She stared at him a long time, shook her head quickly several times, as if to clear it and erase temptation. Finally, she looked down at her bare feet, then lifted her eyes to his again. A curious vulnerability crossed her beautiful face, giving it a haunted look. She sighed and nodded slowly. 'I see you are as lonely tonight as I am, lord,' she said softly. 'Life seems so long when one is bereft. I did not love my late husband. Our marriage was an arranged one, but he was kind to me for a whole year. I suppose he is already a memory, so what have I to be true to, except myself?' She smiled sadly. 'A brief time of forgetting . . . a brief time . . .'

He moved forward slowly into the room, kicking the door shut with his foot. He took her in his arms, felt her trembling. Tired as he was, his penis hardened and he knew that it literally pointed the way towards his finding release from his frustration and stress. He had never had to seek release in sex before. It had always been there, especially after his marriage to Anula.

Anula will kill me if she ever knows, he thought, as he began to caress Sita's cool, soft body.

As they made love on the floor, he discovered that Sita was not a woman of any experience. Yet she was compliant, eager to please and be pleased, so she too could forget. Her body smelled clean, of sandalwood, not of some exotic perfume. He exulted in the pure scent of new sweat beneath her armpits and the youth fragrance of her skin. He had entered a strange new world, a world free of the artifice of the courtesan and the woman of experience. It made him forget his own cool, though passionate, expertise.

215

They clung to each other, in body, mind and spirit, reaching desperately for comfort. He did not try to make her come and come and come. Strangely, with Sita, he did not have to prove anything. So when they were both ready from the exchange of tenderness and comforting, he entered her, moving gently, gazing into her eyes, loving her. He came with her. When it was over, he felt cleansed. He lay upon her yielding body, drowsing, as if she and he were two normal, young lovers. He felt he had discovered his youth and innocence at last.

CHAPTER FIFTEEN
Tuesday, 17 July 1526

Aisha was not surprised when the woman servant brought her the summons to attend her husband in her reception chamber that night. The news these past days had been disastrous and had made her glad that the contingency plan she had suggested was well in place. Abdul Raschid was excellent at getting things done quickly.

Yet as she hastily washed her face, rubbed on her exotic Arabian perfume, she fought down feelings of apprehension. For the first time in her life, her world was crumbling from events over which she had no control.

Ali was with her husband in the chamber. Their grave faces made the sweat break out beneath her dark robes and *chador*, but she was totally in command of herself before she rose from kneeling to her husband and kissing his hand. She acknowledged Ali's salutation, signalled him to resume his seat on the settee while she took her own on the sofa across the room.

'I have tragic news from Sita Waka, wife of mine,' Abdul Raschid informed her. He was sitting very erect, palms on thighs, making no move towards the sweetmeats on the side table. 'King Maya Dunne was severely defeated in a great battle last morning by the combined forces of the Portuguese and the Great King, assisted by an army under the Kandy king.'

King Kumara?' she inquired incredulously. 'What was he doing there?'

'Following through a move organized by Colonel de Albergaria that took King Maya Dunne completely by surprise and probably contributed more than anything else to his defeat.'

Abdul Raschid told her all he knew of the situation, including that King Vidiye had sailed to Batti, undoubtedly to advance overland across the mountains and take King Maya Dunne in the rear. When he had finished, his gaze drifted around the room as if taking in every piece of furniture, every ornament.

'What will happen to us?' she inquired, her voice totally calm and steady.

'My spies tell me that Colonel de Albergaria and the Great King discussed us on the eve before the battle. You were right. They have no evidence of our complicity with King Maya Dunne, but they suspect the truth. The colonel wanted us imprisoned for a time and some of our possessions confiscated, so he could continue to trade with us. He was willing to allow us to retain ownership of this house, as a concession to our past friendship. The Great King, however, insisted that we have been guilty of treason and should be hanged.'

Aisha drew her breath in sharply. A chill hand clutched at her heart. Reprisals, even punishment, she had expected, but this was shattering.

'Never!' The word shot vehemently out of her without any volition. Both men stared at her, Abdul Raschid with brows lifted, her son with a smile of recognition.

'At last we face what life and success are really about,' she declared solemnly. 'it is not all this,' she gestured around the room with her hand, 'but we who enjoy it. It is not riches or amassing more riches, but how we respond to disaster. The very fact that the three of us are here in this room together in a situation of crisis shows that we have what thousands lack, unity as a family.'

She noted a new hope on her husband's face and suddenly realized that what had really bothered him was his concern for her safety and well-being. It pleased her so much that she quickly decided it was important to give him the honour of the lead at this decisive time though she

218

knew they had to flee immediately. 'What do you intend us to do, husband of mine?'

'Go ahead with our escape plan. As you know, everything is ready for us to leave for the east coast. We should do so immediately.'

She hesitated, then decided the time had come to broach something she had been considering recently. 'May I suggest another alternative?'

'Certainly.'

'For years we have gone back and forth, playing with the winning side because we are traders, making winners of losers whenever possible, but never taking a stand in case our wealth and our lives were placed in jeopardy. I suggest that the time has come for us to stay loyal to the man we backed throughout the adversity our very support may have created for him. Should we not remain loyal and true to someone when he is down?'

Abdul Raschid's small mouth fell agape, his eyes so startled that he looked like a fish. He started breathing heavily, the flabby chest rising and falling. Then his mouth started to close, the lower lip out-thrust with determination as her words went beyond the thought process to reach some long-submerged instincts. His fists clenched, the small eyes crinkled. He nodded slowly. 'How do you propose we do this?' he demanded quietly.

'Of all the kings and sub-kings in the country, King Maya Dunne is the only man of principle. Wherever he may be, he will fight back and win. The Portuguese have thousands of miles of ocean routes to protect. They cannot retain their present strength in Lanka for long. The Great King is not a fighter. He will return to Jaya as soon as possible to let others fight his battles. King Kumara has a long way to go before he can obtain support in the low-country. King Vidiye must consolidate his kingdoms in the south and gather enough strength to wield power as prince regent once the Great King dies and his son, Prince

Dharma Pala Dom Juan, succeeds to the throne. I propose that we should join King Maya Dunne wherever he may be.'

'You speak true words, wife of mine.' A note of admiration had entered Abdul Raschid's voice. 'I also commend your idealism.' Tears filled his eyes, the double chin jutted out. 'Let us indeed for once be counted as the true friend of a friend in common disaster.'

She smiled. 'We shall leave tonight then, in disguise. No one will know where we have gone. We shall tell the servants we are fleeing to Calicut. They can remain here, looking after the house under our manager until we return. It will probably be confiscated and occupied by the infidel, but by the grace of Allah we will surely have it back some day. We shall seek out King Maya Dunne wherever he may be and offer him our organization in Ruhuna and on the east coast for his cause.' She noted her husband's shining eyes with a surge of love for him and rose to her feet, smiling. 'Well, what are we wasting time for? Let us hurry.'

Ali had respectfully stood up when she did. Very slim and erect in his close-fitting white pantaloons and dark waistcoat, he looked almost beautiful in that light. 'I shall not be accompanying you, revered parents,' he stated calmly.

'What?' The question shot out of her.

'You heard me.' His voice was deep and firm. 'It is time I became independent. Besides, I have my mission to carry out here.'

Her belly clenched with fear, but she knew she had to let her son go his way.

Tuesday, 17 July 1526

My father paused beside Lord Wickrama Sinha and me, signalling us to remain on our mounts. For once, his sweat-beaded face seemed haggard and drawn. 'We had intended a different welcome for you,' he said. 'But the drummers and dancers, the whip-crackers and *sesath* bearers got lost along the way!'

We listened in silence as he gave us details of the great battle. He had decided to engage the enemy on the plain unaware that King Kumara would attack on his right flank. Almost encircled, his men were simply mown down by cannon fire and muskets frontally and repeated attacks on both flanks. By evening, he had decided to avoid total disaster and ordered the trumpets to sound the retreat. A sword cut on the head and a spear wound on his shoulder, though not serious, explained the bandage and the sling. Fortunately, the enemy had not pressed home their victory, so he had had time to evacuate the capitol, remove much of his treasury and the firearms and withdraw to the eastern mountains. He left the palace draped with the traditional white cloth to signal his desire for a truce, which he had thought to negotiate from strength rather than total weakness because he still had a considerable force of men, cannon and muskets intact.

I was appalled at his request for a truce. Our home, our castle, our palace, left to the mercy of the enemy? I looked down again at the blazing capitol and could not hold back the words. 'Should we not have stayed and fought to the death for hearth and home, Sire?' Even as I uttered the words, I regretted their cruelty in his present plight.

He did not lose his calm. 'If it had been us alone, you would not have had to ask that question, prince. But there is more to ruling a kingdom than dying in the passionate defence of one's home. That home is one of hundreds of thousands throughout the country which we must live to protect.'

A polite cough interrupted him. 'Pardon me, Sire, but may I retire to carry word to our men, who will be anxious for news?' It was Lord Wickrama Sinha, discreet as always, intervening to save us embarrassment.

'Certainly.'

With one last lingering look at the flames in the centre of the valley-bowl below, Lord Wickrama Sinha wheeled his mount around and clip-clopped away.

'I never dreamed that our sacred *charlithraya* would be trampled on and the capitol set on fire.' My father's voice seemed as deep as the night. He had dropped the royal plural to give his words effect. 'I can only conjecture that it is the work of the accursed *parangi*, for my brother would never have committed such an outrage. But even if I had known what was to happen, I doubt that I had any other choice.' He paused, staring into the darkness, haunted by his ghosts. I had no words to offer him.

'Unlike you, I was born in that mansion and spent most of my days there,' he finally resumed. I comprehended what the mansion meant to him. It had originally been built by our great ancestor King Parakrama Bahu VI. My father had converted it into a palace, built the capital around it, created a city out of the township. 'What you see there is more than the end of my hopes, it is the destruction of a lifetime of endeavour.'

His voice rose passionately. 'Yet I know that a house, a home, a palace, a city, are only symbols. You do not die for a symbol, but hold your life sacred for all that it symbolizes. That is the real war, *putha*, my son. We must fight for the cause that will give us the right to life, the pursuit of happiness, the freedom to follow our cherished principles, the establishment of one nation under our revered Doctrine. The cause must always be our first principle.'

'I am sorry I cannot agree with you, *tha*, father and Sire,' I replied, disillusioned, for the first time, by his talk of principles. 'Every man who fights and dies for the principle of hearth and home fights for the cause, which is useless unless it emerges from high principles. Please give me leave to lead my men down to the city and attack it

222

tonight, so we may recapture our sacred places or die in the attempt.'

'We shall neither command nor condone such a fool-hardy, irresponsible move,' he declared harshly. 'You have no right to play with human lives in the pursuit of some noble ideal. You are a prince, a king to be, not a Christian pursuing the Holy Grail.'

They were the first harsh words he had spoken to me and they caused the tears to sting my eyes. 'Very well, Sire,' I retorted bitterly. 'I shall then follow you to whatever death you may lead me, because I also cherish the principle of absolute loyalty and obedience to my leader, my father and my king.'

He was moved but not satisfied. 'We hope you will also be ready to make any sacrifice for our cause.' He paused. 'Our present plan is to wait and see what the enemy will do. We have spies and scouts out and our men are placed in good dispositions, which is how we had word of your arrival and came back here to meet you. You shall have your troops encamp in their present positions and await orders.'

By common consent, we took one last look at the burning capitol. The flames had begun to subside. I was suddenly penitent, emotional. 'How often I have looked up at these mountains from our lawn down there, Sire,' I said softly. 'Looking down from up here, everything seems so different. You should know, at this tragic moment, how much I cherished our conversations every evening.'

'Your words, your loyalty and yes, your love, mean more to me than the loss of any possessions,' he responded gruffly. 'Therein lies the undefeated heart of our nation, so we shall rise from those ashes like that legendary creature of Cathay, the phoenix.'

His face became contorted with pain. My father, openly fighting back tears for the first time in his life? I looked away so he could control his grief with dignity. Within me, rage finally began to boil. I needed desperately to avenge our defeat, our despoliation, to hurl the barbaric invader back to the ocean whence he came. But what was this black, hollow part of me, deep, deep, deep inside my spirit? I sensed it for the first time without feeling it. What can a black hollow hold?

Suddenly, I had the answer. Futility.

At that moment, man seemed to me no more than a worm struggling beneath a pin. My father had been so right when he told me, centuries ago, as we sat on that green lawn down there, now charred ashes, that there was no such thing as success, that when the battles had been won and the cause had seemingly been established, the principle vindicated, a new struggle began for permanency that no one could guarantee. I recognized that least of all would there be such permanence for people like me, who would never even have progeny to leave an inheritance to and who would ensure the continuity of our life form. I thought despondently of Juli and her child by another man. I loved Juli, but did I want to struggle all my life to leave her children and their children an inheritance? I laughed in bitter silence.

The thoughts of Juli faded into the flames below, a reminder that my father and I, who had stood on the threshold of a united Lanka such a short time before, were gazing tonight at the gateway to despair.

I heard the clip-clop of hooves before I saw the ghostly figures of the riders coming up the pass. They soon resolved themselves into three mounted men, carrying white flags and escorted by a group of my father's cavalry which had been guarding our side of the mountains.

The leader of the escort, a young, clean-shaven captain, saluted. 'These three men are emissaries of the Great King, Sire,' he reported. 'They claim to bear an important and urgent message for you.'

'Speak!' my father briefly commanded the white-haired noble, who was obviously the leader of the truce group.

'The Great King desires a meeting with you, this very night, Sire,' the man responded. 'It is of vital importance and urgency that you proceed with us immediately and alone.'

'Alone? What guarantee of safety does the Great King extend to us?'

'His word, Sire.'

'His word?' My father's scornful laugh ripped out to echo along the mountaintop. He pointed down at the capitol. The flames had died down, leaving a smouldering ruin. 'That was once a living, breathing, beautiful capitol. Is that the evidence of the sanctity of your Great King's word?'

'That was the work of the *parangi* barbarians, lord.' The speaker was Lord Siri, a lean-faced young nobleman whom I recognized. 'It is a deed we all abhor.'

My father reflected, scratching his chin. 'Tell the Great King that we shall meet him halfway down this mountain within the hour. Halfway up for him! He is to ride slowly towards us, alone, while we ride slowly down, alone. We shall temporarily withdraw all our outposts on this side of the mountain for two hours and expect that he will similarly pull back all his patrols. There will be no meeting if we discover the slightest signs of treachery, in the event of which our men are well enough in position to retaliate effectively.'

Tuesday, 17 July 1526

Unable to sleep, Julietta rose from her bed, donned a pink silken robe and walked to the window. She sat on her favourite seat looking down at the few remaining lights of the city in the distance and the harbour dotted with the lanterns of the great *nao* and caravels that now crowded it.

She had in her hand a brief letter from Fernao which he had despatched by fast messenger from the battlefield. It told of the great victory over King Maya Dunne's army.

Instead of unalloyed gladness, she was chilled with apprehension. Was Tiki-tiki alive? Surely he had to be, for if he were dead the bleakness of her heart would have been his messenger. She knew that Fernao was not wounded because she had questioned the messenger closely.

All this bloodshed, this killing, was so inhuman, certainly it was unchristian. When would it all end? She stared in the direction of the grove in which Tiki-tiki had made love with her. Would she ever see him again? Would he ever know that Catherina was his baby? If he did, what would his reaction be?

What did the future hold for Fernao's baby, the life stirring in her womb? What did the future hold for little Catherina?

As if to confirm her uncertainty, Catherina whimpered from her cradle beside the bed, then made sucking noises and relapsed into silence. She was teething in earnest.

Fernao stood on the threshold of a great career. The latest word was that the Viceroy would shortly appoint him governor of the Portuguese possessions in Lanka with the rank of general, in recognition of his singular achievements. She owed it to Fernao to extend to him the total love and loyalty due a husband and the father of her unborn child. She knelt by the window and prayed.

'O God, O Blessed Virgin Mary, the forces of death and destruction are all round us. Some men say that it is as much to establish Holy Church as for trade. Others claim they are fighting for their own race and religion. No one knows who is right or what is right any longer. I am as confused as everyone around me in this country seems to be. Forgive us all our sins and cause all men to lay down their arms and their ambitions. Cleanse our hearts. Make us all good, especially me. Lead me not into temptation, but deliver me from evil. Amen.'

Tuesday, 17 July 1526

It had not been a good day for Queen Anula. Indeed the past days since she gagged over her husband's penis had been troubled ones. With her unfailing instinct, she knew that the incident had affected King Kumara more than he had admitted before he departed for the attack on Sita Waka.

Now sitting before her looking-glass in her bedroom at the Kandy palace, watching her attendant brush her long black hair for the night with a gold brush, a gift from King Kumara, she felt glad in a way that her husband was gone. She would get over her sickness by the time he returned, then everything would be beautiful between them once more. Suddenly she felt the craving. 'Olives, Nona,' she told the elderly silver-haired attendant, catching the reflection of the woman's wrinkled eyes in the looking-glass. 'We simply must have some *veralu achcharu*, pickled olives, tonight.'

'That's a far change from your normal delights of the night, my lady,' the woman giggled. 'Unfortunately, olives are as out of season as your royal husband!' She went on brushing the long, curly black locks. 'How about some raw pineapple, though it's a little belated for that!' She giggled again at the belief that raw pineapple can cause abortions.

'Very funny. I should slap your face for giving me your wit instead of my olives.' Queen Anula paused, fell silent as a sudden chill ran through her, causing her to shiver involuntarily.

'What is it, my lady?' Nona inquired anxiously, the brush poised in mid-air. 'Are you feeling sick?'

'No! No! It is nothing.' The queen stared blankly at the

227

mirror. A bleak feeling had taken over her entire being. Oh dear *devas*. I suddenly feel alone, completely alone. Can my beloved be dead? Something told her he was not dead and that he at least was probably not alone. He is being unfaithful to me, she suddenly told herself. And immediately became convinced of the truth of her suspicion. She remembered the lover who had beeen unfaithful to her several years earlier.

Tuesday, 17 July 1526

I watched my father, sitting erect on his horse, disappear downhill into the darkness. With a sigh I turned Rama around and urged him downhill in the opposite direction. Was this somehow symbolic, I wondered dismally. Father and son going downhill in opposite directions.

I handed Rama to a groom to be unsaddled and rubbed down, after which it took about two hours for Lord Wickrama Sinha and I to ensure that our men had eaten their field ration and were settled, however uncomfortably, for the night. I myself was saddlesore and very tired. I wondered what my father must feel like.

Leaving Lord Wickrama Sinha in charge of our sprawling bivouacs, I walked back to the pass on the top of the mountain. The sky was still obscured by smoke from the smouldering capitol, the smell of burning still fractured the night air, but since the fires had died down I could see that the earthworks surrounding the buildings had prevented the fire from spreading into the city. The barking of a dog in the distance was a desolate sound. It was echoed by a monkey's growl from the jungle.

My brain was bright as the absent sun. I knew I would not be able to sleep until my father returned. So many thoughts of the past, so many concerns as to the future.

The sky to the east behind me was beginning to pale when I heard the sentry's challenge below. I rose to my feet, adjusted my sword, stretched cramped limbs, my arms reaching for the skies until I could feel my spine creak.

Before long, I heard the clip-clop of hooves. A dark figure on horseback loomed up alone from the fringe of jungle. My father reined in his horse in front of me and I made obeisance to him. He dismounted stiffly, flung the reins over his mount's neck. The animal was well trained, merely lowered its head and snuffled around for grass, while my father and I stood side by side looking down silently at the city. I wondered gloomily whether we would ever see it again.

'It's all been settled,' King Maya Dunne finally stated. 'To cut a long story short, my brother, the Great King, has agreed to withdraw all his forces commencing at noon tomorrow, so we can return to the city without further hinderance and start to rebuild the capitol. Apparently the *parangi* do not want to remain here much longer, and King Kumara has made a vain bid to take over Sita Waka, which my brother would not permit.'

'Wonderful!' I exclaimed. 'You have scored a victory without firing a single shot, Sire. When will the *parangi* and King Kumara's forces leave?'

'At dawn tomorrow.'

'And they will return whence they came . . . all the way back?' I inquired suspiciously.

'All the way, Prince. Under the Great King's orders. He will follow with his own army once he is sure the others have really gone. So we can return home by tomorrow afternoon and commence the work of reconstruction.' He looked at the sky. 'Or today, I should say.'

'But the conditions, Sire? There must be conditions.'

'Oh yes, the mercenaries must be disbanded and transported back to India without delay. The Great King will arrange for safe passage for the Mouro ships that will take them.'

Something about my father, a stiffness, a tension, a

holding back, suddenly filled me with unease. 'What are the other conditions, Sire?' I demanded.

He looked away into the distance, unable to meet my eyes for the first time in his life. 'The Great King demanded a hostage to ensure that we keep to our borders in future.'

'Whom does he want, Sire?'

'The person we love most in the world.' He looked up at the sky. 'You.'

I stepped back as if he had struck me. The earth seemed to rock beneath my feet. 'Of course you did not agree?' Why then was my heart thudding against my ribs?

'No, we did not.'

I heaved a sigh of relief. The earth became firm again. 'How did you finally settle it?'

'We agreed, on our sacred honour, that you will . . . ah . . . stay with your Aunt Kamini in the town of the five villages, Gam Paha, which is neutral territory twenty miles from Colombo, for five years or until the Great King dies.' He still could not bring himself to look at me. 'You will . . . ah . . . remain in her premises all the time, but you may visit your uncle, Prince Maitri, the governor of the port, in his mansion on the Mutu Vella hill, for one weekend each month. We have committed your own honour to this agreement.'

'How could you do that without my consent, *tha*?' I was trying desperately to find an avenue of escape from this awful fate of virtual exile.

'You promised us unquestioning obedience this very night.'

I heard the sound of a punctured drum. It was the breath leaving my body. Trapped by my own promise! Bartered like some marketable commodity! At first I was stunned, then totally crushed.

'You see, Prince, the cause must come above all else, including individuals,' my father explained. He was still speaking to the dark fringe of trees pressing against the side of the track. His voice was hoarse, I noticed with a strange detachment.

I thought of the promises of the past. My sixteenth birthday when my father assured me that I would ride into battle with him that year, of his dedication to my career and my destiny. I remembered the backbreaking work of training my regiments, day and night, day after day. I recalled the battles I had won, for which I received the rank of general and the title Raja Sinha. The royal lion indeed! Trapped and caged by a promise.

Somewhere out of the depths of me, anguish and despair began to mushroom but a voice whispered insistently, remember your destiny, remember your destiny. I clung to the words. They were my only refuge.

'You will honour this pact, Prince, will you not?' I heard my father speak as if from afar.

'Yes, Sire,' I replied mechanically, then paused, looking blankly down at the earth. 'Please give me leave to withdraw now.'

'You may indeed, Prince, but do not take it hard. We shall prevail if we hold together.'

I made obeisance to him and stumbled back downhill.

I am violated, betrayed, a human sacrifice.

Wednesday, 18 July 1526

I lay alone on my blanket, not to sleep, but to bleed.

I wanted to die rather than face the end of my dreams, the dishonour and shame ahead. What would my men, all my fellow Sinhala, think of me? A national hero one day, an exile the next.

A reverse process of reasoning commenced, simply so that I could save myself from the rawness in my brain, the pressure, the near madness swirling within me.

There would be no shame if I could preserve my pride, hold my head high whatever my plight. Surely there was no dishonour in circumstances only in conduct? Surely most shameful of all would be if I accepted shame or dishonour from the actions of others or from circumstances not of my own creation.

My father was my king. He had a million responsibilities, as I would have some day. He could not avoid placing these responsibilities ahead of individuals, including me. But a king also had a responsibility towards himself, wherein lay his own shame or dishonour.

At least I would be nearer Julietta once a month, if I visited the governor's residence on the Muta Vella hill.

My life had been lonely except for the knowledge of Julietta. She had given me all of herself, even if it had been just for one night. She had the act of love to cherish and perhaps the burden of its guilt to live with for the rest of her life.

I could never give less to the two people I loved most in the world, Julietta and my father, than Julietta had given me that magical night.

Oh, how I loved Julietta. Suddenly that love seemed to be the only certainty in my life. I began to understand what Julietta must have felt during all those years of uncertainty when I abandoned her to follow my destiny.

What was destiny?

King Maya Dunne, the near victor one day, standing outside the walls of the national capital, ready to take it by storm, was tonight a king without a capital or a home. General Prince Tikiri Bandara Raja Sinha, commander of an army and seemingly on his way to becoming a national saviour only two days ago, was but a miserable exile on this grey dawning.

I wanted to bellow and scream with fury and bitterness, to tear my hair, to pound the earth. But the training of a prince denied me the right to such luxuries. Though I was but a nothing prince at this moment, I could never be a non-prince.

What was the meaning of life? I realized with stark clarity that meaning was but a human notion that did not exist in the realm of the eternal and the infinite.

Suddenly, in the light of that knowledge, I again saw that black hole with nothing in it. How could one see nothing? Only by being touched with the utter futility of life. There must be more to my life than a destiny which when fulfilled would prove to be a non-destiny in the light of what would follow. What more could there be?

Tuesday, 24 July 1526

King Kumara had led his troops back to Kandy with rage in his mind. Though he also had gentle thoughts of Sita in his heart, he had resolutely set his mind against any further contact with her. He was committed to Queen Anula, he loved her and would overcome his reaction to her sickness. At a more practical level, he now needed the queen and her Kiri Vella clan's support for the furtherance of his ambitions.

He reached Kandy with his advance guard late in the evening and went straight to the palace, where he immediately sent word to the queen informing her of his return and expressing the hope thay they would be dining together in her quarters.

Since he had returned far sooner than he had expected, there were no urgent matters requiring his attention. He talked to his lord chamberlain and chief minister while he bathed and changed. They were full of praise at the victory over King Maya Dunne, but obviously disappointed that he himself had not remained as the new king of Sita Waka, for it would have extended their own power.

By the time he entered Queen Anula's reception chamber, he was refreshed, in a better mood and eager for her companionship, which he had missed.

Dressed in her favorite colour, blue, her necklace, bracelet, earrings and hair ornaments of aquamarine, she glowed in beauty beneath the golden light of the tapers lining the walls. His absence of a few days made him notice that her cheeks were a little more gaunt than usual, but her figure was fuller, softer. The tall brass lamps had not been lit, so the room had a cool feel to it. They greeted each other formally, as always, and seated themselves opposite each other. King Kumara immediately sensed a difference in her. It was not visible, but there was something around the sides of her eyes.

'We have missed you, beauteous queen,' he said, turning on an intense gaze to test her reaction.

'Oh, have you, Sire?' She seemed cool; the question bore just a hint of a challenge.

This was not what he had expected, but he would not show it. 'Of course. We thought about you night and day.'

'Night, too?'

What could be wrong? For a wild moment he thought that she must somehow know of his infidelity. 'We said night and day.' He curbed his rising impatience, went on to give her details of the campaign and his disappointment that he had not been made King of Sita Waka. It was at this stage that he realized that she had not even expressed surprise at his early return. 'Would you mind telling us why you seem upset?' he inquired gently.

'What makes you think we are upset, Sire?'

He sensed her inner watchfulness. It was like a cat stalking its prey. Cold anger seized him, but he set it aside. 'Nothing, just the feel of you.'

'Why would you think to feel that we are upset?' she pressed.

This was absurd, but he answered her in a similar vein. 'Because you make us feel that we think you are upset.' He grinned. 'We know you, Anula. Is it part of your condition?'

'Does our condition bother you that much, Sire?'

'Only to the extent that it bothers you.' He was being deliberately gentle. Something was indeed wrong, for this was a scene they had never played before, but he wanted to be understanding.

Suddenly she smiled. It was more with her teeth than her eyes. Something about it, some barely perceptible trace of artificiality, bothered him. A lizard went 'thuk . . . thuk . . . thuk . . .' A rustling breeze from the High Forest mountain sighed in through the yellow and red laquer grilles of the window, wafted the scent of sandalwood incense to his nostrils.

'We are happy to have you back, Sire,' she said in her sexiest voice. She rose to her feet. 'Perhaps we should give you a royal greeting to whet your appetite for dinner and of course dessert.' She swayed gracefully towards him, knelt and started on the buttons of his pantaloons. As her cool fingers touched him, his penis started to rise, yet he could not escape the feeling that he was somehow being tested. She fondled him, drew his fully erect penis out and blew on it. 'Have you been in any other mouth?' she inquired of it, her voice soft as if she were talking to a mischievous child.

The truth hit him. She was somehow suspicious of him. The certainty that she was testing him combined with her breath brought back the smell of her vomit from days ago. His penis started to sag.

To his utter amazement, she leapt to her feet. 'You see!' she shouted. 'Do you see that? You are so over-satiated that you cannot even keep it up. You sonofabitch, you have been fornicating with other women.' She was getting hysterical. 'You bastard . . . you bastard . . . I'll kill you . . .'

If he had loved her less, he would have slapped her back to sanity. He had ridden for two days, fought a major battle, endured one of the greatest disappointments in his life then ridden again for another two days. He had been physically and mentally tired. Now his spirit was weary. Something snapped inside him. He knew with a sick horror that this scene was only a beginning. His queen would pursue her suspicions with the same intensity that she brought to bear on the fulfilment of her ambitions. He looked up at her, barely hearing her foul words, only seeing the beautiful features now contorted and ugly, the luminous eyes spitting hatred.

Nothing would be the same again. He thought of the gentle innocent Sita and realized that she had instinctively given him what he needed most in the world, respect, the kind of respect that could only come from innocence.

He buttoned his pantaloons, sighed and rose to his feet. He caused the queen to fall silent by the sheer force of his personality. 'We are leaving now,' he said. 'We shall return when you have composed yourself.' His voice became stern. 'Remember in future that when you address your king, it shall be with respect and that in his presence, you shall at all times conduct yourself with dignity.'

Saturday, 1 September 1526

Fernao had returned to Colombo three days after the firing of Sita Waka, feeling himself on the crest of a wave of success, for now he could consolidate his power in the country before the Portuguese regiments returned to Goa. Even his disappointment at the Great King's truce with King Maya Dunne, including the withdrawal of the Jaya army from Sita Waka, had been offset by Prince Raja Sinha's banishment to Gam Paha. Though he would have preferred his rival dead, the stripping of power and the humiliation of the prince gave Fernao savage satisfaction, though he would never display it to the world, least of all to Julietta.

When he returned home Julietta had been her old sweet self, wanting to know all about the campaign, curious as to his well-being. In the days that followed, he frequently thought of how it had felt in bed on the night of his return, when he held her in his arms, wanting to absorb all of her into all of him. 'Your gentleness is a healing balm after the brutality of battle, Julietta,' he remembered declaring softly. 'God, how I missed you. The thought of coming back to you, of the peace and quiet of our home, was a star above a bloody battlefield at night. I felt so sorry for the men who had only an empty barrack room awaiting them. Even your body feels softer.'

Now here was a despatch from the Viceroy. He had heard rumours of it, but could not believe it had happened. Five years ago, he had the small adjoining office in the tower. Then he took over Captain Oliveira's room. Now, this despatch, the writing beautifully etched on parchment, the red ribbons and seals on the top left-hand corner. Could this have happened to him, Fernao Soarez de Albergaria, aged only twenty-four?

By order of his Imperial Majesty, the King of Portugal, the Viceroy had appointed him governor of the Portuguese possessions in Lanka, with the rank of general.

PART TWO
Women Warriors

CHAPTER SIXTEEN

Extracts from the personal diary of General Fernao Soarez de Albergaria, governor of Portuguese Lanka.

Tuesday, 21 December 1529: . . . My son, named Lopo after his grandfather, turned three years old today. He is a source of immense pride to me. Lopo looks a real de Albergaria already, with the same striking features as my father, from whom I have had absolutely no communication for nearly six years now. He is missing so much by remaining aloof, yet I have begun to understand, through my son, some of what my father felt about me . . .

Thursday, 10 February 1530: The events of the past four years reveal how susceptible we and Lanka are to events in Europe. When Portugal was secure at home, we in the Indies have had all the naval and military support we needed to establish mastery over the various countries with which we trade. Whenever the European rivals went at each other's throats, our support forces were withdrawn, leaving us abandoned. Since it is essential to retain as strong a presence in Goa as possible at all times, Lanka is always first to become the poorer relation. We have therefore existed in a highly sensitive volatile situation. All we can do is our duty by our king and the country of which we are so proud.

I have been thinking of Europe today.

The arch rivals among the great powers of Europe have, for some years, been King Charles V of Spain and King Francis of France. King Henry VIII of England and the Pope keep shifting their support following now one, now the other, to balance power.

Five years ago the Emperor defeated and captured King Francis at the battle of Pavia. This led to the domination of Italy by the Emperor and was followed by the sack of Rome by his unpaid troops in 1527. By 1529, therefore, His Holiness the Pope had become a vassal of the Emperor.

Ships' captains and crews of vessels arriving out of Europe tell us that the Emperor has wielded his power over the Holy Father to prevent the dispensation of the marriage of King Henry VIII to the Emperor's aunt, Queen Catherine of Aragon, although King Henry was on the verge of obtaining it from the Holy See. King Henry has retaliated by summoning a Parliament, which he openly calls the Reformation Parliament, to legalize his independence from the Holy See, so he can obtain the dispensation of his marriage to Queen Catherine of Aragon to pave the way for him to wed the commoner, Anne Boleyn.

What the impact of these events will be on us, I can only conjecture. We are blood-brothers of the Spaniards, need fear no attack from them, but if the other European powers invade the Spanish homeland, we must be ready to defend our own, or to assist Spain. The consequence of the Emperor Charles V's actions has been a pulling back of our forces in the East Indies.

It was this vulnerability that made me take advantage of our strong military presence over the years, which incidentally has contributed in large measure to the years of peace in Lanka, to build a new fort encompassing the entire city of Colombo. Earthworks and battlements now form a great semi-circle along the eastern boundary of the city, from the swamps in the south, which I caused to be converted into a lake, to the Kalyani river in the north. Since the ocean extends along the west, the entire city is now impregnable.

We had built the original fort as a strongpoint to protect our trade in the port of Colombo and to withstand siege, if necessary, until reinforcements arrived from Goa. With the entire city now fortified, I conceive the inner fort to be a last line of defence. If such a desperate situation ever arises, even a single *nao* could dominate the harbour and use its cannon to complement those of the inner fort to keep the besiegers a safe distance away. I then considered that there had to be some way in which to keep the fort directly supplied from the harbour under such dire circumstances. The level of the lake being higher at this point than that of the ocean, which was held back only by a narrow spit of land, I had a canal dug to the south of the inner fort so that ships could sail through a break in the reef along the canal into the lake near the fort's entry bridge. In this way, while there is even one *nao* in the harbour, smaller vessels and boats can supply the inner fort from it, and even if there were no *nao*, such vessels could come through as long as they were not intercepted by an enemy naval force.

The Mutu Vella hill lies within the new fort, so our home is secure, and the original fort remains a citadel within the fortified city, without fear of being starved out as a last resort. Meanwhile, we completed the wooden fort of Galle and garrisoned it fully two years ago. We also established forts in other coastal cities which had good harbours. The ring of iron I had envisaged has been slowly materializing.

This has all been made possible by the years of peace I created by the defeat of King Maya Dunne.

During the past years, King Maya Dunne, with his son as the Great King's hostage, spent most of his time rebuilding his capitol on a more magnificent scale, ignoring King Vidiye's increasing power in the south. From Kandy, I had reports of a rift in the marital lute of King Kumara and Queen Anula, which the birth of their daughter has aggravated rather than healed. Apparently the queen suspected her husband of having taken another woman during the single night we all spent in Sita Waka and belaboured him with her suspicions to the point at which he was so unhappy at home that he sent for this woman and set her up as his mistress near Kandy. Such tales make me thank God for my trusting, gentle Julietta and for our daughter and three-year-old son, who continue to be the special joys of my life.

I had a missive today from Abdul Raschid. He and his wife, Aisha, have moved to the comfort of a small new mansion built especially for them by King Maya Dunne, as a gesture of thanks for their loyal support. I miss the fat Mouro rascal and his so-strong wife. Their son, Ali, reportedly remains in Calicut, following his flight to the home of his uncle, Paichi Marcar, nigh four years ago.

10 February 1530, midnight: I am writing this in my office in the fort almost with a trembling hand.

A most dreadful event occurred this evening. The Great King Bhuvaneka Bahu and his entourage were spending the weekend at the Sinhala border fort in Kalyani, which includes a contingent of Portuguese soldiers. While he watched our men having dinner tonight, a shot rang out from the barracks and the Great King fell dead. We have been unable to trace the identity of the assassin, but the musket-shot would point to one of our own men. Since none of them could have had a grudge against the Great King, the soldier who perpetrated this foul deed must have been hired to do it. But by whom?

God save us all from the possible consequences, especially since we do not have the military strength we had a year ago . . .

CHAPTER SEVENTEEN
Friday, 11 February 1530

Fernao's post in the crisis that had brewed was at his office in the tower of the inner fort, but he had taken time off to go home quickly and endure the security of his family. There was no saying what the Sinhala might do when they heard that the Great King had been assassinated, most likely by a Portuguese musketeer.

The entire household was asleep when he arrived. He woke Julietta and gave her the news. She stood before him listening in shocked silence. 'The Great King was a weak man, but he did not harm anyone personally. I worked well with him.' Fernao cast aside the thought that this was because the Great King had been compliant. 'I'm really sad at the shocking way he died. I mean . . .' He turned away, then strode to the window and stared through the gloom towards the harbour.

'The assassin must have a spare musket which he threw over the fortress walls into the river,' he stated over his shoulder. 'It had to be one of our people. The guard commander ordered a muster of the men and their weapons immediately, but they were all present and correct.'

'The murder was well planned then,' Julietta observed. 'Won't it rouse the entire country against us?'

'Yes, unless we can establish that this was the work of the Sinhala, King Maya Dunne perhaps, or even King Vidiye. They have their motives. Who else could have had it done?' He paused. 'Well, that's the story I shall cause to be spread in any case. We can't afford reprisals against us at a time when our strength in the country has been depleted. It is my duty to protect our own at any cost.'

He sensed her stiffening.

'But that would not be right, Fernao!' she exclaimed.

Her reaction irked him. Did she still retain her loyalty to the Sinhala? 'Certainly, but it is nonetheless desirable,' he replied.

She sighed, shivered once. 'What will happen now? Who will become the Great King?'

'Why, our little Prince Dom Juan,' he stated flatly. 'The boy is under the protection of our own King, Dom João III, and we shall enforce his right to the succession. His father, King Vidiye, will be Regent, and the appointment will place him in a position of great power. I'm afraid our period of peace and calm has ended. This is a situation of crisis, so I intend calling immediately for reinforcements from Goa.'

'You too will be in a position of great power in the country, won't you?'

Fernao could not keep the excitement he felt from his voice. 'Yes, I shall follow the new doctrine evolved by Cardinal Wolsey of England for his sovereign, King Henry VIII. It's called the balance of power. I intend holding it between the various rulers of Lanka, King Vidiye of Jaya and Raigam, King Maya Dunne of Sita Waka and King Kumara of the *uda rata*.' He paused, wondering whether to speak of what was foremost in his mind, then could not resist the urge. 'This means Prince Tikiri Bandara Raja Sinha will now be freed from exile.'

She looked up sharply. The relief on her face somehow angered him. All these years and the thought of his arch rival could still harrow him, but he had learned not to betray any sign of such feelings. 'The prince happens to be at his uncle's residence tonight. I think it in our best interests to capture him secretly before tomorrow, when he will learn of the Great King's death.'

He carefully watched for her reaction. He received none, except for a slight widening of the eyes.

Friday, 11 February 1530

The modest house King Kumara had selected for his new mistress, Sita, in Hangura, about thirty miles south-east of Kandy, had been built close to the palace for a young married nephew of the former sub-king. The town itself consisted of a single street lined by shops and the homes of traders, but was encased in idyllic surroundings, in a grove of mountain apple, jak and breadfruit trees, beside a broad stream rippling over brown sand and black rocks. Located in a long valley in the upper hill country, Hangura was cool throughout the year. Its green paddy, vegetable gardens and fruit orchards spread along the flatlands adjacent to the stream; its cattle grazed on lush mountain pastures.

It had taken King Kumara a whole year of accusations, probing and attempts to be bluffed into a confession before he finally decided that a marriage which did not have consistent peace and oneness must have entered perpetual drought. He knew Queen Anula well enough to believe that she would never give up and that if he did confess to infidelity she could never sustain the truth. So, on the anniversary of his one and only meeting with Sita, he sent a messenger to her asking whether she would like to be his mistress, if she were still free. She was indeed free, so he established her in the house in Hangura, which was far enough from Kandy for gossip not to reach the palace. Here, he spent two days with her on his monthly official visit to Hangura. These latter were important since he had decided after his reversal at Sita Waka to spend three to five years consolidating his kingdom and building up sufficient military, political and economic strength to be independent of anyone else's support. He was young and could afford to wait.

Being furtive was foreign to his sense of dignity and style, so while he was discreet about his relationship with Sita, he was certainly not secretive.

As he sat with Sita this Saturday, it was almost midnight. Strangely, he could spend hours just talking to her because he could be completely natural with her. She was real family to him. He did not have to prove himself to her constantly, as he did with his wife. There was no strain whatever. The past three years had made his visits to Sita the one certain thing in his life. Sita respected him, loved him, desired no further gain from him than to be a part of his life. He had come to love her in a quiet, deep way. Tonight, he reflected with special sadness that even the arrival of the baby girl three years ago had only aggravated his situation with Queen Anula. He had thought that he would be the jealous one, but it turned out that it was his wife who did not want to share him, even with the baby. The result was that Dona Margaridha, dutifully so named at the time as a concession to the Catholic Church and the hope of *parangi* support, had turned out a petulant child, selfish and demanding.

Sita looked stunning tonight. Her bodice and jacket of dark blue showed off her fair skin and classic features to perfection. She never failed to touch him by the way her eyes lit up whenever she saw him and the glad note in her voice when she greeted him, always so grateful to have him.

He had just arrived. Here they were, seated sedately side by side on the settee in the living room, and she had not even pouted at his being so late.

'You must be very tired, Sire,' she said. 'Did you have a hard day?'

'We had dinner with two local noblemen,' he replied. 'We were bored, but as you know, we are never tired. We have been blessed with a quality called stamina. It must have been bestowed on us by the Christian God in anticipation of our conversation.'

'Hush, lord. You should not blaspheme.'

Her large, dark eyes were round and serious. He loved

it when she reproved him for such things. It made him feel like a mischevious child, impelled to shock her more. 'Do you consider such blasphemy, *akusala*, a sin then, my *sundari*, golden one? Being a true Buddhist you do not believe in gods, so where can you find the blasphemy in our words?'

'It is the intention that counts. Even if one does not believe in gods, Lord Buddha said that one should not mock at anything.'

'Now you know you are making that up.'

'Certainly not.'

'All right then, tell us where Lord Buddha said that in his scriptures.'

'The *bhikkus* told me.'

'You are adorable.'

'And you are not very nice, Sire, to laugh at me.' She trust out her lower lip in mock petulance.

'Of course we laugh at you becuase we absolutely adore you.'

A bullfrog croaked from the nearby stream. 'See, the frog contradicts you though I as your loyal subject dare not,' she countered, laughing.

'We shall have that frog executed at dawn tomorrow.'

'But what about his poor mistress then?'

They laughed aloud for the sheer joy of their silly conversation and at being in love. 'Our own belief in religions is confined to one tenet and one alone, which the Christians have discovered,' he stated.

'And what is that, lord?'

'The original sin! It's the only belief that has stood the test of time.' He had taught her the Catholic religion.

She took him seriously and considered that, her eyes round again, head gracefully tilted to one side. 'I don't know enough about religions to test that,' she finally declared. 'But it seems to me that you are being clever with words again and not with the truth.'

He stifled a laugh. 'Tell me, what else is there?'

'*Kharma/vipaka*, cause and effect, which Lord Buddha taught us. Not *kharma* as some sort of fate, destiny or punishment for our sins, but volitional activities that have their effects.' Her eyes misted. 'For instance, I am obviously barren so I can never bear your child, which I would love to have. But I'm also glad I cannot have a child, because I can give all of myself to you and have all of you.'

Her words stirred King Kumara strangely. It brought to mind his earlier mistress, Manel, whose death, he now suspected, had been caused by his queen. Like Manel, Sita realy loved him and cared for his happiness ahead of her own. 'Your being unable to bear children is not a volitional activity,' he declared gruffly, to hide his emotion.

'It would be if I could indeed bear children,' she responded with that strange illogical logic that made her so young, so much a woman in his eyes.

They talked for an hour. He told her more tales of his boyhood. They watched the moths fluttering around the oil lamps, listened to the soughing of a high wind above the splashing of the stream. They had always talked the hours away, the love-making that inevitably followed being from the true closeness that resulted.

He noticed the sand-clock he had given her as a present on the ebony table. 'Ah, it is well past midnight,' he exclaimed, then stretched, yawning. 'Time to go to bed.'

And the front door burst open.

Friday, 11 February 1530

I fell asleep in the governor's mansion that Thursday night rather sad, knowing that my birthday would dawn the next day. I would be twenty-five years old. Life was slipping by and I could not help remembering past birthdays before the three years and more of my exile, especially my sixteenth birthday which I had spent in this very mansion with my father, the day of history. Oh well . . .

Awakened by an unusual sound, I was instantly alert. The darkness inside my upstairs bedroom was accentuated by the two square patches of glowing night sky beyond the open windows. My hand reached out for the hilt of my sword which always slept beside me.

Before I gained my night-sight, I heard the sound again, a familiar scraping rattle just outside the windows which took me back to the night of Julietta's kidnapping. Gravel was being flung from the courtyard window below. Who could it be? An enemy would certainly not want to attract my attention. Yet my heart was beating faster as I grasped my sword, swung out of bed and padded softly to the left-hand window. Standing well-clear of the opening, I peered down at the courtyard.

A great yellow moon draped with wisps of grey cloud was ready to dip into the western horizon, so it must be past midnight. My birthday had arrived! Immediately below me, in the pale light of the deserted courtyard, a dark figure stood looking upwards at my window. He must have known I was there for he beckoned urgently. He might well have been an assassin, inviting me to my doom, but I had to take a chance. I returned to my bedside, quickly changed my sarong for dark pantaloons and tunic. I slipped on and fastened my thonged sandals, wore my sword belt, passed my sword through it for a quick draw. I hastened back to the window, eased out, grabbed the familiar vine that had been my ladder since days long gone and clambered swiftly down the side of the building. I paused about six feet from the ground, drew my sword and leapt down, clearing the base of the vine, landing on bent knees. I sprang sideways and faced the figure, my sword at the ready, the blood pumping in my veins.

'It is I, lord.' The words were quietly spoken, just above a whisper. In a pale shaft of moonlight, I recognized the very ordinary face and nondescript build of Appu, the trained spy I had in Juli's mansion who had been her *major domo* since the day she first resided there.

I straightened up and sheathed my sword, took him by the elbow and guided him along the wall of the building to the shadow of a clump of tall bushes. The reception rooms along the front of the mansion were deserted for the night.

'What is it, Appu?'

'Important news, my lord, and an urgent message from my lady.' The words came out in a soft rush. 'The Great King was shot dead this evening in the Kalyani fort by a *parangi* musket fired from the barracks, while he watched the soldiers having their dinner.'

Shock was followed by dismay, moments of grief and outrage. Then a thrill shot through me. I was free . . . free . . . at last, free after the interminable days of loneliness, hopelessness at times and unfailing rigid self-discipline to keep myself a man. 'That is shocking news.' The questions came out in a jumbled rush. 'Have they caught the assassin? Or was it an accident? How did you get the news?'

'No one knows who did it, or why, but it was not an accident. I had the news from my lady. The general has decided that the boy Prince Dom Juan should become the Great King, with his father, King Vidiye, as Regent, in accordance with the wishes of the dead ruler.'

'That was to be expected.'

The general arrived at the mansion after midnight and gave my lady the news. He returned to the fort and she got me up immediately and sent me to warn you that the general intends having you kidnapped tonight.' He delivered this momentous message as if it were a bundle of groceries! My ears sang with alarm, my heart with joy. 'The Lady Julietta sent you to warn me?' I inquired in amazement.

'Indeed, Prince. No sooner she saw the general off, she spoke to me.' He paused, eyeing me intently. 'She is a great lady in every way, Prince. Forgive me if I am presumptuous, but I must say that you and indeed the Sinhala people are fortunate to have such an ally.'

'Not an ally, Appu, but a friend. The Lady Julietta is too fine a person to be disloyal to her own by taking our side as an ally. Perhaps she is the ally of honour and decency.'

'You are right, Prince, but I repeat we are indeed fortunate.'

You will never know, Appu, just how fortunate I am, for the knowledge that my Juli loves me so deeply has stirred my entire being.

I heard a rustle and a light thud, then a second and a third from across the courtyard. Appu and I froze, merged further into the shadows. He laid a hand on my arm, inclined towards my ear. 'See. It is as I told you,' he murmured.

Hardly daring to breathe, we observed three dark figures, crouching low, steal swiftly across the courtyard, heading towards my bedroom windows. They stood erect at the wall, big men all three, so they could not be Sinhala. They certainly knew the lie of the land, for one of them quietly tested the very vine along which I had just slipped down.

'If we sound the alarm, it might cause the general to wonder how we knew,' I whispered to Appu. 'That could betray the lady. We have no option but to take them.'

He nodded, teeth gleaming white in approval. He drew a black cord from his waist, held it up in both hands. 'Silently then, lord,' he mouthed.

'Wait till the first man is almost at the window,' I breathed into his ear.

When the first figure became a giant dark spider silhouetted half-way up the wall, Appu walked stealthily beside me, I padded silently forward, sword in hand. We edged along the wall. Closer, closer, softly, silently, heart beating rapidly. The two men below were looking up at their comrade, who was now almost at the window. The knife held between his teeth would have been in my ribs within a few minutes.

When we were within five paces of the men, I trod on a dry leaf. The tiniest crackle, but it made the assassins come alert, swinging round in the instant.

Appu sprang like a cheetah at the man nearest him. I hear the swish of his garrotte as I hurtled towards the other man, sword swinging.

This was not a time for delicate swordplay. My mighty slash got the point across his throat. A strangled gurgle escaped him. He stood still, a half-drawn knife gleaming dully in his right hand. I heard the rasp of wind escaping from his torn gullet as I swung round towards the second man. Appu needed no help. His garrotte had the assassin choking, knees bent, hands clawing vainly for the air his windpipe could not find.

I looked up. The third assassin had paused, was peering down, taking in the scene. He must be deciding whether to proceed up or down. I helped him decide. Holding the vine in my left hand, I pulled, slashed at it with my bloody sword, then jumped back.

He came down in a rush, met my sure thrust through his left kidney before he sprawled on the ground. He groaned in agony. Gripping my sword with both hands, I raised it aloft, brought it smashing down with all my strength. A mighty blow, driven by rage, the blade cleft through his skull, ground to a halt at his neck. He collapsed in an untidy heap, nearly tearing my arms loose from their sockets. I placed my foot on his back and tugged. The sword came out with a crunch of bone and gristle. Dark blood and white brains appeared.

Appu's opponent lay sprawled on the ground, very dead. He had a dreadful body odour. Appu hooked the garrotte back in his belt. 'I'm out of practice, lord,' he whispered. 'But this is better than the boredom of domestic service.'

He paused. 'Let me drag these bastards away one by one and hide them in the grove, while you get your things and leave.'

'Not so,' I responded, 'These men are *parangi*. Leave them where they are, so their general will have some explaining to do tomorrow and the Sinhala people will know he is their enemy. You return now to the general's mansion and I shall slip away to freedom.'

He gave me salutation, rose, looked intently into my eyes. 'Farewell, lord. May the *devas* guard you.'

Thank you, Appu. And thank you for saving my life. I shall not forget.'

'I pray that I will have the opportunity to fight the *parangi* under your leadership.'

Suddenly the event and his words made the years of boredom, bitterness and frustration vanish. I had come through them only with a fixity of purpose and a super-human self-control, but they would stand me in good stead when I came to lead men like Appu.

I had bled a long while. Now I could rise and fight again.

CHAPTER EIGHTEEN
Friday, 11 February 1530

King Kumara leapt to his feet, placing himself protectively in front of Sita, his hand reaching for his sword. It was only half-drawn, however, when he recognized the trim figure standing four square at the entrance, hands on hips.

'Anula!' he exclaimed, snapping the sword back.

'Anula!' she mimicked, her lips drawn back in an ugly snarl, her eyes hard with rage. 'I'm surprised you even recognize me, the mother of your three-year-old baby, the woman you service regularly, when you're not out here fucking this whore.' She had abandoned the royal plural in her fury. She took in Sita with a scornful, appraising glance. 'A *young* whore too, I see.'

The king had regained his composure. He had faced up to a confrontation with Queen Anula a hundred times, but never in quite this way. He drew himself to his full height. 'What are you doing here?' he demanded haughtily. 'Wife or mother, you have no right to intrude on our privacy.'

'Only on your private parts, you betrayer?' Something broke loose within her. 'You bastard! You mother-fucking *yakka*, devil. All these years you have kept denying that you had anything to do with this whore. But I *knew* all along. You lied to me, fornicator. You, with your grand talk of fidelity and your romantic promises. You used me.'

'Perhaps we used each other,' he retorted quietly. 'Perhaps we should have loved each other instead.'

She looked as if she would strike him, but suddenly, with an indrawn breath, regained her composure. A slow smile gradually spread over her face, a taut body relaxed. 'Yes indeed, you may be right, lord. Please remain here and enjoy your mating. I shall await you in the palace . . .

with love.' She half-bowed, turned and walked away, her head held high.

Somehow, her tremendous calm conveyed a greater menace to him.

She paused at the door, turned, her eyes glittering like agates. 'Do you realize that without our support, your hopes of becoming the Great King will never be realized?'

Suddenly he knew the answer. It was so simple, he could have laughed aloud with sweet release. 'The hope of a Great King's crown exchanged for a touch of innocence!' he declared. 'Why not? A ruler is first a man.'

She was so taken aback, she clutched the door handle for support. Then the fury intensified, but well controlled now. 'You spoke of love. Understand that each of us loves differently, but all of it is selfishness in the long run.' She nodded to herself. 'You have a streak of idealism in you, Sire, which we never suspected in such a cynic as you made yourself out to be. It makes a hypocrisy of your cynicism. At heart, you are a Kandyan peasant with all a peasant's weakness, but we shall show you the love you need regardless.'

Her words stung him till he quickly realized that she was deliberately trying to wound him. 'Then pray permit a Kandyan peasant to use a peasant's metaphor.' His voice smooth, urbane as he suddenly felt. 'Our experience of people had made a tattered scarecrow of our faith, supported only by the dried sticks of our courage and will. Now that faith has been restored by Sita, a decent human being, whom you have presumed to call a whore.'

'We never thought to hear you speak thus, like a common clown,' she countered, her voice low. 'In you, who never had faith in anyone or anything, even as a child, this new-found faith is pathetic.' Her voice dropped to a reflective whisper. 'You need to be saved from yourself, Sire.'

She turned again, closed the door behind her.

* * *

The moon had set behind the western mountains, so Queen Anula walked from the house through the chill air of darkness, making towards the gate where her two attendants awaited her in the wagon. Her fury had abated, leaving a cold hardness within her that caused a strange detachment from herself, even from life. This was exactly as she had felt the night she discovered that her lover, the man whose son she had borne while she was yet in wedlock with another man, had betrayed and humiliated her; when she poisoned her husband; when she caused Manel, the mistress of Prince Kumara, as he was then, to be killed. Nothing changes, she reflected idly. She paused, turned around to stare at the lamp glow from the house where her husband was perhaps at this very moment comforting the woman who had displaced her. She felt no pain, only a stern resolve which she could not identify, except that its source was a divine role she was destined to play throughout her life. Anula the avenger, Anula commanded by life to remove the frail from her own life.

Her first husband's frailty had been cruelty, her lover's infidelity. The old goat, King Wijayo, had been addicted to drink and sex, the woman Manel, to a special form of whoredom. She had killed her first husband by poisoning the palm wine which caused his druken rages. The poison she had given her lover was on her nipples, which he had been addicted to sucking. A fitting method of punishment for each!

King Kumara was different. She had bared all of herself, including her humanity, to him. He must suffer a different fate, a far worse one.

What was King Kumara's addiction? Nothing, unless it was his newfound whore.

The prattle of the stream intruded upon her senses. A light wind soughed through the branches overhead, brought the cloying scent of green-bug which warned of a cobra. She must use the cobra's stealth and strike as suddenly.

And yet. Streams, branches, wind, cobras, what were they? And what was woman?

We women are all whores, she thought sadly and contemptuously, but without bitterness. We need men to support us, protect us, fuck us, so we sell our bodies and our services through concubinage or wedlock, that more hypocritical, respectable form of concubinage.

What was King Kumara's addiction? What?

His ambition? No. His need to show off? Yes, that was it. Even his addiction to decency came from the desire to show off. The hope of a Great King's crown for a touch of innocence, indeed. One of his clever remarks, but dealing with innocence would make him complacent. Well . . .

A low throaty chuckle escaped her, floated away into the cold darkness. No man addicted to decency ever achieved sovereign power.

Monday, 14 February 1530

It was churlish of me not to bid personal farewell to my aunt in Gam Paha, for she had been marvellously kind and attentive to me during my years of exile under her roof, but after the attempted kidnapping in Mutu Vella, I felt I had a choice between being alive and churlish or well-mannered and dead. The safest place for me and the only place I wanted to get to without delay was Sita Waka, so I left the same night, leaving notes for my uncle, the port governor and my aunt in Gam Paha. What a happy way to start my twenty-fifth birthday, ending my exile and riding back home again, though along a devious route.

I reached the newly built capitol and palace in Sita Waka three evenings later. At the very first glance I saw that my father had learnt his lesson well. The fortifications of the entire city had been augmented, with cleared fields of fire and a moat all round it. Sentry towers had been built at regular intervals. The snouts of cannon protruded from the battlements. Within the city, the new capitol, which had risen on the ashes of our old mansion, had its own moat and fortifications. New life and energy throbbed in the very air, like the drumbeats to which troops were marching on the barrack square. Soldiers in our red and white uniforms were everywhere. There would be no more taking of Sita Waka without the heaviest toll.

I sent word of my arrival ahead to my father. To my surprise, he met me on the *maidan* opposite the capitol. He had aged more than the years of our seperation, the chiselled features rather drawn, the black hair liberally flecked with silver. He embraced me in public and much of my pain and disillusionment were miraculously sloughed away. To my delight and surprise, he had my cavalry regiment assembled on the *maidan*. My inspection of them, the sight of familiar faces, the warmth of their spirits, will remain one of the most thrilling moments of my life.

After the troops were dismissed, my father insisted on taking me personally around the palace, of which he was obviously and justifiably proud. We then retired alone for our usual evening chat, on the palace courtyard now since the front lawn was no more. The feelings that I once experienced whenever I sat there with him, the memories, yes, the renewal of my love for him went too deep to be expressed in words.

I looked up through the dark gold dusk at the green mountains that had teemed with soldiers three and a half years ago. The anguish with which I had looked down at the burning capitol that day returned, caused me to look beyond the sky, pure rose except for the small black sails of bats winging across its early evening light. Was it the same crows that cawed, the same mynahs shrilling against the oncoming night in the banyan trees? A goat bleated from one of the stockades nearby and a rustling breeze brought the faint scent of frying food.

Oh, it was good to be back home again.

We talked first, in hushed tones, about my escape. He thought it fortuitous that I should have fled Colombo on my birthday. When we came to the murder of the Great King, I could see that my father was torn and anguished by it. 'Strange, how none of my brothers and sisters are left,' he stated sadly. 'You are here, thank the *devas*, but it is still a lonely feeling.' He sighed heavily. 'Oh, well, my brother chose to sup with the devil and paid the price.'

I felt myself choking, so I remained silent.

The atmosphere became charged with emotion. 'Do you like the new palace?' my father inquired, abruptly changing the subject.

'Indeed I do, Sire. It is a royal dwelling, worthy of a king.'

I missed the old familiar palace, but how could I complain about the new? The white mountain crystal floors were covered by expensive Pahlava, Persian carpets, which Abdul Raschid had imported; the doors, windows and frames were of carved teak; the furniture was mainly of dark brown tamarind wood, so matured that it was streaked with golden flame; the hanging and many-tiered pedestal lamps were ornamented brass.

I glanced towards the building. As required by traditional Sinhala architecture, it had been erected around a great *meda midula*, central courtyard, which was planted with shady banyans, mountain apple and flowering shower trees, with a young *bodhi* tree as the centrepiece. Under the shade of the *bodhi* tree had been placed a bronze statue of Lord Buddha seated in the lotus pose, served by a shrine at which clay lamps glittered and incense burned. Paved red-brick walkways led past sparkling fountains and cascades, through rusling bamboo and flower beds of yellow *kapuru* and multi-coloured impatience, bushes of white jasmine that scented the air.

'This palace was made possible only by the personal wealth of our family,' my father observed. 'Only the late Great King Bhuvaneka Bahu, and now his grandson and heir, have greater wealth. Those treasures, inherited from generation after generation of Sinhala kings, have become so legendary that they are sure to attract greedy foreigners soon.'

'I should imagine so, Sire.' I too changed the subject. 'Speaking of treasures, I notice you have acquired many of the new instruments called clocks.'

'Abdul Raschid obtained them for us from Europe. We have abandoned our old system of dividing the day into watches and adopted the hours and minutes of Europe. The system was confusing initially but makes good sense now that everyone is familiar with it.'

'I fail to see why a day should have twenty-four hours and each hour sixty minutes, Sire,' I responded smiling. The childhood desire to show off to my father seized me. 'Surely the base of the edifice we call a day is the *thathpara*, or second. Surely too, the 86,400 seconds that make a day could have been more equally sub-divided. But who am I venture into the strange workings of the European mind? They take what belongs to older civilizations and convert it so it can appear to have originated from them. They have even made a new religion of the teachings of Jesus Christ. I believe newer races do this so they can lay claim to the product as being the fruit of their own genius. The truth is that barbaric conquerors become the conquered of their civilized victims.'

My father clapped his hands in mock applause. 'Spoken like a cynic and philosopher, Prince! We fear, however, that our ancient nation may end up aping the manners and customs, institutions and traditions of the West.' A firm note entered his voice. 'This we must prevent at all costs!

Despite using the new inventions of the West, we should remain Aryan Sinhala in our personal lives, so we can be examples to the people and retain our national identity.'

Friday, 29 April 1530

When I answered King Maya Dunne's summons to his audience chamber in the palace at dawn, I never dreamed who would be there. I saw my father smiling at me from behind his great tamarind wood desk, Lord Wickrama Sinha stitting at his left, before noticing the giant, gangling figure dressed in dark blue tunic sitting very erect on my father's right. My pulses quickened. What on earth could King Vidiye be doing here? How could King Maya Dunne be receiving a sworn enemy with such obvious civility?

I cooly sat on the chair to King Vidiye's right.

'Good morning, Prince. We trust you slept well,' the king commenced with his usual pleasantries.

'Thank you, Sire. Indeed I slept well, so well that I had a moment's regret at having to awaken at three A.M., over an hour before my usual time and that of the game cocks, who will surely be sending a deputation to wait on you soon, protesting at your interruption of their regular time-clocks by the introduction of your European models which have ended their monopoly to awaken people at a more respectable hour.'

Eyes twinkling, my father threw back his head and gave his characteristic laugh. King Vidiye's smile showed prominent white teeth but did not reach the huge, fierce dark eyes. 'The prince's exile has not diminished his wit or his agreeable ways.' His voice was deep and rough, seeming to emerge from his stomach.

'You may be surprised to find our cousin King Vidiye here,' the king addressed me. 'He travelled at night and arrived but a few minutes ago. Though he has come for other reasons, he has brought us the latest news.' He looked towards King Vidiye.

'The appointment of our son, Prince Dom Juan Dharma Pala, as the Great King and our appointment as Prince Regent have been confirmed by the Portuguese General de Albergaria under the authority of His Imperial Majesty Dom João III of Portugal.' King Vidiye's large, sunken eyes flamed with anger. 'Why is it that the royal successions of an independent nation need the sanction of a foreign king?' He glanced at each of us in turn. 'King Bhuvaneka Bahu began it all. He sold the nation to the Portuguese, but it is the friar, Father Juan, who now manipulates our affairs from behind the scenes, through his superiors in Lisbon.'

My father shook his head. 'How can that be?'

'All European kings, other than Henry VIII of England who has been driven wild by love for a woman, have a superstitious awe of excommunication from their Church. Look! Others in Lanka, besides us, realize this. King Kumara and his wife, Queen Anula, are having their daughter Dona Margaridha, taught the Catholic religion by the friar, Father Perez.'

'Queen Anula always has deep designs of her own,' my father observed thoughtfully.

'She is a scheming, conniving bitch.' King Vidiye had none of my father's grace or chivalry. 'Meanwhile, General de Albergaria has a thirst for power. He has already forgotten that it was you who calmed our people and prevented them from marching on Colombo to wreak vengeance on the *parangi* for the death of their Great King. He restrained himself for the first few days, probably because of the low level of his military strength, but things have changed since he received word that the Portuguese Viceroy, Don Alfonso de Noronha, will shortly be here with a fleet.' His eyes rolled angrily. 'The Viceroy apparently claims that the object of his visit is to investigate the murder of the Great King, but we believe that it is his well-known greed for wealth that brings him. He is after our treasury.'

'Surely you will not give him access to it?' My father's question was a command.

'Never!' King Vidiye's grin was crooked. 'If it exists!'

'Which brings us to the object of King Vidiye's present visit,' my father stated. 'He feels – and we agree – that the time has come for us to set aside our past differences and present a united front to the Portuguese. We can expect no support from the Kandyans. The Cholas up north have become an island within our island, with virtual autonomy. That leaves King Vidiye and us. He proposes an amicable division of our spheres of influence. His domain as Regent will include the kingdom of Jaya and the Raigam kingdom as far as Galla. Our own will comprise Sita Waka and the Ruhuna region south of Galle. We have accepted these proposals, so Lord Wickrama Sinha will proceed immediately to Matara with three infantry regiments to establish his headquarters there and administer Ruhuna on our behalf. Prince Raja Sinha, you will take over Lord Wickrama Sinha's functions as Chief Minister in addition to your present duties as army commander. Lord Panni will become your deputy army commander.'

'Everybody important moves up under this coalition,' King Vidiye observed, his cunning so obvious it sickened me.

King Maya Dunne cleared his throat. 'Our coalition must be firmly cemented by domestic ties. King Vidiye has graciously accepted the offer we have made to him of the hand of our daughter, the Princess Padma, in marriage. The wedding will take place immediately, without any fuss, as soon as the princess arrives from Anu.'

Murderer of my uncle, King Raigam, yesterday, brother-in-law tomorrow, I thought to myself, bitterly. Such is the ways of princes, kings and pimps.

Friday, 29 April 1530

Aisha Raschid knew that despite her occasional rebellious-
ness, the words of the Prophet Muhammad were ingrained
in her life.

'O you who believe! When the call is made for prayer
on Friday, then hasten to the remembrance of Allah and
leave off all your business; that is better for you if you
know. And when the prayer is ended, then disperse abroad
in the land and seek Allah's grace.'

In Islam, there was neither sabbath, nor a seventh day
for Divine worship or rest. The Muslim left work every
Friday on hearing this call to prayer and resumed work
after the prayer was finished. A special feature of the
Friday service was the sermon, delivered by the *imam*
before the prayer service was held, which dealt with a
subject relating to the welfare of the community.

Aisha had greatly missed the calls to prayer while she
and Abdul Raschid were in virtual hiding in the country.
She had therefore been glad to get to Sita Waka itself,
because it had a small mosque, painted the familiar green
and pink with the fountain for ablutions in front of it.
While she did not need religion to face calamity, she had
discovered the constant reminders of the will of Allah
afforded by Islam to be a source of strength to her.
Acceptance of the inevitable contentedly required as much
strength as the forging of one's own future.

The *imam*'s sermon this Friday had, appropriately
enough, pointed to Allah's rule over every person's destiny
jointly or separately. She returned home more calm than
she had been for some time, but when she learned that
King Maya Dunne's son, Prince Raja Sinha, would be
paying them a visit that night, she was suddenly filled with
intense disquiet. Princes did not call at the abodes of
commoners. Why was Prince Raja Sinha coming to see
them? Abdul Raschid kept asking the question of no one
in particular all through dinner, to the point of monotony.

The murky night outside did not help Aisha's disquiet. An overcast sky seemed to press down on the earth, muffling the creak of crickets. There was not even the hint of a breeze to drive away the smell of *ghee* which she had taught the servants to use in the cooking of *buriyana*, so it clung to the air, pleasant before a meal but cloying when the meal was over.

As soon as she heard the horses' hooves stop at the gate, Aisha withdrew into the main bedroom which adjoined the living room of the four-roomed residence. Abdul Raschid hastened outside to greet the prince. Aisha left the bedroom door slightly ajar, so she could hear the conversation in the living room.

The prince preceded her husband through the entrance foyer. In the golden lamplight, he was taller, leaner, tougher than she remembered him, his features tighter chiselled, making him look more like his father. His skin was lightly tanned, the dark brilliant eyes brilliant. He carried himself with pride, the head held almost arrogantly high, to compensate for suffering and disillusionment, she suddenly thought with a pang for him.

The prince sat on the sofa facing the entry way, so she could only see the clean-cut profile now, wide forehead, full brows, straight nose and firm chin. Her husband gingerly placed his bulk on the edge of a settle facing him.

A lizard chirped in a moment of silence. When the prince began speaking, the world suddenly seemed to recede for Aisha, leaving only him and his words. 'My father, King Maya Dunne, commanded me to deliver this message to you personally as a mark of his appreciation of the devotion that you and your wife, Aisha Raschid, have extended to his cause these many years.' His voice was low, grave. Why? 'He would have come himself except that he has a guest of honour, King Vidiye, Regent of Jaya, visiting him tonight, who brought us the news I am about to give you.'

Aisha fought back the apprehension that churned inside her belly. A moment's dizziness made her place a hand against the wall for support.

'I regret to inform you that your son, Ali, is dead.'

She heard Abdul Raschid's sob, felt the earth spin around her. Prickles broke out over her entire body. These are just words, she thought. The prince is talking about someone else. Then she noted her husband's pudgy face crumpling, the small eyes closing, the tiny mouth agape. The great shoulders sagged. 'Pray tell me how it happened, Prince,' he begged in a hoarse whisper.

'I have the news at second hand from King Vidiye.' The prince's voice hardened, rose. 'Briefly, your son had hired a Portuguese soldier to assassinate the Great King. It is conjectured that part of the murder price was given in advance, the balance to be paid immediately after the deed was done. Your son and the soldier alone knew of the plot and of each other's identities. It is believed that the soldier, in order to protect his own identity, killed your son immediately he made the final payment.'

'When did this happen, lord?' Abdul inquired, fighting back the tears.

'On the very night of the Great King's death, as far as King Vidiye can determine.'

A long pause ensued. 'How was he killed?' Abdul Raschid's voice had dropped to a whisper.

'Do you really wish to know? Why torment yourself with the details now that it is all over and what remains is your inevitable mourning?'

'Begging your pardon, lord, a parent always wishes to know these things. Besides, for us Muslims, there also has to be vengeance.'

'He must have put up a fight in this lonely place, for he was beaten to death.'

'Dear Allah!'

Moments of silence followed, during which Aisha, in a

state of curious suspension from herself, watched a tear role down her husband's cheek. As a Muslim mother, this was the time for her to tear her hair, don sackcloth, smear herself with ashes and wail for her dead. She had no desire to do any of these thigs. She could not claw out the pain, the excruciating pain, the sense of loss. It would be hers for ever. Ali, the joy and promise of her life, was dead. As the *imam* had said today, all of it was the will of Allah. This was Ali's destiny – hers and his father's too. She remembered the killer look in Ali's eyes. Perhaps it was best that Allah took him away. But he had been so alive, so intensely brave and intelligent, so full of promise. Dear Allah, to be beaten to death. Had he been afraid? Had he put up a fight? What of that solitary last moment when he knew death was inevitable?

'This is Allah's punishment!' she heard Abdul Raschid declare in cracked tones. 'My son Ali arranged for other murders too, the conspirator Lord Kandura, the master craftsman Kodi . . .'

'What?' The question had shot from the prince like a bolt from a catapult. 'Kodi?'

Abdul Raschid nodded sadly. 'Yes, Kodi too lord. It was an act performed for the Catholic friars.'

The prince seemed to pull himself away from reflections by an effort of will. 'My father, King Maya Dunne, suspected some of this . . . but Kodi? I never dreamed . . .' The prince shook his head violently, steadied himself. 'Nevertheless, King Maya Dunne bids me inform you that your services to him have closed all past accounts.'

Tears were now pouring down Abdul Raschid's cheeks, but Aisha, dry-eyed, felt only a cold, cold hard knot within her. A red mist swam before her eyes. Her beautiful, beautiful baby, beaten to death. Vengeance! A Portuguese did the deed. Vengeance! Every Portuguese would pay the price. Vengeance! She would spend the rest of her life destroying any and all infidel Portuguese. Vengeance!

'My son's body?' Abdul Raschid inquired.

As if it mattered.

'It was discovered by some fellow Muslims who did not know of your whereabouts and gave it a worthy funeral.'

Suddenly, without volition or realization, the tough descendant of Mahmud of Ghazni fled before the bereaved Mouro mother. Without realizing it, Aisha Raschid started to keen.

CHAPTER NINETEEN
Tuesday, 3 May 1530

Like most people in the Estado da India, Fernao was aware of the greed of the new Viceroy, Don Alfonso de Noronha, who had received his appointment only because he was a great favourite of the King Emperor. The tall, vulture-like figure that had greeted him on the poop-deck of the flagship in the Colombo harbour the previous morning had convinced Fernao that the tales of the Viceroy's greed were true. Avarice and cunning were stamped on his face, and accented by his gaunt frame and hunched shoulders. His love of ostentation was obvious from his dress. The doublet was of the finest velvet, the shirt, of white silk with lace ruffles, was graced by a huge gold necklet studded with rubies, jewelled rings encrusted bony fingers. The lean, gaunt face had deep-set, cunning eyes. A great curved nose, seeming to pause briefly to greet a tight-lipped mouth on its way to the jutting chin, completed the picture of a predator.

The Viceroy had arrived with a flotilla of ten heavily armed *nao* and eight *terco*, regiments of infantry and musketeers. The official reason for his visit was to investigate the murder of the Great King, which could have been the work of a Portuguese soldier, but a few minutes' conversation had convinced Fernao that the Viceroy was really not interested in such an investigation. Fernao had attended the meeting with some trepidation thinking that the Viceroy would also inquire about the three *degredados* he had sent to kidnap Prince Raja Sinha; apart from frustration at realizing that his quarry had escaped, it had been highly embarrassing to him when the men were found dead in the governor's mansion the next morning. He had explained the incident by saying the men were obviously

271

robbers, but he pre-empted any further action from the Sinhala authorities by boldly demanding to know how the Portuguese citizens came to be murdered. The Viceroy had been apprised of the incident, but he had barely touched on it. His principal concerns were obviously to verify the truth about the Great King's treasures and to demand an audience with the Great King the very next day.

Fernao had been walking a tightrope during the past year, balancing the conflicting ambitions of King Kumara, King Vidiye and King Bhuvaneka Bahu. When King Bhuvaneka was killed, he knew that matters would come to a head. So he was not surprised when his spies had told him of King Vidiye's visit to Sita Waka. He had then been officially informed of the king's marriage to King Maya Dunne's daughter, the Princess Padma, who had been hastily summoned to Sita Waka from the ancient capital, Anu, for the purpose. An alliance had obviously been made. He had feared its effects on the balance of power until the Viceroy arrived with such military strength.

The request for an audience was promptly granted. Viceroy Alfonso de Noronha and his delegation, including Fernao, were driven to Jaya in two horse-drawn carriages, with a mounted escort. It was a clear, sparkling morning and they were received at the entrance of Jaya capital by Lord Chamberlain Tammitta Rala, a stout, chubby-faced nobleman, and conducted to the palace with customary pomp. This included a procession of whip-crackers, stilt-walkers, drummers, dancers and twenty-four gaily caparisoned elephants preceding them. The noise was deafening, the smell of human sweat overpowering, the heat from the crush of watching crowds intense.

An armed guard of honour and a great outcry of Sinhala drums, trumpets and firecrackers greeted them in the palace courtyard. Having inspected the guard, cursorily as was the Sinhala custom, they walked up the steps of the assembly hall, which was crowded with princes and nobles.

It was a glittering scene. The men were dressed in finery, pointed shoes of gold or silver, white *dhotis* ballooning from the eighteen yards of linen gathered in pleats at the waist, long-sleeved waistcoats of blue, red or purple velvet, slashed by embroidered cloth-of-gold sashes, long swords at the side. Everyone wore jewelled necklaces, many held gold or silver mounted ebony staffs of office in hand.

Walking steadily at the left of the Viceroy and slightly behind him, Fernao was impressed all over again by the pagentry, it made worthwhile his own heavy sweating beneath rich clothes, red velvet doublet and gold breeches. The price of honour in this country is not death, he thought wryly, but sweat.

The Great King and his entourage were accommodated on the platform at the far end of the hall. Perched on the golden lion throne of the Sinhala kings, beneath a lofty tasselled canopy of burgundy velvet extending on to the platform steps, was the diminutive figure of a thin dark-skinned boy dressed in cloth of gold, a gold turban on his head. His feet barely reached the golden royal footstool. The magnificent jewelled crown of the Sinhala kings, obviously too large for the small head, lay beside the throne on a gold stand, cushioned in burgundy velvet, along with the orb and sceptre. Even at the age of four, the Great King Dom Juan Dharma Pala's broad features, large rolling eyes and gangling frame showed promise that he would grow up to look exactly like his father, the Regent, who stood beside the throne dressed in gold brocade pantaloons and tunic. King Vidiye's nonchalant but haughty bearing showed that he considered himself more than the power behind the throne!

As they paced the red carpeted aisle, to the deafening sound of trumpets and drums which continued unabated outside, Fernao noted the twelve bare-chested men, bearing flaming candles on great silver candlestands, who stood behind the throne, their magnificent muscles rippling in the golden light. He recalled from his first audience in the palace that these were the *pandang karayo*, or candlebearers, a term which had either derived from or had come to mean people who fawned for the favours of the great, literally holding lights for them.

The moment they halted before the steps leading to the platform, the trumpets and drums stopped abruptly, leaving only echoes fading away towards the lofty ceiling. Don Alfonso and Fernao bowed low before the throne. The king merely extended his hands, tips of the fingers together, in acknowledgement.

'On behalf of the princes, noblemen and the people of the illustrious country of Lanka, we are pleased to welcome you,' the little four-year-old king declaimed in schooled Portuguese, his voice high and flutey. He had obviously been carefully tutored to make the brief speech. 'Pray be seated, gentlemen.' He indicated the two chairs on the platform with an innately gracious gesture of his right hand. He nodded once towards Lord Tammitta, obviously relieved that his task was over.

The Chamberlain mounted the stairs and took his place on the right side of the dais. 'Gentlemen, we would like to present you to the honoured Regent of Lanka, King Vidiye Bandara,' he stated in fluent Portuguese.

King Vidiye merely nodded stiffly then sat on the smaller throne, normally reserved for the queen, to the left of his son.

How did one treat a four-year-old king? The Viceroy did not seem the least uncertain. The boy king's knowledge of Portuguese was confined to his welcoming words, but Fernao found Lord Tammitta an excellent interpreter, familiar with both Sinhala and Portuguese languages. The Viceroy's questions sparked the little boy's interest, and his conversation about the latest toys in Europe revealed Don Alfonso to be a seasoned diplomat.

When it seemed that the pleasantries were beginning to

flag, the king reached over for a small golden bell placed on a stool beside him. The echo of the tinkle had barely subsided before attendants, wearing white satin pantaloons and tunic of gold cloth gorgeously belted and slashed in red, entered through the two doors on either side of the platform at the rear of the audience hall. They bore gold trays containing carved goblets of drinks and gold platters laden with a variety of sweetmeats.

'Pray have some refreshments now,' the king invited. 'I would like to tell you a joke while you are having them.' His black eyes brightened. 'We had a king many centuries ago, in our capital city, Anu, who was a great joker. His palace gardener looked exactly like him and he would sometimes make the gardener wear his clothes and the crown and sit on the throne, while he himself stood at the back of the audience hall, laughing at the people bowing to his gardener. One day, as the gardener sat on the throne, he pointed to the real king who was laughing away at the back of the hall. He commanded the guards to seize the rude fellow who dared to laugh out loud in his presence and have him killed. The real king said it was all a joke, but the guards thought he was mad to believe that he was the king and so they killed him. Isn't that funny?'

Fernao and the Viceroy nodded, smiling their appreciation. 'Very funny, Your Majesty,' Don Alfonso declared. 'That is a nice story, thank you.'

The fruit drinks included king coconut water, with tender white kernel in it, red pomegranate juice and the inevitable melon juice with a dash of lime which both Fernao and the Viceroy selected. Fernao also picked up one of the black sweetmeats, called *kalu dodol*, which he loved. It was made of boiled honey, flecked with white cashew nuts, He noticed that the king partook of the same refreshments as his guests, probably in a well-bred gesture to assure them that they were certainly not being poisoned.

More attendants entered bearing small gold basins of

scented water, on which white jasmine petals floated, and linen napkins, for the washing of hands. When they had all finally departed, the king leaned forward on his throne, jerked his head at the senior attendant, a tall muscular man dressed in a red tunic and shiny gold pantaloons, who held the gold staff of office. 'All must leave now,' the king commanded.

The attendant stepped forward to the edge of the platform, banged in it three times with his staff. 'Ahey! Ahey! Ahey!' he called out in stentorian tones. 'By command of our gracious sovereign, His Majesty the Great King Dom Juan Dharma Pala, Lord of Lanka, all those gathered here in this audience hall shall now leave.'

When everyone in the body of the hall had finally backed away, the Great King looked towards his father, King Vidiye, who nodded, then took over. 'You requested this audience, Your Excellency,' King Vidiye stated in his deep, growly voice. 'Please feel free to speak. Lord Tammitta will continue to act as interpreter.'

The Viceroy cleared his throat. 'Your Majesties, I would like to commence these discussions with a most important aspect of your ascension to the throne of Lanka,' he declared in his dry monotone. 'My Emperor sends you and the Regent his felicitations. He has commanded me to convey to Your Majesty that before he officially proclaims you King Emperor of Lanka and your father, King Vidiye, Regent, in Portugal and throughout his territories, he eagerly awaits the fulfilment of the condition of his agreement with your revered grandfather, the late King Bhuvaneka Bahu.'

Fernao was stunned.

'What conditions?' King Vidiye peremptorily demanded after a silence.

The Viceroy's thin lips cracked sideways in the semblance of a smile. 'Your Majesty's baptism in the Catholic faith.'

It was King Vidiye who first recovered from the shock. 'There was no such condition,' he grated.

'On the contrary, my lord.' The Viceroy reached into his doublet and produced a small scroll, bearing broken seals and ribbons. 'I have here a certified copy of the agreement.' He leaned back easily in his chair and proffered the scroll to the Lord Chamberlain.

Long minutes of silence passed as the official scrutinized the document, then read it again while King Vidiye gazed fiercely at him.

The young king merely looked all round the chamber, apparently quite unconcerned. 'We like the Catholic religion,' the boy announced to no one in particular and was rewarded by an angry glare from his father.

The Lord Chamberlain looked quite ill when he finished reading. He held the document limply in his hand. 'You say this is an exact original of the document executed by our late Great King under his seal, Your Excellency?'

'Certainly. It was witnessed as to its authenticity by the Recorder of the Royal Court of Lisbon and despatched to me with the Emperor's approval, His Imperial Majesty commands me to inform Your Majesty that the Royal Proclamation contemplated in that agreement will issue in Lisbon as soon as news of the baptism is conveyed by me to his court.'

'It can never be,' King Vidiye burst forth. 'Any such conversion would destroy the support we have from the Sinhala Buddhist people.'

'But you will have a more than effective substitute,' the Viceroy countered. 'You will have the might of Portugal behind you.'

'From thousands of miles away? We have no doubt as to the effectiveness of your armed might, Your Excellency.' A grim smile crossed King Vidiye's dark visage. 'It is its permanency that we question. If the Great King accepted a foreign faith, it would constitute a betrayal of the people,

277

who are the one permanent source of power in any kingdom.'

'King Kumara has done it with success, in the *uda rata*, we understand,' the Viceroy demurred mildly. 'He would have achieved nothing without our assistance.'

Fernao knew immediately that Father Juan was behind this request from Lisbon.

'And King Kumara only got as far as you would permit him,' King Vidiye retorted bluntly. 'If we accept this condition, we would become a vassal state of Portugal, since our Great King would come under the dominion of the Catholic Church.' A strange gleam crossed King Vidiye's huge eyes and he suddenly relaxed. 'Perhaps we can compromise. Perhaps we have something else to offer that might be ... er ... more valuable to you and your sovereign lord than a conversion.'

The Viceroy nodded towards the scroll which Lord Tammitta still held limply in his hand. 'We would expect you to honour the agreement in any case, my lord. After all, it was made between two sovereign rulers and we stand ready to fulfil our part of it.'

King Vidiye pointed towards the scroll. 'That document is obviously based upon a misunderstanding in the translation. We are aware of the late Great King's intent at the time. He meant that his successor would *acknowledge* the Catholic Church, not that he would accept it. Besides, since no goverment can really bind its successors, agreements between rulers are always subject to change.' King Vidiye's tone was suddenly so conciliatory that it made Fernao suspicious. 'What is important is basic intent. Your Emperor desires to support the succession. We desire your Emperor's support. We understand fully that the Emperor needs the conversion of our Great King as a symbol of our alle ... er ... comradeship, and also as an article of faith to appease the powerful Church in your country. We sugest that, as a compromise, we shall make a substantial payment of tribute to His Imperial Majesty in acknowledgement of our gratitude, from the treasures of the late Great King. We shall also officially announce that our Great King is studying the Catholic religion, and assures freedom of worship to all Catholic converts in our kingdoms. In return, we hope that your King Emperor will graciously proclaim his acceptance of the sovereign succession of our Great King and give us needed military backing from time to time.'

Fernao noted the gleam of avarice that had flitted across the Viceroy's face at the mention of the treasures and the whitening of the knuckles that gripped the arm of the chair. King Vidiye, you are a crafty bastard, he thought.

'That certainly seems like a fair compromise, my lord,' Don Alfonso de Noronha stated. 'I shall personally make His Imperial Majesty aware of the problems confronting you and shall use my good offices to persuade him to accept the modified agreement. It will necessitate our maintaining military forces of sufficient strength for a longer period than we envisaged. So your gracious offer of tribute, provided it is sufficiently substantial, will enable us to secure peace between us on these issues with . . . er . . . honour.'

Friday, 6 May 1530

When he returned from the encounter at Hangura, King Kumara was surprised to find that Queen Anula was her former agreeable, co-operative self. Her sweetness stank of unwonted unctuousness, made him suspicious. Never one to embark on journeys of guilt, notwithstanding the exhortations of the Catholic Church, he set Sita up in a modest home near the palace and began visiting her openly.

When he heard of the assassination of the Great King, his interest had quickened. Somehow this was an opportunity to be seized. But how?

Following dinner with Sita on the night his spies brought word that the Viceroy Don Alfonso de Noronha had arrived in Colombo with a flotilla of ten *nao* and had conferred with the Great King the very next morning, King Kumara sat with her on his favourite sofa. The living room of the house on High Forest Hill was small but luxuriously furnished with bright, locally woven rugs and ebony furniture. He stretched his legs, leaned back and burped politely in acknowledgement of Sita's home cooking. The meal of rice, *polos*, the young breadfruit, curry made Kandyan style, yams fried in chili and lime had been a pleasant change from the palace cooking. Sita had also served ripe *durian* fruit for dessert. Its rich, sweet taste remained in his mouth, but the stench, like the echoes of passed wind, clung faintly to the air.

'My lord does not need to eat *durian* for anything but enjoyment,' Sita sitting beside him, observed mischievously.

She looked so youthful in the golden lamplight, her almond-shaped eyes dark with some mystery, that he reached out involuntarily and stroked her fair hand. 'Why not?' he inquired tenderly, knowing the answer.

She blushed. 'Well . . . lord, they say that men eat *durian* in order to become more aroused sexually,' she volunteered, her gaze down cast.

'Who told you?'

Her blush deepened. 'They.' She shrugged in embarrassment.

'Yes, you said that before, but what "they"?' He was teasing her, his gaze affectionate.

She raised her eyes briefly to his, looked away quickly. 'You are always embarrassing me, lord,' she mock-complained.

'And you love it.'

'Uh-huh.'

'That's no reply to give anyone, least of all your king.'

'"They" are people, lord,' she responded vaguely. 'As the saying warns, I opened the ripe *durian*, which had spilt, in a pail of water, so the stench would pass into the water not into the air. I took out the pulp with the skins still in the water, then carried the pail outside, dug a deep hole and buried the contents.'

'You should have carried it a mile away at night and buried it secretly in the garden of your favourite enemy, so he would have to endure the stench,' he jested, reminding her of the rest of the old admonition.

'I have no enemies,' she replied primly.

'You should have buried it near the queen's quarters in the palace.'

Surprisingly, she took him seriously, half turned towards him. 'Do you really think the queen is my enemy?'

'Yes,' he replied soberly. 'She will not readily give up anything she considers hers and we were her favourite possession.'

'So long as she is kind to you, I don't care what she thinks.'

'I love you,' he said impulsively.

'I love you,' she whispered. 'Oh, so much. If anything ever happened to you, I would take my life.'

His hand tightened on hers while his eyes locked into her gaze. They melted and merged with each other. He gently caressed her hand. Its skin was soft and smooth as velvet. 'Listen,' he bade her.

The faint sound of a flute had emerged from next door. Someone was playing a rolling melody, the sound silver gold. Sita shivered beneath his grasp. 'That is the tune of the devil dancers when they cleanse the house in the morning, having danced all night,' she whispered.

'Nothing wrong with tha.,' he countered. 'Perhaps it's a sign, an omen, for we have been seriously considering the events in Colombo.' He began musing. 'We must move again. Which kingdom should we invade? Sita Waka is too strong for our forces. Jaya will be protected by the *parangi*, who will not want the kind of tough, independent Great King they know we will become. That leaves only a couple of alternatives. Jaffna is one, but it is separated . . . By the *devas*, we have it!' He stood up abruptly. 'We must hasten to the palace, *sundari*, golden one.' His smile was mischievous. 'The effects of the *durian* must await a move we have put off too long already.

Friday, 6 May 1530

Her first reaction to the news of Ali's death, following her involuntary keening, had been a state of numbness. Dimly she had comprehended such numbness to be Allah's way of insulating people against shocking news, like the physicians who administered opium before operating on a patient. She therefore allowed herself to remain in that state. Since there was no physical body to which they could extend religious interment and the finality of Ali's death had not visually registered with her, she avoided accepting it, but oh, the moments when she thought about the manner of Ali's dying. His thoughts, his feelings, his fear, his contempt for his assassin. Her throat would go dry, her mind become raw, her breathing heighten until she thought she would go mad.

That Friday evening, the *imam* had insisted on walking home with her and Abdul Raschid for once, after the last of the five prayer sessions of the day. His name was Mohamed Shafir, the last probably taken by his family since most followers of the Islamic faith in Lanka were of the Shafir'i School of the Sunni followers of the Prophet. He was a little greybeard of a man, with long grey hair, a birdlike face and sharp eyes.

Following a dinner of chicken *pilau*, the *imam* and Abdul Raschid sat in the living room sipping sweet black *copi*, the fragrance of which filled the air. Breaking custom, the *imam* had requested Aisha to sit with them.

'At this sad time, brother and sister, I would commend to you both the tenets of our Islamic faith.' The *imam* had the dry voice which goes with men who pursue subjects dry as withered branches. 'The three terms which express the quality of that faith are *Imam*, belief, *Islam*, the practical consequences of our acceptance of *Imam*, and *Ihsan*, which is the experiental quality of our religious life. You both already have the belief. By accepting and declaring the basic creed at all times, especially in the daily prayer ritual to which you religiously adhere, by paying *zakat*, the wealth tax, by the observance of fasting during the prescribed period of the year and by making the pilgrimage to Mecca, you fulfil the duties of *Islam*. So you are both good Muslims.'

Abdul Raschid bowed his head in silent acknowledgement of the statement. 'So we have always tried to be,' he volunteered solemnly. 'Which is why I for one cannot understand why Allah has visited this . . .' his voice broke and re-emerged in a half-whisper, 'punishment on us.' He paused, squared his great shoulders. 'Yet it is more devout to accept the will of Allah when we don't understand it.'

'That shows that you are indeed good Muslims,' the *imam* responded. 'For it means that you have accepted the true connotation of *Ihsan*, which is the inner realization and acknowledgement of the real meaning of the external forms that are your religious practice, *Islam*. In *Ihsan*, we stress the spirit of worship so that you can feel that you are near Allah at all times, in joy and in adversity.'

'But living it from day to day is so . . . so . . . hard,' Abdul Raschid intervened.

Her husband's words struck an answering cord in Aisha. 'Is there any new wisdom in the world that can help us to cope with our tragedy?' she cried. 'Is there anything besides the incredible faith demanded by all religions to comfort the afflicted?' She noted the startled looks of her husband and the *imam*, but plunged on. 'Islam has its tenet of *kismet*, destiny, which no one can alter, so we must shrug our shoulders and go on, whatever the anguish in our hearts. The Catholic religion has acceptance of God's will. Both faiths promise us re-unification in heaven with our beloved ones. The Buddhists are not supposed to mourn their dead because death is only a change in *kharmic* substance. The Hindus believe in *kharma* in the sense of retribution. Perhaps that is the most appropriate for us today, because of what our son set out to be and the course we allowed him to chart for himself. He received an eye for an eye and a tooth for a tooth. How does any of this help? How hollow are the comforts that religions extend to the bereaved! Why should suffering be good for us?'

The two men continued staring at her, aghast at her blasphemy and her breach of decorum. No one was permitted to speak thus, least of all a woman. She cared not a fig for propriety.

Suddenly, out of the night, out of her grief, certainly from the *imam*'s words, in a great flash of light, the numbness went, the answer was revealed to her. 'I know the truth at last,' she declared solemnly. 'It lies in the words and conduct of the Prophet.'

'What are they?' the *imam* demanded suspiciously.

'*Ihsan* is the converting of our Islamic actions into the spirit. So, an eye for an eye and a tooth for a tooth is not the way of Allah alone. It has to be what we mortals must also do to contain our sorrow. *That* is the example that the Prophet offered us in his own life, with fire, sword and the Holy Koran.' She fixed Abdul Raschid with a deadly gaze. 'Acceptance of our son's death as the will of Allah will not of itself allay our misery. Only when we act as Allah's instruments of vengeance will our pain be soothed. I shall not renounce the *chador*, nor all it signifies, but tomorrow I shall go to the palace to beg King Maya Dunne to allow

284

me to learn the use of weapons so I can fight beside his son to avenge mine. I shall wage my own *jihad*, holy war, against the *parangi*.'

'B . . . but you can't do that, woman!' Abdul Raschid stammered. 'A woman's place . . .' His hands pawed the air helplessly.

She noted reluctant admiration in the *imam*'s gaze. 'Many a woman has ridden to war, husband of mine,' she asserted, 'Rememeber Pooti of the Tharu desert, centuries ago? And Queen Bo-adi-shah of England? Allah must have a similar destiny for me. Why else did I become an expert at horseback riding, sword-play, the use of bow and arrow from the saddle, before I reached the age when I was compelled to take the *chador* and retire?'

'But whom would you ride with?' Abdul Raschid protested feebly. 'I mean, who would have you? And how about the veil?'

'Those are the major practical difficulties,' the *imam* put in. 'But the religious question is more important. How can you reconcile such actions with the teachings of the Prophet? Women are not permitted to play such roles.'

'Where does it forbid us?' she demanded hotly.

'It is implied. We would have to brand you an infidel if you gave up the veil and the robes.'

'I shall not give up robes or veil. What the Prophet commanded was that we women should present a modest mien in public, for our own protection, in lands where both our people and the foreigner were given to kidnapping, raping and murdering women. I shall retain my modest appearance even when I go to battle. Do not our Arabi warriors ride into battle wearing robes and burnous?'

'The veiled woman avenger,' the *imam* remarked drily, but with a hint of excitement in his voice. He stroked his grey beard reflectively. 'Why not? It might cast terror in the hearts of the enemy.'

Aisha noticed that her husband's cheeks had suddenly

begun to tremble. 'I fear for your safety and well-being, wife of mine,' he stated, then gestured inwards to his flabby stomach. 'Besides, I would not be able to ride with you.'

Feeling her eyes smart, Aisha fought back the tears. 'Your concern moves me, revered husband, but mental well-being is more important than physical security.' She paused, nodding slowly at him. 'I know I shall never be accepted individually as part of King Maya Dunne's forces, so I shall raise a troop of cavalry and equip it with our own funds. When it is fully trained, I expect that Prince Raja Sinha will be glad to make it part of his cavalry regiment, for I am a Ghazni and fighting is in my blood. Who knows, I might even lead mixed squadrons of men and women some day.' Already, as determination melded with the spirit of her ancestors, some of the pain had eased.

'You may be killed first,' Abdul ventured, near tears.

'That, husband of mine, would be the will of Allah!'

The *imam* had the last word. 'Certainly if you are killed while fighting the infidel, you will immediately find yourself in paradise.

CHAPTER TWENTY

Saturday, 10 September 1530

The four months of sparring for the promised tribute had been most exasperating for Fernao. The greedy Viceroy had not only kept probing to discover the location of the Great King's legendary treasure, but had also poked his great hooked nose into any of Fernao's work in which he smelt a *cruzado* for himself. When it became evident that King Vidiye was determined to give the least in exchange for the greatest support from the Portuguese, the Viceroy even made an unexpected and quite improper inspection of the Jaya Treasury, which proved to have been stripped by King Vidiye, who had removed its contents elsewhere.

When he was summoned to a conference with the Viceroy on board his flagship on Saturday afternoon, Fernao sensed that Don Alfonso had reached the end of his patience.

Though the stateroom was spacious, the wind had dropped while the fierce afternoon sun had warmed the timbers and the pitch in the seams, so the heat was intense. Fernao held himself very erect on the bolted down bunk-sofa which the Viceroy indicated, so he might not stain the pale cushions with the sweat that was soaking through his burgundy silk doublet. Unlike the staterooms of the flagships to which Fernao was accustomed, this one was furnished with rich mahogany panelling, pale creamy silk, gold brocade trim and burgundy carpeting.

Don Alfonso paced the room, his hand clasped behind his back, hunched shoulders making him look more vulturine than ever. He paused before Fernao. A bead of sweat trickled down from the centre of his domed forehead and poised on the edge of his nose like a dew-drop. Would it fall on his chin or on the jewels studding the gold crucifix he was wearing around his neck? A momentous question! As if to defy speculation, the Viceroy drew a cambric kerchief from the ruffled lace at his sleeve and wiped his nose.

'King Vidiye has created an intolerable situation, General,' he expostulated. 'We executed the amendment to our former agreement and sent a copy to His Imperial Majesty in good faith. We are now made to look foolish, because the tribute King Vidiye continues to offer consists of baubles and trifles.'

'Unfortunately, King Vidiye had too much warning of our intentions,' Fernao commented.

'Yet he keeps pressing us for our Imperial Majesty's proclamation. He has increased that pressure by starting to discriminate against the Catholic converts in the kingdom. Just last week, he caused some of our smaller churches to be looted and burned. Yesterday, he went too far. He had the large church in the township of Mahara, which Father Juan oversees, pillaged and destroyed. The good friar visited us . . . ah . . . privately last night to lodge an official complaint. He demands, on behalf of Holy Church, that suitable action be taken against the Regent. What do you think we should do?'

'We can invade the kingdom and extract reprisals.'

A negative shake of the head made Fernao realize that the Viceroy desired to extract more than vengeance. 'Resorting to military action against the Jaya kingdom might open us up to attack from Sita Waka as well, in view of the new alliance. Your balance of power policy has left us balancing without power, General.'

Fernao flushed. 'What would you have had me do, Excellency?' he demanded, ignoring the immediate issue.

'Align yourself with the real winners and make them succeed in such a manner that they are dependent on you to maintain their success.' The dry voice sounded positively pedagogic. 'That is the real balancing of power.'

Fernao's gorge rose at the thought of backing King Maya Dunne. 'My policy so far has been based upon the exigencies of the situation from time to time,' he temporized.

'We must achieve our aims without resorting to military force. An immediate invasion of Jaya would give us neither the conversion of the boy king nor ... ahem ... the treasure, which King Vidiye controls and would spirit away from wherever he has it hidden.'

Fernao's mind eased, then went into quick reasoning. He had been thinking all along about the treasure of a kingdom when it was the individual that mattered in this case. King Vidiye controlled the treasure! Like the sun flashing out from behind a black cloud, inspiration suddenly dawned on Fernao. 'I have the perfect solution!' he exclaimed.

Sunday, 11 September 1539

He had selected the seven men with care. An obvious choice was the coolest, most resolute man in the fort. If the *fidalgo* Captain Diogo de Mello knew the meaning of the word fear, he never disclosed it. He was a swarthy, slim-hipped man of thirty, with wide shoulders and a triangular face made dashing by a thin, black moustache and pointed beard. His most engaging feature, however, was the look of dare-devil humour in piercing blue eyes.

Apart from Captain de Mello, there was the musketeer, Sergeant Costa, chief of Fernao's personal bodyguard, Aires, Fernao's faithful orderly, and four *degredados* known for their courage and toughness. All of them were lean, tall men, but none of them of such giant size as would attract special attention.

It was Sunday, but the court of the Great King, being officially Buddhist, was carrying out its regular schedule.

As was usual between 6 and 7:30 A.M., the Regent would be present in the small audience chamber, receiving the reports of his ministers and financial advisers.

They rode to Jaya before dawn, at an easy canter. Captain de Mello and Sergeant Costa bore muskets, Fernao and the other five men only carried swords at the side. The group seemed a reasonable escort for their general, especially as Aires was leading a spare mount, a noble Spanish grey with magnificent accoutrements, supposedly a gift for King Vidiye from the Viceroy.

It was just getting light when smiling guards, well accustomed to the frequent visits of the Portuguese general to the Jaya palace, allowed them free entry to the city. The same happened at the capital gates. It must have been almost 6 A.M. when they drew rein in the paved courtyard and Fernao waved aside the grooms who rushed up to take their horses. He dismounted, tossed his reins to Aires, who had ridden up alongside him. Captain de Mello and Sergeant Costa, having dismounted, also tossed their reins to the men riding beside them. The three men formed a line, Fernao in the centre, Captain de Mello, bearing his musket, on the right, the sergeant, similarly armed, on the left. Ignoring the surprised stares of the guards and attendants and the curious looks of the spectators, they strode up the steps to the audience hall and passed into its cool shade. Nobles, courtiers and suppliants were already beginning to fill the hall, well ahead of the 7:30 to 9 A.M. session when the public had access to the ruler. The tapers had not yet been extinguished. Gold ornaments and jewels gleamed and sparkled in their light.

A burly, clean-shaven guard captain, followed by two giant guards, all with drawn swords, rushed up and stood firmly in the aisle. They looked resolute, suspicious. Fernao felt his heart begin to pound. So near to their goal and suddenly it seemed as far away as moonlight. How to meet this unexpected obstacle?

The *fidalgo* gave the answer. 'Don't stop now for anything, General,' he urged under his breath. Fernao, smiling at the guard captain, nodded condescendingly. All eyes were suddenly focused on the event, as an undercurrent of drama swept through the hall. Though the Sinhala were only fifty feet or so away, the intervening space seemed like an infinity to Fernao.

They marched steadily on, with set purpose, as if by royal consent. Twenty paces more to go . . . The Sinhala stood firm . . . Fifteen paces more. Fernao smiled, and nodded again, imperiously this time . . . Ten paces more. The first doubt flickered across the guard captain's eyes . . . Five paces . . . Natural courtesy more than conviction made the captain smile, bow and stand aside. The giant guards followed suit. Fernao quietly released his breath, imagining Captain de Mello's look of dare-devil glee.

They waved aside flustered attendants, opened the door of the audience chamber and entered it, one behind the other, Fernao leading. Only the towering Regent seated at the desk and the portly Lord Tammitta standing at his right, showing him some documents, were in the room. Lord Tammitta's droning voice stopped dead in mid-sentence.

The two men looked up simultaneously. King Vidiye straightened, his large, staring eyes flashing in anger. As planned, Sergeant Costa closed the door and stood before it. Fernao halted in front of the desk, Captain de Mello at his right and slightly to the rear. Both men removed tinder from their doublets.

'How dare you intrude upon us unannounced?' King Vidiye's deep voice made him sound like an enraged bull. He was speaking Portuguese, which he had pretended not to know. His large, staring eyes rolled towards the muskets.

'I dare anything in the name of His Imperial Majesty Dom João III of Portugal,' Fernao responded calmly. 'King

Vidiye, you are accused of crimes against the Holy Church of Lanka, Rome and Portugal and I am here to demand that you accompany me to your place of trial.'

A gasp escaped Lord Tammitta. For a moment, King Vidiye stared uncomprehendingly at Fernao, then his eyes blazed with fury. 'You are out of your mind, General,' he bellowed. 'This is *our* palace. It is alive with *our* guards. Make an end of this foolishness and be gone before we take you seriously and have you arrested and cut to pieces.'

'On the contrary, Regent, I am here, in the name of my Imperial Sovereign, to place *you* under arrest!' Captain de Mello declared firmly.

King Vidiye's massive jaw tightened. In a swift gesture, he pushed away from the desk, his chair grating on the floor of mountain crystal. He reached for his great sword. Swift as a panther, Captain de Mello sprang around the table. Tinder ready, he levelled his musket within inches of the Regent's head. His smile was a white streak between black moustache and beard. 'You draw that sword and I'll blow your brains out,' he warned, his voice so pleasant and easy-going, it carried total menace.

Sunday, 11 September 1530

The *anjanam*, light foreteller, lived in a cave in the High Forest mountain above the Kandy palace. It required early dawn for her to read the past, present and future in the light of a single taper. Queen Anula had visited her before, slipping out of the palace through a secret underground passage, known only to the reigning kings and queens because it was the escape route in case the palace was ever taken by an enemy. It emerged into the forest through a crevice in a rock outcrop, cleverly hidden by vines, so that truant children might not discover it. Since that part of the High Forest was a royal preserve, however, only the foolhardy would venture into it, and even the boldest of these would have been deterred by the story that the area was haunted. Those queens of the past who had lovers knew that the *avatar*, ghost, lights seen glimmering through the dense foliage on occasion at night were the flares of their lovers.

Queen Anula had begun using the secret passageway, which had been shown to her by her husband, King Kumara, years earlier, to make periodic visits to Kusuma, the light foreteller, when her marriage and her goals seemed to be falling apart. The queen was a resolute woman, given to forging her own destiny, but it did no harm to receive some guidance from the powers of light and darkness, especially since her husband had just departed with his army to invade Jaya.

As they emerged from the tunnel into the dense jungle, Nona, her aged attendant, held her flare higher. 'The *avathara devinnanse*, ghost queen, cometh,' she muttered. Servants had a habit of trying to be too familiar when one condescended to share some part of one's private life with them, the queen decided, but she curbed the desire to turn round and slap the woman.

They walked beneath the dense branches, dripping with dew, along a barely perceptible pathway covered with dead leaves. The stench of rotting animal carcass smote them as they entered the better defined lane leading to Kusuma's cave. The city, far below now, still showed an occasional yellow glow through dark branches and grey boles.

They were expected, so a pale light shone at the mouth of the cave. 'One would have to be mad to live here alone,' Nona muttered to herself.

'Kusuma *is* mad,' Queen Anula retorted calmly. 'Else she could not ply her trade.' And, she thought to herself, only those who are mad with desire or passion, grief or fear, uncertainty or hatred, would come to her.

A lean, cadaverous man, with long white hair tied in a knot at the nape of his neck, stood framed at the entrance

293

to the cave, fastening the top button of a black tunic. He placed his palms together in greeting. Nona's flare revealed a gaunt, clean-shaven face, the cheek-bones prominent, the eyes sunken, almost like a death's head. 'Welcome ladies,' he greeted them. He had never questioned the identity of his daughter's clients. 'Kusuma is full of the spirit today.' He held out a horny palm, on which Nona placed three silver coins. 'Ah! This will surely please the god and cause him to reveal the truth.' His dry cackle ending in a hacking cough. He stood aside and gestured towards the cave's interior.

'Wait outside!' Queen Anula directed her attendant.

In the light of a single hanging oil lamp, the cave looked about twenty feet long and ten feet wide. Its high roof could not disguise the musty smell of unwashed linen and the high odour of dry fish, beneath the acrid scent of incense. Joss-sticks glowed on a shelf containing flower offerings to a crude painting of Hanuma, the monkey god of Hindu legend, which adorned the far wall. The furniture consisted of a trestle bed, on which Kusuma was alleged to cohabit with her father, a rough table and two settles. On the table was an unlighted taper on a small brass stand, a circular shade of bright metal behind it. Clay cooking pots and platters were stacked on the floor beside the entrance. A ginger cat mewed, stalked lazily up and began inspecting the queen's bare ankles with a cold, inquisitive nose.

Kusuma emerged from the rear, a thin, almost emaciated figure, with neither breasts nor visible shape, draped in white skirt and jacket. Her face was a replica of her father's, except that it had smaller, more feminine bones. The black eyes were not sunken, but had a faraway look in them, as if she had taken some kind of drug. She greeted the queen with the palms together greeting, then silently indicated the settle at the side of the table. She moved to the door and let down a curtain of some kind of hide, totally obscuring the outside world. She walked back to the table, struck tinder and lit the white taper. She turned, made for the hanging lamp and blew it out, the hiss of her breath, followed by the sizzle of the extinguished wick, a tiny death rattle.

For a few moments, the cave seemed to be in total, overpowering darkness, the feeble taper-light accentuating it. Queen Anula heard the rustle of Kusuma's garment. The woman's form was a shadow as she sat down opposite the taper. She smelled of unwashed body and unaired clothes.

As the queen's eyes became accustomed to the taper-light, Kusuma began to chant to the god Hanuma, pleading with him to appear in the flame and reveal the future. In the narrow confines of the cave, her voice was so strident and piercing it must surely reach her god. She kept staring at the centre of the flame as if she were a hare transfixed by a cobra.

Long minutes elapsed. The taper suddenly began to smoke, emitting a strange, but pleasant odour, soothing to the mind. The queen gazed at the woman's gaunt face, now gleaming with sweat, the large eyes wide. Suddenly the pupils seemed to dilate.

Kusuma broke off in the middle of her chant. 'Oh! Thou hast appeared before me at last?' Her voice had grown softer, taken on a dream-like quality, seeming to come from the roof of the cave rather than from within her. 'In the blue flame of this taper, I see thee swinging from the branch of a tall tree. I offer thee homage, all powerful god Hanuma, who prevailed over the demon Ra-vanna who abducted the lady Sita, wife of the god Ra-ma. Behold our offerings to thee upon thy shrine, the three kinds of flowers, the heady incense. Tomorrow thou shalt also have an offering of fruit, the ripe banana thou dost love so well, if thou wilt reveal the future of this *one* who sits beside me.'

The sudden silence was almost a shock, the faint mew of the cat a witness to it.

'The monkey god beckons,' Kusuma whispered. 'Ask your question.'

'My husband goes to battle. Will he win?'

'The god nods. There will be victory.'

Queen Anula heard the hiss of her own indrawn breath. 'Will he return to me?' She held that breath for the answer.

'The god nods. There will be a return.' Kusuma suddenly stiffened. 'But wait. The god points upwards. He bids me to look. What is this?' The woman shuddered. 'Ah . . . h . . . h! A pair of eyes in the distance. They come closer and closer. Large, black staring eyes, rolling in the large black countenance of a fiend with gangling frame and long arms. O god Hanuma, I am afraid of this devil.'

The queen tensed, leaned forward, watchful, expectant.

Kusuma stiffened, drew a harsh, deep breath. 'This is no devil but a man. Hah! A crown appears above him.' She released her breath sharply, like a pierced drum, slumped forward on the table. The taper flame was suddenly extinguished.

In the stifling darkness, Queen Anula smiled dreamily.

CHAPTER TWENTY-ONE

Sunday, 11 September 1530

King Kumara eased himself in the saddle, stared down the highway, his eyes attempting to pierce the black shadow of the city gates three hundred yards away. The capital city of the Dhamba Deniya sub-kingdom, known as Kuru, lay about twenty-five miles north-west of Kandy along the highway. He noted with satisfaction that there was not a sign of sentries on its earthworks.

He turned his head at the quiet crunch of sand beneath a horse's hooves. General Dunu, commander-in-chief of his forces, rode up, a burly figure carved into his black horse. 'All commanders report their men in readiness, Sire,' he stated. 'General Ratwatte too should be in position by now.'

'Good,' King Kumara responded quietly. 'We still have about half an hour to go.' He looked towards the city again. 'Do you know how the Dhamba clan came by its name, General?'

'I have always assumed that it is from the place known as Dhamba Deniya, the parkland of the Dhamba clan, which is nearby.'

'No. The clan was not originally from here, and at the time its ancestors became the Great Kings of Lanka this area was merely called the Deniya. It was after they ruled Anu, later Polon, centuries ago, that the family took to itself the title Dharma, or Dhamma, meaning righteous. The name stuck, so when they created a new capital south-west of Polon, they called it Dhamba Ulla and when that capital was in danger from the Cholas, they moved south-west again, to the Deniya, which they renamed Dhamba Deniya.'

'You are a fountain of knowledge, Sire.'

'We are all compelled to study many irrelevant facts as children. It seems to me that teachers are a special breed of witchdoctors who have to assemble every possible bit of hocus-pocus to supplement their ignorance, so they can force it into the minds of the only breed more ignorant than they, children. The particular irrelevancy which we have just imparted to you was, however, confirmed by the present King Vikrama's grandmother, when we visited the palace years ago. The old matriarch's dead now.' His mouth tightened. 'We hope her grandson will prove compliant and spare us the need to have him join her!'

'With due deference, Sire, King Vikrama is better known for his piety than his valour, which is why he elected to remain in the palace at a time when his entire army is in the Anu area on manoeuvres. Your timing of this move was a stroke of genius.'

'We thank you. King Vikrama will undoubtedly have sent frantic messages to his army to return the moment he learned that we were on the move from Kandy, but it will arrive too late. As for your confidence in King Vikrama's piety, always remember that the truly pious can be the most dangerous of all opponents. Piety is a pose, and like all people who pose, the pious end up ignorant of who they really are. This makes them develop an almost maniacal addition to martyrdom. We do not wish King Vikrama to end his ancient dynasty. We need his support before we are joined by our Queen Anula's Kiri Vella army.'

The general laughed shortly, then grew serious. 'What guarantee do you have that the Kiri Vella army will join us, Sire?'

'We shall know soon enough, after Lord Unan delivers my message to the queen. Realistically, however, the Kiri Vella clan has no option unless it desires to face opponents on two flanks, Jaya and ourselves, and as the new rulers of Dhamba we would be the more formidable foe. They will support us, not out of love for our queen but from the desire for self-preservation that has governed their policies for generations. The queen's request would merely give them an opportunity to save face in their haste to align themselves with our victory.'

The general nodded slowly. 'Your planning of this move was so secretive. We all thought our objective was Jaya. We did not even guess at Dhamba when we practised this operation on the barrack square and the sand table. It was only when we encamped at the Polgaha junction last night that you ordered us to veer north to the Dhamba capital instead of continuing west to Jaya. I must confess that, as your commander-in-chief, I felt somewhat humiliated. Yet I do understand your reticence.'

'No offence was meant, General, but no other living soul knew our real plan, not even our queen, nor even those who infiltrated this city two days ago, who had their final orders by messenger only after we began our move today. Total secrecy was essential, which is why we positioned men just outside the city last night, to prevent anyone from entering through either of its gates and carrying the news once we had issued our orders.'

'Brilliant!' the general exclaimed.

'Brilliance means shine,' King Kumara retorted drily. 'Secrets are dark!' He paused, his eyes keen on the cleared ground on either side of the highway leading to the distant city gates. It was lightening faintly. He reflected a moment. 'We might as well tell you now to . . . er . . . spare you added humiliation, General.' He grinned. 'We have been in communication with the king of Jaffna, who will become our ally against Jaya and Sita Waka as soon as we demonstrate sufficient strength by capturing Dhamba.'

'The Cholas! Our allies? Surely you jest, Sire. The Cholas have been our hereditary foes for almost two thousand years.'

'Which is why they made this alliance, General, in order

to divide the Sinhala nation and survive. The Cholas are an entity that we cannot sweep away. So long as we give them equal status for their religion and language, their culture and their traditions, they will not mind token acknowledgement of the Great King of Lanka. Today, they will happily join a Catholic king against their gravest threat, King Maya Dunne, a rabid Sinhala Buddhist nationalist.'

He came alert at a 'Ho . . . oo . . . ooo . . .' sound from the direction of the capital. 'That's our signal!'

He drew his sword, began waving it aloft. When he sensed that he had the attention of the column of cavalry massed behind him, he silently pointed the gleaming blade in the direction of the capital. He dug urgent heels into the flanks of his bay. His charger took off like a gust of wind. Behind him, the column burst from the cover of the trees and hit the open highway, thundered towards the fort, with never a whoop or a war cry.

They were within a hundred yards of their objective before King Kumara saw that the gates were open. His plan had worked. He laughed aloud, the first human sound above the awesome thunder of the charge. He soon saw armed men lined up on either side of the entrance. These were his infiltrators who had jumped the guards at their sleepiest hour and open the gates. Galloping through the entrance, he saluted the men with his sword.

Fierce exultation seized him. His cavalry could now seize the city with hardly any opposition to the entire Kandyan army, complete with war elephants, battering rams, catapults, infantry and horsemen, baggage trains and camp followers. If the other band of infiltrators at the far northern gate had done their job equally well, General Ratwatte and his men would converge with him at the palace exactly as planned. The masterpiece of planning, co-ordination and execution appealed to his intellect.

Sunday, 11 September 1530

If King Vidiye felt any fear, he did not show it. Instead, he suddenly smiled, as if in response to Captain Diogo de Mello's seeming pleasantry. Fernao could not restrain a flash of admiration for the man's courage.

Ignoring the captain, King Vidiye directed his large, staring eyes at Fernao. 'It would appear that you give us no option but to accede to your dictates, General,' he said, his growly voice low. 'We wish we could give you some credit for originality, but as you know, one of your seafaring captains did precisely this to a sultan in the Middle Eastern regions – was it in Dui? – not many years ago. What do you now have in mind?'

He leaned back in his chair. Captain de Mello tautened, shoved the musket closer to his head.

'Oh, do put that thing away, Captain,' King Vidiye said calmly. 'You are nervous. Brandishing such a fearsome weapon, you might just cause it to go off.' His glance at Fernao became as ironic as the tone of his voice. 'Surely we can discuss your desires in the manner of civilized men.'

'Any discussion will take place in our fort, where His Excellency the Viceroy awaits you,' Fernao gritted, suddenly sweating with tension.

'You surely w-would not d-dare have a ruling m-monarch d-dragged before . . .' Lord Tammitta stuttered, before his voice quavered off into silence.

'These are desperate men who dare anything for wealth and personal ambition, Lord Chamberlain,' King Vidiye interrupted. A hint of scorn had entered his voice. 'Think of the Viceroy and the general as adventurers, *degredado* of the realm of morality in the guise of noblemen, with no roots in any country and no loyalty even to themselves.'

Captain de Mello tensed at the insult. Fernao shot him a warning glance.

'You are in a somewhat difficult situation,' King Vidiye stated calmly. 'So few of you and hundreds of our men in the palace. Will you carry the tinder for your muskets openly, like statues in a procession? You got safely in. Can you get safely out?'

Fernao regained full control of himself. 'We will leave this chamber together, Regent, you leading, Lord Tammitta at your left and to the rear, all very proper. I shall be immediately behind you with Captain de Mello on my right and Sergeant Costa bringing up the rear. It takes but seconds to place a tinder fuse. Even the hint of a false move and your heads will be blasted.'

Fernao's eyes swept to Lord Tammitta, who was sweating profusely, his plump cheeks quivering. 'You should take special care, Lord Tammitta. Do not attempt to play the hero. The life of the Regent is in your hands.' Knowing that the seconds of time it would take to fire the muskets could make or end the operation, he injected menace into his voice, but kept his words light. 'He might be very annoyed if his golden brains splattered his body. As he has just observed, Captain de Mello is very nervous. Besides, it would take less than two seconds for me to run your Regent through with my sword.'

'Do as the general says, Lord Chamberlain,' the king commanded.

'Certainly, Your M-majesty.'

'One final admonition, Lord Chamberlain,' Fernao warned. 'We have a mount awaiting the Regent in the courtyard, ostensibly a present for him, but we will need a horse for you. As soon as we are outside, you will summon a groom to bring you a horse. We shall chat pleasantly until it arrives, after which we will ride away in the friendliest fashion for the Regent to try out the new horse.'

'You have thought of everything, General,' King Vidiye volunteered. 'You are to be congratulated. But have you considered the consequences should any harm befall us after we get to your fort?'

'Certainly. But we are strong enough militarily at present, not only to cope with trouble but to administer it.' Fernao straightened his shoulders. 'All right now. On your feet, Regent. You will lead, smiling, relaxed, reassuring. Let's go!'

King Vidiye placed his hands on the desk and rose slowly to his feet. Lord Tammitta move deferentially aside. They all formed up as Fernao had directed.

'Open the door now, Sergeant,' Fernao directed.

Sergeant Costa reached for the door handle.

'Smile, Regent,' Fernao quietly bade the towering figure. 'Remember, your life for a smile!'

A cluster of excited voices, from a gaggle of flustered guards and attendants standing in the hallway, greeted them no sooner the door was opened, but everyone relaxed at seeing the smiling Regent, bowed low as he passed them.

Lord Tammitta cleared his throat. 'Our Regent has just received a present of a horse from the King Emperor of Portugal,' he announced, trying to sound grand, while they proceeded forward. 'He desires to try it out immediately.' He jerked his head at one of the attendants. 'Run ahead, Goda, and have the grooms bring me a horse, so I can accompany him. We shall not need an escort.'

They entered the hall. Fernao's nerve-ends began screaming silently. This was the final round. The audience hall was more crowded now. As the attention of those nearest the aisle became directed towards the group, the echoes of their voices were replaced by a hush that slowly rippled toward the front entrance.

'No false moves' Fernao hissed, a gracious smile on his face.

Each step was a manacled moment of time. Thank God for obeisance, Fernao thought, his eyes scanning the crowd for the slightest sign of suspicion.

As he strode along, Fernao became aware of his fear-sweat, the reeky odour of oil from Captain de Mello's musket, scents of sandalwood. Then he saw dazzling sunlight at the far end of the hall, a bright blue sky relieved by a single fleecy white cloud, above a contour line of dense green branches. Light at the end of a tortuous tunnel.

His attention was caught by vibrations from a tall, brown-skinned nobleman, with regular features and bright eyes. Fernao locked into the man's imperious gaze. His condescending nod was of no avail. The nobleman's lean body tightened, preparatory to stepping forward. The Regent stopped dead in his tracks.

Sunday, 11 September 1530

Early the same morning, in the king's audience chamber of the Sita Waka palace, Aisha Raschid and her husband sat facing King Maya Dunne and Prince Raja Sinha, awaiting the royal response to Aisha's plea. The king had readily granted the Raschids' request for a private audience. Though it was Aisha's first visit to the palace, she had barely noticed its splendour, her sole concern being the task in hand. Her request had been met with stunned silence. For once she was grateful for the black *chador* which hid her anxious look.

King Maya Dunne glanced across at the prince, his younger double. Aisha recalled the day, centuries ago, when she had first encountered them together in the governor's mansion on the Mutu Vella hill. Life had been uncomplicated till that fateful day the Portuguese fleet arrived. Ali, her beloved Ali, had been alive then. Her throat cracked into raw edges at the recollection and tears gushed to her eyes.

In that instant, King Maya Dunne's eyes sought hers above her veil with such a penetrating glance that she felt he could see right through her. The tension in the room built up. When he finally spoke, it was quietly, but thunder seemed to be rumbling in a dark sky. 'We too have lost loved ones, but without the comfort of vengeance, which Lord Buddha's teaching forbids,' he declared, his brilliant eyes unwavering on her. 'We understand your request fully, madam, because it springs from your creed, an eye for an eye and a tooth for a tooth. Yet that philosophy is totally contrary to all our Buddhist beliefs.' A smile touched the corners of the firm mouth. 'Then again, we are reminded of the Hindu doctrine of *dharma*, the duty of one's station. What is the duty of our station to you, our subject? It makes us recall a saying of Jesus Christ, when he was criticized for picking and eating corn on the holy day of the week, "The sabbath was made for man, not man for the sabbath." Would we be right to force our sabbath on you when you are hungry? According to Lord Buddha's Doctrine, each of us makes our own *kharma*. Though no one can be responsible for the *kharma* of others, you face us with the eternal dilemma of whether we should encourage or permit others to commit *akusala* – evil – *kharma*. In this instance we are inclined to the dictates of *ashima*, compassion. It is apparent that you must find the outlet to your grief or be consumed by it. We have therefore decided to welcome you to our cause. There will be tremendous difficulties ahead, not the least the reaction of our soldiers and indeed the entire country to a group of Muslim women warriors in a Sinhala army.' His gaze drifted to his son's face. 'Yet we are sure that Prince Raja Sinha will gladly accept into his cavalry regiment anyone who can help him fulfil his cherished ideals.

Sunday, 11 September 1530

Through the years, Queen Anula had retained most of her contacts in the Jaya palace, keeping them on her payroll as informers rather than spies. Fully believing that her husband was headed for Jaya, she had sent her message through a trusted servant to her best contact in Jaya, a courtier named Lord Dissa, with instructions that it should be passed to the right person. This would create the direct link-up necessary to further her plan. The nature of her information, its promptitude and the source, herself, would then produce the result she desired.

Sitting alone in her chamber after her morning meal, she wondered for the thousandth time what response she would receive from Jaya. It was a sleepy kind of dawn outside. The green leaves seemed to be at rest, quietly awaiting the first glimmer of sunlight. The hum of an early bee reached her through the open windows, followed by a sharp rasping of its wings as it tried to enter the room but encountered the yellow and red lacquered grilles. It must be a male bee, she thought idly, possibly attracted to me, the Queen Bee! The thought amused her.

She rose to her feet, walked to the window. The bee was departing, its buzzing now faint. She heard the click of the door opening, but remained staring in fascination at the dew sparkling like *diamanthi* on the fresh green grass.

'Lord Unan awaits Your Majesty's pleasure,' the voice of Nona her chief attendant broke into her brown study. 'He bears a message from your royal husband.'

What message could her husband have sent her while on his way to Jaya?

Lord Unan was an oval-faced, oval-bodied man of about thirty-five, with a pale complexion and small, shifty eyes that kept blinking. His dusty white tunic covered a slim upper body, but the red pantaloons were tight over pudgy thighs, making him look like a gourd. She had never liked or trusted the man.

'*Ayubowan*, my lord.' The queen's greeting was formal, unsmiling. 'We understand you have a letter for us?'

'Not a letter, my lady.' Lord Unan's voice was soft, almost effeminate. 'A message intended only for your ears.'

'Please be seated then.' She indicated a settle opposite her usual sofa, sat down, gestured to Nona to depart.

Lord Unan took the settle with a grunt of satisfaction. 'My lord commanded me to inform you of a change of plan,' he began.

A quick tremor of apprehension fibrillated through the queen, but she remained silent, a lift of delicate eyebrows asking her question.

'Instead of marching of Jaya, he is proceeding against Kurune Gala, the capital of the Dhamba sub-kingdom, at this very moment.'

She tried not to betray her consternation. 'But Dhamba kingdom had always been inviolate because it belongs to the ancient ruling family of Lanka,' she countered keeping her voice calm. 'Why the change in His Majesty's plans?'

Lord Unan grinned. 'The Dhamba kingdom is not inviolate any more.' He sounded smug. 'Fighting could be raging in that capital even at this moment. My lord requests that you send messengers to Kiri Vella to alert your clansmen, so they can rally to him at the place he has selected when he sends for them.'

'This is great news, Lord Unan,' she lied. 'We presume that you will personally convey back to His Majesty our assurance that we shall certainly alert our Kiri Vella supporters.'

Sunday, 11 September 1530

The dead bodies of guardsmen lying askew on the paved courtyard bore silent testimony to the success of his infiltrators. The blood pounding in his veins, King Kumara, followed by the centre line of his cavalry, trotted directly along the main street, which led to the palace on top of the *Kuruné Gala*, no small rock, while the other two lines of cavalry veered right and left along the roads that circled the city at the base of the rough earthwork ramparts that surrounded it.

To the right of the street, the long high rock was plainly visible in the distance. Curious city dwellers, roused by the clatter of hooves, tumbled out of their houses to stare open-mouthed at the intruders. As always, the bare-bodied men scratched hairy chests, a few of the tousle-haired children had fingers up their noses. Three basket women paused in their swaying strides, necks slightly twisted to stare from beneath the tiers of baskets they carried on their heads. A milkman hastily pulled his cart aside to give them passage. No one comprehended what had happened.

Within minutes, King Kumara reined in at the base of the great rock, isolating the palace and the Dhamba king from the city. Moments later, the shrill trumpeting of elephants reached King Kumara's ears. His main body too had entered the city.

He gazed up the sheer rock face at the palace buildings on top, their white walls and red-tiled roofs now lit up by silver-grey glimmers of dawn. I need not lay a hand on your inviolate person, King Vikrama, scion of the Dhamba dynasty, he thought, for I have your city and your kingdom.

Sunday, 11 September 1530

As he paused behind the Regent, Fernao's blood ran cold, his heart skipped a beat. This was it. King Vidiye would expose the plot and he and his men would be surrounded and massacred. He sensed Captain Diogo de Mello's hands tensing on the tinder and had to use all his own self-control not to reach for his sword.

'Ah, Lord Senaratna, we see you have come all the way from Alutgama, the new village,' King Vidiye observed pleasantly. 'We regret we shall have to keep you waiting, but we have been unexpectedly summoned to an affair of

308

state, the surprise presentation to us of a new Spanish stallion by His Excellency the Viceroy of Portugal. We have not been given much notice, but we do not wish to be an ally to rudeness by keeping foreign guests waiting. After all, we must defer to their strange customs, must we not? But we shall be back soon.' He half-turned towards Fernao, his glance positive, then resumed his stride.

Fernao's entire body was in a sweat. Bowing courteously to the tall lord, he followed King Vidiye.

Never had the morning sunlight felt so good. The waiting Portuguese guards brought forward the horses. Fernao could sense their relief, Aires' special glance of gladness. Theirs may have been the harder role, simply waiting.

Within minutes, Lord Tammitta's horse was brought up. Countless eyes swept over them from the audience hall above. A cool breeze swept the courtyard. They mounted their horses and broke into a slow trot.

King Vidiye's presence, literally under their guns, assured that the rest of the journey was uneventful. Proceeding at an easy canter, they reached the fort in two hours. Fernao breathed easily only when the great gates closed behind them. Soldiers exercising in the square barely gave the party a curious glance.

They dismounted at the tower door. Fernao thanked Captain de Mello and the men for their brave performance. He bowed to the king, gestured towards the office. Aires led Lord Tammitta away. The king stalked into the tower, loose-jointed, stooped at the entry-way and entered. Fernao followed while the rest of the raiders dispersed.

Nothing had changed in the office since Captain Oliveira and he first occupied it. Yet today a king of Lanka was there for the first time and as a prisoner. It was a historic occasion, demonstrating Portuguese brains, daring and power. Thrills of pride ran through Fernao.

The Viceroy rose from behind the desk to greet them. In

a rich blue velvet doublet, with white lace ruffs, the small room made him look like a dressed up vulture in a cage. He bowed to King Vidiye. 'Welcome to our humble office, Your Majesty,' he rasped. He sneezed violently, reached for the cambric hankerchief in his sleeve. 'I beg your pardon. Royalty is not to be sneezed at, but I am coming down with a cold.'

'We are neither concerned with nor amused by the state of your health, Viceroy,' King Vidiye rejoined. 'We demand to know the meaning of this ... this outrage committed by your lackey.' He half-turned, gesturing contemptuously towards Fernao.

The Viceroy stiffened. 'That is no lackey, sir, but a nobleman who also happens to be the General Officer Commanding His Imperial Majesty's troops in Lanka.' His voice was chill as frozen metal. 'As for outrage, it is you who have committed outrage against the Holy Church and State of Portugal and you are here to answer for it.' He relaxed. 'But why do we not sit down and discuss this like civilized people?' He indicated a settle opposite the desk.

'State your business, Viceroy, so we can return to our palace and our duties. We have neither the time nor the inclination for niceties in the present situation.' The Regent remained standing.

The Viceroy went white with anger. He was obviously not accustomed to being spoken to in this manner. He was a cruel man and Fernao hoped that the Regent would not push him too far. Curiously, for the first time, he began to feel the tiniest twinge of sympathy for King Vidiye.

'Since you seek direct dealing, let us give it to you,' the Viceroy stated. 'You have fooled us long enough as to the extent and whereabouts of the Great King's treasure. Our patience is at an end. You will be detained until you deliver all of it as tribute to our king.'

'What of the conversion of our son, King Dharma Pala? Would you insist on that too as a condition of our release?'

'No.'

'So it comes down to a commercial transaction, like buying dry fish in a market.'

'We would hardly call Your Majesty dry fish,' the Viceroy commented. 'On the contrary, let us say that the price of a king's freedom must of necessity be . . . er . . . a king's ransom!'

'Well put, How will we know that the treasure will reach your king?'

'You will not.'

The Viceroy's gaze had turned so merciless that Fernao knew that most of the treasure, perhaps all of it, would never reach Lisbon. Had he played into the Viceroy's hands with his daring plan? Had he, the *fidalgo* and their men risked their lives merely for the Viceroy's personal enrichment? His sense of fair play intruded. He should not pre-judge the man.

'If we direct you to the treasure, will we and Lord Tammitta be released?' King Vidiye inquired stiffly.

'You will have fulfilled the spirit of the terms of the treaty and we shall have no cause to hold you on that account, Regent.'

For a moment, the statement went over Fernao as it obviously had over King Vidiye, then suddenly he wondered at the Viceroy's choice of words. He pulled them back to his recollection, went sick at the hidden meaning.

'You have a contract, Viceroy.' Fernao heard King Vidiye's statement in a daze. 'We shall reveal the location of the treasure to you.'

CHAPTER TWENTY-TWO
Monday, 12 September 1530

My father, King Maya Dunne, and I were duelling with swords in the arena of the Sita Waka palace that afternoon. An expert and aggressive swordsman, he had kept me almost on the run, forcing me to use all my energy and skills to prevent him from getting under my guard. The pounding of urgent hooves in the distance caused an almost imperceptible shift of his fierce and total concentration, for a fraction of a second. I took advantage of that instant with the reflex of practice. Tightening my grip so my blade circled left, I went under his guard. My lunge was swift and smooth as the flight of a bird. I pulled back just when my point might have pierced his black leather breast plate. I was elated because I so seldom beat him. He acknowledged my victory by saluting me, hilt of upraised sword to lightly panting mouth. A smile of genuine pleasure broke through the sweat droplets on his face. He never minded losing to me.

Attendants rushed up with linen squares. Wiping my face, I followed my father to the entrance door of the arena. We stood on the open verandah, looked across fierce sunshine towards the gates.

The galloping hooves had diminished to the more sedate rhythm of a slow canter; the horseman had swerved from the grey cobbles of the central roadway and was crossing the dry green grass of the deserted barrack square. Dressed in red pantaloons and a white tunic, riding a black Scindhi charger, he was revealed in the pitiless afternoon sunlight as a bearded captain of the Jaya army. A messenger from Jaya in such an obvious hurry could only be the bearer of ill news. Indeed, the captain's dust-stained, wet uniform and his mount's foam-flecked mouth showed that he had ridden hard. As he slowed to a trot, the horse sneezed violently.

The captain was a lean, brown-skinned Sinhala of medium height, with regular features, black eyes and high forehead. He dismounted a few paces away, flung his reins over the neck of his horse and sank in obeisance.

My father acknowledged his greeting. 'You must have urgent news for us?'

'Indeed I do, Sire. I am Captain Asoka of King Vidiye's bodyguard. His queen, your daughter, directed me to seek your assistance. Her husband, King Vidiye, was arrested in the Jaya palace yesterday morning by a small group of Portuguese soldiers headed by General de Albergaria and Captain Diogo de Mello. He and the Lord Chamberlain, Tammitta Rala, were taken to the Colombo fort.' He bowed his head. 'I beg your forgiveness, Sire, for bringing you bad news.' He was referring to an old Sinhala custom which gives a king the right to execute the bearer of ill tidings.

We were both so thunderstruck that words failed us. My father was the first to recover. 'The news is the news and you are not to blame for it, Captain. Since you say this happened yesterday morning, your ride here in such a short time is a fine example of dedication. Come inside now and tell us the whole story.'

Captain Asoka walked stiffly behind us into the arena. He smelled of horse-sweat and wet leather. The king ordered refreshments, directed his aides to have the captain's mount watered, rubbed down, stabled and fed.

I listened with mounting fury as the captain unfolded his tale of how the Portuguese arrested the man who was now my brother-in-law. The truth had been discovered in the palace only after Lord Tammitta was permitted by the Viceroy to return in the afternoon while King Vidiye was still being held to ensure the good conduct of the Jaya army. Meanwhile, the Viceroy had appointed himself Lord Protector of the Great King and demanded the promised tribute.

'This is the most outrageous insult ever extended against the Sinhala nation,' King Maya Dunne asserted when the captain ended his story. 'Was there no sense of alarm when King Vidiye left so abruptly?'

'No, Sire. After all, he himself stated to Lord Senaratna that he was going to try out the magnificent Spanish horse, which the Viceroy had presented to him and which had already been brought to the palace courtyard.'

'But the king was away so long.'

'Who would dare to question an occasional oddity in a sovereign's behaviour?' Captain Asoka grinned wryly to rob his words of offence.

'Well put, Captain.' My father reflected a moment. 'We are powerless to intervene without risking King Vidiye's life. H'mm. Did Lord Tammitta bring back any word as to the Viceroy's intentions? Will King Vidiye be released as soon as he has paid the price in gold for his alleged misdeeds against the State of Portugal and the Catholic Church?'

'That was Lord Tammitta's impression.'

'Where is King Vidiye being held?'

'In the fort, Sire.'

'H'mm . . .' My father tapped his knee rapidly with a forefinger.

I was hard put to it not to demand that the joint armies of Jaya and Sita Waka should attack the greedy, arrogant *parangi* immediately.

'We must proceed with caution,' my father counselled. I knew he was directing a warning at me.

'Sire, these foreign invaders once violated our territory and burned down our capitol,' I burst out, finally unable to contain myself. 'Now they have violated the sacred person of a ruling regent, arresting him as if he were some common criminal.'

'What would you have us do, Prince? The Viceroy will not hesitate to kill King Vidiye at the first sign of violence on our side. Your sister seeks our help. There must already be hot-headed clamour for action in the Jaya palace. We must not add firewood to the blaze. We must first discover what the Viceroy wants for King Vidiye's safe return. Meanwhile, Captain Asoka must be tired. Why don't you tell one of our aides to organize a room for him?' He turned towards the captain. 'We shall have more questions for you, when you have eaten and had a few hours' sleep.' He nodded, smiling agreeably. 'Your effort was magnificent, Captain Asoka.'

I returned to find the king swaying back and forth on his settle as he was wont to do when working out a plan. He gestured towards my seat.

'Here is what we shall do,' he stated. He expressed his solutions briefly and succinctly. 'There is only one person who can carry out this mission successfully,' he concluded. 'You must leave immediately to meet your sister in Jaya.'

Monday, 12 September 1530

It was so unusual for Fernao to come home during the afternoon siesta hour on a weekday that Julietta did not need to look at his face to know something was wrong. She was resting in her upstairs bedroom when he arrived. He paced to the window like an angry panther, stood there gazing out through the afternoon sunlight at the warships in the distant harbour.

She walked up to him, laid a gentle hand on his shoulder. 'What's the matter, Fernao?'

He kept staring out, made no reply.

'Is it something I've done?' she inquired tremulous.

He swung round then, took her in his arms. 'Oh no, my

darling. How could you even imagine that? You are the only decent, noble person in my life.' He bent down and kissed her passionately. She felt her lips bruise, but clung to him regardless, knowing his need, sensing a kind of despair beneath his anger.

Presently he released her, looked into her eyes, shook his head. 'What would I do without you?'

'Don't, Fernao.' She guessed that his anger had to do with the Viceroy and yesterday's arrest of King Vidiye.

'You may be sure I won't.' He paused. 'Just holding you has made me feel clean already. Here, let's sit down and I'll tell you about it.' He made for their favourite chair beside the window and patted his lap. 'Right here.'

She sat down and felt the warmth of his body. He drew her head against his shoulder. She looked out at the burnt sky, completely cloudless above the familiar contoured border of green branches. The querulous grumble of a crow spiralled through the silence, a puppy started yapping in the servants' quarters. Unusually, a small band of monkeys loped on the top of the giant *etamba*, seed mango, tree which was covered by a green creeper, making it look like a hillock.

She turned her face towards Fernao, laid a finger on his cheek. 'What has made you so angry, my love?'

His eyes flashed ice. 'It's that vulture de Noronha,' he gritted. 'Despicable, vile, greedy bastard.'

'What has he done?'

'He was shown the real treasure early today by King Vidiye, who believed that he would be free once he paid the ransom. I'm not sure that it was the entire treasure, but it had been hidden in a private room of the Kalyani temple and is certainly a king's ransom. You remember I told you last night that I didn't like the reply the old vulture gave when the Regent demanded to know whether they were in agreement?'

Julietta could feel her stomach knotting in anticipation

of the news. 'He broke the king's understanding of the agreement, didn't he?'

'Oh God, if that were all. He had the treasure, consisting of gold and silver, jewellery, ornaments and precious gems, one a perfect blood ruby the size of a pigeon's egg, carried on board his flagship. I doubt that our King Emperor will see any of it.'

Out of the blue, Julietta decided what she must do. 'Was King Vidiye not released, then?' she inquired, without divulging her decision.

'He was. The Viceroy told him that, as the temporal obligation for having broken the treaty had been satisfied, he was released from arrest. His son, Dom Juan Dharma Pala, would be declared rightful Great King of Lanka under the divine protection of our King Emperor. But there was a little matter of King Vidiye's offences against Holy Church, for which he had to be rearrested. Oh the despicable, crafty bastard! This is what comes of appointing a commoner to a noble position. You cannot make a silken doublet out of flea-skin.'

Inside her, Julietta felt the sting of it. Somewhere deep within Fernao birth still counted. 'How dreadful!' she exclaimed politely.

'The worst is yet to come,' Fernao ground out savagely. 'He ordered King Vidiye consigned to a dungeon.'

'A dungeon?'

'Yes, a pitch dark, filthy dungeon, with stale air and rats for company.'

'But where's the dungeon, Fernao? There is no dungeon in the fort.' Then she remembered. 'Not the mine shaft, surely not the mine shaft? You would not send the worst of your *degredados* there for any crime. You would rather have them executed.'

'Exactly. That bastard, bastard, bastard. Oh Juli, you should have heard how smug, smooth and arrogant he

317

sounded. Is this what becomes of us when we have unlimited power?'

Hope clutched at Julietta's heart. Fernao had said 'us'. She knew that he, the wealthy factor and army general, also had unlimited power and that its exercise had made a lesser person of him. Would this example open his eyes to what he was making of himself?

'And now the Viceroy is determined to extend his power at all costs,' Fernao continued. 'We will march against Sita Waka at the end of the month. I have advised against it because the monsoon is imminent and our cannon, which alone give us superiority since we are heavily outnumbered in manpower, may get bogged down, but the man is mad with lust for wealth. I believe he wants to take Sita Waka only to lay his hands on King Maya Dunne's treasury as well.'

Monday, 12 September 1530

Aisha knew that the decision to include her in the Sita Waka army had been received with derision in some quarters. 'King Maya Dunne's *gānu-toku*, women's head-knocks,' some chortled behind the palms of their hands. 'He must be hard-up for real men.' But the king and Prince Raja Sinha obviously did not care and she herself certainly did not.

She had planned to raise a unit of sixty troopers, with herself as captain, and two lieutenants. Her choice of the junior lieutenant was a recently widowed woman named Sithy Amin. Sithy had lived in the Arab deserts as a child and had become such an expert horsewoman that she had even participated in some of her tribe's raids. Lieutenant Nanda, a grizzled Sinhala veteran, the father of four children, was the senior officer. Already six women with girlhood horseback riding experience, all of whom hated the Portuguese, had enlisted as troopers.

King Maya Dunne had placed one of his private parks on the outskirts of the city of Sita Waka at her disposal. She was there this afternoon with fifteen male troopers, recruited in the brief time since her plan was approved. These fifteen had been men enough to have no belief in male superiority. They had found the new concept intriguing, especially at Aisha's wage rates.

Aware of Prince Raja Sinha's rigorous requirements, Lieutenant Nanda insisted that all his pupils, as he called them, start from scratch as if they had never ridden a horse before. He first made them practice on the lunge, riding bareback, without stirrups or reins, hands locked together behind their backs. Sithy Amin had excelled because this was how she had ridden in the desert. Aisha too soon found herself in perfect motion with her black Arab.

'You have the natural grace of a born rider,' the lieutenant commented, when she finally stood with him in the shade of a tall tamarind tree which he had made their outdoor headquarters. 'Still, it's a good thing you ladies are Muslims and wear pantaloons beneath your black robes!'

'I'm glad you approve.' Aisha hesitated, then decided to be blunt. 'I have formulated a new theory I want to put into action immediately.'

'Let's not start with new theories,' Lieutenant Nanda retorted. 'You must learn to ride before you can gallop.'

'I can gallop as well as anybody. Remember I am not unfamiliar with the smell of horse-sweat.'

'Every groom knows the smell of horse-sweat, but not just anybody can be a cavalryman.' The lieutenant paused, looked at her firmly with piercing eyes. 'Being an expert horseman, or even having experience in raids, is not enough. You need patience, special skills, discipline and training. I cannot emphasize enough the training and discipline required for the charge, the thrusting lance, the

319

swordplay, the wheeling back, the withdrawal to decoy, the sudden flanking movement.'

He was talking to the descendant of Mahmud of Ghazni who had invented some of these cavalry tactics. 'That, sir, is part of my plan,' Aisha assured him quietly. 'Will you please do me the honour of listening to me for a few minutes?'

Lieutenant Nanda's glance became impatient. While she awaited his response, a shrilling mynah bird took off from an overhead branch. A tiny plop announced its droppings on the green grass. She turned at a hissing sound to find one of the Arab greys urinating on the earth.

The lieutenant grinned at her. 'See what one hears when one listens,' he observed drily.

Aisha flushed beneath her *chador*. She would have to teach these males that she was their equal or better if she was to survive in their world. She would learn anything she could from this man, then take command. Only brains and courage make a leader and men did not have a monopoly of those. Aloud she said, 'My plan is simple and could be an adjunct to barrack square training. I would call it battle drill. Today, the individual trooper receives orders from his immediate superior and carries them out without any knowledge of the final object of the battle. He is merely one of a pack executing a series of movements. He gives no thought as to how he, as an individual, can use his god-given brains to achieve that final object. You say, "Charge!" – he charges. You command him to withdraw and he withdraws. These are intelligent human beings on horseback, not chickens to cluck around a battlefield when they become lost. I say, let us give our men the entire battle picture, so if they become isolated they can use their initiative to assist with the final victory. After you have finished giving our troop all the training necessary to make them good cavalrymen, I want you to teach them field tactics on the barrack square.'

'And what are those, madam?' He was all good-natured tolerance now, humouring her.

'What more can tactics be than a frontal attack, or attacks on either or both flanks, or the rear, or a combination? Let us divide our sixty troopers into five sections, so they can practice making each type of attack during their training.'

Lieutenant Nanda's dark eyes widened as he thought it out. 'You mean, practice all those tactics in separate sections on the barrack square, so if the squadron becomes detached each man will know how to achieve the final object as an individual?'

'Why not?'

'Why not, indeed.' His eyes were gleaming now. 'It's a splendid idea. We teach our section leaders and troopers not only to be good cavalrymen, but also tacticians.' He smacked his pantaloons with his riding whip. 'We shall recommend this to Prince Raja Sinha for all his cavalry regiments.'

Aisha's eyes flashed, her temper rising at the hint of condescension. 'More importantly, sir, I hope you find the idea to be worthy of the mere woman who shall lead this troop into battle.'

CHAPTER TWENTY-THREE
Monday, 12 September 1530

Conveniently located near the base of the *Kuruné Gala*, a large house belonging to one of the Dhamba nobles had been commandeered for King Kumara's use the previous day, soon after the take over of the capital, which had been achieved remarkably peacefully. The bulk of the Kandyan army was encamped on the open plain to the north of the city, conveniently disposed to give battle to the Dhamba army when it returned.

It was now late evening, almost thirty-six hours after the city was taken, and there was still no word from King Vikrama.

'The worst part of a military campaign is its discomfort,' King Kumara observed to the stocky General Dunu who was seated very erect on a settee opposite him. He deliberately stretched out full length on the pale green cushions of his satinwood couch, stuck one of the cushions behind his head and surveyed the room. It had red-brick paved floors covered with thick white handwoven rugs of local weave, creamy satinwood furniture and bright-coloured tapestries adorning the walls. His eyes drifted to the two great ivory elephant tusks set in carved ebony stands on either side of the entrance door, forming a kind of archway. When would King Vikrama come through them?

Meanwhile, the residence was not a palace, but he was living in reasonable style. His ancient chief attendant had even obtained his favourite sandalwood incense for the burners and its scent was being wafted to him by the breeze created by a slow-moving punkah.

'War is hell, General,' he bared white teeth, 'luxury is sheer hell!' he added. He heaved a sigh, half pretence, half contentment, crossed one ankle over the other and inspected his slim legs in their tight, dark-blue pantaloons. 'Now if only the food and palm wine remain as hellish as the delectable meal we had last night!'

The burly general grinned, revealing white teeth beneath his natty moustache. 'I suppose King Vikrama must be suffering too in the hellish luxury of his palace, Sire. Else, why has he not come out to greet his conquerors? I must confess to feeling some sympathy for him.'

'Always keep your sympathy to yourself, General. Never display it to its source, for sympathy only encourages the poor afflicted to wallow in their affliction as if it were some kind of riches. And never forget that compassion extended to others is the last refuge of the scoundrel we call conscience.'

'Do you have neither sympathy nor conscience then, Sire?' the general inquired incredulously.

The king knew General Dunu to be a simple soldier and a typical Kandyan aristocrat. 'Sympathy is but the poor relation of compassion,' he responded airily. 'It is at best a product of religious philosophies, calculated to cause the "haves" to lose or so to diminish enjoyment of their possessions that they will disgorge some or all of them to the "have nots". At worst, it is a form of condescension. As for conscience . . . ah now, that is a product of the Christian ethic, for Buddhists extend compassion without conscience which the Christian Church alone uses to impose moral blackmail on the human soul. All these religions have complicated existence, which is essentially simple if one lives it like the birds of the air or the lilies of the field, into the intricacy of a chimpanzee clothed in pink warp and purple weft, mostly warped.'

The general gaped at him, slack-jawed in partial comprehension. King Kumara was about to launch into a witty attack against conventional concepts like responsibility and stability as the means leaders use to enslave subjects, when

323

he suddenly realized that he needed these very virtues from his general! He had best not condemn them to such a person. Besides, it was useless trying to engage this simple-minded soldier in the kind of cynical dialogue in which he loved to indulge. Regardless of the deterioration in their relations, his wife, Queen Anula, was the best foil for such bouts of the intellect.

The silence was interrupted by a hesitant knocking on the door. 'That must be dinner,' King Kumara stated. 'About time, for we are starving.'

'Enter!' the general called out.

The white-haired chief attendant opened the door, made obeisance. 'Pray forgive the intrusion, Sire, but a messenger who claims to bring urgent news for you from Jaya has arrived under escort of one of the captains of the gate-guard. He says his name is Prema and that you will grant him immediate audience.'

'From Jaya?' the king demanded. 'How did he know so soon that we are in Kuru?'

'He was on his way to our capital, Sire, on a fast horse, he says, but had news of your royal presence here when he reached Polgaha.'

'It would appear that we cannot find a secret hiding place anywhere, not even in a flea's rump. Bid him enter.'

The nondescript-looking man of small stature who hurried in was clad in drab tunic and pantaloons, covered with dust from his ride. He made obeisance while the attendant backed out of the room and closed the door.

King Kumara swung his feet off the couch and assumed a sitting position. 'You sought immediate audience!' he exclaimed. 'What are your credentials?'

Prema glanced at the general, then said quietly, 'The dumb can speak.'

King Kumara became alert. The password was one used by his master spy in Jaya, a man whose voice box had been severed by a nobleman as punishment for refusing to give his wife to the lord. 'Tell us your news,' the king bade the visitor.

'My news is terrible, Sire. King Vidiye was arrested in his audience chamber in the Jaya palace early yesterday morning by a small group of *parangi* armed with muskets, led by their commander, General de Albergaria and a Captain Diogo de Mello.'

King Kumara felt a spurt of elation. Could it be that . . .? No, that was not possible. He noticed that General Dunu was staring at him, pale under his tan. 'Where is King Vidiye now?'

'In the Colombo fort, Sire.'

'All right, tell us all you know.'

King Kumara listened while Prema told his story, only asking questions when it was necessary to bring out details. By the time the man finished, King Kumara had the entire picture. He was aware of Viceroy Don Alfonso de Noronha's reputation for greed. King Vidiye would be released upon paying the ransom . . . or would he be? If he, King Kumara, could ensure that King Vidiye was kept confined, the weakened kingdom of Jaya would be easier prey for him. If he could, in addition, direct the Portuguese against King Maya Dunne, the Great King's crown would be within his grasp. As a Catholic, he had the greatest claim on the Portuguese. Now was the time to lay that claim. In a trice, he knew how this could be achieved.

The faint sound of trumpets pierced his reflections. He cocked an ear in its direction. 'Seems to be coming from the top of the rock,' he remarked.

'I believe it is from the palace grounds, Sire,' General Dunu replied. 'The Dhamba king's paean, as I recall.'

King Kumara straightened in his seat. 'Of course. King Vikrama must be leaving the palace to visit us.' he chuckled, waved Prema away. 'You may retire now,' he directed the man. 'We thank you for bringing us the news. Our *kollu*, servant boy, will look after you. Be on call to us, however, for further questioning.' He rose to his feet, the general with him. 'Conduct the king here, present him and leave us alone,' he directed the general.

He took up his position at the far side of the room facing the entrance door and waited. It would take all of twenty minutes for King Vikrama to proceed down the rock slope, curve around its base and reach the mansion. The palms of his hands crossed behind his back, balancing on the balls of his feet, King Kumara filled those minutes thinking and planning, planning and thinking, until he finally knew how he should proceed.

The sound of trumpets, now underlaid by drumming, had grown louder and louder until it paused at the gates in a final deafening medley of sound.

Most kings are ostentatious to the point of vulgarity, King Kumara decided. They are like the insane, who need devil-dancing, chanting and drumming to drive away their malady, which in the case of kings is terror at being considered ordinary!

Announced by General Dunu, King Vikrama paused at the entrance to the room. He was as King Kumara remembered him from a visit to Kuru several years earlier. A tall man of spare build and austere countenance, his black eyes were strangely gentle. He was simply dressed in a white tunic and pantaloons of homespun linen. He wore no ornaments. His head was completely shaven and shone with oil in the yellow taper light.

'*Ayubowan*, cousin.' King Vikrama's greeting, even before the door closed behind the attendant, neatly pre-empted King Kumara. The senior king always spoke first. He crossed the room with a slow, dignified stride.

The first round to you, King Kumara thought. I must win the next. He stood his ground, waiting for his visitor to come up to him. The tiniest hint of amusement in King Vikrama's black eyes conceded the second round.

King Vikrama stopped, opened his arms to his host. 'Ah,

we are so happy to see you here,' he stated. 'Such an unexpected pleasure, but nonetheless most welcome.'

For once in his life, King Kumara was nonplussed and at a loss to know how to proceed. Fleetingly acknowledging the value of centuries of kingship in the man's blood, bones and training, he quickly decided to fence according to the rules of this undoubted expert. He stepped forward and embraced his kinsman far removed. The king smelled of incense.

'Such a grief not to have been able to give you more notice, cousin,' King Kumara declared, releasing himself from the embrace. 'How charming of you to visit us in our humble abode. Pray be seated.' He indicated the couch which he had just vacated.

They stood side by side, then sat down together on the same couch, as if playing some kind of game, which indeed they were. You will learn that you are not visiting the royal kennels, you son of a bitch, King Kumara thought, moved by a sudden flaring of impatience. He would rather have stormed the palace and seized it without all this nonsensical waste of time. 'Would you like some refreshments?' he inquired.

'No, thank you. We have already dined.'

It reminded King Kumara that he had not. He heard his stomach growl grr . . . in complaint and wished he could indeed cut this whole thing short. 'A *sara bulath vita* perhaps, then?' He gestured towards the green betel leaves, brown shredded areca nut, white *chunam*, dried *adathoda* leaves and spices on the inevitable gold salver on a low satinwood table beside the couch.

King Vikrama raised a gentle hand in refusal. 'No thank you, cousin. Can't stand the stuff. It reddens the mouth and blackens the teeth, Good enough for peasants, not for royalty, don't you agree?'

Damn you, King Kumara thought. You have to be cut down to size. Aloud, he said, 'It is the privilege of royalty to behave as Great Kings, in their flatulence . . . or . . . er peasants in their manners.'

Again the appreciative gleam flickered in King Vikrama's eyes. 'How true. It reminds us of Lord Buddha's maxim, "Not by birth is a Brahman made".' he paused, mock apologetic. 'But of course you would not wish to be reminded of our national religion, now that you are a Catholic. So perhaps we should quote your scriptures to you. "Consider the lilies of the field. They toil not, neither do they spin. Yet Solomon in all his glory was not arrayed as one of these."' he paused long enough to see that his barb had struck, then proceeded quickly to prevent a response. 'Did you know that the Jewish King Solomon actually sent to our Lanka for precious gems to adorn his Queen of Shaybah?'

'So the peasants claim,' King Kumara retorted, his smile above the thrust pleasant. 'But we kings are not impressed by the brambles of history. We *make* history.'

'Talking of peasants, how did your Kandyan kingdom manage to survive the floods last year?'

'Through resourcefulness and the gathering of our crops in anticipation of the rains.'

'We heard that an earthslip in the high hill country had caused over a hundred deaths.'

'Probably peasant gossip that does not reach our palace. How did your kingdom survive the drought this year?'

'Through wisdom and the united efforts of all the people.'

'Strange, how fast unity can dry up in the dry zone around Anu and give way to uprisings,' King Kumara replied brutally. Now that they had entered on the battle of words, at which he could more than match his fellow monarch, he suddenly tired of it. 'Enough of this, cousin,' he declared, his tone abrupt. 'We have paid our respects to the rules of decorum. Now let us proceed to business.'

The rude words were met by the lift of what could have

been a single eyebrow if King Vikrama had eyebrows. 'Certainly, cousin.' His smile was slightly scornful. 'After all, you are the host!'

King Kumara held back the expletive that rose to his lips only with a tremendous effort. 'We are glad you recognize that fact in what was once your territory,' he declared. 'We are now the victors and shall dictate our terms.'

'Oh, so that was your aim.' King Vikrama paused. 'Well, you need not have indulged in all this elaborate drama, including the assassination of the guards at our gates, if you had notified us of your plans. The bulk of our army is away in the Anu area putting down the uprising you mentioned. You could simply have sent us word of your desires and we would have given you control of the kingdom.'

'What?'

'Certainly. Ruling a minor kingdom like Dhamba becomes tiresome after a while, especially for someone who is more interested in Lord Buddha's Doctrine. We would gladly have let you share our game of ruling, or permitted you to play it alone.'

'Are ... you ... telling us that ... that your kingdom is available to anyone, just anyone who marches in?' Each word came out staccato, King Kumara's finger stabbing for emphasis.

'Not just anyone. Not just *any* peasant!'

'Anyone strong enough to take the kingdom by force?' King Kumara found himself compelled to ignore the thrust.

'No. Anyone strong enough to *hold* it.' King Vikrama half turned in his seat, gazed dreamily at the tapestries on the opposite wall. 'You see, cousin, there is never any security ruling a kingdom like Dhamba. You know our geographical situation. We have the Cholas of Jaffna to the north, Jaya to the west, Sita Waka to the south and you to the east. We keep on ruling only because we must fulfil our duties, pay our debts to history. All those ancestors, you know, holding their demanding palms towards us, an unending chain of beggars needing to have their dynasty perpetuated because they died like ordinary people and failed to achieve immortality! Our personal philosophy is simple. Let any king strong enough to hold power in the sub-kingdom take it over. Such a man may remove us and face the opposition of our princes, our noblemen and our people, as well as the threats from other kingdoms, all of which would demand a strong rule. If he is wise, however, he would rule through us, for what does he need from our kingdom after all? Wealth and power. What else is there? What drives such an adventurer? Ambition. A vaulting ambition that makes him leap for stars that turn out to be only glittering tinsel in his hot, sweaty grasp, before he falls to earth's ground again. As for us, we have shed all ambition, all desire for wealth. We sleep more comfortably on a wicker mat on our austere bed of planks than we would on a golden couch. We rule but to fulfil a pledge to our ancestors which was intrinsic to our birth!' He laughed shortly. 'People talk of *birthright*. Faugh! All of it, including selfish ambition, is birth *duty*. This knowledge has shaped our personal philosophy. We shall leave it to the more foolhardy of our dynasty who follow to overthrow an usurper, so the whole silly game can keep going on and on.' His black eyes focused back on his host, suddenly became magnetic.

This man has opened a whole new dimension to me, King Kumara thought. He has reduced his office, his position and his philosophy to the most simple terms. He will not allow himself to become a chimpanzee clothed in pink warp and purple weft. 'Why then have you sent your army to Anu to quell the uprisings?' he demanded, but the words were merely a defensive motion.

'We did not send our army out. We really have no army of our own. The princes and nobles of Dhamba decided that the uprisings, which were merely an expression of the needs of a drought-stricken people, could be easier quelled than their hunger pangs. Who are we to hold back those who desire to exercise the influence of power rather than the power of influence?'

'You have no responsibility towards your starving people?'

'On the contrary, we had arranged food convoys for them from Jaffna and Batti. Our princes and noblemen desired to teach those people who dared to rebel and seize the royal granaries, thereby depriving others in the area of food that would have been distributed to all, the lesson of their lives through death!'

Thoughts were tumbling around in King Kumara's mind, but only one quickly surfaced. 'Will you then acknowledge our overlordship over the kingdom of Dhamba?'

'Certainly.'

'Will you place your army at our disposal?'

'We told you we have no army.'

'Will you swear eternal allegiance to us?'

A smile touched the firm mouth. 'Eternal is a long time. Like our ancestors, we do not have the gift of immortality.' King Vikrama smiled broadly now. He glanced around the room. 'Really, cousin, you should maintain a life-style more in keeping with your rank and station. This house, worthy as it is for a nobleman, hardly befits the stature of a Great King, which you have now become. Please move to our palace immediately. After all, life is so transient, and change, unlike allegiance, is so ... uh ... eternal, that you should live your rank whenever you can, moment by moment.'

You superior bastard, King Kumara thought, I should run you through with my sword. Then he remembered the Yakka King Tikka who slew the Kalyani *bhikku* king, Sri-Rahula, with his sword two thousand years earlier. He made an immediate decision. 'We must accept a fallen king on his own terms,' he declared.

King Vikrama shook his head. His dark eyes were now full of knowledge. 'How can we be a fallen king when we never wanted a throne?' he inquired softly. 'But you, cousin, do you not realize that every man who leaps up must come down? Conquerors are like frogs. They leap higher and higher until they finally collapse or die. You thought you were on your way up when you seized the small kingdoms of Pera, Gampola and Hangura some years ago. In reality, you had taken the first steps towards your end. So welcome to our palace, O Great King. For a shining hour, you shall wear the royal donkey's head in the *nadagama*, village play, we call rulership.'

Monday, 12 September 1530

Julietta could not distinguish the features of the priest sitting in the darkened confessional enclosure of the Mutu Vella church that evening after Vespers, but the voice emerging from behind the heavy burgundy drapes was unmistakably Father Juan's. God had sent this particular friar to her so she could be exposed to eternal damnation, purgatory at least, for having used the sacred confessional for a secular purpose. She stoutly reassured herself with the belief that it was the duty of Holy Church to promote justice and of every true Catholic to ensure the Church was rendered its rightful dues.

Having gone through the ritual of confessing her sins, she now approached her purpose with some trepidation, but no less decisiveness. 'Father, I have sinned in not conveying promptly, to Holy Church and the authorities, knowledge I possess of an attempt most insidious, by one in an exalted place, to rob Holy Church and its Lord Protector, our revered King Emperor, of their rightful dues.'

She did not have to hear any response from the priest to detect the sudden tremor of interest from within the enclosure. After all, public sins are more important to clever men than petty private peccadilloes, she reflected.

'And what place can be so exalted?' the booming voice inquired.

She pretended to hesitate. 'Can I not . . .' she began, then paused.

'Are you afraid that your confidence might be betrayed, my child? Remember the secrets of the confessional are totally inviolate, even by the King Emperor.'

She gave the appearance of making up her mind by heaving an audible sigh of relief. 'No less an exalted personage than His Excellency the Viceroy.' She paused, as if scared, plunged on. 'He has obtained much of the treasure of the rulers of Jaya from the Regent, King Vidiye, part of which at least is meant to be compensation for the Regent's destruction of Church property. Yet he continues to keep the Regent imprisoned for crimes against Holy Church, probably in order to demonstrate that he has not yet obtained all the treasure, but I am aware that he made no official accounting and has already sent some of what he seized on a small vessel to his palace in Goa. Meanwhile, Holy Church has received nothing for the losses it has suffered at the Regent's hands.'

A pregnant silence was her first response. 'You have sinned by your delay in making this confession, my child,' the friar finally stated. 'You have made yourself an accessory after the fact. You must offer penance on earth, but you shall be rewarded in heaven. Say ten Our Fathers, ten Hail Marys and ten Creeds every day for the next thirty days.'

I pray that there will be reward on earth too, she thought as she heard the words of the absolution and made the sign of the cross.

To His Excellency Admiral Lopo Soarez de Albergaria,
her father by the law,

Julietta de Albergaria née de Brito sends respectful and filial greetings. Your silence through the years has but confirmed your deep displeasure at your son's choice of wife.

I presume to address you now only because of the new life in our world, our son, whom we have named Lopo Soarez de Albergaria after his illustrious grandfather.

You will note from the painting I have done of Lopo, which I enclose as my humble gift to you, that he already reveals the classical features of the noble de Albergarias.

I pray you in the name of Sweet Jesus and the Blessed Virgin to take your grandson to your heart.

You are now, by the grace of God and your indomitable endeavours, the Lord High Admiral of the Fleet of our King Emperor. Please accept our most cordial invitation to visit us in this far-flung outpost of the Empire. There are tragic events taking place here which it would be in the public interest for you to witness at first hand without delay, so you can determine whether or not to intervene on behalf of His Majesty.

Please also visit your grandson, for by God's will you are today his living connection with the de Albergaria family, while he is your link with future generations.

You are now a grandfather. I respectfully beseech you to be grand towards our son even if you continue to disown,

Your humble servant,
Julietta de Albergaria

Signed in Colombo, capital of the island of Lanka, this twelfth day of September in the year of grace fifteen hundred and thirty.

She handed the manuscript and the rolled painting of her son to Appu for delivery to Prince Tikiri Raja Sinha, who would see that it reached the trader Abdul Raschid, thus ensuring its secret passage to Lisbon. Vague stirrings of concern as to whether it was right and honourable for her to have passed information to Father Juan and now Admiral de Albergaria, were stilled before the knowledge that she was using her only weapon, a woman's wisdom, for the public good. After all, she was setting in motion the two forces available to her, Holy Church and the Lord High Admiral, to intervene on behalf of Portuguese justice.

CHAPTER TWENTY-FOUR
Tuesday, 13 September 1530

On the instructions of my father, King Maya Dunne, I left unaccompanied for Jaya that same evening on my secret mission to meet my sister, now Queen Padma, in the Jaya palace. I reached a village called Kadu, a few miles east of the capital of Jaya, very late that night, where I knew I would be given lodging at the home of Sene, a petty chief who was secretly one of 'our' men. His son, an important official in the Jaya palace, was also one of our contacts. Sene's spacious single-storey brick house was located in a large grove of coconut, arecanut, jak and wild breadfruit trees, and surrounded by his paddyfields, now lying brown and fallow. The crop had been gathered and the fields awaited the monsoon rains due shortly in the month of October for sowing. Sene and his household, consisting of his pretty, silver-haired wife, Chandra, and their three other grown-up sons, not only made me welcome, but the elder son, who was about my age, left for Jaya well before dawn to carry my message to his brother who was a principal aide to the Lord Chamberlain in the Jaya palace and therefore had ready access to my sister. My message requested her to meet me that morning at the beginning of the pre-noon watch in the home of one of the palace goldsmiths, Mundi, another of our secret connections, who lived in the capital city's street of goldsmiths. Tradesmen's homes were built attached to each other and were served by stout wooden entrance doors set into a wall that ran along the entire street, all of which ensured security. This, combined with the lay-out of Mundi's own house with his shop in the ante-room and a private room at the rear adjoining the *meda midula*, centre courtyard, would enable me to meet my sister unobserved.

Dressed in homespun white pantaloons and *kurtha*, overshirt, I arrived at Mundi's home soon after he opened his shutters for the day. Mundi was a middle-aged man, so short he was almost a dwarf. He had a large shaggy head poised on his shoulders, so his chin was almost level with his chest. He was of an amiable disposition, wore a perpetual smile and had the sharp eyes of a master crafts-man.

He must have noted my curious glances towards the verandah where his two sons and a nephew apprenticed to him normally worked. 'I received a message from your royal sister at the palace, lord, so I sent everyone away on various errands,' he reassured me. 'The house is empty, and you can await my lady in the private room we use for royalty at the back of the house. Her attendants can remain in the shop without knowing you are here.' This was as I had hoped.

I glanced at the sand-clock placed on a shelf by the entrance to the ante-room. Since my sister was due at the commencement of the pre-noon watch, ten o'clock by the new *parangi* time-pieces, I had an hour to wait. 'I'll take a stroll, so I don't disturb you,' I replied.

'Whatever you wish, lord. You are welcome to remain here. You will certainly not be disturbing me.'

'Your time is precious – precious metal! – I shall not take up any more of it than necessary. Meanwhile, it will be good to see this part of the city unescorted for once.'

It was a hot time of the year when any city, especially along streets that had been stripped of trees to make way for boundary walls and buildings, could become like an oven. As I stepped back on to the cobbled street, the morning in Jaya gave the assurance of an oven-hot afternoon.

Since the days of the early Arya, many centuries ago,

city streets in the quarter set aside for tradesmen had been allotted to the members of the eighteen craftsmen's guilds. The word 'quarter' as a place of residence derives from the Arya custom of dividing cities into four main parts, separated by two intersecting cross streets running north and south, east and west respectively. One quarter was reserved for princes and noblemen, one for temples, temple schools and priests, one for tradesmen and inns and the last for people. In the Jaya tradesmen's quarter, goldsmiths, silversmiths, batten makers, basket-weavers and the like all lived in their separate side streets. They intermarried to keep their business and prosperity within the family, a form of greed or economic self-preservation created by the caste system which in turn helped perpetuate the system.

As I walked aimlessly through hurrying crowds, I found myself headed for the poorer quarter of the city, which I had never visited before. Increasing squalor, dirt and foul smells confronted me. Before long I was jostling my way past bare-chested children in unwashed sarongs using the street as their playground, their wild screams and cries polluted the foetid air. Two boys were teasing a mangy pi-dog in a gutter meant to carry refuse, others paddled in its filthy water. Most of them should be at school, but times seemed to have changed since the days of King Dharma Parakrama. Today, nobody seemed to care. The dwellings were unpainted, run-down. Rotting garbage, its stench overpowering, lay in heaps, attracting flies that kept alighting on me for a quick inspection. I was shocked. What could kings and princes know about their people unless they knew how the poor lived? How could this breeding ground of disease and discontent produce valiant patriotic Sinhala? I realized then that the power I sought should not be for creating a unified Sinhala nation, but to end deprivation and want.

My eyes fell on them because they were apart from the other children, almost as if they were lepers to be shunned.

338

A little boy of about four, clad only in a filthy half-sarong worn low around his spindly waist, knelt, scrawny buttocks on heels, before a naked mite of a girl. Not more than two years old, she was seated on the dirt, legs spread, finger to snotty nose, crying her heart out in quiet, jerking sobs. The ribs of both children protruded through dusky skin covered with red sores. The boy's face was gaunt; his large black eyes were set in dark hollows. 'Don't cry, *chuti*,' he soothed the girl, in a thin, dry voice full of tenderness. 'See, *aiya* has brought you something to eat.'

The 'something' was the remains of a rotten banana, obviously foraged from one of the garbage heaps.

Dear *devas*, what in your name is this? Is my beloved Lanka no more than a garbage heap in which children eat refuse? What have I missed in my splendid isolation as a prince living in a luxurious palace?

Pity and horror tore at my throat.

I approached the two children and paused. When my shadow fell on them, they both glanced up fearfully. Other children nearby ceased their playing, moved towards us but did not approach too close. 'Don't go near the boy, *lokka*, older person. He is an animal. He bites and kicks,' one of them called out. 'And the girl will infect you with the bloody-shit disease.'

Ignoring them, I squatted on my haunches before the boy. 'Where is your home?' I asked him.

He cowered back in fear, the hand holding the corpse of that rotten banana raised to ward off a blow. 'We . . . we were doing no harm, master,' he responded. The girl began wailing in earnest. 'Please . . . please don't beat us. Beat me, not my sister. She is so tiny.'

Oh gods of our fathers! Tears sprang to my eyes. I gazed upon that pleading gaze, the emaciated face already defeated except by the desire to protect his young sister. 'No, I am not here to hurt or harm you.' I was barely able to get the words through my aching throat. 'I want to help

339

you.' I swallowed, struggling for control. 'Where do you live?'

'Here, master.'

'Have you no home?'

'No.'

'Where are your parents?'

'My mother died so Lord Buddha could give life to *nangi*, little sister, but then our father left us.' He scratched a red, pink-rimmed ulcer on his dark chest, waved away the eye-flies settling on his sister's sores, stroked back the matted hair on her head. 'Don't cry, *nangi*, the gentleman ain't a *goni billa*, sack monster. He will not harm us.' He turned pleading eyes to me. 'You will not harm us, no?'

My eyes hot-prickled again with the burning rush of tears which I desperately held back. 'No, I will not harm you. What is your name?'

'Bandula.'

'That is a nice name. And what is your sister's name?'

'She is *nangi*.'

'I know she is your younger sister, but what is her real name?'

'That is her name.'

A sick, starving, homeless, nameless waif, ended before she ever began.

Oh my country, my country, how much more there is to your destiny than becoming a united kingdom? Tell me more, little Bandula, tell me in a few minutes all I should have known and never sought to learn during my entire past lifetime. Tell me of the real anguish, the true needs of the nation, the gnawing stomachs, the cries of the helpless, the despair of the hopeless. Tell me, so I can be punished for my selfishness and ignorance. Wound me even more deeply so I can realize what it really means to be whole, as a king should be.

'How do you feed yourselves?' I inquired hoarsely.

'I look in the garbage heaps. Sometimes I find good

340

things, like yesterday rice and dhall curry.' His old eyes lit up at the recollection. '*Nangi* and I ate and ate till our stomachs puffed up. So . . . o.' He showed how much by holding out an almost withered little hand. He eyed his sister who had stopped crying and was reaching out tiny fingers for the rotten banana. He held the fruit while she ate it, making slurpy noises. 'Tasty, no?'

She nodded solemnly. The snot from her nose mingled with the banana pulp around her lips.

'Don't people feed you at all, the temple . . .?' I found myself shrugging helplessly.

'*Aney*. People do not like us to come near them. Sometimes they throw scraps, but there are lots of beggars. The beggar king is very rich. He tells all his people where to beg, how to steal and takes his share.' He looked around furtively in case he had been overheard. 'He does not like anyone to beg on their own, so he gives us beeg trouble. He can use me, but my sister is too small. I will never leave *nangi*.'

'The *bhikkus* . . .' I persisted.

'*Aiyo*! They just drive us away.'

'What do you do when it rains?' I thought of the approaching monsoon.

'We go here, there.' He sounded vague. His little sister started to cough, hacking away with wide, staring eyes.

I could have broken down and wept. I could have screamed and sobbed, pounded the earth, banged my head on the ground, not for these two destitute waifs, but for myself. How blind I had been through the years, with my grandiose ambition for the nation, when so many who made it up were in this plight.

With true loyalty and devotion to his baby sister, this little boy, Bandula, whom I was seeing through the tear-glisten of my eyes, had opened my mind to a new reality. I recalled words from the Christian Bible . . . 'And a little child shall lead them' . . . 'Suffer the little children to come unto me . . .'

'You and your sister are coming with me,' I said firmly.

'Where?' He was immediately defensive, suspicion causing goose-bumps to rise on his dark, dirty skin. 'We have done no harm.'

I gentled my eyes as never before, needing desperately to reassure him. 'I want to give you and your sister a home, food and clothes.'

'Why?'

'Lies, he is telling you lies,' one of the little children who had been silent witnesses interrupted. 'He is a *goni billa*, sack monster. He wants to take you both to his home and make soup of you.'

Too heartsick to be angry, I ignored the interruption and kept looking at little Bandula with some feeling pouring out of me that I could not identify – perhaps it was human love for the first time in my life. 'You know I would never harm you. I want to take you to a new home.'

Conflict swept to and fro across his pinched face and puzzled the sunken eyes. He had survived thus far in a cruel world through tenacity and cunning. What I offered was much to easy a way. There had to be a catch. I felt as if my whole life was hanging in the balance of his reply. As the moments stretched out, I was blind to all else save the need for him to agree, a prince silently pleading for his life with a beggar boy.

'We will come,' he finally said. And relief flooded me so intensely I released my breath. 'But *nangi* and I must always be with each other.'

'You will be together as long as you want, I promise you.' I rose to my feet. 'Let us go now.'

'*Nangi* can't walk too well.' He bent, placed his hands beneath her armpits, straining to haul her up.

I should be the one to carry the little girl. I looked closely at her puny body for the first time. It was covered with dirt and those runny, festering sores that looked alive. Her snot-streaked face, her matted hair, filled me with revulsion. I was facing her and her brother as physical entities for the first time. Suddenly, I wanted to run away.

Some deeper feeling, I knew not what, perhaps it was the instinct to survive, held me back. I reached down. 'Here, let me carry your sister.'

My decisiveness swept aside his mistrust. I raised up that tiny, filthy body to carry it, awkwardly, for I had never carried a child before. Her sores rubbed against my white *kurtha*, overshirt.

By that single act, I crossed a threshold of my life. A whole new world seemed to extend before me, its throb against my chest the beating of a baby's tiny heart.

My sister, Padma, was small and fair, with masses of black curls framing a delicately boned face. She had sable eyes that vanished into the unlined folds of the lids when she smiled. She was not smiling today, as we sat across from each other, alone in the little room at the back of Mundi's house. The sunlight was bright in the centre courtyard across the open verandah, the hum of bees was soothing, but Padma's eyes were clouded and the room vibrated with her pain and anger.

Having seen each other so seldom over the years, my sister and I barely knew each other, but I felt a sense of kinship with her today, partly because of the way she was seated, very much the princess breed, erect, with straight back and slender relaxed neck, her hands primly folded across her lap, but mostly because of our shared concern.

We had barely exchanged small formal talk when a child's wailing reached us from the bathroom across the courtyard. 'Who is that?' my sister demanded, her eyes darting suspiciously in the direction of the sounds. 'Mundi has no small children.'

A smile touched my lips. 'That is probably *nangi* protesting at being given a bath by Mundi.'

'Who is *nangi*?'

I told her briefly. As I spoke I noticed some of the pain and anger leaving her expression, to be replaced by pity and approbation. 'So I brought the two children here,' I ended. 'Having bathed and fed them, Mundi will put them to bed, after which the physician will call on them.'

'What will you do with them?'

'I shall adopt them, take them to the palace. Bandula is a gallant little boy. He must grow up to be a gallant gentleman.'

'You will not do anything of the kind.' My sister's voice was sharp. I could detect the Maya Dunne authority in it. 'You have always been an idealistic fool, given to acting on impulse. Can you imagine what it will be like for them to grow up in that enviroment, especially with you away so often? You want to transplant wild flowers into a palace garden?'

Hot words of protest rose to my lips, but a sudden flash of good sense made me hold them back. 'You were for ever bossing me, when you were little,' I muttered. 'I used to humour you in the old days because you were my little sister.'

'Like Bandula with *nangi*,' she declared, sweet and low, causing me to melt.

'All right, what would you have me do? Mundi cannot keep them here for more than a few hours without arousing suspicion.'

'Take them to our friend, Sene,' she responded. 'I do not know him, but he and his wife have a large home and no small children. From what I have gathered in conversations with the oldest son in the palace, the mother is a kindly matron. It will be the perfect place for the two children, at least for the present.'

'Wonderful. You have brains as well as beauty. Family

failings, I might add! Now that's settled, let us get on with our real task.'

She smiled, wanly now. 'Did you know that the Viceroy, may his own God consign his soul to the Christian hell, has consigned my husband to a dungeon?'

'What?'

'You heard me. King Vidiye gave up a large portion of the family treasure in exchange for a promise of freedom from his arrest for alleged crimes against Portugal. That . . . that greedy shark took it all, then re-arrested him for crimes against their Church.'

I became deadly quiet. 'Tell me everything you know.'

It was not much more, but by the time she finished speaking, I had identified the dungeon to which she had referred. 'I know that dungeon,' I observed gloomily. 'It's a deep mine-shaft, abandoned fifty years ago, with a single access located at the northern end of the fort.'

I did not wish to add to my sister's grief by saying that the dungeon was filthy, dark, noisome and infested with rats and vermin. Then, anger knifed through me, reached into my brain scraping it raw. 'Our only hope is to smash these accursed *parangi*, destroy their fort. Why in hell didn't our *thatha* listen . . .'

'I told you just now that you are impulsive,' my sister quietly admonished me.

I leapt to my feet. '*Devas, devas, devas,*' I shouted, raising clenched fists in frustration. 'You . . .'

'Quiet please, Prince.' My sister interrupted again. 'My attendants might hear you. Calm down and listen to me quietly, will you?'

'You keep interrupting me,' I protested. 'Are these the manners they teach you in the Anu court?'

'You should not interrupt me when I interrupt you,' she retorted, with a cheeky grin. Then her expression grew serious. 'Sit down and listen to me.' I subsided sulkily on to my settle.

'Have you ever heard of a mine-shaft without a mine?'

'N-n-no . . .' I began, then inspiration flooded me, like rainwater in a mine. 'By the *devas*!' I pounded on my thigh. 'Of course. I have even played in the mine as a boy. It extends beneath the entrance gates of the fort to . . .'

'Precisely.' The little lady seemed determined to keep interrupting me, but this time I did not complain. She leant down and produced an old scroll from her little wicker-work satchel. She opened the scroll and held it out to me. 'Look, here is a map of the mine. The entrance from the shaft has been blocked for so long that few people remember it even exists. Certainly, the *parangi* cannot know. I have already found loyal men who will dig through the blockage and rescue my husband.'

'By all that I hold sacred, *you* are the real Maya Dunne,' I breathed, light-headed with admiration for her. 'Brains, cunning, speed where necessary. What did you need our father and me for?'

'To create the necessary diversion,' she replied, sweet and low. 'You must advance against Colombo in full force without delay. The *parangi* will then move out to Sita Waka in maximum strength. This will ensure fewer guards while the rescue takes place.'

'How do you know that they will move to Sita Waka instead of defending Colombo, or fighting nearer home?'

'Because I have caused word to be confidentially passed on to the avaricious Viceroy that King Maya Dunne's treasures far exceed those of the late King Bhuvaneka Bahu! There is nothing like a large bait to lure a great white shark.'

I was astonished. 'You are a devil!' I shook my head in wonder. Her reasoning was faultless. 'When do they want us to move?'

'Immediately. Every day's delay could mean death to my husband . . .' She paused deliberately. 'And an end to

346

the sanctity of royal personages.' Oh, the cunning of this little family devil. 'You must have had the news that King Kumara has seized the Dhamba kingdom?'

'Yes, I heard just this morning from Sene. I'm not surprised that King Kumara decided to violate the sanctity of the Dhamba kings. He is an adventurer.'

'You had better get the *parangi* to move before King Kumara links up with them.' Her smile was charming and white, but it was the baring of a female cheetah's teeth. 'You would not want history to repeat itself, would you? Exile does not go well with your complexion!'

The *devas* forbid that this sister of mine should ever compete with me for the succession! 'But the monsoons are imminent,' I feebly protested.

'The Viceroy is so greedy, he will take the risk, hoping the rains will be delayed. You must advance before the *parangi* leave Colombo, choosing the route most likely to be flooded, through Mulleri, for instance. Give them ample warning of this route. According to our astrologer, the monsoons will come within a week. With their cannon bogged down in the mud, their gunpowder wet . . .' Even thinking about the prospects of achieving her goal caused a momentary crumpling of her face.

CHAPTER TWENTY-FIVE

Saturday, 1 October 1530

Upon learning that King Maya Dunne was about to advance against Jaya or Colombo, Don Alfonso de Noronha had decided to accelerate his plans to move against Sita Waka. Fernao was surprised that the Sita Waka king had not waited until the monsoon was over. He suspected some hidden motive, but did not pursue that line of thought because the Viceroy was adamant. The Portuguese force, consisting of twenty troops of artillery under Major Nantes, as his rank now was, and ten infantry regiments, had left Colombo that morning and made good speed.

Just before noon, dark grey storm clouds had started mushrooming from the south-west, backgrounded by glimmers of lightning followed by thunder rumbling like the growl of a distant giant's stomach. Fernao half-turned in the saddle of his great bay, caught the eye of the Viceroy plodding hunched beside him. 'These are the classic heralds of the monsoon, Your Excellency,' he remarked. 'Sparkling clear mornings, clouds beginning to pile up by noon, heavy rain early evening. It is still not too late to turn back.'

Don Alfonso merely flickered hooded eyes back in his direction, did not even deign to glance at the sky. 'Poetically put, General, but we are well aware of the symptoms of the rainy season.' He transferred his reins to his left hand, reached in his sleeve for the handkerchief tucked in it, mopped the beads of sweat from his face. 'But we do not turn back when we are on the king's business. As you know, our scouts have reported that the enemy is encamped east of Mulleri. We shall press on and defeat him in battle on the plain tomorrow. You have done it before, with far less firepower and fewer brave Portuguese soldiers. We shall beat your performance. By the time the monsoon breaks, we shall be victorious in Sita Waka.'

The Viceroy's pig-headedness and the oppressive heat were beginning to irritate Fernao. 'Somehow I sense a trap, Your Excellency,' he persisted.

'Come now, General, your defeatist attitude hardly becomes a soldier. Oh, we forgot. You're really a naval man, aren't you?'

Fernao flushed at the covert insult, but held back the hot words that rose to his lips. This man, clod though he was, happened to be the *vice roi*, the personage 'on behalf of the king'. He forced a smile instead. 'Any good military commander, of whichever arm of the services, must evaluate the strength and intention of an enemy he is about to engage in battle, the nature of the terrain and the weather, Your Excellency,' he responded, firm. 'We shall arrive at the Mulleri plain tonight. It is less familiar to us than to the enemy, but from my recollection the plain is mostly low-lying swamp and . . .'

'The might of Portugal will prevail over any native chief with his obsolete weapons,' the Viceroy interrupted. 'Your King Maya Dunne is a pygmy compared to the giants of India we have defeated. Have no fear. When we camp on the west of the plain this evening, we shall send out scouting patrols to check on enemy dispositions. We can then assess what, if any, traps have been laid.'

What if we have blinding monsoon rain tonight? Fernao thought helplessly. Our patrols won't be able to see beyond their noses. But there was no way in which one could get through to the Viceroy once the man had made up his mind. This stubborness had its compensations. Fernao had admired the tenacity of purpose and the military skills with which the Viceroy had got the army ready for the attack against Sita Waka. He was meticulous in planning and a stickler for perfection in every detail, whether it was the men's morale, the arms and equipment, the artilllery and wagons, or the support units and supply train. The confidence of His Imperial Majesty in Portugal had obviously been well earned on the home front, where Don Alfonso had helped reorganize the imperial army so successfully that the posting to Goa had been his reward.

Black clouds were now scurrying across the blue sky with incredible swiftness. The air darkened and was suddenly rippled by breezes, yet the earth was hushed. The fallow brown fields through which they rode were devoid of human life, no birds rode the sky. All the people had withdrawn to their homes in anticipation of the deluge and perhaps to avoid trouble from foreign troops. In that setting, a man and a boy tying up cattle in a wayside grove seemed unreal. Suddenly, Fernao found the clip-clop of horses' hooves, the creak of leather and the distant squeak and rattle of the horsedrawn cannon way behind to be non-sounds. Ten thousand cavalry, musketeers and supporting artillery, a mighty force because of its firepower, all unreal. The royal standard of Portugal borne by his standard-bearer brought reality back as it flapped madly on its pole when the first rain, large separate drops of crystal, hurried earthwards, cooled his face.

Sunday, 2 October 1530

The rain ceased during the night, but the men had been soaked to the skin in the bivouac tents, with no way of lighting fires to keep warm or get dry. Dinner had been a dismal meal of soggy flour cakes and cold meat. Yet both *degredados* and regulars had been in cheerful spirits, spoiling for the fight, and there was always the consolation that the enemy, reported by scouting patrols to be massed on the eastern end of the plain, were enduring the same discomforts.

Now it was dawn. There was that hint of silver in the

first glint of daybreak that betokened a clear morning. Cockerels began to crow lustily and the air smelt of dank leaves. Fernao's clothes were beginning to dry on his body, but were damp and cold beneath his leather armour and thigh greaves.

All the commanders had received battle orders from the Viceroy before retiring for the night. When Fernao had all their state of readiness reports, he conveyed these to Don Alfonso. They mounted their horses and slow-trotted to the line of trees bordering the western edge of the plain. They reined in beneath the overhanging branches, to study the terrain.

'There they are!' The Viceroy pointed to the long dark mass at the far end of the plain, seperating north and south like a fringe of low trees in the distance.

Fernao leaned forward, peering more closely. 'They have elephants up front.'

A grim smile crossed the Viceroy's face, his hooked nose twitched. 'No matter. We've faced them before. A couple of salvoes from our cannon and the creatures will turn against their own.'

'Shall I have the artillery advance within range, Excellency?' They would need heavy artillery support against the massive manpower of the enemy.

'Let's see! The enemy are still beyond range. We shall need to move the cannon at least five hundred yards up front. Our battle plan shall remain unchanged, cavalry charges to soften them up and spread confusion, with pikemen and infantry following.' He paused, nodded with satisfaction. 'But first, the kind of artillery barrage from two hundred cannon that will strike terror in their hearts. Yes, certainly have the cannon moved up, General.'

Fernao turned and gave the order to Captain Diogo de Mello who, though a cavalry commander, had become his chief aide in recent days.

Before long, a cacophony of squeaks and rattles, drown-

ing the screech of birds in alarm, announced the approach
of field pieces which artillery officers were leading over the
carpet of leaves and the muddy soil. The officers saluted as
they moved past the headquarters group. Then came the
cannon. Drawn by horses whose bridles were held by
uniformed men, the weapons trundled along in extended
line, poking their ugly snouts between the trees like
prehistoric monsters. The horses began straining against
mud.

'The ground is more treacherous that I thought,' Fernao
muttered. He remembered his fear of a trap and it crystal-
lized into a cold knot in the pit of his stomach. He wished
they had mules, as in Europe, instead of horses, to haul the
artillery pieces. He glanced to his left. His eyes following
the slight upward slope of the land, paused at the faint
glimmer of a broad ribbon of water in the distance. That
would be the river. In the lightening air, what appeared to
be a wide channel headed from the river in the direction of
the plain. Strange! The river did not have a tributary at this
point. As the truth hit him, the knot in his stomach seemed
to explode.

Sunday, 2 October 1530

Having declined King Vikrama's invitation to move to the
palace – he loved ostentation and luxury, but wanted to be
around to enjoy it! – King Kumara now eyed Father Juan
across the reception room of the Dhamba mansion. Except
for streaks of grey in his hair and the pointed beard, the
years had not aged the friar, but he had grown a little more
plump with eating Portuguese food as a regular diet. His
olive skin was unwrinkled and the yellow eyes sparkled
like topaz, even in the pale light of dawn. King Kumara
thought of earlier times, recalled without satisfaction his
original assessment that the Catholic Church would
become a power to be reckoned with. Since the growth of

the temporal power of Portugal in Lanka and coastal India, the Catholic Church had indeed extended its grip on the region, to convert the heathen and share his wealth or whatever charity could be extracted from his indigence. Why had the friar come on a Sunday?

They had spent some time fencing, before Father Juan thrust. 'You suggest that it is time Holy Church caused the temporal power of Portugal to ally itself openly with the most powerful of this country, Sire,' he stated. The once unctuous friar now spoke like a man conscious of his power. He steepled long, ruthless fingers. 'I am inclined to agree with you. But *who* is the most powerful of the kings of Lanka today: King Maya Dunne, the boy king of Jaya, the king of Jaffna, or . . . er . . . you?'

King Kumara restrained his irritation. 'We are aware of the overtures you have made to the Jaffna king, Father, in order to establish Holy Church in his kingdom.' He leaned back, deliberately relaxing on the high satinwood chair that substituted for a throne. 'But the Cholas will never again win any part of the other kingdoms, so their only use to you will be as a dagger pointed at the heartland of the Sinhala. Unfortunately, our capitals have for centuries now been farther than dagger-thrust distance from the north! As for the boy king of Jaya, your Viceroy has drawn his teeth by consigning the real power behind his throne to King Vidiye, then emasculating the king by consigning him to a dungeon – a favour for which we thank the Viceroy.' He paused, watching with seeming carelessness the hard black pinpoints of the friar's eyes for a reaction.

Father Juan gestured with both hands in the manner of the benediction. 'True, Sire. But what about the Sita Waka king?'

'Your army will surely defeat him in the battle which we understand may be joined even at this moment.'

'It might be prudent for us to use King Maya Dunne as a puppet after defeating him in battle.'

'He will be no one's puppet.'

'Would you, Sire?'

King Kumara was momentarily taken aback, but did not show it. 'Not to the temporal power. Only to the Church. After all, we are Catholic.'

'Are you, Sire?' The voice had suddenly become as hard as the black points of the keen eyes.

'You know we are,' the king responded firmly. 'We go to Church regularly, say our prayers, attempt to convert our nobles. We are as good a Catholic as any, perhaps better than some.'

'But what about your innermost convictions?'

A sudden disquiet surfaced within the king. Did the friar know more than he should? If so, how? Could Queen Anula have blabbed to Father Perez? Or was Father Juan just an exceptionally clever man who understood people? After all, this was an arch plotter who had in recent times managed to manipulate some of the policies of Portugal in Lanka through Holy Church.

'Our innermost convictions are between us and God,' King Kumara replied solemnly. He seemed to remember having made this point before.

'Ah yes, but I am God's representative on this earth.'

'Then you should have God's power to know the truth of our convictions.'

The friar bowed his acknowledgement of the riposte. 'How do you see the political situation following today's battle?' he inquired, changing the subject.

'Your forces will win, provided the monsoon rains do not intervene. King Maya Dunne will then retire to the mountains and wage guerilla warfare, regrouping until your troops leave Sita Waka. You cannot afford to stay there for ever, you know. If your people had only kept their word and let me take over as king of Sita Waka four years ago, you would not have had to face these problems today. As it is, events in Europe, which have always governed the strength you maintain in Lanka, will cause you to withdraw at some point of time. You can then command the coast with your firepower, but the hinterland, never.'

'His Imperial Majesty gives Lanka priority over all other countries in this region.'

'A wise decision since we are giving His Imperial Majesty the greatest prosperity. Yet retaining forces in Sita Waka for too long will be both expensive and unproductive. You need, as an ally, a king who can keep King Maya Dunne and his son, Prince Raja Sinha, on the run in the high country, while you command the low country where more produce is available. We therefore remain your only choice.' His grin was feral. 'It is still not too late to honour your former promises, you know.'

The friar's eyes twinkled. 'And if the Viceroy loses the imminent battle, Sire?'

'Then you will need us more than ever.'

Sunday, 2 October 1530

The news of King Vidiye's arrest and subsequent imprisonment in a dungeon had been a definite setback to Queen Anula's plans. It had caused her many a sleepless night. Now, the monsoon had arrived. Heavy rain thundering on the roof and squalling winds last night had not helped. The very elements seemed to be in disarray, like her mind. Now it was dawn and she paced her reception room, prickly-eyed. The pale grey air outside the open window was clear, the earth a carpet of brown and green leaves blown by the high winds, the first crows were cawing hungrily.

How to proceed? Having received satisfactory reports from her Kiri Vella relations, she must persuade her husband to accept her plan. What was the key? Ah yes, his new found decency which would have bred some faith

355

within him. Now, if she could only find the right connection, all would be well. Where could she find it?

She swung round as the door opened abruptly. Her daughter, now nearly four, stood at the entrance, Nona, the silver-haired chief attendant wringing impotent hands behind her.

'*Aiyo mathini*, your little daughter cannot be restrained,' the woman cried. 'She demanded to see you and here she is. She is a queen already.'

Queen Anula looked at the fair-skinned child standing imperiously at the entrance, tiny arms akimbo, dark curly head proudly raised, brown eyes, so like her father's, flashing.

'I wanted to see you because I have a pain in my tummy, yet Nona said I couldn't come,' the child lisped. She stamped her foot. 'But I came anyway.'

I came anyway, the child had said. She already had the attributes of a queen. Inspiration dawned.

'We shall get you some medicine,' she told her daughter. 'Remain in the outside room.' She glanced at Nona. 'Come in and close the door behind you,' she commanded.

The quiet thud of the closing door was followed by a sudden throb of drumming from the Buddhist temple adjoining the palace. 'We trust you, Nona,' she said, pleasantly menacing. 'We are about to entrust an important task to you. If you ever betray us, even to the king, we shall have you tortured.'

The old woman's pale eyes gazed back with gentle amusement. 'If you feel you need the threats, my lady, you should not place your trust in me.'

Just like Nona to attempt quiet defiance, all in the name of overt respect. The queen dropped her voice. 'We want you personally to carry a secret message to their Catholic friar, Father Perez. We need to meet his fellow-priest, Father Juan, urgently and secretly. Also tell Father Perez that we desire to have our daughter baptized as soon as possible. Do you understand?'

'Yes, my lady.'

The queen smiled to herself. She was taking the first step for her daughter's future, as a spare arrow to her bow. She liked to cover all bases. She had to find the right connection for her major move.

CHAPTER TWENTY-SIX

Sunday, 2 October 1530

Spurring his bay forward on the instant into the open ground, Fernao wheeled to face the lumbering cannon. He raised a warning hand. 'Halt!' he commanded.

'What the fuck goes on?' Major Nantes, the senior gunnery officer at the head of his command, had lost neither his disposition nor his love of invective.

Fernao pointed towards the plain. 'Marshy land ahead. Your guns will get bogged down beyond the range of the enemy.'

'Shit!' Major Nantes turned around to pass the orders.

'General!' the Viceroy thundered, cantering forward.

Fernao swung his horse back. 'Your Excellency?'

Don Alfonso dropped his voice so no one else could hear. 'Do not exceed your authority. *We* are in command here.'

Fernao flushed, but restrained his anger. 'What are your orders?' he quietly demanded.

'The brave armies of Portugal never run away from a little water. We leave that to the navy. Let the advance continue.'

'You give them the order then,' Fernao gritted back. He would have liked to challenge this vulture who was prepared to risk men's lives for personal greed to a duel for the insults, but this was not the time. He did not want to be cashiered and shot for mutiny.

'Major Nantes!' the dry voice of the Viceroy crackled. 'General de Albergaria has reconsidered his last order. Continue your advance.'

Rage and frustration boiling within him, Fernao looked fixedly to his front while the guns lumbered slowly past him, creaking and squeaking, rattling and thumping, the horses straining harder to pull their burdens over the softer ground. They broke cover, extending in two long lines across the plain, the gunners grim-faced at the prospect of action, followed by the barrows hauling the cannonballs.

The two lines proceeded slowly but steadily forward, dark outlines in the greying light. Had he made an error of judgement, Fernao wondered. Was the terrain not as marshy as he had thought? Please God, confirm my observation. And he immediately flushed with shame at his selfishness. No, no, God, please let the ground be firm so we can prevail today. Please make your representative on earth, my King Emperor, triumph, so Holy Church may spread its wings from this battleground. Nothing like bribing God. He flushed again.

The first line of artillery reached much softer ground. The horses' hooves began to plod. Dirt was flung back from slithering wheels, muddy water splashed, but the movement continued, slower now.

Fernao's breath caught. The gunners behind the cannon began shoving, three men to each piece. Would they make it?

The air was suddenly rent by the sharp whinnying of horses. The lead animals shied, pulling their bridle-men.

'Halt!' Fernao screamed, spurring his mount forward, hooves squelching in the mud.

But he was too late. The horses had sensed what the artillery men could not see in the muddy waters. The ground shelved steeply downwards into a deep channel, obviously cut by the enemy. Animals and men were suddenly in a welter of confusion, brimming with shouts, whinnying and neighs. Cannon slowly began tilting over or subsiding inside the channel. Major Nantes was screaming obscenities.

Before he even reached the barrows, Fernao heard the distant blare of trumpets followed by the roar of the enemy. He reined in, saw the long spread of elephants and men advancing. With the artillery slowly bogging down, their numbers now seemed legion. In a flash, Fernao concluded that his one hope was to rescue the cannon, then use the channel as a moat against the advancing enemy.

'Attack!' the Viceroy screamed frenziedly.

Fernao could not believe his ears. 'No . . .!' he exploded. But once again he was too late. Musketry officers began crackling the order to their companies. Mounted musketeers trotted forward in two ranks. The front rank broke cover, leather creaking, hooves thudding, headed towards the artillery. Swarthy-faced musketeers grinned from ear to ear at the prospect of being first into action. The second rank flowed by, smooth as a stream, men's jaws set, eyes intent on the plain ahead.

Don Alfonso de Noronha rose in his stirrups, his eyes blazing, the vulturine face aglow. He drew his long sword. 'Men of Portugal, the time has come for you to fight against all odds for your king, your country and your faith!' he roared. He pointed his sword in the direction of the advancing enemy. 'We attack according to plan. Forward!'

This was madness. Fernao had lost control over a situation over which he never had command. All that was left to him was to go along with the stream. He took his place beside the trotting Viceroy, who nodded his acknowledgement, the great hooked nose dipping in a grin of fierce optimism.

The slow advancing enemy was but a few hundred yards away now. Fernao could distinguish the standard bearers with the bright red, green and orange flags of the noble families. He tried vainly to spot the gold Sinhala lion rampant on a scarlet field that would be the herald of the man he sought, Prince Tikiri Bandara Raja Sinha. Trumpeters and drummers were following the Sinhala standard bearers, then armoured elephants, bright canopied *how-*

dahs swaying on their backs, and massed cavalry, hiding the inevitable pikeman, foot-soldiers and bowmen. This was the classic Sinhala order of battle.

The first rank of Fernao's mounted musketeers had filtered through the artillery, which Major Nantes was miraculously reassembling on the near side of the channel. Weapons raised high, the mounted musketeers began fording through the muddy water. The hastily constructed channel could not have been very deep, for the men soon emerged on the other side, the rear hooves of their horses slipping and slithering in the black mud. They dismounted, ran forward and took the kneeling position in extended line. Then Fernao was threading his way through men, horses and cannon, leaning slightly back as he headed downslope into the murky water of the channel.

'Fucking shithole mud!' Major Nantes exclaimed as he rode past the gunner. Fernao could not help but echo the sentiment while he spurred his reluctant bay, leaning forward to ease it upslope. Then he too was on firmer ground once more.

The sun broke cover. The enemy trumpeters and drummers began to back away, allowing their troops to filter past them. Fernao could distinguish the faces of the enemy champions, gigantic men in leather breast armour cavorting ahead of the Sinhala hosts. They brandished great swords, screamed and shouted insults to boost the morale of their troops. Drawing rein at the rear of the second rank of his musketeers, who were priming their muskets, Fernao could distinguish the brown faces of the Sinhala mahouts guiding the battle elephants with their tridents, even the features of the spearmen and dart throwers in the *howdahs*. The great, grey elephants continued lumbering forward, trunks upraised, now trumpeting fearfully.

'Prepare to fire!' The order crackled through the din.

'Fire!'

Musket fire sputtered and rattled along the line in flashes, smoke erupted. Elephants squealed, mahouts slithered off the beasts, some shrieking. The familiar stink of gunpowder, the odour of power, assailed Fernao's nostrils.

The enemy elephants continued advancing steadily. They must have been trained to withstand musket fire. Something else strove to surface in Fernao's mind, some warning, but it vanished as his blood began to pound, sparkling through his veins. This was reality at last, bright, cool, hot, fervid. This was the enemy. Kill or be killed. Fierce delight, the savage lust for violence, mushroomed through Fernao's being, flinging aside all doubt and fear. He could even taste raw blood in his dry mouth.

'Prepare to fire!'

'Fire!'

The thunderous rattle from the standing rank of musketeers erupted while the kneeling rank was still reloading. The trumpet-screech of elephants filled the air again. This time, one of the beasts broke ranks, shook the *howdah* off its back as if it were a feather. Men screamed as they were hurled to the ground. The line of elephants wavered.

'Prepare to fire!'

'Fire!'

Crackling above the confusion, the third volley finally created panic in the ranks of the advancing elephants. Their line broke. More *howdahs* and mahouts tumbled to the ground. Some of the beasts turned, began lumbering back, throwing the enemy cavalry into disarray.

Fernao was quick to seize the advantage. He drew his sword, brandished it aloft, pointed. 'Cavalry, prepare to charge!' he thundered.

Upright lances, pennants fluttering, were levelled at the Sinhala enemy.

'Ch . . . aa . . . arge!' Fernao dug his heels into the flanks of his bay. It shot forward through the double ranks of musketeers. The thunder of the hooves of his regiment caused his blood to sing and dance in his veins. He yelled his hatred.

The hail of arrows came whooshing down, a total surprise. He had forgotten the enemy bowmen. Wounded horses neighed shrilly, men groaned, some fell, but he pounded on regardless. The enemy cavalry sped towards them, lances couched. Fernao swerved to his right to avoid an enemy trooper, transferred his sword to his left hand, slashed sideways at the bearded face. A shock ran through his arm. He nearly lost his sword. His opponent began slowly toppling sideways. He quickly shifted his sword back to his right hand. Then he was in the thick of a blind battle, filled with insensate rage, guiding his horse expertly, cutting, chopping, thrusting. The clang of steel, red, gouting blood, the shrilling of horses, the screams of men became a dazed part of his hot, sweating body, his fevered mind. He killed four men before he broke through the ranks of enemy cavalry.

He stared uncomprehending at the double rank of muskets facing him. Sinhala musketeers. A triple trap, he comprehended, the channel, the pretended attack, the give, all to lead him and his men into . . .

Muskets flashed in unison, smoke spurted. He heard the crackle of the volley, felt a sharp pain in his right arm. He stared in dismay at his nerveless hand, from which the sword had dropped. Warm blood began seeping through his sleeve. He clenched his fist, relieved to find it had feeling. Aires rode up on his left, flung another sword to him. He grasped it. Hatred exploded in his head.

Sword pointing, he bellowed aloud and spurred his bay forward. Heedless of the second row of flashes from the enemy musketeers, he thundered at their twin lines. Sword swinging, he struck a swarthy veteran, saw a necklace of blood, noted the fear and surprise in the widened eyes before the body sagged. A backward slash with the sword felled a dark-skinned giant with the sheer ferocity of the blow.

A mass of Sinhala infantrymen stood ahead, but soon all orderliness ceased. He caught glimpses of the Viceroy, a fearless figure of doom, his great sword flaying death. The fighting broke up into groups. Fernao rode from group to group, wielding his sword mightily. And always, his faithful Aires rode beside him. His men followed his crazed leadership, the *degredados* revelling in the battle, the brutality.

The fighting eased. He had killed or downed two dozen men, but the flame in his heart remained unquenched. The pain in his arm became a quick burn, his entire body was aching, yet he was a man demented. Sweat-strewn, bloody, thirst-wrenched, he plunged forward again, his men, as crazed as he, behind him. The enemy began to give.

Suddenly he had a clear space around him, blood-stained grass, littered with weapons, wounded men and corpses, a blue sky appeared. Time to press home the victory. Renewed energy burst through him.

Where was Price Tikiri? His murderous eyes had repeatedly sought the prince's standard, but in vain.

At first, he thought it was the thunder of the monsoon. His eyes swept up to the south-west, briefly noted the dark rain clouds pluming swiftly towards the battlefield. In seconds, he identified the sound as the drumming of hooves to his right. He swivelled his bay round.

The shock of the first impact of the enemy cavalry charge sent waves through the *degredado* ranks. Fernao felt it physically before his gaze locked on to the standard he had sought all morning. A gold lion rampant on a scarlet field, held high above the Sinhala flank attack.

At that moment, the enemy pretending to retreat on the front turned round and renewed their attack with stunning ferocity. Behind them, more Sinhala hordes were pouring down the hill to reinforce the counterattack.

Another trap! Damn the accursed Sinhala! Damn their duplicity.

With a roar of rage, Fernao spurred his horse towards the hated lion standard. All he wanted was to meet Prince Tikiri face to face and kill him. Blood in his eyes, madness in his heart, murder in his spirit, 'Kill the Sinhala bastards!' he screamed. 'Men of Portugal, rally to victory!'

His men took new heart, plunged forward anew, but taken on two fronts, they were helpless. Try as he might, Fernao could not even push through to the front ranks of the Sinhala cavalry. Black spots appeared before his eyes. He blinked to clear his vision, but the spots only became larger, started to spin. The pain from his wound was unbearable. His right sleeve was soaked with blood. He became dizzy, men seeming to swim around him. The earth revolved. He was slipping from his horse, powerless to stop himself. Oh God, why have you deserted your chosen?

An arm steadied him, let go, seized the bridle of his horse. 'Aires!' he muttered.

He felt himself being turned around, and led away.

Oh, the bitterness of defeat! How many of us will live to taste it?

The air darkened. Thunder crackled and rolled above the clash of weapons, the roar of battle. Vivid flashes of lightning-glow penetrated Fernao's closed lids. The first huge raindrops began to fall, cool on his face. Crystal teardrops from the weeping heavens on my body, he thought. Will you receive my own tears back, O heavens? Will that product of my anguish comfort you?

Sunday, 2 October 1530

When he came to, Fernao found himself on a pallet bed in a small room lit by dim lamplight. Where was he? Recollection flooded, merged with the bitter taste of defeat that

365

had lain within his spirit while he was unconscious. His eyes drifted upwards to a thatched roof on which rain was drumming with unabated fury. His whole body ached, his arm throbbed violently. He still wore his soaked uniform, but the helmet and leather armour had been removed. Had he been taken prisoner? The thought was so alarming that he sat up on the instant. A flood of dizziness submerged him, forced him back. His half-closed eyes roved round the room, noted mud walls.

A shadow fell across his face and his eyes widened. Don Alfonso de Noronha, Viceroy, stood above him, gaunt weary, more predator-like than ever in the uncertain light.

'Are we prisoners, Excellency?' He brought the words out with effort.

'No, thank God.'

'We lost the battle, didn't we?'

'Yes.' Hard pinpoints of madness glinted in the Viceroy's eyes, or was it just Fernao's imagination?

'How many of our men are dead?'

'Over three thousand . . . but we killed three times that many enemy.'

Oh God of our fathers! Fernao felt sick enough to vomit. The poor men, some he had known for years, the widows, parents, children. And the shame of it all would be written in history. 'How many badly wounded?'

'Several hundred.'

'Where are we?'

'Encamped three miles from the battleground. Being heavily outnumbered, we retreated intending a box-defence in the grove until nightfall, when we could safely retreat. We were saved by Major Nantes. Having salvaged most of his cannon while we fought, he already had them lined up at the edge of the grove to cover our passage back across the channel, which then became our moat. So we were able to re-group and withdraw after dark. We have promoted Major Nantes to the rank of Colonel for his outstanding conduct. Your aide, Captain Diogo de Mello, is also now a colonel. His conspicuous bravery and leadership have earned him command of one of our regiments, the senior officers of which have all been killed.'

'How did I get back, Excellency? I remember being about to fall off my horse, then everything went blank.'

'Your man, Aires, saved you. A splendid fellow. He got off his horse, mounted behind you and led both horses back. By the way, your wound is deep but not serious, though complications can always set in.'

'What are your plans?'

'We shall return to Colombo before dawn. Our defences there are strong enough to withstand any assault. I myself shall sail back to Goa in a few days, leaving two *nao* and two additional regiments to protect you, but I shall be back with reinforcements to avenge this defeat.' In the dim light, the Viceroy's expression was diabolical. 'We shall smash Sinhala utterly for having dared to take up arms against our King Emperor.'

And for denying you King Maya Dunne's treasure, Fernao thought.

Sunday, 2 October 1530

We had been compelled to draw back from the devastating barrage of the *parangi* cannon. How they had managed to keep their powder dry and fire the weapons in that pouring rain was a mystery of experience and ingenuity.

Now, as we sat our horses in the centre of the Mulleri plain, with rain pouring down in bucketfuls, droplets dripping off our eyelids, I was stunned to hear King Maya Dunne's decision not to press home our victory. The tattered remnants of the enemy would be permitted safe passage back to Colombo. The entire strategy for battle had been mine; the victory belonged to the thousands of our troops who were crowding the plain, all equally soaked, but all eager to annihilate the foe.

'Why, Sire?' I cried out through the rain. 'A withdrawal is the most complicated of all military operations, as you know. If we push home our victory, we can decimate the retreating enemy before they reach Colombo, perhaps even capture some of the two hundred cannon!'

'If we destroy them further we are likely to kill or capture the two representatives of the King Emperor of Portugal, his Viceroy and his governor,' King Maya Dunne stated soberly. 'Such an insult would invite reprisals. Let us follow the example of the Zamorins of Calicut and the other rajas of India and hold the Viceroy's person inviolate.'

I saw the wisdom of his judgement, but it went hard, because my blood was up. Besides, he and I had fought side by side today, as he had promised on my sixteenth birthday over nine years ago, and I wanted more!

'It was your plan that gave us this historic victory,' my father added, noting my disappointment. Then, characteristically, he abruptly changed the subject. 'By the way, your new troop commander, Aisha Raschid, and her women struck terror into the hearts of the enemy. They made up in ferocity what they lacked in experience, especially Aisha Raschid. There is no being more ferocious than a mother fighting for her young, or to avenge them.'

'Oh yes, Sire, they were terrific. I shall give command of a squadron to Aisha soon. No one in our army can say it was not earned.'

'Good!'

I was still moved by the hunter's instinct to go for the kill. 'Why should we restrain ourselves as to the Viceroy's sacred person?' I demanded. 'He certainly did not hold King Vidiye inviolate!'

He smiled tolerantly as me through the blood, sweat and grime that caked his chiselled features. 'Instinct dictates it,' he replied tolerantly. 'Besides, we have a much more important foe to engage.'

'Who, Sire?'

'King Kumara. Having seized the inviolate,' he crinkled his eyes at the word, 'kingdom of Dhamba, he has made overtures to the Cholas of Jaffna for an army and to Father Juan for Portuguese support. With the Cholas undecided and the Portuguese forces in some slight disarray, the time is absolutely right for us to strike at the Kandyan. He will never be more vulnerable.'

'Give me leave to proceed against him immediately, Sire.'

'You are bloodthirsty! That is good. But we have selected another leader for the expedition.'

My heart sank with disappointment. 'Have I not proved myself today?' I inquired, crushed.

He interrupted me with an upraised palm. 'You did more than prove yourself, General Prince Raja Sinha. You planned and ensured our victory. But the decision as to who should lead our armies against Kandy must also be political.

Politics, politics. Would I ever have an end to politics? 'Who can better lead our men, Sire?'

'King Vidiye.' He paused, eyed me gravely. 'The good news which was brought to us at our headquarters during the heat of battle, is that he escaped from his dungeon prison this morning, as your sister and you so cleverly planned.'

Monday, 3 October 1530

A messenger had galloped from the fort at dawn to give Julietta news of the massacre of Portuguese forces at Mulleri and the resounding Sinhala victory. She was thankful that Fernao was alive, though wounded. The news brought a blinding flash of realization. Supposing Fernao had been killed? What would her position be? A widow with two children in a country that was not her own. For the first time in her life, awareness of her dependency on Fernao struck her with a force that no defences could withstand. She had taken Fernao, his protection, his position, his kindness, his love so much for granted. She went down on her knees on the *prie-dieu* in her bedroom and prayed to God and the Blessed Virgin for Fernao's safe return. She had long given up trying to reconcile her love for her husband with her love for Prince Tikiri. Each love was entwined in her life. Both loves were God-inspired, divine, but her daily responsibility in this life was to Fernao.

She spent most of the morning in prayer before the altar containing the painted statue of the Virgin Mary carrying the infant Jesus. Lit by the glow from two small tapers, the black wicks floating in their own melted wax in small white china bowls, the statue seemed to smile at times. On occasion, she heard the clatter of horses' hooves on the driveway outside. Each time she excused herself from the Blessed Virgin, crossed herself and hastened to the window, only to be disappointed. Guards and tradesmen always called at this time of day.

Finally, she prayed . . . 'Holy Mary, Virgin Mother of Jesus, I pray thee to listen to a mother's prayers. I placed my husband, Fernao, in thy divine protection before he left on his campaign. Bring him safely back to me, as thou wouldst have protected thy husband, Joseph. May my two children never become fatherless . . .' Even as she uttered the words, she remembered, as always, that little Catherina had another father, so she hastily added, 'O Mother of the Virgin conception, thy daughter may have sinned in conceiving her own first-born, but thou, more than any mortal, dost surely understand the separation of parenthood from conception, of conception from virgin birth. My husband, Fernao de Albergaria, is the parent and protector of my daughter, Catherina, as thy husband Joseph was of our Lord, Jesus Christ. I do indeed pray thee, save her and my son, little Lopo, from becoming fatherless. Not for myself, but for them, O Blessed Virgin . . .'

Was this sacrilege? Surely the Blessed Virgin would understand.

'Hail Mary, full of grace . . .'

She heard the clip-clop of horses' hooves again, this time accompanied by the creak and squeak of wheels. She finished her Hail Mary, rapidly crossed herself and sped to the window. Her eyes fell on Aires riding ahead of a small covered wagon. Blood-stained, lean features tight, the scar on his face livid in the bright sunlight, he held himself erect in the saddle only with the greatest effort. Her heart started to pound. She turned on the instant and ran downstairs, calling Appu to have the servants prepare a hot bath and to the governess to keep the children in their nursery.

Something of love, something of compassion, something of guilt choked her when she saw Fernao being helped from the wagon. His face was gaunt and unshaven, his hair matted. The lines on his face were etched with dark grime. The sleeve of his doublet had been cut away and a great blood-stained bandage was wrapped around his right upper arm and strapped around his chest and neck. He smiled wanly at her. She longed with all her soul to rush to him and take him in her arms.

She fought back the impulse and her tears. This time, more than ever in her life before, she had to behave like a lady. She owed it to her wounded husband.

'It's good to be back home.' Fernao said, his voice weak and hoarse. He stood swaying on the step, assisted by Aires.

'It's good to have you back,' she responded steadily. 'Now upstairs with you. A warm bath and some hot food is what you need most.' She glanced at Aires. 'How bad is the general's wound?'

'Deep, but not serious if looked after, my lady.'

'Aires saved my life,' Fernao interjected. 'He'll need some food and rest.' He smiled wryly at his man. 'So off with you, Aires. And get a bath too. I swear by the saints that you smell like a sewer.'

While Fernao was being bathed, changed and put to bed, Julietta listened to his story of the great battle. He then asked for both children. They came into the bedroom and stood on either side of his bed. Propped up on the pink cushions, Fernao told them briefly what had happened. Julietta noted he carefully avoided making any reference to victory or defeat.

Catherina understood that her father had been wounded and started to cry, but little Lopo merely stood firm on both feet in a stance that reminded Julietta of his grand-father. He listened gravely to Fernao's explanation. When it was over, he said very quietly, 'I shall fight the men who hurt you, when I grow big.'

Then the Viceroy's personal physician, Armando Juarez, arrived from the flagship to examine and dress Fernao's wound, before hastening back to the fort to minister to the train of wounded soldiers who had been arriving since midnight. He gave Fernao a foul-smelling medicine to drink. Fernao fell alsleep almost before the physician had left the house.

He slept through the day. Julietta was seated close to his bed, sewing in the bright lights of the oil lamps, when he awoke that night. She knew the moment his eyes opened without having to look up. He smiled at her, reached out for her hand, squeezed it gently. 'My love,' he whispered. 'I regained consciousness last night to find myself in a mud hut with a thatched roof and the Viceroy's face above. How wonderful to open my eyes and see you glowing in beauty beside me tonight. As always, but especially after the horror of battle, you are my symbol of white purity.'

She felt herself blush. 'Oh Fernao, my much loved husband, there is no greater poet than you.' She shook her head. 'You would utter beautiful words even if you were dying.' She realized the inappropriateness of her remark under the circumstances and smiled ruefully. 'I could say that because you are alive and will be well soon,' she hastened to explain. 'you are not going to get away with dying merely by uttering beautiful words!'

Fernao turned towards her, winced at a stab of pain. 'You should have heard me swearing yesterday.'

'Even your swearing would be poetic,' she retorted. 'Aires gave me details of the battle, which you carefully avoided. You were so gallant. I'm proud of you.'

Her eyes grew moist, her nose tickled with emotion. She sniffed and blew into her hankerchief. 'What happens now, Fernao? Will King Maya Dunne attack Colombo?'

'If he intended doing so, he would be outside the city walls by now. He could have pressed home his victory last night, or at least this morning. Why didn't he? It is probably because he feared reprisals from Goa and Lisbon. Or perhaps he has other goals. What they are, we'll know soon enough. Now we can easily hold the city until the Viceroy sends reinforcements.' He grew thoughtful. 'The Don departs in a few days,' he continued. 'What will he do with King Vidiye? He can't kill him. I shall free him before Don Alfonso's flagship leaves the harbour, regardless of the consequences.' Julietta had avoided giving Fernao the news in case it upset him more. His words brought a gush of love within her. 'You do not have to worry about taking on the responsibility for freeing King Vidiye,' she assured him.

His eyebrows lifted, the ice-blue eyes inquiring. 'How so?'

'King Vidiye escaped the night before the battle.'

'Escaped! How did that happen?'

'No one on the fort knows. When the guards took his

breakfast to the dungeon yesterday morning, there was not a trace of him, nor any evidence as to how he had managed to escape.'

She had chosen her words with care. 'No one in the fort knows . . .' She had been tempted to tell Fernao the truth about the mine, which she had learned from Appu, but its access into the dungeon had been carefully covered up again by the Sinhala and some blind instinct held her back.

Fernao fell asleep immediately, as if a load had been removed from his mind. She was thankful that Prince Tikiri's name had never ever been mentioned during the day. She knew from Appu that the prince was safe.

CHAPTER TWENTY-SEVEN

Wednesday, 5 October 1530

Prince Kumara had news of the crushing defeat of the Portuguese at Mulleri the very next evening, by fast messenger. Although this was a blow to his hopes of Portuguese military support, he deemed it good fortune from his ascendant star when a delegation consisting of the army commander of the Dhamba army and the senior officers, all noblemen, arrived from Anu the same night and pledged their allegiance to him. Since he could not expect support from the Portuguese for the time being and since the Chola king in the north of Lanka was still being non-commital, he decided to watch events unfold while consolidating his grip on the Dhamba sub-kingdom. Meanwhile, the logical decision was to pull back the bulk of his troops to the safety of Kandy, leaving a token force and administrators in the Dhamba capital, and to see what King Maya Dunne's next move would be. Why had the Sita Waka army not followed up their victory and demolished the entire Portuguese task force while it was on the run? Reports indicated that King Maya Dunne would be heading for Jaya instead. Why?

King Vikrama of Dhamba and his court were being so agreeable that King Kumara saw no reason to dissipate his strength by leaving a large army of occupation in the sub-kingdom; he rejected a momentary qualm at the too-ready co-operation he was receiving in Dhamba. After all, King Vikrama was a decent human being, who had abdicated all desire for material possessions, and he would continue his rule under Kandyan suzerainty instead of that of the Great King in Jaya.

King Kumara had found Queen Anula in such a good mood on his return to Kandy that evening, almost her former self, bright, witty, cynical and a good listener, that he decided to postpone the visit he had intended paying his mistress Sita to the following day and had dinner with Queen Anula instead. He needed her both as a sounding board for his future plans and for the support she could command from her Kiri Vella clan, which had now become crucial to him.

They sat opposite each other in the queen's chamber after dinner and it was almost like old times again. The crickets still creaked from the darkness beyond the yellow and red lacquered grilles of the open window. A high wind rustled the dark branches carpeting the High Forest hillside. The blue night sky seemed to glow with promise.

'You are not visiting your young whore tonight, Sire,' Queen Anula teased him. 'We are flattered. We missed you while you were were away.'

He was touched by her pleasant acceptance of the situation, even grateful. He decided to be sincere, decent to her. 'When you came into our life – it seems like ages ago – we had a mistress, Manel,' he stated. 'Do you remember?'

She nodded, her gaze suddenly inscrutable.

'We then requested your understanding to include her in your life and ours, just as we were willing to help you with your son, Prince Deva Raja, a fact of your own life. The need for such understanding on each of our parts became moot when Manel died and you decided to leave your son in Kiri Vella. Ours became a perfect marriage.' He paused, leaned forward on his settle. 'Your suspicions and mistrust drew veils between us when we returned from Sita Waka. We ourselves admit to having given you probable cause.'

He sat back and studied her reaction. Had the large eyes flashed at his near admission of guilt, or had it been a trick of the light?

'We have a bright future ahead of us, beloved wife, if we work together harmoniously, for we now command a geographic area larger than that of any of the other kingdoms through our alliance with Jaya created by the betrothal of our daughter to King Dom Juan Dharma Pala, a product of your master mind. With our daughter also a Catholic we are better assured of Portuguese support when their reinforcements arrive; there is no reason why we should not become King Regent of Jaya in the interim, since King Vidiye is out of favour with the Portuguese state and Church. Why don't we both set aside our personal differences and work together as loving partners for the future?'

She had listened mainly with downcast eyes. Now she lifted them to his face and they were brilliant. 'Partners in bed too, Sire? Not just for the future, but tonight?' She was indeed her old self again.

'Tonight and every night, for ever,' he declared solemnly. Though he had his reservations, this was not the time to express them. 'How else could it be with the most magnificent bed partner in the land?'

She shook her head from side to side. 'You uplift us,' she stated.

'More importantly, it is you who can uplift us with the merest glance from your beautiful, dark eyes,' he responded, with a spontaneous return to his former self.

'We missed you so much while you were gone. We faced up to the fact that, whether as a woman or a queen, we were nothing without you, who *are* our future. We therefore took the liberty of setting in motion plans for supporting you unreservedly, so you could know how much we love and need you. As a result, our cousin Prince Ratna of Kiri Vella has three thousand men already under arms, awaiting your command. Also, being closely related to the Dhamba army commander, General Lord Gima, we have been able to arrange for two thousand of his men to move on your orders.'

'You did all this when you were so bitterly hurt and disappointed with us?' he inquired with wonder. 'How utterly decent of you!'

Her face hardened momentarily. 'We did it all because we love you.'

'As we told you on that sad night in Hangura, true love begets decency.'

'They discussed the future far into the night, then retired to the queen's bed-chamber. It was a sparkling love-making, but King Kumara kept seeing Sita's innocent beauty in his mind's eye and deep inside him felt he was betraying the one decent human being in his life.

Wednesday, 5 October 1530

Fernao slept intermittently for over forty hours, sitting up only to eat and have his wound dressed by the physician, who called again the next day. He was dozing propped up on the cushions when he heard the clatter of horses' hooves on the driveway outside. He glanced at the clock, his wedding present from Admiral Vasco de Gama. It read 3:55. The afternoon air outside was bright, but infused with the inner quietude that heralds the end of the day. At precisely 4 o'clock, the Viceroy was announced by Appu.

Don Alfonso was richly garbed as usual, in a high-necked slashed doublet of burgundy velvet, caught up with frilly golden lace at the throat and sleeves, embroidery being currently out of fashion. He wore puffed black breeches and burgundy nether-hosen. His heavy gold chains were studded with rubies, matching the inlaid hilt of the dagger at his waist, His vulturine face somehow matched the sombre richness, the fashion of the times, which he exuded.

He sat down on the chair beside the bed. 'We are glad to see you on the road to recovery, General.' He nodded, the great curving nose seeming to reach down towards his voice box.

'I shall be up and about in no time, Your Excellency. I am honoured by your visit.'

'It is our pleasure to visit our gallant general.' Was there a note of sarcasm in the dry voice?

The Viceroy talked idly for a few minutes before coming to the real reason for his visit. 'The extent of the defeat we have suffered must be minimized,' he stated. 'This is but a minor set-back. We and we alone will send despatches to His Majesty and the departments involved in Lisbon. There must be none from you. Understood, General?'

Fernao stiffened. Thousands of the king's men dead and only a minor set-back? 'I hear your words, Excellency.'

'And will carry out our order,' the parchment voice had become a warning growl.

'Are you directing me to join you in a conspiracy to withhold information from the King Emperor and the departments of state?'

'No.' The Viceroy climbed down visibly. He fingered his bony jaw with talon-like fingers. 'We are merely directing that we alone do the necessary reporting.'

Fernao pondered that. 'I suppose I cannot object to that.'

'Very well, then.' The dry voice became almost pleasant. 'King Vidiye's escape from the dungeon was nothing short of miraculous. We have still not worked out how it happened.'

Your treasure hunt was aborted, Fernao thought savagely. Perhaps God wrought the miracle.

'No matter,' the Viceroy proceeded. 'We have a request, channelled through Father Juan, for support against King Maya Dunne from that ruler . . . what's his name?'

'King Kumara of Kandy?'

'Yes, King Kumara. An odd fellow but seemingly quite clever. Of course, we are in no position at the moment to help anyone but ourselves, so we gave him a promise for the future.' The Viceroy's face turned hard and cruel. 'You will need quite literally to hold the fort in Colombo until we return, General. Our spies and those of the Church report that King Maya Dunne may attempt to take Jaya, but will refrain from any attack against us. We have therefore sent a whole regiment to help defend the capital city. The boy king, Dom Juan, must be safeguarded at all costs. You will need to keep lines of communication open between the fort and the city, a sort of corridor. Meanwhile, a formal ceremony of betrothal between King Dom Juan and the little daughter of King Kumara, Princess Dona Margaridha, has been arranged in our cathedral.' The Viceroy's smile was smug. 'That clever lady, Queen Anula, requested us to arrange the betrothal and we did so promptly.'

'What?' Fernao was stunned. What kind of mad cunning was this?

'You heard us. Father Perez was the intermediary. Holy Church has its uses. This betrothal makes everything fall into place for the future. It will be a blow to King Maya Dunne. He will not be able to take the Jaya capital, and we shall manipulate the boy king as ruler of the Jaya kingdom. Lanka shall remain divided and we shall rule it.'

Fernao could not fault the plan. Queen Anula, she would connive in her grave, he thought. She had obviously wanted her husband to become the Regent of Jaya since King Vidiye was imprisoned. But King Vidiye had escaped. He would not go back to Jaya. What would happen? As he contemplated, the Viceroy's harsh whisper interrupted Fernao's thought.

'But that is not the end of it,' the narrow eyes were glittering. 'We shall return and wreak vengeance on this country.'

King Kumara had been stunned to learn that King Vidiye was leading an army group of King Maya Dunne's forces against Kandy. But only for a brief while. Since no one in Sita Waka could know of the ready support available to him from Kiri Vella and Dhamba, he decided to take the offensive. He and Queen Anula had discussed details of the plan he had conceived, his most brilliant as the queen had enthusiastically described it, and she has sent trusted messengers to Prince Ratna in Kiri Vella and Lord Gima in Dhamba, who had returned with confirmation that they would participate in the plan and mesh in with its timing.

He had therefore set out from Kandy before dawn the previous morning, in order to reach the gorge by evening. Known as Kegalla, some thirty miles to the west, he had selected it as the battleground. King Vidiye would have to pass through it on his way to Kandy, so King Kumara had the opportunity to scout the ground, entrench his troops and have his bowmen test for range before battle was joined. His army of cavalry, bowmen and infantry was headed by forty armoured elephants. With the Kiri Vella and Dhamba groups, he heavily outnumbered King Vidiye's force, reportedly of five thousand men.

He had always been confident in battle. The fear he knew until an engagement commenced, he accepted as the natural expression of an intelligent, imaginative mind. It brought forth courage, generated true fearlessness during an action, helped a man take care. Only clods knew no fear, and only the stupid indulged in bravado.

But although totally satisfied with his plan, some deep instinct warned King Kumara this morning of some weak link in it which he could not identify.

Everything had gone smoothly so far, perhaps too smoothly.

King Vidiye now faced him at the far end of the green

gorge on one side of which a muddy river chattered over black rocks. Sitting firmly astride his favourite chestnut, King Kumara glanced up at the grey crags that sloped sharply down the valley. He could detect no sign of movement there. Good! His Dhamba allies were well hidden from view.

The sun had not yet risen, but the sky beyond the hills to the east was rosy with the promise of dawn. The countless bats that hung like tiny black sacks from the brown branches of the tall trees fringing the river did not even stir, though the air was filled with cawing crows.

King Kumara had a pain at the nape of his neck and his cheekbones hurt. He knew this was caused by the humidity of the gorge. He turned to the general, his stocky figure seeming to be carved like granite into the bay charger. 'You are sure the Kiri Vella force is in position, ready to move?' he inquired.

'Prince Ratna sent me word of it, Sire.'

'And the Dhamba army?' Could that be the weak link?

The general glanced towards the hilltops. 'They are already in position, with our officers to ensure that they fulfil their task and don't run away. Your plan to draw King Vidiye into the gorge by pretending to withdraw last night was brilliant, Sire. Being neither strategist nor a tactician but a fighting man, King Vidiye obviously decided to pursue us relentlessly.'

At that moment enemy trumpets blared in the distance, their drums shuddering in a long roll before breaking out into a deafening rattle. The shouts, screams and curses of men arose.

General Dunu smiled, his tan-pink cheeks glowing. 'Your trap is set, Sire. When the rats have walked in, Prince Ratna will close it from the rear and the Dhamba army will pour down those hills to the enemy flank.' He placed his hand on the pommel of his saddle and turned round to survey his men, drawn up in massed column behind them.

King Kumara followed his glance, noted with satisfaction the bright coloured standards of the Kandyan noblemen fluttering in a light breeze blowing down the valley, the cavalry twenty abreast, pennants on lances. He had placed the pikeman immediately behind the cavalry, then the bowmen, with the infantrymen in the rear, ready to filter through for the kill.

He turned back to face the advancing enemy. 'They are playing their own funeral march,' he stated. But the stab of disquiet within him persisted.

The enemy approached closer and closer. Fortified war-elephants began to trot, *howdahs* swaying. Four hundred yards, three hundred . . . Now!

What had happened? Anxiously, King Kumara's eyes sought the hilltops from which the Dhamba force should be sending boulders crashing down to make the elephants stampede.

Had they misunderstood the timing? A sick sensation clawed at the pit of King Kumara's stomach, sent chills through it.

Then he heard the rumble from above him on both sides of the valley and released his breath, glanced towards the enemy to witness the chaos in their ranks.

Dear *devas*!' General Dunu cried, He pointed. 'Look Sire!' His voice cracked. 'We are betrayed.' He drew his sword.

The boulders were not hurtling down at the enemy, but at his own troops.

Within moments, there was utter confusion in the Kandyan ranks, but King Kumara suddenly became cool as mountain air. Only one alternative remained, to attack and drive the enemy back towards the Kiri Vella force.

He whipped out his blade, raised it aloft, pointed in the direction of the enemy. 'Death or glory, all you loyal Kandyans!' he roared. 'Ch . . . ar . . . ge!'

He dug fierce heels into his horse's flanks. The animal

shot forward. Deadly silent, King Kumara made for the enemy. His blood sang when he heard the thunder of hooves behind him. His men were sweeping to the attack, regardless of the rocks and boulders hurtling down on them.

He galloped between the enemy elephants, taking darts from the men in the *howdahs* on his shield and his leather armour. He crashed into the line of cavalry, a wall of stunned faces. He saw the giant figure of King Vidiye on a great horse. Take the snake's head, some instinct within him urged. He began hacking his way towards his opponent.

'Clear a space!' King Vidiye's deep roar resounded through the clash and din of battle. 'Clear a space. Let this be mortal combat between us two kings.'

As if by magic, his men responded. Within minutes, a space was cleared. The two kings faced each other on horseback. The sounds of battle died down. Even the rumble of the falling boulders became a mere background to the silence of the little arena.

'How does a proud man like you become a Maya Dunne lackey?' King Kumara demanded half wondering, half insulting, across the yards that separated him from King Vidiye.

'How does one of royal birth like you offer your arse to the white man?' King Vidiye growled back. 'And to the friars. It is heroes like you who divide our nation. Never trust a Kandyan.' He threw back his head, the large fierce eyes rolled, his bitter laugh echoed to the skies.

'Your point is well taken, cousin.' King Kumara remembered the words of the Dhamba ruler. What is it all for, he wondered. I shall kill this man today. And what will he and I have gained, for we are worse than lackeys, we are both roadside prostitutes, as all kings are, dependent upon the common people for their livelihood. 'Let us now decide who is the superior lackey,' he grated. Sword at the ready, he urged his mount forward.

Suddenly fresh screams arose to his rear, a thudding, the swell as of a wave, the clash of metal. King Kumara reined in immediately, his attention distracted.

Seizing the opportunity, King Vidiye charged.

King Kumara swung back too late. He had expected his opponent to attack towards his left. Instead, King Vidiye swerved at the last moment, crossing in front of him. The great upraised sword crashed down before King Kumara could raise his own weapon high enough to parry the blow.

First, an explosion of crushing pain that shot downwards from his skull, driving his head into his neck, then blackness interspersed by a dozen stars. Sword and shield dropped from his nerveless hands. He swayed in the saddle, heard General Dunu's cry from a great distance away. 'The Kiri Vella men have betrayed us too. They are attacking our rear. Fight for your lives, you loyal Kandyans.'

In a flash of comprehension, King Kumar saw it all. A split second, during which he thought with wonder, Anula, you have won. You played on the faith of a man who developed a spark of decency. The croak that escaped him before he hit the ground was meant to be a laugh.

Wednesday, 19 October 1530

When King Kumara came to, he could not lift his eyelids. At first he wondered at the numbness that was his entire being, then recollection flooded him. He knew he was mortally wounded. He would not see the sky again, nor hear the sound of laughter before he died. Could he speak?

'Any . . . anyone there?' He croaked the words, barely hearing them himself.

'This is General Dunu, Sire.' The voice reached him faintly, as if from another world. 'We are both prisoners,

385

awaiting the return of King Vidiye from pursuing our troops. I have failed you, my king. I shall take my own life as punishment.'

'Not so!' Some reserve of superhuman strength brought the words out sharply. 'We give you back your life.' He felt the need to speak. In a few words, he mumbled out what had just happened to him. 'You . . . will find our . . . our diaries . . . with the Chief Bhikku of the Temple of the Tooth . . . People may find them interesting. Now . . . p . . . please write down what we say and seal it with our ring.'

In halting phrases he gave his message. Finally it was ended. 'General . . . a life for a l . . . life,' he directed. 'Your l . . . life in exchange for giving us a release from our life.'

'Never, Sire!' The general's voice was hoarse.

'We have always been . . . d . . . different from other men. One final proof now . . . we beg you . . . so you can . . . t . . . tell the world: where others awaited the visitor, death, we visited death instead!' His voice weakened, without faltering. 'You alone can give us that immortality.'

'No, no, no . . .'

'It is a matter of honour. We command you.'

A long silence. Too long for the king with so much at stake . . . 'Time is running . . . out.'

Finally, the welcome words. 'Very well, Sire. They took away my sword, but overlooked my knife. My stroke will be swift and sure through your great heart, O Great King.'

Miraculously, a scornful laugh escaped the king. The words came out clear and strong, with the old cynical tone to them. 'Instant heaven. Ha! You know, General, I never thought that death could be so . . . amusing!'

Wednesday, 19 October 1530

In the Kandy palace, Queen Anula selected a silk sari of pale blue, the Buddhist's alternative colour of mourning.

She was a widow again and must portray the right image, sad and brave, to the world and especially to the man who would send for her. But beautiful, always beautiful. Consternation had reigned in the palace, especially among the younger princes, the older chieftains and the Catholics, after the breathless, dust-stained messenger had arrived from Kegalla that evening bringing the news of her husband's defeat and death. Only she remained calm. It was a noble role and coldly, cynically, she enjoyed playing it. Now at 8 P.M. by the timepiece Father Juan had given King Kumara as a baptism present, she calmly awaited the head of the victorious low-country forces. King Vidiye, she knew, had worshipped briefly at the sacred temple outside the palace and was now holding audience in the great hall. When it was over, he would send for her.

There had been a few moments of nostalgia while she dressed. She remembered the Prince Kumara of old, a fair-faced boy with silken skin, sparkling brown eyes and slender build, who possessed unique sexual power and stamina. His wit and charm had touched her heart. He had been the only man to reach into the hidden depths of her, to probe her mystery as he had described it.

But recollection of the pain, the shame of his infidelity had swiftly intruded and she had smoothly, naturally, thrust aside the beautiful memories. All men were alike, ready to humiliate and exploit women by physical force and superior station. It was for women to use their brains and their very position as the sex objects men made them, in order to exploit those same men!

She had betrayed the betrayer by exploiting his new weakness, a growing addiction to and belief in decency. The secret plan for the Kiri Vella forces and the Dhamba army to turn against King Kumara had been hers. She too had been the contact with King Vidiye, assuring him of the betrayal. She would have loved to extend her vengeance to her husband's mistress, Sita. Unfortunately, on hearing the news of King Kumara's death, the whore had taken her own life by drinking poison.

Her pulses quickened when the knock on the door finally came and Nona informed her that King Vidiye requested her presence in the audience chamber. Since she'd had her daughter, Dona Margaridha, betrothed to his son, Dom Juan, the Great King, she and King Vidiye were now family connections too. Through foresight and cunning, she had once again placed herself in a unique position.

The flare-lit corridors were thronged with older nobles, speaking in hushed voices. She swept past them, eyes downcast so as to ignore men such as the silver-haired dandies, Prince Surya Bandara and Lord Ellawela, who were about to offer their condolences.

Her mind was completely clear when she entered the room and saw the giant King Vidiye seated on the familiar divan. He looked bigger and more menacing than she remembered him. He did not rise to greet her, merely acknowledged her salutation. Hot and sweaty from the morning's battle, he exuded a power that stimulated her. When she was seated, he fixed her with those large, fierce eyes. 'Madam, we extend you our sincere thanks,' he growled. 'The support you afforded us today helped us achieve a victory that would have been ours in any event, with a greater degree of ease and less bloodshed.'

'It was no more than our duty, Sire,' she responded, her glance lowered. 'Painful as it was, we responded to a higher call.' She lifted moist eyes to meet his gaze, slowly fluttered her lashes to convey sorrow, then looked down again. She had been unable to fathom his thoughts.

'A higher call! Like a call of nature? Piss on that!' He laughed without mirth. 'In that event, we shall avoid the hypocrisy of offering you our sympathies.' He was mocking her and it dawned on her that he knew her of old. 'You obviously have some object in mind, madam. Would it not be best for us to talk openly about it, as two people who might have a common purpose, instead of insulting each other by fencing.' His dark eyes were boring into her, but she would not meet his gaze. He was a rough, tough man who would take whatever he wanted. 'What do you want in exchange for the support you have extended?'

'Perhaps it would be better for us to tell you first what further support we can extend to you, lord, before we get down to a dry-fish trade!' She allowed a tight smile to touch the corners of her mouth. 'You are the only man strong enough to create a united kingdom in Lanka. We can help you achieve that goal.' She looked at him squarely then.

The large, dark eyes with their haunted look widened. 'Are you suggesting, madam, that we turn against our wife who rescued us from a Portuguese dungeon, and her father who restored an honoured place to us by entrusting us with an army?'

'They all helped you in order to achieve their own objectives,' she retorted bluntly. Her gaze became piercing, dominant. 'We thought you wanted to talk frankly, lord. If you are not willing to do so, we shall gladly accept your sympathies and beg your leave to return to our grief!'

Their glances locked in a silent battle. Which way would it go? Either way she had nothing to lose, except power if he rebuffed her.

To her surprise, he suddenly grinned, revealing large white teeth. 'We always knew you to be a unique lady,' he stated. 'But you have grown with experience.' He paused, musing. 'And why not? After all, you had one of the cleverest men ever for a husband, the late King Kumara.' His voice became sharp again. 'What help can you give us to achieve national unity?'

'The continued support of the entire Kiri Vella clan, plus that of the Dhamba army, plus full assistance from the Kandyan people. In short, everything which our late husband organized and thought he possessed. The Kiri

389

Vella clan turned against him at my behest. The Dhamba army were never his, because they resented his violation of their king's sacred position. They would, however, join you at our request. We have family connections with them. Add to those the isolationist policy of the Chola king in the north and the loyalty of those who believe in your son's right of succession and you will command a geographic area far greater than that of Sita Waka.'

'The Kiri Vella clan we can understand, but how could you, a *pathaya*, low-country person, ever presume to obtain the backing of the Kandyans?'

'They consist of two groups, those who have become Catholics, who are loyal to Holy Church, and the old, established Sinhala Buddhist up-country families, who will support a strong succession in order to avoid a return to feuding amongst themselves.'

'And will you be that strong successor, madam?'

Was he mocking her again? 'No, *you* will be, Sire.'

His great eyes rolled. He leaned forward on his seat. 'How can that happen without the backing of King Maya Dunne?'

'By your setting aside your present marriage to his daughter and marrying us.'

His great jaw dropped momentarily. Then his eyes widened as the possibilities of such a union slowly dawned on him. 'You are a lady after our own heart!' he finally declared. His tone became sober. 'It is our mind that warns.' He hesitated, pondering. 'Assuming that we are willing to consider what appears at first hearing to be a preposterous proposal, madam, how will it be achieved?'

She told him.

CHAPTER TWENTY-EIGHT
Wednesday, 19 October 1530

On the third day after the battle, Fernao's wound had turned septic. The flesh around it swelled, the skin became an angry red. The wound began to throb, aching outwards and inwards as if the bone were on fire. Two days later, he was running such a fierce temperature that his mouth was always dry, his lips were parched and his thirst became insatiable. The physician ordered leeches to bleed him, applied unguents, gave him noxious mixtures, all to no avail, the infection had entered his body.

Whenever he had opened his eyes, Julietta had been there, soaking his head with a cooling liquid, feeding him or on her knees beside his bed praying.

How could he tell her that, following the battle, he had lost some of his will to live? That he blamed himself for the loss of his men, that the bitterness of defeat had finally overtaken him and was searing his soul? How could he reveal the horrible recurring nightmare he had begun to experience whenever he fell asleep?

Ghostly white skeletons, teeth grinning fiendishly, reach me with claw-like fingers, fiercely gripping my wounded arm, pulling me towards them so they can tear out my flesh. Behind them, living beings clad in black robes kneel with outstretched arms that are but whitened bones, piteously imploring me to do something, something, I know not what, to save them and I know not from what.

I struggle to ward off my attackers. A giant figure emerges from the dark, horrible depths of nowhere. My terror-drenched spirit tells me it is the Devil, for it is dressed in black and red, has horns on its head and cloven feet. The face reveals itself as that of the dead rapist Sergeant Correa.

Why then does it have live, burning coals for eyes and mad, slavering jaws? The figure starts increasing in size, imprisoning me by its presence, so I am powerless to move.

Its chest is at my eye level, palpitating, shimmering, like a bull's liver on a platter, now its stomach, the belly button an ugly red blob. Now, oh God, its crotch. Ulcerous, obscene, the crotch comes closer and closer to me, balls to eyeballs. Bones rattle, talons tear my helpless quivering flesh. A wailing shatters my ears. Horror-stricken I see that the crotch is empty, torn and bleeding. No penis, just a whirlpool of stinking blood sucking me in, sucking me in, sucking me in . . .

He would wake with a cry, trembling, hot, bathed in sweat, terrified. And always, Julietta was there, comforting him.

Though he did not know it, Fernao's life hung in the balance for eleven days. On the eleventh night, he opened feeble eyes from a tortured sleep to find Father Juan beside his bed, a silver crucifix held in both hands. In the golden lamplight, the priest's silken vestments gleamed as if from another world. Rain pounding on the roof and against the window shutters intruded into Fernao's senses. His flesh was numb, but his bones ached and the bedclothes were damp with sweat. His eyelids drooped against the light.

'*Indulgentiam, absolutionem, et remissionem peccatorum tuorum tribuat tibi omnipotens et misericors Dominus . . .*

'May the almighty and merciful Lord grant you pardon, absolution and remission of your sins.'

At first, he could not comprehend what the priest was saying. The prayer was strange to him, the meaning of the Latin words would not penetrate his fogged brain.

The booming voice went on and on. He wished its droning would end, so he could sleep in peace . . . for ever.

'*Si vivis, per istam sanctam Unctionem, indulgeat tibi Dominus quidquid delquisti. Amen.*'

'If you are alive, may the Lord forgive you by this holy anointing whatever sins you have committed. Amen.'

The coolness of the oil on his forehead seemed to go through his skull and penetrate his brain. Suddenly he knew that he was hearing the words of Absolution, from the Last Rites.

So he was going to die. And it did not really matter, because he was weary unto death.

Why?

He did not know the answer. All he wanted was to make his confession and die in peace.

A child's cry, quickly hushed, intruded into his consciousness. Who was that? Some child he knew, someone close to him? Ah yes, his son, little Lopo, flesh of his tortured flesh, his aching blood. The boy he loved, whose mother he loved. Somewhere in his restless, confused mind, a thought stirred.

Can I die in peace? Sweet Jesu help me. God of my fathers give me strength.

As if in answer to his prayers, inspiration exploded suddenly in a flash of whiteness within his brain. 'Father, I am going to die,' he muttered. 'There is poison within me, but not in my body alone. It can only be removed through confession.'

A moment's silence. As in a mist, he caught the gleam of understanding in the pale yellow eyes. 'Kneel in your spirit then before God and His Son, Jesus Christ and before the Holy Ghost, and reveal your sickness to them through their minister on earth. In the name of the Father, the Son . . .'

His whispered confession included how he had plotted to coerce Julietta into marrying him and the way in which he had misused his military power to still the ache of jealousy in him, the bombardment of helpless civilians in Galle, the hanging of innocents, the betrayal of the Abdul Raschids, his many breaches of the code of *cavaleiro*, the suspicions that had made him moody at home, his guilt about the defeat at Mulleri.

When it was over, Fernao felt drained, totally exhausted, yet he was cleansed. During the entire ceremonial, Father Juan had been strong as a rock, conveying the peace, consolation and hope of the Church. And through that symbol, Fernao discovered the truth and the agelessness of his Christian belief. He had walked through the valley of the shadow of death. But now he feared no evil.

Father Juan's parting words to him became embedded in his mind: 'You owe it to your wife, Julietta, to live. Therefore live and offer penance for your sins by dedicating your future life to your family in the Christian way, with unfailing love and understanding.'

Friday, 28 October 1530

The battle of Mulleri had been savagely satisfying to Aisha Raschid. Every time she struck down a Portuguese soldier, watching the eyes widen, the white face contort with pain and terror, she was striking a blow for her dead son, Ali. She could see his smile of approval as she spurred her horse to the next enemy and the next, sword raised aloft, a figure of doom in the black *chador* she wore over the leather corselet. Her troop had acquitted itself honourably, the women being especially ruthless and daring. They had stilled the male critics, struck a blow for womankind. Now there was talk of giving her command of a squadron. But it was vengeance, vengeance, vengeance ... balm she needed for her lonely tortured spirit. Why then did the ache remain?

Even the temporary alleviation of her anguish was, however, short-lived. When it became apparent that a *status quo* had been established, with the Portuguese in command of the cities of Jaya and Colombo, King Kumara dead, King Vidiye in control of the Kandy kingdom and

Dhamba, the Chola king neutral and the Sita Waka forces supreme elsewhere, King Maya Dunne departed for his capital with the bulk of his army. Although Prince Raja Sinha remained encamped in a great arc near Kadu, well away from the capital, Jaya, Aisha and her cavalry troop had been directed to return with King Maya Dunne to Sita Waka, where she resumed the training that had been interrupted by the campaign. But training alone would no longer be enough.

Aisha noticed that her husband, Abdul, had lost weight and seemed to have aged somewhat during the three weeks she had been away. He had appeared tired, listless, at dinner. She had decided to ask him about it later. Now, as they sat in their living room, there were other things to discuss. The servants had retired to the kitchen quarters and the inevitable clatter of platters intruded upon the stillness of the room, ripe with the rich odour of the *biriyani* remaining in the dining room. So different from campfires, Aisha thought. And yet, there had been something about those campfires that had appealed to the nomadic blood in her veins.

Seated on his usual divan, Abdul began cleaning his teeth with an ivory pick. 'King Maya Dunne's victory has changed everything for us,' he observed. 'We can even go back to our old home in Colombo by an arrangement I have been able to make.'

'Are we not still under sentence of death in Colombo?' Aisha inquired. Somehow she did not want to return to Colombo. Sita Waka alone could give her the action for which her soul craved.

'The Portuguese want us back. With King Bhuvaneka dead, King Maya Dunne has obtained a full pardon for us from King Vidiye and the restoration of all our property.' He eyed her hopefully, his small eyes almost pleading.

She felt fiercely resolute. 'This is now our home, husband of mine.'

'It was meant to be but a temporary refuge,' he reminded her quietly. 'You wish to remain here so you can go into battle again and ease your torment. Was not the one occasion enough?'

She looked at him squarely over the veil, her dark eyes glittering. 'It was enough for the time being, but there is something inside, a burning anguish that can never be quenched.'

'You will not quench such anguish by killing the enemy on the battlefield. Its end must come from within you.'

'For me, I think the end will only come from outside, in death. I am not merely fighting for revenge. This is my private *jihad* against the infidel Christians.'

'Are not the Buddhists and Hindus infidels?'

'They are unbelievers, not infidels. Christians are the offshoot of the Jews who denied our Prophet and his heirs much needed support. Besides, it is Christians who persecuted our people through their so-called Crusades. By killing them, I wreak my private vengeance as well as that of my faith.'

'And what about me, your husband? I have never spoken about this before, but you know how I have suffered, wondering how you were, whether you were dead or alive, wounded or taken prisoner, while bearing my own load of sorrow?'

'Whenever I have thought about it, my grief has increased. It has torn me apart at times. But now, this is my life. As I once minded the house while you fought your battles in the world of trade, it is your turn to let me fight my own battles on the field.'

'You might be killed.' His eyes definitely pleading now, but gave way before her relentless stare, drifted to a moth hopelessly fluttering its wings around the single oil lamp on its brass stand.

'Then I shall go to heaven instantly.'

'Supposing you are never killed, but go on fighting untill there are no battles left?'

'I shall have become at least the commander of a regiment by then and will go down in history, a woman unique as Pooti of the Tharu desert.'

'Will that ease the torment within you?' he inquired shrewdly.

She dropped her gaze. This was something she had wondered about too. She did not really want to die, only to fill her aching void. 'Perhaps the knowledge that I have struck a blow for womankind will compensate.'

As she spoke the words she knew that they were untrue. Only death would heal her wounds. She had a moment's inspiration. 'We have not made love to each other since we learnt of our son's death,' she stated quietly. 'Your concern for me tonight has freed me of some fear of loving that held me back. I would like to give myself to you now.'

His gaze softened, became compassionate. 'Fear of making love to someone whom I could lose otherwise than through natural causes holds *me* back,' he responded gently. 'Besides, I was told by the physician, while you were gone, that some of the symptoms I have, which I never brought to your notice, arise from a wasting disease. I do not have much longer to live.'

Following his confession, Fernao had fallen into a deep untroubled sleep, which lasted through that night, the whole of the next day and all the following night. When he awoke to birdsongs on a grey dawn, weak as a kitten, his drowsy eyes had fallen on Julietta sleeping on the carpet beside him. He had known a deep gratitude, a rush of love for her, such as he had never experienced before. She loved him without reserve and that was what marrige was all about. Nothing she might have done or could do mattered, so long as she loved him. He could not possess her

397

immortal soul. She was God's creature, acting out of God's will for her and answerable only to God.

The poison in his mind and spirit had vanished. He could get back to being his true self again.

He began falling asleep again to the imagined fragrance of queen-of-the-night from the open window.

Or had it been Julietta's scent? . . .

Now, ten days later, the monsoon had ended and he was on his feet again. A late moon had arisen following the full moon four nights earlier. The scent of queen-of-the-night was real. So was the jasmine scent that Julietta, seated on the floor beside his chair, was wearing. So was the deep, deep love in his heart. So was the peace of his spirit.

Sunday, 30 October 1530

I took advantage of the inaction following the monsoon to visit Sene and his wife Chandra, with whom my two wards, Bandula and his little sister, Nangi, were living. Since their home was within the broad area of our encampment, I sent word ahead and rode there alone that afternoon. A sudden flurry of rain nearly soaked me just as I slid off my black horse, Rama. I hurried into the house wiping the rain off my clothes.

'We are disappointed that you could not share the noon meal with us, Prince,' the motherly Chandra said. 'Camp food is not that good even for a general and you would have enjoyed some home cooking.'

'I certainly would, but when campaigning, the king and I make it a point to eat only what the men do.'

'Why, how nice of you,' she responded. 'It's a good idea to make your men more loyal.'

I merely shrugged, for such was not my motive.

'Would you like some hot coriander tea?' Chandra inquired. 'And some sweetmeats perhaps? We have oil-cakes and *kokkis*.'

'Just some coriander tea. My throat is beginning to tickle. I have avoided colds this monsoon. I'd hate to get one now.'

'Then you must inhale some of the steam first. I'll get it ready for you.' Chandra bustled into the house.

Sene smiled tolerantly at her receding figure. 'She is a real treasure. You should think of getting married, Prince. You need someone to look after you.'

I grinned. 'A palace does not permit that kind of mothering. You know our routines.'

'Ah, true, true. You have to pay a price for your station in life. Everything balances out in the long run.' He nodded towards water still trickling down the inner wall of the verandah. 'A homeless beggar does not have to worry about a leaking roof.' He paused. 'Which reminds me, you will want to meet your wards.'

'How are they doing?'

'Very well, as you shall see for yourself.'

'Have they settled down comfortably to their new station?'

'Physically, yes. But you must understand that Bandula is a wild one, used to the freedom of a hare. It will take him time to become disciplined.'

'I thought his wildness was only for survival.'

'However it starts, wildness becomes a part of a person's character, Prince. It scurries inside the mind to meet the basic wildness of the animal that lies within all human beings. But you must not worry. Bandula will adjust with time and . . . er . . . the affection we will give, of which he is suspicious at present. His sister has, however, adapted more easily to routine and she is a good influence on him, like the tame elephant with the noosed one in the *kraal*.'

'H'mm.' All this was new to me. It seemed rather more complicated than the upbringing of princes in a palace, which was difficult enough. I was glad I had taken the vow of *brachmachariya* and would never have children. I simply could not cope! And yet . . . why had I looked forward with such eagerness to seeing the two children again?

'Shall we go into the sitting room, lord?' Sene gestured with his hand.

We sat in the spacious living room. It was lit against the darkness outside from heavy clouds and rain that had begun to gather, a final lash of the monsoon's tail before it curled up and died. Many-tiered brass lamps, their multi-wicks fluttering and smoking, bathed us with a warm, golden glow. The two children entered. They had obviously been schooled for the occasion, for they greeted me with obeisance.

Bandula was dressed in a blue *kurtha* and white *dhoti*, Nangi wore a pink cloth and jacket. Their hair washed, oiled and combed, their faces scrubbed, they looked like two little children from any decent home, quite different from the grubby waifs I had picked up. I scanned their faces and arms as they stood in front of me, Nangi goggling. Their sores had almost healed, the scars would disappear with time, but a certain wariness in the boy's downcast eyes warned me that the wounds in his spirit remained a part of his inner being.

At that moment, I realized with amazement that I had only just become an adult. Waging war, winning battles, having noble aims does not make an adult. It is feeling personally responsible for some other human being, especially a child, that causes the transition. Up to now, I had not been responsible for a plant or a dog, not even my horse. A desire for family mushroomed within me, identi-fied itself with Julietta.

Deliberately, coldly, my reflexes took over, caused me to thrust aside all sentiment. For others, a lifetime of family. For me, duties of my station and my destiny. *Dharma*. The killing, maiming, blood-letting lay within me, needing more reason for being there than a hope of salvation. *Dharma!* The Hindu doctrine which alone could

400

permit me to live with compassion, but without compassion.

Meanwhile, all the family life I might experience had to be concentrated on these two children.

I cleared my throat to break the awkward silence that had fallen on the room. 'You both seem very well,' I remarked.

'Are you a real prince?' Bandula inquired, looking squarely at me for the first time.'

'Yes.'

'My sister is learning to talk. She doesn't know what a prince is, but I do. You live in a palace, wear fine clothes, have lots of servants and tell people what to do.'

'Not always,' I laughed. 'The king frequently tells me what to do. And the people point the way to him. I also have to fight sometimes, or wait in the rain for a fight to start.'

'Like now,' he ventured shrewdly. 'Your clothes are wet.' He paused, looked me in the eye, his gaze suddenly moist. 'I don't want you to get wet and become sick. I will work hard when I become big to see you don't get wet any more.'

Dear *devas*, concern from this wayside waif such as I had never experienced before. I fought back emotion. The obvious love of this child sparked a new need which some intuition told me would have a dramatic effect on me some day.

Sunday, 6 November 1530

One week later, Fernao was well enough to sit by the window of his upstairs bedroom, reading his correspondence, catching up with the daily reports that Captain Diogo de Mello had submitted and issuing written orders at last. He felt curiously at peace with himself this morning, but his interest quickened when Julietta entered the room.

401

She was dressed in pale yellow, which accented her auburn hair. She gave him her sweetest smile and he realized with wonder that it had always been his to evoke. 'Ah, the great general is himself again, riding his favourite *chaise-longue*,' she remarked. She grew serious on the instant. 'Well, at least that's better than riding the wings of sickness . . . or . . . or . . .' Her voice faltered. 'I think it must have been my prayers to the Blessed Virgin that saved you.' It was the first time she had broached his near-escape from death.

He stared out of the window again and spoke into the distance. 'It could have been, Juli, because the turning point was a cry from our son,' he responded soberly. 'There was indeed a great sickness within me. My confession, the absolution of Holy Church and your love saved me. Now there can be no going back, because God has given me a second chance and I must not misuse it.'

The time was right. He told her all, holding back nothing, still speaking into the distance, knowing it to be the distant past.

'The jealousy and suspicion, the feeling of being humiliated was like the great hot winds that arose from the flames of the Sita Waka capitol when it burned down,' he concluded quietly. 'They swirled back to fan the hellish flames of cruelty and ambition. I know that I am no longer the idealistic young midshipman who first sailed into Colombo harbour. Yet it is not too late for me to dedicate myself to what is right.'

He glanced at her for the first time, noted with wonder the tears streaming silently down her fair cheeks. She simply stood there, her staring eyes shedding tears like monsoon rain. Something held him back, some knowledge that her weeping was from a source so deep that words would never reach it. It seemed like hours before she stopped. She sniffed once, wiped her cheeks, brushed away the last teardrops from her eyes with a kerchief, volunteered no comment as to why she had cried.

'How will you carry out your duties and still retain your ideals?' she inquired steadily.

'I have thought that out. Our real objectives in Lanka and the Indian Ocean have become clouded by personal aims. We came here for trade, not for conquest. Holy Church wants conquest. It is an easy way to spread the gospel and satisfy the lust of clerics for wealth and power. I no longer believe that trade and religion should be advanced by coercion.'

'What you say is true, Fernao, but is it not by military force that we are able to obtain the most favorable terms in trade and to safeguard our religion once it is established?'

'Certainly. That is why we build forts around our factories, but our real quest should be to create fair competition. Before Vasco da Gama came out to the Indies, local producers were exploited by their rulers, who in turn were being cheated by the Mouro. Vasco da Gama established fair prices to be paid by decree of our king, which he enforced with our naval might. I intend to follow a similar policy.'

'But what of the Viceroy? Surely his greed . . .' She looked at him fearfully.

'Will lead us to a clash.' He concluded her sentence with a tight smile. 'That is a risk I have to take. While I have the power, however, I shall cease all interference in the internal affairs of this country. We shall maintain strong forts, especially in Colombo and Galle. We are committed to keeping the regiment in Jaya so the succession of the Great King is ensured. We will be compelled to protect Holy Church, especially now that the Franciscans are due to arrive and establish schools, convents and churches here, but all this will be from a defensive posture. The policy of domination which I conceived died when God gave me life again. You were his instrument, Juli, and I will not do you the dishonour of thanking you for your devotion. I shall instead try to live my thankfulness.'

'Oh Fernao,' was all she could say, except for the tears that gushed into her beautiful eyes again.

His jaw tightened with resolve. 'Many years ago, I resigned my naval commission on a principle, because my father would have separated you and me,' he continued. 'If I am ordered to act contrary to my conscience, I shall resign my army commission.'

She dimpled, her smile mischievous through tear-sparkled eyes. 'Men and history will say that you made a habit of resigning commissions.'

'And what will my wife say?'

'That she loves you, respects you, admires you more than ever before for your integrity.' She paused. 'Would they allow you to remain as trade factor if you resigned your commission?'

'They might. But even if they asked me to resign as factor, I would have the choice of remaining here as a private citizen or returning to Portugal, living the life of a wealthy landowner and . . .' He looked at her hopefully. '. . .becoming a writer at long last, while my wife paints.' He reached out his hand to her. 'Would you be willing to share such a decision?'

She hesitated. obviously troubled.

'I realize that this is your country,' he stated quietly, no longer jealous, full of new understanding. 'But think of our children too. They will have no real future here.'

She made up her mind on the instant. 'Whither thou goest, I go.' Her smile was brave, but sad.

PART THREE
The Real Victory

CHAPTER TWENTY-NINE

Extracts from the personal diary of General Fernao Soarez de Albergaria.

Thursday, 26 December 1532: Sickness from my wound interrupted my habit of maintaining this personal diary. Now, three years later, after a Merry Christmas indeed, I am eager to write again.

This has been a most dramatic year for all of us in Lanka . . .

Before King Vidiye returned to Jaya after his defeat of King Kumara and the annexation of the Kandyan kingdoms, he arbitrarily appointed Dona Margaridha, the infant daughter of King Kumara, Queen of Kandy, with Queen Anula as Regent. Since the little lady was betrothed to his son, the Great King Dom Juan, this gave King Vidiye that control over Jaya, the Kandyan kingdoms, Dhamba and Kiri Vella which King Kumara had sought to establish for himself before he died. Thus did Queen Anula prevail in her plans. King Maya Dunne was reluctant to overrule King Vidiye, who was after all his son-in-law, so the widowed queen became a power in her own right. As soon as my new policy of non-alignment became apparent, King Vidiye moved back to the Jaya palace. Having once established himself there as the real ruler, he moved again and occupied the Raigam kingdom in the south. King Maya Dunne still held back out of loyalty. Finally, King Vidiye sent his wife, Queen Padma, King Maya Dunne's daughter, back to her former home in Anu. He pretended that this was a prudent move to protect her against reprisals he alleged that he feared from a Portuguese agent of the Viceroy, who, he claimed, had discovered that his wife had masterminded his escape from the dungeon. The truth became apparent, however, when he began visiting Kandy frequently to consort with Queen Anula.

King Maya Dunne acknowledged at last that King Vidiye did not return his loyalty and posed a real threat to him, but he still held back, in spite of Prince Raja Sinha's pleas.

King Vidiye finally flung down the gauntlet when, at the urging of Queen Anula, he divorced his wife, Padma, under Kandyan law, by which he was not governed either by birth or marriage. He wed Queen Anula under the same law, which did not govern her either. Within one week of consecrating his illicit cohabitation with the queen, he moved south through Raigam, his thrust obviously being to take the sub-kingdom of Ruhuna and encircle Sita Waka completely. Many of the southern nobles rallied to his banner.

I became convinced that King Vidiye was such a threat to our presence in Lanka that it was time to intervene. I was supported in this conviction by the new Bishop of Lanka, no less a person than the former friar, Father Juan, who had never forgotten King Vidiye's hatred of the Church and the sacrilegious acts of the past.

When King Maya Dunne requested military support from me, I therefore abandoned my policy of non-alignment and readily gave it to him in the form of a large contingent of musketeers and artillery to augment Prince Raja Sinha's army group.

The opposing forces met in battle near the village of Deni in the southern hill country, about thirty miles south-east of Galle.

Throughout the whole of a day, Prince Raja Sinha, that master-strategist, held off from any major attack, feinting and giving before King Vidiye's fierce thrusts. Finally, in the evening, when the enemy was frustrated and exhausted, the prince led a cavalry charge along the entire front. After a fierce fight, he pretended to retreat. His move had the desired effect of drawing out the enemy cavalry, led by King Vidiye, into swampy ground, whereupon the prince made a surprise counter-attack on both flanks in a pincer movement that isolated the enemy cavalry, which he massacred. King Vidiye was one of the few survivors. He lost his mount and escaped under cover of darkness, carried on the shoulders of some of his men.

Prince Raja Sinha thereupon turned on the main body of the enemy and scattered them, killing thousands. Thus, in a single battle, he re-established the ascendancy of the Sita Waka king over the entire south and west of the island.

King Vidye fled to Kandy. Not unexpectedly, Queen Anula rejected him and sought the protection of King Maya

Dunne, claiming that she had been forced into the marriage. Still hoping for a reconciliation between his daughter and King Vidiye, King Maya Dunne forgave her, on condition that she renounced the marriage.

As I look on all the actions of the three brothers, King Maya Dunne, the Great King Bhuvaneka Bahu and King Raigam, I now see that despite any differences that may have arisen between them due to conflicting ambitions, they were bound by a deep feeling for the blood-ties of their families.

Another feature of King Maya Dunne's actions was his anxiety not to deplete the country of its heroic leaders. He actually sent messengers requesting King Vidiye, who had been given refuge by the pious Dhamba King Vikrama to return to the fold.

Instead of accepting this gracious offer, being well-established in Dhamba, King Vidiye turned on his host. He killed King Vikrama and seized power in the Dhamba kingdom, then proceeded to Jaffna to enlist the aid of the Chola sub-king for a joint effort against Sita Waka. Yes, he was a man of insensate ambition who cared not with whom he consorted, even Queen Anula and the Devil, so long as he could propel himself to power. In truth, however, he was allied with the devil within himself!

The people of Jaffna believed that their visitor had in his possession those parts of the fabled family treasure he had held back from our Viceroy Don Alfonso de Noronha. A group of Tamil princes and chieftains, having decided to seize the treasure, therefore attacked him in their capital city. One of his followers, Lord Nadiye, leapt forward to place himself between his leader and the assassins. Though he nobly sacrificed his life in the attempt, it was futile. King Vidiye and his companion, Prince Viyaya Pala, were slain and the treasure was seized.

Thus did the mighty warrior king with the huge gangling body and fierce rolling eyes become the victim of his own dishonesty. Desiring to take over an entire land instead of being content to serve the cause of his people, he died on alien soil without a single grain of sand to hold in his grasp. So the devil within him triumphed in the end.

With King Vidiye's death, the entire country of Lanka began to settle down again, all of it, excepting the Jaya kingdom, under King Maya Dunne, who adopted a very wise policy. So long as a region or sub-kingdom offered him allegiance by paying his taxes, he chose not to occupy it, but used most of the taxes to improve the lot of the people. He built or endowed Buddhist temples, schools and hospitals. He constructed new roads, reservoirs, irrigation works. He never attempted to penetrate militarily the Kandyan mountain fastness or the north.

Since I have extinguished all personal antagonism towards Prince Raja Sinha with the absolution of my sins, my co-operation with King Maya Dunne began to earn rewards in the form of mutual trust and more favourable trade for my own king, the latter channelled once again through the now ailing Abdul Raschid to whom King Maya Dunne owed a debt of gratitude. It seemed that Aisha Raschid, who had been a she-devil in the fateful battle of Mulleri, gave up her desire for vengeance once she discovered that her husband had not long to live. She obviously decided to let the dead bury their dead!

As for Prince Raja Sinha, once my hated rival and arch-enemy, I view him now with detachment. Poor man, Juli is mine and he has no one. It is rumoured that he is actively studying Hindusim.

We are all enjoying the unique peace, which only this island – called Serendib, the isle of serendipity, by the ancient Arabs, Taprobanus by the Greeks and Romans, Lanka from time immemorial and more recently, Ceilan by us newcomers from Europe – can afford . . .

CHAPTER THIRTY

One should never make a pilgrimage to the Kataragama shrine in Ruhuna, the southernmost region of Lanka, as part of some other, lay, purpose to which the pilgrimage is but incidental. The shrine goes back almost to the origins of the Sinhala nation. Its first exposure to politics was in the fourth century before Christ, when the ten *kshashtryas*, holy ruler-priests from India who administered it, gave refuge to the Sinhala King Mahanaga. He had fled the capital city of Anu because his brother's wife coveted the throne of her son and had attempted to eliminate the king by poisoning him. King Mahanaga later turned on his benefactors and caused them to be foully murdered, so that he could consolidate his grip on the southern sub-kingdom of Ruhuna which he had adopted as his own, but his descendants attempted to expiate this impious deed of their ancestor by venerating the temple and endowing it.

The Kataragama god proved to be very jealous of his exclusivity. He smote whomever slighted him. There were hundreds of examples. People who went hunting in the adjacent jungles with the intention of visiting the shrine incidentally, on their way back, were killed or wounded before they ever got to the shrine. Others who undertook the pilgrimage on a fixed time schedule were never able to keep to it because misfortune befell them.

There is more to this belief than the god's pride. If one cannot accord an exclusive place in one's life, with total priority of purpose, for the things one holds sacred, then true sanctity, which is essential to the success of that purpose, is missing and its absence will bring the purpose to naught. Jesus Christ could never have died on the cross for mankind, Lord Buddha would never have attained Nibbhana, Muhammad would never have created Islam, without this unswerving integrity towards the purposes each of them held sacred.

I had believed for a long time that I was under the divine protection of the Kataragama god. It seemed to me significant that the shrine, located in the Ruhuna jungles, had originated as a Hindu temple and that the daily *poojas* conducted there should follow the Hindu ritual to this day. Of all the world's great religions, Hinduism alone recognizes no leader or teacher who created it, or from whom it emerged. It has been handed down from the mists of time, more specifically from the Vedic period of Sanskrit literature a thousand years or more before the birth of the Christ. Unhampered by founder, dogma or priestly hierarchy, it consists of the contributions of sages through the centuries, the basic philosophies of which one could interpret freely according to one's own reasoning.

Against this background, it was therefore no wonder that I inclined to Hinduism and made the pilgrimage to Kataragama at every opportunity.

To me, the most attractive element of Hindu belief was *dharma*, the duty of one's station, which must be fulfilled even if it means slaying others. Thus did the Chola King Elara, seventeen hundred years ago, have his only son and heir executed for heedlessly killing a sacred white cow-calf on a sacred day, in violation of King Elara's law. I was spellbound by such unbending compliance with one's own law in fulfilment of the duty of the king's station.

No other religion offered me moral right to support me on the road to my destiny, which must necessitate my committing what would otherwise be regarded as wrongdoing. I simply could not accept the double standard of some *bhikkus*, monks, and say that killing for the establishment of Sinhala Buddhist rule was justifiable when there was no moral principle in the Buddhist's Doctrine to support it, any more than I could condone the supposed Christian ethic behind the Crusades, or the Muslim belief in *jihad*, holy war. If actions are deemed wrong by the religion in the first place, promotion of the religion cannot justify them. Nor can one offset evil actions by subsequent good works. I needed a religion that gave me the moral right – or more, cast a moral duty upon me – to fulfil my destiny and the duty of my station, so long as I retained my personal honour.

It was my father, then General Prince Maya Dunne, who first opened my mind, on my sixteenth birthday, to the way in which the basic character of people made them choose a major religion. A very wise man, my father, though himself a militant Sinhala Buddhist.

December 1532/January 1533

With peace in the country following the death of King Vidiye, I decided to make a pilgrimage to the Kataragama shrine, taking my wards, Bandula and Nangi, with me as an offering of thankfulness to the god for bringing them into my life. Buddhist pilgrimages are great levellers. The moment that word of my intention got around, as always, devout people asked to be able to join me. More would spontaneously join us along the way, but when we finally set off from Sita Waka on 20 December by the Christian calendar, we were already a convoy – thirty bullock-drawn wagons with thatched roofs, most of them carrying pilgrims seated on yellow mats, a few laden with provisions and supplies for the journeys out and back. One never bought anything on these sacred missions, but depended on one's own resources or the charity of people on the route, who would acquire merit by providing *dana*, meals, in order to share in the merit of the pilgrimage. *Dana* is not the giving of food alone, but every kind of alms, including the offering of flowers and light and the bestowing of temples and schools. We slept in the shade of our wagons during the worst heat of the day and made good progress at night, our sacred chants rising above the trundle-creak of the wagons, the clatter of the bullocks' hooves and the jingling of the bells around their necks. I like these chants because they are tuneless and I cannot sing tunefully!

As we drew nearer to Kataragama, we passed other pilgrims, for this was the season for pilgrimage. Some of them were actually walking all the way. One devotee was rolling sideways along the edge of the highway to fulfil a vow. The last twenty miles lay through dense jungle. How many millions of pilgrims had taken this route through the ages? We passed the shining silver sheet of the great Tissa reservoir and offered flowers and worship at the huge Tissa *dagoba*, built seventeen hundred years before by King Kakkavan the father of King Abhaya Gamini. Ten miles beyond, to our right, the saddle of a hill rose sharply to the looming greeny-blue top of the tall mountain that Lord Buddha had visited. It is called *Va'di-hitti-kande*, meaning the mountain on which he lingered longer.

We left our wagons in a clearing and walked the last four miles, as was mandatory. Neither king nor chieftain, commoner or priest would build a road to the sacred place.

When we reached the Menik, jewel, river on the evening of 25 December we were at journey's end. I recalled that it was Christmas Day for Christians and wondered how Julietta was celebrating it. With her family no doubt. All I desired for her was happiness. Even if I were normally otherwise disposed, I could feel nothing but *maitriya*, loving kindness, for everyone in this holy place, which had an atmosphere that excluded evil of any kind.

We awoke well before dawn the next morning in order to attend the early *pooja*. We first performed our ablutions at the river. A bath and the wearing of fresh white garments is essential. The level of water was low enough for us to

414

step into it. The roots of the tall, green *kumbuk* trees that bordered the river kept the water cool during the warmest seasons. The light brown sand was clean to our bare feet, at which small fish took an occasional nibble. This being the colder season, the water was cool as mountain dew to our bodies and as refreshing, the work of the god.

Once across the river, we were accosted by vendors from the thatched booths that lined the bank, a form of commercialism that some of the lay heads of the shrine had encouraged. Trinkets, bead necklaces, baubles hanging on strings glittered in the pre-dawn flare-light. Bandula and Nangi were entranced. I would have liked to buy them some souvenirs, but it would not have been proper when we were all so seriously dedicated to the purpose of our visit. Therefore, we obtained *thattu*, platters of cane-weave, instead. On these we placed votive offerings of cut fruit, yellow bananas, ripe red guavas, sliced golden pineapple, puffed rice and incense, all of which we also bought, since the proceeds would go to the shrine. Our final purchase was husked coconuts to be smashed against the ancient black rock opposite the *kovil*, temple.

I will not describe the ritual of the *poojas* lest I offend the god. We emerged into the grey dawn from the close confines of the *kovil*, with our heads anointed by sacred oil, the holy ash on our foreheads.

Certain remarkable features of the shrine must be noted.

First, it is a place where the devout can observe penance, or people can mortify their flesh in order to fulfil a vow or as an offering for some favour sought. None of this was Buddhist practice. Many Hindus also carried the heavy *kavadi*, decorated wooden archways symbolizing the entrance to devotion, dancing the while. Others had stuck shiny metal hooks through the flesh of their backs, a fresh green lime affixed to the pointed ends as an antiseptic. Their tortured flesh quivered with the pain, but the devotees gave no evidence of feeling it. When the hooks were finally withdrawn, miraculously there would not even by a scar on the body.

Since the *pooja* was over, we proceeded the half-mile or so to the *Kiri Vihare*, milk-white temple, built by King Abhaya Gamini in the second century B.C. We walked along a narrow track running straight as an arrow between tall jungle trees, mainly wood-apple and *sal*, on either side of which were long lines of beggars and little booths selling lotus-blossoms and waterlilies. The beggars were all professionals, though they included blind men and cripples, women with tiny babies at their breasts and small children. The dark jungle, filled with creaking, rustling and the occasional ho . . . ro . . . ho . . . ro of monkeys, pressed on both sides. Just where booths, beggars and the jungle ended at the clearing in which the temple had been built, a strange hush greeted us, so peaceful that it seemed as if gods and men, birds and animals, had fallen silent in awe.

We offered flowers and incense at the altars that marked the four corners of the great platform on which the exquisite white, bell-shaped *dagoba* had been built, paused in meditation on the grey stone paving before the central altar. I could tell that the spirit of the shrine had entered Bandula and Nangi, young as they were.

During the first watch before sundown, I strolled alone around the *dagoba*. The near-setting sunlight tinged the air a pale gold. The scent of burning incense was wafted to my nostrils by a light rustling breeze from the jungle beyond. I paused at the north-western altar, beside which a bare-chested man was seated in the lotus pose, legs crossed, hands on thighs, the palms upwards. His skin was almost black, wrinkled but with a glossy smoothness that made it glow. His long white hair and beard fluttered in the breeze, his upper body was very erect. His eyes were closed. He was obviously in a trance. As I watched him, fascinated, a sudden gust of wind swept the temple. His torso moved with the wind, from the waist up; the rest of him was completely still. I realized with wonder that in this state, his body was light as a leaf. I believe that if one had placed him in a trough of water, he would not have sunk, because all of him was lighter than air.

That night we watched the fire-walking. The same sort of humble devotee, whose faith permitted the offering of such incredible penance, walked across the glowing embers of a fire-pit some forty feet long and ten feet wide. These were not showmen or magicians, but people of deep faith. May the god forgive me, but I could not help thinking that if I could harness such faith to my cause, our country would be unified in short order. Of course, almost all the devotees performing these miracles were Hindus!

Thursday, 2 January 1533

Famous last words! Fernao could not help recalling the last entry in his diary when, without any warning, Don Alfonso de Noronha, who was still Viceroy of India, sailed on a grey January tide into Colombo harbour with twelve great *nao* and ten *terco*. The sun was well up and glinting off the calm grey harbour waters by the time Fernao's barge settled against the tall sides of the flagship. The Don awaited Fernao by the rail of the poop deck. Disapproval literally hung in the air around him as he acknowledged Fernao's salute.

'Good morning, Your Excellency,' Fernao conjured a cheerful smile. 'Welcome to Lanka.'

The Viceroy made no response until they were alone in his stateroom. 'We doubt that either Lanka or you would really welcome us,' he finally retorted, openly rude. 'You and the natives have been so loving and comfortable here that our presence will be an intrusion.'

The cold scorn of the well-bred man for a boor chilled Fernao's mind. 'Nonetheless, we should observe these little

417

niceties of a civilized existence, should we not, your Excellency?'

'We did not come to discuss philosophy with you, young man. We are here for action.'

Fernao stiffened. 'In that case, I will thank you to address me according to my rank, your Excellency. I am not your young man, but an officer of his Imperial Majesty's army, bearing His Majesty's commission, with the rank of general.'

The Viceroy straightened his hunched shoulders. 'And we are his Majesty's Representative in the East Indies . . .'

'And must therefore conduct yourself as His Majesty would have done,' Fernao interrupted.

'Very well then, General de Albergaria, supposing we act as His Majesty would have done and strip you of your rank and commission?'

'His Majesty would never act in such an intemperate fashion. As for you, Excellency, why ask the question if that is really your intention?' Fernao could scarcely keep the contempt from his voice.

The Viceroy backed off. 'Since we are to observe the niceties of decorum, pray be seated.' He indicated the built-in divan. 'Would you care for a glass of Madeira, *General*?' He placed ironic emphasis on the last word.

'No thank you, Excellency.' Fernao moved to the divan.

'All right then, let us come to the point.' The Viceroy sat on the straight-backed red leather chair, cleared his throat. 'We have observed that your policies since our departure from these shores have been diametrically opposed to our wishes.'

'In what respects?'

'You are well aware of them, General, but let us outline them to you. First, you have not only permitted the traitorous Mouro Abdul Raschid and his bloodthirsty wife to return to their home in Slave Island and resume their business, but are actually using the Mouro once more as middle men, sharing in our profits. Why?' Don Alfonso was glaring at him now.

'My best answer is in the results. I have bettered our volume by forty per cent this past year and our local profits alone are up twenty per cent. Further, the cinnamon and other spices now being provided are uniformly of such superior grades that we are commanding much higher profits in Europe.'

The Viceroy had obviously not expected such a rebuttal from the facts. 'That's as may be, but the principle is wrong,' he demurred. 'You had no right to act unilaterally.'

'I was given full power in my duties by your predecessors in office.' Fernao deliberately stretched the truth.

'You gambled . . .'

'And won. As for allowing the Mouro to return to his home, it was part of the same gamble which, I repeat, we won.'

'You joined forces with our arch enemy, King Maya Dunne, to attack the father of the Great King, when the Great King is under our protection.'

'I sent troops to augment those of King Maya Dunne, in order to defeat the most bitter man in this country, King Vidiye. This is the king you imprisoned, Excellency. Remember? He held particular grudges against you, me and Holy Church. I had the full support of Bishop Juan in my actions.'

'The insult to His Imperial Majesty and to Portugal at the battle of Mulleri cannot be wiped out by alliances, however noble their purpose. Only blood and ashes can atone for what we endured. We are here today to extract vengeance. We shall teach these barbarian heathens a lesson they will never forget. We shall demonstrate the power and might of Portugal, then subjugate the entire country and establish the Portuguese presence permanently in every coastal town.'

Fernao blanched. Instinctively glancing out of the porthole, he saw the great *nao* anchored in a staggered line. 'What do you have in mind, Excellency?'

The Viceroy's vulturine face broke into a smile, caused the great hooked nose to dip even further downwards. But the eyes remained malignant as a devil's. 'You shall see how Don Alfonso de Noronha deals with his enemies.'

Wednesday, 8 January 1533

We reached Sita Waka on the return journey of our pilgrimage early in the morning. The city seemed quite normal, right down to the cawing of crows by a hint of sewage. But as the bullock wagon parted from the convoy and was driven to the capitol I sensed that something was wrong before we reached the entrance gates. I directed the wagoner to hurry.

'*Juk-pita-muk!*' he cried, nudging the rear of the bullock with his bare toes. The clip-clop of hooves became a clatter. The bull's neck began swinging, bells jingled, wheels rattled and we sped towards the palace.

I was not surprised to find a summons from my father awaiting me. Requesting Sene and Chandra to look after the two children, I made my way, still clad in the white cotton *dhoti* and *kurtha* of the pilgrim, through the crowd of courtiers and suppliants awaiting the public audience hour. Grim tension hung like a pall on the air. The tall, handsome Prince Senerat seemed about to say something as I passed him, but held back obviously unwilling to delay me.

Although my father was outwardly his usual calm self, I could feel his suppressed anger even before I rose from my obeisance. Lord Wickrama Sinha, his lean, fair face tight and slightly pinched, stood on the left of the king's brown and yellow tamarind wood desk. I took my usual place on the settle at its right.

'Welcome back, Prince,' my father opened the conversation. 'Did you find peace on your pilgrimage?'

'Yes, Sire. It was balm for the spirit to be away from civilization.'

His eyes twinkled. 'But we Buddhists do not believe in the spirit, so balm must be for some other of your *kharmic* composition!'

'Wherever it lies, I felt the balm, Sire.' I grinned back at him, happy at our easy communion.

'Did your two wards enjoy their first journey to the shrine?'

'Oh yes!' I told him briefly about the pilgrimage, sticking to bare facts because I was anxious to get to the reason for his summons.

When I had done, he grew serious. 'Have you heard the news, Prince?'

'No, Sire.'

'Viceroy Don Alfonso de Noronha arrived in Colombo, leading a fleet of twelve *nao*, the day after the Christian New Year. He sailed south to Beruwala the next day. The town, as you know, is populated chiefly by Mouro. He bombarded the town mercilessly, after which he personally led a landing party of troops ashore. While he robbed the jewellers, his men raped the women and set fire to most of the buildings.' His dark eyes flashed. 'The Viceroy then proceeded south to Galle, Matara and Tangalla, repeating the process in each city before returning to Colombo and heading north, doubtless to the other seabased towns. We have been promised more of the same medicine all along the coast. Only Christian converts were spared. The man is driven mad by his lust for treasure and vengeance, in whichever order.'

'What have we done to stop him, Sire?' I burst out, shaking with rage, no longer the placid pilgrim.

'Nothing. What would you have us do?'

'Attack the murderous barbarians. Destroy them. Give

me leave, Sire ...' I was about to utter my favourite sentence when I suddenly realized that my anger was futile. My shoulders sagged helplessly. I turned to Lord Wickrama Sinha, who merely stared bitterly into space.

'We have no fleet,' my father reminded me sadly. 'We can only attack the Viceroy on land, but even there, we have no way of knowing where he will proceed next.'

Inspiration emerged. I looked at the king bright-eyed. 'We could attack the Colombo fort.'

He shook his head. 'General de Albergaria commands the fort. It is reported that he furiously opposed the Viceroy's plan, called it barbaric and refused any part of it.' His voice became firm. 'We cannot attack our friends, Prince.'

The blood rushed to my face. 'I did not know,' I volunteered lamely.

It was bad enough that I had had to choke down all personal feeling and pride and accept my rival's contingent of musketeers and artillery men when I went after King Vidiye. As a matter of fact, I made sure that our victory that historic day was won without the aid of the general's contingent. To have him protected by my father as an ally was yet another bitter cup I had to swallow. But I was a prince and I could never show my personal feelings in any extravagant way, still less allow them to cloud my judgement.

'The Viceroy is an evil man!' Lord Wickrama Sinha's high voice seemed to float quietly on the silence that had ensued. 'We must find some method of destroying him.'

'He will destroy himself,' my father asserted with certainty.

'We cannot wait for that, Sire,' the lord responded. 'We should help him on his way.'

'With the utmost respect, I agree, Sire.' I gladly echoed the lord's words.

'The Viceroy may well have given us the means to unite

the whole country against the Portuguese presence,' my father declared. 'Our people needed a cause more fundamental to their survival than race, language or religion. The Viceroy's wanton acts of destruction will force them to fight for their lives.'

Wild elation flooded me, for I knew he spoke the truth. I glanced at Lord Wickrama Sinha whose eyes had lit up. 'That's absolutely . . .' I began, when I heard my father gasp. His hand was clamped on his upper chest, his eyes were staring, his jaw had dropped. His open mouth clawed vainly for breath.

'*Tha!*' The affectionate diminutive of my youth escaped me as a shout. For a moment, I was petrified with fear that swept through me like the chill of ague. I leapt towards him. He stood up, swayed on his feet, vainly attempting to breathe. His eyes crossed in an attempt to draw me into his line of vision. Sweat poured down his face. His eyelids drooped and closed.

I swept past the desk, held him before he could slump to the floor. My face close to his, I remembered how Prince Rodana saved the life of King Kakkavan long ago. I placed my lips on my father's mouth, sent my breath into him. Dear *devas*, let my life-force save my father's life. Lord Wickrama Sinha rushed out, calling for the physicians. Attendants flustered into the room.

In minutes, my father's laboured breathing eased, but the fine features had sagged. Suddenly, his eyes fluttered open. Relief flooded my being. Drawing back, I gazed at his tired eyes.

'Nothing, no one must come between you and your destiny,' he commanded hoarsely. He held my glance with a sudden, superhuman effort of will. 'Swear it!'

My anguished eyes searched his face. In despair, I knew the time was short. 'I swear it, O Great King, my father.'

He smiled wearily. His eyes closed. With a sigh, his body relaxed in my arms.

My hero and my only friend, the *Maha Raja*, Great King Maya Dunne, was dead. I had always thought him to be invincible, indestructible.

CHAPTER THIRTY-ONE

Friday, 10 January 1533

Standing before her easel in the bright, airy studio on the upper floor of the Mutu Vella mansion, Julietta hummed the melody of a religious chant as she carefully studied the scene outside the window. She had to mix the colours just right to recreate the different blues of the morning sea and sky, the browns of the branches and the greens of the leaves as a background to the figures of Catherina and Lopo who were seated on the lawn with their tutor, having their lesson on Nature. In quiet elation that she had become inspired to paint again, she looked up at the heavens silently thanking God for this mercy. It was God's will that Fernao should have a near escape from death, resulting in a changed outlook that had given her back the man she had tried to love as her husband until the morning following the attempted rape by Sergeant Correa. So much had happened since that fatal day, the good, the bad, the ugly, but she preferred to remember only the beautiful. There was one hideous memory, however, that she still had not been able to overcome completely, the terror that clutched at her throat, tightened her chest and made her mind demented when something brought recollection of that nightmare. It could be a dark night when she was alone in her bedroom and her awakening eyes saw a shadow that looked like a man looming over her, or a sudden jolt from the creak of crickets. Always, always, it was the knowledge of her rescue and what had followed that calmed her.

All this was her secret world, for life in the mansion had been almost idyllic this past year, until the arrival of the Viceroy followed by his barbaric acts against the coastal towns of Lanka threw up dark clouds. When Fernao firmly refused to permit his garrison to participate in those actions, Julietta was convinced that their marriage was on solid bedrock at last. She had never been more proud of him than at this time, when he risked his whole career for his principles. It had inspired her to paint a ship in full sail leaving the Colombo harbour, on a rosy-gold evening, heading west into the sunset. If that was what Fernao now wanted, to leave Lanka for good and settle in Portugal, she would support him wholeheartedly, despite her sick pangs at the thought of being so impossibly far away from Tiki-tiki, at leaving the dear, familiar places, the people she had known since birth. Her rendezvous with Tiki-tiki would have to wait until they met in heaven. She had no doubt that Tiki-tiki would go straight to heaven even though Holy Church said that non-Catholics had first to enter Purgatory.

She had just begun mixing colours on her palette, when she heard the clip-clippity-clop of fast hooves on the driveway. She glanced through the windows again to see Fernoa cantering his bay round the bend. Unusually, he was alone.

Her heart fluttered. Fernao never came home during working hours unless the news was bad. A closer look at his set face confirmed her fears. He glanced up at her window, caught her gaze and waved. He called a greeting to the children and the tutor.

She awaited Fernao upstairs, her pulse quickening. He strode into the room, magnificent in his general's uniform, the gold braid on his white doublet gleaming. He had the same bouncing step he had as a young midshipman. When he held her in his arms, it was with no less eagerness.

He released her, took her by the hand and guided her down on to her settle, sat on a footstool beside her without releasing her hand. 'I have good news and bad news,' he announced gravely, his grip tightening, 'Which do you want to hear first?'

Her stomach knotted. 'The bad news,' she answered.

'All right then . . . King Maya Dunne is dead.'

She had been hit on the head with a hammer. 'Dead? Dear sweet Jesu . . . when . . . how . . . ?' She gestured helplessly with her free hand.

'Yesterday morning, in the Sita Waka palace. He died of a heart attack.'

'Oh, how sad, sad.'

Somehow she felt bereft. And suddenly the knowledge that an era was ended chilled her whole body, causing her to shiver. 'Wasn't it sudden?'

'Completely unexpected. One moment he was talking to his son and Lord Wickrama Sinha in his chamber, the next he collapsed and died.'

'So he didn't suffer much?'

'No.'

'That is merciful. I never really knew him, but he was so handsome, cleancut, alive, somehow indestructible, if you know what I mean. Like your father . . . like you, Fernao. He gave the impression of being a stern, aloof aristocrat, but he was kindly inside. He would bring me an occasional present when I was a little girl. He must have known of . . .' she nearly said 'of my feelings for his son,' but bit back the words in time,' . . . my isolation. He was a man of instinctive compassion, real courage and honourable conduct, one of the truly great.'

'I agree. Even when he was our enemy, plotting to achieve his goals, there was a basic honour to his conduct and all he did was not for himself but for the country.' Fernao paused. 'I wonder what history will say of him?'

'That he was a brilliant politician, an enlightened monarch and a great patriot.' Try as she might, Julietta could not keep the tears from stinging her eyes and she wondered how much of her grief was at the king's death, how much of it for Tiki-tiki. She knew with a woman's understanding that Tiki-tiki's one lifeline had been his father. Now that

427

lifeline was cut, how would her dear Tiki-tiki fare on the dark, deep waters of loneliness?

'History may evaluate some of King Maya Dunne's actions differently.' Fernao broke into her reflections, his voice sober. 'People have a habit of ascribing ideals only to those who, like Joan of Arc, embark on gallant but futile crusades. Since King Maya Dunne was a master of timing, a man who knew when to attack and when to withdraw, a man who would treat, if necessary, to safeguard his position, he may be accused of an overriding personal ambition.'

'But we know differently, don't we, Fernao?' She was surprised at the note of pleading in her voice.

'Indeed.' He hesitated. 'When I told you just now that I had bad news, I was not referring merely to the fact of the king's death, but to the consequences.'

'You mean the likely uncertainties of the succ . . . Surely, Prince Tik . . . er . . . Raja Sinha will succeed to the throne and will rule wisely and well? After all, if nothing else, he is aware of Christian principles. Besides, will he not retain his father's loyalty to us for our support against King Vidiye? We must send him a message of sympathy.' Inside, she was beginning to wish that she could be alone with Tiki-tiki at this time.

'I've already sent a courier with a message of condolence.' He released her hand, reached out and touched her cheek gently, his eyes clouding. 'There are always uncertainties with a new succession. As for loyalty to us, our gallant Viceroy's actions have cancelled any past debts.' He paused. 'But enough of that. Now for the good news.'

'Oh yes, I forgot. Tell me quickly.'

'Not until I get a reward for it.'

'That's blackmail, but what else can a poor lady do but succumb to it? What is your demand, blackmailer?'

'A kiss now, or the promise of more immediately after the news!'

'You never let go an opportunity, do you? Trying to catch up on all the virtue of your boyhood, I suppose!' She smiled. 'All right, the promise then, you have it.'

'Good,' His eyes were sparkling again. 'It is not often a lady will accept the fate worse than death with such remarkable fortitude!'

Julietta felt herself blush.

'Oh the lightnings of her blush,' Fernao commented. 'Now, the news. We are to have a distinguished visitor from abroad soon. I have received a despatch to this effect from His Imperial Majesty's Commander of the Home Fleet, Grand Admiral Lopo Soarez de Albergaria.'

Julietta's heart quickened. 'Your father? Oh Fernao, that's wonderful. It's an answer to my prayers.' Also to my written plea, she thought silently, relieved that the admiral had obviously not mentioned her private letter in his despatch. 'How did you get the news? When does he arrive?'

'Any day now, because the captain of the mail packet said he was leaving a week after the packet sailed from Lisbon for Goa. The visit is an official one, by the way, undertaken on behalf of His Majesty.' There was grim satisfaction in his voice.

Monday, 20 January 1533

Ten days later, on a blustery Monday morning, Fernao, surrounded by his aides, stood on the wharf watching his father's flagship, the *Santa Maria*, followed by two great *nao*, sail slowly into Colombo harbour. His mind went back to the day he first arrived in Lanka, a midshipman on board his father's ship. Young, idealistic, he had no idea as to what lay ahead for him. It was surely God's mercy that denied the human race knowledge of the future.

A great clattering from the anchor chains of the *Santa Maria* sent a flock of seagulls soaring into the air with creaks of alarm. For the thousandth time since receiving news of the visit, he wondered what his father looked like. Had the twelve years aged him? Or was he the same craggy, powerful personality?

The Viceroy had decided, to Fernao's delight, that he should go on board alone to welcome his father and conduct him to Don Alfonso's own flagship, the *Santa Caterina*. It was proper protocol for the fleet commander to call on the king's representative.

As his barge rode the murky waters smoothly towards the flagship, Fernao's searching eyes detected the tall figure of his father standing alone on the poop deck. Some warmth from way back broke through his mind, forced him to blink back tears. Leaving his aides chatting with the ship's officers on the main deck, Fernao strode across to the ladder leading up to the poop deck, carefully avoiding any upward glance. Only when he finally faced the admiral and saluted him, did Fernao look him in the eye, note his face.

Admiral Lopo Soarez de Albergaria was in his mid-sixties now but, strangely, he was almost exactly as Fernao remembered him, except for added white in the blond hair and beard, a deepening of the wrinkles on the craggy face and more looseness of the skin of the neck above the white ruffles of his shirt. He had the same erect, haughty bearing, great red-veined nose and piercing, ice-blue eyes.

'It's good to see you, General,' the admiral declared gruffly. He withdrew a handkerchief from his sleeve and blew his nose violently. 'Damned tropical climate,' he explained.

Knowing his father lied to cover his emotion, Fernao felt that warmth stirring within him again. 'It's good to see you, sir. I had given up hope that we would ever meet again.' He was grateful for the breeding that would make them both avoid any reference to their past differences.

'Indeed. We must thank the Almighty and his agent . . .

hrmph . . . His Excellency the Viceroy for making it possible.' He paused. 'How is your family?'

'Very well, thank you, sir. They eagerly await your stay with us, your grandson especially.'

The white eyebrows lifted. 'I'm to stay with you?'

'Yes, sir. If that is your pleasure, we would be honoured. As you know, His Excellency has no residence here and since you were likely to remain a while, we thought . . .'

'Indeed, indeed.' The old man blew his nose again, more violently this time. 'You are all most kind. I'd be delighted, I'm sure.' He replaced the handkerchief, the gesture unexpectedly graceful in one so stiff and formal. 'Well, come on into my cabin, so we can talk. I take it His Excellency is awaiting me?'

'I'm to escort you on board his flagship immediately, sir.'

'Oh?' The admiral seemed surprised, the ice-blue eyes glinted dangerously. 'Well, we must not keep His Imperial Majesty's representative waiting, must we?'

'I suppose not.' Fernao caught his father's mood. 'Will you follow me, if you please, sir.'

'First my cap, General. It's very important to have one's cap to doff to royalty or . . . er . . . its shadow!'

The formal pleasantries, those necessary hypocrisies of society, were over. The three of them were alone in the Viceroy's stateroom and it was obvious to Fernao that both the king's representative and the king's commissioner, which His Majesty's sealed mandate had disclosed the admiral to be, were eager to get on to the business at hand.

'His Majesty's commission,' Don Alfonso rasped, glancing at the roll of white parchment with red ribbons which he had placed on his desk after reading, 'speaks of certain improprieties. May we inquire who has accused us of improprieties?'

'No one,' the admiral responded blandly.

The Viceroy's browless eyes lifted, the great beak nose tightened. 'Then what . . .?' he began.

The admiral's smile did not extend to his gaze. 'Your Excellency, for there to be accusers, there must be crimes. His Majesty's mandate refers to alleged irregularities.'

The Viceroy seemed relieved. 'May I know the nature of those . . . er . . . irregularities, Admiral?'

'Indeed. I have brought along a list of them, which we can doubtless go into privately later on. For the present, let me say that the most important of them relates to the treasure of the late Great King of Lanka.'

'As to that, we were holding what little was made available to us by the late Regent at Goa . . . er . . . in trust for His Imperial Majesty who has elected to honour us with his friendship.'

A timely reminder of the Viceroy's personal influence, Fernao thought.

'His Majesty is gracious enough to bestow not only his patronage, but also his friendship to certain of his subjects,' the admiral countered, obviously unimpressed. 'But these are the products of his personal esteem.'

'Are you insinuating, sir, that we have lost His Majesty's esteem?' Don Alfonso demanded, bridling.

'I am stating, Your Excellency, that my inquiries could well result in the loss of His Majesty's esteem and patronage.' The admiral's deep voice had grown cold and hard as his frosty look. 'My mandate is far-ranging, so I shall also inquire into other matters that were brought to my notice while we were anchored in Calicut.'

'And what are those matters, sir?' the Viceroy demanded haughtily. He was taking high ground.

'The bombardment of coastal villages in this country without cause, rape and pillaging, arson and looting.'

'The bombardments were necessary reprisals and an essential deterrent. But these are matters of royal policy for which I am answerable to His Majesty alone.'

432

'Indeed. But while you are responsible to His Majesty alone, I am here to observe and report on all these matters.' The admiral leaned forward and tapped his knee for emphasis. 'You must also realize, Your Excellency, that Holy Church will influence His Majesty's judgement on any conduct by his representatives that might render their missionary efforts in the East abortive.'

'We respect and revere Holy Church, Admiral, but you are surely aware that there are those who use cassock and robe to cloak their lust for power and their greed.'

'Indeed. Not uncommon characteristics of the entire human race, Your Excellency.'

He would remember the afternoon scene as long as he lived. Julietta and the two children awaited his father in the formal dining room, furnished with gilt French furniture, a great Persian carpet and crystal glass chandeliers, in the mansion on the Mutu Vella hill. He viewed them with special pride today.

The blue dress Julietta had specially made for the occasion was an exact replica of the one she had worn to the dinner party on the admiral's flagship the night she first met him. It saddled her wasp-waist, fitted the full breasts and flaring hips to perfection. She showed not a trace of child-bearing and held herself with the grace of a princess.

Catherina, in a similar blue dress, was an exact miniature of her mother, except for those dark brown eyes with the blue rims. Those eyes. Once he had grown to accept them and her, he had found peace and a new joy in the girl, because she had opened to him, came to adore him, even fussed over him.

As for his son, here was a true de Albergaria, already carrying his small frame with the family haughtiness, the features and colouring showing promise that he would one day be a replica of his grandfather. Dressed in red doublet

433

with white ruffs, white breeches and nether-hosen, he looked every inch a young aristocrat.

Some instinctive, undefinable feeling between grandfather and grandson broke through the formal restraint of the occasion as they sat on the settees in the drawing room. Little Lopo even placed himself next to the admiral on a love-seat facing the front entryway, as if it were his right.

The admiral glanced at the little boy in surprise, gave a 'Hrmph . . .' of satisfied approval. 'The young man seems to know his place,' he stated. The ice-blue eyes twinkled. 'Which is more than I can say for his father.'

'As to that, sir,' Julietta intervened boldly, much to Fernao's astonishment, 'it seems to be a family trait, which all three de Albergarias have now overcome, thanks to your generosity.'

'Hrmph . . . hrmph . . . I'd say someone should teach you *your* place, young lady,' he retorted, then twinkled again, 'were it not for the fact that you are echoing precisely my sentiments.' He turned towards his grandson. 'Well, now that we all understand each other, tell me about yourself, young man.'

'I want to be an admiral, just like you,' little Lopo piped. 'Would you like to see my ship? It is sailing on our pond.'

'Before I leave.'

Had the cold, ice-blue eyes become soft? Suddenly the truth hit Fernao. This was no haughty aristocrat but a lonely old man, impenetrable by anyone who loved him. Children seldom see their parents as other human beings. There are invisible, almost biological barriers. Was that why grandchildren were so often closer to grandparents?

From then on, Fernao was content to let the beautiful play unfold before him. Occasionally his mind drifted from the piping of his son, the deep tones of his father and the saffron gold of Julietta's voice to other matters. Now that there was no love lost between the Viceroy and the chief guest, how would the official dinner party the Viceroy was

434

throwing on board his flagship that night go? His mind drifted to the list of things he had yet to do for the grand ball he and Julietta were giving in the mansion the next evening.

'Fernao, your father is asking you a question.' Julietta's voice broke into his reflections.

'What? I'm sorry, sir.'

'You never listen to me, do you?' The admiral inquired good-humouredly.

'Oh, I do. Indeed I do, sir.' He felt almost like a little boy caught in some social omission.

'Oh, he listens to everyone, but he doesn't necessarily do what they want him to,' Julietta intervened cheekily.

'I asked you why you did not bring the seizing of the treasure and the tragic defeat at Mulleri to the notice of the State Department,' the admiral inquired.

'I was under orders not to, sir.'

'That's what I thought.' The admiral pondered a while, his strong fingers tapping his knee. 'Well, all I can do is report the facts.'

'Which reminds me that I have a confession to make to my husband,' Julietta intervened calmly. 'Run along children. It's your tea-time.'

'But I want to talk to my grandpapa,' little Lopo demurred.

'You go upstairs now. You can talk to him before he dresses for dinner.'

To Fernao's surprise, his son plonked a kiss on the admiral's cheek before bustling away with his sister. The admiral's eyes widened. 'Hrmph ... humph,' he went, eyes grown soft on the boy's receding figure.

'Now, your dire confession,' Fernao bade Julietta. He listened in amazement as Julietta told of the letter she had sent his father. When she had finished, a silence fell on the room. He glanced at his father, noted his approving eyes

435

on Julietta. It caused his own immediate irritation to subside.

Some imp made him look at his father with a severe expression on his face. 'And you, sir, made no mention of this to me?' he demanded.

The admiral actually avoided his gaze. How wonderful. He had his father on the defensive. 'Indeed, indeed . . . well . . . you know . . . the question never arose . . .'

'I can see that I am going to need allies when we get back to Portugal,' Fernao stated.

'You mean you have actually decided to move to Portugal?' The admiral's eyes almost bulged with wonder and disbelief.

'It will take time, sir, but that is certainly our intention.'

'Thank God. Since I shall have to spend a great deal of time teaching my grandson to become a de Albergaria, I shall retire from the navy as soon as you get home.'

CHAPTER THIRTY-TWO
Monday, 10 February 1533

Fernao found that his father, Admiral de Albergaria, wore two faces, one by day, when he was the keen investigator with a mind like iron fetters and the other during the social events of the night, when the courtly aristocrat emerged. The social events included an evening audience and dinner with the boy king of Jaya, Dom Juan Dharma Pala, at which the admiral conveyed the assurances of the protection of his sovereign lord, the Emperor of Portugal.

By tacit agreement, Fernao and his father never discussed the investigation, either informally or in private. It took almost four weeks, because the admiral also checked on the naval and military condition of the fort garrisons, including Galle, and visited the coastal towns that the Viceroy had bombarded.

On that cool February afternoon, it was with a heavy heart that Fernao attended a final meeting between the admiral and the Viceroy on board the latter's flagship, *Santa Caterina*. That meeting signalled the end of his father's stay in Lanka, which had drawn all five of them really close as a family. Fernao had actually come to enjoy his father, who had proved to be a different person in the home environment from the shipboard martinet of Fernao's teens. Having won all their hearts, his father would be sailing for Lisbon the following day.

Following the admiral into the richly furnished stateroom of the Viceroy's flagship, Fernao reflected on his father's words at dinner the previous night over his own intended resignation from the army, in order to return to Portugal and become a writer. 'We de Albergarias have always been navy,' he had declared. 'So better you become a writer, slogging through words than over mud! Your decision may be fortuitous. Just before I left Lisbon I extended my patronage to an enterprise there, the new printing process. I can therefore have your work published. If you dedicate it to His Majesty, you will be widely read.' He had paused, seemed to feel obliged to volunteer an explanation for an investment that represented an entry into the world of crass commerce, foreign to the landed gentry. 'We are in an era when people can be more effectively bombarded with words than with cannon or musket fire. Witness the power exerted by the treatises of the heretics Luther and that new young man Calvin. What better way for a retired admiral to continue exercising authority?' His smile had been as embarrassed as his customary 'Hrmph . . . hrmph.'

Fernao would have liked to inquire about the timing of his father's interest in the printing process. Perhaps the old mariner had intended belatedly giving his son an opportunity to fulfil his boyhood dreams when he left Lanka!

Once seated on the creamy cushions of the bunk-bed, Fernao took stock of the two opponents, as the Viceroy and the admiral would be today. His white-uniformed father, a craggy-faced giant with dominant nose and piercing eyes, was an eagle, while the beak-nosed Viceroy was a vulture dressed up in burgundy and gold finery.

The Viceroy came quickly to the point. 'We trust you have satisfactorily concluded your inquiries here, Admiral. Is there anything more we can do to assist you?'

'Indeed, Your Excellency.' To Fernao's surprise, Admiral de Albergaria's voice was curt. 'You can return the treasure of the Great Kings of Lanka to its rightful owners.'

For a moment, the Viceroy stared back flabbergasted, but he quickly recovered; his small eyes sparked with anger and he squared his boy shoulders. 'Those treasures, sir, were royal property acquired for the royal Treasury of Portugal,' he declaimed haughtily.

A good attempt to pre-empt any interference from a mere admiral, even of royal blood, Fernao thought.

'The owner of the royal Treasury of Portugal commands you to return the treasure,' the admiral countered drily. 'Those were my instructions even before I left Lisbon.'

'The spoils of war,' the Viceroy began.

'Are different from the despoiling of private property,' the admiral cut in harshly. His head lifted, the downward slant of his eyes made them more piercing. 'Your Excellency may refuse to carry out His Majesty's command and face the consequences.'

Slighty embarrassed but greatly elated, Fernao watched the struggle of pride and greed with self-preservation reflected in the Viceroy's face. Finally, the thin lips curved in a smile. He nodded, his nose and voice-box converging like two crescent moons. 'His Majesty's command is the breath of our life,' he declared.

More so than you think, Fernao reflected sardonically, for if you refuse, the breath of your life may be extinguished!

'The treasure is safely stored in our . . . er . . . the royal vault in our Goa palace,' the Viceroy continued. 'We took it over for safe-keeping and shall certainly return it, as the Emperor commands.' He paused to sneeze violently, removed a lace handkerchief from his sleeve and blew his nose. 'Pardon me, but my nose is running,' he said, causing Fernao a shiver of repulsion at the thought of the monumental run that great nose was capable of producing. 'Now do you have any royal directives as to our future policy in this part of the world, Admiral?

'The storm clouds in Europe, created by the continued adventurism of the Emperor Charles V and the actions of King Henry VIII of England, make it imperative that all our available military resources be concentrated on the home front. The Reformation Parliament of England has declared King Henry supreme head of the English Church.

I doubt that his real religious convictions will extend to supporting the Reformation movement in Europe so long as his sex life and his Treasury are in surfeit.' A smile cracked the admiral's craggy features. 'After all, he is probably in spirit still the good Catholic who earned the title *Fidei Defensor*, Defender of the Faith, for the English kings by his treatise in support of the Holy Father, although his heart seems to have run away from his spirit of late. In consequence of these circumstances, however, all *nao* not immediately necessary to maintain our trade in the East Indies and to protect our military and civilians will be returned to Lisbon without delay.'

Fernao's immediate concern was dissipated somewhat by the knowledge that before long he would not be involved in these political/military seesaws.

The Viceroy grunted as if he had been hit in the stomach. 'Weakness could expose some of our enclaves in this country, especially Colombo, to the risk of attack,' he protested, his dry voice crackling. 'You know the state of local politics here. The new king of Sita Waka, being young, hot-headed and a rabid nationalist, will attempt to exploit any military weakness on our part.'

'Indeed, but that is a risk we have to take in the interests of domestic security,' the admiral responded. 'Be assured, however, that His Majesty has no intention of diminishing his power in this region. Our response from the home base to any threat here will be swift and effective.'

'The lives of your son and his family would be in danger.'

'Hardly a consideration that would influence royal policy.' The admiral suddenly became stiff and haughty. 'Besides, these are His Majesty's commands.'

'You could advise His Majesty.' Fernao felt contempt at the pleading note in Don Alfonso's voice.

'I do not allow personal concerns to guide such advice,' the admiral retorted, a hint of anger in his voice. 'You may be relieved to know, however, that any danger of which General de Albergaria and his family may be exposed will be short-lived. The general will relinquish his command and return home as soon as a successor is appointed.'

Fernao stared at his father in amazement. The old man had neatly converted his intentions into reality, for he could not protest at such a definite statement without embarrassing them both. The de Albergarias certainly go after what they want, he thought with reluctant admiration, starting with the head of the family.

Tuesday, 11 February 1533

A slight chill in the morning air heralded a warm, bright day, but an inner feeling of gloom pervaded the Mutu Vella mansion. Before nightfall, Admiral de Albergaria would be miles away on the ocean. Breakfast over, the admiral went upstairs to wash his hands while Fernao and his family remained in the formal drawing room, where they would say their farewells.

Fernao turned from staring blankly through the French windows to gaze at the sad little group. Julietta wore a long dress of her favourite powder blue. His son, holding himself like a man, wore a red doublet and pantaloons, while Catherina was dressed in the same colour and style as her mother.

'The last time I parted from my father,' Fernao mused quietly to Julietta, so the children might not hear, 'I was glad to get away from him. Anger is such a debilitating emotion. It can destroy what is precious, and the individual who experiences it. My father was wrong and has acknowledged his error. Now it is my turn to acknowledge my errors and express my love for him freely.'

Julietta smiled tearfully. 'I feel as you do. It was a humiliating experience, almost shattering, to be rejected because of my birth. Do you remember my outburst on the ramparts that night you returned from Goa? Poor Fernao, you took it so well, but I could tell how hurt and disappointed you were. It must have left you feeling so alone, so hopeless. And I'm still sorry about it.' She gazed at him tearfully. 'But it is today that matters. And I am happy to have your father's love and respect as a person rather than as his prospective daughter-in-law. I hate to see him go.'

'At least we shall be together again before the year's end.' Fernao surveyed the room, glanced outside. 'How to give all this up is another problem. In the navy, my house was my bunk, all my possessions were in my seabag. This is the first real home I have known.'

'Home is where the four of us are a family,' Julietta stated firmly. 'We will make a home again wherever we may be.'

The tread of his father's footsteps on the stairs crept through the subdued sounds of the household. The giant figure in white uniform strode briskly into the room. 'Ah, there you are, General, with your lovely wife and children, ready to see me off on my journey. How kind of you.' His tone of well-bred pleasure at their presence, as if he had not expected it though it was really a foregone conclusion, touched Fernao. 'Since my luggage has gone on ahead, it only remains for me to . . . er . . . bid you good-bye.' He paused. 'Hrmph . . . hrmph . . . er . . . regretfully.'

'Can I come with you to the ship, please, Grandpapa?' little Lopo pleaded. 'I want to be with you as long as possible and to see you off properly.'

'Hrmph . . . h'rmph . . .' The admiral cleared his throat again to hide his emotion, shot a quick glance at Julietta as being the person who could give the boy permission, but recalled himself. 'There is nothing better I would like on this . . . er . . . sad occasion, but don't you think it would evidence a display of emotion to the public that we should avoid?'

The boy understood. 'Yes, sir!' he agreed, straightening his little shoulders, standing more stiffly at attention.

Fernao felt a tightness in his chest. A man's station always brings with it certain duties and restraints, he reflected. It was especially hard at times for a little boy to be a de Albergaria.

'Remember, we shall meet before the end of the year, never to be parted again,' the admiral responded.

'How long is that, sir?' the boy inquired.

'About nine and one-half months . . . er . . . exactly three hundred and twenty-three days to the new year.'

So the stern old man had actually counted the days! Fernao was deeply moved.

'I shall be watching your ship from my window,' the boy declared. 'So look up when you leave.'

'I too,' Catherina intervened.

'And I,' Jullietta added, a catch in her voice.

'H'rmph . . . h'rmph.' The admiral's eyes misted. He drew himself to his full height, left hand on his sword hilt. 'I shall do more than look up as we leave port,' he declared. 'I shall salute you . . . er . . . my dear family . . . from the poop deck.'

'I would like that,' little Lopo replied firmly.

The grandson had appropriated the grandfather for his own from the first moment they had met and a strange bond of affection had instantly been established between them. As for Fernao, he could not have spoken if he wanted to.

'I thank you for the hospitality, the kindness and . . . er . . . yes, the love you have showered on me,' the admiral stated quietly, his eyes taking each of them in turn. He abruptly started his formal leave-taking.

There were no tears. The family did not even come out to the front verandah as Fernao saw his father into the coach.

Finally, they stood on the wharf. The bile was bitter in

Fernao's throat as his father inspected the guard that had been drawn up in his honour. Then it was time for leave-taking. The admiral turned to Fernao and shook his hand formally. 'I shall see you and your family again before year's end, General,' he declared firmly, the words almost a command. His eyes drifted in the direction of the Mutu Vella hill, clouded. He drew himself to his full height. 'Be assured that a good ship will arrive soon to speed you all back home to Portugal.'

CHAPTER THIRTY-THREE
Wednesday, 11 February 1534

For weeks after my father died I felt low and depressed. Though the feeling had eased with time, I could not bear to write my personal diary until today, the second birthday on which I was a king. The arduous duties of a ruler, based upon the daily schedule of the Arya kings, filled my days and most of my nights, but my heart had been empty and I had been a hollow man. It was difficult to forget my father, King Maya Dunne, even for a moment when I kept being confronted by daily evidence of how magnificently he had ruled our kingdom. The order and discipline, the efficient administration, the clear-cut fiscal policies so fair to the ruler and the people alike, were a source of wonder to me.

But mostly I missed the man, with a stark desolation in my heart.

So much for my grief, which is a private thing.

Part of my father's work had reminded me of King Kakkavan Tissa, sire of our first national liberation hero, Abhaya Gamini, who made the winds of Sinhala blow across the entire island of Lanka. It was King Kakkavan who created the military production machine necessary to support a long and arduous campaign. My father had not only built a similar machine, but also included in it modern weapons, muskets and cannon, which were admittedly not as advanced as those of the Portuguese but nonetheless augmented our military power.

Those who have not had to finance and support wars could never understand the monumental difficulties involved. However noble the cause, war steadily destroys a nation's economy, even though it gives an immediate boost to the employment of soldiers, people in the support services and the production machine. Everyone has to be paid, everything has to be paid for. The only sources of such payment are taxes imposed on the people, the king's private treasury and whatever spoils of war can be extracted from the enemy, whom one has to support if one is victorious! I soon came to discover that my father's wise endeavours included the equitable tax base he had established, which not only supported the day-to-day government of the realm but was also capable of sustaining a war. It made me wonder whether King Maya Dunne, reputedly a man of immense personal ambition, had not been content merely to set the stage for the performance by me, his son, as lead actor in the Sinhala national drama.

All I needed to do was to expand and train my army. Ironically, from the moment I grasped the reins of office, I had seen the wisdom of my father's restraint at long last and had curbed my rash impulses to proceed at a gallop on a glorious war of national unity. This in spite of the weakened state of the Portuguese forces.

I had organized the kingdom simultaneously on several fronts.

I strengthened my ties with the nobles and with community leaders like the *bhikkus*, the *ayurvedic* physicians, the school teachers. I improved, extended and smoothed the military production machine. I built on the tax base, causing more funds and goods to flow into the general treasury.

As for the armed forces, I reorganized them so they could efficiently and effectively function as a team. I increased their total strength to one hundred thousand men, dividing them into ten groups, each under a general: intelligence, cavalry, chariots, infantry, artillery, engineers, supply, transportation, fiscal and medical. The fiscal group was an innovation to keep the troops paid regularly and ensure the ready availability of funds for other military purposes.

I had sent for my sister, Queen Padma, the widow of King Vidiye, to assist me with the government. She came immediately from Anu and I soon discovered her to be as sharp, forceful and loyal as I had assessed her to be. She brought some semblance of family to my life. I resisted the temptation to add my two wards, Bandula and Nangi, to my retinue, since Queen Padma had disapproved of my adopting them in the first place.

All this took over one year, because the monsoon rains failed and a drought affected the Yala, the first paddy crop. The Maha crop at the end of last year was, however, bountiful.

Then, since I was completely ready, I struck. What better way to mark my birthday.

Monday, 16 February 1534

One year after the departure of his father, and Fernao was thankful that peace still prevailed in Lanka, not least because, with the Viceroy's departure soon after his father, he had available only two great *nao* in the harbour, one for the protection of Colombo, the other to answer any urgent summons for help from Galle or one of the coastal forts. The only setback that year had been the command of King Dom João III that Fernao should delay the relinquishment of his rank and his return to Portugal. Yet Fernao had been able to take this in his stride because the first pangs from his father's departure and the urgency of the need to start a new life in Portugal had abated.

Julietta seemed wistful at times, but Fernao told himself that was only to be expected. She was an utterly loyal soul. He could not expect her to carve out and fling aside other loyalties that had lain within her almost since birth. If she had any personal conflicts because of her feelings for King

447

Raja Sinha, which God forbid, it was up to her to solve them within her God-given conscience. He could only stand by to help her with love and understanding. There were times when he marvelled at his own new attitudes, although he realized that these were not far from the ideals of his boyhood.

Since King Raja Sinha had not rushed to the fray, even the government departments at home had relaxed over the Lanka situation and correspondence with them had slackened off. The Sita Waka king was reportedly consolidating his kingdom and building up mighty military strength, but there was no evidence of any militant moves in the offing. Meanwhile the Great King Dom Juan in Jaya had soon become the puppet of Fernao's administration and Holy Church.

Things had been dull in the office of late. In the absence of regal interference, trading had become almost routine, thanks to the efficient organization of the Abdul Raschids. There was still an hour to go before he went home for the day, so Fernao welcomed the diversion when his orderly, Aires, now a sergeant, knocked on the door and entered to announce Bishop Juan.

Fernao rose to greet the cleric. The bird-like figure had acquired a new dignity, not only because it was clothed in the rich scarlet vestments of his new office, the cap on the head, but also by virtue of some power his position exuded. The hair and pointed beard had more silver in them, but the pale yellow eyes remained like pebbles.

'Ah, my lord, it is good to see you!' Fernao exclaimed.

Bishop Juan looked grave as he made the sign of the cross. 'It is good to see you too, General. We only wish we were the bearer of better tidings.'

A stab of apprehension streaked through Fernao. He searched the lean face for some hint as to the nature of the news. 'Please sit down.' He indicated the chair opposite his desk, waited for the bishop to take it before seating himself.

'The news is so grave that we decided to bring it to you ourselves,' Bishop Juan stated flatly. 'King Raja Sinha invaded and took Kandy two days ago.'

Fernao coldly held back any sign of reaction, but his mind began spinning rapidly. 'The move was well and secretly timed,' he observed.

'Of course. The king obviously built up his strength and his intelligence system, which seems to be perfect, before he struck.'

'He was undoubtedly opposed by the Kandyan forces?'

'Unfortunately the Kandyans were totally unprepared and put up only token resistance.'

Real fear attacked Fernao. 'The Kandyan army has been disunited for a long time, following King Kumara's death,' he volunteered. 'Queen Anula made her only wise military move when she reappointed General Dunu to command the army last month, but she waited too long.' He could not restrain a philosophic thought. 'The Buddhists say it is all cause and effect. We Catholics might believe in God's punishment for the murder of the Catholic King Kumara.'

'King Raja Sinha struck with the speed, silence and savagery of a lion.' Bishop Juan obviously had no inclination to debate God's punishment. 'He sent Lord Wickrama Sinha with the main body of his army on a frontal assault against the Kandyan forts at the passes of Kadu and Balane, while he himself attacked from a totally unexpected direction. He moved his cavalry west then north in groups through the most difficult mountain terrain, overwhelmed the city and the palace in a carefully planned and co-ordinated night assault, then dashed foward to take the forts from the rear. Queen Anula is a cunning and able woman but, alas, she is not cast in the heroic mould needed to rally troops.'

Fernao was tempted to remark that the queen was more heroic in the bedroom than on the battlefield, but chivalry and respect for his guest's clerical robes made him hold back. 'Where is the queen?' he questioned.

'She is reported to be secluded in the palace.' The bishop's discoloured teeth were bared in a grin, his short laugh sent a whiff of his bad breath across the desk, and caused Fernao to squirm inwardly. 'The question is, should we not intervene, General?'

'Why should we?' Fernao resented the arrogation of authority implied by the word 'we', but kept his tone civil. 'This is purely an internal affair of the Sinhala. Besides, we no longer have the strength of intervene even if it had accorded with His Majesty's policies.'

'Surely, but don't you think we should at least take steps to bare our teeth against any further expansion of King Raja Sinha's power? Remember he has a military machine the like of which this country has not witnessed for a hundred years.'

A thought struck Fernao. 'We could use the trader, Abdul Raschid, as an intermediary with the new king, who likes the Mouro and respects his wife, Aisha, because she acquitted herself so well in the king's cavalry regiment.'

The cleric's pale yellow eyes became hard as those of an inquisitor. 'You are concerned with lay purposes, General; we are here today representing Holy Church. If we solicit the help of an infidel we will lose our influence. Holy Church is in danger and we demand your protection.'

'What can I do with the small forces now at my disposal?' Fernao questioned irritably. 'Besides, unlike the late King Vidiye, King Raja Sinha has never been known to attack Holy Church. He is a most tolerant man.'

'You can reinforce the power of the Great King of Jaya, who holds office by divine favour and with the sanction of the Holy Father and His Imperial Majesty. He is a Catholic sovereign married to a Catholic lady, the daughter of Queen Anula and under the protection of Holy Church.'

Mention of Queen Anula revealed to Fernao why the

cleric was trying to persuade him to proceed against King Raja Sinha. 'We have no forces for an offensive campaign,' he retorted bluntly. 'We would not even have the strength to hold Colombo were it not for the protection offered by the guns of our warships in the harbour.'

The bishop nodded. 'We shall ensure that you receive the necessary troops,' he declared. His voice suddenly acquired a note of authority. 'God has also willed that, after the first barren years of near-despair, our activities in this country should become fruitful and multiply.' The bishop's deep voice began to boom with religious fervour. 'Driven by missionary zeal, our clerical brethren have flocked in increasing numbers to the Indies on their divine quest to bring light to the darkness of heathen religions.'

Not to mention the hope of acquiring riches from the bounty of the converted barbarians, Fernao thought cynically. He resented any slur on the ancient native people of the country.

'The missionary endeavours have been crowned by the arrival of the Franciscan monks,' Bishop Juan continued. 'Soon our saintly Father Francis Xavier hopes to commence his personal mission in the East by establishing a seminary in Goa and then visiting Japan to have the gospel carried to the native peoples by men of their own race.' His voice had continued rising and he now paused for effect, his pale yellow eyes gleaming fanatically. 'Our blessed Father Francis has agreed to establish a seminary in Kandy as well, upon his return from the Far East. It is imperative therefore that our Christian mission should have a firm base in that capital city. This is why you must intervene in Kandy, General.'

Fernao did not try to hide his expression of astonishment. 'But why build the seminary in Kandy, my lord? Why not in Colombo? And how does Father Francis even know of the best location for a seminary in this country?'

The bishop leaned back, stroked his silver grey beard

smugly. 'Father Francis has had our personal advice. We chose Kandy for a variety of reasons. First, it has a strong Catholic element among the royalty, beginning with Dona Margaridha, the rightful Queen of Lanka, and the nobles. Kandy will also give us an enclave in the heartland of the country which it is virtually impossible to penetrate militarily. Finally, the population of Kandy is ... er ... more charitably disposed to us than that of the low country.'

Fernao had given up wondering as to how the cleric came by his information. The confessional yielded its secrets and those who came to it frequently remained the eyes and ears of the friars. Whatever the saintly Father Xavier's intentions, the decision to establish the seminary in Kandy was purely political, signifying the beginning of direct power play by the Church in Lanka. Shrugging aside his anger, he raised his eyes to the bishop. 'Any religious mission deserves more forethought than a mere lay purpose,' he declared non-committally.

'The Holy Father in Rome has graciously taken note of our own humble endeavours, and desires to support them even more than in the past.' There was nothing humble in Bishop Juan's tone. 'Upon our recommendation, he has placed the dioceses of Goa and Lanka under the apostolic Archbishop of Lisbon who in turn is responsible to the Cardinal Administrator in Rome.'

Fernao's heart sank. He knew what was coming even before the bishop uttered the words.

'Our parishes in Colombo, Kandy, Galle, Jaffna and the coastal towns will be organized under a single fiscal control.' Bishop Juan sounded pompous and arrogant now. 'They will be administered by Father Perez as Procurator. They will not only have to function independently but will also be required to contribute towards the work of the archbishopric, the cardinalate and the Vatican. A people, especially a religious people, must not depend on the charity of the Mother Church.'

So the whole rotten system of the Vatican was to be introduced into Lanka. It always started with the idealism of the clerics, but the system would corrupt most of those who administered it. Fernao's gaze caught the flash of something in the bishop's pale eyes, identified it. Somewhere along the road, had the idealism of this man also become corrupted? At least by the desire for power?

Bishop Juan must have known that Fernao had guessed at the secret, for a cruel gleam entered his eyes. 'You must remember that you hope to depart these shores soon, General. Why should you of all people thwart our purposes?' The threat was implicit: If you wish to return home, do not oppose our policies. 'If you assist us, you will know your reward both now' – the promise was explicit – 'and in heaven.'

Fernao was suddenly filled with disgust. Peter's Pence translated into Sinhala and Tamil. Tithes, alimony, the sale of indulgences, the forgiveness of sins for a few *cruzados*, the creation of a religious power parallel to that of the civil and military presence without the shedding of a single drop of priestly blood, with no sweat except the body odour emanating from the cassocks of unbathed friars and no tears save that of a cruelly exploited flock.

'Baptism has already identified the loyal and faithful Sinhala and Tamil by the use of Christian names instead of those of heathen origin,' Bishop Juan concluded triumphantly. A curiously harsh chuckle escaped him, caused Fernao to realize the deep bitterness within this man against the Sinhala because of the slights, indignities and frustrations he had endured in the early days of his mission in Lanka. 'People in and around the towns and cities are adopting a new way of life, our European way. They speak our language, sing our songs, imitate our dances, follow our customs. It is fascinating to watch God move powerfully to change an entire nation. Make no mistake about it, General. That is what we intend.' He paused for breath, wiped a flicker of saliva from the side of his mouth with a silk kerchief he removed from his sleeve.

'What of the Muslims?' Fernao demanded impulsively.

The brown eyes gleamed with hatred, a cheek twitched. 'They have never responded to our call. Like the Jews who betrayed and reviled our Lord, they are accursed.'

What is going to happen to the Sinhala people who have kept their race, language, religion and culture pure for centuries? Fernao wondered.

Almost as if he had heard the question, Bishop Juan gave him the answer.

'We are in Lanka to rescue its people from the dead hands of Hinduism and the Buddha. Even those we fail to convert shall end up lesser in their own faiths and be changed into brown Europeans, who even if they won't worship God, shall reverence the white man.'

CHAPTER THIRTY-FOUR

Monday, 16 February 1534

In her upstairs studio, Julietta was painting the morning scene outside when the quiet knocking on the door, two long taps, one short, two long, interrupted her. It was Appu's signal. 'Come in!' she called.

Appu glided silently in and quietly closed the door behind him. Though the capacity to move unobtrusively was part of his training as a spy, it also made him the perfect domestic servant. His face was inscrutable as usual, but there was an inner excitement.

'You have some news?' she inquired. It was their practice to come directly to the point.

'Yes, my lady. King Raja Sinha invaded the *uda rata* and seized the capital city of Kandy and the royal palace two days ago. He now controls the entire sub-kingdom and is indeed a Great King.'

'How wonderful!' A thought struck her. 'What has happened to the Regent, Queen Anula?' Unaccountably, she found herself fearful of what that man-eater might do to Tiki-tiki.

'As far as I know, she is a prisoner in her quarters.'

'I hope . . .' Realizing the impropriety of expressing her concern that King Raja Sinha might fall into the queen's clutches, Julietta changed tack, '. . . the Great King is safe and well.'

A mischievous glint flickered in Appu's eyes. He knows that I would not want his king to bed with the queen, Julietta thought, her cheeks warming with a blush.

'The Great King is indeed safe and well,' Appu responded. 'He is in the Kandy palace, accepting the fealty of the nobles and having the administration of the *uda rata* reorganized. He is reported to have Queen Anula confined to her quarters and had not deigned to give her audience when I last had news.'

Thank God for that, Julietta thought, but an undefinable concern for Tiki-tiki's wellbeing remained.

Monday, 16 February 1534

Strong woman that she was, Aisha found her helplessness to do anything about her husband's illness totally frustrating. He was shrivelling away before her very eyes. The Muslim medical men and the Sinhala *ayurvedics* knew the symptoms but had no cure for the disease. King Raja Sinha's court physicians and General de Albergaria's European doctor were equally helpless. Abdul Raschid had now reached a stage where he was tired of all the purgings, the *cassayas*, the decoctions, the *guli*, pills, the *patthu*, poultices and the leeching. His skin had become drier and more itchy. If he scratched himself too vigorously, lacerations sometimes resulted that turned into ulcers. Black patches had appeared on his body. He urinated frequently, was always thirsty and tired easily. Someone had even suggested a devil dancing ceremony to drive away the evil spirit that must have entered Abdul Raschid's body through the *hooniyam*, charm, of an enemy, but Abdul Raschid was too good a Muslim to resort to black magic. He merely shrugged now-bony shoulders on which his clothes flapped and murmured. 'It is the will of Allah.'

More recently, when numbness of the extremities and blurred vision had developed, Aisha had been forced to accept that the only man she had ever loved was dying and that her indomitable will was helpless in the face of his affliction.

Abdul Raschid took to lying more often on the divan in her reception room. It was as if he needed the security of her presence. So in recent months, unknown to the world, she had handled their entire business herself from his private office at the rear of the Slave Island house. It had prospered beyond measure, but she took good care to ensure that everyone believed that her husband was responsible for its success.

Like a miser counting treasure against the possibility of losing it, she went to her husband as frequently as she could during the day, just to sit on her sofa in silent communion with him, or to watch him while he dozed.

This morning, when she hurried to him from her office, the whistle of the lovebirds from their cages in the centre of the courtyard irritated her, the two great ivory tusks in her reception room seemed an archway to doom, and the smell of incense from the brass burners on their ebony stands were overpowering.

Abdul Raschid lay back on the divan, eyes closed. His lids fluttered open at her quiet entrance and he smiled weakly. We are so close to each other, he knows without seeing me when I have entered the room. Months ago, she had given up asking him how he felt because his only reply was, 'Better,' I wish that Allah would grant me one divine miracle and really make my husband better, she thought as she knelt her greeting, kissed his hand and sat on her sofa facing him.

'What will you do when I am gone?' His words were barely above a whisper, but she heard him.

'Whatever you would have me do, beloved husband of mine.' The reply was totally out of character for her and yet, why not, she reasoned fiercely. My love for this man is as strong as my character and unwavering as my spirit.

'You must do whatever will sustain your life,' Abdul Raschid murmured. 'Like all truly strong leaders, you will never find peace within your station. Such is not the gateway to contentment, but when your life is done, you will make your way to heaven and I shall meet you there.'

The words stabbed her heart with the ferocity of a sharp

457

blade, but in a flash she comprehended their truth. And from that comprehension, she knew what her husband would have her do. In his gentle way, he had pointed the direction. 'You and I both know that I shall do as you would want me to, beloved husband of mine,' she stated steadily. 'I shall run our business and try to find peace within myself.'

'It is good. I can go in that peace then.'

Aisha barely heard the words. Overcome by terror, she watched his trembling hand reach out for another sweet-meat, watched it hover in the air like a wounded bird uncertain of its landing, then flop helplessly against the side of the divan.

The keening rose from the depths of her being, fluttering at first as if that same wounded bird were now in her throat. Then it soared free and shrill on grief-stricken wings. She was not even aware of the sound, only of its dread source.

Wednesday, 18 February 1534

I deliberately refrained from granting Queen Anula an audience after I occupied the Kandy palace. Cool as usual she made no request for an audience either, simply waited it out, probably knowing that I would have to send for her at some time.

After my successful takeover of the Kandyan kingdom, I reconfirmed the appointment belatedly made by Queen Anula, of the veteran General Dunu, King Kumara's former chief of staff, as commander of the Kandyan forces, and despatched a strong column under him and Lord Wickrama Sinha to take over the Gampola and Hangura sub-kingdoms. Gampola was taken in a day, following a brief battle. Three days later, I had word that the column had won a bloodless victory in Hangura. It appeared to me that the proud Kandyan people were ready for strong leadership again, even from a *pathaya*, low-country fellow!

I nonetheless allowed one more day to elapse before summoning Queen Anula to a private audience in the same chamber in which she had first met the two former kings, her husband, Prince Kumara as he had been then, and King Wira.

Seated on the divan, I could see through the open door. The courtyard was bathed in pale golden morning sunlight of the hill country laced by the shadow tracery of branches. The splash of the fountain and the cooing of wood pigeons provided pleasant background music, rendering the heartbeat of the palace somehow remote. The peaceful scene partly compensated for the garish red and gold furnishings within the chamber.

The silver-haired attendant, Kolla, announced the queen. She glided into the room wearing a blue sari, ornamented by a necklace, earrings, hair-pins and bracelets of dark blue sapphires set in heavily worked gold. Though she glittered, sparkled, shimmered, my first impressions were of an innate, subdued dignity, the remarkable grace of the slender, well-formed body and an elegance of posture that was unique. She did not make obeisance, but bowed low as befitted her rank and station. Even before she rose, the fragrance of her perfume, which I recognized as a distillate of the temple flower, reached my nostrils.

Then I saw her face, the flawless, dusky beauty that no ornaments could subdue, the exquisite oval mould of delicate facial bones, a perfect setting for her dark, magnetic eyes. I had last met her when I was but a boy in the Jaya palace, totally unconcerned about any female save Juli. Now I was a man, responding without thought to a physical vibrance which went beyond sex appeal.

She was immediately aware of my reaction, for an enigmatic smile of knowledge, of recognition, of unspoken intimacy, briefly lit her eyes.

459

'Pray be seated, madam,' I bade her.

She moved to the settle on my left, sat down, gracefully arranged the pleats of her sari. She looked up at me, her gaze suddenly lustrous, compelling. The warmth she was projecting caused my eyes to widen. What had happened to make me, the *brachmachariya*, so responsive to any woman?

As was proper, she waited for me to open the conversation, but not having dealt with queens before, for a moment I was at a loss as to how to proceed. Then the training of years and my latent power to overcome any circumstance took over. 'We trust you have been extended every courtesy due your rank and station by our staff, madam?' My voice was firm, controlled.

A mischievous smile twitched the sides of her mouth, revealing a glimpse of pearly white teeth. 'Your *staff* has treated us with great consideration, my lord.'

She had emphasized the word 'staff' and I realized that she was delicately chiding me for the delay in granting her this audience.

Her expression swiftly changed. She became serious, earnest. 'Our only loss is that we have been so long denied the joy of your presence, the only royal lion, Raja Sinha by name and deed, in our country.'

The words were spoken with such complete sincerity that they robbed her earlier reprimand of any offence and removed her poetic phrases from the realm of flattery. No woman had ever spoken like this to me before. Once again, I could only look deep into her eyes, enjoying their intimacy, until an unwonted gallantry took over. 'Seeing you now, madam, we know the loss has been ours, we can only hope that you will permit us to make up for that loss in the days ahead.' The words emerged without thought. This woman had the rare ability to evoke them.

Only after she acknowledged my tribute with a shy smile, eyes quickly downcast, did a fragment of knowledge appear in my mind. The gallantry was mine, the intimacy had been willed by her. This was her power. She had exercised it over many a man before. Now it was my turn and I had no desire to resist her or to curb the unusual physical stirrings of my manhood. I had made love to a woman only once in my life, to Juli beneath the dark branches of a grove on the Mutu Vella hill canopied by the paling stars of the night sky. That love-making had been a spontaneous product of love, of loving, an act as natural and crystal pure as dew on the morning grass. Queen Anula stirred me with a powerful lust.

I briefly wondered where our relationship would lead. Innate caution warned against the queen's total deceit and the ill fortune she unfailingly brought the men in her life. I saw the sad expression on the face of my grandfather, King Wijayo, as he told his three sons of her betrayal of him. Yet if the end was tragic, how pleasant the journey, I thought, as our conversation drifted to current events. Witty, observant, with an acute mind and surprising knowledge, she soon had me relaxed, laughing, chatting as if I had known her all my life. I even began to wonder whether the stories of her machinations could be completely true. After all, I had never heard the story from Queen Anula's point of view. My grandfather had been a lecherous old goat. When he named her son, Prince Deva, to the succession, it need not have been at her urging, but might well have been caused by a desire to show off combined with antipathy towards his own sons. King Kumara was a thoroughly amoral man. How terribly he must have wounded his wife by taking a younger mistress.

Queen Anula finally brought me back to present reality. She glanced at the clock on the wall. 'It is almost the hour for your public audiences in the great hall, lord. Pray forgive us for having kept you from your subjects. Time ceased to exist when we entered your presence.' Her long eyelashes fluttered once, were quickly lowered.

'Madam, your beauty is timeless,' I responded. 'Your reminder of our duty but enhances you in our eyes.' Not being given to making gallant speeches to ladies, I could not believe what I was hearing! Could this be me speaking?

Her eyes misted. She nodded acknowledgement. 'No one has ever spoken to us as you do, Sire.' She had used my honorific at last. 'Most men merely desire to grab what they consider desirable. Otherwise ... perhaps ...' She shrugged sad shoulders, then became brisk. 'Well, enough of conjecture, for these moments are reality. *You* are reality. To you, we offer everything, the fealty of our kingdoms which you have conquered, the strength of our Kiri Vella clan, the overlordship of the Jaya kingdom of which our daughter is the queen-elect, the support of the Catholic Church.'

'You can offer all that?' I inquired, disbelieving at last.

'Certainly, lord,' She paused, her expression serious. 'Our influence may by itself be small, but combined with your military power ... why ... we can control the whole island, except the north, and with the entire Sinhala race behind us, the Cholas would soon accept our dominion.'

A despairing voice within me inquired, Is this the bargain you made with King Vidiye? But it was momentarily lost in the grand vista of possibilities that her words had opened. A shortcut to the achievement of my ideals, with this beautiful woman thrown in to complete my fulfilment. 'What are your conditions, madam?' I inquired seriously.

Her eyes flashed. 'Are we dry-fish vendors haggling over a salted catch, lord?' Her voice took on a sad note. Incredibly, she looked like a hurt child. 'Please do not let your mind mar the beauty of what we have just discovered by instinct. And please do not deem us less than we are.' She lifted a proud head. 'Our offer has no conditions. It is a gesture of thankfulness to one who has acknowledged us as a queen, a lady,' she eyed me directly, 'and a woman. It is also a humble submission to your awesome majesty.'

Her voice and manner, the emanation of her spirit, were so convincing that I was moved to the depths of my being. She must be speaking the truth, for my father had that same majesty and I had always desired to inherit it. More, for the first time in my life, someone had offered me something merely because of who I was. This surely was a dream. I closed my eyes briefly and opened them to see her still sitting before me, her eyes lustrous with promise and something deeper, a wonderment at herself. She made me feel very much a worthwhile man. 'Sire, we have need of the person you are,' she whispered huskily. 'We meet on common ground. Your spirit is virgin for love. So is ours. We human beings have a hunger of which we are not completely aware until we glimpse its appeasement. The tenderness of your spirit is unique. You honour and fulfil us with the communion which you hold unfulfilled.' She paused, smiling wryly. 'There, we have broken every rule of decorum and deportment, but we are not ashamed. If we have transgressed, you may inflict on us the worst possible punishment, exile for ever from your presence.'

'Beauteous queen, it is not fitting for rulers to punish themselves.'

'Then we may see you again.' Excitement made her eyes sparkle.

'Of course.'

Her expression became bright and merry. 'In that event, Sire, since we know that your schedule is a busy one today and tomorrow, we invite you to dine with us in our private quarters on the night after. Just the two of us, suitably chaperoned by our trusted lady-in-waiting.'

Her eyes held the promise of more communion than mere words. For a moment, I saw myself as a hare transfixed by a sinuous, swaying cobra. Her magnetism erased the thought. I *wanted* all that she could offer me. Suddenly, out of the blue, I saw Juli, young, without guile, fairer than moonlit air. I saw her slender build, her auburn hair, the white of goodness gleaming in her skin. Why did the aquamarine eyes gaze at me imploringly? Juli had a husband and children. Why should she care about my feelings for another woman?

'This is no dream from the past, lord. It is present reality.'

How did the queen know that a ghost from the past had haunted me then? Was she a witch? In any case, she was right. Juli belonged to someone else. She would soon be gone from Lanka, for ever. Yet . . .

'Will you honour us, lord?' The queen's voice, crystal clear, removed the image of Juli like water obscuring a windowpane.

'Of course. The honour will be ours.' Boldness took over. 'We trust that we shall both be fulfilled.'

Wednesday, 18 February 1534

Fernao was later than usual coming home for dinner, so Juli stood by her bedroom window gazing our at the driveway beneath her and the city lights. Though she had grown accustomed to the uncertainties of Fernao's routine, she still worried whenever he was late. The faint hiss of the flares lighting the driveway brought the consciousness of resin tincturing the night air. Her eyes drifted to the gleaming patch in the distance, pricked by lights, that was the Colombo harbour, to the two great *nao* riding at anchor.

Her attention was suddenly drawn sideways to the blackness of the grove beneath the governor's mansion. Evil had once attended her there, followed by moments of incredible beauty that had altered her entire life. Where was Tiki-tiki? In Kandy of course, in the palace.

The knowledge of evil lurking somewhere hit her with such blinding blackness that a short gasp escaped her. She perceived the existence of this evil with the same stunning clarity as when she had known that she had conceived Tiki-tiki's child. Her entire being screamed with the urge to race blindly to wherever Tiki-tiki was and help him. but how could she?

Could she appeal to Fernao? No. To Appu? How?

Now the undefinable evil that Tiki-tiki faced was slithering all over him, choking him. Fear tightened Julietta's chest, gripped her by the throat.

Oh dear God, sweet Jesu, beloved Virgin Mother, help Tiki-tiki.

Only God could help.

She ran to her *prie-dieu*, knelt down. The flames from the burning candles brought life to the Madonna's face, but the eyes of the Saviour on the brown cross were muted with anguish. She directed the fierce concentration of desperation to God the Father.

Oh God, please protect my Tiki-tiki from the evil that is about to befall him, which the love Thou gavest me for him has brought to my knowledge.

Oh Blessed Virgin, I beg thee to intercede with Our Father on behalf of my virgin man, Tiki-tiki.

Oh dear Jesu, Prince of Peace, I beg thee to give peace, purity and security to my earthly prince . . .

CHAPTER THIRTY-FIVE

Friday, 20 February 1534

Standing by the windows of her reception chamber that afternoon, Queen Anula reflected on her situation with satisfaction. Her beauty and brains had placed her on the threshold of a far greater future than she had ever known. King Wijayo had been a Great King only in name, King Kumara and King Vidiye merely in their aspirations to the title. This young man, King Raja Sinha, was, at the age of twenty-nine, a Great King already. If she handled him right, the entire nation would be at her feet. It gave her a feeling of power, her only love, so sensual it was almost orgasmic. It came from her childhood desires when she had been ignored because she was dusky and not fair. She recalled being totally unable to attract her parents or family. How she wished that those who rejected her could see her now. But if they could not witness her approaching triumph, it was only because their eyes were sightless while hers were alive, vibrant, able to sway the most powerful man in the land. So she had won.

Her thoughts shot back to King Kumara, the only man who had been able to reach the innermost depths of her. His very brains had caused his downfall. He had been too clever to have had to fall back on the reflexes of conventional morality, but he had done so and lost.

'You rejected me, but I beat you in the end,' she called to him, for he was somewhere in the green jungle of the sharply sloping mountainside. 'With King Vidiye and you both dead, your successor will never know that I am playing an old role again. You men! Pah! I hold you to scorn.'

Her quiet laughter echoed throught the open window, seemed to filter up the mountainside.

Friday, 20 February 1534

The meal over, they returned from Queen Anula's private dining quarters to her reception chamber. King Raja Sinha sat on King Kumara's favourite settle. Her eyes strayed briefly through her visitor to the past. Memories are wonderful, she thought, casting out the recollection, so long as they are the stepping stones to achievement through the swamp of sighs.

She studied her guest in the golden flarelight. He was younger than King Kumara and different in most respects. The shiny black hair, dark eyes, the chiselled features with the cleft chin made him look sexually desirable. This was not a pretty Kandyan boy growing up, but a quiet, reserved man of great inner strength, totally without cynicism, earnest, sincere, sensitive. He had eaten sparingly of the sumptuous meal she had served him, contenting himself with boiled rice, chicken and dark *polos*, young breadfruit curry. He refused the *rasa kavili*, dessert sweets, the wine and *ra*, drank only water, sipped some pomegranate juice. Altogether a temperate young man, with a quiet inner regality which she found most attractive. She could think of two ways of getting him into her power, tempting him with her body, but denying it until he became so consumed by desire that he would do anything to couple with her, or giving the *brachmachariya* such a taste of the joys of sex that he would slaver for more and end up her slave.

Which was it to be? Since he would soon be leaving to occupy Dhamba and the north, time was short.

She directed a brilliant gaze at King Raja Sinha, injecting lust into it. She was rewarded by his response, a quick blink of the eyes followed by a searching scrutiny. A lizard's chirp broke the stillness of the night outside. Did it warn of danger to the king? She continued to hypnotize him with an unfettered outpouring of desire.

'You are such an alone person, lord,' she commenced, her voice soft and low. She placed into her glance the intimacy that is generated between the lonely. 'You may think that we are not lonely. After all, we have two children. But how can the young fill the aching voids in the lives of grown-ups?'

He half-smiled, wistfully she thought. 'We also have two children,' he replied. 'So we know what you mean.'

She was stunned, dismayed, but did not show it. 'We are so glad, lord. But how . . .? You have never wed. Perhaps these are children of some concubine?'

His eyes glinted with mischief satisfied. 'Oh no, madam. We adopted two children some years ago. Their names are Bandula and Nangi.'

She sighed with huge relief. 'Please tell us about them.'

He told her the story of how he had discovered his two wards, conveyed his feeling that to him they represented all the people of the country, told her that they were the one love and personal responsibility of his life. 'So you see, they live with their foster parents, Sene and his wife, in Kadu,' he concluded. 'We see very little of them, but . . . er . . . the love remains.'

She had listened in silence, making mental notes. 'Just as we thought, you care for the helpless. Oh, you arouse feelings in us that were repeatedly stifled through the laughter and sneers of those who should have cared.' Her voice was a caress, soft as the gold of the lamplight. 'You are so different, a sensitive, perceptive, gentle human being. Such qualitites belong to the truly strong. They are more important than military conquest, for they can conquer a woman's heart.' She paused, half-smiling, shaking her head. 'Before we met you two days ago, we were afraid . . . so afraid that we would face a ruthless conqueror. Now . . .

now, we only want to serve you in every way possible . . . in *every single* way.' Her look conveyed her meaning.

He responded head-on. 'Madam, we have led the life of the *brachmachariya* from our earliest days. Having met you, we believe that you have been much maligned. No one so exquisite could possibly have aught but beauty of mind and heart.' He paused to look more deeply at her. 'For instance, no one has ever thought to give us a private meal before. Your kindness has touched us. The *brachmachariya* now asks, how best can *we* serve *you*?'

She made up her mind on the instant. 'By permitting a queen to render you a woman's service,' she whispered hoarsely. She rose to her feet, advanced slowly and knelt before him. 'So we can serve the *brachmachariya* as no other woman has in his lifetime.' She forced tears to her eyes.

She saw his nostrils flare, heard the catch of his breath. His eyes took in her face, dropped to her breasts, deliberately remained there, then returned to her eyes. He reached out slowly, gently, to touch her face with his fingers, took a poised tear-drop on his forefinger and gazed at it with wonder. He shook his head. 'You weep for me?' Having dropped the royal plural, he raised the finger to his lips, kissed it tenderly.

'For myself, lord,' she whispered, moved in spite of herself.

He leaned forward, caressed her face with both hands, his touch so light it made her tremble. His hands reached up to stroke her forehead, her hair. He rose to his feet and she with him, standing close to he could not escape the softness of her body. Several inches taller than her, he bent his head cupped her face in his hands, looked deep into her eyes. 'When we invaded the Kandyan kingdom perhaps we had an even greater date with destiny than we realized,' he stated quietly.

She raised her lips to him. He brushed them with his

mouth. Then the pent-up feelings of an entire lifetime broke loose. With a groan, he crushed her in his arms. He was very strong, smelled of sandalwood. She felt the thrust of his erection against her abdomen. Young, virile, hard, he was so large she shivered involuntarily with desire. Swept by the old daze, she had to use all her power to stop herself from floating away.

Time for such surrender later. Tonight must be handled with care.

Relaxing her lips, she opened her mouth to him, moaned, rubbed her abdomen against his penis. She reached to unloose his belt buckle, thrilled to the heaviness of his breathing . . .

At first she barely heard it. The knocking was so quiet. But its insistence soon penetrated her senses.

King Raja Sinha drew back, re-buckling his belt. He sat down on his settle, still breathing heavily, nostrils flaring, but the eye-daze was replaced by sudden coolness. He smiled wryly. 'It seems that the gods will otherwise, madam,' he observed quietly. Did he believe in divine intervention?

'We are sorry to be disturbed, lord,' she whispered. 'But whatever it is will go away. Please be patient.'

She smoothed her hair, walked across the room, resumed her seat. 'Enter!' she called.

The door opened, revealing her silver-haired chief attendant, Nona, making obeisance. 'What is it?' the queen demanded sharply. 'We told you we were not to be disturbed.'

'I beg my lady's pardon,' Nona responded as she scrambled to her feet. 'But high-ups crave immediate audience with His Majesty.'

'Who?' King Raja Sinha was obviously annoyed.

'Lord Wickrama Sinha and General Dunu, lord.'

'Then it must be urgent,' the king responded. 'Tell them

470

we shall meet them at the audience chamber ... er... soon.'

'They are already here, lord. In the waiting chamber ... They crave Your Majesty's leave to enter.'

The king exchanged a quick glance with the queen. He hesitated, but only for a moment. 'With my lady's permission?'

The queen felt an unaccountable stab of apprehension. 'Of course, Your Majesty. Your wish is our command.' Her faint smile promised him more than his wish of the immediate moment.

Though she had appointed him commander of the Kandyan army recently, it had been a long time since she had met General Dunu. In fact, she had not seen him since the day before her late husband had set off on his ill-fated campaign, which her brains had manipulated into King Kumara's sorry end. General Dunu knew nothing about the part she had personally played in the betrayal by the commanders of the Dhamba and Kiri Vella forces in the battle of Kegalla, because she had let the world believe that they acted against King Kumara on their own initiative. After that battle, General Dunu was merely a defeated ex-army commander who had been permitted by King Vidiye, her consort, to retire to his country estate.

She therefore greeted the general and Lord Wickrama Sinha with an open smile. She noted the general's bow to her was stiffly formal, but then he was by nature a dour man, always playing the stern soldier.

'Pray be seated.' King Raja Sinha indicted settles beside him.

'If it please Your Majesty, the matters that have arisen are so urgent that we do not have time to sit down.' Lord Wickrama Sinha sounded grim and tense. 'We beg you to accompany us to your chamber so we can discuss them.'

A puzzled frown creased King Raja Sinha's brow. He looked at the queen briefly, seemed to make up his mind.

'Pray be seated, gentlemen,' he reiterated firmly. 'Queen Anula has just become our ally, so you may speak freely in her presence.'

She thrilled at his words, was hard put to keep a hint of triumph from her expression. 'Begging your pardon, my lord,' she began. 'If these gentlemen desire to have private discussion with their sovereign, to which an ignorant woman, notwithstanding her rank, can hardly contribute . . .' She paused, shrugging shapely shoulders, inviting his acceptance of her self-dismissal.

The king gave her the answer she had expected. 'Madam, you are the soul of courtesy and thoughtfulness. For that very reason it would be churlish of us to exclude you. Besides . . .' he looked at her with eyes suddenly brilliant, meaningful. 'We shall need to finish our business with you before retiring for the night.' He half-turned towards the two men, gestured imperiously for them to be seated.

She watched them take their seats with secret amusement. 'Now, gentlemen, your news. It had best be of momentous importance for you to have broken in on our private meeting.'

Lord Wickrama blanched at the king's words and their peremptory tone as if he had been smacked across the face with a dead fish. 'General Dunu and I returned a few minutes ago from taking the Hangura kingdom,' he responded. 'Messengers from the north awaited us, with news that King Ratnes Waram of Jaffna, heading a strong force estimated at twenty thousand men and reinforced by an army of some fifteen thousand mercenaries from South India, has seized our ancient capital of Anu. The entire operation was carried out so secretly that the ruling council of Dhamba had no time to boost its forces in Anu. The Chola are expected to march on Polon next, before moving against the Dhamba capital.'

'Fifteen thousand mercenaries! Did you say *fifteen thousand*?' King Raja Sinha sounded incredulous.

'Yes, Sire.'

'How on earth could that have happened without our knowing it? Has our foreign intelligence system collapsed?'

'When our spies reported the assembling of a force in Tiruvandum, you may recall we thought it was intended for an internal war against the Raja of Calicut.'

An initial spurt of alarm at the news merged into questions whirling through the queen's head. How could she use this development to get King Raja Sinha into her clutches? She had been on the verge of seducing the arch *brachmachariya* when these two donkeys came blundering in. Would the king yet take his pleasure with her as his words, 'finish our business with you', had promised? How could she bend the turn of events to her advantage?

She looked at the lithe figure of the king, sitting with straight back and squared shoulders, but very relaxed. Unaccountably, a raw urge to finish the business she had began stabbed inside her abdomen. She had not had a man for a long time. She knew she was in the full flowering of her fertile period. If she could become pregnant . . .

'With our combined strengths, we are more than a match for the Chola.' King Raja Sinha had obviously been assessing relative strengths. 'The only question is where to give him battle. We could meet him headlong or allow him to enter into the heart of Sinhala territory, where he will have no local support and his lines of communication will be stretched.'

If you wait, we can finish our business tonight, the queen thought. Then inspiration seized her. 'Would you please grant a foolish woman leave to make a suggestion, lord?' she inquired with seeming timidity.

'Yes, madam.'

The king was all courteous attention, but she had felt the other two men stiffening. 'Why not follow your brilliant analysis to its conclusion?' she inquired. 'By having the

Chola harrassed along the way, then cutting him off in the rear from his home base?'

'And how can that be achieved?' the king demanded.

'We could arrange for the armies of Dhamba and our Kirir Vella clan to take the offensive.' Wanting to impress, the words were out of her without serious thought. 'After all, you have just done us the honour of counting us your ally.'

'Well, gentlemen, what do you think of that for a strategic concept?' The king turned to his two generals. 'It would appear that the queen complements beauty with brains and loyalty.'

General Dunu actually snorted, his round face reddening, the black moustache bristling. 'Sire, the allies that Her Majesty speaks of are quite literally a deadly combination to which I can personally testify,' he rumbled.

'Your words have a hidden meaning, General,' the king stated sharply. 'Your explanation, please.'

The atmosphere in the room had suddenly turned cold, taut as a new drum. Even the lights of the tapers were unwavering, as if to listen. A breeze stirring the leaves in the darkness outside was a harsh instrusion, the hooting of an owl from the jungle a lonely sound. She shivered.

'Sire, at the risk of incurring your displeasure, I must respectfully inform you that I would never trust military arrangements made by the queen.' The general ground out the words slowly, heavily, his gaze on her so fierce she was compelled for once to drop her glance. 'My former sovereign lord, King Kumara, died because of the so-called allies provided by his queen. I myself am only alive today through the intervention of the *devas* and a promise I made to the late King Vidiye on my honour, as a condition of his releasing me after the Kegalla battle. He did not wish the world to know how he came by his victory and I thought I would carry the secret to my grave, but now I see old evil bubbling afresh from its pits, unseen by you,

474

hidden by beauty, and I am compelled to ask myself, what is honour?'

The queen knew, with sick horror, what he was about to reveal. She sought desperately for something to say, some method of diverting the conversation. Before she could interrupt, the stern-faced general had proceeded. 'Living honour commands the breaking of a cowardly oath given to save myself from death or imprisonment. It was this same queen, Sire, who arranged with King Vidiye for the betrayal of her husband and her fellow Kandyans, so she could become his consort and marry him. King Kumara gave me the details just before he died.'

'We are aware that King Kumara was betrayed, General, but what proof do you have that the queen arranged it?' the king demanded. 'You had best . . .' He must have noted her expression, because he stopped abruptly, his eyelids widening. Suddenly his dark gaze seared into her very *atman*, her life essence and she finally knew the power of him.

'Sire, King Kumara's last command was that I deliver him his death blow so he could die without shame.' The general's deep voice broke. 'He gave me the proof of his wife's perfidy before he died, commanding me to use it when the time was right. He obviously knew his queen.'

'That was a long time ago, General,' the king responded, half-impatiently now. 'We understand your concern, but events move on, alliances change, new loyalties develop.'

The queen looked up at him gratefully. Stand by me and I will show you a new world, she thought.

'We must shed the past, cast aside old fears and unite on every front for the greater glory of Lanka,' the king continued earnestly. He was deliberately side-tracking the issue. 'The Chola king's invasion is the best thing that could have happened to our country. At long last, he has given our people a cause.' The strong, deep voice became animated, the black eyes gleamed with excitement. 'We are finally on the threshold of achieving national unity. Today the Chola. Tomorrow, Jaya. Finally, the Portuguese.'

'Sire, with due respect, I repeat, the real enemy is in our midst,' General Dunu quietly protested. 'How can we have untity with people of known perfidy, people whom we should not trust?'

General Dunu's bitter glance was directed at her. She caught it and her stomach churned.

'I humbly beg private audience with you before you make any decision on this matter.' The general's voice had become guttural.

'For what?'

'To give you, my sovereign, a written message from another sovereign which I have carried far too long.'

Puzzled, King Raja Sinha glanced at the general then questioningly at the queen. She shrugged her shapely shoulders again. Harsh anger against the portly general flamed within her. 'All we can do is to beg that any representations the general makes against our people be made in our presence,' she grated.

'That would seem appropriate,' the king observed.

'Not when it is a private missive from one sovereign lord, especially one now dead, to another,' the general insisted soberly. 'Besides, we would not want to embarrass Her Majesty.' She could not miss the sarcasm he injected into the honorific.

Tensely, she watched desire for her struggle with native caution in the king's mind. Which would win? He looked at her anew, deeply again instead of incisively. His eyes softened. A thrill of triumph shot through her, for she had won.

'We also have a message from an old friend of your lordship, from the days when you were Prince Tiki-tiki . . . er . . . Tikiri.' Lord Wickrama Sinha had intervened for the first time. Somehow she knew he had done it deliberately and framed his words with care.

On the instant, a shining blade slashed through the connection between her and the king. Bewildered, she saw his eyes widen, noted an invisible haze leaving them. He was alert, aloof again, staring at her as if she were a stranger.

'Madam, you will forgive us, but we are summoned by urgent affairs of State.' His voice was cold, formal. 'With your leave, we shall depart to attend to them.'

'You will return tonight, lord?' She found herself almost pleading and hated him for it.

'That is unlikely, madam.'

The words sent chill dread through her. 'Some other time perhaps, lord?' she persisted.

The king rose to his feet, she and the generals with him. '*That* would be impossible.' He saluted her and strode through the door, Lord Wickrama Sinha following. General Dunu paused briefly, eyeing her with savage contempt. 'My former sovereign lord has returned from the grave to win the final battle,' he declared quietly. 'It has been a long time, but as you know, he always *was* the cleverest man of his day . . . and he *always won*.' He saluted courteously, hastened out.

She gazed after him, fighting the desire to race behind him and tear his tongue out. A sob escaped her. She raised a hand to her mouth. She turned abruptly, her gaze fell on the settle on which King Kumara had always sat. His dominating brown eyes appeared before her. The room began to spin with memories, the tenderness, the cynicism, the clever words, the gallantry. Suddenly, she could stand it no longer. She needed fresh air.

She rushed to the window. King Kumara's face came racing towards her from the dark mountain slope, stopped before her. The brown eyes, mocking as when she first met him, grew larger and larger, spinning. His cynical laughter resounded in her ears. He had returned from the grave to mock her.

'We have won.' His voice was soberly triumphant. 'We *always win*. You have run your course, Anula. You no longer have a future. You are dead, more dead than us, the physical dead, because you are alive. You have wrought your own evil. *Kharma/vipaka*, cause and effect, for the Buddhist side of you, God's punishment for the Christian side. You will live a long, long time, wrinkled within and wrinkling without, swinging between tragic sanity and the relief of madness, a female monkey on the tightrope of your lust for power, a dowager queen mother . . . ha! ha! ha! . . .' His laughter echoed and re-echoed up the dark mountainside. She clapped her hands to her ears but could not shut out the sound.

'Damn you, Kumara!' she suddenly exploded. 'Damn you to hell! Damn your black soul for ever. I curse you, I curse you . . .' The words ended in a wail. She realized with dread that it was the wailing of a lost soul. Desperately she strove to overcome the madness that was taking over her brain.

CHAPTER THIRTY-SIX
Friday, 20 February 1534

The night was cool on the palace verandah, but my shivers as I strode away from the queen's chamber, followed by Lord Wickrama Sinha and General Dunu, were from within me. They emanated from a man who had had a near escape from the worst form of death. I was no stranger to fear, which I regarded as the buckler of survival, its sword, courage. The greater the fear, the mightier the courage needed to ovecome it. Thus, to me deeds of valour alone were not the true measure of courage. One who overcomes quaking fear merely to do his duty has more courage than the fearless man who excels in battle.

Having escaped the gaping jaws of death on many an occasion, I knew with startling clarity that the fate from which I had just been rescued would have been worse than death, for being in sexual bondage to Queen Anula would have meant the death of my ideals. As I had observed it, there can be no more dread slavery than sex. It emanates from an elemental hunger created by love or bare lust, then enthralls even those who seek it through love in the delights of its sensations, which then take over erotically to symbolize the sacred act. Any pleasurable sensation creates hunger that clamours for satisfaction, feeding on its own appetite, ever insatible. As the Jains believe, sex diminishes one's judgement and God-consciousness to the point of total erosion. Ironically, its arch-devil is the sex object, man or woman. How do I, a *brachmachariya*, know these things? I do not have to be able to lay an egg to know that it is addled, hence the chicken-skin bumps on my skin in the flare-lit verandahs through which I returned to the audience chamber, thankful that I had not broken my oath.

My feelings were not exaggerated. Queen Anula was one of those rare women who can destroy their men, a female praying-mantis gobbling up the male after giving him the ecstasy of copulation. Was it her power to entice, or the power of men to succumb to her, or both, that created the mating?

In a state of heightened reaction, I saw that what saved me from her was the loyalty of two people, General Dunu and Juli. Both broke oaths, the general to the dead King Vidiye, Juli to a living husband, to save me from evil. When Juli sent me the code word Tiki-tiki, her love reached out from the bondage of marriage and family, rescued me from slavery. Had it been her prayers, therefore her God, that had timed my rescue? Suddenly, I felt that a god or gods must govern our destinies, that only faith in divine guidance could help us survive. A voice from our history echoed in my ears: Does true strength lie within a man, so he needs no gods, or does a man derive his strength from gods? The Hindu pantheon of gods beckoned, ironically when I was about to plan battle against a Hindu king!

By the time the two generals and I were seated in my chambers I was calm again, yet I recalled that it was here, in this very room, that my seduction had begun two days earlier.

'The Chola King Ratnes Waram's timing is perfect,' I asserted. 'He has struck when our feet are off the ground with the need to regroup and consolidate.'

'Now that he has taken Anu, with the adjoining sub-kingdom of Dhamba being of uncertain temper, he has a large geographical area, much of it almost no-man's-land, in which to move,' Lord Wickrama pointed out.

'This move also affects our own battle-plan,' General Dunu rumbled. 'We must be wary of any promised support from the Dhamba kingdom, as you will see from this message.' He stood up, proffered me an *ola*. 'You will note that it bears King Kumara's seal.' He cleared his throat, blinked rapidly to fight down his emotion. 'I wrote down the words as he spoke them, his last royal act before he died.' He sat down abruptly.

I examined the seal, opened the *ola*, read the message which had been directed to me personally. The words must remain secret, but King Kumara's foresight had been incredible, even bizarre. How well he had known and understood his wife. How well he had comprehended the politics of our country. I placed the *ola* in my tunic pocket, chicken-bumps on my skin again at its affirmation of my near escape from Queen Anula's talons.

I glanced at Lord Wickrama Sinha. 'You mentioned that a messenger had arrived from Colombo?'

'Yes, Sire. The message is that the Portuguese, inspired by Bishop Juan, will give King Ratnes Waram every possible support. Though it is not much militarily, the Chola has agreed, in return, to receive missionary friars into his capital, with total freedom to propagate their religion.'

I exploded with fury. 'Lanka is being manipulated,' I cried out passionately. 'We will only know true freedom when the accursed *parangi* are driven from our shores. It will surely be their turn after we have conquered the Chola.' As I uttered the words, I remembered with a shock that Juli was a *parangi*.

'We are your men, Sire!' General Dunu exclaimed.

'Now let us deal with the present,' I stated. 'We shall not allow the Chola threat to stampede us into action. We shall consolidate our victory over the three Kandyan kingdoms, establish a grip over their administration. Lord Wickrama Sinha, you will work out the same kind of plan you used so successfully in Ruhuna. It will ensure us the support of the Kandyan princes and nobles by permitting them their normal independence, while we remain independent of their support.' I paused, turned to General Dunu. 'You, General, shall garrison and provision the capital cities of Kandy, Pera, Gampola and Hangura with our own men and resources. General Weera, our service corps commander, has already commenced firming up our lines of supply and communication. We shall, however, need additional supply bases to serve our attack route north when we do advance against the Chola. We ourself shall enlist aid from all loyal Sinhala in the areas occupied by or under threat from the Chola. We shall need loyalists to sabotage the Chola's supply lines and whittle away at his armed forces.'

We discussed details far into the night. Early tomorrow, the commanders would be briefed so battle plans could be drawn up. I was about to grant the two men leave to retire when a thought struck me. 'We have been discussing the Chola threat and what we should do about it,' I declared. 'But we ignored the most important question of all. Why did the Chola strike?'

'Because the timing was right,' General Dunu replied. 'Just as you said, Sire.'

Lord Wickrama Sinha had grown thoughtful. 'We should look beyond King Ratnes Waram's own timing,' he responded. 'What really caused him to decide to invade the Sinhala kingdoms after all these years of peaceful co-existence? He is a devout Hindu, a man with no grand ambitions. He has never been interested in territorial expansion. Why would such a man plan an ambitious invasion?'

'The Cholas always coveted the fertile lands to the south of their barren wastes,' General Dunu declared.

'It must go beyond that, with a man like King Ratnes Waram.' Lord Wickrama Sinha's narrowed eyes held the beginning of comprehension. 'It could only be survival, Sire. King Ratnes Waram is driven by fear.'

'Fear of whom?' I demanded.

'Obviously of you, Sire.'

'Fear of what? Surely he knows that all we desire is

suzerainty, with him remaining a sub-king? He cannot possibly think that we would act as a tyrant. There must be something King Ratnes Waram is afraid of . . . something . . . something . . .' Feverishly, my mind searched for other causes.

'Could it be there is something he is afraid *for*?' Lord Wickrama Sinha inquired quietly.

My thoughts started spinning in that direction like an acrobat's flame. 'What does the Chola treasure most?' I mused aloud. 'The Hindu religion, integral to which is a family system, the Dravid language, the culture, customs, traditions of the ages. But why would the Chola fear for these now?' The spinning stopped as brighter knowledge illuminated my mind. 'We have it!' I chopped the air with an extended palm in my excitement. 'King Maya Dunne's power base, which we have inherited, is a combination of Buddhist *bhikkus*, *ayurvedic* physicians and village school teachers, all of whom have tremendous influence over the Sinhala people, especially our women. Most of them are rabid Sinhala Buddhist nationalists. Hungry for personal power and influence, these extremists seize on the cause to satisfy their craving. They inflame the people to tread on and destroy the rights of other races, other languages, other religions. *That* is what the Chola fears.'

'One race, one language, one religion,' General Dunu rolled out.

Even my father had echoed this ancient battle cry, knowing that it could never be achieved, for the groups that make up a nation must be one *in* all races, one *in* all languages, one *in* all religions, unified in their own pluralities by the singular bond of one nation.

'King Ratnes Waram undoubtedly fears that the forces that combined to propel me to be *maha raja*, the Great King of Lanka, will end up like a charging herd of elephants, destroying all he holds dear before its path,' I stated softly.

'What will you do about it, Sire?' Lord Wickrama Sinha alone knew my secret views of nationhood.

What is the duty of a king? To rule a contented people. I thought of my two little wards, Bandula and Nangi, who symbolized what this country really was about, hundreds of thousands of other children, Sinhala, Tamil, Muslim, Catholic, all of whom might need more protection from their Sinhala mentors than from the Chola enemy. Only I could give them that protection.

'I shall think on it,' I replied briskly. 'Meanwhile, we should all get some sleep. General Dunu, we shall attend a full staff session in the briefing room at 6 A.M. tomorrow.' I glanced at the wall clock, which read 1:40 A.M. 'Today, it would seem.'

When the two generals left, I repaired to my bed-chamber, not to sleep but to think soberly of possibly ways of removing the causes of the Chola initiative.

Tuesday, 24 February 1534

The large house had become a lonely place. Aisha was wise enough, however, to know that it was not the house but her whole life that was lonely because the loneliness was in her heart.

During the long hours of each night, she had time to reflect on the nature of a person's wholeness. We are like night and day, she once thought. The sun is with us for a few brief hours when we experience human communion and find joy in our interactions. Then the shadows of evening inevitably fall. Soon it is night and we are alone, even when we have a loved one lying asleep beside us. It is the will of Allah. Like unfailing night, Death too is his will.

The stark knowledge that the light had gone from her days had finally settled in Aisha Raschid's mind only when

Abdul Raschid's body was finally removed from the house. Then, more that ever before in her life, she had to use her natural strength to survive. She meticulously performed her business duties, sustained the day-to-day, hour-to-hour, minute-to-minute acts of living without permitting despair to change her. Yet all desire to conquer, to dominate, had gone with Abdul's huge body. His death was such a great loss to her that even Ali's murder paled before it, so the need to ease the wound created by the murder had ceased to exist. It was as if Allah had used Abdul as the instrument to excise her wound, leaving an aching void instead. And she was glad that she had finally come to love Abdul, for without that love, the old wound would have remained. She wondered at the change in her, though. Could it have been that her former ambitions were caused by her husband's presence in her life, the Muslim woman's constant reminder of her inferior position? Whatever the answer, with her days full, it was the nights she had come to dread.

Not even the news of King Raja Sinha's invasion of Kandy had warmed her cold, listless spirit. When information that the Chola king had taken Anu reached her that morning, she had felt some stirrings of loyalty towards King Raja Sihha, but in a curiously objective way. Now it was noon and she awaited the promised messenger from her brother, Paichi Marcar, with instructions as to how to proceed in the light of Abdul Raschid's death.

Seated alone on her usual divan, waiting for the noon meal to be served, she could see the white-gold fire of pitiless sunlight beating down so fiercely on the courtyard that the green leaves drooped before it and the love-birds in their cage were somnolent. She was so jaded with the heat that even the pleasant smell of frying *ghee*, cooking oil, announcing *biriyani* from the dining room, could not titillate her appetite.

She did not look up at the soft clatter of sandals on the verandah, or at hearing the high voice of her bare-chested eunuch bodyguard presenting the newcomer as Deen, a messenger from the illustrious lord, Paichi Marcar of Calicut. Only when the eunuch began backing away did she gaze incuriously at the visitor from above her *yashmak*.

She suddenly stiffened, suppressed the gasp that had nearly escaped her. Incredibly, she was staring into the eyes of Ali, her son.

And yet this was not Ali but a young man who looked almost exactly as Ali would have done had he been alive. The same clear, fair complexion, accented by shiny black hair, the same well-shaped, oval face and delicate, almost feminine features, the same slender build except that this young man was taller than Ali had been. He even favoured Ali's dress, cream-coloured *dhoti* and short, dark-brown waistcoat.

'Who are you?' she demanded, puzzled.

The bright eyes crinkled in a smile, the firm chin lifted. 'As the attendant said, my name is Deen. I am the younger son of your brother, Paichi Marcar, my lady.' The young man had a soft, melodious voice. 'That makes me your nephew by blood.'

Which explained the resemblance, for Ali too had looked very like her brother.

Impulsively, she held out her hand. He advanced, took it in his, knelt to kiss it. She could feel her heart beating faster. Had the will of Allah brought her a glimpse of daylight again?

'Sit down,' she bade. Some inner compulsion made her indicate the divan on which her husband used to sit.

Deen walked across the room with a springy step, sat down gracefully. His every move was lithe, clean as a cheetah's.

Once again, she was moved by impulse. 'Try some of those sweetmeats.'

'No thank you, my lady.'

'Aren't you hungry? Have you had your noon meal?'

'Not yet.'

'You must be starving.' Much to her surprise, feelings long dormant since the days she had looked after Ali when he was her little boy had begun stirring within her. She found them pleasing.

It is not enough to have a full day's work, she thought, whether in battle, on the field, or in trade. After all, when I had Ali, I didn't need a battlefield. In order to be completely whole, a real human being must have responsibility for others, for their welfare and well-being. 'The noon meal will be served shortly. You can have it with me. How long are you here for?'

'For as long as you need me. My father desires you to carry on the business as before, using your own initiative and enterprise. He sent me to help you, now that Uncle Abdul is dead.'

A great calm seized her in which she heard the flutter of bird-wings of joy, or had it been the love-birds in their cage? The demands of her character and temperament had prevented her from finding the contentment which her husband had mentioned just before he died. Perhaps the time had come for her to steer a new course with the same indomitable will she had shown in other aspects of her life. Perhaps Allah was showing the way, using her wise brother, Paichi Marcar, as the instrument? 'Then you had best be prepared for a long stay,' she declared, smiling to herself beneath her *yashmak*.

He must have sensed the smile, for he grinned back companionably. 'I have no ties, my lady. Helping my father in his business has been my whole life.' The brown eyes flashed, as Ali's were wont to do when he felt indignant. 'As you can imagine, however, I have no real future back home because my brother, Majid, will always stand ahead of me. And rightly so. He is not only the eldest son, but is also extremely competent and a brilliant trader.'

'So you think you can take over here some day?'

'Yes.' The tone of his voice was emphatic, his gaze-level. He reminded her so much of Ali.

'Good,' she responded, amazed at having discovered once again where real strength lies. 'I shall teach you all I know. When I am convinced that you are ready to take over, I shall step aside and remain to support you the rest of my life.'

The tears that sprang to his eyes told her of some of the frustrations he must have endured back home. Her own eyes went moist. What was happening to her? Why did she feel such a great peace? Reasoning told her that it was because what she was now doing required more strength than anything she had ever done before. Yet the feeling was so familiar that she quickly identified it. She had known this strength and contentment from it when she had her baby and helped him to grow. 'We can talk while we eat,' she said aloud. 'Meanwhile, do have one of those sweetmeats. They were always kept there for the head of the household.'

He grew grave on the instant, stared at her, trying to make sure she was serious. Finally, he nodded, laughed lightly. He reached out long, sensitive fingers for a square of red Turkish delight from the gold salver and popped it in his mouth.

Tuesday, 24 February 1534

Holding Juli's hand, Fernao slowly paced the lawn of the Mutu Vella mansion. Across the golden evening air, the sound of the two children's voices, singing a Portuguese folk song, floated from their study room on the ground floor. His son had a clear, silvery treble voice, sang in the church choir and was always ready with a solo during their musical evenings at home. Catherina could only just about carry a tune in her head.

The scorching heat of the afternoon had left behind a pungent smell of baked grass. Fernao paused in his stride to sniff it appreciatively. He slipped his arm around Juli's slender waist and looked down towards the sunlight bouncing off the waters of the harbour in the distance. 'All this has been so much our life, Juli,' he observed soberly. 'It is strange . . . and rather sad . . . to think of leaving it for ever.'

She turned her head to look at him. The westering sun made her aquamarine eyes seem to shimmer like the ocean. 'We can only look forward,' she responded. 'We have made our plans and must not alter them. What's important is for you, the children and me to be together.' She hesitated, a sigh escaping her. 'Something tells me though that we face serious obstacles before we reach our goals, very serious obstacles.'

'Like what?'

'I don't know, Fernao. I sometimes see a black cloud hanging between us and our departure.' A piteous note in her voice made him draw her closer to him. A gust of wind from the ocean swept up the hillside, caused the branches to rustle and sway, sent dried brown leaves floating to the ground. He turned, gripped her upper arms and stared deep into her eyes. 'What do you fear?'

'I wish I knew, Fernao.'

'Perhaps you want so much to leave that you fear it will not happen?' Receiving no response other than a frightened stare, he pretended to laugh. 'That's it,' he declared with a firmness he did not feel. 'Let me be your magician. The black cloud is really your own fear that your heart's desire will not materialize.'

She shook her head slowly, cocked it sideways and stared over his shoulder. 'I don't know, Fernao. I wish I did. You and I don't matter, because we have lived most of our lives. It's the children I'm concerned about.'

He made up his mind quickly, wheeled round and

pointed down towards the harbour. 'You see those two great *nao*? With their big guns, they are the most powerful machines on earth. They can get us out of anything, take us wherever we want to go.' He paused, sobering. 'Unless God wills it otherwise.'

'I wish I had your confidence, my darling.' Her voice was troubled. 'It's God's will that bothers me. What does He have in store for us?'

'Portugal, home and beauty,' he declared with a low laugh. He suddenly ached with love for her. He had to get her out of this mood. 'You are depressed,' he asserted. 'It must be that time of the month.'

He watched with delight the blush mantling her cheeks. So many years of married life and her blush could still arouse poetic feelings in him.

'Now General Fernao de Albergaria, I *do* declare,' she stated with mock gravity, snapping out of her mood. 'That surely is no way for a gentleman to talk to a lady. Unless he loves her. Dost thou?'

'I do indeed love thee.'

She laughed lightly. 'In spite of my black clouds?'

'To dispel all black clouds and dragons that beset thee whom I do love.'

'Thou art crazy.'

'About thee.'

Her eyes, filled with love, locked into his with such startling force that he felt the air between them shimmer. 'Tonight,' she whispered.

He felt his organ harden. 'Why not here and now?' he teased.

'Oh sir, you are indeed too forward,' she demurred.

'You really do have the gift of second sight if you can see beneath my codpiece.'

This time she flushed. 'It doesn't take much to cause pressure on your codpiece, does it?'

'Not with you.'

490

'Oh Fernao, I love you so much.' She melted into his arms, laid her head on his shoulder. Her auburn hair, shining in the sun, smelled of musk. 'Let's not talk about sad things.' She snuggled her nose against his chest. 'Tell me the news.'

He released her, his face serious. 'It's not good, Juli. King Ratnes Waram, having captured Anu, has taken Polon and is making for Dhamba. Worst of all, the Chola king's Indian mercenaries have broken loose and are pillaging the countryside, robbing, murdering and raping.'

'What are *we* doing about it, Fernao?'

'Nothing,' he muttered bitterly. 'We are helpless in the face of orders, initiated by Holy Church, to give tacit support to King Ratnes Waram.'

'Surely we can help him control his own mercenaries.'

'Only if he seeks our help. And even then, we dare not deplete our numbers in Colombo too much. If only the situation in Europe weren't so tense, a few *nao* with half a dozen *terco* would solve all our problems.'

'Since we don't have them, what help can King Raja Sinha expect from his own people? I hope he does not fall into the same trap as King Kumara did with that dreadful Queen Anula.'

Fernao sensed what was close to Juli's heart. When he set aside his jealously of King Raja Sinha many years earlier, a miracle had resulted. Not only had he freed himself from the bondage of self-torture, but it had brought Julietta closer and closer to him. He had learned the lesson that for Julietta to love him freely, he had to let her be herself, and to achieve this, to rid her mind of apprehensions she might have about his rival's welfare. He told her all he knew about what had transpired between Queen Anula and King Raja Sinha in the Kandy palace. 'The final result, according to reports, is that the queen seems to have gone mad,' he ended.

'Gone mad? Why?. . . How? You mean actually *mad*?'

'Only God knows, Juli. All I can say is that her conduct always had the stuff of insanity in it. She is now reported to alternate between lucidity, ravings about her late husband, King Kumara, and covert threats against King Raja Sinha. She is a pitiful creature with no future except as the mother of Dona Margaridha, queen consort of the Jaya king.'

Juli's small chin was out-thrust. 'She is an evil woman. This must be God's punishment.'

'How is a person judged evil, except for repeatedly offending the laws of conventional morality?'

'There are people who do more than that, people who coolly and deliberately offend the laws of humanity and holiness because they can neither feel, think nor act in any other way. Since they have the power to corrupt and destroy others, they are the anti-Christ. They are of Satan, who was once God's chief angel.'

He was surprised at her unusual vehemence.

'They are all human beings,' he protested.

'No, Fernao. Like the rogue elephant, or better still, like the serpent in the garden of Eden, such people are not human, but devils.'

Fernao shrugged. 'Perhaps you are right. Meanwhile, we have to prepare for the day when King Raja Sinha disposes of the Chola and turns against Jaya.'

'Will he defeat the Chola?'

'With such a powerful Sinhala army, it is only a question of time.'

'How long do you think that will take?'

'At least six months.'

'Will we defend Jaya against him?'

'With our present strength, we can only defend the capital city, not the entire kingdom. But it could be Colombo next, instead of Jaya, so I have asked urgently for reinforcements from Goa.'

'Will we get the reinforcements?'

'Certainly. But of course you and the children and I will have set sail for Portugal before then.' Fernao gazed into the red-gold west, towards which their ship would sail. A black cloud hung above the fort. It was there one moment, gone the next. Had it been reality, or a trick of his eyes, or of the light?

CHAPTER THIRTY-SEVEN
Tuesday, 3 March 1534

The best position to negotiate from is strength. Having decided not to move against the Chola king until I had consolidated my hold on the Kandyan kingdoms, I had sent a secret emissary to King Ratnes Waram, suggesting a private meeting in a neutral area to discuss peace, while putting into effect my plans to harass the Chola forces and sabotage his supply lines.

Meanwhile, the Chola king was slowly weakening himself by remaining in Anu and allowing his commanders to move outwards in groups to control the entire region. In consequence, he had also lost control of his mercenaries, whose raping, looting, arson and murder were hardening the Sinhala people of the region and giving them a cause. The consolidation of my hold on Kandy and my plan to set up supply points along the proposed route of my advance against the Chola had proceeded so smoothly that within two weeks I had a task force, to be commanded by Lord Wickrama Sinha, moving in small groups to an assembly point on the east coast. Once assembled the force was to proceed north along the coast, then unexpectedly veer sharply west so as to cut off the Chola's rear from his base in Jaffna. The main body of my army was being readied to move to the Kahagalla plain, where I had decided to give battle to King Ratnes Waram, because it was there that our hero King Abhaya Gamini had finally defeated the Chola seventeen hundred years ago.

I had chosen a Hindu priest who ministered to the small group of Cholas in Kandy, mostly shopkeepers, jewellers and scavengers, to make secret contact with King Ratnes Waram. This priest was known to the king and would be a credible witness to the powerful military forces I had at my disposal, which gave me a position of strength from which to negotiate. Also, I had devoted some time during those busy weeks to learning even more about the Hindu religion from this priest and had even commenced practising the Hindu *pooja* rituals daily in the privacy of my chambers, where I had installed statues of Lord Kataragam and Lord Shiva. Strange for a man who practised *brachmachariya*, abstinence from sex, to accept a god whose symbol was the *lingam*, the giver of life! Inevitably, word of my interest in the Hindu religion had leaked out to the *bhikkus*, Buddhist monks, but none of them had ever dared even question a strong ruler. Moreover, my own position was doubly secure at this time, when the people needed a saviour from the threat of the advancing Cholas regardless of his religious leanings.

My secret meeting with King Ratnes Waram was set to take place at a Hindu *kovil* in the former rock capital of Dambulla, which lies between Kuru and Polon, about forty miles north of Kandy. It was part of the no man's territory at this time. The land around the massive rock, which houses a Buddhist temple, was flat, so any movements of troops, should either of us have intended betrayal, could have been observed. The time of the meeting was noon, when the *kovil* would be deserted and the hours of daylight before and after the meeting would afford a greater assurance of security to both of us in our movement to and from the site.

It is no easy accomplishment for a king to vanish from his palace, alone, unaccompanied, for two nights and a day. I pretended to my closest aides that I was departing alone for secret negotiations with the Dhamba king and instructed Colonel Wickram, my chief aide, to cover my absence by saying that I would be in meditation for twenty-four hours. I was especially concerned that Queen Anula, who had reportedly become the victim of her own insanity, should not learn of my whereabouts. Though direct rule was always effected by the king wherever he might be, in his palace, on the move or on the battlefield, the administration can go on without him, if he is a capable ruler.

I rode through the night, without an escort, using relays of horses from the residences of trusted chieftains along the way, slept for a few hours in the home of Lord Alu in Alu Vidhare and was in Dambulla during the pre-noon watch.

I hid my horse in a copse and changed my clothes, emerging disguised in the orange robes of a *sannyasi*, holy mendicant. My hair was loose, holy ash was liberally smeared on my forehead, a yellow bag was slung over one bare shoulder. I even held a staff of gnarled white wood in my hand.

The fierce glare of noonday sunlight bounded off the giant spread of black rock, shaped like a sleeping lion, casting waves of warmth on the village that was once the city of Dambulla, briefly the capital of Sinhala kings. As with many a sacred area, like Kataragama and Kandy, the *kovil* adjoined the Buddhist temple: peaceful co-existence, destroyed only by the bigot, the extremist, the opportunist and the idiot. Unlike temples, which are bell-shaped and generally shaded by a spreading *bodhi*-tree, the small rectangular *kovil* was built in the centre of a sandy clearing. Its ornate architecture was embellished by orange and red brickwork. Catholics, Hindus and Buddhists all have the same idea, that church and temple must be as striking to the physical senses as the doctrines are to the spirit. Hence perhaps the violent bell-ringing too!

Standing isolated, the building inspired reverence, probably for the very reason that its sandy courtyard was deserted save for the inevitable beggars leaning back against the wall, most of them dozing, their small wicker begging baskets idle for once. The inevitable mangy pi-dogs lay somnolent in the heat, chins on extended forepaws, their posture like that of crocodiles. An ancient cripple, his bare body blackened by the sun, sensed my approach with the sure instinct of his profession. He opened a rheumy eye, but closed it again when he noted my indigence. A snotty-nosed little beggar boy, his ribs like a brown bird-cage, stared incuriously at me. He was already old before his time. His mother, gaunt and toothless, clutched her red rags closer to her emaciated breasts in a concession to modesty. I thought of my first meeting with Bandula and Nangi, but I knew I could do nothing for this lot. They were living the life they had chosen, beggary had become their disease and they would run away from a doctor.

I paused at the entrace to the *kovil*, glanced with seeming indifference along the path, taking in the scene. Any one of the beggars could be an assassin, or riders could hurtle down the path if King Ratnes Waram had set a trap. My heart beat faster as I spotted movement about a hundred yards away, then settled when I saw another *sannyasi*, dressed exactly like me, approaching. This was a giant, his bulk more fitted to the role of champion warrior than of ascetic devotee. His walk was slow and stately, his staff was wielded with haughty authority rather than as a support. I had never met the Chola king, but I would not have needed the descriptions I had received to recognize this as my man. I walked into the courtyard, quickly and unobtrusively scanning each beggar. Satisfied, I prostrated myself before the temple. Through the open doorway, I noted that the cool, shady interior was obviously empty. I gazed at the roof, the branches of nearby trees, for those who forget to check above eye-level often end up very dead.

I entered the building. A garish painting of the goddess Luckshimi adorned a canvas curtain at the front of the shrine. After going through the ritual *asanas*, movements, of prayers to her, I moved outside, beneath the shade of a coconut palm at the rear of the courtyard. This was where King Ratnes Waram and I had agreed to meet, pretending that we were sharing a meal of rice and dhall curry from our begging bowls while we conversed.

Oddly enough, except for his black colour, King Ratnes Waram looked like a huge Buddha as he sat in the lotus pose facing me. He had the same cast of features, round face, broad cheekbones. Only the eyes were different. Almost as black as his skin, they were depthless yet enormously penetrating. Also, he smelled of sesame oil.

Sweating profusely in spite of the cool shadow tracery of coconut branches on our bodies, we had our meal without uttering a single word. At one point, a crackling of leaves made us both look upwards. Two red-brown *rilawa* monkeys had leapt on to the coconut tree and were inspecting us, or probably our food.

Although I outranked him and had the right to speak first, hoping to throw him off balance, I deliberately waited for him to start the discussion. As a result, no word was spoken until we had washed our hands and begging bowls at the well and resumed our seats.

'You desired a secret meeting, Great King.' His voice was rich, pitched rather high, but with an unmistakable undercurrent of strength. His use of the Tamil language, undoubtedly meant to give me a message, amused me. 'We have gone through this elaborate drama to satisfy your wishes. We hope that whatever you have to propose proves worthwhile.'

His tone was so arrogant, I had to set him in his place. 'We are the Great King, not a marriage broker,' I declared pleasantly in classical Tamil, which I had studied from boyhood. 'We make no proposals.'

Astonishment at my fluent use of his language overcame any resentment he may have felt at my reply. 'You speak our language in the classical manner. Your grammar is more refined than ours. How is that?'

'We have taken the trouble to do more than learn the language of our Chola fellow countrymen. We have made a study of it. Do you speak Sinhala, *raja*?'

From above us, one of those monkeys emitted a snarl.

Why did you study our language?' he demanded, ignoring my question.

I concluded that he did speak Sinhala but would not admit to it. 'We wanted to honour your race,' I replied. 'We despise foreigners who come to our land and acquire smatterings of our languages so they can show off, or learn it just sufficiently to be condescending.' Unaccountably, I thought of General de Albergaria who spoke Sinhala so fluently.

I had not only gained King Ratnes Waram's fullest attention but I had also seized the initiative. He looked down, thoughtful awhile, nodded to himself several times. Then the dark eyes were suddenly raised to mine. 'In the *kovil* just now, you went through our Hindu ritual as if you had been trained to it. Did you learn it just for this occasion?'

'If we had, you would have noted it.'

The bushy black eyebrows were raised in astonishment. 'You have had instruction in our religion?'

I merely nodded, slowly.

'You speak our language, you know our religion. We had a different image of you.'

'You saw us as the leader of rabid Sinhala Buddhist factions. You feared our rapid rise to power and the forces it could release to harm you and your people because of the intolerance of the leaders of our civilian power base. You therefore collected all your resources and hired fifteen thousand mercenaries at great cost to defend your people.'

It was his turn to nod, gravely.

'How will you defend them against your mercenaries?' I was hard put to keep my voice low because of my passionate hatred of what this king's mercenaries were

499

doing to my people. 'These Indian soldiers of fortune have less identity with you than the Sinhala people with whom you share common bonds of territory and communal living. Your people and ours have reached a stage where they can co-exist comfortably side-by-side, like sand and rock, tree and boulder. You have the reputation for being a scholar, *raja*, so you must know from history that disparate factions who unite merely to overthrow a common oppressor generally end up in greater conflict with each other, once they seize power, than they had with the oppressor in the first place.'

'True, true. But if we had the choice of an oppressor we would choose one who would give us the pride of our language and who is at least of our own religion.'

His words made me reflect sombrely on the nature of man. He is naturally born of woman of the same species, yet he sets up artificial barriers of territory, race, culture, language and, worst of all, religion, which after all is only belief, to create conflict with his fellow man.

King Ratnes Waram sensed my thoughts with uncanny instinct.

'Language is our link, our means of communication with our fellow man,' he urged. 'Likewise, religion is our link, our means of communication with our special gods.'

'A nation is not linguistic, cultural, or territorial, but spiritual,' I countered, low and intense.

'Religion is of the spirit alone,' he retorted fiercely.

I looked at him with eyes suddenly so calm, serene, that he was taken aback. 'Is it principally religion then, not language, that separates Chola and Sinhala?'

He hesitated. 'Yes,' he finally conceded.

'If we removed that barrier, would you withdraw your forces to your former territory, send back your mercenaries and acknowledge our suzerainty as your Great King, while retaining your customs, institutions and traditions?'

His gaze became penetrating, the dark eyes boring into

my soul. Long moments passed as I held his gaze, too much aware of my own sincerity of purpose to attempt to display it. The monkeys above us started gibbering at each other. A hot wind riffled through the coconut branches, rolled little curtains of sand, brought odours of stale food, the scent of incense from the temple and the stink of some dead creature. Still he held my gaze and I returned his look, calm, untroubled.

'How . . .?' he began, then took off on another tack, this time the practical, shrewd Chola. 'Our mercenaries will need to be paid off,' he asserted. 'It will be impossible for us to find the means without the spoils of war and the fruits of occupation.'

'How would you pay them when we have defeated you in battle?' I questioned with gentle strength. 'You hired them, you pay them off.'

He was taken aback, then a broad smile flashed across his face revealing even teeth, so white against the blackness of his skin that it brightened his whole aura. 'No wonder you have got thus far,' he declared. 'Beneath the smoothness, you are a tough ruler.'

'We can afford to be tough, because we are here in a position of strength.' My voice was still gentle as the rustle of the palm branches overhead. 'Let us explain. As of this moment, our army of over fifty thousand men, with fifty cannon and two hundred musketeers, is poised to advance against you. Meanwhile, a huge task force under General Lord Wickrama Sinha has already cut off your rear. You and your armies face annihilation.'

'Treachery while we negotiate,' he ground out, dark eyes flashing. He started to rise. 'We knew we could not trust the Sinhala.

'Sit down,' I commanded him. 'Did you stop your advance these last few days? No? Then how can you blame us for continuing with our own plans?'

He was nothing if not fair. He grinned wryly. 'It would

seem as if you have placed yourself in a position to make demands.'

'Yes.'

'Very well. What are they?'

'We merely agreed that we are in a position to make demands. We did not say we are here to make them.' I noted his puzzlement with delight, for I had placed him exactly where I had planned during many days of careful thought. 'First, if you withdraw immediately, we ourselves shall pay off your mercenaries.'

'What?' Even his royal breeding could not prevent the amazed expletive form bursting forth.

'You heard us.'

'That is . . . that is . . . very generous of you.'

'But it will not give you a lasting sense of security.' I paused, my entire being now glowing. 'So if you accept our terms, we promise you on our sacred honour, by conviction and not from political expediency, that as soon as we have driven the foreign *parangi* from our shores and consolidated our grip on the entire island of Lanka, we shall use the Tamil language in our court for Tamil-speaking subjects and we ourself shall convert to the Hindu religion.'

Friday, 13 March 1534

Fernao was in his office in the fort, going through plans for the Portuguese community to celebrate Easter. He tapped a foot to the rhythm of an Easter hymn being practised by the army choir on the sun-baked parade ground outside instead of drill.

'Sweet Jesu rose from the dead,' the deep, granite voices of the basses proclaimed triumphantly, 'and ascended into heaven,' went the higher, rich gold tenors.

The spirit of Easter already pervaded the fort. The plan was to set up a cross in the centre of the parade ground and enact the crucifixion on Good Friday and the Easter scene on Sunday. Christmas and Easter were pleasant changes for everyone from the eternal succession of arms drill, individual training, section training, platoon training, company training, regimental manoeuvres, that formed the deadly routine of the soldier year in year out, with only battle or perhaps death to relieve the dreadful monotony.

An urgent knocking on the door interrupted Fernao's pleasant duty. Sergeant Aires stood at the doorway saluting. 'Urgent messenger for sir . . . sir!' His tight features were grim, the scar down his face taut.

'From whom, Sergeant?'

'Father Perez in Kandy, sir!'

A thrill of alarm shot through Fernao, but he remained outwardly calm, placed his elbows on the teakwood desk. 'Show him in.'

The Sinhala who entered was small and birdlike. His long black hair was tied in a knot at the nape of his neck and held tight on his head by a semi-circular tortoiseshell comb. He was dressed in blue pantaloons and a white tunic, covered with dust. The brown face was strewn with sweat. He wore a small silver crucifix on a black cord around his neck.

Fernao opened the conversation. 'You are from Kandy? You seem to have ridden hard. Have you eaten this morning?'

The man's pointed features twitched in surprise. ' N . . . no, Sire. I have barely eaten since I left Kandy the night before last.' He recovered himself, bowing low, hands together at his forehead. 'Let me introduce myself. My name is Rana Tunga, Pedro Rana Tunga.' A note of pride when he announced his Christian name moistened the thin, dry voice. 'I'm a Catholic,' he added unnecessarily.

'Sit down *a senhor* Pedro Rana Tunga,' Fernao bade him. 'Let me first order you some food.' He reached out and tugged at the bell-rope while his visitor sat gingerly on the edge of a settle.

The door creaked open to reveal Sergeant Aires.

'A plate of food and a glass of melon juice for *a senhor,*' Fernao bade him. He waited till the door had closed again behind Sergeant Aires. 'Now sit down comfortably and tell me your story.'

'Honoured sir, Father Perez commanded me to ride night and day to you. King Ratnes Waram started withdrawing his army back to Jaffna some days ago. His mercenaries are heading for Mantota, where ships wait to take them back to the continent.'

'How? Why?' Fernao tried not to show his bewilderment.

'King Raja Sinha was unavailable for a whole day recently. Father Perez conjectures that he was away at a secret meeting with the Chola king. We have absolutely no idea as to what agreement, if any, was reached, but the Great King advanced against the Chola last week with fifty thousand men and fifty cannon to give battle on the Kahagalla plain, while Lord Wickrama Sinha was already in position at the northern causeway to cut off the Chola's rear. When the Chola unexpectedly started to withdraw, the Great King simultaneously carried out a turning movement. He headed south to sweep through the Dhamba sub-kingdom, which he took without a single arrow being fired, and is now headed west, reportedly for Jaya. Meanwhile, Lord Wickrama Sinha has begun moving south along the west coast, to give the Chola a clear passage back home, including King Ratnes Waram's mercenaries who are probably even at this moment boarding ship at Mantota. It is also our understanding that another task force of ten thousand men has moved from Sita Waka, its target Jaya, which thus has three Sinhala army groups converging on it from different directions.'

Lord Wickrama Sinha moving south towards Jaya along

the west coast, the task force from Sita Waka advancing westwards towards the capital, King Raja Sinha with his main body proceeding south-west from Dhamba, all of it posing a terrible threat to the main kingdom, Jaya. It could be the turn of Colombo next. The knowledge stunned Fernao with the force of cannonballs. He had counted on King Raja Sinha being fully occupied with the Chola for at least three months and requiring at least another three to consolidate his assured victory, to regroup and organize the administration of the occupied northern sub-kingdom, before directing his attention to Jaya. During this time, it was entirely possible that the situation in Europe would have righted itself sufficiently for a strong flotilla to be despatched from Portugal, in which his father could have included the ship to carry him and his family back home.

Now those hopes were shattered. Juli's black cloud had materialized, ironically, on Friday the thirteenth. Even the hopes for a happy Easter had been dashed.

In that instant, as the cold horror of certainty caused chills to go through him, the old antagonism between himself and King Raja Sinha burst into flame. It had sparked the moment they set eyes on each other when they were both still boys in their teens. He had thought it dead, but it had been there all the time, though he had erased it from his consciousness after his skirmish with death from the wound he took in the battle of Mulleri. He had once believed that the conflict had been a herald of his jealousy, but he had been wrong. What lay between him and King Raja Sinha went far beyond any woman to a primitive, elemental, struggle for survival between two living creatures. He recognized the primitivism of it with a shudder that let loose an immediate reflex of cold, hard determination to oppose his ancient antagonist. He would fight to the death if need be, taking the enemy with him. He had become too soft. Now the de Albergaria had to emerge: No man seizes what is mine with impunity.

'Sir . . . sir . . .' Pedro had become agitated at the sudden ferocity of his stare.

'I'm sorry to have alarmed you,' Fernao apologized. 'But your news has made me very angry.'

He was about to reach for the bell-rope when he heard the knock on the door and saw Sergeant Aires at the entrance again, this time holding a metal tray containing a plate of cold meat, bread and cheese and a clay goblet of milk.

'Best I could do, sir!' Aires announced cheerfully.

'Good enough, Sergeant,' Fernao replied. He noted how Pedro's eyes lit up at the sight of the food and the smell of fresh bread and aged cheese. 'Set it down on my desk, there's a good man.' He waited till the tray was clanked down. 'Have Colonel de Mello and Major Nantes attend me immediately.'

'Aye, aye, sir!' Sergeant Aires touched his forehead with two fingers in salute. 'Ooops, sorry, sir. Keep thinking we're still in the navy. Very well, sir!' He avoided Fernao's pretence of a cold stare, hesitated. 'Begging your pardon, sir, why do bloody army say "very well" when it isn't well at all but only aye, sir?' He caught the stare. 'Immediately, sir!' he exclaimed and fled.

Fernao watched in silence as Pedro wolfed down his meal. It gave him the opportunity to think clearly. He considered his options and began to see the glimmering of hope. His main object should be to defend Colombo, but attack was the best form of defence. By the time the two senior officers arrived and took their seats, Pedro had almost finished his meal and Fernao had considered how best to utilize the resources and firepower at his disposal. He introduced Pedro, briefed the officers, watched for their reactions.

Colonel de Mello had taken the news with his usual devil-may-care calm. Major Nantes, on the other hand, exploded. 'Son of a fucking cock-sucker! You can never trust these native bastards. One moment they are clutching each other's balls, the next each of 'em is trying for a hole in the same fucking bitch. "Which one will you take, sir?" one of 'em asks. "You fucking first, sir," the other replies, very polite. "Since it's *fucking* you want from me, why don't I take the cunt, while you take the shit."' He shook his head. 'It's we foreign buggers who get fucked in the long run.'

Fernao glanced briefly at Pedro. The crude outburst had put the Sinhala in a state of shock, the dropped jaw revealing a sponge of bread and cheese in his mouth. The Sinhala started chewing again mechanically, barely aware of what he was doing, brown eyes still popping out of his head.

It was time to dismiss the man. 'We shall take appropriate action, *a senhor*,' he informed Pedro. 'Thank you for bringing us the news in such a timely manner. You may retire now – Sergeant Aires will look to your needs – but please remember that we expect the support of all loyal Catholics, especially those in the Kandyan kingdoms that have been seized by a low-country usurper.'

When the door had closed behind the Sinhala, Fernao turned his gaze on the two officers. 'Well, gentlemen, that is the situation. Now for my appreciation of it. First, as to our object. Having seriously considered all possibilities, I have decided that our object shall be to hold Colombo against the enemy at all costs.'

'Colombo?' Major Nantes questioned. 'I thought that King Raja Sinha was heading for Jaya?'

'So it is reported, but our concern should be for our ultimate responsibility, which must remain the lives and well-being of our fellow-countrymen and countrywomen and the safeguarding of his Imperial Majesty's possessions and interests in Lanka.'

Noting the affirmation in both men's eyes, he led the discussion to relative strengths, logistics, timing and all other factors affecting the attainment of the object, including preparation for a long siege of as much as six months.

When they had thrashed out every aspect of the situation, Fernao summed up. 'Remember, gentlemen, the defences of Colombo are impregnable. The lake acts as a moat to our south, extending east up to the rampart walls. The enemy cannot use it for an assault without coming within reach of our cannon. We regularly man the rampart walls up to the river in strength and that constitutes another sound water defence, overlooked by our two forts. We have hundreds of cannon. It will primarily be your task, Major Nantes, to keep the enemy at bay.'

Major Nantes grinned wolfishly. 'Let the mother-fuckers come,' he asserted.

'Now, gentlemen, we come to the protection of Jaya.' Fernao concentrated on Colonel de Mello. 'We shall attempt to achieve this by establishing a corridor between Colombo and Jaya, protected by mobile firepower. But please realize that we can only hold the corridor just so long against the tremendous forces assembled by the enemy. When the pressure becomes too great, we shall use the corridor to bring the boy King Dom Juan to the safety of Colombo, from where he can rule.'

'As a fucking puppet,' Major Nantes muttered.

'As anything, so long as he is the titular head of the Jaya kingdom,' Fernao retorted firmly. 'He shall rule according to *my* dictates. I shall use him to rally the people of the Jaya kingdom to his cause. Divide and rule shall be our policy. Sinhala against Sinhala, Catholic against Buddhist, now that our attempt to pit Chola against Sinhala has failed.'

'You can't trust them bloody natives to chew each other's balls, General,' Major Nantes warned.

'Well, gentlemen, that is a broad appreciation of the situation,' Fernao concluded. 'Summon your commanders immediately and prepare final defence plans for my approval. Keep in mind that the struggle ahead may well be won by our ability to keep Colombo supplied.'

'I hate defensive battles,' Colonel de Mello interjected. 'We've got to find some way of taking the offensive.'

Fernao smiled, remembering the ideas that had struck him. 'Have no fear, for I have a couple of other interesting options in mind,' he assured the colonel. 'The Sinhala forces are of necessity split into three. It's obvious that we cannot take on the main body, but the other two groups, especially the one advancing along the west coast, are vulnerable. I will brief you when we have got our main plan hammered out and under way. Meanwhile, I shall need up-to-date intelligence on the movements of each of the enemy groups.'

Fernao's smile was confident, but the full realization of the massive forces converging against the small band of Portuguese suddenly hit him. For the first time in his life, he experienced a feeling of isolation, the isolation of the white man many thousands of miles from home, on a foreign strand teeming with hostile brown people.

CHAPTER THIRTY-EIGHT

Wednesday, 18 March 1534

My plan for peace with honour between the Chola and Sinhala people had worked. Within ten days of my meeting with King Ratnes Waram, the Chola army had withdrawn within the former borders of the sub-kingdom, and the mercenaries, having received their pay, departed for India on cargo ships provided with astonishing speed by a young Mouro named Deen who had joined the household of Aisha Raschid.

Lord Wickrama Sinha had begun moving his task force along the west coast, heading south for Jaya, while the main body, under me, moved west towards the capital. I had given command of our Sita Waka corps to General Dunu as a gesture of solidarity with the Kandyans. General Lord Senerat, the prince from Alut Gama, would be his chief of staff. We were therefore converging on Jaya from three directions.

The first night of our advance found our main body encamped by a lake near the village of Rada Wana, so called because only people of the *dhobi*, washerman, caste resided there. I was in my tent preparing to go to bed when my aide, Colonel Wickram, burst in on me, almost unceremoniously. Even in the uncertain light of a single taper on my white *gini sapu* table, I noted that his broad features were set, the thin-lipped mouth tight.

'What is it, Colonel?' I inquired.

'Please forgive me for disturbing you, Sire, but this is a grave emergency. I have just received reports that the Jaya army, under General Lord Tammitta and reinforced by Portuguese cannon and muskets, is advancing rapidly towards Sita Waka.'

I rose from my settle, ignoring the whine of a mosquito I had disturbed. 'A bold, shrewd move aimed at our vitals!' I declared grimly. I pondered awhile. The strategy was certainly not that of the boy king Dom Juan or of Lord Tammitta. 'I see the fine hand of General de Albergaria behind this,' I declared.

'They can roll General Senerat back by sheer weight of numbers.' Colonel Wickram had stated the obvious. 'Then Sita Waka will be exposed.'

I made no comment. I had anticipated this possibility and that Lord Wickrama Sinha too could be in danger from a Portuguese strike force, but had not thought the General would leave Jaya depleted and exposed to me. Now I also had to consider the possible treachery of King Ratnes Waran if he sensed that we were in jeopardy.

Thinking deeply, I stared at the darkness outside the open tent flap as if penetrating it would bring daylight to my problem.

Thursday, 19 March 1534

Sitting his tall bay motionlessly, Fernao waited in the dark grove of cashew trees for the first glimmerings of dawn. Behind him, his cavalry squadrons quietly moved into position. He could not suppress a feeling of self-satisfaction at his strategy. Here he was, ready to strike a stunning blow at Lord Wickrama Sinha's task force, while Lord Tammitta and the Jaya army was probably preparing to engage the Sita Waka army group under General Dunu near the village of Boralu at this very moment.

Lord Wickrama Sinha's task force, whose movements faithful Sinhala fishermen converts to the Catholic Church had been following and reporting for the past two days, had encamped for the night on a long spit of land in Negombo. With the ocean on one side and the lagoon on the other, the location was well selected and should have offered double protection, but Fernao had planned to turn it into triple jeopardy!

The spies had estimated the enemy force to number about twenty thousand men. Since he had provided a contingent to reinforce the Jaya army that was advancing against the Sita Waka army group led by General Dunu, Fernao's force consisted of only a thousand men, but he had superior firepower and the bloodthirsty *degredados* on his side.

Staring into the darkness, Fernao though of Juli. For once, not wanting to alarm her with such a reckless plan, he had not told her of his intentions until it was almost time for him to leave. He smiled tenderly at recalling her concern when she learned that he was off to battle again.

Although he had not slept all night, he felt curiously alert, his mind white-bright, his senses sharp. Directly ahead, across the intervening strip of open land scattered with a few graceful coconut palms, he could make out the red embers of the enemy watchfires. To his left, the lightening sky barely revealed the ocean, but he could hear its continuous roar, the splash and thump of waves above the more gentle lapping of lagoon waters. A sudden breeze brought the odour of dry fish.

Aires materialized soundlessly on foot, raised a hand to signal that all their forces were in position.

I wish the cockerels would start crowing at the false dawn, Fernao thought, for then the time will be right. Waiting for battle to start tensed his nerves. It was the worst time for most soldiers, especially when a surprise attack was to be launched.

And in that instant, a sudden illusion of dawn-light in the air was followed by the shrill crowing of a cockerel . . . *Couk . . . ou-ouk-ooook*! . . . it went again. The sounds had barely died down before he glimpsed sparking tinder on the opposite side of the lagoon. In seconds, the muzzle flashes of the cannon ripped through the darkness, then thunder rolled across the waters almost in unison with the crump-thump of cannonballs. Screams and yells broke loose from the enemy encampment. On target! Major Nantes had gauged his distances perfectly. Before the enemy had time to recover, the crash of the second salvo rolled through the air. Louder screams and frenzied curses arose from the encampment.

Then, from his left came the deep booming of the great guns of the *nao*. A series of whistles overhead heralded the cannonballs. 'O lord God, destroy Thy heathen enemies!' Fernao prayed. Dozens of crash thumps, a crescendo of screams and shouts told him his prayers had been answered.

The enemy were in confusion. Stentorian voices barked orders, were swamped by the thunder of the next salvo from the land cannon. Rapid fire, in alternate succession, had been his orders to Major Nantes, during the time it would take for the *nao* to tack and present its larboard guns to the target.

'Long moments passed, the land cannon continuing to boom with ear-splitting regularity. Fernao's pulse quickened. The familiar sparkling bloodlust thrilled through his being. Then the *nao*'s larboard cannon boomed and he was seized by a holy ecstasy. 'For thee, O Lord!'

He drew his sword, raised it aloft, silently pointed in the direction of the enemy encampment. He felt the line of mounted musketeers behind him tense in response.

'Cha . . . aa . . . rge!' he roared and dug his spurs into his bay's flanks.

Thursday, 19 March 1534

Speed was essential if I was to save General Dunu's army group. Only cavalry could achieve that speed. Moving ten cavalry regiments, each consisting of a thousand men, at short notice is not as easy as a hundred men leaping on their steeds and dashing off on a raid! But our fighting machine had begun to operate so smoothly that I was able to leave with the regiments, one of which included a company of mounted musketeers, well before daybreak. Why only one company of musketeers? During all the years we had produced muskets and cannon, the weapons had been plagued by technical imperfections and hampered by shortages of metal and gunpowder, the latter being part of the price we paid for the security of being an island nation. Otherwise by now we would have had enough firepower to drown an invader in the ocean!

I had ordered our main body to continue its move westwards to invest Jaya, while I led the ten cavalry regiments on our rescue operation. In spite of my natural apprehensions, the thunderous drumming of slow-cantering hooves in the clear morning air, the beauty of perfect motion with my new black Scindhi, Rama II, filled me with sensuous delight. Rama I, having served me nobly, was now in the honourable retirement of a Sita Waka pasture. How many times he had watched out for me since he had protected my rear when I dismounted and fought on foot during the first battle in Galle. I missed him but his successor gave promise of matching him.

As morning approached, the blue hills in the distance drew closer, became more sharp-etched. People in the villages came rushing from their cottages to the roadside to see us pass. We had ridden for about three hours when I heard a rumbling from afar. My first thought was that a storm was approaching. I glanced anxiously at the clear blue sky, but before I spied a single cloud, the truth hit me in the stomach. It was not thunder I had heard, but the sound of cannon-fire. The Jaya forces had already joined battle with my Sita Waka army group, which had no cannon.

I turned to Colonel Wickram, sensed his anxiety. 'Have the regiments maintain the same speed,' I directed him, overcoming the desire to gallop madly to the rescue. 'The battle has commenced on the Boralu plain beyond those hills.' I pointed towards the range of hills, now about a mile away. 'We shall ride on ahead to reconnoitre. You see the copse to the right of the bare brown saddle between those two green hill features? We should be able to get a good look at the battle from that point. Join us there with the commanders.'

Colonel Wickram saluted, reined his horse sideways to relay my orders. I urged Rama II to a fast canter. My escort squadron followed closely behind me.

Our vanguard had been proceeding in double lines on either side of the highway. I rode between them, up the slope along which the highway ran straight as an arrow through open green parkland scattered with dark bushes. The bouts of thunder that continued to rumble became louder and louder. Fearing no ambush, we made for the gap between the hills. The blood pounded in my veins in time with the drumming of hooves. The knowledge of invincibility suddenly seized me.

On reaching the copse, I found that it sloped sharply down beneath dark timber on the other side. The copse itself consisted mainly of mountain apple trees, whose lush green foliage provided perfect cover from the valley below. Even before I reined in my horse, I could see the battle beneath me as clearly as if it were taking place on a sand-table model in one of the Sudaliye or Maravila staff schools. Only these players were not chips of painted wood representing companies to be shifted with a pointer, but flesh and blood human beings moving to the dictates of a live battle. The open plain consisted mainly of fallow brown paddy fields, interspersed by the silver threads of irrigation channels and relieved by green hedgerows of *kanda* trees and small groves of coconut palms. A great basin in the hills, it would have been the ideal battleground for forces of equal strength and armament, but I immediately saw why Lord Tammitta, or perhaps General de Albergaria in distant Colombo, had selected it. The evil snouts of cannon gleaming dully in the silver morning sunlight, had been hidden in two diagonal lines half-facing General Dunu's group at the western edge of the basin. The cannon were visible from up here but would be completely invisible from the front. Glinting iron helmets beside the guns announced the presence of the Portuguese manning the guns.

Even as I watched, flames erupted from the dragon-snouts, followed by puffs of smoke and the rumble of their thunder. Screams, curses, shrill neighs, the sounds of battle reached me. Our advancing men were falling like trees before the axe.

With a sinking heart, I knew what had happened. The two forces had advanced conventionally towards each other, cavalry massed in the centre. Obviously unaware of the cannon, General Dunu had positioned his own cavalry in the shape of an arrowhead to punch a hole through the enemy lines. This very shape made our cavalry fit snugly, like a wedge in a sleeve, into the positioning of the Portuguese cannon. General Dunu's advance must have been slowed by the very first salvo from the big guns. When it had been halted by repeated salvoes, General Tammitta's cavalry had punched a hole though its centre, veered around in two arcs to take our cavalry in the rear. A classic battle plan, it could only have been conceived by General de Albergaria. My arch-rival had struck from behind the scenes again.

My eyes returned to those evil cannon. Some of them were now being wheeled so they could pound our flanks.

These were *my* men being pulverized.

My hand reached for my sword hilt, my heels were about to dig into Rama's flanks so I could rush to the rescue when good sense intruded. I was an army commander, not a raider. I relaxed in the saddle, gritting my jaw, but cool again.

My regimental commanders rode up. I gave them their orders. Soon, though it seemed like hours to me because of the sickening slaughter I was forced to watch, I headed for the steep slope below me, followed by my crack cavalry and three other regiments. As I carefully clip . . . clop . . . clip . . . clopped downwards, the tense moments dragged by. Total secrecy was essential. Yet our comrades were being butchered on the plain below. The tension and frustration of the men hung so tangibly in the air that for an instant I had the absurd feeling that it might roll down the hillside and warn the enemy.

Slow step, slither, I pulled up Rama II's head. The crunch of a hoof on a rock, the snort of a horse. I hoped the noises of battle would drown out these sounds of our approach. I had started to sweat beneath my leather armour, but it was not from the heat alone, or the closeness of the air beneath the heavy branches of the great tamarind trees lining the hill-slope.

The clamour of battle, clashing weapons, screams of the wounded, groans of the dying, the steady roar of voices, became louder and louder. The big guns had stopped booming by the time I got a glimpse of the battlefield again through the grey-brown tree trunks. Rank upon rank of the enemy infantry were advancing with steady step, the pikemen in front, foot soldiers with drawn swords behind. Whispering whooshes told of a flight of arrows arcing towards our troops, like hawks for their targets.

I reached flat ground at last. I reined Rama in. Burning with impatience, I allowed my men time to get into position. I silently prayed to Lord Kataragam to have the two regiments on my right flank reach their positions unobserved. Theirs was a key role, the task of the two regiments on my left flank being only to cover a regrouping of the retreating Sita Waka forces.

The sun was now well risen above the trees. The sky was a pale, cloudless blue. Light and shadow dappled our armour. The rich scent of ripe, sweet olives tinged the air. A flock of swifts darted above the green branches. What did they think of the battle going on beneath them? Or did they care?

The time was right. I drew my sword. The cold of its metal sent that feeling of invincibility coursing through all of me again.

'Cha . . . aa . . . arge!' I screamed and dug my heels into Rama II's flanks.

CHAPTER THIRTY-NINE
Thursday, 19 March 1534

The perimeter outpost of the Sinhala strike force on the spit of land had barely recovered from the shock of the artillery barrage. Pikemen were desperately reaching for their weapons. As Fernao's mount hurtled foward through the semi-gloom, for an instant he recalled his brush with death after the Mulleri battle and fear sliced through him. Then the excitement of battle took over, fear fled and he screamed with the exhilaration of the charge. His cavalry smashed through the milling humanity like a gigantic battering ram, scattering all before them. Men were hurled aside, shrieking or trampled beneath wild hooves. Pandemonium broke loose. Horses whinnied shrilly, men roared, yelled, groaned, arms clashing and rang.

A giant figure tried to grab at his bridle. Fernao swung his sword in a classic sweep. It sliced through the bull neck, jarring in his hand when metal met bone. The resistance shot up his arm to sudden pain from his old wound. He tugged the sword out before the man's collapsing weight could pull it from his grasp. His mount plunged ahead. Someone reached for his left stirrup. He released his foot, kicked viciously at a bearded, snarling face, was rewarded by a scream of pain. Mists of blood-lust swirled before his eyes, reality spun, his whole being became an insane urge to kill. His singing ears filled with red silence, he barely heard the wild yells that broke loose from within him as he laid about him mightily, swinging, thrusting, chopping. Men cowered before his mad approach. He lost count of time and the number of lives he took.

His horse began to lose momentum. The urge to plunge

ahead regardless, to dismount and lay about him right and left for ever, consumed him, but only for a second. He remembered the rest of his plan. The mists cleared. Through the lightening gloom, he found that he had reached open ground. Ahead a solid wall of men was massing. He swung his horse around, bellowed the order, 'Withdraw! Withdraw!'

The clash and clangour of battle resounded again. Then it was swing, withdraw ... chop, withdraw ... thrust, withdraw. The way back was easier because the enemy were confused by the manoeuvre.

Immediately they broke through to the front again, Fernao dug his spurs into his horse's flanks. The bay took off, racing through the twin ranks of his musketeers, the front rank kneeling, the rear rank standing. Bloody, sweating, panting, he slowed to a trot and swung back to face the enemy. He felt the weight of his reddened sword in his hand, the throb of the old wound. He relaxed his shoulder.

The enemy had regrouped. These were seasoned veterans. They began advancing at the double, screaming like dervishes. Now he could distinguish brown faces, bearded, clean-shaven, all distorted with hate and a deadly purpose.

'Prepare to fire!' he roared. With the striking of steel on flint, tiny flames flared along the line.

'Fire!'

The blast of two hundred muskets crackled along the entrance to the spit of land. Puffs of grey smoke emerged from the line of musketeers. Not even a raw recruit could miss the mass of the enemy at this range. Gaps appeared in the front ranks. Burnt cordite stung his nostrils.

'Line one, reload. Line two, prepare to fire!' Again the scrape of tinder, again the tiny flares.

'Fire!' Again the flashes, the puffs, the rattle of muskets. The Sinhala were closer, but this time the volley had even more deadly effect. The enemy front rank wavered.

'Prepare to fire!'

'Fire!'

The enemy broke and ran before the murderous volley deliverd at almost point blank range.

The roar of cannon from across the lagoon and from the ocean now glimmering with the first light of dawn commenced again.

'Calvary! . . . For King Dom João and Portugal . . . Char . . . arr . . . rge!' Screaming like a deathwind, Fernao led his men into the mass of enemy once more. Now only this final strike remained before a quick withdrawal to Colombo, under the protection of the cannon, completed his daring operation.

Thursday, 19 March 1534

We broke cover, red and gold lion banner of the Sinhala streaming. With the wind in my face, the enemy ahead of me, my men behind me, invincibility fired my being. As we thundered across the open fields in arrow formation, heading for the centre of Lord Tammitta's left flank, the only sounds I heard were the pounding of hooves and the creak of leather echoing the thudding of my heart. My men were bent low, lances levelled, pennants fluttering. I alone galloped erect in classic cavalry fashion, seat just high enough for Rama's motion from powerful thrusting rear legs to ripple beneath me like a succession of wavelets.

We were on them before they could recover from their surprise. I took a grizzled veteran with a sweep of my sword. His eyes crossed before he went down. Then a burly youth, red blood gouting from his stomach, then a giant . . .

Within the hour, we had turned the tide of battle. The absence of cannon fire had told me that my two cavalry regiments had surprised the Portuguese artillery, silenced it and attacked the enemy rear as I had planned. My own flank attack had cut the enemy column down the middle.

Relieved of pressure, the retreating Sita Waka men had turned around and re-engaged the enemy's front.

By noon, a stubborn enemy had made the Boralu plain a charnel house. Only shortly after did they break and run with us in hot pursuit.

Why tell of the dead stacked up for mass cremation? Why speak of the wounded needing attention, the men who begged comrades for a quick end to unbearable pain?

General Dunu was dead. He had been killed, while leading his troops, by an enemy cannonball before we even arrived on the scene. It was the way the gallant soldier would have wished it.

The hero of the day was General Lord Senerat, who had taken over command and kept rallying our Sita Waka forces against immense odds. He had personally led every counter attack, refusing to submit or yield. As a reward, I received him in my tent that night and appointed him co-commander of my armies, equal in rank to Lord Wickrama Sinha. Since he was of royal blood, I also named him ruler of the Raigam sub-kingdom.

However tired I might be, I could never fall immediately asleep on the night following a battle. My mind white-bright, I would go over the details of the enemy's tactical plan and mine, probing for defects and weaknesses. When that analysis was over, the dead, the dying, the wounded, especially my men, marched before my fevered gaze. Their wounds gouted red blood, their eyes were piteous, their death screams tormented me. They were all human beings, with wives, children, friends. What had they thought of at their moment of death? Had these thoughts propelled them to a better re-birth?

'Sire! Sire!' The first drowse of uneasy sleep was disturbed by Colonel Wickram's agitated voice. An attendant accompanied my aide, placed a lighted flare on a sconce in the upright of the tent-frame. In its red-gold light, Colonel Wickram's face contorted with pain.

'Speak!' I commanded him.

'I deeply regret having to be the bearer of evil tidings once more, Sire, but this time the news is personal.'

What personal news could I have? Was my sister dead, or injured?

The colonel turned towards the tent flamp. 'Come in!' he called.

A tall, lean man, his face lined, greying hair tied in a knot at the nape of the neck, entered and made obeisance.

I recognized him instantly, saw the tears streaming down his face. Sick horror reached for my stomach. 'Sene, what are you doing here?'

'My lord! My lord! I come with tragic news! He remained kneeling, tears streaming down his grief-stricken face.

Bandula and Nangi, my wards. My innards knotted. 'Come on, man, speak up.'

'Sire, Bandula and Nangi were kidnapped from my house last night. We have discovered them this morning in one of my fields ... with their ... with their ...' He broke down sobbing.

Rage seized me, 'With their what?' I roared. 'Stand up, man and tell me the worst, else ...' I could not utter the threat.

'... throats cut.' He managed the words in a strangled whisper. His face crumpled, he broke down sobbing uncontrollably. Still kneeling at my feet, he kissed them. 'Pardon, lord ... pardon ...'

Behind closed lids, I saw my two children lying dead, gashes across their slender throats. I heard the roar of a wounded animal in mortal agony and realized that it had escaped from me. I clenched my eyelids to hold back the tears.

'Kill me, lord, for I deserve death. I have failed in my

523

responsibility. Have my throat slashed, as those poor children were done to death.'

My eyes flickered towards the great sword in its golden sheath lying beside my bed. To slash this man's scrawny neck would indeed be a fitting punishment, give me release. The sword had been my father's, his father's before him, gold-handled in token of royalty. Ah, royalty!

From somewhere deep inside me, duty called. I was the Great King, not an executioner. I opened my eyes, reached down and raised Sene to his feet. 'Stand up and tell me quietly who did it.' I looked so calmly into his eyes, willing him to regain his composure, that his sobs subsided. I felt for him then, for he too must suffer.

He wiped the tears and snot from his face with the back of his hand. 'Sire, we have no evidence whatever as to who did it, or why.'

'No evidence at all?'

'None, my lord. The children went to bed as usual. They were missing in the morning. Whoever kidnapped them must have known our routine and the lay-out of our house perfectly.'

Only one person could have done it so perfectly. General Fernao de Albergaria. 'Then it was planned and directed against us,' I declared quietly. 'It was not your fault, Sene. This was an act of vengeance and a warning.' I paused, felt my eyes glittering. 'For this, I shall have two thousand Portuguese throats slit.'

I gave Colonel Wickram a level glance. 'Have the commanders report to me immediately. We leave at dawn tomorrow.'

'For Jaya, Sire?'

'No, for Colombo.'

CHAPTER FORTY
Sunday, 22 March 1534

Julietta had heard the distant booming of the big guns and the fainter rattle of musket fire all evening. It seemed especially wrong with Easter only two weeks away. Besides, the present situation was unlike anything she had experienced in the past. Fernao and Tiki-tiki, two men of military genius, were finally confronting each other. Why had Tiki-tiki moved the Sinhala armies lightning-fast against Colombo instead of Jaya? Was it to avenge Fernao's massive blow against Lord Wickrama Sinha?

Unable to sleep all night, Julietta had alternated between tossing in bed, gazing out at the starlit night, and kneeling on her *prie-dieu* in prayer before the statue of the Blessed Virgin. Now, standing beside her bedroom window in the cool grey of morning, her fears were less vivid, but she still stared anxiously towards the east. The cannon began to boom again, more insistently than last night. The Sinhala must be near the city wall. She wished the green tree line did not block her view of the eastern ramparts, so she could see what was going on.

Tiki-tiki was out there, with one of the most powerful Sinhala armies ever assembled, intent on driving the white man from his homeland. Did he want to drive her away too? And what of little Catherina? How could she allow Tiki-tiki, all unknowing that he was banishing his own flesh and blood, to drive his daughter away? Or did royalty care about family?

She remembered King Wijayo's murder. Had King Maya Dunne and Tiki-tiki killed him, as some people said? Though she did not believe the story, she shuddered, for the plots of princes, their ruthlessness in achieving their

525

ambitions, were diabolical. Even her beloved Fernao, bred
to the ideals of the *cavaleiro*, still veered at times between
the winds of expediency and the calm of honour. Like
now?

She jerked herself away from the truth. Fernao was a
good man. He was out there defending her and his children
with his life. Against whom? The man she loved, Tiki-tiki.
This must be God's punishment on her.

Appu had told her of the murder of Tiki-tiki's two
wards. How dreadful! Was that God's punishment too?
Who could have done it? Supposing he caused the death of
Catherina, his natural child? Poor Tiki-tiki, she wished she
could comfort him.

It was all so tangled; her eyes sought the harbour and
the ocean beyond. There lay the means of escape to some
distant refuge. But when she had physically escaped, what
of her mind, her heart, her immortal soul?

Sunday, 22 March 1534

Queen Anula was seated, as she spent most of her time
nowadays, on her favourite sofa in her chamber in the
Kandy palace. It was one of her lucid days, when she
calmly tried to fill in the blank periods within her mind.
At first, the loss of memory had worried her tremendously,
but she had used her strong will to overcome the surges of
panic that swept her as she tried vainly to penetrate the
walls of nothingness. Any probing had to be done alone,
for she was a queen and could not ask anyone. Something
had happened to her. Since she did not know what it was,
she had taught herself to welcome the blanks, the times
when nothing bothered her.

This morning, having finished breakfast early, she found
her thoughts racing as she considered the opportunities
which the political situation in Lanka might still afford her.
She had received regular reports from Father Perez, whose

spy system was almost fool-proof, of all the recent political and military events. The friar had visited her personally the previous evening to bring her up to date with regard to General de Albergaria's victory over General Lord Wickrama Sinha's task force in Negombo, and the plan to trap General Dunu and the Sita Waka army simultaneously. Exhilarated, she pondered as to how she could exploit these events to her advantage. She had already taken steps to wreak vengeance on King Raja Sinha for his rejection of her. As for General Dunu and Lord Wickrama Sinha, her curse would destroy them if the *booniyam*, charm, she had caused Kusuma the light-foreteller to place on them failed.

The morning was cold and damp. She wore a dark blue silken shawl around her bare shoulders against the chill. The ceaseless drip of rain on the leaves trapped between the building and the green mountainside irritated her.

She recognized the discreet knock on the door as that of her chief attendant, Nona. 'Enter!' she called.

Even before the silver-haired woman rose from her obeisance, the queen noted the look of anguish on her face. Surely it could not be bad news? She simply could not stand any more bad news.

'What is it?' she inquired sharply.

'*Aiyo*, my lady, such terrible news. Those two wards of King Raja Sinha have been foully murdered. *Aney* their throats have been cut. What fiend would want to harm innocent children?' A sob escaped her. She began snivelling, tears pouring down her cheeks. 'The Great King believes that the Portuguese general is behind it. He has moved with his whole army against Colombo in revenge.'

So it had happened. The planning and bribing had been worth it. The queen hid her elation. If King Raja Sinha suspected the Portuguese general, so much the better. This was *her* vengeance, not that of the Portuguese. No one, but no one, would ever reject her without suffering the consequences. A pity she could not receive due recognition of her brains and cunning, but one could not have everything. And of course by now the assassin would have been disposed of as well. 'Is there any news of that battle between Lord Tammitta and the Sita Waka forces?' If her hopes were realized on that front too, all her immediate desires would be satisfied.

'Yes, my lady. The people are telling that King Raja Sinha somehow got there in time to save his men. The king is not a human being, he is a *deva*, blessed of the stars. Having won the battle, he has gone with his entire army to take Colombo. This is a great day for the entire Sinhala nation.' She wiped her cheeks with the back of a horny hand. 'But General Dunu was killed in the battle.'

The sharpness of the queen's disappointment was relieved by the news of the general's death. Another enemy gone. Now if only her plan to kill Lord Wickrama Sinha would work . . . 'Stop your accursed blabbing and finish your story. What has happend to the Great King of Jaya, our royal daughter's betrothed?'

'I beg my lady's pardon. It seems that when King Raja Sinha headed for Colombo, the *parangi* general had King Dom Juan and most of his army removed to safety in that city.'

'We have told you not to call the Portuguese *parangi*,' the queen admonished in severe tones. 'Well, thank the *devas* King Dom Juan is safe.' Thank the *devas* indeed, for he was her one remaining instrument with which to wield power. She started questioning Nona for details.

When she finally dismissed the woman, her mind started to churn. Events had backfired on her and she no longer had any control over them. Pressure began building up in her mind so physically that she felt it would burst through her temples. She raced to the window, needing fresh air to relieve it. That damned, dead Kumara had caused all this. 'I am a greater schemer than you, mother-fucker,' she screamed at the green mountainside which she knew he inhabited. 'King Raja Sinha thinks his arch-enemy, the Portuguese general, is responsible for the murders of his wards, when it is I ... I ...' She repeatedly gestured inwards with her fingers. 'It is I who had it done. How cleverly I obtained the information about the two brats from King Raja Sinha! And discovered all about the routine of their house. I'll have you know, I had the assassin killed as well, so no once could ever connect me with the murders.'

Her husband's mocking voice pealed back from the mountainside. 'You kill without thought of the ultimate future, Anula. Look where it has brought you. Now you have lost your last hope of power. Your daughter's bethrothed, the Great King Dom Juan, is virtually a prisoner, with no power at all. You silly bitch, you are so clever, you keep planning yourself out of your own aims ... Ha! ... ha! ... ha!'

She clapped her hands to her ears, as always, to shut out the maddening sound of his mocking laughter. 'Curse you and damn you to hell, Kumara!' she shrieked, as always.

'*You* are already accursed,' his voice came back. 'You have thrice damned yourself. The difference between you and me is that I am not only clever, I am a genius. You are not merely stupid, you are insane!'

Her mind dimly comprehended that she was hallucinating, that her knowledge of King Kumara was thrusting into her senses the counterpoints which she knew he would make to her points had he been alive. It must be some kind of defensive mechanism, an acknowledgement of errors which she could never consciously admit.

Then her mind snapped again.

News of the near-massacre of Lord Wickrama Sinha's strike force in Negombo had awaited me in Kadu, to which I had rushed on hearing of the murder of my two wards.

Numbed as I was by the news, the sense of personal loss lay like a chill pall within me.

The truth is that we human beings bear our grief alone, especially in the dark recesses of night. Even if we have someone to share it with, no human being can ever comprehend or live another's grief or pain.

I cannot describe my feelings at seeing the dead bodies of Bandula and Nangi, their small faces distorted in spite of the best efforts of the embalmers. As I stood alone before the two silver-mounted, brown *nadun* wood coffins in the hall of their home, the desire to open their closed eyelids clamoured within me. I had promised Bandula that he and his sister would never be separated in this life and they had not been, even in death.

Had they been afraid at the time they were killed, or had the assassin mercifully stunned them before the kidnap? I needed so desperately to know. Would their eyes have told me? Instead, I forced myself to recall the love and adoration in those trusting eyes. The tears of my heart flowed freely, but I had fought down those that clawed at my eyes. It was not because I was a king, or a prince, but because we Maya Dunnes do not cry.

When my father died, I had known the depths of grief. This time, somehow it was different. Pity and the feeling of responsibility kept overwhelming me. Was I right to have removed Bandula and Nangi from their environment? What kind of security had I provided them? Would they not be alive today if I had not taken them under my protection? Had I done right to make them the victims of my compassion and my need?

From that day on, the sickly sweet scents of the embalming unguents that are used to hide death-stink would remain in my nostrils, and the soft moans of the mourner women would haunt me for ever. Vengeance! A clamour. I now understood what Aisha Raschid had felt. Only vengeance would give me relief. When I saw the terror of

Bandula and Nangi in the eyes of the murderous *parangi*, I would know some peace again.

Oh devas, hear my cry. I have saved myself from death in a dozen battles, but my own two children I could not save. What kind of power have you given me? Why does your cynical laughter ring in my ears?

Hatred was burning me up, I knew. I was a king, a Great King. I could not let emotion destroy me. Instead, I would destroy General de Albergaria, who had my children murdered.

Some instincts of nobility, some dictates of princely breeding brought my father's words to me from across the years . . . 'Above all else, honour.'

In the event, we took the capital city of Jaya without a fight, then encamped in a tight ring around the Colombo city walls. There were fleeting moments when I regretted spoiling Julietta's Easter celebrations, but the rest of the time, the cold anger within me brought only grim satisfaction at bottling up the enemy during the time of one of their most important festivals. If nothing else, they were in our country on a mission of which the Prince of Peace would hardly have approved.

For days we probed the enemy walls without being able to find a weak spot. Their water defences made them impregnable; their deadly cannon fire compelled us to remain outside range of the ramparts. General de Albergaria had done his work well. Moreover, thousands of Sinhala soldiers from the Great King Dom Juan's army, including bowmen and infantry, lined their walls. My natural instincts as a soldier and a general held me back from making the rash moves anger dictated.

As the days passed, I realized that the only way in which I could take the city was by starving it into submission. Already no supplies could reach it from land. The high sea lanes were patrolled by Piachi Marcar's ships, organized by Aisha Raschid and her nephew, Deen, whose escape from the city of Colombo to a mansion I owned on the ocean-front about nine miles south I had arranged before investing the city. Only the occasional Portuguese supply sloop could now get in under the protection of their two local *nao*, whose guns were needed to help defend the port as well. These supplies would hardly be enough to feed the thousands of people living in the city, a demand now vastly increased by the presence of the Jaya court and most of its standing army. I also hoped that the local inhabitants would turn against the *parangi* and then surrender. The one uncertain factor was whether or not Portuguese reinforcements would arrive from across the seas, but this was a chance I had to take. Meanwhile, I could afford to wait.

Tuesday, 31 March 1534

A loyal Sinhala nobleman had placed a mansion owned by him in the suburb known as Demata at my disposal. I used it for my military headquarters, but only for official purposes, because I ate the same food as the men and slept in a tent like them. None of my troops were ever billeted in houses or schools, or permitted to live off the land, creating hardship for the local people.

That morning, I was working in a room at the rear of the mansion which I used as my audience chamber, when General Lord Wickrama Sinha was announced, seeking a private audience. I had found him thoughtful and withdrawn during our planning sessions and had attributed it to hurt pride and humiliation at his defeat in Negombo. I had never taken him to task for his selection of an encampment that had bottled him up and made him an easy prey for the raiders. As far as I was concerned, he always remained my comrade-at-arms, a superb general and one of the finest soldiers in the country.

When he entered the room, I was surprised at his

appearance. His lean, fair face looked almost gaunt, the normally sparkling eyes were smaller, with black circles around them.

I came to the point without the usual banalities, knowing he would want it that way. 'Please sit down, General, and tell us why you wanted this audience.'

He looked down, remained standing, then raised his eyes to mine. 'Sire, I desire to be relieved of my command. I also request your permission to retire to my family lands.'

'What?' I demanded, my shock and bewilderment evident. 'Why?'

'Surely you must know, Sire, but since you ask me I shall tell you with humble submission.' He paused to clear his throat, then the words came out in a rush. 'The defeat of my force at Negombo has been a severe blow to my pride and reputation.'

'Is that all?' I laughed with relief. 'Every general knows defeat. Do you not remember our own defeat in Sita Waka when we were given away as a hostage? Can you do better for humiliation and loss of reputation? Please be assured our confidence in you is unshaken.'

'True, my lord king, but I beg to state that my greatest humiliation is that which I have suffered at your royal hands.' He hesitated again, then set his jaw. 'Sire, it is not for me to question the appointments of my sovereign lord, but you and I once fought together as comrades so I owe you the truth. Your appointment of Lord Senerat as co-general with me, I could have accepted, though it wounded me. But I cannot bow down without protest to your appointment of him as overlord of the district which I and my family have owned for centuries.'

How thoughtless I had been, how insensitive to the needs of my closest friend and comrade-at-arms in his direst moments! What are we mortals if we cannot be sensitive, perceptive human beings? Surely, the totally civilized man is the totally aware man – aware of the feelings of others. What was I, who should be an example, when I had so poorly timed any action of mine?

The damage had been done and there was no way to repair it. I could not rescind Lord Senerat's appointment. I wondered for a moment whether I could not appoint Lord Wickrama Sinha a sub-king elsewhere, but though he was a nobleman, he was not of royal blood. In our feudal system such an appointment would create a few dozen complications instead of one.

My expression must have told him of my guilt and of the pain in my heart, for tears sprang to his eyes. Even at his moment of great loss, his noble nature came to the fore. 'It is too late to rectify the situation, my lord,' he quietly assured me. 'I am glad I came to you in person, for I now see that you have not acted to punish me. Regardless, I wish you well. I pray that perhaps someday, when we have both paid the price, me for my over-confidence and you . . .' he paused and smiled wryly, 'because the king can do no wrong, we may be able to fight a final battle side by side again.'

'We wish that with all our heart. You are the most generous man we have ever known. We shall miss you deeply.'

Erect and proud, he backed away from the room. The emptiness of the lonely gripped my heart. I wished I could have torn out my raw, aching brain. Something told me that he and I would never fight side by side again, that I would never more see that lean, fair face, the kindly twinkling eyes.

Lord Wickrama Sinha was assassinated two days later when he had almost reached his home in the south. Once again, I believed it to be the work of Portuguese agents. They had dug a trap for him along the highway, covered it up so he would fall into it, like a beast in the jungle, then slain him where he lay and left his body inside. They would never have got him in a fair fight.

I had one more cause for vengeance against General de Albergaria.

CHAPTER FORTY-ONE
Tuesday, 21 April 1534

Fernao walked up the steps of the ramparts opposite the tower in the fort. Colonel de Mello had been staring across the lake that stretched from beneath the rampart wall. For once, the colonel was not smiling when he turned around and saluted. The dare-devil blue eyes held cold anger and the laughing mouth beneath the thin black moustache was tight-lipped.

'Anything special irritating you?' Fernao inquired, with a lift of his eyebrows.

'No, sir, but what wouldn't I give for ten more *terco*, infantry regiments, and a few more companies of artillery. I'd clear those damned natives out of there in seconds.'

By common accord they leant against the parapet. The morning sun, which had just climbed the tree-line to the east of the ramparts, had begun to absorb the dewdrops that glistened like tiny diamonds on tufts of grass sprouting from the walls. His hope of leaving for Portugal had proved as illusory as the dew. Now, even if a ship called for him, there was no way in which he could relinquish a beleaguered command and leave.

Fernao tried to distinguish the enemy, dark figures out of artillery range moving easily in open compounds and dark groves. 'Ten regiments might not be enough,' he commented. 'We are facing the entire Sinhala army. One hundred thousand men all told. If their cannon had the range of ours, we'd be in real trouble.'

Colonel de Mello shrugged. 'Worth a try if we had the men. Better than being trapped in here. I can't stand the thought of anyone having the power to bottle up me and the might of Portugal.'

'You shouldn't let yourself feel bottled up when there's nothing you can do about it.'

'Ah, philosophy, General! Unfortunately I have neither your patience nor your spiritual fortitude.'

'Make no mistake about it, Colonel, I cultivate those virtues only because I need them for survival. I too live for the day when I can remove this scourge that threatens our lives. King Raja Sinha has unified this island as no other king before him, except the well-known hero kings of Sinhala history. He and his father, King Maya Dunne, have, however, extended a unique legacy to posterity.'

'And that?'

'Firearms! How they obtained them, heaven only knows, but while they have cannon and muskets, no foreigner can really conquer them. Oh yes, we can make forays in strength into the interior, but how to hold on to our gains will always be the question. From now on, foreign powers may build and hold forts, maintain spheres of influence in limited areas like the coasts, the Church may have its special spheres of influence, but the nation will never be taken in its entirety without the consent of its rulers.'

'I don't mean to contradict you, General, but surely the Sinhala people are still divided. Look at those soldiers manning our walls by the thousand. They belong to the Sinhala King of Jaya who rules from Colombo.'

'A Great King with a great treasury but no territory.' Fernao paused, struck by an idea. 'There *is* another way in which we can render King Raja Sinha powerless,' he slowly continued. 'We must find a like hero to contend with him for power.'

'You mean another Sinhala Buddhist hero.' The colonel's eyes widened as he caught on. He slapped his thigh with his hand, the blue eyes sparkling with excitement. 'What a splendid idea. We have been blindly accepting the *status quo* of Sinhala succession all this time. Let us now determine King Raja Sinha's weaknesses and exploit them.'

Fernao's heart was beating faster. 'And the weaknesses are there,' he rejoined. 'He started with a Sinhala Buddhist base, but is now studying the Hindu religions, opposes caste distinctions, tries to look after the poor at the expense of the rich.' He placed his elbows on the parapet, leaned against it. 'But . . . he has eliminated all likely opponents. To whom can we turn?'

'There is no one in Lanka,' Colonel de Mello responded, with a reversion to gloom.

'Perhaps whoever had his two wards murdered would be cunning and powerful enough, a bitter enemy with strength enough to have the deed done.' A thought struck Fernao. 'Dear God, that's it . . . that's the reason he suddenly came charging down to Colombo like an enraged lion.'

'What, General?'

'He believes that I was responsible for those murders,' Fernao replied bleakly.

'Surely you can send him word that you had no part in it?'

Fernao shook his head slowly. 'You of all people will surely agree that pride forbids it. Besides, the king would never believe me.' He shrugged. 'Oh, well. No matter. He would eventually have headed for Colombo anyway. He is a man who feels driven by destiny and we stand in his way.'

'Surely there must be someone in all the millions of Sinhala in this country whom we can raise against him?' the colonel reiterated.

Fernao struck his forehead with his palm. 'You said, "in this country", Colonel. Surely here too I have been blind! I have been looking within the country, when such a man exists abroad. Remember the Sinhala fencing champion who fled to Goa when King Maya Dunne was bent on arresting him for some act of treason? You know . . . the man who challenged the Great Warrior of India, Gaja Bahu, to a duel and clove the Great Warrior's head in two with one stroke of his sword?'

Colonel de Mello nodded, his eyes beginning to shine. 'Yes indeed, Lord Kon Appu Bandqara. He is a Sinhala Buddhist of royal blood who exiled himself to India. A trained military commander, superb fighter, he is the sort of hero who will capture the imagination of the Sinhala people.'

'I shall send for him,' Fernao responded.

They looked at each other, smiling.

Friday, 24 July 1534

Almost four months had gone by, during which I tightened my grip on the city of Colombo. All my attempts to force entry, including two direct frontal assaults, one all along the line and one concentrated on the main city gate, were beaten back, with heavy losses to me. I tried night attacks and sneak raids just to be able to get a foothold within the city, but these too were abortive.

On the other hand, the occasional enemy sorties had been masterpieces of tactics and timing which added to our losses. I came to realize that our vastly superior numbers could not overcome superior firepower and a resolute enemy. The Portuguese were finely trained, battle experienced, well stocked with food and ammunition behind well-nigh impregnable defences. I had to concede again and again that General de Albergaria had shown remarkable imagination and military skill. A foe indeed worth of my steel.

My only recourse, to starve the garrison into submission, proved easier conceived than done. As the weeks slipped by, my troops became restive with inaction. Besides, they had to be fed, clothed, given shelter, trained and kept busy.

When the monsoon broke, their living conditions deteriorated, sickness set in, our field hospitals overflowed. Then there were the civil repercussions. Already our presence in the area, spread many miles around the principal port, was disrupting the lives of the local people. The artificial boost to their economy was not offset by the interruption of a free flow of trade and the end of commerce through the port.

It was not surprising therefore that I felt a tinge of anxiety at what I saw through the trees when I rode my black Rama II on inspection that afternoon.

Dark clouds pluming in the south-west on an otherwise speckless sky of deep burnt blue were undoubtedly headed in our direction. 'I hope those are merely rain clouds and not the heralds of another monsoon,' I joked over my shoulder to Lord Senerat, Colonel Wickram and my aides who were riding behind me.

'Not another monsoon, I beg you, Sire,' Lord Senerat, sub-king of Raigam, responded fervently. He was a slim, tall man with wide shoulders, narrow hips and a most beautiful speaking voice.

I shrugged and rode on past our men, most of them bare-chested. The day was so warm that sweat glistened on their sunburnt bodies. Even the occasional bird-call was querulous and the branches overhead drooped and seemed to crackle faintly with dryness.

The men were easy with me. A tall, gangly youth with broad features straightened up, saluted. A wide smile broke across his broad features, 'We're just cleaning out a nest of termite white ants, Sire,' he remarked, sticking his pick in a hole he had just dug. 'But this is boring work. When can we have another crack at the white termites inside the city?'

From the way the men crowding around him grinned, he had to be the company wit. 'You must be cracked in the head to want to go after termites that bite, merely because

540

you're bored. Why not play it safe and become our court jester?'

The men's laughter rippled through the air. A king, a commander, or any person in authority for that matter, never knows whether he has been really witty or whether such laughter is sycophantic! I had found, however, that with emotion, be it laughter or tears, it is an expression that regenerates the state of the person experiencing it. Ripples of laughter expand to creat waves of cheerfulness, gusts of sorrow generate tempests of grief. So if we control joy and pain, we are left with a much less acute experience, merely the essence of that which the stimulus first generated. I wished I could be equally clever about the deepest grieving of my life, the deaths of Lord Wickrama Sinha, my father, Bandula and Nangi.

We rode until we came to the edge of the lake. I stared at the sheet of water for long moments. At its far end rose the city walls, spreading south until they reached the distant ramparts of the inner fort, the final bastion of the *parangi*. A supply ship was tied up alongside the bridge of the fort. 'If we could only get across the lake,' I observed, 'we could smash through the city to the inner fort and no ship would be able to supply it.'

'The enemy firepower makes a water-crossing impossible, Sire,' Lord Senerat countered. 'You have already discounted that as a practical alternative in our battle plans. General de Albergaria knew what he was doing when he created the lake.'

A sudden breeze made the water tremble, sent tiny wavelets in my direction. General de Albergaria had created the lake. The *devas* were sending wavelets in my direction! I knew in a flash what had to be done.

Sunday, 20 September 1534

Within an hour of receiving the urgent summons from Colonel de Mello, Fernao strode up the rampart steps, returning the salutes of the officers and men. He had arranged for Appu to take Juli and the children to Sunday Mass in order to answer the summons.

He stood beside Colonel de Mello and stared over the parapet.

The morning sun had cleared the distant blue hills and the eastern treetops, and was casting pale golden light on the scene. What lay before him was far worse than he had expected. The supply ship had left, but it would never return, for the lake was baring its breast. What had been a sheet of green-brown water created by him, was now half-drained, even staring to show brown mud-flats. Hundreds of small figures at the far end of the lake like a horde of ants, some digging, others moving around carrying loads, told what was happening.

Never before had Fernao faced such danger. 'Dear, sweet Jesus, what a clever bastard!' The grudging words came out of him involuntarily. 'You're right, Colonel. King Raja Sinha is draining the entire lake. All that talk of cutting channels for a massive irrigation work as compensation for the local people who are suffering from the military operations was intended to deceive us.'

He pounded the wall with a clenched fist. 'I might have known that brackish lake water would never support cultivation. Now, no supply ships can readily reach us, and within two or three days, when the mud-flats are dry, he'll come charging in with his army. We cannot disperse our fire-power along a wide enough front to defend the entire city.'

'The ship's guns,' the colonel began, then stopped with a wry grin. 'Barely sufficient, especially since we'll never know where his attacks will be mounted.'

As always, once the initial sick panic was over, Fernao was at his best in a crisis, his head cool, all his faculties directed towards solving the problem. He stared grimly at the lake. Already the smell of slime from patches of dark

542

ooze was assailing his nostrils. He turned north to stare at the city walls. Where water had once lapped against them, black soil lay exposed. The glances his men lining the walls cast at him showed that they shared his concern. They were his responsibility.

Suddenly everything fell into place.

He turned to the colonel. 'We have only one option,' he stated. 'Forget about the city. Withdraw to the inner fort, into which we can concentrate all our cannon and fire-power. Combined with the guns of the *nao*, they will enable us to withstand any attack.'

'But, General, how can we accommodate the Jaya troops in here when there is hardly room for our own men? And what about our families?'

Fernao looked at de Mello squarely. 'Colonel, my first duty is the protection of Portuguese lives and property,' he quietly asserted. 'All else takes second place. We simply do not have room for the food and supplies necessary to look after the Jaya troops. We will therefore have to arrange suitable surrender terms for them. Only the Great King Dom Juan shall remain in our custody, as a hostage. When we have come through all this, he will be useful in restoring our position. Meanwhile, all supplies available in the city must be concentrated inside the inner fort without delay.' Brave words from a sinking heart. The plan would mean the Portuguese giving up their homes and possessions.

'Why couldn't that damned Viceroy have sent us rein-forcements, blast him?' Colonel de Mello swore impotently.

Fernao was too loyal and disciplined to be critical of his superiors and his king in public. 'His Excellency's hands are tied by our King Emperor, who knows best where his armies should be dispersed. Meanwhile, we shall send his Excellency an even more urgent summons for help. Thank God, the sloop has not yet left. Perhaps it will be more effective when the Viceroy learns that we are to be imprisoned within the inner fort.'

He smiled at Colonel de Mello's growl, looked at the cloudless blue sky. Swarms of cawing black crows were flying in the direction of the labouring Sinhala, whose camps were a ready source of food. He could not find even a trace of cloud. 'Why can't those clouds that approached a few days ago return?' he muttered to himself. 'Rain would create a swamp.'

'We'll simply have to play for time,' Colonel de Mello responded.

'Our decision to concentrate in the fort should buy us that time.' Fernao's gaze returned to the patches of shimmering water and dark mud. 'Have the commanders assemble in the briefing room for orders, Colonel. Time is short and we have much to accomplish with the next forty-eight hours.'

It is funny about life, Fernao thought, as he returned Colonel de Mello's salute. One moment you have it well in hand, the next, everything has slipped from your grasp. It would be so dreadfully hard on Juli and the children to leave their beautiful home. Yet it was a loss they had faced anyway because of their plan to return to Portugal. He felt sorry for the other officers and civilians who would have to give up their houses.

Sunday, 20 September 1534

It had been a good day, with my acceptance of the surrender of the Jaya army. I understood why General de Albergaria had held King Dom Juan Dharma Pala back. I would have done the same thing in his place.

With Lord Wickrama Sinha gone, Colonel Wickram had become my closest confidant. Strong rulers lean on no one. My father, King Maya Dunne, was always a loner and I am my father's son. But it was good to have someone to share thoughts and ideas with, so long as such sharing did not become a dependence.

Colonel Wickram had come to my tent in the grounds of the mansion in Demata to see whether I needed anything before retiring for the night. As we sat at the white *gini sapu* wood table conversing, I noted that the years had made him more grizzled than ever; the lines of his face had deepened, giving it added strength and dignity, not age. The hushed voices of my immediate guard from their tents in the nearby grove of coconut palms were part of the murmuring of night. Within the tent, the occasional whine of a mosquito in the taper light disturbed the stillness. I love darkness and silence, especially silence, of which a king has too little, and hushed voices can be a part of silence.

We had been discussing the draining of the lake. 'The past two days have been momentous,' I observed. 'We have made history. And all because Lord Senerat reminded us that the lake was man-made and at that very moment the *devas* sent a sudden breeze that made the sheet of water tremble, sending wavelets away from the ramparts as if pointing the direction in which the waters should move!'

'The winds of Sinhala, Sire, blowing in the direction of your destiny.'

A sudden restlessness seized me. I rose from my seat and started pacing the tent. Six short steps up, six down, the very limits of the space increasing my desire to break out of its confines. I paused to observe the colonel. His look was quizzical. He had never been afraid of me, the mark of a truly honest man. 'You speak of destiny,' I stated. 'We have always had other aims than becoming a Great King. Even when the last foreign soldier has been driven from our shores, we shall never be satisfied until all the people in this land, of whatever race of religion, live happily in it.'

'The end is in sight, Sire. Since you accepted the surrender of the Jaya army today, it only remains for us to drive

545

the foreigner from the inner fort. They may well board their *nao* and depart.'

'It will not be enough,' I declared abruptly. 'The Portuguese commander, General de Albergaria, organized the foul murders of my two wards and Lord Wickrama Sinha. He must be tried and executed.'

'But, Sire, the king's law requires satisfactory evidence of guilt before a man can be brought to justice,' he protested mildly. 'Also, our kings have prescribed court procedures for an accused person to be tried. With due respect, you are the law-giver today, Sire, and you must obey your laws or change them. Since we have no evidence whatever that the general organized the murders, you are hamstrung by your own power!'

A long speech indeed for my normally laconic aide. I stared at him, frowning. No one had dared to speak to me thus before, but he had raised doubts in my mind. He could be right, but I did not want to be convinced. 'General de Albergaria is the most dangerous enemy of Lanka.' I kept stabbing downwards with my index finger for emphasis. 'Our entire country is in danger while he commands the Portuguese garrisons.'

'That has nothing to do with the murders you speak of, Sire. It is said that he will leave Lanka for good as soon as a ship arrives to transport him and his family to Portugal. Why not just let him go?'

This was the first time I had heard someone else mention Julietta's departure since I had had the news. It brought me the shock of reality. I knew that Julietta and her children would have had to move from their home on the Mutu Vella hill to the inner fort, but had shoved the thought aside because I could not afford to let sentiment guide my policies. I shrugged helplessly. 'We shall see. Meanwhile, we move into position as planned tomorrow morning and attack the inner fort the day after.'

Fortunately, the fort had been built to accommodate two regiments. Fernao secretly blessed Captain Oliveira for his foresight and for the lay-out, which would enable the fort to withstand a long siege. In spite of this, noise and confusion were the order of the day. Apart from the activity caused by moving Portuguese families inside, cannon had been brought up and now lined the rampart fronting the lake at about six-foot intervals, poking their snouts throught the embrasures Fernao's men had hammered through the walls in record time.

Fernao had allocated Julietta and the two children her father's former quarters, with Appu to look after them. It had torn his heart to see the backward glances the two children had cast when they were finally driven away from the mansion in the waggon containing the few belongings they were able to take away. Ironically, the bells of the church had been ringing, as usual on a Sunday, as they drove past it to the fort. What would become of the church, or their home with all its elegant furniture and furnishings? Would they ever see any of it again? Perhaps the owner of the house would obtain a wealthy local tenant.

'It only goes to show how valueless possessions are,' Julietta had remarked as they took a last look at the mansion. 'The only valuable thing we have is our love for each other as a family. And thank God, unlike so many people, we also have a roof over our heads.'

Among the few possessions they had brought with them were some of Julietta's paintings. The rolled-up canvases included the one she had done as a girl of the knight rescuing the lady from a dragon that Prince Tiki had returned as a wedding present and the recent painting of a white-sailed ship sailing into the sunset. Vasco da Gama's clock adorned the small dining room. Julietta placed her statue of the Madonna on a stand in the bedroom which had once been her father's. The two children were to share her former room.

All day long, King Raja Sinha's troops moved closer and closer to the fort in orderly lines. Whenever he stood on the ramparts, Fernao could distinguish the separate regiments by their bright banners. It was like a gaudy net tightening around the fort and he was one of the fishes.

Infantry, bowmen, artillery, finally halted just out of range of the fort's cannon and started the routine of the day, the sounds drifting towards the fort.

His own men, lining the battlements, had not been so silent. Jeers, catcalls and obscenities were flung at the enemy, but beneath it all the undercurrent of tension was a common bond.

He made love to Julietta that night, a sweet, tender lovemaking, as much an act of mental and spiritual need for both of them as of the body's demands. When it was over, his body felt one with the air around him and his mind was at ease.

As he had directed, the fort's trumpets had blared the stand-to at 4 A.M. Sounds of activity began breaking through the shuttered windows of the quarters. He washed, dressed, said his prayers in the light of the brass lamps which Appu had lit. He sat alone with Julietta at a breakfast of bread and cheese, while the children, typical of the young, continued to sleep through the near-din of the fort's activities.

They ate in silence, in perfect communion but deliberately avoiding any reference to the situation. He felt more love for Julietta than he had ever known before and it brought black depression. He drank in her aquamarine eyes, mysterious in the lamplight, sparkling as always, her auburn hair shining like burnished copper, wanting to engrave the image of her into his consciousness so it would be his for ever if he died.

Breakfast over, he leaned forward to place a hand over her long pale fingers. 'You know, Juli, you have been a true soldier's wife always, but especially these past days,' he stated quietly. 'You have not uttered one word of complaint. No one could have asked for better. I thank God for you. The children are lucky to have you for a mother.'

Tears sprang to her eyes. She looked at him deeply for long moments, saying nothing, her love reaching out but with an undercurrent of some inner pain. She rose to her feet, stumbled to kneel beside him. She placed her head on his lap. 'You are my refuge and my strength, beloved husband,' she whispered. She sniffed back her tears, then grew quiet while he tenderly stroked her hair. It felt silken to the touch. He wished with every fibre of his being that these moments would never end. Would he die in battle today? Would he be wounded? Would the fort be overrun? His love for her now brought determination. Never! He would stop the enemy at all costs. He and his men were fighting for hearth and home, even if it were only in a barracks.

The Vasco da Gama clock on the wall told him it was time to go. He sighed. Somehow, it was always time to go. In that instant, he longed so unbearably for the release that the normal life he had planned for them all in Portugal could give that it seemed almost real to him. Distant memory came to the fore with a vivid recollection of the gracious old family mansion, its spacious gardens, the rolling lawns, the green groves, pasture lands with black and white cattle grazing on them. Mooing cows and braying mules, birdsong and the first woodpecker's rat-tat-tat, the fragrance of new-mown hay and the scent of lilac. And fantasy thrust in, with Juli, him and the children riding their horses across green meadows.

The blare of trumpets blasted away the images, brought

549

him back to grim reality. A fierce determination to make the fantasy come true seized him.

Juli stirred, raised her eyes to him. 'It's time you went, my love,' she said. A true soldier's wife. 'Wherever you go, you take my heart with you. There is not one moment of the day or night when you are not in my consciousness. Whatever I may be doing, thinking, saying, you are always there, ever-present. If harm should come to you, I would surely die, but remember at that moment that you would have my thoughts and my love. May the Blessed Virgin keep you.'

His eyes went moist. Releasing her, he pushed back his settle, stood up and raised her to her feet. He held her close. Her hair smelled sweet of spice. 'Lovest thou me?' he whispered in her ear.

'I do indeed love thee' She paused. 'Dost thou love me?'

'I do indeed love thee. With all my heart.'

He felt her tremble. For a moment, he thought she would break down and weep. But she held steady. Eyes closed, she raised her face to his and he kissed her soft lips very gently, resisting a violent urge to crush her to him so fiercely that she would for ever remain physically merged to his body, a part of him.

He released her and she drew back, opened her eyes, smiling tenderly at him. 'Oh, General de Albergaria, I do declare. Is this what you do with all your women? Fie for shame, you are only about to step outside and you behave as if you are off to the wars. You do know how to take advantage of a woman's tender heart, don't you, Sir General?'

He loved it when she talked like this. He shook his head in wonderment. 'You're really a unique human being, my Juli,' he breathed. He laid a gentle hand on her soft cheek, then turned away to get his iron helmet. 'Will you please do me the honour of walking the ramparts with me this evening, so we can watch the sunset?' They had resumed their former practice the previous day.

'I would be delighted, sir.'

He closed the door behind him, thinking, where there is love, there is no war. A scrubby bush of wild jasmine grew at the entrance of the quarters. Remembering the first day he went on a campaign, before he married Juli, he stooped and picked a sprig of the white flowers. He walked back to the door. To his surprise, it opened before he could grasp the handle. Juli stood at the entrance, smiling. She held a white cambric handkerchief edged with lace in her hand as she had done on that same occasion years ago. How different everything was today. On that day, he had no apprehension of real danger, but he did not have Juli's deepest love. Today, when he finally had her love . . .

CHAPTER FORTY-TWO
Monday, 21 September 1534

Fernao emerged from his quarters to find the heavy darkness that precedes dawn. In the gloom, the silhouettes of men and cannon lining the southern wall seemed like a regularly spaced, well-trimmed hedgerow. He was glad they were human beings and metal instead, behind granite, an invincible combination. Sergeant Aires emerged as if from nowhere, teeth white, saluting with his usual 'Good morning, Sir General!' then fell into step behind him.

Fernao strode past the tower, standing stark and square against the sky, with patches of golden light from the open windows. The cool air was balmy, bearing a hint of humidity, promising a warm day. This was one of the hottest times of the year. He and the men teeming in the fort would all suffer in their leather cuirasses and iron headgear. The barrels of the cannon and the breeches would become too hot to touch.

Moments later, he stood beside Colonel de Mello on the ramparts, surveying the scene of impending battle. The bed of the lake stretched dark before him. His eyes quickly caught the lights in the middle distance. Flares flickered yellow, the dying embers of campfires glowed red, golden patches from open tent-flaps stretched across his line of vision, floating endlessly north on what had been the lake-bed. A quiet peaceful scene, its beauty heightened rather than diminished by the sounds being wafted from the enemy above the roar of the sea and the beating of surf. The background of many men's voices, that always seemed to blend into a single hum when coming from a distance, was punctured by the tentative notes of a trumpet, an occasional drumbeat and the shrill, intermittent neighing of horses. The rotten reek of the mud remained, but it was a thinner, dried-up smell, mingling with odours of gun-oil and cordite from within the fort.

His eyes soon acquired their dark-sight. He focused them on the foreground, sweeping slowly from left to right, then moved into the middle distance from right to left . . . and stopped . . . at a darker patch that should not have been there. He closed his eyes, opened the lids quickly and in the resulting flash of extra-sight, saw what appeared to be a hedge of some sort. Forcing himself to scan carefully, he moved his vision left. The hedge stretched on and on until it ended in the dark, impenetrable cloud of the groves lining what had formerly been the northern border of the lake.

He jerked his head towards Colonel de Mello, standing lean and tall on his left. 'Do you see . . .?' he began. He was interrupted by a flash from the dark mass. Before he could swivel his gaze back, other flashes spread along it. Men beside him started exclaiming, arms pointing. Flames broke out spreading sideways to join each other.

'Egad!' Colonel de Mello gritted from clenched teeth. 'The bastards have moved up brushwood and set it alight.'

'You're right,' Fernao agreed tersely.

Within moments the blaze had spread to become a long thick line of fire circling their sector of the rampart walls.

'But they're over two hundred yards from us,' the colonel interjected. 'What the hell have they got to gain?'

In the shocked silence that held the men lining the ramparts in its grip, he had his answer. Furrows of fire came snaking towards them, smoke billowing upwards. The roar of flames arose, interspersed by the sputtering of damp wood.

On the instant, Fernao recognized the tactic. 'Smoke-screen!' He bellowed, 'Artillery, prepare to fire! Muskets ready!'

His orders went rattling down the line along the rampart

walls. Men were instantly alert, as tangibly as the clang of metal. 'Kill the mother-fuckers! Blast their goddamn balls!' It was Major Nantes shouting.

A pounding of hooves arose across the lake bed. Fernao tried vainly to penetrate the gloom behind the smoke and the long line of the blaze, to see from where the enemy cavalry would break through. He noted the gaps. 'Artillery, direct your fire at the gaps!' he cried. The squeaking of wheels being frantically turned pierced his ears. Too late. The cannon could not be concentrated on those gaps in time.

The pounding of hooves changed to a tremendous drumming. Columns of cavalry shot through the dark, each line briefly highlighted by the flames, an endless stream of ghost-riders of the Apocalypse. They fanned out as they passed the flames, advancing in thundering masses between the furrows of light.

'Artillery, prepare to fire at will! Fire!' It was Major Nantes screaming the order. Good man, Fernao thought wildly. This is no time to be taking aim. He heard the scrape of flint on steel, noted the sparking, the flames out of the corners of his eyes.

'Fire! . . . Fire! . . . Fire!'

Roar upon roar rocked the rampart walls. His ears sang. Smoke belched. He though he heard the whistle of cannon balls. Riders tumbled in the firelit darkness, horses neigh-shrieked. Gaps appeared in the charging line. But it came on, unwavering. The stink of burnt gunpowder mingled with a curious taste of raw blood in Fernao's throat. The enemy cavalry would be below the depressing range of the cannon. This was total danger. Cold chills ran up Fernao's spine.

'Musketeers, prepare to fire! . . . Fire! . . . Fire!' he roared.

The rattle of muskets filled the air. More enemy fell, but still they came. Instinctively, Fernao drew his sword. The feel of the cold steel sent resolution racing through his blood. Smoke and flashes in confusion, but his men were steady.

The lines of enemy cavalry were almost beneath the rampart walls. They slowed to a canter, began to wheel in perfect precision.

'Musketeers prepare to fire! . . . Fire! . . . Fire! . . . Fire!'

More enemy fell, soundlessly. For a flash second Fernao admired their deadly discipline. Horses squealed in agony. Darkness below. Flames roaring behind the enemy. A scene from hell.

A soughing whoo . . . oosh! . . . overhead, sparkling, like a vast array of shooting stars. Fire-tipped arrows rained against armour, clanked against metal. Men fell, pierced by flaming arrows, some of them screaming in agony. Dear God the enemy had brought their bowmen within range . . .

A great clattering arose. Hooks soared to the walls, were tested. His men rushed to tear them loose. Who . . . oosh . . . whoo . . . oosh . . . More arrows pierced soft leather, clanged against metal helmets, glanced off granite. Now came the flash and rattle of enemy muskets firing at short range. More of his men fell, others took over. He himself bore a charmed life. 'Spears and swords!' he roared.

A groan beside him. Sergeant Aires was collapsing, wildly clawing at a chance arrow . . .

He darted to his man, now lying slumped on his back, an arrow sticking obscenely out of his throat. 'Sergeant!' he screamed. He sheathed his sword, reaching for the arrow in a single motion. He placed his boot on his man's heaving chest, stopped abruptly. Pulling the arrow out would only speed Aires' death. The sergeant's eyes opened wide, instantly veiled over in agony. A pleading look entered them as he clawed vainly for breath, tired to raise a feeble hand and point at the arrow.

Fernao understood. 'God forgive me?' he prayed.

'Good-bye Aires, my dearest, most devoted friend.' He stamped hard on the near-bursting chest, tugged fiercely. The arrow came out swift and sure, crunching through gristle and tendon. Aires grunted. His eyes closed. Dark blood came gouting from the gaping hole in his neck. With a fierce effort, he raised his head, opened his eyes wide. He smiled his thanks, gave a single sigh, like a child. His head went limp, thudded on the paving, slanted grotesquely sideways.

Tears sprang to Fernao's eyes. He let them flow for once. He closed the dead man's lids, folded his hands across his breast. He picked up his sword, leapt to his feet. The roar of battle smote him again. Arrows were still raining down. Muskets were firing at random on either side of him. His men were cursing, screaming obscenities. They hacked away with their swords at the scaling ladders flung between the embrasures, trying to dislodge the enemy who were clambering up, short swords in their teeth. The entire attack was perfectly timed, the enemy knew the defences like the furrows of their paddy fields.

With Aires' death, there was only cold fury in Fernao. He ran to an embrasure. A dark head appeared above the wall. He swung with his sword. A mighty cut. The head simply disappeared. He knew the body would topple soon, hoped it would dislodge some of those who were following so silently that it was unnerving. He heard the roar of cannon on the lake-bed and his blood ran cold. His first thought was for Juli and the children. Then the soldier took over as cannon balls whistled, crashed, pounded, thudded within the fort. More of his men fell. The roof of a building collapsed.

He heard Major Nantes screaming out orders for range and rapid fire. The gunnery officer was bent on knocking out the enemy cannon. Another enemy head appeared. Fernao slashed at it. The head vanished. Two of his men reached out, trying to grab the grappling hooks. One of them shrieked wildly, groping at the bloody mess that had been his face before the musket ball had hit him. Fernao himself had escaped that one.

Sinhala broke over the ramparts, fierce shadows. Hand-to-hand fighting, at which the *degredados* excelled, commenced. Fernao lost count of the enemy he killed.

The fighting went on through dawn, to the thunder of cannon, the rattle of muskets, the screaming of men, the clashing of arms. Fernao's wounded arm burned. He barely saw that the sun was well risen over the eastern treetops, but felt its warmth beneath his armour.

Suddenly, in the dimness of his consciousness, he heard the blare of trumpets from the lake-bed breaking above the din of battle. The enemy instantly broke off the fighting, turned round to retreat. His men took advantage of the lull, roared in with screams, curses and swinging swords. Within minutes the ramparts were bare.

Fernao rushed to the walls. The enemy were streaming back, cavalry in columns, bowmen and infantry loping along through the firescreen that had died down to smouldering embers. 'Give them all you've got!' he bellowed.

Orders crackled, muskets rattled, the deep roar of his cannon rose again. Flame, smoke, din. Enemy went down, but their retreat was still orderly.

Finally, it was over. A great hush settled over the battle scene, like a flame dowsed with water hissing to its death. The blood-stink remained. Men were groaning on the ramparts. Dead bodies littered the walls and the lake-bed. Fernao became conscious of his aching muscles and tight chest, of the stinking sweat that soaked his body.

A breeze sprang up from the south, whipping burnt leaves and grey ashes across the intervening space. Dead leaves, dead ashes. Fernao remembered Sergeant Aires lying nearby in death.

The attack had almost succeeded. The only thing I had not taken into account was the resolution and desperate fighting skill of the Portuguese *degredado*.

The defeat caused huge losses, was bitter in my mind. Nearly two thousand of my men were dead, over a thousand seriously wounded, dozens of horses had been killed or maimed, thirty-one of our cannon were smashed by deadly artillery fire from the fort.

I sent a truce party to my hated enemy, General de Albergaria, so we could collect our dead from the fort and battlefield and give them decent cremation. He agreed, but stated his position in a letter:

> To the Great King Tikiri Bandara Raja Sinha, General de Albergaria sends greetings.
>
> You have from dawn till dusk tomorrow to remove your dead from the battlefield. We shall throw the corpses within the fort over the rampart walls. There are no wounded, for let it be known that we do not take prisoners.
>
> I make this concession to you not on humanitarian grounds or moral considerations, but only so that we Portuguese can avoid discomfort and disease from your rotting corpses.
>
> Realize, Great King, that we shall never submit or yield, so ours is a battle unto death
>
> (Signed) Fernao de Albergaria
> General Officer Commanding
> the Armed Forces in Lanka of His Imperial Majesty,
> the King of Portugal

My enemy had told me no more than I had fully believed for a long time.

It took us all that day to gather our dead from the fort and the battlefield. The next day, we observed Buddhist rites and cremated the corpses in great funeral pyres. Their billowing smoke carried the odour of death far and wide.

It would take long for the smell of burnt flesh to ease. It

would take more than my lifetime to erase the wound in my heart.

Wednesday, 23 September 1534

In a fort that barely had space for the living, what room was there for burying the dead?

That was the problem which Fernao had to overcome.

Bishop Juan had been permitted by King Raja Sinha to remain in residence in the city of Colombo and to carry on with his religious duties. In keeping with the king's policy of free religion the bishop was now given special permission to enter the fort and conduct services for the dead.

Following the service there would be mass burials of three hundred and eleven corpses in great pits that Fernao had caused to be dug at the northern end of the fort, with a thick layer of quick-lime made of crushed coral at the bottom as an antiseptic. We used crushed coral to bond the granite blocks of the fort's rampart wall many years ago in an attempt to repel invasion forces, now it is being used to repel another kind of invasion, disease, Fernao reflected sadly, as he stood in full dress uniform at the head of his men.

It was early evening on the day following the battle. The garrison was drawn up on the parade ground, forming three sides of a square, in the hollow of which the bodies of the dead, including that of Fernao's faithful Sergeant Aires, all wrapped in canvas, were neatly laid out in four ranks: soldiers on parade, close enough to the pits to be easily dumped inside them! Carrion crows, attracted by the death-smells, soared overhead, black sails against a grey-smoke sky, cawing plaintively above the roar and splash of surf.

How pitiful! These dead bodies were those of *degredados*, criminals from the prisons of Portugal, bonded into the service of their king abroad, bonded into exile so they could escape from the bitter alternative of noisome dungeons and filthy jails. Most of them had been the victims of their own senseless brutality, which in turn had become the remorseless instrument of their punishment. Crowded as children in city slums or with cattle in country hovels, herded together as prisoners when they became young adults, almost chained to each other in barrack rooms as grown men, at this moment they were receiving life's crowning climax. They were being dumped into burial pits, still clumped together, as the dead.

When all the canvas bags had been slid into the pit, Fernao watched Bishop Juan in his splendid robes, cloth of gold, crimson silk, the tall mitre on his head gleaming like the proud prow of a king's flagship, sprinkle handfuls of soil into each pit, his booming voice declaiming:

'Dust to dust, ashes to ashes . . .'

Fernao's mouth went dry; bitter bile rose at the back of his throat, his chest ached. Oh God, could I have avoided these battles? Was I responsible for the deaths of these men? His head swam with guilt and compassion.

The shovels of the burial detail hacked at the dry earth like the coughs of a hundred tubercular men, the slap of sand on the canvases in the pits sounded like death rattles.

A burial service for the Portuguese dead, while smoke from the Buddhist cremations of the enemy was wafted overhead by steady south-eastern winds. Suddenly, deep inside him, a part of Fernao understood and respected what the Sinhala were fighting for. Would he not do the same if a foreigner invaded Portugal? Sinhala and Portuguese on common ground at last, as the dead. Yet he also knew, with sadness, that the living Portuguese and Sinhala, white man and brown skin, east and west, would meet only in death, never in life.

In a moment of dazzling clarity, Fernao realized what his father had been trying to achieve. The de Albergarias belonged to the soil which they owned to no less degree

560

than their tenants and serfs who were chained to it. The nation spirit of a Portuguese could be anywhere, but the body had to yield itself to the soil of Portugal. He must get Julietta and his children home to Portugal, whatever the cost. Especially his son, the ultimate hope of continuing the de Albergaria line for the glory of Portugal.

He should have left Lanka for Portugal with his family long ago.

CHAPTER FORTY-THREE

Extracts from the private diary of General Fernao de Albergaria.

Friday, 16 October 1534: There has been no enemy activity since the last battle. Having penned us into the fort, they are simply waiting. The Mouro fleet continued to blockade the approaches to Colombo, so only one sloop has sneaked into a harbour once alive with shipping, now virtually dead. I recall how busy it was the day we first arrived almost fourteen years ago. The sloop brought grand promises from the Viceroy and sparse supplies! Even the two *nao* are almost locked in and can barely supply themselves from the north and east coasts. Gossip has it that our problems are due to the situation in Europe, where the power of the Emperor, Charles V, is threatened and requires the fullest support from every Catholic and Hispanic.

None of this gives us food and water, both of which we have started rationing. Even the monsoon rains have been delayed . . .

Monday, 16 November 1534: The monsoon rains did come. While they eased the water shortage, problems of disease had arisen because we have to man our walls and remain at our stations regardless of the rain. If it is not one thing, it's another in our present situation. Many of our men have colds and coughs, some have developed bronchitis and pneumonia. Twenty-nine have died of the ague. Our hospital facilities are limited, medical supplies sparse. All our floors are damp, so we cannot even make our sick dry and comfortable. By the grace of God and the Blessed Virgin, my family and I remain untouched.

Meanwhile the enemy still sits outside . . .

Tuesday, 1 December 1534: The rains ceased, but our final toll from disease was fifty-six dead. All of them have been given Christian burial. We have now been under siege within the fort for almost three months without relief and our food supplies are running very low.

Since today is the first day of December, I cannot help wondering what kind of a Christmas we will have! . . .

God forgive me, but when the rationing of our rotting meat became low as I dared allow it, I ordered the oldest horses killed. Poor creatures, their death screams will remain in my ears for ever. But I am determined to survive this siege. Though Julietta and I give some of our rations to the two children, they are beginning to look as gaunt and hollow-eyed as the rest of us. My main concern is Julietta. She has times of intense thoughtfulness when she simply sits and stares into space, withdrawn into a world of her own, but one that must be very real to her because she is obviously thinking deeply. I know her so well. I must let her reveal her thoughts to me in her own time, for she remains unfailingly loving and devoted to me and the children. We are indeed blessed in her.

Saturday, 5 December 1534: Today, disaster really struck. I had orders from His Excellency the Viceroy, on a supply sloop that managed to slip the ocean blockade, that the two great *nao* are to return to Goa forthwith, to help cope with some serious problems with the local *raja*. Not only did the *nao* afford us the protection of their guns, but they were also useful in bringing us some supplies at least . . .

Julietta and I watched from the ramparts this evening as our one link with the security of the outside world sailed into the sunset. Lack of food heightens imagination. It seemed to me the sails of the *nao* were blood-red. I shivered involuntarily, wondered whose blood it would be. Will Julietta, the two children and I ever sail for Lisbon on such an evening?

The speed and dimension of adversity is unbelievable, but I know this is the way with life, one moment elation, the next despair. I am somewhat depressed tonight, but am determined to continue unyielding, undaunted!!!!

Thursday, 10 December 1534

In the pale light of early morning, the three men standing to attention before him, staring straight ahead, their faces expressionless, seemed to crowd Fernao's office room in the tower of the fort. It was their smell that he found most overpowering. He guessed what was on their minds. Funny how men of different appearance were selected to speak for such a group, as if a more representative picture of spokesmen would justify their unacceptable requests.

Sergeant Souza in the centre was a strapping great fellow, with a heavy bearded face and deep-set, black eyes, one of the toughest men in the garrison. On his right, Gunner Sergeant Fonsecka, his death's-head face rendered mournful by a long moustache, the ends of which trailed sadly downward, looked cadaverous. The small birdlike man of Sergeant Souza's left was Corporal Diaz of the supply regiment, a normally cheery soul with mischievous brown eyes, but looking deadly serious at the moment. All three men bore visible signs of the privations of the past months in their gaunt faces, black circles around sunken eyes and that terrible odour of unwashed, unhealthy bodies.

Fernao leaned back in his chair, eyed the three men, deliberately allowing the silence to make them nervous. He could not help feeling sorry for them because all three were products of the harrowing shortages of food and water.

The seconds scratched away on the clock against the far wall. Only when he thought that the men were beginning to feel uncomfortable did Fernao speak. 'You requested an interview, Sergeant Souza?'

'Yes, sir.' The response was firm, the deep voice steady.

'What is it you want?'

'Sir, we are all trapped in this fort, starving to death. The men feel we should not sit here doing nothing.'

Fernao's eyebrows shot up. This was so much more daring than he had anticipated that he could feel the ancestral frost enter his eyes. 'The men?' he inquired sharply. 'What men?' He already knew.

'All the troops in the fort, sir.'

'Are you their spokesman, Sergeant?'

'Yes, sir.'

'And your two companions?'

'They are with me, sir.'

'So I observe. So I observe.' Fernao paused deliberately. 'Since when do you have the authority to speak for all troops in the fort, Sergeant?'

'Sir, you are the general. The men told me to speak to you . . . sir.'

'You understand the consequences of this act, Sergeant . . . all three of you?' His cold eyes swept each of the men in turn, but deep inside he was somehow beginning to feel disquiet. 'Let me explain to you. It is illegal for anyone in or outside His Majesty's military forces to discuss grievances in a group, to organize such a group without the approval of their commanding officer, or to act as a spokesman for any group not under his direct command. Any person so doing is held to be spreading disaffection amongst the troops and can be brought before his commanding officer for summary trial. If he is found guilty of the offence, he shall be flogged, imprisoned, or even hanged. Now that I have warned you, do you wish to proceed or would you prefer that I give you leave to retire?'

The answer emerged without hesitation. 'I for one still wish to speak up, sir.'

'You, Sergeant Fonsecka?'

'Me too, sir.'

'Corporal Diaz?'

'Sir!'

Fernao sighed inwardly. He had no wish to punish these men. They were merely fellow sufferers who had obviously been driven to desperation. 'Proceed, Sergeant.'

'Sir, we are soldiers, but in this fort, we are only rats in a trap. We beg you, sir, get one of the *nao* back and send us to some other duty station, or negotiate with the Sinhala.

565

Better that we die in battle or imprisoned by our enemies than starve to death in here . . . sir.'

'That is for me to decide. Anything else?'

'Yes, sir. We think that otherwise we had better surrender the women and children, sir, so that the available food will last a longer time.'

A feeling of desolation gripped Fernao.

You gave me the wrong reason, he thought. Why did you not say it would be better to save the women and children, that this was the reason you are here? 'Do you have anything else to add, Sergeant?'

'No, sir.'

'Then, you have my answer. I reject your requests.'

Sergeant Souza did not hesitate even for a second. 'I regret to inform you, sir, that we have taken over the fort. All the officers are already in the dungeons.'

Thursday, 10 December 1534

Julietta watched the two children seated at the table in the living room of their quarters, engrossed in their regular morning studies. Her daughter was beginning to show signs of flagging, but little Lopo was putting on a good show. Both children looked like the sad products of famine. She too had felt the weakness, the easy exhaustion, the listlessness that made it easy just to lie back and sleep, but she had kept driving herself for the sake of Fernao and the children. To add to their discomfort they were all smelling high since the water rationing made even minimum standards of cleanliness well nigh impossible. Washing frequently in salt water caused sores.

Where would it all end?

Evening after evening, when they took their regular walk on the ramparts, she and Fernao would gaze out across the ocean, their eyes searching the distant horizon for the speck of sail that would announce the arrival of the rescue fleet. From dawn till dusk the lookouts on the tower scanned the seas. But to no avail.

A fierce feeling of protectiveness towards her family swept over Julietta. She looked more closely at Catherina. With her dark hair, slim build and chiselled face, now pinched, she was a constant reminder of the Tiki-tiki of her childhood days in the Jaya palace. At that moment, she heard an authoritative rapping on the door. Appu was out, visiting a sick soldier in the infirmary. The children looked up at her. 'Shall I answer it, *a mae*?' the boy inquired.

'No, *o filho*,' she replied, rising to her feet. 'You carry on with your studies. *A mae* will answer it.'

She opened the door and was hard put to it to stifle a gasp. A rough looking soldier in dirty uniform, his hair and beard unkempt, stood at the entrance, silver sunlight gleaming on the naked sword in his hand. Behind him, about twenty men with drawn swords crowded the flag-stone walk.

Instinctively, she tried to slam the door shut, but a huge booted foot was already wedged inside. 'Not so fast, pretty lady,' the soldier said in a drink-coarsened voice. She remembered her rapist, panicked.

She pushed harder, hoping to hurt his foot so he would withdraw it, kept pushing with all her might, then realized that it was useless. She let go and stood aside. The door flew wide open.

'You hurt me,' the man growled, now standing in the doorway.

'You have no right in here,' she replied acidly. 'The general will have you shot for this.' She became aware of the children's presence.

Little Lopo stepped forward, haughty and erect, block-ing the entrance. 'Get out!' he ordered. He looked every inch a de Albergaria.

A thrill of pride at her son's fearlessness and nobility ran through Julietta. Then the stark truth hit her. These were mutineers. She trembled for Fernao. Where was he? Was he safe? Had he been killed? She would have known in her heart if he were dead. She took a deep breath, forced resolution into her stomach. She would show these men how the general's lady behaved.

'Oh, it's the general's whelp, is it?' The soldier was sneering now, pale brown eyes flashing evil in the sunlight.

'Sir, you have come to the wrong residence, for whelps live in kennels.' The icy de Albergaria stare was evident in the boy's eyes. 'We have kennels outside these quarters for dogs and their whelps. And prison and yardarms for insolent men.'

The soldier was taken aback by the boy's boldness, but in a moment his fists clenched. He started forward, stopped when a man in the support group called to him. 'Hey, Moniz. Don't harm the woman or kids. We are here only to keep 'em prisoner.

Thursday, 10 December 1534

Following the noon meal, I was in my audience chamber at army headquarters in the Demata mansion when the truce party from the fort was announced. My eyebrows shot up with pleasure, but Colonel Wickram soon disillusioned me. 'Sire, this is no ordinary truce party,' he stated. 'It consists of two sergeants and a corporal.'

'What?'

'I have the impression that there has been a mutiny in the fort and that the men have taken over from their officers.'

Strangely, my first thought was for Julietta's safety. 'Have they harmed anyone?'

Colonel Wickram readily comprehended the source of my concern. 'We don't know, Sire. May I usher the party in?'

I nodded towards the door. My heart was pounding against my chest, alarm struggling with anticipation.

The three men who entered with the spears of my guards at their backs were rough and tough, especially the giant in the centre, who was obviously their leader. They showed the terrible effects of deprivation and stank like outhouses. All of them had cruel mouths.

'Sire, allow me to present Sergeant Souza, Sergeant Fonsecka and Corporal Diaz.' Colonel Wickram gestured to each man in turn. 'They have been searched for weapons.' He stood to a side, his sword drawn.

'Good.' I did not like these men. They were obviously mutinous dogs who had turned on their masters. 'This is an unusual embassy,' I remarked coldly. 'Whom do you represent?'

'We are spokesmen for all the Portuguese in the fort,' Sergeant Souza stated.

'You are obviously unaccustomed to the manners and protocol of a Court. It is necessary to use a title when addressing a king, or even one of his commanders. How is it that General de Albergaria selected men of such little breeding to speak for his Imperial Majesty?'

The sergeant flushed. He hesitated, not liking the thought of giving in, but wisdom dictated that he make a concession. 'We are in command of the fort now, Majesty.'

'By whose authority?'

'By the authority that superior force has given us.'

'H'mm. We see.' The blood was chill in my veins. 'Have any of your superior officers been harmed or killed?'

'No, Majesty. They are in custody in the dungeons.'

'Or the women and children?' Anxiety awaited his response.

'We do not wage war against women and children. They are in their quarters, not with their husbands.'

I breathed more easily. 'That at least is to your credit.' For a moment, I was tempted to ask him what he proposed, but felt contempt at myself for even having the thought. 'Kings only treat with other kings or their generals,' I stated grimly. 'This is a palace, not a trading store where human lives or possessions are bartered by the public. You have come here under a flag of truce, so you shall not be harmed. You shall be treated with every courtesy, but as the rules of war permit, you shall be detained indefinitely until you can be handed over to the justice of your superiors.'

The men were obviously stunned. 'Majesty, how can you detain us?' Sergeant Souza cried.

'By the authority that superior force has given us,' I reminded him, smiling with my teeth but not with my eyes.

'We can deliver the fort to you,' Corporal Diaz intervened.

I cut him short curtly. 'We shall take the fort without the help of traitorous dogs.'

Curious that at that moment I should have felt such an identity with my mortal enemy, General de Albergaria.

Thursday, 10 December 1534

Colonel Wickram remained for my instructions after the three-man Portuguese delegation was led away.

'Send a fast horseman carrying a white truce flag to the main gate of the inner fort with a message on *pola* from us to the leaders of the mutiny,' I commanded. 'Have him fling the *pola* over the bridge of the moat and ride away. The message shall state that the members of the truce party are being detained as hostages for the safety of the Great King Dom Juan.' His eyes lit up in approval at my desire to protect the man who was once my rival king. 'Also the safety of all Portuguese women and children in the fort, the general and the officers. If one single hair of the head of the Great King or any woman or child is harmed, we shall bring down the fort brick by brick if necessary and tear every mutineer limb from limb.'

The intensity of my feelings was based on concern for Julietta. Suddenly, after all these years, the danger to her filled my whole being. I remembered Sergeant Correa, thought of him multiplied a thousand times by the *degredados* in the fort and shuddered at what my Juli's fate might be.

'Sire, may I respectfully ask a question?'

I returned from my thoughts to meet Colonel Wickram's inquiring gaze. 'Certainly.'

'We have reached the end of a long campaign to create a united Lanka, free of foreign domination. If you accept the surrender of the Colombo fort, we would have achieved our goal. If I may say so without being presumptuous, I know that your decision has been made on grounds of honour. You are the Great King. You do not treat with mutineers. But have you given due weight to the practicalities involved, with the lives of many Sinhala at stake?'

'We need men who can speak up honestly,' I asserted, then paused, eyeing him steadily. 'Consider three practical factors, Colonel. First, surrender by these mutineers does not bind their masters in Goa or Lisbon. On the contrary, if we collaborate with them and any harm befalls their officers in consequence, His Imperial Majesty would be compelled to send the largest possible fleet to teach us the kind of lesson that Admiral Vasco da Gama administered to the Zamorin years ago.'

My aide's eyebrows lifted with comprehension. 'I never thought of that, Sire. A clean-cut victory over the garrison here, on the other hand, would make his Imperial Majesty pause. In that event, there would be hurt feelings, a loss of territory, certainly, but not of face. There would not even be cause for righteous anger, because you would have spared the Catholic Church. It reminds me of the decision your royal father took, years ago, to spare the persons of the Viceroy and the governor, General de Albergaria, after the Mulleri battle. You have inherited his widom, Sire.' Another long speech from the colonel!

At long last, I thought, remembering my earlier impulsiveness. 'Precisely! And all Europe will respect us for having protected the women and children.' He knew I would have protected the women and children in any case. 'In addition, remember that the surrender of the Colombo fort will not mean automatic capitulation of the other Portuguese forts in Lanka. We shall have to take them one by one. Meanwhile, each of them is a bridgehead for the return of the Portuguese in full force. Only if we take the mighty Colombo fort by force of arms can we expect the other forts to surrender.'

He was nodding in full accord now. I did not wish to tell him how tempted I had been to set all considerations of honour aside and accept surrender from the mutineers. I suppose no man, however noble, and no prince, however well-bred, automatically follows the code of honour. It is overcoming the temptation to be base that creates nobility. In the process of time, many such decisions may result in the sort of man who is never tempted again, the man of complete nobility.

Colonel Wickram was waiting for me to proceed. 'The final reason for our decision is that if we encourage mutineers it could come back to haunt us. Only the harshest response can ensure the same thing will not happen in the Sinhala ranks.'

Colonel Wickram was not a man given to fulsome praise, but I could see from the expression on his face that he was impressed by my reasoning and it pleased me. 'You will personally ensure that the three hostages are well treated,' I concluded. 'Now summon our generals to attend a planning conference at sunset. They can be our guests at dinner.'

The Great Pahlava, the Persian Emperor Dha-roos, built

highways with relay stations at regular intervals in the wake of his expanding empire, to connect the far-flung outposts with his capital cities. Despatches reached him in record time, so he was able to deal promptly with defeat and ruthlessly with disaffection. I did not have the Emperor's problems of distance, but I had messengers with fast horses right down to company level for speedy intercommunication, so even those of my generals who were at the far ends of the sectors encircling Colombo could reach me within two hours.

I had made no changes in the administration of the Jaya kingdom. I believed that what follows victory must be carefully regulated, and this belief had been proved when I took over the low country sub-kingdoms, Kandy, the hill country sub-kingdoms, and Dhamba. In the case of Jaya, all I had to do was to appoint Lord Tammitta its Regent, thus keeping a popular figure in the seat of power, ensuring continuity of administration and relieving me and my staff of our responsibilities.

The generals arrived on time and we retired immediately to the staff room. This was the former reception chamber of the mansion and we had set it up with a yellow jakwood conference table and chairs in the centre, maps and plans on the walls and a model of the inner fort and its defences on a side table.

When I had outlined my plan to them, I could tell the generals were pleased. 'Our attacks must by systematic, to keep the enemy occupied,' I concluded. 'Let them waste their energies and their fire-power. Now that the *nao* are gone they will run out of cannonballs and gunpowder at some point of time.'

'Ahey! Ahey! . . .' There was some table thumping.

'It will be good for the men to get back into action,' General Lord Senerat observed.

'We should have recommended such action before,' General Veera Sena, my new cavalry commander, stated.

He was the lean, dashing type, with a thin moustache and piercing black eyes. 'The best way to deplete a starving garrison is to keep pressure on it. Assaulting the fort daily, at frequent irregular intervals, varying the nature and scope of the attacks but building up to a climax the day before the Portuguese Christmas, is the best way to drain their reserves.'

'The reason we did not even think of it was the possiblility of a drain on our own men and resources.' General Surya was a stout balding man, with fair, oily skin. His pomposity was somewhat diminished by a belch. He turned to me with a sycophantic smile. 'It takes the genius of a wise king to come up with such a brilliant idea.'

General Senerat summed up. 'Sire, the enemy is so short of food and ammunition that they will run out of horses to eat within two weeks. Your decision today will certainly shorten their ...' He smiled grimly ... 'Shall we say deadline?'

There was neither day nor night, still less time, in the darkness of the dungeon. The harsh scrape of the daily food platter, which contained less and less, and the clatter of the mug of water being pushed through the trap at the bottom of the door almost hurt his ears because they burst through the sounds of silence. Yet he was grateful for an event that marked some element of time. The sounds occurred with regularity, helped him identify time-spans from their intervals. Though he never knew the time of day, he guessed from his knowledge of the fort's routine that the food was given him around noon each day.

He became accustomed to the darkness, learned to identify the tiny skittering of rats, ignore the cockroaches. He had even grabbed one of the rats and killed it. Gagging, he had eaten the flesh raw, sucking at the blood, not to satisfy his hunger, but to keep his strength, impelled by a grim determination to survive. He now lived mainly to bring the mutineers to justice and to triumph over his archenemy, King Raja Sinha, whom he blamed for the torture he was undergoing. The return of his family had become secondary.

He had been sick after eating the raw rat's meat. Unbearable cramps in his stomach made him vomit. His thirst then became dry agony. Since he had only his hands to wipe his stubbly beard, his bare chest and filthy pantaloons, the stench was incredible.

He kept himself sane by planning his vengeance, deliberately shutting out feelings of guilt and shame that this should have happened to his command and excluding all thought of the possible fate of Julietta, the two children and his fellow officers.

Sometimes he escaped from reality by dreaming of the future in Portugal. He took many a wild ride on horseback with his son through the fresh air of the countryside, many a walk with Julietta through cool moonlight, blessed by the scent of honeysuckle and the nightingale's song.

Always he had to return to the unbearable heat and closeness, the stench of his own faeces in the bucket and the awful sounds of silence. Then he used every trait of his character, every part of his training, every in-breeding of pride, to maintain rigid self-control, until his mind became raw from the exertion. He gently exercised his body by muscle control, his voice by speaking aloud. He regulated his breathing so that he used up as little as possible of the noisome air. He organized a pattern for eating and sleeping. He disciplined himself to resist the unbearable craving to gobble up his food, to grab the water mug and drain its contents instead of taking a sip at long intervals merely to moisten his cracked lips. Fighting the overpowering drowsiness, forcing his eyelids open when they seemed weighted by iron shackles, was one of his most difficult battles, but he won every time and each victory strengthened him.

Most important of all, he managed to break through the

seemingly impenetrable barrier of rebellion in his mind against his situation. He overcame frustration and rage, alternating hope and despair. He kept his faith in God, but controlled the abject desire to belabour the gates of heaven with beseeching and lament. Abandoning both hope and hopelessness, he made himself one with his dreadful life and was able to sustain it. He said his normal prayers each time the meal platter was shoved through the trapdoor, observing wryly that each day he had less and less on the platter for which to be thankful.

And he survived.

Thursday, 24 December 1534

The big guns of the fort had suddenly started booming in rapid succession. Fernao could not hear the sounds, merely felt their vibration and detected the cracker-like rattle of muskets. His first response had been a spurt of interest, a desire to be in the fight, but he quickly became apathetic. He had begun living each moment for that moment. Only the iron need for vengeance was permanent.

CHAPTER FORTY-FOUR
Friday, 25 December 1534

At first it was merely a new sound for Fernao's numbed senses vaguely to identify. Then he realized what it was. The dungeon door had opened. Seated on the stinking pallet bed, his back to the wall, legs outstretched, he would normally have risen quickly to his feet, but in his weakened condition he just sat there, looking. The pale golden glow of lantern light suffusing the dark gloom hurt his eyes. He quickly shut them, then looked incuriously at the intruders through mere slits of eyelids shaded by his lashes.

There were two of them. From the morning of his detention, he recognized the rough, loose-limbed giant, Sergeant Moniz, as one of the leaders of the mutiny. The man behind the sergeant was a vague shadow.

'General, I have come to offer you limited freedom.' The coarse voice of Segeant Moniz was the first human sound Fernao had heard in weeks. It hurt his ears. The sergeant essayed a weak grin. 'Though we are not celebrating, it is Christmas Day and maybe this is a Christmas present for you!'

So today was Christmas Day. Merry Christmas Julietta! Merry Chrismas Catherina! Merry Christmas Lopo! Fernao had to force comprehension through the fog of his mind. 'What does limited freedom mean?' He spoke with an effort, his voice rusty.

'We are hard-pressed by repeated enemy attacks. We need officers to direct the defence.'

Fernao's first instinct was to sneer bitterly at this traitorous dog and his pathetic offer of a Christmas present, but the stronger instinct for survival triumphed. 'What do you propose?'

'You come out now, look at the battle situation and give us a defence plan. We are running out of ammunition for the cannon and the muskets. Only you will know how we can best use them.'

'Then return to this dungeon after you have used me? You must be mad.' He wished the words could come out stronger. He was sorely tempted to ask about Julietta and the children, but held back from displaying such weakness.

'No, General.' The man sounded almost humble. 'We will move you to better quarters. We will let you out once a day for two hours. We will give you better food, even though we don't have much horsemeat left.' The man scratched his bristly chest in a circular motion, wiped the sweat pouring down his face with the palm of his hand. 'We will need you to plan our defence and to come out every time the enemy attacks.' He paused, obviously searching for more bait. 'You can also wash and have clean clothes.'

This last was sheer temptation to Fernao. Anything to get clean again. In his mind, he allowed himself blessed, shiny white moments of cleanliness, removing his filthy underpants, his body no longer itching with dirt, crawling with vermin, the scent of new-washed clothes. Then he trapped out the thoughts in an instant. 'What else?'

'You can see your wife and children, but from a distance. You may not talk to them.'

So Juli, Catherina and Lopo were safe. Thank God for that. He had known inside. If anything had happened to his beloved, his heart would have told him before it broke. Tears rushed to Fernao's eyes, but he fought them back. Seeing his beautiful family even from a distance would be a glimpse of heaven.

Once again, he steeled himself against the soul-devouring temptation. He pondered awhile, deliberately keeping the man in suspense. He leaned forward. 'Listen to me, Sergeant,' he finally said, making his voice as cold and terse as his condition would permit. 'And listen well. You and your comrades rebelled against the king. For that, you will surely die, whether at the hands of the Sinhala or by order of His Imperial Majesty. You had hoped to treat with the Sinhala king, surrender the fort, pull down our flag. That plan has obviously fallen through.' He had to pause and recover his breath. 'You created this situation. You get yourselves out of it. Only death awaits you. And may our souls rot in hell.' He fell back totally exhausted.

A gasp escaped the sergeant, turned into a strangled sob. His heavy shoulders slumped. He was about to run away when he suddenly stopped short, thinking. He studied Fernao's face; his eyes gleamed with cunning, a hooded triumph in them. 'You spoke of the flag, General. You have a duty as our commanding officer . . .' he hesitated, cleared his throat, his larynx wobbling . . . 'and a de Albergaria, to defend and uphold the flag at any cost.'

You've got me, Fernao thought listlessly. He suddenly felt too weak to argue. 'All right, Sergeant, I'll tell you my terms. All senior officers shall be released. They shall be accorded the same freedom, food and other privileges as you have offered me. We can work out the details. But let us understand each other, you and I. I promise you no mercy. If we come out of this alive, you'll end up dead.'

'Since we no longer have the option of surrendering to the Sinhala, sir, my comrades and I would rather die fighting fair, or even at the end of a rope, than of starvation.'

Friday, 25 December 1534

There were times during the two weeks of Fernao's imprisonment when Julietta had wondered whether it would not be better to kill herself and the children, rather than watch them slowly waste away. Only thoughts of the mortal sin and of poor Fernao locked away in the dungeons made her push the temptation aside. Day by day, the children had become more gaunt and haggard, bones showed pitifully beneath skin tight drawn over their ribs. The eyes stared, the expressions were listless. Worse, the lack of water meant matted hair, dirt on their bodies, grime on their faces. Appu was in worse shape than any of them, because the mutineers barely gave him a ration. But he remained unfailingly cheerful, refusing Julietta's offer to share her morsels with him. Last night, having free access anywhere in the fort, he had trapped a lizard, which made a delicious if leathery meal for them all.

If this was her condition, how much worse must Fernao's be? Only her prayers and her faith in God kept her sanity from snapping.

When the Sinhala forces started daily attacks on the fort, the mutineers were kept busy and their limited energy was drained, so they were less watchful. Surely something could be done, but what?

Appu's expression when he walked slowly into the reception room where she sat alone that noon, quickened her interest, but her body remained apathetic.

'Some good news, for once, lady,' he announced. 'General master will remain in the dungeons and cannot see you or the small master and missy, but the men need him and the other officers to show them how to beat back the Sinhala attacks, so he will be free during those times.' He went on to give her details of the agreement between Fernao and the mutineers.

'Oh praise God, the saints and the Blessed Virgin Mary,' Julietta said, her heart fluttering with joy. She had to summon energy even to speak nowadays.

She raised her voice, so it would carry to the children's room. 'Did you hear all that children?'

The two children came slowly in, tired eyes shining. 'The first ray of hope,' Julietta continued. 'Let us kneel and thank God for His blessing.'

So weak had he become, he was hard put to it not to reach out to the sides of the corridor walls for support as he walked out of the dungeon. A fierce pride kept him erect, head high, but even so he lurched once or twice because his knees were weak.

The smell of fresher air, though still rank, the ceaseless crash of the ocean, men's voices, were an unbelievable experience after the silence of the dungeon. He even heard the rustle of the wind before he felt it on his grimy skin. His first flimpse of sunshine through the open entrance door of the prison was so fantastic, it had to be a dream, but he closed his eyes not wanting to risk hurting them through sudden exposure to bright light.

Finally, he stood in the open again. Not caring that the sunshine hurt his eyes, he took in the familiar scene. His gaze strayed to his quarters. Julietta and the children would be there. Oh God, vouchsafe me just a sight of them. Tears stung his eyes.

The men lining the rampart walls were unkempt and bedraggled. Dear God, are these soldiers of His Imperial Majesty? There was no excuse for this even at the worst of times. They could at least use seawater to keep clean. His first task would be to restore the appearance of the garrison and with it their morale and self-respect. A spurt of optimism gave him new stamina. He found himself looking forward to meeting his officers again, especially Colonel de Mello and Major Nantes, and to fighting against terrible odds that lay ahead.

Two soldiers came slowly towards him, carrying a dead comrade. The body, held by the head and the feet, hung limply. It stank of old sweat, dried faeces and new blood. 'Top of the morning to you, General,' one of the men greeted him with a diffident smile.

'Good morning.' The smell of the corpse reminded him

of the rat that he had killed and eaten. Suspicion seized him. 'Whose is that body?'

'It's our *compadre*, Paulo,' the soldier replied. 'He was killed in the enemy attack this morning.'

'Lay the body down.'

The men hesitated, uncertain. Questioning with their eyes, their glances shifted to Sergeant Moniz.

'I said, lay the body down,' Fernao rapped out, command in his voice. 'You are taking your orders from me again.'

The men obediently laid the body on the sandy soil.

Fernao walked up to the corpse. It was clad in a torn, bloodied uniform, with no helmet, the filthy, black beard and hair tousled. The face was gaunt, but the body was well formed. 'What were you going to do with it?'

The men looked down, guilt on their faces.

'General, we've been salting the dead bodies so they can be preserved for those who care to eat 'em,' Sergeant Moniz intervened. 'In our present situation, nothing can be wasted.'

Fernao swung round on him. 'By the blood of the saints, have we become savages, cannibals, then?' A wave of giddiness swept over him from the sudden effort. Horror choked him momentarily, then the breeding came out. 'This practice will cease forthwith. We are civilized Christians. Any man who desires to stoop so low will be hanged and his body fed to the fishes. Now, have Colonel de Mello and Major Nantes report to me in the orderly room immediately.' He stumped towards the tower, using every ounce of willpower to ensure that the men gazing at him from the parade ground and ramparts were seeing an undefeated general.

Saturday, 26 December 1534

The night meal was over and I was seated on a settle at the white *gini sapu* table in my tent. Having said my silent

582

prayers to my special Hindu gods, I was about ready for the yellow *kenaf* mat I slept on, like my men. I stood up, yawned and stretched mightily, became conscious of the sounds of the encampment.

Camp sounds have a special pattern and content. At dusk, there is the chatter of conversation, punctuated by raucous laughter. Spaces of sudden silence may be filled by the tinkling strains of a *sitar* filtering into the night like pure, crystal water from a spring, offered up as it were by the thump of *tabla* drums. A horse may whinny or neigh, pans will definitely clatter. Sometimes a donkey brays, a man sings, a trumpet essays tentative notes. All of it is welded together into a single symphony. By dinner time, these sounds fade away. Then, single voices call out, a joke raises hoots of mirth. Finally, the subdued hum of conversation arises from stomachs replete, slowly tapering off to silence, like the flames of the campfires now dwindling to glowing embers.

This last was the moment I had caught and it was sheer magic to me. All the thousands of men around me, merged into one single cause, were giving way to their common humanity by satisfying the demand for sleep. Then how could death be more than sleep uninterrupted by the humanity of awakening? Is it not death, rather than birth, that makes us immortal?

My reflections were interrupted by Colonel Wickram who stood at the entrance to the tent, his expression serious. 'Forgive me for intruding on your time of rest, Sire, but I have an unexpected visitor for you.'

At first, I did not recognize the man who entred the tent. Clad in soiled white pantaloons and *kurtha*, overshirt, he made obeisance and stood up respectfully before me, eyes downcast, awaiting permission to speak. Even if the lamplight had not been so dim, I doubt that I would have identified him immediately, for he looked like a walking corpse risen from a cemetery. When recognition dawned, I could not believe my eyes. The death's head of a face belonged to Appu.

A message from Julietta, or perhaps bad news of her. That was it! Julietta had died. Otherwise Appu would never have left his charge and come to me. Oh dear *devas*, what had I done? Two children, my wards, who gave me their trust, were foully murdered because of me and now I had killed the only woman I ever loved. The stark truth of my feelings for Julietta struck me again, left me dizzy. Black spots shimmered before my eyes. From our earliest days, there had been some tangible connection between Julietta and me that made us one. We understood each other perfectly, we knew there was such deep love in our hearts that it passed all human understanding. Such love did not require marriage, or the normal fulfilments of human beings living together. It was a perpetual communion, the expression of which remained ever bright even after years of separation. She and I were a simple truth, shorn of the complications of human desire, two halves of a spirit whole that had come together. While she was alive, I was not alone. Now she was gone and I was alone, completely, utterly alone.

'Permission to retire, lord.' Colonel Wickram was displaying his rare sensitivity.

'Granted.' My voice was hoarse. I had to use all my princely training to restrain myself from shaking.

The tent flap closed behind my aide. 'You may speak,' I directed Appu, my voice level, dread in my stomach.

'Sire, pray forgive me for taking up your time, but my mistress requests that you accompany me for a meeting with her.'

A meeting with her, the man had said. My Juli was alive. Joybells started ringing in my brain, my nostrils dilated with the effort to calm my quickened breathing. 'Yes, yes, of course. When? Where? How? Surely she has not left the fort?' I had not been able to keep the eagerness from my voice. Suddenly, I was not a conquering king but a teenager ready for his first tryst with the maiden of his dreams.

'No, Sire,' he responded sadly. 'She is still in the fort, virtually a prisoner.'

'Then how can we meet?' Comprehension dawned and I clicked my fingers. 'Of course! The secret passageway to the mine, the shaft, the dungeon from whence King Vidiye escaped. That's how you got here, isn't it?'

Since the day we invested the city of Colombo, I had wondered how to use this secret entry-way to sneak men into the fort, so they could spike the big guns and open the gates to my main body. Such operation required the most careful planning and co-ordination. Also, the passageway would have had to be improved to admit a large body of men, even in single file. This last posed the danger, for if the Portuguese ever became aware of the manoeuvre, they could pick our men off one by one with their muskets as they emerged from the tunnel, destroying them as one would a nest of termites. I had not divulged my thoughts to anyone, not even to Colonel Wickram, but I had contacted my sister to get in touch with the two men she had hired to rescue her husband from the dungeon. Unfortunately, they could not be found, so I had kept the possibility at the back of my mind, to be used as a last resort.

Appu picked up the drift of my thoughts immediately and shook his head. 'Perhaps the *devas* willed that entry-way to be used for a more important mission first, Sire. I do not know what my lady intends, but I suspect it is something desperate.'

'Why did she not think of this meeting-place before?'

'Once the officers were imprisoned in the dungeons, it became impossible with so many guards around. But the officers were released yesterday in order to organize the defence of the fort more effectively.' He gave me details of the arrangements with the mutineers. 'Since the officers have given their word of honour not to escape, there are no guards in the dungeons.'

I suddenly became aware again of Appu's physical state. 'You have been almost starved for months. You must have food, drink, a bath, a change of clothes.'

'No, thank you, Sire. I could not explain cleanliness when I return to the fort. As for food and drink, I cannot eat while my mistress and her children are starving.'

His words hit me with a force of a thunder-clap. This humble man had so much loyalty for his adopted mistress, while I had been responsible for starving her and her children near to death. Dear gods, what is this all about? What good is *dharma*, the duty of one's station, if it must destroy one's beloved? What had seemed so clear minutes earlier became blank as the darkness of the night outside the tent.

'We respect and admire your loyalty, Appu,' I declared, my voice shaking. 'You are a king among men and we are humble before your dignity.'

Since I would return well before dawn, it was not too difficult for me to slip out of the encampment in disguise. Only Colonel Wickram knew that I was not in my tent.

The entrance to the mineshaft had been so carefully concealed that Appu and I were able to enter it without being detected. We groped our way in the dark to the first bend of the passageway, where he had hidden a lantern. Though it was slippery underfoot, the going was easy, but eerie from the occasional drip of water, the squeak of rats and, once, the flapping of a bat's wings.

We finally came to a circular hole in a mass of debris where the other end of the shaft had obviously collapsed. 'I dug through to get out, Sire,' Appu informed me, speaking low. 'Please forgive me, but it was the best I could do. You will have to crawl through.'

It's a miracle you found the strength to dig at all, I reflected, and at that moment a new discovery illuminated my mind like brilliant shaft of lightning. Only love could have produced such strength. Appu had been in love with Julietta all these years.

My first reaction was anger. How dared he raise his eyes to my Julietta? Then it struck me that he had never raised his eyes to her, but merely loved her silently, without her ever knowing it, without hope of a reward.

Everything is relative. As in birth, in my love I had more than Appu.

As I stared at him in the shaded lampglow, his eyes widened. He knew I had bared his secret. At first, fear widened his eyes. When he saw that I was not angry, tears sprang in them. He turned abruptly to the hole in the debris. 'This way, Sire,' he said quietly and wriggled through.

I followed, thinking, indeed there are many ways in which I can follow this remarkable man.

By the time I entered the small dungeon room and stood erect, Appu, carrying the lantern, had almost vanished at its entrance.

The room was small, lit by the dim yellow-gold glow of a lantern placed on a stone shelf jutting from one of the granite walls. The stink of ancient faeces and stale rodent fur hung heavily on cool but humid air. The silence was intense.

As I straightened up, I saw her. My Juli stood to one side of the entrance, facing me. Beneath her dark, hooded cloak, she was clad in a shabby blue dress. I immediately recognized it as a replica of the one she had worn so long ago in the Jaya palace, in a carefree lifetime.

She threw back her hood and a gasp escaped me. This gaunt, droopy figure, its skin drawn so tightly over the bones that her cheeks were hollow, the eye-sockets deep and black-ringed. Even in that light, I saw the hint of grey in her auburn hair, the red veins in the whites of the aquamarine eyes. She had tried her best to look groomed, but it was pitiful.

Yet the love was there, linking us both, regardless of appearance or circumstance. This was my Juli, whom I alone had brought to such a sorry pass.

In that instant, I knew with stunning, sad clarity that it could not have been any other way. The destiny of the millions in my country was more crucial than hers and mine. Her eyes told me that she knew it too. So the farce that commenced so many years ago, when I made my choice, had to drag on while our love soared. And life and the destinies of others would continue to make a farce of our love.

Only then did I see the smaller figure standing behind Juli.

Noticing my glance, Juli, direct as always, did not wait for permission to speak but came to the point. 'I am happy to see you, Sire, though I wish I could have looked better and met you under more auspicious circumstances.'

'Meeting you again is the auspicious circumstance, Juli,' I replied tautly, not caring about her companion or the royal plurals. 'It has always been so and I am an unfortunate wretch to have had so few auspicious circumstances in my life. As for looking better, the beauty of your spirit gives you radiance. I would also have you know that there is no Sire here, only your humble, obedient servant.'

'Oh Tiki-tiki.' She sighed, her whole expression softening through all the toughness created by her suffering. 'Can you say that to this old hag, this bag of bones?' She was about to say something more, but pulled back. 'As you can see, you have another visitor.'

She stepped aside and the face of her companion emerged into the lantern-glow.

At first, I was puzzled. I knew this girl. Through the gauntness and hollows of her face, I knew her. When? Where? I blinked, trying to turn the familiarity into recognition. Then it struck me with incredulity that I was staring at the chiselled, but feminine, features of a Maya

Dunne. How could it be? Something stirred deep within me, something I could not identify, an itch that could not be scratched. 'Step forward,' I commanded.

The girl moved into the brigher glow of the lamp. With a sick feeling within me, I realized why she walked so shakily, but that was not why my heart had started beating faster, thumping against my chest. I peered at her eyes. Unmistakably brown, the blue rims. 'The Maya Dunne eyes!' I exclaimed still puzzled. 'How did she get them?' I turned to Juli.

'Sire, allow me to present your daughter, Catherina Julietta Menika, who bears the de Albergaria name.'

The words exploded in my brain, the blast shattered my senses. The room rocked about me. My world became tormented fragments through which my mind went reeling back through the years to a night of magic in a dark grove, beneath a blue starlit sky. The eternity of the earth, the infinity of the heavens had brought forth life? This creature standing before me was my daughter, flesh of my flesh, blood of my blood, bone of my bone, fruit of the purest love a man and woman could ever know. I was no longer alone. Juli had sacrificed her entire life to confer on me something more precious than the heartbeat that suddenly starts a life. She had given me immortality.

And the moment deserved my finest. 'Come to me, *mage dhoo*, my daughter.' I opened my arms to her.

The girl slipped into my embrace as naturally as a spring merging into a mountain stream. I held my daughter's bones to me. There was only one body, ours. I felt the pounding of her heart and it was the echo of mine. I stroked her dark hair, murmured endearments I had never used before. The tears flowed unchecked for the first time in my life.

What takes place between families at their most intimate times has to be secret. All I will say is that when I pulled away from my daughter, it was as if a part of my body had been torn away from me. I clung to her hand. Soft and dry, it vibrated inside mine.

'I told our daughter the truth only this evening,' Juli informed me softly. 'She understood immediately. Strangely, she had known she was different for a long time.' She paused, looked searchingly at me. 'The reason I requested this meeting and brought her here was that I could not let you destroy your own child. I could never do that to you. Please take her and look after her as your own. She was too loyal to leave us, but finally agreed when I told her that God the Father would want her to do this for her earthly father.'

I was stunned, but elated. 'What will your husband say?'

'I have hidden the truth from him too long. He will have to accept it at last, but I believe he already knows. He is a good man.'

Thoughts were racing furiously through my brain, scraping it raw. Conflicting desires clashed within my spirit. I stared at Juli, but I was not seeing her physical presence. I was with the Juli I loved. Suddenly, her total unselfishness became an example to me. She had sacrificed her whole life to keep our secret, now she was ready to reveal the secret and sacrifice her life again. Another lesson in dignity learned tonight by the Great King, only this one left me in awe.

'What of you?' I inquired through the husk in my throat.

'I hope my husband will permit me to do my duty by him and our son.'

'What will you tell people about giving the little one to me?' I pressed my daughter's hand and she clasped mine tightly in response.

'That you graciously and chivalrously agreed to spare the life of a young lady.'

I shook my head. 'Such things must not be done in a hurry,' I said. 'I must think on it. You shall have my answer tomorrow. I shall have word conveyed to you somehow. Meanwhile, go back with our daughter and please do nothing.'

'Very well.' A sob escaped her. The large eyes were glistening with tears. She looked more beautiful than I had ever seen her before, somehow so virginal that I had clear knowledge that virginity is not a physical condition ended by the piercing of a veil.

What we said to each other, the three of us, is private. What Juli and I said to each other after we had excused our daughter, is private too. Suffice it to say that we told each other everything and that Juli and I finally spoke of the true nature of our love, which we had lived without life.

Our parting is the most private of all. I shall not bare my torment to anyone. After all, I am the Great King, Tikiri Bandara Raja Sinha, the son of the man who was General Prince Maya Dunne when I first loved Julietta.

Monday, 28 December 1534

The night was very dark. Most of the sentries and lookouts slept through sheer exhaustion. As in the past, Fernao was up with the first crowing of roosters at the false dawn. He had a little more food in his stomach. A bath in seawater drawn up by buckets left his body sticky, but heavenly clean like his clothes. He was beginning to feel the first stirrings of a return of strength.

A skeletal but unvanquished Colonel de Mello and Fernao slowly paced the ramparts. 'It was so wonderful just to be able to see Julietta and the children even from a distance,' Fernao remarked. 'They have obviously been ravaged by conditions here, but thank God we are all alive and together.'

'I felt the same at seeing my wife,' Colonel de Mello responded. 'Thank God, she and I have no children.' Though wan from hollow cheeks, even in the semi-gloom his dare-devil blue eyes were brilliant, slightly amused as always.

Strange, how common adversity has allowed two normally reticent men to open up to each other, Fernao thought.

They paused by the rampart wall and stared across the dry lake-bed. The Sinhala campfires had died down, merely glowed like a red-gold pattern on a vast black carpet. Fernao stared about him, remembering many things, the building of the fort, Captain Oliveira, Abdul Raschid, Aires, his walks with Juli on those very walls in happier times. The sky to the east lightened. An aura of rose spread above the tree-line to merge into the grey of the sky. Slowly, the darkness was absorbed into pale silver light. A cock crowed in the distance. The whistle of distant birds arose, the mewing of seagulls over the western sea, which gave back its dank odour of seaweed.

'The earth will keep coming to life each morning, long after we are dead and gone,' Fernao remarked. He caught Colonel de Mello's nod. 'The fires of man have died down too.' His eyes drifted towards the dying campfires, across the lake-bed, sightlessly because he was lost in bitter-sweet contemplation. Something intruded into his consciousness. He shook his head violently, stared, his gaze sharp. He pointed a shaking hand. 'Look!' he gasped.

On either side of him the ramparts were coming to life, with men exclaiming, shouting. 'Look! . . . look! . . . look! . . .'

The entire area of the lake-bed was devoid of life. Teeming tents, soldiers, guns had vanished overnight, leaving a desolate wasteland.

'They have fled, leaving behind wagonloads of food!' a sentry from the tower shouted.

A westerly wind sprang up, sending countless small flurries of dry dust inland in the wake of the departed Sinhala lion.

Friday, 1 January 1535

Having withdrawn my forces to Jaya, I took up residence in the palace. I had given up the certainty of conquest for love of a woman and my newly found and lost daughter, whose people would have been defeated by the force of my armies had I not been consumed by the tenderness of their arms!

The following day Appu delivered a package from Juli. It contained her painting of the knight in shining armour, riding a white horse, slaying a dragon in defence of his lady. This was the present she had given me so many years ago on my birthday, 11 February 1521, which I had caused to be framed and sent to her as a wedding gift. She had now returned it with a note that simply said: 'This is sent back to whom it rightfully belongs.'

Her gesture touched me deeply, but could not ease the pain of having given up my daughter, the gnawing ache at parting from her and Juli.

Saturday, 2 January 1535

A Portuguese fleet consisting of twelve great *nao* sailed into Colombo harbour today. I was so glad that I had withdrawn my army before I had any knowledge of the arrival of this fleet, but it did provide my commanders with a reason after the event to which they could ascribe my decision. My reputation for foresight soared in consequence!

Wednesday, 10 February 1535

Not wishing a confrontation, Admiral de Albergaria, the father of the general, who commanded the fleet, made no attempt to re-take the city of Colombo, but contented himself with dealing with the mutineers. The justice he meted out was harsh and summary. Many conspirators were manacled, chained and sentenced to the dungeons for life. Others were fined and denied pay and privileges. The ring-leaders, including the three-man delegation which had been escorted back to the inner fort on my orders, were publicly flogged and hanged.

Bishop Juan and Father Perez, who had emerged through all this unscathed, were hailed as Christian heroes. I had never considered conferring martyrdom on them but, who knows, if they continue to perform such miracles of survival, they may even be canonized as saints by the Holy Father!

Meanwhile, my gesture in not accepting the surrender of the mutineers had pleased Admiral de Albergaria greatly and had made all the Portuguese officers well-disposed towards us.

Now that order and military discipline had been restored, I received word that the Portuguese desired to resume trade on the same basis as when they first landed. They would withdraw all military forces from their forts, which they would retain as trading posts. I readily agreed, so peace was restored and Aisha Raschid and her new partner, Deen, returned to their Slave Island mansion with the knowledge of prosperity ahead.

I even released the waters of the lake so the inner fort was protected once again.

Now I had my most patriotic mission to fulfil, the payment of the debt I owed my two dead wards, Bandula and Nangi – the regeneration of the poor of my country. Meanwhile, it seemed as if all the sound and fury, the countless dead and wounded, had only caused the wheel to turn full circle to where it had been shortly after my birthday fourteen years before, when it all began.

I received word today from Juli, through Appu, that she, her husband, their son and my daughter are sailing to Portugal for good tomorrow evening.

Thursday, 11 February 1535

I stood alone on a rocky promontory just south of the lake and watched the single great *nao* emerge from the harbour. Proudly bearing the Portuguese flag, it headed majestically west. Gathering speed, it became a dark silhouette with sails that looked like great patches of red blood. Juli had told me about her painting. Perhaps she had the gift of prescience.

The distant horizon bore the dark line of approaching night. Seagulls mewed mournfully overhead. A steady sea-breeze fluttered against me like the flapping of a bird's wings. I imagined I could hear the creak of the ship's timbers and the soughing of its sails.

Juli was on that ship, being borne away from me for ever. Suddenly, I was completely crushed, utterly weary, totally desolate.

Fourteen years before, to the day, the Portuguese sailed into Colombo harbour. During this period, I had succeeded in pushing them back to where they started from but this was not the end. As I recalled my father's words, *Our war will never end ... the old feeling of futility overwhelmed me.

Today is my birthday. Yet the part of me that never lived has died. I am no longer invincible.

Julietta leaned against the rail of the main deck of the great *nao* as it glided away from the Colombo harbour. It was good to feel physically whole again and to see Fernao and the children, neat, clean, groomed, though their clothes hung on their bodies. The rest of her was empty.

The red-gold rays of the setting sun turned the heaving waters of the ocean into a blood-red mirror. She looked up at the sails. They were exactly like those she had visualized when she did her painting of a ship sailing home into the sunset so many years ago. Whose blood was it?

She gazed towards the land. In the distance, she saw the speck of a solitary figure standing just south of the lake. It must be a fisherman.

Where was her Tiki-tiki? He was the Great King. He would be in the Jaya palace. As he had once cast her aside because he had set his sails towards his horizons, so today he could not even see her off. She had lost him for ever in this life. Yet it was he that had given her life, once from the claws of a rapist, now from the talons of his own war.

She stifled a sob. She was leaving her whole life behind. Yet, in little Catherina, she as least would have part of Tiki-tiki with her in the years ahead. Poor Tiki-tiki, what did he have? Once again, only loneliness from his noble gestures. Vaguely she knew that he would at least have nobility always, an almost tangible possession.

Suddenly a stunning physical connection jolted her. She stared at the tiny figure on the shore. It looked so forlorn.

Oh God, that is Tiki-tiki!

Fernao slowly paced the poop-deck with his father. Wind and wave slid past the sides of the great *nao*, the timbers creaked. The mate's voice ripped throught the air, giving orders.

'You and I sailed into that harbour fourteen years ago,' Admiral de Albergaria stated. 'Do you remember?'

Fernao nodded. His chest felt tight with emotion, a mixture of nostalgia at the recollection and sadness at leaving what had been his home for so long. 'Thank God you arrived in time,' he said. 'You scared the Great King away.' In his mind he secretly asked himself why the Sinhala had left the food wagons behind, if they had really run away.

The admiral's craggy face softened. 'Indeed. You have acquired much wisdom since we first came here, General.' He spoke gruffly to cover his embarrassment. 'Your suggestion that we resume trade on the old basis until the

Sinhala champion we brought in from Goa can establish himself as the Great King's opponent is statesmanship indeed.'

'Indeed.' Fernao found himself repeating his father's favourite word. 'The fencing champion, Lord Kon Appu Bandara, who challenged and defeated our warrior captain in Goa by cleaving his head in two, is a man of royal blood. He can rally Sinhala Buddhists to his cause against a liberal king who practises the Hindu religion.'

'Divide and rule,' the admiral asserted.

'Give the man time,' Fernao declared. He glanced at Juli, standing alone by the rail below him, staring towards the shore, and was swept by a sudden access of rage for all they had endured. 'When Kon Appu overthrows the Great King, I will have won at last.'

He noticed a shudder run through Juli's frame. Had she heard his words?

EPILOGUE

Extracts from a private diary maintained by *a senhora* Julietta de Albergaria after her return to Portugal.

11 February 1546: Today is Tiki-tiki's birthday. Eleven years have gone by without any news from Lanka. My father-in-law, Admiral de Albergaria, is now bedridden and spends all his time in his suite. My husband, Fernao, has become a writer of renown through the patronage of His Imperial Majesty, King Dom João III, who still rules our country. Our son is already a lieutenant in the navy and our daughter has married a prince of the royal family, which I secretly deem only proper since she is herself of royal blood.

Out of the blue, I have just received a letter, written in Portuguese, from Appu, our former major-domo in Lanka and once my loyal contact man with Tiki-tiki

Most revered lady,

This letter is written under command of His Majesty the Great King Tikiri Bandara Raja Sinha, who appointed me his personal aide shortly after you set sail for Portugal.

Two weeks ago, the Great King defeated the pretender, Lord Kon Appu Bandara, in the hill country and caused the enemy forces to retreat. This was his first major battle since the sad ones before you left our shores. One of its lesser but significant outcomes was the Great King's discovery from an informer that it was Queen Anula and not General de Albergaria who had caused the murders of his two wards Bandula and Nangi and of Lord Wickrama Sinha, but the Great King was somehow too listless to mete out punishment to the queen.

After the battle was over, the Great King was injured in the foot by a bamboo splinter. Men say that one of his physicians then poisoned the wound, so the king became much weakened. Yesterday, he spoke thus to me in private: 'I fought my first battle when I was eighteen years old and have been fighting ever since. No king has been able to stand against me. But he who has appeared in the hill country this time is the new favourite of fortune. The power of my merits has declined. My invincibility has gone to him.'

'Convey my words to the one who made me invincible,' he finally commanded me. 'Tell her that I shall await her on the other side.'

He then gave a tired sigh and died.

Revered lady, our Great King was the last of the Sinhala lions. Undefeated in battle, he brought our country under one royal rule. This beautiful Lanka will never be supreme again.

You may not be surprised to learn that a few years ago, the Great King openly professed the Hindu religion, as he had promised the Chola King Ratnes Waram. It has united Chola and Sinhala as never before, but I fear this most supreme act of greatness will cause the Buddhist *bhikkus* who maintain our historical chronicle, the Chula Vamsa, to belittle him for posterity, as will the Catholic chroniclers.

Upon the Great King's death, Lord Kon Appu Bandara took over his title and suzerainty, under the name King Vimala Dharma Surya.

You may be aware that, after you departed from our shores, King Dom Juan Dharma Pala lived in a palace in Colombo which your own king graciously placed at his disposal, maintaining all the external symbols of royalty without any power. He dressed in Portuguese style, spoke the Portuguese language and of course practised the Catholic religion. He even wrote a will leaving his throne, upon his death, to Portugal. When your armed forces recently returned to Colombo, they seized the Sita Waka kingdom and bestowed it on this son of King Vidiye, King Dom Juan Dharma Pala, who rules over it only in name. Confrontation between your garrisons and King Vimala Dharma Surya is therefore inevitable.

Our wars will never end!

It is no wonder that my lord, King Raja Sinha, frequently spoke of the futility of it all. Conscious of this, I myself have decided to retire to the country estate which he generously bestowed on me, because I can never find another leader worthy of serving in such a sacred cause.

Maya Dunne, Vidiye, Kumara, Raigam, finally Raja Sinha. We have seen the last Sinhala lions.

May the blessings of the Triple Gem and the God you so devoutly worship ever be with you.

Your humble, obedient servant,
Appu

When her son-in-law, the titular Great King, Dom Juan, died in suspicious circumstances, he had named his wife,

Dona Margaridha, his heir. An heiress without a fortune, Queen Anula thought cynically, but at least I have paved the way to a kingdom.

Then came the news of King Raja Sinha's death. Gloating, Queen Anula immediately contacted Bishop Juan with a request that the Church use its influence with the King of Portugal to confirm her daughter's station. Ever eager to support a policy of divide and rule, he readily agreed. Instinct and her *anjanam*, light-foreteller, told the queen that Dona Margaridha would one day be a Great Queen. Queen Anula decided to plot for it and become the power behind the throne. Strangely, now she had a visible purpose once more, her moments of lucidity began to increase.

It was not long before the day came when, seated in her chamber, she awaited the visit of the new champion, Lord Kon Appu Bandara, who had adopted the tile King Vimala Dharma Surya and had also grandiosely arrogated to himself a Christian title, in addition, Dom Juan of Austria. With beating heart she prepared her approach battle . . .

Julietta was in her bedroom in the family manor, red-eyed from weeping, her lids swollen, when Fernao returned that evening.

'What is it, my love?' he inquired anxiously.

She told him about the death of King Raja Sinha.

'So he finally lost his power when he faced the man I sent against him,' Fernao declared, savage satisfaction in his voice. 'He did everything possible to destroy me. I've waited many years to win. My only regret is that it had to be by proxy, but nonetheless I've won.'

She looked at him appalled. This was a part of the husband she loved which she had thought buried for ever. 'Fernao, you speak of King Raja Sinha wanting to destroy you. He pulled back when he was poised for the kill.'

'Rubbish. He pulled back because he had advance warning that our fleet was homing in to the rescue.'

'Oh, you are wrong,' Her mouth twisted, her voice was low. She shook her head slowly from side to side. 'So wrong.'

'What do you know about war?' he demanded, unwonted anger in his voice.

Does it take a man to know war? Do women not live it more vividly in their hearts and minds? The very last Sinhala lion seemed to stand before her, glowing with the youth of that night beneath the stars. When faced with the final outcome, he had chosen honour, love over ambition. She owed him the last victory, through the truth which only she could reveal.

Needing Fernao as never before, she calmly, steadily told him all, from the very beginning. Would Fernao's valour and love finally match those of the dead Sinhala lion?

AUTHOR'S NOTE

Many of the events of this novel actually took place, although not always exactly as I describe them. Portuguese records of the time claim that King Raja Sinha I was as great a general as Hannibal Barca, Alexander the Great or Julius Caesar. It is the Buddhist and Catholic historians of Ceylon that have failed to accord him his true greatness.

As some of the characters in this story had foreseen, Dutch vessels appeared in the Indian Ocean before the turn of the century. They eventually captured the coastal regions of Lanka that the Portuguese held, only to be ousted in the eighteenth century by the British.

The names of most of the characters in this novel have come from the history books, including *Portugal* by John Dos Passos; the *Rajavaliya*; the *Chula Vamsa* (Wm Geiger's translation); and Father S. G. Perera's *History of Ceylon, Portuguese and Dutch Periods*.

Portuguese characters: King Dom Manuel I; King Dom João III; Vasco da Gama; de Albergaria; the de Almeidas; de Albuquerque; de Noronha; de Mello; de Souza.

Sinhala characters: King Dharma Parakrama Bahu; King Wijayo; his consort, whom I have named Queen Anula, and her son, Prince Deva Raja; King Bhuvaneka Bahu; King Jaya Wira Bandara; Prince Kumara; Prince Vidiye; King Maya Dunne; King Raja Sinha I; King Dom Juan Dharma Pala; Queen Dona Margaridha; and Prince Kon Appu, who succeeded King Raja Sinha with the name Vimala Dharma Surya.

Indian/Moorish characters: the Zamorin(s) of Calicut; Paichi Marcar.

Also some historical events: Vasco da Gama's discovery of the sea route to India in 1498 and his subsequent appointment as Viceroy; the planting of the stone cross in Galle by Lorenzo de Almeida; the establishment of Portuguese forts in Colombo, Galle and other costal cities; the looting of King Wijayo's treasury and his assassination; the assassination of King Bhuvaneka by a Portuguese musketeer; the arrival of the Franciscans; King Maya Dunne's triumphs and defeats, including the sacking of Sita Waka after he had draped the palace in white and withdrawn from it; the battle of Mulleri (*yawa*); Captain Diogo de Mello's daring arrest of Prince Vidiye, the imprisonment in a dungeon and his rescue from it by his wife, King Maya Dunne's daughter; Don Alfonso de Noronha's greed; the merciless bombardments of coastal towns in Lanka and elsewhere by the Portuguese; the naval battle between Portuguese and Mouro forces, including the battle of Vedalai; the draining of the lake by King Raja Sinha and his establishment of a single kingdom.

The actual events spanned over sixty years. King Raja Sinha I was a much older man when he became the Great King. I have telescoped time, juxtaposed dates, altered actual events, created characters, all in the interest of a more readable story.

This was an era of extreme cruelty and ruthlessness. Save for some of the methods, however, it is no different from the modern scene, with the exception that today honour is scorned and the meaning of nobility is unknown to many. I pray that this book will inspire those who still have such ideals to cherish them, whatever the price.

Colin de Silva
Honolulu, Hawaii, 1987

The world's greatest novelists now available in paperback from Grafton Books

Eric van Lustbader

Jian	£3.50	☐
The Miko	£2.95	☐
The Ninja	£3.50	☐
Sirens	£3.50	☐
Beneath An Opal Moon	£2.95	☐
Black Heart	£3.50	☐

Nelson de Mille

By the Rivers of Babylon	£2.50	☐
Cathedral	£1.95	☐
The Talbot Odyssey	£3.50	☐

Justin Scott

The Shipkiller	£2.50	☐
The Man Who Loved the Normandie	£2.50	☐
A Pride of Kings	£2.95	☐

Leslie Waller

Trocadero	£2.50	☐
The Swiss Account	£2.50	☐
The American	£2.50	☐
The Family	£1.95	☐
The Banker	£2.50	☐
The Brave and the Free	£1.95	☐
Gameplan	£1.95	☐

David Charney

Sensei	£2.50	☐
Sensei II: The Swordmaster	£2.50	☐

Paul-Loup Sulitzer

The Green King	£2.95	☐

To order direct from the publisher just tick the titles you want
and fill in the order form.   **GF781**

The world's greatest novelists now available in paperback from Grafton Books

Angus Wilson

Such Darling Dodos	£1.50	☐
Late Call	£1.95	☐
The Wrong Set	£1.95	☐
For Whom the Cloche Tolls	£2.95	☐
A Bit Off the Map	£1.50	☐
As If By Magic	£2.50	☐
Hemlock and After	£1.50	☐
No Laughing Matter	£1.95	☐
The Old Men at the Zoo	£1.95	☐
The Middle Age of Mrs Eliot	£1.95	☐
Setting the World on Fire	£1.95	☐
Anglo-Saxon Attitudes	£2.95	☐
The Strange Ride of Rudyard Kipling (non-fiction)	£1.95	☐
The World of Charles Dickens (non-fiction)	£3.95	☐

John Fowles

The Ebony Tower	£2.50	☐
The Collector	£1.95	☐
The French Lieutenant's Woman	£2.50	☐
The Magus	£2.95	☐
Daniel Martin	£3.95	☐
Mantissa	£2.50	☐
The Aristos (non-fiction)	£2.50	☐

Brian Moore

The Lonely Passion of Judith Hearne	£2.50	☐
I am Mary Dunne	£1.50	☐
Catholics	£2.50	☐
Fergus	£2.50	☐
The Temptation of Eileen Hughes	£1.50	☐
The Feast of Lupercal	£1.50	☐
Cold Heaven	£2.50	☐

To order direct from the publisher just tick the titles you want and fill in the order form.

Outstanding fiction in paperback from Grafton Books

Nicola Thorne
Yesterday's Promises	£3.50 ☐
A Woman Like Us	£1.25 ☐
The Perfect Wife and Mother	£1.50 ☐
The Daughters of the House	£2.50 ☐
Where the Rivers Meet	£2.50 ☐
Affairs of Love	£2.50 ☐
The Enchantress Saga	£3.95 ☐
Never Such Innocence	£2.95 ☐

Jacqueline Briskin
Paloverde	£3.50 ☐
Rich Friends	£2.95 ☐
Decade	£2.50 ☐
The Onyx	£3.50 ☐
Everything and More	£2.50 ☐

Barbara Taylor Bradford
A Woman of Substance	£3.95 ☐
Voice of the Heart	£3.95 ☐
Hold the Dream	£3.50 ☐

Alan Ebert and Janice Rotchstein
Traditions	£3.95 ☐
The Long Way Home	£2.95 ☐

Marcelle Bernstein
Sadie	£2.95 ☐

To order direct from the publisher just tick the titles you want and fill in the order form.

All these books are available at your local bookshop or newsagent, or can be ordered direct from the publisher.

To order direct from the publishers just tick the titles you want and fill in the form below.

Name _____

Address _____

_____

Send to:
Grafton Cash Sales
PO Box 11, Falmouth, Cornwall TR10 9EN.

Please enclose remittance to the value of the cover price plus:

UK 60p for the first book, 25p for the second book plus 15p per copy for each additional book ordered to a maximum charge of £1.90.

BFPO 60p for the first book, 25p for the second book plus 15p per copy for the next 7 books, thereafter 9p per book.

Overseas including Eire £1.25 for the first book, 75p for second book and 28p for each additional book.

Grafton Books reserve the right to show new retail prices on covers, which may differ from those previously advertised in the text or elsewhere.